The Ghastly Gothic Tomes

Vol. 6

The Ghastly Gothic Tomes

Vol. 6

Published by NRM Books.

ISBN: 978-1-965179-09-3

CREDITS
Cover Art by: Nathan Reese Maher

COPYRIGHT

The Ghastly Gothic Tomes are protected under the copyright laws of the United States of America. Any reproductions or unauthorized use of the contents herein including, but not limited to, artwork and text is prohibited without written permission from the author. Novels, poems, plays and short stories published herein are part of the public domain.

Copyright 1st Edition October 14th, 2024, all rights reserved.

Table of Contents

"Frankenstein; or, The Modern Prometheus"
by Mary Wollstonecraft (Godwin) Shelly
Published 1818, p. 2-177

"Presumption; or, The Fate of Frankenstein"
by Richard Brinsley Peake
Published 1823, p. 178-229

"The Private Memoirs and Confessions of a Justified Sinner"
by James Hogg
Published 1824, p. 230-410

"The Legend of Sleepy Hollow"
by Washington Irving
Published 1824, p. 411-437

"Berenice"
by Edgar Allan Poe
Published 1835, p. 438-445

"Ligeia"
By Edgar Allan Poe
Published 1838, p. 446-460

"Masque of the Red Death"
By Edgar Allan Poe
Published 1842, p. 479-484

"The Oval Portrait"
By Edgar Allan Poe
Published 1842, p. 485-487

"The Pit and the Pendulum"
By Edgar Allan Poe
Pub. 1835, p. 488-500

"The Black Cat"
By Edgar Allan Poe
Published 1843, p. 501-509

"The Tell Tale Heart"
By Edgar Allan Poe
Published 1843, p. 510-514

"A Christmas Carol"
by Charles Dickens
Published 1843, p. 515-593

Frankenstein; or, The Modern Prometheus

By Mary Wollstonecraft (Godwin) Shelly

Letter 1

To Mrs. Saville, England.

St. Petersburgh, Dec. 11th, 17—.

You will rejoice to hear that no disaster has accompanied the commencement of an enterprise which you have regarded with such evil forebodings. I arrived here yesterday, and my first task is to assure my dear sister of my welfare and increasing confidence in the success of my undertaking.

I am already far north of London, and as I walk in the streets of Petersburgh, I feel a cold northern breeze play upon my cheeks, which braces my nerves and fills me with delight. Do you understand this feeling? This breeze, which has travelled from the regions towards which I am advancing, gives me a foretaste of those icy climes. Inspirited by this wind of promise, my daydreams become more fervent and vivid. I try in vain to be persuaded that the pole is the seat of frost and desolation; it ever presents itself to my imagination as the region of beauty and delight. There, Margaret, the sun is for ever visible, its broad disk just skirting the horizon and diffusing a perpetual splendour. There—for with your leave, my sister, I will put some trust in preceding navigators—there snow and frost are banished; and, sailing over a calm sea, we may be wafted to a land surpassing in wonders and in beauty every region hitherto discovered on the habitable globe. Its productions and features may be without example, as the phenomena of the heavenly bodies undoubtedly are in those undiscovered solitudes. What may not be expected in a country of eternal light? I may there discover the wondrous power which attracts the needle and may regulate a thousand celestial observations that require only this voyage to render their seeming eccentricities consistent for ever. I shall satiate my ardent curiosity with the sight of a part of the world never before visited, and may tread a land never before imprinted by the foot of man. These are my enticements, and they are sufficient to conquer all fear of danger or death and to induce me to commence this laborious voyage with the joy a child feels when he embarks in a little boat, with his holiday mates, on an expedition of discovery up his native river. But supposing all these conjectures to be false, you cannot contest the inestimable benefit which I shall confer on all mankind, to the last generation, by discovering a passage near the pole to those countries, to reach which at present so many months are requisite; or by ascertaining the secret of the magnet, which, if at all possible, can only be effected by an undertaking such as mine.

These reflections have dispelled the agitation with which I began my letter, and I feel my heart glow with an enthusiasm which elevates me to heaven, for nothing contributes so much to tranquillise the mind as a steady purpose—a point on which the soul may fix its intellectual eye. This expedition has been the favourite dream of my early years. I have read with ardour the accounts of the various voyages which have been made in the prospect of arriving at the North Pacific Ocean through the seas which surround the pole. You may remember that a history of all the voyages made for purposes of discovery composed the whole of our good Uncle Thomas' library. My education was neglected, yet I was passionately fond of reading. These volumes were my study day and night, and my familiarity with them increased that regret which I had felt, as a child, on learning that my father's dying injunction had forbidden my uncle to allow me to embark in a seafaring life.

These visions faded when I perused, for the first time, those poets whose effusions entranced my soul and lifted it to heaven. I also became a poet and for one year lived in a paradise of my own creation; I imagined that I also might obtain a niche in the temple where the names of Homer and Shakespeare are consecrated. You are well acquainted with my failure and how heavily I bore the disappointment. But just at that time I inherited the fortune of my cousin, and my thoughts were turned into the channel of their earlier bent.

Six years have passed since I resolved on my present undertaking. I can, even now, remember the hour from which I dedicated myself to this great enterprise. I commenced by inuring my body to hardship. I accompanied the whale-fishers on several expeditions to the North Sea; I voluntarily endured cold, famine, thirst, and want of sleep; I often worked harder than the common sailors during the day and devoted my nights to the study of mathematics, the theory of medicine, and those branches of physical science from which a naval adventurer might derive the greatest practical advantage. Twice I actually hired myself as an under-mate in a Greenland whaler, and acquitted myself to admiration. I must own I felt a little proud when my captain offered me the second dignity in the vessel and entreated me to remain with the greatest earnestness, so valuable did he consider my services.

And now, dear Margaret, do I not deserve to accomplish some great purpose? My life might have been passed in ease and luxury, but I preferred glory to every enticement that wealth placed in my path. Oh, that some encouraging voice would answer in the affirmative! My courage and my resolution is firm; but my hopes fluctuate, and my spirits are often depressed. I am about to proceed on a long and difficult voyage, the emergencies of which will demand all my fortitude: I am required not only to raise the spirits of others, but sometimes to sustain my own, when theirs are failing.

This is the most favourable period for travelling in Russia. They fly quickly over the snow in their sledges; the motion is pleasant, and, in my opinion, far more agreeable than that of an English stagecoach. The cold is not excessive, if you are wrapped in furs—a dress which I have already adopted, for there is a great difference between walking the deck and remaining seated motionless for hours, when no exercise prevents the blood from actually freezing in your veins. I have no ambition to lose my life on the post-road between St. Petersburgh and Archangel.

I shall depart for the latter town in a fortnight or three weeks; and my intention is to hire a ship there, which can easily be done by paying the insurance for the owner, and to engage as many sailors as I think necessary among those who are accustomed to the whale-fishing. I do not intend to sail until the month of June; and when shall I return? Ah, dear sister, how can I answer this question? If I succeed, many, many months, perhaps years, will pass before you and I may meet. If I fail, you will see me again soon, or never.

Farewell, my dear, excellent Margaret. Heaven shower down blessings on you, and save me, that I may again and again testify my gratitude for all your love and kindness.

Your affectionate brother,

R. Walton

Letter 2

To Mrs. Saville, England.

Archangel, 28th March, 17—.

How slowly the time passes here, encompassed as I am by frost and snow! Yet a second step is taken towards my enterprise. I have hired a vessel and am occupied in collecting my sailors; those whom I have already engaged appear to be men on whom I can depend and are certainly possessed of dauntless courage.

But I have one want which I have never yet been able to satisfy, and the absence of the object of which I now feel as a most severe evil, I have no friend, Margaret: when I am glowing with the enthusiasm of success, there will be none to participate my joy; if I am assailed by disappointment, no one will endeavour to sustain me in dejection. I shall commit my thoughts to paper, it is true; but that is a poor medium for the communication of feeling. I desire the company of a man who could sympathise with me, whose eyes would reply to mine. You may deem me romantic, my dear sister, but I bitterly feel the want of a friend. I have no one near me, gentle yet courageous, possessed of a cultivated as well as of a capacious mind, whose tastes are like my own, to approve or amend my plans. How would such a friend repair the faults of your poor brother! I am too ardent in execution and too impatient of difficulties. But it is a still greater evil to me that I am self-educated: for the first fourteen years of my life I ran wild on a common and read nothing but our Uncle Thomas' books of voyages. At that age I became acquainted with the celebrated poets of our own country; but it was only when it had ceased to be in my power to derive its most important benefits from such a conviction that I perceived the necessity of becoming acquainted with more languages than that of my native country. Now I am twenty-eight and am in reality more illiterate than many schoolboys of fifteen. It is true that I have thought more and that my daydreams are more extended and magnificent, but they want (as the painters call it) keeping; and I greatly need a friend who would have sense enough not to despise me as romantic, and affection enough for me to endeavour to regulate my mind.

Well, these are useless complaints; I shall certainly find no friend on the wide ocean, nor even here in Archangel, among merchants and seamen. Yet some feelings, unallied to the dross of human nature, beat even in these rugged bosoms. My

Frankenstein

lieutenant, for instance, is a man of wonderful courage and enterprise; he is madly desirous of glory, or rather, to word my phrase more characteristically, of advancement in his profession. He is an Englishman, and in the midst of national and professional prejudices, unsoftened by cultivation, retains some of the noblest endowments of humanity. I first became acquainted with him on board a whale vessel; finding that he was unemployed in this city, I easily engaged him to assist in my enterprise.

The master is a person of an excellent disposition and is remarkable in the ship for his gentleness and the mildness of his discipline. This circumstance, added to his well-known integrity and dauntless courage, made me very desirous to engage him. A youth passed in solitude, my best years spent under your gentle and feminine fosterage, has so refined the groundwork of my character that I cannot overcome an intense distaste to the usual brutality exercised on board ship: I have never believed it to be necessary, and when I heard of a mariner equally noted for his kindliness of heart and the respect and obedience paid to him by his crew, I felt myself peculiarly fortunate in being able to secure his services. I heard of him first in rather a romantic manner, from a lady who owes to him the happiness of her life. This, briefly, is his story. Some years ago he loved a young Russian lady of moderate fortune, and having amassed a considerable sum in prize-money, the father of the girl consented to the match. He saw his mistress once before the destined ceremony; but she was bathed in tears, and throwing herself at his feet, entreated him to spare her, confessing at the same time that she loved another, but that he was poor, and that her father would never consent to the union. My generous friend reassured the suppliant, and on being informed of the name of her lover, instantly abandoned his pursuit. He had already bought a farm with his money, on which he had designed to pass the remainder of his life; but he bestowed the whole on his rival, together with the remains of his prize-money to purchase stock, and then himself solicited the young woman's father to consent to her marriage with her lover. But the old man decidedly refused, thinking himself bound in honour to my friend, who, when he found the father inexorable, quitted his country, nor returned until he heard that his former mistress was married according to her inclinations. "What a noble fellow!" you will exclaim. He is so; but then he is wholly uneducated: he is as silent as a Turk, and a kind of ignorant carelessness attends him, which, while it renders his conduct the more astonishing, detracts from the interest and sympathy which otherwise he would command.

Frankenstein

Yet do not suppose, because I complain a little or because I can conceive a consolation for my toils which I may never know, that I am wavering in my resolutions. Those are as fixed as fate, and my voyage is only now delayed until the weather shall permit my embarkation. The winter has been dreadfully severe, but the spring promises well, and it is considered as a remarkably early season, so that perhaps I may sail sooner than I expected. I shall do nothing rashly: you know me sufficiently to confide in my prudence and considerateness whenever the safety of others is committed to my care.

I cannot describe to you my sensations on the near prospect of my undertaking. It is impossible to communicate to you a conception of the trembling sensation, half pleasurable and half fearful, with which I am preparing to depart. I am going to unexplored regions, to "the land of mist and snow," but I shall kill no albatross; therefore do not be alarmed for my safety or if I should come back to you as worn and woeful as the "Ancient Mariner." You will smile at my allusion, but I will disclose a secret. I have often attributed my attachment to, my passionate enthusiasm for, the dangerous mysteries of ocean to that production of the most imaginative of modern poets. There is something at work in my soul which I do not understand. I am practically industrious—painstaking, a workman to execute with perseverance and labour—but besides this there is a love for the marvellous, a belief in the marvellous, intertwined in all my projects, which hurries me out of the common pathways of men, even to the wild sea and unvisited regions I am about to explore.

But to return to dearer considerations. Shall I meet you again, after having traversed immense seas, and returned by the most southern cape of Africa or America? I dare not expect such success, yet I cannot bear to look on the reverse of the picture. Continue for the present to write to me by every opportunity: I may receive your letters on some occasions when I need them most to support my spirits. I love you very tenderly. Remember me with affection, should you never hear from me again.

Your affectionate brother,

Robert Walton

Letter 3

To Mrs. Saville, England.

July 7th, 17—.

My dear Sister,

I write a few lines in haste to say that I am safe—and well advanced on my voyage. This letter will reach England by a merchantman now on its homeward voyage from Archangel; more fortunate than I, who may not see my native land, perhaps, for many years. I am, however, in good spirits: my men are bold and apparently firm of purpose, nor do the floating sheets of ice that continually pass us, indicating the dangers of the region towards which we are advancing, appear to dismay them. We have already reached a very high latitude; but it is the height of summer, and although not so warm as in England, the southern gales, which blow us speedily towards those shores which I so ardently desire to attain, breathe a degree of renovating warmth which I had not expected.

No incidents have hitherto befallen us that would make a figure in a letter. One or two stiff gales and the springing of a leak are accidents which experienced navigators scarcely remember to record, and I shall be well content if nothing worse happen to us during our voyage.

Adieu, my dear Margaret. Be assured that for my own sake, as well as yours, I will not rashly encounter danger. I will be cool, persevering, and prudent.

But success shall crown my endeavours. Wherefore not? Thus far I have gone, tracing a secure way over the pathless seas, the very stars themselves being witnesses and testimonies of my triumph. Why not still proceed over the untamed yet obedient element? What can stop the determined heart and resolved will of man?

My swelling heart involuntarily pours itself out thus. But I must finish. Heaven bless my beloved sister!

R.W.

and
Letter 4

To Mrs. Saville, England.

August 5th, 17—.

So strange an accident has happened to us that I cannot forbear recording it, although it is very probable that you will see me before these papers can come into your possession.

Last Monday (July 31st) we were nearly surrounded by ice, which closed in the ship on all sides, scarcely leaving her the sea-room in which she floated. Our situation was somewhat dangerous, especially as we were compassed round by a very thick fog. We accordingly lay to, hoping that some change would take place in the atmosphere and weather.

About two o'clock the mist cleared away, and we beheld, stretched out in every direction, vast and irregular plains of ice, which seemed to have no end. Some of my comrades groaned, and my own mind began to grow watchful with anxious thoughts, when a strange sight suddenly attracted our attention and diverted our solicitude from our own situation. We perceived a low carriage, fixed on a sledge and drawn by dogs, pass on towards the north, at the distance of half a mile; a being which had the shape of a man, but apparently of gigantic stature, sat in the sledge and guided the dogs. We watched the rapid progress of the traveller with our telescopes until he was lost among the distant inequalities of the ice.

This appearance excited our unqualified wonder. We were, as we believed, many hundred miles from any land; but this apparition seemed to denote that it was not, in reality, so distant as we had supposed. Shut in, however, by ice, it was impossible to follow his track, which we had observed with the greatest attention.

About two hours after this occurrence we heard the ground sea, and before night the ice broke and freed our ship. We, however, lay to until the morning, fearing to encounter in the dark those large loose masses which float about after the breaking up of the ice. I profited of this time to rest for a few hours.

In the morning, however, as soon as it was light, I went upon deck and found all the sailors busy on one side of the vessel, apparently talking to someone in the sea. It was, in fact, a sledge, like that we had seen before, which had drifted towards us in the night on a large fragment of ice. Only one dog remained alive; but there was a human being within it whom the sailors were persuading to enter the vessel. He was not, as the other traveller seemed to be, a savage inhabitant of some undiscovered island, but a European. When I appeared on deck the master said, "Here is our captain, and he will not allow you to perish on the open sea."

On perceiving me, the stranger addressed me in English, although with a foreign accent. "Before I come on board your vessel," said he, "will you have the kindness to inform me whither you are bound?"

You may conceive my astonishment on hearing such a question addressed to me from a man on the brink of destruction and to whom I should have supposed that my vessel would have been a resource which he would not have exchanged for the most precious wealth the earth can afford. I replied, however, that we were on a voyage of discovery towards the northern pole.

Upon hearing this he appeared satisfied and consented to come on board. Good God! Margaret, if you had seen the man who thus capitulated for his safety, your surprise would have been boundless. His limbs were nearly frozen, and his body dreadfully emaciated by fatigue and suffering. I never saw a man in so wretched a condition. We attempted to carry him into the cabin, but as soon as he had quitted the fresh air he fainted. We accordingly brought him back to the deck and restored him to animation by rubbing him with brandy and forcing him to swallow a small quantity. As soon as he showed signs of life we wrapped him up in blankets and placed him near the chimney of the kitchen stove. By slow degrees he recovered and ate a little soup, which restored him wonderfully.

Two days passed in this manner before he was able to speak, and I often feared that his sufferings had deprived him of understanding. When he had in some measure recovered, I removed him to my own cabin and attended on him as much as my duty would permit. I never saw a more interesting creature: his eyes have generally an expression of wildness, and even madness, but there are moments when, if anyone performs an act of kindness towards him or does him any the most trifling service, his whole countenance is lighted up, as it were, with a beam of benevolence and sweetness that I never saw equalled. But he is generally melancholy and despairing, and sometimes he gnashes his teeth, as if impatient of the weight of woes that oppresses him.

Frankenstein

When my guest was a little recovered I had great trouble to keep off the men, who wished to ask him a thousand questions; but I would not allow him to be tormented by their idle curiosity, in a state of body and mind whose restoration evidently depended upon entire repose. Once, however, the lieutenant asked why he had come so far upon the ice in so strange a vehicle.

His countenance instantly assumed an aspect of the deepest gloom, and he replied, "To seek one who fled from me."

"And did the man whom you pursued travel in the same fashion?"

"Yes."

"Then I fancy we have seen him, for the day before we picked you up we saw some dogs drawing a sledge, with a man in it, across the ice."

This aroused the stranger's attention, and he asked a multitude of questions concerning the route which the dæmon, as he called him, had pursued. Soon after, when he was alone with me, he said, "I have, doubtless, excited your curiosity, as well as that of these good people; but you are too considerate to make inquiries."

"Certainly; it would indeed be very impertinent and inhuman in me to trouble you with any inquisitiveness of mine."

"And yet you rescued me from a strange and perilous situation; you have benevolently restored me to life."

Soon after this he inquired if I thought that the breaking up of the ice had destroyed the other sledge. I replied that I could not answer with any degree of certainty, for the ice had not broken until near midnight, and the traveller might have arrived at a place of safety before that time; but of this I could not judge.

From this time a new spirit of life animated the decaying frame of the stranger. He manifested the greatest eagerness to be upon deck to watch for the sledge which had before appeared; but I have persuaded him to remain in the cabin, for he is far too weak to sustain the rawness of the atmosphere. I have promised that someone should watch for him and give him instant notice if any new object should appear in sight.

Frankenstein

Such is my journal of what relates to this strange occurrence up to the present day. The stranger has gradually improved in health but is very silent and appears uneasy when anyone except myself enters his cabin. Yet his manners are so conciliating and gentle that the sailors are all interested in him, although they have had very little communication with him. For my own part, I begin to love him as a brother, and his constant and deep grief fills me with sympathy and compassion. He must have been a noble creature in his better days, being even now in wreck so attractive and amiable.

I said in one of my letters, my dear Margaret, that I should find no friend on the wide ocean; yet I have found a man who, before his spirit had been broken by misery, I should have been happy to have possessed as the brother of my heart.

I shall continue my journal concerning the stranger at intervals, should I have any fresh incidents to record.

August 13th, 17—.

My affection for my guest increases every day. He excites at once my admiration and my pity to an astonishing degree. How can I see so noble a creature destroyed by misery without feeling the most poignant grief? He is so gentle, yet so wise; his mind is so cultivated, and when he speaks, although his words are culled with the choicest art, yet they flow with rapidity and unparalleled eloquence.

He is now much recovered from his illness and is continually on the deck, apparently watching for the sledge that preceded his own. Yet, although unhappy, he is not so utterly occupied by his own misery but that he interests himself deeply in the projects of others. He has frequently conversed with me on mine, which I have communicated to him without disguise. He entered attentively into all my arguments in favour of my eventual success and into every minute detail of the measures I had taken to secure it. I was easily led by the sympathy which he evinced to use the language of my heart, to give utterance to the burning ardour of my soul and to say, with all the fervour that warmed me, how gladly I would sacrifice my fortune, my existence, my every hope, to the furtherance of my enterprise. One man's life or death were but a small price to pay for the acquirement of the knowledge which I sought, for the dominion I should acquire and transmit over the elemental foes of our race. As I spoke, a dark gloom spread over my listener's countenance. At first I perceived that he tried to suppress his emotion; he placed his hands before his eyes, and my voice

Frankenstein

quivered and failed me as I beheld tears trickle fast from between his fingers; a groan burst from his heaving breast. I paused; at length he spoke, in broken accents: "Unhappy man! Do you share my madness? Have you drunk also of the intoxicating draught? Hear me; let me reveal my tale, and you will dash the cup from your lips!"

Such words, you may imagine, strongly excited my curiosity; but the paroxysm of grief that had seized the stranger overcame his weakened powers, and many hours of repose and tranquil conversation were necessary to restore his composure.

Having conquered the violence of his feelings, he appeared to despise himself for being the slave of passion; and quelling the dark tyranny of despair, he led me again to converse concerning myself personally. He asked me the history of my earlier years. The tale was quickly told, but it awakened various trains of reflection. I spoke of my desire of finding a friend, of my thirst for a more intimate sympathy with a fellow mind than had ever fallen to my lot, and expressed my conviction that a man could boast of little happiness who did not enjoy this blessing.

"I agree with you," replied the stranger; "we are unfashioned creatures, but half made up, if one wiser, better, dearer than ourselves — such a friend ought to be — do not lend his aid to perfectionate our weak and faulty natures. I once had a friend, the most noble of human creatures, and am entitled, therefore, to judge respecting friendship. You have hope, and the world before you, and have no cause for despair. But I — I have lost everything and cannot begin life anew."

As he said this his countenance became expressive of a calm, settled grief that touched me to the heart. But he was silent and presently retired to his cabin.

Even broken in spirit as he is, no one can feel more deeply than he does the beauties of nature. The starry sky, the sea, and every sight afforded by these wonderful regions seem still to have the power of elevating his soul from earth. Such a man has a double existence: he may suffer misery and be overwhelmed by disappointments, yet when he has retired into himself, he will be like a celestial spirit that has a halo around him, within whose circle no grief or folly ventures.

Will you smile at the enthusiasm I express concerning this divine wanderer? You would not if you saw him. You have been tutored and refined by books and retirement from the world, and you are therefore somewhat fastidious; but this only renders you the more fit to appreciate the extraordinary merits of this wonderful man. Sometimes I have endeavoured to discover what quality it is which he possesses that elevates him so immeasurably above any other person I ever knew. I believe it to be an intuitive discernment, a quick but never-failing power of judgment, a penetration into the causes of things, unequalled for clearness and precision; add to this a facility of expression and a voice whose varied intonations are soul-subduing music.

August 19th, 17—.

Yesterday the stranger said to me, "You may easily perceive, Captain Walton, that I have suffered great and unparalleled misfortunes. I had determined at one time that the memory of these evils should die with me, but you have won me to alter my determination. You seek for knowledge and wisdom, as I once did; and I ardently hope that the gratification of your wishes may not be a serpent to sting you, as mine has been. I do not know that the relation of my disasters will be useful to you; yet, when I reflect that you are pursuing the same course, exposing yourself to the same dangers which have rendered me what I am, I imagine that you may deduce an apt moral from my tale, one that may direct you if you succeed in your undertaking and console you in case of failure. Prepare to hear of occurrences which are usually deemed marvellous. Were we among the tamer scenes of nature I might fear to encounter your unbelief, perhaps your ridicule; but many things will appear possible in these wild and mysterious regions which would provoke the laughter of those unacquainted with the ever-varied powers of nature; nor can I doubt but that my tale conveys in its series internal evidence of the truth of the events of which it is composed."

You may easily imagine that I was much gratified by the offered communication, yet I could not endure that he should renew his grief by a recital of his misfortunes. I felt the greatest eagerness to hear the promised narrative, partly from curiosity and partly from a strong desire to ameliorate his fate if it were in my power. I expressed these feelings in my answer.

"I thank you," he replied, "for your sympathy, but it is useless; my fate is nearly fulfilled. I wait but for one event, and then I shall repose in peace. I understand your feeling," continued he, perceiving that I wished to interrupt him; "but you are mistaken, my friend, if thus you will allow me to name you; nothing can alter my destiny; listen to my history, and you

Frankenstein

will perceive how irrevocably it is determined."

He then told me that he would commence his narrative the next day when I should be at leisure. This promise drew from me the warmest thanks. I have resolved every night, when I am not imperatively occupied by my duties, to record, as nearly as possible in his own words, what he has related during the day. If I should be engaged, I will at least make notes. This manuscript will doubtless afford you the greatest pleasure; but to me, who know him, and who hear it from his own lips — with what interest and sympathy shall I read it in some future day! Even now, as I commence my task, his full-toned voice swells in my ears; his lustrous eyes dwell on me with all their melancholy sweetness; I see his thin hand raised in animation, while the lineaments of his face are irradiated by the soul within. Strange and harrowing must be his story, frightful the storm which embraced the gallant vessel on its course and wrecked it — thus!

Chapter 1

I am by birth a Genevese, and my family is one of the most distinguished of that republic. My ancestors had been for many years counsellors and syndics, and my father had filled several public situations with honour and reputation. He was respected by all who knew him for his integrity and indefatigable attention to public business. He passed his younger days perpetually occupied by the affairs of his country; a variety of circumstances had prevented his marrying early, nor was it until the decline of life that he became a husband and the father of a family.

As the circumstances of his marriage illustrate his character, I cannot refrain from relating them. One of his most intimate friends was a merchant who, from a flourishing state, fell, through numerous mischances, into poverty. This man, whose name was Beaufort, was of a proud and unbending disposition and could not bear to live in poverty and oblivion in the same country where he had formerly been distinguished for his rank and magnificence. Having paid his debts, therefore, in the most honourable manner, he retreated with his daughter to the town of Lucerne, where he lived unknown and in wretchedness. My father loved Beaufort with the truest friendship and was deeply grieved by his retreat in these unfortunate circumstances. He bitterly deplored the false pride which led his friend to a conduct so little worthy of the affection that united them. He lost no time in endeavouring to seek him out, with the hope of persuading him to begin the world again through his credit and assistance.

Beaufort had taken effectual measures to conceal himself, and it was ten months before my father discovered his abode. Overjoyed at this discovery, he hastened to the house, which was situated in a mean street near the Reuss. But when he entered, misery and despair alone welcomed him. Beaufort had saved but a very small sum of money from the wreck of his fortunes, but it was sufficient to provide him with sustenance for some months, and in the meantime he hoped to procure some respectable employment in a merchant's house. The interval was, consequently, spent in inaction; his grief only became more deep and rankling when he had leisure for reflection, and at length it took so fast hold of his mind that at the end of three months he lay on a bed of sickness, incapable of any exertion.

Frankenstein

His daughter attended him with the greatest tenderness, but she saw with despair that their little fund was rapidly decreasing and that there was no other prospect of support. But Caroline Beaufort possessed a mind of an uncommon mould, and her courage rose to support her in her adversity. She procured plain work; she plaited straw and by various means contrived to earn a pittance scarcely sufficient to support life.

Several months passed in this manner. Her father grew worse; her time was more entirely occupied in attending him; her means of subsistence decreased; and in the tenth month her father died in her arms, leaving her an orphan and a beggar. This last blow overcame her, and she knelt by Beaufort's coffin weeping bitterly, when my father entered the chamber. He came like a protecting spirit to the poor girl, who committed herself to his care; and after the interment of his friend he conducted her to Geneva and placed her under the protection of a relation. Two years after this event Caroline became his wife.

There was a considerable difference between the ages of my parents, but this circumstance seemed to unite them only closer in bonds of devoted affection. There was a sense of justice in my father's upright mind which rendered it necessary that he should approve highly to love strongly. Perhaps during former years he had suffered from the late-discovered unworthiness of one beloved and so was disposed to set a greater value on tried worth. There was a show of gratitude and worship in his attachment to my mother, differing wholly from the doting fondness of age, for it was inspired by reverence for her virtues and a desire to be the means of, in some degree, recompensing her for the sorrows she had endured, but which gave inexpressible grace to his behaviour to her. Everything was made to yield to her wishes and her convenience. He strove to shelter her, as a fair exotic is sheltered by the gardener, from every rougher wind and to surround her with all that could tend to excite pleasurable emotion in her soft and benevolent mind. Her health, and even the tranquillity of her hitherto constant spirit, had been shaken by what she had gone through. During the two years that had elapsed previous to their marriage my father had gradually relinquished all his public functions; and immediately after their union they sought the pleasant climate of Italy, and the change of scene and interest attendant on a tour through that land of wonders, as a restorative for her weakened frame.

From Italy they visited Germany and France. I, their eldest child, was born at Naples, and as an infant accompanied them in their rambles. I remained for several years their only child.

Much as they were attached to each other, they seemed to draw inexhaustible stores of affection from a very mine of love to bestow them upon me. My mother's tender caresses and my father's smile of benevolent pleasure while regarding me are my first recollections. I was their plaything and their idol, and something better—their child, the innocent and helpless creature bestowed on them by Heaven, whom to bring up to good, and whose future lot it was in their hands to direct to happiness or misery, according as they fulfilled their duties towards me. With this deep consciousness of what they owed towards the being to which they had given life, added to the active spirit of tenderness that animated both, it may be imagined that while during every hour of my infant life I received a lesson of patience, of charity, and of self-control, I was so guided by a silken cord that all seemed but one train of enjoyment to me.

    For a long time I was their only care. My mother had much desired to have a daughter, but I continued their single offspring. When I was about five years old, while making an excursion beyond the frontiers of Italy, they passed a week on the shores of the Lake of Como. Their benevolent disposition often made them enter the cottages of the poor. This, to my mother, was more than a duty; it was a necessity, a passion—remembering what she had suffered, and how she had been relieved—for her to act in her turn the guardian angel to the afflicted. During one of their walks a poor cot in the foldings of a vale attracted their notice as being singularly disconsolate, while the number of half-clothed children gathered about it spoke of penury in its worst shape. One day, when my father had gone by himself to Milan, my mother, accompanied by me, visited this abode. She found a peasant and his wife, hard working, bent down by care and labour, distributing a scanty meal to five hungry babes. Among these there was one which attracted my mother far above all the rest. She appeared of a different stock. The four others were dark-eyed, hardy little vagrants; this child was thin and very fair. Her hair was the brightest living gold, and despite the poverty of her clothing, seemed to set a crown of distinction on her head. Her brow was clear and ample, her blue eyes cloudless, and her lips and the moulding of her face so expressive of sensibility and sweetness that none could behold her without looking on her as of a distinct species, a being heaven-sent, and bearing a celestial stamp in all her features.

    The peasant woman, perceiving that my mother fixed eyes of wonder and admiration on this lovely girl, eagerly communicated her history. She was not her child, but the daughter of a Milanese nobleman. Her mother was a German and had died on giving her birth. The infant had been placed with these good people to nurse: they were better off then. They had not been long married, and their eldest child was but just born. The father of their charge was one of those Italians nursed in the memory of the antique glory of Italy—one among the schiavi ognor frementi, who exerted himself to obtain the liberty of his country. He became the victim of its weakness. Whether he had died or still lingered in the dungeons of Austria was not known. His property was confiscated; his child became an orphan and a beggar. She continued with her foster parents and bloomed in their rude abode, fairer than a garden rose among dark-leaved brambles.

When my father returned from Milan, he found playing with me in the hall of our villa a child fairer than pictured cherub—a creature who seemed to shed radiance from her looks and whose form and motions were lighter than the chamois of the hills. The apparition was soon explained. With his permission my mother prevailed on her rustic guardians to yield their charge to her. They were fond of the sweet orphan. Her presence had seemed a blessing to them, but it would be unfair to her to keep her in poverty and want when Providence afforded her such powerful protection. They consulted their village priest, and the result was that Elizabeth Lavenza became the inmate of my parents' house—my more than sister—the beautiful and adored companion of all my occupations and my pleasures.

Everyone loved Elizabeth. The passionate and almost reverential attachment with which all regarded her became, while I shared it, my pride and my delight. On the evening previous to her being brought to my home, my mother had said playfully, "I have a pretty present for my Victor—tomorrow he shall have it." And when, on the morrow, she presented Elizabeth to me as her promised gift, I, with childish seriousness, interpreted her words literally and looked upon Elizabeth as mine—mine to protect, love, and cherish. All praises bestowed on her I received as made to a possession of my own. We called each other familiarly by the name of cousin. No word, no expression could body forth the kind of relation in which she stood to me—my more than sister, since till death she was to be mine only.

Chapter 2

We were brought up together; there was not quite a year difference in our ages. I need not say that we were strangers to any species of disunion or dispute. Harmony was the soul of our companionship, and the diversity and contrast that subsisted in our characters drew us nearer together. Elizabeth was of a calmer and more concentrated disposition; but, with all my ardour, I was capable of a more intense application and was more deeply smitten with the thirst for knowledge. She busied herself with following the aerial creations of the poets; and in the majestic and wondrous scenes which surrounded our Swiss home — the sublime shapes of the mountains, the changes of the seasons, tempest and calm, the silence of winter, and the life and turbulence of our Alpine summers — she found ample scope for admiration and delight. While my companion contemplated with a serious and satisfied spirit the magnificent appearances of things, I delighted in investigating their causes. The world was to me a secret which I desired to divine. Curiosity, earnest research to learn the hidden laws of nature, gladness akin to rapture, as they were unfolded to me, are among the earliest sensations I can remember.

On the birth of a second son, my junior by seven years, my parents gave up entirely their wandering life and fixed themselves in their native country. We possessed a house in Geneva, and a campagne on Belrive, the eastern shore of the lake, at the distance of rather more than a league from the city. We resided principally in the latter, and the lives of my parents were passed in considerable seclusion. It was my temper to avoid a crowd and to attach myself fervently to a few. I was indifferent, therefore, to my school-fellows in general; but I united myself in the bonds of the closest friendship to one among them. Henry Clerval was the son of a merchant of Geneva. He was a boy of singular talent and fancy. He loved enterprise, hardship, and even danger for its own sake. He was deeply read in books of chivalry and romance. He composed heroic songs and began to write many a tale of enchantment and knightly adventure. He tried to make us act plays and to enter into masquerades, in which the characters were drawn from the heroes of Roncesvalles, of the Round Table of King Arthur, and the chivalrous train who shed their blood to redeem the holy sepulchre from the hands of the infidels.

No human being could have passed a happier childhood than myself. My parents were possessed by the very spirit of kindness and indulgence. We felt that they were not the tyrants to rule our lot according to their caprice, but the agents and

Frankenstein

creators of all the many delights which we enjoyed. When I mingled with other families I distinctly discerned how peculiarly fortunate my lot was, and gratitude assisted the development of filial love.

My temper was sometimes violent, and my passions vehement; but by some law in my temperature they were turned not towards childish pursuits but to an eager desire to learn, and not to learn all things indiscriminately. I confess that neither the structure of languages, nor the code of governments, nor the politics of various states possessed attractions for me. It was the secrets of heaven and earth that I desired to learn; and whether it was the outward substance of things or the inner spirit of nature and the mysterious soul of man that occupied me, still my inquiries were directed to the metaphysical, or in its highest sense, the physical secrets of the world.

Meanwhile Clerval occupied himself, so to speak, with the moral relations of things. The busy stage of life, the virtues of heroes, and the actions of men were his theme; and his hope and his dream was to become one among those whose names are recorded in story as the gallant and adventurous benefactors of our species. The saintly soul of Elizabeth shone like a shrine-dedicated lamp in our peaceful home. Her sympathy was ours; her smile, her soft voice, the sweet glance of her celestial eyes, were ever there to bless and animate us. She was the living spirit of love to soften and attract; I might have become sullen in my study, rough through the ardour of my nature, but that she was there to subdue me to a semblance of her own gentleness. And Clerval—could aught ill entrench on the noble spirit of Clerval? Yet he might not have been so perfectly humane, so thoughtful in his generosity, so full of kindness and tenderness amidst his passion for adventurous exploit, had she not unfolded to him the real loveliness of beneficence and made the doing good the end and aim of his soaring ambition.

I feel exquisite pleasure in dwelling on the recollections of childhood, before misfortune had tainted my mind and changed its bright visions of extensive usefulness into gloomy and narrow reflections upon self. Besides, in drawing the picture of my early days, I also record those events which led, by insensible steps, to my after tale of misery, for when I would account to myself for the birth of that passion which afterwards ruled my destiny I find it arise, like a mountain river, from ignoble and almost forgotten sources; but, swelling as it proceeded, it became the torrent which, in its course, has swept away all my hopes and joys.

Natural philosophy is the genius that has regulated my fate; I desire, therefore, in this narration, to state those facts which led to my predilection for that science. When I was thirteen years of age we all went on a party of pleasure to the baths near Thonon; the inclemency of the weather obliged us to remain a day confined to the inn. In this house I chanced to find a volume of the works of Cornelius Agrippa. I opened it with apathy; the theory which he attempts to demonstrate and the wonderful facts which he relates soon changed this feeling into enthusiasm. A new light seemed to dawn upon my mind, and bounding with joy, I communicated my discovery to my father. My father looked carelessly at the title page of my book and said, "Ah! Cornelius Agrippa! My dear Victor, do not waste your time upon this; it is sad trash."

If, instead of this remark, my father had taken the pains to explain to me that the principles of Agrippa had been entirely exploded and that a modern system of science had been introduced which possessed much greater powers than the ancient, because the powers of the latter were chimerical, while those of the former were real and practical, under such circumstances I should certainly have thrown Agrippa aside and have contented my imagination, warmed as it was, by returning with greater ardour to my former studies. It is even possible that the train of my ideas would never have received the fatal impulse that led to my ruin. But the cursory glance my father had taken of my volume by no means assured me that he was acquainted with its contents, and I continued to read with the greatest avidity.

When I returned home my first care was to procure the whole works of this author, and afterwards of Paracelsus and Albertus Magnus. I read and studied the wild fancies of these writers with delight; they appeared to me treasures known to few besides myself. I have described myself as always having been imbued with a fervent longing to penetrate the secrets of nature. In spite of the intense labour and wonderful discoveries of modern philosophers, I always came from my studies discontented and unsatisfied. Sir Isaac Newton is said to have avowed that he felt like a child picking up shells beside the great and unexplored ocean of truth. Those of his successors in each branch of natural philosophy with whom I was acquainted appeared even to my boy's apprehensions as tyros engaged in the same pursuit.

The untaught peasant beheld the elements around him and was acquainted with their practical uses. The most learned philosopher knew little more. He had partially unveiled the face

Frankenstein

of Nature, but her immortal lineaments were still a wonder and a mystery. He might dissect, anatomise, and give names; but, not to speak of a final cause, causes in their secondary and tertiary grades were utterly unknown to him. I had gazed upon the fortifications and impediments that seemed to keep human beings from entering the citadel of nature, and rashly and ignorantly I had repined.

But here were books, and here were men who had penetrated deeper and knew more. I took their word for all that they averred, and I became their disciple. It may appear strange that such should arise in the eighteenth century; but while I followed the routine of education in the schools of Geneva, I was, to a great degree, self-taught with regard to my favourite studies. My father was not scientific, and I was left to struggle with a child's blindness, added to a student's thirst for knowledge. Under the guidance of my new preceptors I entered with the greatest diligence into the search of the philosopher's stone and the elixir of life; but the latter soon obtained my undivided attention. Wealth was an inferior object, but what glory would attend the discovery if I could banish disease from the human frame and render man invulnerable to any but a violent death!

Nor were these my only visions. The raising of ghosts or devils was a promise liberally accorded by my favourite authors, the fulfilment of which I most eagerly sought; and if my incantations were always unsuccessful, I attributed the failure rather to my own inexperience and mistake than to a want of skill or fidelity in my instructors. And thus for a time I was occupied by exploded systems, mingling, like an unadept, a thousand contradictory theories and floundering desperately in a very slough of multifarious knowledge, guided by an ardent imagination and childish reasoning, till an accident again changed the current of my ideas.

When I was about fifteen years old we had retired to our house near Belrive, when we witnessed a most violent and terrible thunderstorm. It advanced from behind the mountains of Jura, and the thunder burst at once with frightful loudness from various quarters of the heavens. I remained, while the storm lasted, watching its progress with curiosity and delight. As I stood at the door, on a sudden I beheld a stream of fire issue from an old and beautiful oak which stood about twenty yards from our house; and so soon as the dazzling light vanished, the oak had disappeared, and nothing remained but a blasted stump. When we visited it the next morning, we found the tree shattered in a singular manner. It was not splintered by the shock, but entirely reduced to thin ribbons of wood. I never beheld anything so utterly destroyed.

Before this I was not unacquainted with the more obvious laws of electricity. On this occasion a man of great research in natural philosophy was with us, and excited by this catastrophe, he entered on the explanation of a theory which he had formed on the subject of electricity and galvanism, which was at once new and astonishing to me. All that he said threw greatly into the shade Cornelius Agrippa, Albertus Magnus, and Paracelsus, the lords of my imagination; but by some fatality the overthrow of these men disinclined me to pursue my accustomed studies. It seemed to me as if nothing would or could ever be known. All that had so long engaged my attention suddenly grew despicable. By one of those caprices of the mind which we are perhaps most subject to in early youth, I at once gave up my former occupations, set down natural history and all its progeny as a deformed and abortive creation, and entertained the greatest disdain for a would-be science which could never even step within the threshold of real knowledge. In this mood of mind I betook myself to the mathematics and the branches of study appertaining to that science as being built upon secure foundations, and so worthy of my consideration.

Thus strangely are our souls constructed, and by such slight ligaments are we bound to prosperity or ruin. When I look back, it seems to me as if this almost miraculous change of inclination and will was the immediate suggestion of the guardian angel of my life — the last effort made by the spirit of preservation to avert the storm that was even then hanging in the stars and ready to envelop me. Her victory was announced by an unusual tranquillity and gladness of soul which followed the relinquishing of my ancient and latterly tormenting studies. It was thus that I was to be taught to associate evil with their prosecution, happiness with their disregard.

It was a strong effort of the spirit of good, but it was ineffectual. Destiny was too potent, and her immutable laws had decreed my utter and terrible destruction.

Chapter 3

When I had attained the age of seventeen my parents resolved that I should become a student at the university of Ingolstadt. I had hitherto attended the schools of Geneva, but my father thought it necessary for the completion of my education that I should be made acquainted with other customs than those of my native country. My departure was therefore fixed at an early date, but before the day resolved upon could arrive, the first misfortune of my life occurred—an omen, as it were, of my future misery.

Elizabeth had caught the scarlet fever; her illness was severe, and she was in the greatest danger. During her illness many arguments had been urged to persuade my mother to refrain from attending upon her. She had at first yielded to our entreaties, but when she heard that the life of her favourite was menaced, she could no longer control her anxiety. She attended her sickbed; her watchful attentions triumphed over the malignity of the distemper—Elizabeth was saved, but the consequences of this imprudence were fatal to her preserver. On the third day my mother sickened; her fever was accompanied by the most alarming symptoms, and the looks of her medical attendants prognosticated the worst event. On her deathbed the fortitude and benignity of this best of women did not desert her. She joined the hands of Elizabeth and myself. "My children," she said, "my firmest hopes of future happiness were placed on the prospect of your union. This expectation will now be the consolation of your father. Elizabeth, my love, you must supply my place to my younger children. Alas! I regret that I am taken from you; and, happy and beloved as I have been, is it not hard to quit you all? But these are not thoughts befitting me; I will endeavour to resign myself cheerfully to death and will indulge a hope of meeting you in another world."

She died calmly, and her countenance expressed affection even in death. I need not describe the feelings of those whose dearest ties are rent by that most irreparable evil, the void that presents itself to the soul, and the despair that is exhibited on the countenance. It is so long before the mind can persuade itself that she whom we saw every day and whose very existence appeared a part of our own can have departed for ever—that the brightness of a beloved eye can have been extinguished and the sound of a voice so familiar and dear to the ear can be hushed, never more to be heard. These are the reflections of the first days; but when the lapse of time proves the reality of the evil, then the actual bitterness of grief commences. Yet from whom has not that rude hand rent away some dear connection? And why should I describe a sorrow which all have felt, and must feel? The time at length arrives when grief is rather an indulgence than a necessity; and the smile that plays upon the lips, although it may be deemed a sacrilege, is not banished. My mother was dead, but we had still duties which we ought to perform; we must continue our course with the rest and learn to think ourselves fortunate whilst one remains whom the spoiler has not seized.

My departure for Ingolstadt, which had been deferred by these events, was now again determined upon. I obtained from my father a respite of some weeks. It appeared to me sacrilege so soon to leave the repose, akin to death, of the house of mourning and to rush into the thick of life. I was new to sorrow, but it did not the less alarm me. I was unwilling to quit the sight of those that remained to me, and above all, I desired to see my sweet Elizabeth in some degree consoled.

She indeed veiled her grief and strove to act the comforter to us all. She looked steadily on life and assumed its duties with courage and zeal. She devoted herself to those whom she had been taught to call her uncle and cousins. Never was she so enchanting as at this time, when she recalled the sunshine of her smiles and spent them upon us. She forgot even her own regret in her endeavours to make us forget.

The day of my departure at length arrived. Clerval spent the last evening with us. He had endeavoured to persuade his father to permit him to accompany me and to become my fellow student, but in vain. His father was a narrow-minded trader and saw idleness and ruin in the aspirations and ambition of his son. Henry deeply felt the misfortune of being debarred from a liberal education. He said little, but when he spoke I read in his kindling eye and in his animated glance a restrained but firm resolve not to be chained to the miserable details of commerce.

We sat late. We could not tear ourselves away from each other nor persuade ourselves to say the word "Farewell!" It was said, and we retired under the pretence of seeking repose, each fancying that the other was deceived; but when at morning's dawn I descended to the carriage which was to convey me away, they were all there—my father again to bless me, Clerval to press my hand once more, my Elizabeth to renew her entreaties that I would write often and to bestow the last feminine attentions on her playmate and friend.

Frankenstein

I threw myself into the chaise that was to convey me away and indulged in the most melancholy reflections. I, who had ever been surrounded by amiable companions, continually engaged in endeavouring to bestow mutual pleasure—I was now alone. In the university whither I was going I must form my own friends and be my own protector. My life had hitherto been remarkably secluded and domestic, and this had given me invincible repugnance to new countenances. I loved my brothers, Elizabeth, and Clerval; these were "old familiar faces," but I believed myself totally unfitted for the company of strangers. Such were my reflections as I commenced my journey; but as I proceeded, my spirits and hopes rose. I ardently desired the acquisition of knowledge. I had often, when at home, thought it hard to remain during my youth cooped up in one place and had longed to enter the world and take my station among other human beings. Now my desires were complied with, and it would, indeed, have been folly to repent.

I had sufficient leisure for these and many other reflections during my journey to Ingolstadt, which was long and fatiguing. At length the high white steeple of the town met my eyes. I alighted and was conducted to my solitary apartment to spend the evening as I pleased.

The next morning I delivered my letters of introduction and paid a visit to some of the principal professors. Chance—or rather the evil influence, the Angel of Destruction, which asserted omnipotent sway over me from the moment I turned my reluctant steps from my father's door—led me first to M. Krempe, professor of natural philosophy. He was an uncouth man, but deeply imbued in the secrets of his science. He asked me several questions concerning my progress in the different branches of science appertaining to natural philosophy. I replied carelessly, and partly in contempt, mentioned the names of my alchemists as the principal authors I had studied. The professor stared. "Have you," he said, "really spent your time in studying such nonsense?"

I replied in the affirmative. "Every minute," continued M. Krempe with warmth, "every instant that you have wasted on those books is utterly and entirely lost. You have burdened your memory with exploded systems and useless names. Good God! In what desert land have you lived, where no one was kind enough to inform you that these fancies which you have so greedily imbibed are a thousand years old and as musty as they are ancient? I little expected, in this enlightened and scientific age, to find a disciple of Albertus Magnus and Paracelsus. My dear sir, you must begin your studies entirely anew."

So saying, he stepped aside and wrote down a list of several books treating of natural philosophy which he desired me to procure, and dismissed me after mentioning that in the beginning of the following week he intended to commence a course of lectures upon natural philosophy in its general relations, and that M. Waldman, a fellow professor, would lecture upon chemistry the alternate days that he omitted.

I returned home not disappointed, for I have said that I had long considered those authors useless whom the professor reprobated; but I returned not at all the more inclined to recur to these studies in any shape. M. Krempe was a little squat man with a gruff voice and a repulsive countenance; the teacher, therefore, did not prepossess me in favour of his pursuits. In rather a too philosophical and connected a strain, perhaps, I have given an account of the conclusions I had come to concerning them in my early years. As a child I had not been content with the results promised by the modern professors of natural science. With a confusion of ideas only to be accounted for by my extreme youth and my want of a guide on such matters, I had retrod the steps of knowledge along the paths of time and exchanged the discoveries of recent inquirers for the dreams of forgotten alchemists. Besides, I had a contempt for the uses of modern natural philosophy. It was very different when the masters of the science sought immortality and power; such views, although futile, were grand; but now the scene was changed. The ambition of the inquirer seemed to limit itself to the annihilation of those visions on which my interest in science was chiefly founded. I was required to exchange chimeras of boundless grandeur for realities of little worth.

Such were my reflections during the first two or three days of my residence at Ingolstadt, which were chiefly spent in becoming acquainted with the localities and the principal residents in my new abode. But as the ensuing week commenced, I thought of the information which M. Krempe had given me concerning the lectures. And although I could not consent to go and hear that little conceited fellow deliver sentences out of a pulpit, I recollected what he had said of M. Waldman, whom I had never seen, as he had hitherto been out of town.

Partly from curiosity and partly from idleness, I went into the lecturing room, which M. Waldman entered shortly after. This professor was very unlike his colleague. He appeared about fifty years of age, but with an aspect expressive of the

Frankenstein

greatest benevolence; a few grey hairs covered his temples, but those at the back of his head were nearly black. His person was short but remarkably erect and his voice the sweetest I had ever heard. He began his lecture by a recapitulation of the history of chemistry and the various improvements made by different men of learning, pronouncing with fervour the names of the most distinguished discoverers. He then took a cursory view of the present state of the science and explained many of its elementary terms. After having made a few preparatory experiments, he concluded with a panegyric upon modern chemistry, the terms of which I shall never forget:

"The ancient teachers of this science," said he, "promised impossibilities and performed nothing. The modern masters promise very little; they know that metals cannot be transmuted and that the elixir of life is a chimera but these philosophers, whose hands seem only made to dabble in dirt, and their eyes to pore over the microscope or crucible, have indeed performed miracles. They penetrate into the recesses of nature and show how she works in her hiding-places. They ascend into the heavens; they have discovered how the blood circulates, and the nature of the air we breathe. They have acquired new and almost unlimited powers; they can command the thunders of heaven, mimic the earthquake, and even mock the invisible world with its own shadows."

Such were the professor's words—rather let me say such the words of the fate—enounced to destroy me. As he went on I felt as if my soul were grappling with a palpable enemy; one by one the various keys were touched which formed the mechanism of my being; chord after chord was sounded, and soon my mind was filled with one thought, one conception, one purpose. So much has been done, exclaimed the soul of Frankenstein— more, far more, will I achieve; treading in the steps already marked, I will pioneer a new way, explore unknown powers, and unfold to the world the deepest mysteries of creation.

I closed not my eyes that night. My internal being was in a state of insurrection and turmoil; I felt that order would thence arise, but I had no power to produce it. By degrees, after the morning's dawn, sleep came. I awoke, and my yesternight's thoughts were as a dream. There only remained a resolution to return to my ancient studies and to devote myself to a science for which I believed myself to possess a natural talent. On the same day I paid M. Waldman a visit. His manners in private were even more mild and attractive than in public, for there was a certain dignity in his mien during his lecture which in his own house was replaced by the greatest affability and kindness. I gave him pretty nearly the same account of my former pursuits as I had given to his fellow professor. He heard with attention the little narration concerning my studies and smiled at the names of Cornelius Agrippa and Paracelsus, but without the contempt that M. Krempe had exhibited. He said that "These were men to whose indefatigable zeal modern philosophers were indebted for most of the foundations of their knowledge. They had left to us, as an easier task, to give new names and arrange in connected classifications the facts which they in a great degree had been the instruments of bringing to light. The labours of men of genius, however erroneously directed, scarcely ever fail in ultimately turning to the solid advantage of mankind." I listened to his statement, which was delivered without any presumption or affectation, and then added that his lecture had removed my prejudices against modern chemists; I expressed myself in measured terms, with the modesty and deference due from a youth to his instructor, without letting escape (inexperience in life would have made me ashamed) any of the enthusiasm which stimulated my intended labours. I requested his advice concerning the books I ought to procure.

"I am happy," said M. Waldman, "to have gained a disciple; and if your application equals your ability, I have no doubt of your success. Chemistry is that branch of natural philosophy in which the greatest improvements have been and may be made; it is on that account that I have made it my peculiar study; but at the same time, I have not neglected the other branches of science. A man would make but a very sorry chemist if he attended to that department of human knowledge alone. If your wish is to become really a man of science and not merely a petty experimentalist, I should advise you to apply to every branch of natural philosophy, including mathematics."

He then took me into his laboratory and explained to me the uses of his various machines, instructing me as to what I ought to procure and promising me the use of his own when I should have advanced far enough in the science not to derange their mechanism. He also gave me the list of books which I had requested, and I took my leave.

Thus ended a day memorable to me; it decided my future destiny.

Chapter 4

From this day natural philosophy, and particularly chemistry, in the most comprehensive sense of the term, became nearly my sole occupation. I read with ardour those works, so full of genius and discrimination, which modern inquirers have written on these subjects. I attended the lectures and cultivated the acquaintance of the men of science of the university, and I found even in M. Krempe a great deal of sound sense and real information, combined, it is true, with a repulsive physiognomy and manners, but not on that account the less valuable. In M. Waldman I found a true friend. His gentleness was never tinged by dogmatism, and his instructions were given with an air of frankness and good nature that banished every idea of pedantry. In a thousand ways he smoothed for me the path of knowledge and made the most abstruse inquiries clear and facile to my apprehension. My application was at first fluctuating and uncertain; it gained strength as I proceeded and soon became so ardent and eager that the stars often disappeared in the light of morning whilst I was yet engaged in my laboratory.

As I applied so closely, it may be easily conceived that my progress was rapid. My ardour was indeed the astonishment of the students, and my proficiency that of the masters. Professor Krempe often asked me, with a sly smile, how Cornelius Agrippa went on, whilst M. Waldman expressed the most heartfelt exultation in my progress. Two years passed in this manner, during which I paid no visit to Geneva, but was engaged, heart and soul, in the pursuit of some discoveries which I hoped to make. None but those who have experienced them can conceive of the enticements of science. In other studies you go as far as others have gone before you, and there is nothing more to know; but in a scientific pursuit there is continual food for discovery and wonder. A mind of moderate capacity which closely pursues one study must infallibly arrive at great proficiency in that study; and I, who continually sought the attainment of one object of pursuit and was solely wrapped up in this, improved so rapidly that at the end of two years I made some discoveries in the improvement of some chemical instruments, which procured me great esteem and admiration at the university. When I had arrived at this point and had become as well acquainted with the theory and practice of natural philosophy as depended on the lessons of any of the professors at Ingolstadt, my residence there being no longer conducive to my improvements, I thought of returning to my friends and my native town, when an incident happened that protracted my stay.

Frankenstein

One of the phenomena which had peculiarly attracted my attention was the structure of the human frame, and, indeed, any animal endued with life. Whence, I often asked myself, did the principle of life proceed? It was a bold question, and one which has ever been considered as a mystery; yet with how many things are we upon the brink of becoming acquainted, if cowardice or carelessness did not restrain our inquiries. I revolved these circumstances in my mind and determined thenceforth to apply myself more particularly to those branches of natural philosophy which relate to physiology. Unless I had been animated by an almost supernatural enthusiasm, my application to this study would have been irksome and almost intolerable. To examine the causes of life, we must first have recourse to death. I became acquainted with the science of anatomy, but this was not sufficient; I must also observe the natural decay and corruption of the human body. In my education my father had taken the greatest precautions that my mind should be impressed with no supernatural horrors. I do not ever remember to have trembled at a tale of superstition or to have feared the apparition of a spirit. Darkness had no effect upon my fancy, and a churchyard was to me merely the receptacle of bodies deprived of life, which, from being the seat of beauty and strength, had become food for the worm. Now I was led to examine the cause and progress of this decay and forced to spend days and nights in vaults and charnel-houses. My attention was fixed upon every object the most insupportable to the delicacy of the human feelings. I saw how the fine form of man was degraded and wasted; I beheld the corruption of death succeed to the blooming cheek of life; I saw how the worm inherited the wonders of the eye and brain. I paused, examining and analysing all the minutiae of causation, as exemplified in the change from life to death, and death to life, until from the midst of this darkness a sudden light broke in upon me—a light so brilliant and wondrous, yet so simple, that while I became dizzy with the immensity of the prospect which it illustrated, I was surprised that among so many men of genius who had directed their inquiries towards the same science, that I alone should be reserved to discover so astonishing a secret.

Remember, I am not recording the vision of a madman. The sun does not more certainly shine in the heavens than that which I now affirm is true. Some miracle might have produced it, yet the stages of the discovery were distinct and probable. After days and nights of incredible labour and fatigue, I succeeded in discovering the cause of generation and life; nay, more, I became myself capable of bestowing animation upon lifeless matter.

Frankenstein

The astonishment which I had at first experienced on this discovery soon gave place to delight and rapture. After so much time spent in painful labour, to arrive at once at the summit of my desires was the most gratifying consummation of my toils. But this discovery was so great and overwhelming that all the steps by which I had been progressively led to it were obliterated, and I beheld only the result. What had been the study and desire of the wisest men since the creation of the world was now within my grasp. Not that, like a magic scene, it all opened upon me at once: the information I had obtained was of a nature rather to direct my endeavours so soon as I should point them towards the object of my search than to exhibit that object already accomplished. I was like the Arabian who had been buried with the dead and found a passage to life, aided only by one glimmering and seemingly ineffectual light.

I see by your eagerness and the wonder and hope which your eyes express, my friend, that you expect to be informed of the secret with which I am acquainted; that cannot be; listen patiently until the end of my story, and you will easily perceive why I am reserved upon that subject. I will not lead you on, unguarded and ardent as I then was, to your destruction and infallible misery. Learn from me, if not by my precepts, at least by my example, how dangerous is the acquirement of knowledge and how much happier that man is who believes his native town to be the world, than he who aspires to become greater than his nature will allow.

When I found so astonishing a power placed within my hands, I hesitated a long time concerning the manner in which I should employ it. Although I possessed the capacity of bestowing animation, yet to prepare a frame for the reception of it, with all its intricacies of fibres, muscles, and veins, still remained a work of inconceivable difficulty and labour. I doubted at first whether I should attempt the creation of a being like myself, or one of simpler organization; but my imagination was too much exalted by my first success to permit me to doubt of my ability to give life to an animal as complex and wonderful as man. The materials at present within my command hardly appeared adequate to so arduous an undertaking, but I doubted not that I should ultimately succeed. I prepared myself for a multitude of reverses; my operations might be incessantly baffled, and at last my work be imperfect, yet when I considered the improvement which every day takes place in science and mechanics, I was encouraged to hope my present attempts would at least lay the foundations of future success. Nor could I consider the magnitude and complexity of my plan as any argument of its impracticability. It was with these feelings that I began the creation of a human being. As the minuteness of the parts formed a great hindrance to my speed, I resolved, contrary to my first intention, to make the being of a gigantic stature, that is to say, about eight feet in height, and proportionably large. After having formed this determination and having spent some months in successfully collecting and arranging my materials, I began.

No one can conceive the variety of feelings which bore me onwards, like a hurricane, in the first enthusiasm of success. Life and death appeared to me ideal bounds, which I should first break through, and pour a torrent of light into our dark world. A new species would bless me as its creator and source; many happy and excellent natures would owe their being to me. No father could claim the gratitude of his child so completely as I should deserve theirs. Pursuing these reflections, I thought that if I could bestow animation upon lifeless matter, I might in process of time (although I now found it impossible) renew life where death had apparently devoted the body to corruption.

These thoughts supported my spirits, while I pursued my undertaking with unremitting ardour. My cheek had grown pale with study, and my person had become emaciated with confinement. Sometimes, on the very brink of certainty, I failed; yet still I clung to the hope which the next day or the next hour might realise. One secret which I alone possessed was the hope to which I had dedicated myself; and the moon gazed on my midnight labours, while, with unrelaxed and breathless eagerness, I pursued nature to her hiding-places. Who shall conceive the horrors of my secret toil as I dabbled among the unhallowed damps of the grave or tortured the living animal to animate the lifeless clay? My limbs now tremble, and my eyes swim with the remembrance; but then a resistless and almost frantic impulse urged me forward; I seemed to have lost all soul or sensation but for this one pursuit. It was indeed but a passing trance, that only made me feel with renewed acuteness so soon as, the unnatural stimulus ceasing to operate, I had returned to my old habits. I collected bones from charnel-houses and disturbed, with profane fingers, the tremendous secrets of the human frame. In a solitary chamber, or rather cell, at the top of the house, and separated from all the other apartments by a gallery and staircase, I kept my workshop of filthy creation; my eyeballs were starting from their sockets in attending to the details of my employment. The dissecting room and the slaughter-house furnished many of my materials; and often did my human nature turn with loathing from my occupation, whilst, still urged on by an eagerness which perpetually increased, I brought my work near to a conclusion.

Frankenstein

The summer months passed while I was thus engaged, heart and soul, in one pursuit. It was a most beautiful season; never did the fields bestow a more plentiful harvest or the vines yield a more luxuriant vintage, but my eyes were insensible to the charms of nature. And the same feelings which made me neglect the scenes around me caused me also to forget those friends who were so many miles absent, and whom I had not seen for so long a time. I knew my silence disquieted them, and I well remembered the words of my father: "I know that while you are pleased with yourself you will think of us with affection, and we shall hear regularly from you. You must pardon me if I regard any interruption in your correspondence as a proof that your other duties are equally neglected."

I knew well therefore what would be my father's feelings, but I could not tear my thoughts from my employment, loathsome in itself, but which had taken an irresistible hold of my imagination. I wished, as it were, to procrastinate all that related to my feelings of affection until the great object, which swallowed up every habit of my nature, should be completed.

I then thought that my father would be unjust if he ascribed my neglect to vice or faultiness on my part, but I am now convinced that he was justified in conceiving that I should not be altogether free from blame. A human being in perfection ought always to preserve a calm and peaceful mind and never to allow passion or a transitory desire to disturb his tranquillity. I do not think that the pursuit of knowledge is an exception to this rule. If the study to which you apply yourself has a tendency to weaken your affections and to destroy your taste for those simple pleasures in which no alloy can possibly mix, then that study is certainly unlawful, that is to say, not befitting the human mind. If this rule were always observed; if no man allowed any pursuit whatsoever to interfere with the tranquillity of his domestic affections, Greece had not been enslaved, Cæsar would have spared his country, America would have been discovered more gradually, and the empires of Mexico and Peru had not been destroyed.

But I forget that I am moralizing in the most interesting part of my tale, and your looks remind me to proceed.

My father made no reproach in his letters and only took notice of my silence by inquiring into my occupations more particularly than before. Winter, spring, and summer passed away during my labours; but I did not watch the blossom or the expanding leaves—sights which before always yielded me supreme delight—so deeply was I engrossed in my occupation.

The leaves of that year had withered before my work drew near to a close, and now every day showed me more plainly how well I had succeeded. But my enthusiasm was checked by my anxiety, and I appeared rather like one doomed by slavery to toil in the mines, or any other unwholesome trade than an artist occupied by his favourite employment. Every night I was oppressed by a slow fever, and I became nervous to a most painful degree; the fall of a leaf startled me, and I shunned my fellow creatures as if I had been guilty of a crime. Sometimes I grew alarmed at the wreck I perceived that I had become; the energy of my purpose alone sustained me: my labours would soon end, and I believed that exercise and amusement would then drive away incipient disease; and I promised myself both of these when my creation should be complete.

Chapter 5

It was on a dreary night of November that I beheld the accomplishment of my toils. With an anxiety that almost amounted to agony, I collected the instruments of life around me, that I might infuse a spark of being into the lifeless thing that lay at my feet. It was already one in the morning; the rain pattered dismally against the panes, and my candle was nearly burnt out, when, by the glimmer of the half-extinguished light, I saw the dull yellow eye of the creature open; it breathed hard, and a convulsive motion agitated its limbs.

How can I describe my emotions at this catastrophe, or how delineate the wretch whom with such infinite pains and care I had endeavoured to form? His limbs were in proportion, and I had selected his features as beautiful. Beautiful! Great God! His yellow skin scarcely covered the work of muscles and arteries beneath; his hair was of a lustrous black, and flowing; his teeth of a pearly whiteness; but these luxuriances only formed a more horrid contrast with his watery eyes, that seemed almost of the same colour as the dun-white sockets in which they were set, his shrivelled complexion and straight black lips.

The different accidents of life are not so changeable as the feelings of human nature. I had worked hard for nearly two years, for the sole purpose of infusing life into an inanimate body. For this I had deprived myself of rest and health. I had desired it with an ardour that far exceeded moderation; but now that I had finished, the beauty of the dream vanished, and breathless horror and disgust filled my heart. Unable to endure the aspect of the being I had created, I rushed out of the room and continued a long time traversing my bed-chamber, unable to compose my mind to sleep. At length lassitude succeeded to the tumult I had before endured, and I threw myself on the bed in my clothes, endeavouring to seek a few moments of forgetfulness. But it was in vain; I slept, indeed, but I was disturbed by the wildest dreams. I thought I saw Elizabeth, in the bloom of health, walking in the streets of Ingolstadt. Delighted and surprised, I embraced her, but as I imprinted the first kiss on her lips, they became livid with the hue of death; her features appeared to change, and I thought that I held the corpse of my dead mother in my arms; a shroud enveloped her form, and I saw the grave-worms crawling in the folds of the flannel. I started from my sleep with horror; a cold dew covered my forehead, my teeth chattered, and every limb became convulsed; when, by the dim and yellow light of the moon, as it forced its way through the window shutters, I beheld the wretch—the miserable monster whom I had created. He held up the curtain of the bed; and his eyes, if eyes they may be called, were fixed on me. His jaws opened, and he muttered some inarticulate sounds, while a grin wrinkled his cheeks. He might have spoken, but I did not hear; one hand was stretched out, seemingly to detain me, but I escaped and rushed downstairs. I took refuge in the courtyard belonging to the house which I inhabited, where I remained during the rest of the night, walking up and down in the greatest agitation, listening attentively, catching and fearing each sound as if it were to announce the approach of the demoniacal corpse to which I had so miserably given life.

Oh! No mortal could support the horror of that countenance. A mummy again endued with animation could not be so hideous as that wretch. I had gazed on him while unfinished; he was ugly then, but when those muscles and joints were rendered capable of motion, it became a thing such as even Dante could not have conceived.

I passed the night wretchedly. Sometimes my pulse beat so quickly and hardly that I felt the palpitation of every artery; at others, I nearly sank to the ground through languor and extreme weakness. Mingled with this horror, I felt the bitterness of disappointment; dreams that had been my food and pleasant rest for so long a space were now become a hell to me; and the change was so rapid, the overthrow so complete!

Morning, dismal and wet, at length dawned and discovered to my sleepless and aching eyes the church of Ingolstadt, its white steeple and clock, which indicated the sixth hour. The porter opened the gates of the court, which had that night been my asylum, and I issued into the streets, pacing them with quick steps, as if I sought to avoid the wretch whom I feared every turning of the street would present to my view. I did not dare return to the apartment which I inhabited, but felt impelled to hurry on, although drenched by the rain which poured from a black and comfortless sky.

I continued walking in this manner for some time, endeavouring by bodily exercise to ease the load that weighed upon my mind. I traversed the streets without any clear conception of where I was or what I was doing. My heart palpitated in the sickness of fear, and I hurried on with irregular steps, not daring to look about me:

Like one who, on a lonely road,

Doth walk in fear and dread,

Frankenstein

> And, having once turned round, walks on,
>
> And turns no more his head;
>
> Because he knows a frightful fiend
>
> Doth close behind him tread.

[Coleridge's "Ancient Mariner."]

Continuing thus, I came at length opposite to the inn at which the various diligences and carriages usually stopped. Here I paused, I knew not why; but I remained some minutes with my eyes fixed on a coach that was coming towards me from the other end of the street. As it drew nearer I observed that it was the Swiss diligence; it stopped just where I was standing, and on the door being opened, I perceived Henry Clerval, who, on seeing me, instantly sprung out. "My dear Frankenstein," exclaimed he, "how glad I am to see you! How fortunate that you should be here at the very moment of my alighting!"

Nothing could equal my delight on seeing Clerval; his presence brought back to my thoughts my father, Elizabeth, and all those scenes of home so dear to my recollection. I grasped his hand, and in a moment forgot my horror and misfortune; I felt suddenly, and for the first time during many months, calm and serene joy. I welcomed my friend, therefore, in the most cordial manner, and we walked towards my college. Clerval continued talking for some time about our mutual friends and his own good fortune in being permitted to come to Ingolstadt. "You may easily believe," said he, "how great was the difficulty to persuade my father that all necessary knowledge was not comprised in the noble art of book-keeping; and, indeed, I believe I left him incredulous to the last, for his constant answer to my unwearied entreaties was the same as that of the Dutch schoolmaster in The Vicar of Wakefield: 'I have ten thousand florins a year without Greek, I eat heartily without Greek.' But his affection for me at length overcame his dislike of learning, and he has permitted me to undertake a voyage of discovery to the land of knowledge."

"It gives me the greatest delight to see you; but tell me how you left my father, brothers, and Elizabeth."

"Very well, and very happy, only a little uneasy that they hear from you so seldom. By the by, I mean to lecture you a little upon their account myself. But, my dear Frankenstein," continued he, stopping short and gazing full in my face, "I did not before remark how very ill you appear; so thin and pale; you look as if you had been watching for several nights."

"You have guessed right; I have lately been so deeply engaged in one occupation that I have not allowed myself sufficient rest, as you see; but I hope, I sincerely hope, that all these employments are now at an end and that I am at length free."

I trembled excessively; I could not endure to think of, and far less to allude to, the occurrences of the preceding night. I walked with a quick pace, and we soon arrived at my college. I then reflected, and the thought made me shiver, that the creature whom I had left in my apartment might still be there, alive and walking about. I dreaded to behold this monster, but I feared still more that Henry should see him. Entreating him, therefore, to remain a few minutes at the bottom of the stairs, I darted up towards my own room. My hand was already on the lock of the door before I recollected myself. I then paused, and a cold shivering came over me. I threw the door forcibly open, as children are accustomed to do when they expect a spectre to stand in waiting for them on the other side; but nothing appeared. I stepped fearfully in: the apartment was empty, and my bedroom was also freed from its hideous guest. I could hardly believe that so great a good fortune could have befallen me, but when I became assured that my enemy had indeed fled, I clapped my hands for joy and ran down to Clerval.

We ascended into my room, and the servant presently brought breakfast; but I was unable to contain myself. It was not joy only that possessed me; I felt my flesh tingle with excess of sensitiveness, and my pulse beat rapidly. I was unable to remain for a single instant in the same place; I jumped over the chairs, clapped my hands, and laughed aloud. Clerval at first attributed my unusual spirits to joy on his arrival, but when he observed me more attentively, he saw a wildness in my eyes for which he could not account, and my loud, unrestrained, heartless laughter frightened and astonished him.

"My dear Victor," cried he, "what, for God's sake, is the matter? Do not laugh in that manner. How ill you are! What is the cause of all this?"

"Do not ask me," cried I, putting my hands before my eyes, for I thought I saw the dreaded spectre glide into the room; "he can tell. Oh, save me! Save me!" I imagined that the monster seized me; I struggled furiously and fell down in a fit.

Frankenstein

Poor Clerval! What must have been his feelings? A meeting, which he anticipated with such joy, so strangely turned to bitterness. But I was not the witness of his grief, for I was lifeless and did not recover my senses for a long, long time.

This was the commencement of a nervous fever which confined me for several months. During all that time Henry was my only nurse. I afterwards learned that, knowing my father's advanced age and unfitness for so long a journey, and how wretched my sickness would make Elizabeth, he spared them this grief by concealing the extent of my disorder. He knew that I could not have a more kind and attentive nurse than himself; and, firm in the hope he felt of my recovery, he did not doubt that, instead of doing harm, he performed the kindest action that he could towards them.

But I was in reality very ill, and surely nothing but the unbounded and unremitting attentions of my friend could have restored me to life. The form of the monster on whom I had bestowed existence was for ever before my eyes, and I raved incessantly concerning him. Doubtless my words surprised Henry; he at first believed them to be the wanderings of my disturbed imagination, but the pertinacity with which I continually recurred to the same subject persuaded him that my disorder indeed owed its origin to some uncommon and terrible event.

By very slow degrees, and with frequent relapses that alarmed and grieved my friend, I recovered. I remember the first time I became capable of observing outward objects with any kind of pleasure, I perceived that the fallen leaves had disappeared and that the young buds were shooting forth from the trees that shaded my window. It was a divine spring, and the season contributed greatly to my convalescence. I felt also sentiments of joy and affection revive in my bosom; my gloom disappeared, and in a short time I became as cheerful as before I was attacked by the fatal passion.

"Dearest Clerval," exclaimed I, "how kind, how very good you are to me. This whole winter, instead of being spent in study, as you promised yourself, has been consumed in my sick room. How shall I ever repay you? I feel the greatest remorse for the disappointment of which I have been the occasion, but you will forgive me."

"You will repay me entirely if you do not discompose yourself, but get well as fast as you can; and since you appear in such good spirits, I may speak to you on one subject, may I not?"

I trembled. One subject! What could it be? Could he allude to an object on whom I dared not even think?

"Compose yourself," said Clerval, who observed my change of colour, "I will not mention it if it agitates you; but your father and cousin would be very happy if they received a letter from you in your own handwriting. They hardly know how ill you have been and are uneasy at your long silence."

"Is that all, my dear Henry? How could you suppose that my first thought would not fly towards those dear, dear friends whom I love and who are so deserving of my love?"

"If this is your present temper, my friend, you will perhaps be glad to see a letter that has been lying here some days for you; it is from your cousin, I believe."

Chapter 6

Clerval then put the following letter into my hands. It was from my own Elizabeth:

"My dearest Cousin,

"You have been ill, very ill, and even the constant letters of dear kind Henry are not sufficient to reassure me on your account. You are forbidden to write—to hold a pen; yet one word from you, dear Victor, is necessary to calm our apprehensions. For a long time I have thought that each post would bring this line, and my persuasions have restrained my uncle from undertaking a journey to Ingolstadt. I have prevented his encountering the inconveniences and perhaps dangers of so long a journey, yet how often have I regretted not being able to perform it myself! I figure to myself that the task of attending on your sickbed has devolved on some mercenary old nurse, who could never guess your wishes nor minister to them with the care and affection of your poor cousin. Yet that is over now: Clerval writes that indeed you are getting better. I eagerly hope that you will confirm this intelligence soon in your own handwriting.

"Get well—and return to us. You will find a happy, cheerful home and friends who love you dearly. Your father's health is vigorous, and he asks but to see you, but to be assured that you are well; and not a care will ever cloud his benevolent countenance. How pleased you would be to remark the improvement of our Ernest! He is now sixteen and full of activity and spirit. He is desirous to be a true Swiss and to enter into foreign service, but we cannot part with him, at least until his elder brother returns to us. My uncle is not pleased with the idea of a military career in a distant country, but Ernest never had your powers of application. He looks upon study as an odious fetter; his time is spent in the open air, climbing the hills or rowing on the lake. I fear that he will become an idler unless we yield the point and permit him to enter on the profession which he has selected.

"Little alteration, except the growth of our dear children, has taken place since you left us. The blue lake and snow-clad mountains—they never change; and I think our placid home and our contented hearts are regulated by the same immutable laws. My trifling occupations take up my time and amuse me, and I am rewarded for any exertions by seeing none but happy, kind faces around me. Since you left us, but one change has taken place in our little household. Do you remember on what occasion Justine Moritz entered our family? Probably you do not; I will relate her history, therefore in a few words. Madame Moritz, her mother, was a widow with four children, of whom Justine was the third. This girl had always been the favourite of her father, but through a strange perversity, her mother could not endure her, and after the death of M. Moritz, treated her very ill. My aunt observed this, and when Justine was twelve years of age, prevailed on her mother to allow her to live at our house. The republican institutions of our country have produced simpler and happier manners than those which prevail in the great monarchies that surround it. Hence there is less distinction between the several classes of its inhabitants; and the lower orders, being neither so poor nor so despised, their manners are more refined and moral. A servant in Geneva does not mean the same thing as a servant in France and England. Justine, thus received in our family, learned the duties of a servant, a condition which, in our fortunate country, does not include the idea of ignorance and a sacrifice of the dignity of a human being.

"Justine, you may remember, was a great favourite of yours; and I recollect you once remarked that if you were in an ill humour, one glance from Justine could dissipate it, for the same reason that Ariosto gives concerning the beauty of Angelica — she looked so frank-hearted and happy. My aunt conceived a great attachment for her, by which she was induced to give her an education superior to that which she had at first intended. This benefit was fully repaid; Justine was the most grateful little creature in the world: I do not mean that she made any professions I never heard one pass her lips, but you could see by her eyes that she almost adored her protectress. Although her disposition was gay and in many respects inconsiderate, yet she paid the greatest attention to every gesture of my aunt. She thought her the model of all excellence and endeavoured to imitate her phraseology and manners, so that even now she often reminds me of her.

"When my dearest aunt died every one was too much occupied in their own grief to notice poor Justine, who had attended her during her illness with the most anxious affection. Poor Justine was very ill; but other trials were reserved for her.

"One by one, her brothers and sister died; and her mother, with the exception of her neglected daughter, was left childless. The conscience of the woman was troubled; she began to think that the deaths of her favourites was a judgement from heaven to chastise her partiality. She was a Roman Catholic; and I believe her confessor confirmed the idea which she had

44

conceived. Accordingly, a few months after your departure for Ingolstadt, Justine was called home by her repentant mother. Poor girl! She wept when she quitted our house; she was much altered since the death of my aunt; grief had given softness and a winning mildness to her manners, which had before been remarkable for vivacity. Nor was her residence at her mother's house of a nature to restore her gaiety. The poor woman was very vacillating in her repentance. She sometimes begged Justine to forgive her unkindness, but much oftener accused her of having caused the deaths of her brothers and sister. Perpetual fretting at length threw Madame Moritz into a decline, which at first increased her irritability, but she is now at peace for ever. She died on the first approach of cold weather, at the beginning of this last winter. Justine has just returned to us; and I assure you I love her tenderly. She is very clever and gentle, and extremely pretty; as I mentioned before, her mien and her expression continually remind me of my dear aunt.

"I must say also a few words to you, my dear cousin, of little darling William. I wish you could see him; he is very tall of his age, with sweet laughing blue eyes, dark eyelashes, and curling hair. When he smiles, two little dimples appear on each cheek, which are rosy with health. He has already had one or two little wives, but Louisa Biron is his favourite, a pretty little girl of five years of age.

"Now, dear Victor, I dare say you wish to be indulged in a little gossip concerning the good people of Geneva. The pretty Miss Mansfield has already received the congratulatory visits on her approaching marriage with a young Englishman, John Melbourne, Esq. Her ugly sister, Manon, married M. Duvillard, the rich banker, last autumn. Your favourite schoolfellow, Louis Manoir, has suffered several misfortunes since the departure of Clerval from Geneva. But he has already recovered his spirits, and is reported to be on the point of marrying a lively pretty Frenchwoman, Madame Tavernier. She is a widow, and much older than Manoir; but she is very much admired, and a favourite with everybody.

"I have written myself into better spirits, dear cousin; but my anxiety returns upon me as I conclude. Write, dearest Victor, — one line — one word will be a blessing to us. Ten thousand thanks to Henry for his kindness, his affection, and his many letters; we are sincerely grateful. Adieu! my cousin; take care of yourself; and, I entreat you, write!

"Elizabeth Lavenza.

"Geneva, March 18th, 17—."

"Dear, dear Elizabeth!" I exclaimed, when I had read her letter: "I will write instantly and relieve them from the anxiety they must feel." I wrote, and this exertion greatly fatigued me; but my convalescence had commenced, and proceeded regularly. In another fortnight I was able to leave my chamber.

One of my first duties on my recovery was to introduce Clerval to the several professors of the university. In doing this, I underwent a kind of rough usage, ill befitting the wounds that my mind had sustained. Ever since the fatal night, the end of my labours, and the beginning of my misfortunes, I had conceived a violent antipathy even to the name of natural philosophy. When I was otherwise quite restored to health, the sight of a chemical instrument would renew all the agony of my nervous symptoms. Henry saw this, and had removed all my apparatus from my view. He had also changed my apartment; for he perceived that I had acquired a dislike for the room which had previously been my laboratory. But these cares of Clerval were made of no avail when I visited the professors. M. Waldman inflicted torture when he praised, with kindness and warmth, the astonishing progress I had made in the sciences. He soon perceived that I disliked the subject; but not guessing the real cause, he attributed my feelings to modesty, and changed the subject from my improvement, to the science itself, with a desire, as I evidently saw, of drawing me out. What could I do? He meant to please, and he tormented me. I felt as if he had placed carefully, one by one, in my view those instruments which were to be afterwards used in putting me to a slow and cruel death. I writhed under his words, yet dared not exhibit the pain I felt. Clerval, whose eyes and feelings were always quick in discerning the sensations of others, declined the subject, alleging, in excuse, his total ignorance; and the conversation took a more general turn. I thanked my friend from my heart, but I did not speak. I saw plainly that he was surprised, but he never attempted to draw my secret from me; and although I loved him with a mixture of affection and reverence that knew no bounds, yet I could never persuade myself to confide in him that event which was so often present to my recollection, but which I feared the detail to another would only impress more deeply.

M. Krempe was not equally docile; and in my condition at that time, of almost insupportable sensitiveness, his harsh blunt encomiums gave me even more pain than the benevolent approbation of M. Waldman. "D—n the fellow!" cried he; "why, M. Clerval, I assure you he has outstript us all. Ay, stare if you

Frankenstein

please; but it is nevertheless true. A youngster who, but a few years ago, believed in Cornelius Agrippa as firmly as in the gospel, has now set himself at the head of the university; and if he is not soon pulled down, we shall all be out of countenance. — Ay, ay," continued he, observing my face expressive of suffering, "M. Frankenstein is modest; an excellent quality in a young man. Young men should be diffident of themselves, you know, M. Clerval: I was myself when young; but that wears out in a very short time."

M. Krempe had now commenced an eulogy on himself, which happily turned the conversation from a subject that was so annoying to me.

Clerval had never sympathised in my tastes for natural science; and his literary pursuits differed wholly from those which had occupied me. He came to the university with the design of making himself complete master of the oriental languages, and thus he should open a field for the plan of life he had marked out for himself. Resolved to pursue no inglorious career, he turned his eyes toward the East, as affording scope for his spirit of enterprise. The Persian, Arabic, and Sanskrit languages engaged his attention, and I was easily induced to enter on the same studies. Idleness had ever been irksome to me, and now that I wished to fly from reflection, and hated my former studies, I felt great relief in being the fellow-pupil with my friend, and found not only instruction but consolation in the works of the orientalists. I did not, like him, attempt a critical knowledge of their dialects, for I did not contemplate making any other use of them than temporary amusement. I read merely to understand their meaning, and they well repaid my labours. Their melancholy is soothing, and their joy elevating, to a degree I never experienced in studying the authors of any other country. When you read their writings, life appears to consist in a warm sun and a garden of roses, — in the smiles and frowns of a fair enemy, and the fire that consumes your own heart. How different from the manly and heroical poetry of Greece and Rome!

Summer passed away in these occupations, and my return to Geneva was fixed for the latter end of autumn; but being delayed by several accidents, winter and snow arrived, the roads were deemed impassable, and my journey was retarded until the ensuing spring. I felt this delay very bitterly; for I longed to see my native town and my beloved friends. My return had only been delayed so long, from an unwillingness to leave Clerval in a strange place, before he had become acquainted with any of its inhabitants. The winter, however, was spent cheerfully; and although the spring was uncommonly late, when it came its beauty compensated for its dilatoriness.

The month of May had already commenced, and I expected the letter daily which was to fix the date of my departure, when Henry proposed a pedestrian tour in the environs of Ingolstadt, that I might bid a personal farewell to the country I had so long inhabited. I acceded with pleasure to this proposition: I was fond of exercise, and Clerval had always been my favourite companion in the ramble of this nature that I had taken among the scenes of my native country.

We passed a fortnight in these perambulations: my health and spirits had long been restored, and they gained additional strength from the salubrious air I breathed, the natural incidents of our progress, and the conversation of my friend. Study had before secluded me from the intercourse of my fellow-creatures, and rendered me unsocial; but Clerval called forth the better feelings of my heart; he again taught me to love the aspect of nature, and the cheerful faces of children. Excellent friend! how sincerely you did love me, and endeavour to elevate my mind until it was on a level with your own. A selfish pursuit had cramped and narrowed me, until your gentleness and affection warmed and opened my senses; I became the same happy creature who, a few years ago, loved and beloved by all, had no sorrow or care. When happy, inanimate nature had the power of bestowing on me the most delightful sensations. A serene sky and verdant fields filled me with ecstasy. The present season was indeed divine; the flowers of spring bloomed in the hedges, while those of summer were already in bud. I was undisturbed by thoughts which during the preceding year had pressed upon me, notwithstanding my endeavours to throw them off, with an invincible burden.

Henry rejoiced in my gaiety, and sincerely sympathised in my feelings: he exerted himself to amuse me, while he expressed the sensations that filled his soul. The resources of his mind on this occasion were truly astonishing: his conversation was full of imagination; and very often, in imitation of the Persian and Arabic writers, he invented tales of wonderful fancy and passion. At other times he repeated my favourite poems, or drew me out into arguments, which he supported with great ingenuity.

We returned to our college on a Sunday afternoon: the peasants were dancing, and every one we met appeared gay and happy. My own spirits were high, and I bounded along with feelings of unbridled joy and hilarity.

Chapter 7

On my return, I found the following letter from my father:—

"My dear Victor,

"You have probably waited impatiently for a letter to fix the date of your return to us; and I was at first tempted to write only a few lines, merely mentioning the day on which I should expect you. But that would be a cruel kindness, and I dare not do it. What would be your surprise, my son, when you expected a happy and glad welcome, to behold, on the contrary, tears and wretchedness? And how, Victor, can I relate our misfortune? Absence cannot have rendered you callous to our joys and griefs; and how shall I inflict pain on my long absent son? I wish to prepare you for the woeful news, but I know it is impossible; even now your eye skims over the page to seek the words which are to convey to you the horrible tidings.

"William is dead!—that sweet child, whose smiles delighted and warmed my heart, who was so gentle, yet so gay! Victor, he is murdered!

"I will not attempt to console you; but will simply relate the circumstances of the transaction.

"Last Thursday (May 7th), I, my niece, and your two brothers, went to walk in Plainpalais. The evening was warm and serene, and we prolonged our walk farther than usual. It was already dusk before we thought of returning; and then we discovered that William and Ernest, who had gone on before, were not to be found. We accordingly rested on a seat until they should return. Presently Ernest came, and enquired if we had seen his brother; he said, that he had been playing with him, that William had run away to hide himself, and that he vainly sought for him, and afterwards waited for a long time, but that he did not return.

"This account rather alarmed us, and we continued to search for him until night fell, when Elizabeth conjectured that he might have returned to the house. He was not there. We returned again, with torches; for I could not rest, when I thought that my sweet boy had lost himself, and was exposed to all the damps and dews of night; Elizabeth also suffered extreme anguish. About five in the morning I discovered my lovely boy, whom the night before I had seen blooming and active in health, stretched on the grass livid and motionless; the print of the murder's finger was on his neck.

"He was conveyed home, and the anguish that was visible in my countenance betrayed the secret to Elizabeth. She was very earnest to see the corpse. At first I attempted to prevent her but she persisted, and entering the room where it lay, hastily examined the neck of the victim, and clasping her hands exclaimed, 'O God! I have murdered my darling child!'

"She fainted, and was restored with extreme difficulty. When she again lived, it was only to weep and sigh. She told me, that that same evening William had teased her to let him wear a very valuable miniature that she possessed of your mother. This picture is gone, and was doubtless the temptation which urged the murderer to the deed. We have no trace of him at present, although our exertions to discover him are unremitted; but they will not restore my beloved William!

"Come, dearest Victor; you alone can console Elizabeth. She weeps continually, and accuses herself unjustly as the cause of his death; her words pierce my heart. We are all unhappy; but will not that be an additional motive for you, my son, to return and be our comforter? Your dear mother! Alas, Victor! I now say, Thank God she did not live to witness the cruel, miserable death of her youngest darling!

"Come, Victor; not brooding thoughts of vengeance against the assassin, but with feelings of peace and gentleness, that will heal, instead of festering, the wounds of our minds. Enter the house of mourning, my friend, but with kindness and affection for those who love you, and not with hatred for your enemies.

"Your affectionate and afflicted father,

"Alphonse Frankenstein.

"Geneva, May 12th, 17—."

Clerval, who had watched my countenance as I read this letter, was surprised to observe the despair that succeeded the joy I at first expressed on receiving new from my friends. I threw the letter on the table, and covered my face with my hands.

"My dear Frankenstein," exclaimed Henry, when he perceived me weep with bitterness, "are you always to be unhappy? My dear friend, what has happened?"

I motioned him to take up the letter, while I walked up and down the room in the extremest agitation. Tears also gushed

Frankenstein

from the eyes of Clerval, as he read the account of my misfortune.

"I can offer you no consolation, my friend," said he; "your disaster is irreparable. What do you intend to do?"

"To go instantly to Geneva: come with me, Henry, to order the horses."

During our walk, Clerval endeavoured to say a few words of consolation; he could only express his heartfelt sympathy. "Poor William!" said he, "dear lovely child, he now sleeps with his angel mother! Who that had seen him bright and joyous in his young beauty, but must weep over his untimely loss! To die so miserably; to feel the murderer's grasp! How much more a murdered that could destroy radiant innocence! Poor little fellow! one only consolation have we; his friends mourn and weep, but he is at rest. The pang is over, his sufferings are at an end for ever. A sod covers his gentle form, and he knows no pain. He can no longer be a subject for pity; we must reserve that for his miserable survivors."

Clerval spoke thus as we hurried through the streets; the words impressed themselves on my mind and I remembered them afterwards in solitude. But now, as soon as the horses arrived, I hurried into a cabriolet, and bade farewell to my friend.

My journey was very melancholy. At first I wished to hurry on, for I longed to console and sympathise with my loved and sorrowing friends; but when I drew near my native town, I slackened my progress. I could hardly sustain the multitude of feelings that crowded into my mind. I passed through scenes familiar to my youth, but which I had not seen for nearly six years. How altered every thing might be during that time! One sudden and desolating change had taken place; but a thousand little circumstances might have by degrees worked other alterations, which, although they were done more tranquilly, might not be the less decisive. Fear overcame me; I dared no advance, dreading a thousand nameless evils that made me tremble, although I was unable to define them.

I remained two days at Lausanne, in this painful state of mind. I contemplated the lake: the waters were placid; all around was calm; and the snowy mountains, "the palaces of nature," were not changed. By degrees the calm and heavenly scene restored me, and I continued my journey towards Geneva.

The road ran by the side of the lake, which became narrower as I approached my native town. I discovered more distinctly the black sides of Jura, and the bright summit of Mont Blanc. I wept like a child. "Dear mountains! my own beautiful lake! how do you welcome your wanderer? Your summits are clear; the sky and lake are blue and placid. Is this to prognosticate peace, or to mock at my unhappiness?"

I fear, my friend, that I shall render myself tedious by dwelling on these preliminary circumstances; but they were days of comparative happiness, and I think of them with pleasure. My country, my beloved country! who but a native can tell the delight I took in again beholding thy streams, thy mountains, and, more than all, thy lovely lake!

Yet, as I drew nearer home, grief and fear again overcame me. Night also closed around; and when I could hardly see the dark mountains, I felt still more gloomily. The picture appeared a vast and dim scene of evil, and I foresaw obscurely that I was destined to become the most wretched of human beings. Alas! I prophesied truly, and failed only in one single circumstance, that in all the misery I imagined and dreaded, I did not conceive the hundredth part of the anguish I was destined to endure.

It was completely dark when I arrived in the environs of Geneva; the gates of the town were already shut; and I was obliged to pass the night at Secheron, a village at the distance of half a league from the city. The sky was serene; and, as I was unable to rest, I resolved to visit the spot where my poor William had been murdered. As I could not pass through the town, I was obliged to cross the lake in a boat to arrive at Plainpalais. During this short voyage I saw the lightning playing on the summit of Mont Blanc in the most beautiful figures. The storm appeared to approach rapidly, and, on landing, I ascended a low hill, that I might observe its progress. It advanced; the heavens were clouded, and I soon felt the rain coming slowly in large drops, but its violence quickly increased.

I quitted my seat, and walked on, although the darkness and storm increased every minute, and the thunder burst with a terrific crash over my head. It was echoed from Salêve, the Juras, and the Alps of Savoy; vivid flashes of lightning dazzled my eyes, illuminating the lake, making it appear like a vast sheet of fire; then for an instant every thing seemed of a pitchy darkness, until the eye recovered itself from the preceding flash. The storm, as is often the case in Switzerland, appeared at once in various parts of the heavens. The most violent storm hung exactly north of the town, over the part of the lake which lies between the promontory of Belrive and the village of Copêt. Another storm enlightened Jura with faint flashes; and another darkened and sometimes disclosed the Môle, a peaked mountain to the east of the lake.

While I watched the tempest, so beautiful yet terrific, I wandered on with a hasty step. This noble war in the sky elevated my spirits; I clasped my hands, and exclaimed aloud, "William, dear angel! this is thy funeral, this thy dirge!" As I said these words, I perceived in the gloom a figure which stole from behind a clump of trees near me; I stood fixed, gazing intently: I could not be mistaken. A flash of lightning illuminated the object, and discovered its shape plainly to me; its gigantic stature, and the deformity of its aspect more hideous than belongs to humanity, instantly informed me that it was the wretch, the filthy dæmon, to whom I had given life. What did he there? Could he be (I shuddered at the conception) the murderer of my brother? No sooner did that idea cross my imagination, than I became convinced of its truth; my teeth chattered, and I was forced to lean against a tree for support. The figure passed me quickly, and I lost it in the gloom. Nothing in human shape could have destroyed the fair child. He was the murderer! I could not doubt it. The mere presence of the idea was an irresistible proof of the fact. I thought of pursuing the devil; but it would have been in vain, for another flash discovered him to me hanging among the rocks of the nearly perpendicular ascent of Mont Salêve, a hill that bounds Plainpalais on the south. He soon reached the summit, and disappeared.

I remained motionless. The thunder ceased; but the rain still continued, and the scene was enveloped in an impenetrable darkness. I revolved in my mind the events which I had until now sought to forget: the whole train of my progress toward the creation; the appearance of the works of my own hands at my bedside; its departure. Two years had now nearly elapsed since the night on which he first received life; and was this his first crime? Alas! I had turned loose into the world a depraved wretch, whose delight was in carnage and misery; had he not murdered my brother?

No one can conceive the anguish I suffered during the remainder of the night, which I spent, cold and wet, in the open air. But I did not feel the inconvenience of the weather; my imagination was busy in scenes of evil and despair. I considered the being whom I had cast among mankind, and endowed with the will and power to effect purposes of horror, such as the deed which he had now done, nearly in the light of my own vampire, my own spirit let loose from the grave, and forced to destroy all that was dear to me.

Day dawned; and I directed my steps towards the town. The gates were open, and I hastened to my father's house. My first thought was to discover what I knew of the murderer, and cause instant pursuit to be made. But I paused when I reflected on the story that I had to tell. A being whom I myself had formed, and endued with life, had met me at midnight among the precipices of an inaccessible mountain. I remembered also the nervous fever with which I had been seized just at the time that I dated my creation, and which would give an air of delirium to a tale otherwise so utterly improbable. I well knew that if any other had communicated such a relation to me, I should have looked upon it as the ravings of insanity. Besides, the strange nature of the animal would elude all pursuit, even if I were so far credited as to persuade my relatives to commence it. And then of what use would be pursuit? Who could arrest a creature capable of scaling the overhanging sides of Mont Salêve? These reflections determined me, and I resolved to remain silent.

It was about five in the morning when I entered my father's house. I told the servants not to disturb the family, and went into the library to attend their usual hour of rising.

Six years had elapsed, passed in a dream but for one indelible trace, and I stood in the same place where I had last embraced my father before my departure for Ingolstadt. Beloved and venerable parent! He still remained to me. I gazed on the picture of my mother, which stood over the mantel-piece. It was an historical subject, painted at my father's desire, and represented Caroline Beaufort in an agony of despair, kneeling by the coffin of her dead father. Her garb was rustic, and her cheek pale; but there was an air of dignity and beauty, that hardly permitted the sentiment of pity. Below this picture was a miniature of William; and my tears flowed when I looked upon it. While I was thus engaged, Ernest entered: he had heard me arrive, and hastened to welcome me: "Welcome, my dearest Victor," said he. "Ah! I wish you had come three months ago, and then you would have found us all joyous and delighted. You come to us now to share a misery which nothing can alleviate; yet your presence will, I hope, revive our father, who seems sinking under his misfortune; and your persuasions will induce poor Elizabeth to cease her vain and tormenting self-accusations.—Poor William! he was our darling and our pride!"

Frankenstein

Tears, unrestrained, fell from my brother's eyes; a sense of mortal agony crept over my frame. Before, I had only imagined the wretchedness of my desolated home; the reality came on me as a new, and a not less terrible, disaster. I tried to calm Ernest; I enquired more minutely concerning my father, and here I named my cousin.

"She most of all," said Ernest, "requires consolation; she accused herself of having caused the death of my brother, and that made her very wretched. But since the murderer has been discovered—"

"The murderer discovered! Good God! how can that be? who could attempt to pursue him? It is impossible; one might as well try to overtake the winds, or confine a mountain-stream with a straw. I saw him too; he was free last night!"

"I do not know what you mean," replied my brother, in accents of wonder, "but to us the discovery we have made completes our misery. No one would believe it at first; and even now Elizabeth will not be convinced, notwithstanding all the evidence. Indeed, who would credit that Justine Moritz, who was so amiable, and fond of all the family, could suddenly become so capable of so frightful, so appalling a crime?"

"Justine Moritz! Poor, poor girl, is she the accused? But it is wrongfully; every one knows that; no one believes it, surely, Ernest?"

"No one did at first; but several circumstances came out, that have almost forced conviction upon us; and her own behaviour has been so confused, as to add to the evidence of facts a weight that, I fear, leaves no hope for doubt. But she will be tried today, and you will then hear all."

He then related that, the morning on which the murder of poor William had been discovered, Justine had been taken ill, and confined to her bed for several days. During this interval, one of the servants, happening to examine the apparel she had worn on the night of the murder, had discovered in her pocket the picture of my mother, which had been judged to be the temptation of the murderer. The servant instantly showed it to one of the others, who, without saying a word to any of the family, went to a magistrate; and, upon their deposition, Justine was apprehended. On being charged with the fact, the poor girl confirmed the suspicion in a great measure by her extreme confusion of manner.

This was a strange tale, but it did not shake my faith; and I replied earnestly, "You are all mistaken; I know the murderer. Justine, poor, good Justine, is innocent."

At that instant my father entered. I saw unhappiness deeply impressed on his countenance, but he endeavoured to welcome me cheerfully; and, after we had exchanged our mournful greeting, would have introduced some other topic than that of our disaster, had not Ernest exclaimed, "Good God, papa! Victor says that he knows who was the murderer of poor William."

"We do also, unfortunately," replied my father, "for indeed I had rather have been for ever ignorant than have discovered so much depravity and ungratitude in one I valued so highly."

"My dear father, you are mistaken; Justine is innocent."

"If she is, God forbid that she should suffer as guilty. She is to be tried today, and I hope, I sincerely hope, that she will be acquitted."

This speech calmed me. I was firmly convinced in my own mind that Justine, and indeed every human being, was guiltless of this murder. I had no fear, therefore, that any circumstantial evidence could be brought forward strong enough to convict her. My tale was not one to announce publicly; its astounding horror would be looked upon as madness by the vulgar. Did any one indeed exist, except I, the creator, who would believe, unless his senses convinced him, in the existence of the living monument of presumption and rash ignorance which I had let loose upon the world?

We were soon joined by Elizabeth. Time had altered her since I last beheld her; it had endowed her with loveliness surpassing the beauty of her childish years. There was the same candour, the same vivacity, but it was allied to an expression more full of sensibility and intellect. She welcomed me with the greatest affection. "Your arrival, my dear cousin," said she, "fills me with hope. You perhaps will find some means to justify my poor guiltless Justine. Alas! who is safe, if she be convicted of crime? I rely on her innocence as certainly as I do upon my own. Our misfortune is doubly hard to us; we have not only lost that lovely darling boy, but this poor girl, whom I sincerely love, is to be torn away by even a worse fate. If she is condemned, I never shall know joy more. But she will not, I am sure she will not; and then I shall be happy again, even after the sad death of my little William."

"She is innocent, my Elizabeth," said I, "and that shall be proved; fear nothing, but let your spirits be cheered by the assurance of her acquittal."

"How kind and generous you are! every one else believes in her guilt, and that made me wretched, for I knew that it was impossible: and to see every one else prejudiced in so deadly a manner rendered me hopeless and despairing." She wept.

"Dearest niece," said my father, "dry your tears. If she is, as you believe, innocent, rely on the justice of our laws, and the activity with which I shall prevent the slightest shadow of partiality."

Chapter 8

We passed a few sad hours until eleven o'clock, when the trial was to commence. My father and the rest of the family being obliged to attend as witnesses, I accompanied them to the court. During the whole of this wretched mockery of justice I suffered living torture. It was to be decided whether the result of my curiosity and lawless devices would cause the death of two of my fellow beings: one a smiling babe full of innocence and joy, the other far more dreadfully murdered, with every aggravation of infamy that could make the murder memorable in horror. Justine also was a girl of merit and possessed qualities which promised to render her life happy; now all was to be obliterated in an ignominious grave, and I the cause! A thousand times rather would I have confessed myself guilty of the crime ascribed to Justine, but I was absent when it was committed, and such a declaration would have been considered as the ravings of a madman and would not have exculpated her who suffered through me.

The appearance of Justine was calm. She was dressed in mourning, and her countenance, always engaging, was rendered, by the solemnity of her feelings, exquisitely beautiful. Yet she appeared confident in innocence and did not tremble, although gazed on and execrated by thousands, for all the kindness which her beauty might otherwise have excited was obliterated in the minds of the spectators by the imagination of the enormity she was supposed to have committed. She was tranquil, yet her tranquillity was evidently constrained; and as her confusion had before been adduced as a proof of her guilt, she worked up her mind to an appearance of courage. When she entered the court she threw her eyes round it and quickly discovered where we were seated. A tear seemed to dim her eye when she saw us, but she quickly recovered herself, and a look of sorrowful affection seemed to attest her utter guiltlessness.

The trial began, and after the advocate against her had stated the charge, several witnesses were called. Several strange facts combined against her, which might have staggered anyone who had not such proof of her innocence as I had. She had been out the whole of the night on which the murder had been committed and towards morning had been perceived by a market-woman not far from the spot where the body of the murdered child had been afterwards found. The woman asked her what she did there, but she looked very strangely and only returned a confused and unintelligible answer. She returned to the house about eight o'clock, and when one inquired where she had passed the night, she replied that she had been looking for

Frankenstein

the child and demanded earnestly if anything had been heard concerning him. When shown the body, she fell into violent hysterics and kept her bed for several days. The picture was then produced which the servant had found in her pocket; and when Elizabeth, in a faltering voice, proved that it was the same which, an hour before the child had been missed, she had placed round his neck, a murmur of horror and indignation filled the court.

Justine was called on for her defence. As the trial had proceeded, her countenance had altered. Surprise, horror, and misery were strongly expressed. Sometimes she struggled with her tears, but when she was desired to plead, she collected her powers and spoke in an audible although variable voice.

"God knows," she said, "how entirely I am innocent. But I do not pretend that my protestations should acquit me; I rest my innocence on a plain and simple explanation of the facts which have been adduced against me, and I hope the character I have always borne will incline my judges to a favourable interpretation where any circumstance appears doubtful or suspicious."

She then related that, by the permission of Elizabeth, she had passed the evening of the night on which the murder had been committed at the house of an aunt at Chêne, a village situated at about a league from Geneva. On her return, at about nine o'clock, she met a man who asked her if she had seen anything of the child who was lost. She was alarmed by this account and passed several hours in looking for him, when the gates of Geneva were shut, and she was forced to remain several hours of the night in a barn belonging to a cottage, being unwilling to call up the inhabitants, to whom she was well known. Most of the night she spent here watching; towards morning she believed that she slept for a few minutes; some steps disturbed her, and she awoke. It was dawn, and she quitted her asylum, that she might again endeavour to find my brother. If she had gone near the spot where his body lay, it was without her knowledge. That she had been bewildered when questioned by the market-woman was not surprising, since she had passed a sleepless night and the fate of poor William was yet uncertain. Concerning the picture she could give no account.

"I know," continued the unhappy victim, "how heavily and fatally this one circumstance weighs against me, but I have no power of explaining it; and when I have expressed my utter ignorance, I am only left to conjecture concerning the probabilities by which it might have been placed in my pocket.

But here also I am checked. I believe that I have no enemy on earth, and none surely would have been so wicked as to destroy me wantonly. Did the murderer place it there? I know of no opportunity afforded him for so doing; or, if I had, why should he have stolen the jewel, to part with it again so soon?

"I commit my cause to the justice of my judges, yet I see no room for hope. I beg permission to have a few witnesses examined concerning my character, and if their testimony shall not overweigh my supposed guilt, I must be condemned, although I would pledge my salvation on my innocence."

Several witnesses were called who had known her for many years, and they spoke well of her; but fear and hatred of the crime of which they supposed her guilty rendered them timorous and unwilling to come forward. Elizabeth saw even this last resource, her excellent dispositions and irreproachable conduct, about to fail the accused, when, although violently agitated, she desired permission to address the court.

"I am," said she, "the cousin of the unhappy child who was murdered, or rather his sister, for I was educated by and have lived with his parents ever since and even long before his birth. It may therefore be judged indecent in me to come forward on this occasion, but when I see a fellow creature about to perish through the cowardice of her pretended friends, I wish to be allowed to speak, that I may say what I know of her character. I am well acquainted with the accused. I have lived in the same house with her, at one time for five and at another for nearly two years. During all that period she appeared to me the most amiable and benevolent of human creatures. She nursed Madame Frankenstein, my aunt, in her last illness, with the greatest affection and care and afterwards attended her own mother during a tedious illness, in a manner that excited the admiration of all who knew her, after which she again lived in my uncle's house, where she was beloved by all the family. She was warmly attached to the child who is now dead and acted towards him like a most affectionate mother. For my own part, I do not hesitate to say that, notwithstanding all the evidence produced against her, I believe and rely on her perfect innocence. She had no temptation for such an action; as to the bauble on which the chief proof rests, if she had earnestly desired it, I should have willingly given it to her, so much do I esteem and value her."

A murmur of approbation followed Elizabeth's simple and powerful appeal, but it was excited by her generous interference, and not in favour of poor Justine, on whom the

Frankenstein

public indignation was turned with renewed violence, charging her with the blackest ingratitude. She herself wept as Elizabeth spoke, but she did not answer. My own agitation and anguish was extreme during the whole trial. I believed in her innocence; I knew it. Could the dæmon who had (I did not for a minute doubt) murdered my brother also in his hellish sport have betrayed the innocent to death and ignominy? I could not sustain the horror of my situation, and when I perceived that the popular voice and the countenances of the judges had already condemned my unhappy victim, I rushed out of the court in agony. The tortures of the accused did not equal mine; she was sustained by innocence, but the fangs of remorse tore my bosom and would not forgo their hold.

I passed a night of unmingled wretchedness. In the morning I went to the court; my lips and throat were parched. I dared not ask the fatal question, but I was known, and the officer guessed the cause of my visit. The ballots had been thrown; they were all black, and Justine was condemned.

I cannot pretend to describe what I then felt. I had before experienced sensations of horror, and I have endeavoured to bestow upon them adequate expressions, but words cannot convey an idea of the heart-sickening despair that I then endured. The person to whom I addressed myself added that Justine had already confessed her guilt. "That evidence," he observed, "was hardly required in so glaring a case, but I am glad of it, and, indeed, none of our judges like to condemn a criminal upon circumstantial evidence, be it ever so decisive."

This was strange and unexpected intelligence; what could it mean? Had my eyes deceived me? And was I really as mad as the whole world would believe me to be if I disclosed the object of my suspicions? I hastened to return home, and Elizabeth eagerly demanded the result.

"My cousin," replied I, "it is decided as you may have expected; all judges had rather that ten innocent should suffer than that one guilty should escape. But she has confessed."

This was a dire blow to poor Elizabeth, who had relied with firmness upon Justine's innocence. "Alas!" said she. "How shall I ever again believe in human goodness? Justine, whom I loved and esteemed as my sister, how could she put on those smiles of innocence only to betray? Her mild eyes seemed incapable of any severity or guile, and yet she has committed a murder."

Soon after we heard that the poor victim had expressed a desire to see my cousin. My father wished her not to go but said that he left it to her own judgment and feelings to decide. "Yes," said Elizabeth, "I will go, although she is guilty; and you, Victor, shall accompany me; I cannot go alone." The idea of this visit was torture to me, yet I could not refuse.

We entered the gloomy prison chamber and beheld Justine sitting on some straw at the farther end; her hands were manacled, and her head rested on her knees. She rose on seeing us enter, and when we were left alone with her, she threw herself at the feet of Elizabeth, weeping bitterly. My cousin wept also.

"Oh, Justine!" said she. "Why did you rob me of my last consolation? I relied on your innocence, and although I was then very wretched, I was not so miserable as I am now."

"And do you also believe that I am so very, very wicked? Do you also join with my enemies to crush me, to condemn me as a murderer?" Her voice was suffocated with sobs.

"Rise, my poor girl," said Elizabeth; "why do you kneel, if you are innocent? I am not one of your enemies, I believed you guiltless, notwithstanding every evidence, until I heard that you had yourself declared your guilt. That report, you say, is false; and be assured, dear Justine, that nothing can shake my confidence in you for a moment, but your own confession."

"I did confess, but I confessed a lie. I confessed, that I might obtain absolution; but now that falsehood lies heavier at my heart than all my other sins. The God of heaven forgive me! Ever since I was condemned, my confessor has besieged me; he threatened and menaced, until I almost began to think that I was the monster that he said I was. He threatened excommunication and hell fire in my last moments if I continued obdurate. Dear lady, I had none to support me; all looked on me as a wretch doomed to ignominy and perdition. What could I do? In an evil hour I subscribed to a lie; and now only am I truly miserable."

She paused, weeping, and then continued, "I thought with horror, my sweet lady, that you should believe your Justine, whom your blessed aunt had so highly honoured, and whom you loved, was a creature capable of a crime which none but the devil himself could have perpetrated. Dear William! dearest blessed child! I soon shall see you again in heaven, where we shall all be happy; and that consoles me, going as I am to suffer ignominy and death."

"Oh, Justine! Forgive me for having for one moment distrusted you. Why did you confess? But do not mourn, dear girl. Do not fear. I will proclaim, I will prove your innocence. I will melt the stony hearts of your enemies by my tears and prayers. You shall not die! You, my playfellow, my companion, my sister, perish on the scaffold! No! No! I never could survive so horrible a misfortune."

Justine shook her head mournfully. "I do not fear to die," she said; "that pang is past. God raises my weakness and gives me courage to endure the worst. I leave a sad and bitter world; and if you remember me and think of me as of one unjustly condemned, I am resigned to the fate awaiting me. Learn from me, dear lady, to submit in patience to the will of heaven!"

During this conversation I had retired to a corner of the prison room, where I could conceal the horrid anguish that possessed me. Despair! Who dared talk of that? The poor victim, who on the morrow was to pass the awful boundary between life and death, felt not, as I did, such deep and bitter agony. I gnashed my teeth and ground them together, uttering a groan that came from my inmost soul. Justine started. When she saw who it was, she approached me and said, "Dear sir, you are very kind to visit me; you, I hope, do not believe that I am guilty?"

I could not answer. "No, Justine," said Elizabeth; "he is more convinced of your innocence than I was, for even when he heard that you had confessed, he did not credit it."

"I truly thank him. In these last moments I feel the sincerest gratitude towards those who think of me with kindness. How sweet is the affection of others to such a wretch as I am! It removes more than half my misfortune, and I feel as if I could die in peace now that my innocence is acknowledged by you, dear lady, and your cousin."

Thus the poor sufferer tried to comfort others and herself. She indeed gained the resignation she desired. But I, the true murderer, felt the never-dying worm alive in my bosom, which allowed of no hope or consolation. Elizabeth also wept and was unhappy, but hers also was the misery of innocence, which, like a cloud that passes over the fair moon, for a while hides but cannot tarnish its brightness. Anguish and despair had penetrated into the core of my heart; I bore a hell within me which nothing could extinguish. We stayed several hours with

Justine, and it was with great difficulty that Elizabeth could tear herself away. "I wish," cried she, "that I were to die with you; I cannot live in this world of misery."

Justine assumed an air of cheerfulness, while she with difficulty repressed her bitter tears. She embraced Elizabeth and said in a voice of half-suppressed emotion, "Farewell, sweet lady, dearest Elizabeth, my beloved and only friend; may heaven, in its bounty, bless and preserve you; may this be the last misfortune that you will ever suffer! Live, and be happy, and make others so."

And on the morrow Justine died. Elizabeth's heart-rending eloquence failed to move the judges from their settled conviction in the criminality of the saintly sufferer. My passionate and indignant appeals were lost upon them. And when I received their cold answers and heard the harsh, unfeeling reasoning of these men, my purposed avowal died away on my lips. Thus I might proclaim myself a madman, but not revoke the sentence passed upon my wretched victim. She perished on the scaffold as a murderess!

From the tortures of my own heart, I turned to contemplate the deep and voiceless grief of my Elizabeth. This also was my doing! And my father's woe, and the desolation of that late so smiling home all was the work of my thrice-accursed hands! Ye weep, unhappy ones, but these are not your last tears! Again shall you raise the funeral wail, and the sound of your lamentations shall again and again be heard! Frankenstein, your son, your kinsman, your early, much-loved friend; he who would spend each vital drop of blood for your sakes, who has no thought nor sense of joy except as it is mirrored also in your dear countenances, who would fill the air with blessings and spend his life in serving you — he bids you weep, to shed countless tears; happy beyond his hopes, if thus inexorable fate be satisfied, and if the destruction pause before the peace of the grave have succeeded to your sad torments!

Thus spoke my prophetic soul, as, torn by remorse, horror, and despair, I beheld those I loved spend vain sorrow upon the graves of William and Justine, the first hapless victims to my unhallowed arts.

Chapter 9

Nothing is more painful to the human mind than, after the feelings have been worked up by a quick succession of events, the dead calmness of inaction and certainty which follows and deprives the soul both of hope and fear. Justine died, she rested, and I was alive. The blood flowed freely in my veins, but a weight of despair and remorse pressed on my heart which nothing could remove. Sleep fled from my eyes; I wandered like an evil spirit, for I had committed deeds of mischief beyond description horrible, and more, much more (I persuaded myself) was yet behind. Yet my heart overflowed with kindness and the love of virtue. I had begun life with benevolent intentions and thirsted for the moment when I should put them in practice and make myself useful to my fellow beings. Now all was blasted; instead of that serenity of conscience which allowed me to look back upon the past with self-satisfaction, and from thence to gather promise of new hopes, I was seized by remorse and the sense of guilt, which hurried me away to a hell of intense tortures such as no language can describe.

This state of mind preyed upon my health, which had perhaps never entirely recovered from the first shock it had sustained. I shunned the face of man; all sound of joy or complacency was torture to me; solitude was my only consolation—deep, dark, deathlike solitude.

My father observed with pain the alteration perceptible in my disposition and habits and endeavoured by arguments deduced from the feelings of his serene conscience and guiltless life to inspire me with fortitude and awaken in me the courage to dispel the dark cloud which brooded over me. "Do you think, Victor," said he, "that I do not suffer also? No one could love a child more than I loved your brother"—tears came into his eyes as he spoke—"but is it not a duty to the survivors that we should refrain from augmenting their unhappiness by an appearance of immoderate grief? It is also a duty owed to yourself, for excessive sorrow prevents improvement or enjoyment, or even the discharge of daily usefulness, without which no man is fit for society."

This advice, although good, was totally inapplicable to my case; I should have been the first to hide my grief and console my friends if remorse had not mingled its bitterness, and terror its alarm, with my other sensations. Now I could only answer my father with a look of despair and endeavour to hide myself from his view.

Frankenstein

About this time we retired to our house at Belrive. This change was particularly agreeable to me. The shutting of the gates regularly at ten o'clock and the impossibility of remaining on the lake after that hour had rendered our residence within the walls of Geneva very irksome to me. I was now free. Often, after the rest of the family had retired for the night, I took the boat and passed many hours upon the water. Sometimes, with my sails set, I was carried by the wind; and sometimes, after rowing into the middle of the lake, I left the boat to pursue its own course and gave way to my own miserable reflections. I was often tempted, when all was at peace around me, and I the only unquiet thing that wandered restless in a scene so beautiful and heavenly—if I except some bat, or the frogs, whose harsh and interrupted croaking was heard only when I approached the shore—often, I say, I was tempted to plunge into the silent lake, that the waters might close over me and my calamities for ever. But I was restrained, when I thought of the heroic and suffering Elizabeth, whom I tenderly loved, and whose existence was bound up in mine. I thought also of my father and surviving brother; should I by my base desertion leave them exposed and unprotected to the malice of the fiend whom I had let loose among them?

At these moments I wept bitterly and wished that peace would revisit my mind only that I might afford them consolation and happiness. But that could not be. Remorse extinguished every hope. I had been the author of unalterable evils, and I lived in daily fear lest the monster whom I had created should perpetrate some new wickedness. I had an obscure feeling that all was not over and that he would still commit some signal crime, which by its enormity should almost efface the recollection of the past. There was always scope for fear so long as anything I loved remained behind. My abhorrence of this fiend cannot be conceived. When I thought of him I gnashed my teeth, my eyes became inflamed, and I ardently wished to extinguish that life which I had so thoughtlessly bestowed. When I reflected on his crimes and malice, my hatred and revenge burst all bounds of moderation. I would have made a pilgrimage to the highest peak of the Andes, could I, when there, have precipitated him to their base. I wished to see him again, that I might wreak the utmost extent of abhorrence on his head and avenge the deaths of William and Justine.

Our house was the house of mourning. My father's health was deeply shaken by the horror of the recent events. Elizabeth was sad and desponding; she no longer took delight in her ordinary occupations; all pleasure seemed to her sacrilege toward the dead; eternal woe and tears she then thought was the just tribute she should pay to innocence so blasted and destroyed. She was no longer that happy creature who in earlier youth wandered with me on the banks of the lake and talked with ecstasy of our future prospects. The first of those sorrows which are sent to wean us from the earth had visited her, and its dimming influence quenched her dearest smiles.

"When I reflect, my dear cousin," said she, "on the miserable death of Justine Moritz, I no longer see the world and its works as they before appeared to me. Before, I looked upon the accounts of vice and injustice that I read in books or heard from others as tales of ancient days or imaginary evils; at least they were remote and more familiar to reason than to the imagination; but now misery has come home, and men appear to me as monsters thirsting for each other's blood. Yet I am certainly unjust. Everybody believed that poor girl to be guilty; and if she could have committed the crime for which she suffered, assuredly she would have been the most depraved of human creatures. For the sake of a few jewels, to have murdered the son of her benefactor and friend, a child whom she had nursed from its birth, and appeared to love as if it had been her own! I could not consent to the death of any human being, but certainly I should have thought such a creature unfit to remain in the society of men. But she was innocent. I know, I feel she was innocent; you are of the same opinion, and that confirms me. Alas! Victor, when falsehood can look so like the truth, who can assure themselves of certain happiness? I feel as if I were walking on the edge of a precipice, towards which thousands are crowding and endeavouring to plunge me into the abyss. William and Justine were assassinated, and the murderer escapes; he walks about the world free, and perhaps respected. But even if I were condemned to suffer on the scaffold for the same crimes, I would not change places with such a wretch."

I listened to this discourse with the extremest agony. I, not in deed, but in effect, was the true murderer. Elizabeth read my anguish in my countenance, and kindly taking my hand, said, "My dearest friend, you must calm yourself. These events have affected me, God knows how deeply; but I am not so wretched as you are. There is an expression of despair, and sometimes of revenge, in your countenance that makes me tremble. Dear Victor, banish these dark passions. Remember the friends around you, who centre all their hopes in you. Have we lost the power of rendering you happy? Ah! While we love, while we are true to each other, here in this land of peace and beauty, your native country, we may reap every tranquil blessing—

what can disturb our peace?"

And could not such words from her whom I fondly prized before every other gift of fortune suffice to chase away the fiend that lurked in my heart? Even as she spoke I drew near to her, as if in terror, lest at that very moment the destroyer had been near to rob me of her.

Thus not the tenderness of friendship, nor the beauty of earth, nor of heaven, could redeem my soul from woe; the very accents of love were ineffectual. I was encompassed by a cloud which no beneficial influence could penetrate. The wounded deer dragging its fainting limbs to some untrodden brake, there to gaze upon the arrow which had pierced it, and to die, was but a type of me.

Sometimes I could cope with the sullen despair that overwhelmed me, but sometimes the whirlwind passions of my soul drove me to seek, by bodily exercise and by change of place, some relief from my intolerable sensations. It was during an access of this kind that I suddenly left my home, and bending my steps towards the near Alpine valleys, sought in the magnificence, the eternity of such scenes, to forget myself and my ephemeral, because human, sorrows. My wanderings were directed towards the valley of Chamounix. I had visited it frequently during my boyhood. Six years had passed since then: I was a wreck, but nought had changed in those savage and enduring scenes.

I performed the first part of my journey on horseback. I afterwards hired a mule, as the more sure-footed and least liable to receive injury on these rugged roads. The weather was fine; it was about the middle of the month of August, nearly two months after the death of Justine, that miserable epoch from which I dated all my woe. The weight upon my spirit was sensibly lightened as I plunged yet deeper in the ravine of Arve. The immense mountains and precipices that overhung me on every side, the sound of the river raging among the rocks, and the dashing of the waterfalls around spoke of a power mighty as Omnipotence—and I ceased to fear or to bend before any being less almighty than that which had created and ruled the elements, here displayed in their most terrific guise. Still, as I ascended higher, the valley assumed a more magnificent and astonishing character. Ruined castles hanging on the precipices of piny mountains, the impetuous Arve, and cottages every here and there peeping forth from among the trees formed a scene of singular beauty. But it was augmented and rendered sublime by the mighty Alps, whose white and shining pyramids and domes

Frankenstein

towered above all, as belonging to another earth, the habitations of another race of beings.

I passed the bridge of Pélissier, where the ravine, which the river forms, opened before me, and I began to ascend the mountain that overhangs it. Soon after, I entered the valley of Chamounix. This valley is more wonderful and sublime, but not so beautiful and picturesque as that of Servox, through which I had just passed. The high and snowy mountains were its immediate boundaries, but I saw no more ruined castles and fertile fields. Immense glaciers approached the road; I heard the rumbling thunder of the falling avalanche and marked the smoke of its passage. Mont Blanc, the supreme and magnificent Mont Blanc, raised itself from the surrounding aiguilles, and its tremendous dôme overlooked the valley.

A tingling long-lost sense of pleasure often came across me during this journey. Some turn in the road, some new object suddenly perceived and recognised, reminded me of days gone by, and were associated with the lighthearted gaiety of boyhood. The very winds whispered in soothing accents, and maternal Nature bade me weep no more. Then again the kindly influence ceased to act—I found myself fettered again to grief and indulging in all the misery of reflection. Then I spurred on my animal, striving so to forget the world, my fears, and more than all, myself—or, in a more desperate fashion, I alighted and threw myself on the grass, weighed down by horror and despair.

At length I arrived at the village of Chamounix. Exhaustion succeeded to the extreme fatigue both of body and of mind which I had endured. For a short space of time I remained at the window watching the pallid lightnings that played above Mont Blanc and listening to the rushing of the Arve, which pursued its noisy way beneath. The same lulling sounds acted as a lullaby to my too keen sensations; when I placed my head upon my pillow, sleep crept over me; I felt it as it came and blessed the giver of oblivion.

Chapter 10

    I spent the following day roaming through the valley. I stood beside the sources of the Arveiron, which take their rise in a glacier, that with slow pace is advancing down from the summit of the hills to barricade the valley. The abrupt sides of vast mountains were before me; the icy wall of the glacier overhung me; a few shattered pines were scattered around; and the solemn silence of this glorious presence-chamber of imperial Nature was broken only by the brawling waves or the fall of some vast fragment, the thunder sound of the avalanche or the cracking, reverberated along the mountains, of the accumulated ice, which, through the silent working of immutable laws, was ever and anon rent and torn, as if it had been but a plaything in their hands. These sublime and magnificent scenes afforded me the greatest consolation that I was capable of receiving. They elevated me from all littleness of feeling, and although they did not remove my grief, they subdued and tranquillised it. In some degree, also, they diverted my mind from the thoughts over which it had brooded for the last month. I retired to rest at night; my slumbers, as it were, waited on and ministered to by the assemblance of grand shapes which I had contemplated during the day. They congregated round me; the unstained snowy mountain-top, the glittering pinnacle, the pine woods, and ragged bare ravine, the eagle, soaring amidst the clouds—they all gathered round me and bade me be at peace.

    Where had they fled when the next morning I awoke? All of soul-inspiriting fled with sleep, and dark melancholy clouded every thought. The rain was pouring in torrents, and thick mists hid the summits of the mountains, so that I even saw not the faces of those mighty friends. Still I would penetrate their misty veil and seek them in their cloudy retreats. What were rain and storm to me? My mule was brought to the door, and I resolved to ascend to the summit of Montanvert. I remembered the effect that the view of the tremendous and ever-moving glacier had produced upon my mind when I first saw it. It had then filled me with a sublime ecstasy that gave wings to the soul and allowed it to soar from the obscure world to light and joy. The sight of the awful and majestic in nature had indeed always the effect of solemnising my mind and causing me to forget the passing cares of life. I determined to go without a guide, for I was well acquainted with the path, and the presence of another would destroy the solitary grandeur of the scene.

    The ascent is precipitous, but the path is cut into continual and short windings, which enable you to surmount the perpendicularity of the mountain. It is a scene terrifically desolate. In a thousand spots the traces of the winter avalanche may be perceived, where trees lie broken and strewed on the ground, some entirely destroyed, others bent, leaning upon the jutting rocks of the mountain or transversely upon other trees. The path, as you ascend higher, is intersected by ravines of snow, down which stones continually roll from above; one of them is particularly dangerous, as the slightest sound, such as even speaking in a loud voice, produces a concussion of air sufficient to draw destruction upon the head of the speaker. The pines are not tall or luxuriant, but they are sombre and add an air of severity to the scene. I looked on the valley beneath; vast mists were rising from the rivers which ran through it and curling in thick wreaths around the opposite mountains, whose summits were hid in the uniform clouds, while rain poured from the dark sky and added to the melancholy impression I received from the objects around me. Alas! Why does man boast of sensibilities superior to those apparent in the brute; it only renders them more necessary beings. If our impulses were confined to hunger, thirst, and desire, we might be nearly free; but now we are moved by every wind that blows and a chance word or scene that that word may convey to us.

> We rest; a dream has power to poison sleep.
>> We rise; one wand'ring thought pollutes the day.
> We feel, conceive, or reason; laugh or weep,
>> Embrace fond woe, or cast our cares away;
> It is the same: for, be it joy or sorrow,
>> The path of its departure still is free.
> Man's yesterday may ne'er be like his morrow;
>> Nought may endure but mutability!

It was nearly noon when I arrived at the top of the ascent. For some time I sat upon the rock that overlooks the sea of ice. A mist covered both that and the surrounding mountains. Presently a breeze dissipated the cloud, and I descended upon the glacier. The surface is very uneven, rising like the waves of a troubled sea, descending low, and interspersed by rifts that sink deep. The field of ice is almost a league in width, but I spent nearly two hours in crossing it. The opposite mountain is a bare perpendicular rock. From the side where I now stood Montanvert was exactly opposite, at the distance of a league; and above it rose Mont Blanc, in awful majesty. I remained in a recess of the rock, gazing on this wonderful and stupendous scene. The sea, or rather the vast river of ice, wound among its dependent mountains, whose aerial summits hung over its recesses. Their icy and glittering peaks shone in the sunlight over the clouds. My heart, which was before sorrowful, now swelled with something like joy; I exclaimed, "Wandering spirits, if indeed ye wander, and do not rest in your narrow beds, allow me this faint happiness, or take me, as your companion, away from the joys of life."

As I said this I suddenly beheld the figure of a man, at some distance, advancing towards me with superhuman speed. He bounded over the crevices in the ice, among which I had walked with caution; his stature, also, as he approached, seemed to exceed that of man. I was troubled; a mist came over my eyes, and I felt a faintness seize me, but I was quickly restored by the cold gale of the mountains. I perceived, as the shape came nearer (sight tremendous and abhorred!) that it was the wretch whom I had created. I trembled with rage and horror, resolving to wait his approach and then close with him in mortal combat. He approached; his countenance bespoke bitter anguish, combined with disdain and malignity, while its unearthly ugliness rendered it almost too horrible for human eyes. But I scarcely observed this; rage and hatred had at first deprived me of utterance, and I recovered only to overwhelm him with words expressive of furious detestation and contempt.

"Devil," I exclaimed, "do you dare approach me? And do not you fear the fierce vengeance of my arm wreaked on your miserable head? Begone, vile insect! Or rather, stay, that I may trample you to dust! And, oh! That I could, with the extinction of your miserable existence, restore those victims whom you have so diabolically murdered!"

"I expected this reception," said the dæmon. "All men hate the wretched; how, then, must I be hated, who am miserable beyond all living things! Yet you, my creator, detest and spurn me, thy creature, to whom thou art bound by ties only dissoluble by the annihilation of one of us. You purpose to kill me. How dare you sport thus with life? Do your duty towards me, and I will do mine towards you and the rest of mankind. If you will comply with my conditions, I will leave them and you at peace; but if you refuse, I will glut the maw of death, until it be satiated with the blood of your remaining friends."

"Abhorred monster! Fiend that thou art! The tortures of hell are too mild a vengeance for thy crimes. Wretched devil! You reproach me with your creation, come on, then, that I may extinguish the spark which I so negligently bestowed."

My rage was without bounds; I sprang on him, impelled by all the feelings which can arm one being against the existence of another.

He easily eluded me and said,

"Be calm! I entreat you to hear me before you give vent to your hatred on my devoted head. Have I not suffered enough, that you seek to increase my misery? Life, although it may only be an accumulation of anguish, is dear to me, and I will defend it. Remember, thou hast made me more powerful than thyself; my height is superior to thine, my joints more supple. But I will not be tempted to set myself in opposition to thee. I am thy creature, and I will be even mild and docile to my natural lord and king if thou wilt also perform thy part, the which thou owest me. Oh, Frankenstein, be not equitable to every other and trample upon me alone, to whom thy justice, and even thy clemency and affection, is most due. Remember that I am thy creature; I ought to be thy Adam, but I am rather the fallen angel, whom thou drivest from joy for no misdeed. Everywhere I see bliss, from which I alone am irrevocably excluded. I was benevolent and good; misery made me a fiend. Make me happy, and I shall again be virtuous."

"Begone! I will not hear you. There can be no community between you and me; we are enemies. Begone, or let us try our strength in a fight, in which one must fall."

"How can I move thee? Will no entreaties cause thee to turn a favourable eye upon thy creature, who implores thy goodness and compassion? Believe me, Frankenstein, I was benevolent; my soul glowed with love and humanity; but am I not alone, miserably alone? You, my creator, abhor me; what hope can I gather from your fellow creatures, who owe me nothing? They spurn and hate me. The desert mountains and dreary glaciers are my refuge. I have wandered here many days; the caves of ice, which I only do not fear, are a dwelling to me, and the only one which man does not grudge. These bleak skies I hail, for they are kinder to me than your fellow beings. If the multitude of mankind knew of my existence, they would do as you do, and arm themselves for my destruction. Shall I not then hate them who abhor me? I will keep no terms with my enemies. I am miserable, and they shall share my wretchedness. Yet it is in your power to recompense me, and deliver them from an evil which it only remains for you to make so great, that not only you and your family, but thousands of others, shall be swallowed up in the whirlwinds of its rage. Let your compassion be moved, and do not disdain me. Listen to my tale;

when you have heard that, abandon or commiserate me, as you shall judge that I deserve. But hear me. The guilty are allowed, by human laws, bloody as they are, to speak in their own defence before they are condemned. Listen to me, Frankenstein. You accuse me of murder, and yet you would, with a satisfied conscience, destroy your own creature. Oh, praise the eternal justice of man! Yet I ask you not to spare me; listen to me, and then, if you can, and if you will, destroy the work of your hands."

"Why do you call to my remembrance," I rejoined, "circumstances of which I shudder to reflect, that I have been the miserable origin and author? Cursed be the day, abhorred devil, in which you first saw light! Cursed (although I curse myself) be the hands that formed you! You have made me wretched beyond expression. You have left me no power to consider whether I am just to you or not. Begone! Relieve me from the sight of your detested form."

"Thus I relieve thee, my creator," he said, and placed his hated hands before my eyes, which I flung from me with violence; "thus I take from thee a sight which you abhor. Still thou canst listen to me and grant me thy compassion. By the virtues that I once possessed, I demand this from you. Hear my tale; it is long and strange, and the temperature of this place is not fitting to your fine sensations; come to the hut upon the mountain. The sun is yet high in the heavens; before it descends to hide itself behind your snowy precipices and illuminate another world, you will have heard my story and can decide. On you it rests, whether I quit for ever the neighbourhood of man and lead a harmless life, or become the scourge of your fellow creatures and the author of your own speedy ruin."

As he said this he led the way across the ice; I followed. My heart was full, and I did not answer him, but as I proceeded, I weighed the various arguments that he had used and determined at least to listen to his tale. I was partly urged by curiosity, and compassion confirmed my resolution. I had hitherto supposed him to be the murderer of my brother, and I eagerly sought a confirmation or denial of this opinion. For the first time, also, I felt what the duties of a creator towards his creature were, and that I ought to render him happy before I complained of his wickedness. These motives urged me to comply with his demand. We crossed the ice, therefore, and ascended the opposite rock. The air was cold, and the rain again began to descend; we entered the hut, the fiend with an air of exultation, I with a heavy heart and depressed spirits. But I consented to listen, and seating myself by the fire which my odious companion had lighted, he thus began his tale.

Chapter 11

"It is with considerable difficulty that I remember the original era of my being; all the events of that period appear confused and indistinct. A strange multiplicity of sensations seized me, and I saw, felt, heard, and smelt at the same time; and it was, indeed, a long time before I learned to distinguish between the operations of my various senses. By degrees, I remember, a stronger light pressed upon my nerves, so that I was obliged to shut my eyes. Darkness then came over me and troubled me, but hardly had I felt this when, by opening my eyes, as I now suppose, the light poured in upon me again. I walked and, I believe, descended, but I presently found a great alteration in my sensations. Before, dark and opaque bodies had surrounded me, impervious to my touch or sight; but I now found that I could wander on at liberty, with no obstacles which I could not either surmount or avoid. The light became more and more oppressive to me, and the heat wearying me as I walked, I sought a place where I could receive shade. This was the forest near Ingolstadt; and here I lay by the side of a brook resting from my fatigue, until I felt tormented by hunger and thirst. This roused me from my nearly dormant state, and I ate some berries which I found hanging on the trees or lying on the ground. I slaked my thirst at the brook, and then lying down, was overcome by sleep.

"It was dark when I awoke; I felt cold also, and half frightened, as it were, instinctively, finding myself so desolate. Before I had quitted your apartment, on a sensation of cold, I had covered myself with some clothes, but these were insufficient to secure me from the dews of night. I was a poor, helpless, miserable wretch; I knew, and could distinguish, nothing; but feeling pain invade me on all sides, I sat down and wept.

"Soon a gentle light stole over the heavens and gave me a sensation of pleasure. I started up and beheld a radiant form rise from among the trees. [The moon] I gazed with a kind of wonder. It moved slowly, but it enlightened my path, and I again went out in search of berries. I was still cold when under one of the trees I found a huge cloak, with which I covered myself, and sat down upon the ground. No distinct ideas occupied my mind; all was confused. I felt light, and hunger, and thirst, and darkness; innumerable sounds rang in my ears, and on all sides various scents saluted me; the only object that I could distinguish was the bright moon, and I fixed my eyes on that with pleasure.

"Several changes of day and night passed, and the orb of night had greatly lessened, when I began to distinguish my sensations from each other. I gradually saw plainly the clear stream that supplied me with drink and the trees that shaded me with their foliage. I was delighted when I first discovered that a pleasant sound, which often saluted my ears, proceeded from the throats of the little winged animals who had often intercepted the light from my eyes. I began also to observe, with greater accuracy, the forms that surrounded me and to perceive the boundaries of the radiant roof of light which canopied me. Sometimes I tried to imitate the pleasant songs of the birds but was unable. Sometimes I wished to express my sensations in my own mode, but the uncouth and inarticulate sounds which broke from me frightened me into silence again.

"The moon had disappeared from the night, and again, with a lessened form, showed itself, while I still remained in the forest. My sensations had by this time become distinct, and my mind received every day additional ideas. My eyes became accustomed to the light and to perceive objects in their right forms; I distinguished the insect from the herb, and by degrees, one herb from another. I found that the sparrow uttered none but harsh notes, whilst those of the blackbird and thrush were sweet and enticing.

"One day, when I was oppressed by cold, I found a fire which had been left by some wandering beggars, and was overcome with delight at the warmth I experienced from it. In my joy I thrust my hand into the live embers, but quickly drew it out again with a cry of pain. How strange, I thought, that the same cause should produce such opposite effects! I examined the materials of the fire, and to my joy found it to be composed of wood. I quickly collected some branches, but they were wet and would not burn. I was pained at this and sat still watching the operation of the fire. The wet wood which I had placed near the heat dried and itself became inflamed. I reflected on this, and by touching the various branches, I discovered the cause and busied myself in collecting a great quantity of wood, that I might dry it and have a plentiful supply of fire. When night came on and brought sleep with it, I was in the greatest fear lest my fire should be extinguished. I covered it carefully with dry wood and leaves and placed wet branches upon it; and then, spreading my cloak, I lay on the ground and sank into sleep.

"It was morning when I awoke, and my first care was to visit the fire. I uncovered it, and a gentle breeze quickly fanned it into a flame. I observed this also and contrived a fan of branches, which roused the embers when they were nearly

Frankenstein

extinguished. When night came again I found, with pleasure, that the fire gave light as well as heat and that the discovery of this element was useful to me in my food, for I found some of the offals that the travellers had left had been roasted, and tasted much more savoury than the berries I gathered from the trees. I tried, therefore, to dress my food in the same manner, placing it on the live embers. I found that the berries were spoiled by this operation, and the nuts and roots much improved.

"Food, however, became scarce, and I often spent the whole day searching in vain for a few acorns to assuage the pangs of hunger. When I found this, I resolved to quit the place that I had hitherto inhabited, to seek for one where the few wants I experienced would be more easily satisfied. In this emigration I exceedingly lamented the loss of the fire which I had obtained through accident and knew not how to reproduce it. I gave several hours to the serious consideration of this difficulty, but I was obliged to relinquish all attempt to supply it, and wrapping myself up in my cloak, I struck across the wood towards the setting sun. I passed three days in these rambles and at length discovered the open country. A great fall of snow had taken place the night before, and the fields were of one uniform white; the appearance was disconsolate, and I found my feet chilled by the cold damp substance that covered the ground.

"It was about seven in the morning, and I longed to obtain food and shelter; at length I perceived a small hut, on a rising ground, which had doubtless been built for the convenience of some shepherd. This was a new sight to me, and I examined the structure with great curiosity. Finding the door open, I entered. An old man sat in it, near a fire, over which he was preparing his breakfast. He turned on hearing a noise, and perceiving me, shrieked loudly, and quitting the hut, ran across the fields with a speed of which his debilitated form hardly appeared capable. His appearance, different from any I had ever before seen, and his flight somewhat surprised me. But I was enchanted by the appearance of the hut; here the snow and rain could not penetrate; the ground was dry; and it presented to me then as exquisite and divine a retreat as Pandæmonium appeared to the dæmons of hell after their sufferings in the lake of fire. I greedily devoured the remnants of the shepherd's breakfast, which consisted of bread, cheese, milk, and wine; the latter, however, I did not like. Then, overcome by fatigue, I lay down among some straw and fell asleep.

"It was noon when I awoke, and allured by the warmth of the sun, which shone brightly on the white ground, I determined to recommence my travels; and, depositing the remains of the peasant's breakfast in a wallet I found, I proceeded across the fields for several hours, until at sunset I arrived at a village. How miraculous did this appear! The huts, the neater cottages, and stately houses engaged my admiration by turns. The vegetables in the gardens, the milk and cheese that I saw placed at the windows of some of the cottages, allured my appetite. One of the best of these I entered, but I had hardly placed my foot within the door before the children shrieked, and one of the women fainted. The whole village was roused; some fled, some attacked me, until, grievously bruised by stones and many other kinds of missile weapons, I escaped to the open country and fearfully took refuge in a low hovel, quite bare, and making a wretched appearance after the palaces I had beheld in the village. This hovel however, joined a cottage of a neat and pleasant appearance, but after my late dearly bought experience, I dared not enter it. My place of refuge was constructed of wood, but so low that I could with difficulty sit upright in it. No wood, however, was placed on the earth, which formed the floor, but it was dry; and although the wind entered it by innumerable chinks, I found it an agreeable asylum from the snow and rain.

"Here, then, I retreated and lay down happy to have found a shelter, however miserable, from the inclemency of the season, and still more from the barbarity of man. As soon as morning dawned I crept from my kennel, that I might view the adjacent cottage and discover if I could remain in the habitation I had found. It was situated against the back of the cottage and surrounded on the sides which were exposed by a pig sty and a clear pool of water. One part was open, and by that I had crept in; but now I covered every crevice by which I might be perceived with stones and wood, yet in such a manner that I might move them on occasion to pass out; all the light I enjoyed came through the sty, and that was sufficient for me.

"Having thus arranged my dwelling and carpeted it with clean straw, I retired, for I saw the figure of a man at a distance, and I remembered too well my treatment the night before to trust myself in his power. I had first, however, provided for my sustenance for that day by a loaf of coarse bread, which I purloined, and a cup with which I could drink more conveniently than from my hand of the pure water which flowed by my retreat. The floor was a little raised, so that it was kept perfectly dry, and by its vicinity to the chimney of the cottage it was tolerably warm.

Frankenstein

"Being thus provided, I resolved to reside in this hovel until something should occur which might alter my determination. It was indeed a paradise compared to the bleak forest, my former residence, the rain-dropping branches, and dank earth. I ate my breakfast with pleasure and was about to remove a plank to procure myself a little water when I heard a step, and looking through a small chink, I beheld a young creature, with a pail on her head, passing before my hovel. The girl was young and of gentle demeanour, unlike what I have since found cottagers and farmhouse servants to be. Yet she was meanly dressed, a coarse blue petticoat and a linen jacket being her only garb; her fair hair was plaited but not adorned: she looked patient yet sad. I lost sight of her, and in about a quarter of an hour she returned bearing the pail, which was now partly filled with milk. As she walked along, seemingly incommoded by the burden, a young man met her, whose countenance expressed a deeper despondence. Uttering a few sounds with an air of melancholy, he took the pail from her head and bore it to the cottage himself. She followed, and they disappeared. Presently I saw the young man again, with some tools in his hand, cross the field behind the cottage; and the girl was also busied, sometimes in the house and sometimes in the yard.

"On examining my dwelling, I found that one of the windows of the cottage had formerly occupied a part of it, but the panes had been filled up with wood. In one of these was a small and almost imperceptible chink through which the eye could just penetrate. Through this crevice a small room was visible, whitewashed and clean but very bare of furniture. In one corner, near a small fire, sat an old man, leaning his head on his hands in a disconsolate attitude. The young girl was occupied in arranging the cottage; but presently she took something out of a drawer, which employed her hands, and she sat down beside the old man, who, taking up an instrument, began to play and to produce sounds sweeter than the voice of the thrush or the nightingale. It was a lovely sight, even to me, poor wretch who had never beheld aught beautiful before. The silver hair and benevolent countenance of the aged cottager won my reverence, while the gentle manners of the girl enticed my love. He played a sweet mournful air which I perceived drew tears from the eyes of his amiable companion, of which the old man took no notice, until she sobbed audibly; he then pronounced a few sounds, and the fair creature, leaving her work, knelt at his feet. He raised her and smiled with such kindness and affection that I felt sensations of a peculiar and overpowering nature; they were a mixture of pain and pleasure, such as I had never before experienced, either from hunger or cold, warmth or food; and I withdrew from the window, unable to bear these emotions.

"Soon after this the young man returned, bearing on his shoulders a load of wood. The girl met him at the door, helped to relieve him of his burden, and taking some of the fuel into the cottage, placed it on the fire; then she and the youth went apart into a nook of the cottage, and he showed her a large loaf and a piece of cheese. She seemed pleased and went into the garden for some roots and plants, which she placed in water, and then upon the fire. She afterwards continued her work, whilst the young man went into the garden and appeared busily employed in digging and pulling up roots. After he had been employed thus about an hour, the young woman joined him and they entered the cottage together.

"The old man had, in the meantime, been pensive, but on the appearance of his companions he assumed a more cheerful air, and they sat down to eat. The meal was quickly dispatched. The young woman was again occupied in arranging the cottage, the old man walked before the cottage in the sun for a few minutes, leaning on the arm of the youth. Nothing could exceed in beauty the contrast between these two excellent creatures. One was old, with silver hairs and a countenance beaming with benevolence and love; the younger was slight and graceful in his figure, and his features were moulded with the finest symmetry, yet his eyes and attitude expressed the utmost sadness and despondency. The old man returned to the cottage, and the youth, with tools different from those he had used in the morning, directed his steps across the fields.

"Night quickly shut in, but to my extreme wonder, I found that the cottagers had a means of prolonging light by the use of tapers, and was delighted to find that the setting of the sun did not put an end to the pleasure I experienced in watching my human neighbours. In the evening the young girl and her companion were employed in various occupations which I did not understand; and the old man again took up the instrument which produced the divine sounds that had enchanted me in the morning. So soon as he had finished, the youth began, not to play, but to utter sounds that were monotonous, and neither resembling the harmony of the old man's instrument nor the songs of the birds; I since found that he read aloud, but at that time I knew nothing of the science of words or letters.

"The family, after having been thus occupied for a short time, extinguished their lights and retired, as I conjectured, to rest."

Chapter 12

"I lay on my straw, but I could not sleep. I thought of the occurrences of the day. What chiefly struck me was the gentle manners of these people, and I longed to join them, but dared not. I remembered too well the treatment I had suffered the night before from the barbarous villagers, and resolved, whatever course of conduct I might hereafter think it right to pursue, that for the present I would remain quietly in my hovel, watching and endeavouring to discover the motives which influenced their actions.

"The cottagers arose the next morning before the sun. The young woman arranged the cottage and prepared the food, and the youth departed after the first meal.

"This day was passed in the same routine as that which preceded it. The young man was constantly employed out of doors, and the girl in various laborious occupations within. The old man, whom I soon perceived to be blind, employed his leisure hours on his instrument or in contemplation. Nothing could exceed the love and respect which the younger cottagers exhibited towards their venerable companion. They performed towards him every little office of affection and duty with gentleness, and he rewarded them by his benevolent smiles.

"They were not entirely happy. The young man and his companion often went apart and appeared to weep. I saw no cause for their unhappiness, but I was deeply affected by it. If such lovely creatures were miserable, it was less strange that I, an imperfect and solitary being, should be wretched. Yet why were these gentle beings unhappy? They possessed a delightful house (for such it was in my eyes) and every luxury; they had a fire to warm them when chill and delicious viands when hungry; they were dressed in excellent clothes; and, still more, they enjoyed one another's company and speech, interchanging each day looks of affection and kindness. What did their tears imply? Did they really express pain? I was at first unable to solve these questions, but perpetual attention and time explained to me many appearances which were at first enigmatic.

"A considerable period elapsed before I discovered one of the causes of the uneasiness of this amiable family: it was poverty, and they suffered that evil in a very distressing degree. Their nourishment consisted entirely of the vegetables of their garden and the milk of one cow, which gave very little during the winter, when its masters could scarcely procure food to support it. They often, I believe, suffered the pangs of hunger very poignantly, especially the two younger cottagers, for several times they placed food before the old man when they reserved none for themselves.

"This trait of kindness moved me sensibly. I had been accustomed, during the night, to steal a part of their store for my own consumption, but when I found that in doing this I inflicted pain on the cottagers, I abstained and satisfied myself with berries, nuts, and roots which I gathered from a neighbouring wood.

"I discovered also another means through which I was enabled to assist their labours. I found that the youth spent a great part of each day in collecting wood for the family fire, and during the night I often took his tools, the use of which I quickly discovered, and brought home firing sufficient for the consumption of several days.

"I remember, the first time that I did this, the young woman, when she opened the door in the morning, appeared greatly astonished on seeing a great pile of wood on the outside. She uttered some words in a loud voice, and the youth joined her, who also expressed surprise. I observed, with pleasure, that he did not go to the forest that day, but spent it in repairing the cottage and cultivating the garden.

"By degrees I made a discovery of still greater moment. I found that these people possessed a method of communicating their experience and feelings to one another by articulate sounds. I perceived that the words they spoke sometimes produced pleasure or pain, smiles or sadness, in the minds and countenances of the hearers. This was indeed a godlike science, and I ardently desired to become acquainted with it. But I was baffled in every attempt I made for this purpose. Their pronunciation was quick, and the words they uttered, not having any apparent connection with visible objects, I was unable to discover any clue by which I could unravel the mystery of their reference. By great application, however, and after having remained during the space of several revolutions of the moon in my hovel, I discovered the names that were given to some of the most familiar objects of discourse; I learned and applied the words, fire, milk, bread, and wood. I learned also the names of the cottagers themselves. The youth and his companion had each of them several names, but the old man had only one, which was father. The girl was called sister or Agatha, and the youth Felix, brother, or son. I cannot describe the delight I felt when I learned the ideas appropriated to each

Frankenstein

of these sounds and was able to pronounce them. I distinguished several other words without being able as yet to understand or apply them, such as good, dearest, unhappy.

"I spent the winter in this manner. The gentle manners and beauty of the cottagers greatly endeared them to me; when they were unhappy, I felt depressed; when they rejoiced, I sympathised in their joys. I saw few human beings besides them, and if any other happened to enter the cottage, their harsh manners and rude gait only enhanced to me the superior accomplishments of my friends. The old man, I could perceive, often endeavoured to encourage his children, as sometimes I found that he called them, to cast off their melancholy. He would talk in a cheerful accent, with an expression of goodness that bestowed pleasure even upon me. Agatha listened with respect, her eyes sometimes filled with tears, which she endeavoured to wipe away unperceived; but I generally found that her countenance and tone were more cheerful after having listened to the exhortations of her father. It was not thus with Felix. He was always the saddest of the group, and even to my unpractised senses, he appeared to have suffered more deeply than his friends. But if his countenance was more sorrowful, his voice was more cheerful than that of his sister, especially when he addressed the old man.

"I could mention innumerable instances which, although slight, marked the dispositions of these amiable cottagers. In the midst of poverty and want, Felix carried with pleasure to his sister the first little white flower that peeped out from beneath the snowy ground. Early in the morning, before she had risen, he cleared away the snow that obstructed her path to the milk-house, drew water from the well, and brought the wood from the outhouse, where, to his perpetual astonishment, he found his store always replenished by an invisible hand. In the day, I believe, he worked sometimes for a neighbouring farmer, because he often went forth and did not return until dinner, yet brought no wood with him. At other times he worked in the garden, but as there was little to do in the frosty season, he read to the old man and Agatha.

"This reading had puzzled me extremely at first, but by degrees I discovered that he uttered many of the same sounds when he read as when he talked. I conjectured, therefore, that he found on the paper signs for speech which he understood, and I ardently longed to comprehend these also; but how was that possible when I did not even understand the sounds for which they stood as signs? I improved, however, sensibly in this science, but not sufficiently to follow up any kind of conversation, although I applied my whole mind to the endeavour, for I easily perceived that, although I eagerly longed to discover myself to the cottagers, I ought not to make the attempt until I had first become master of their language, which knowledge might enable me to make them overlook the deformity of my figure, for with this also the contrast perpetually presented to my eyes had made me acquainted.

"I had admired the perfect forms of my cottagers—their grace, beauty, and delicate complexions; but how was I terrified when I viewed myself in a transparent pool! At first I started back, unable to believe that it was indeed I who was reflected in the mirror; and when I became fully convinced that I was in reality the monster that I am, I was filled with the bitterest sensations of despondence and mortification. Alas! I did not yet entirely know the fatal effects of this miserable deformity.

"As the sun became warmer and the light of day longer, the snow vanished, and I beheld the bare trees and the black earth. From this time Felix was more employed, and the heart-moving indications of impending famine disappeared. Their food, as I afterwards found, was coarse, but it was wholesome; and they procured a sufficiency of it. Several new kinds of plants sprang up in the garden, which they dressed; and these signs of comfort increased daily as the season advanced.

"The old man, leaning on his son, walked each day at noon, when it did not rain, as I found it was called when the heavens poured forth its waters. This frequently took place, but a high wind quickly dried the earth, and the season became far more pleasant than it had been.

"My mode of life in my hovel was uniform. During the morning I attended the motions of the cottagers, and when they were dispersed in various occupations, I slept; the remainder of the day was spent in observing my friends. When they had retired to rest, if there was any moon or the night was star-light, I went into the woods and collected my own food and fuel for the cottage. When I returned, as often as it was necessary, I cleared their path from the snow and performed those offices that I had seen done by Felix. I afterwards found that these labours, performed by an invisible hand, greatly astonished them; and once or twice I heard them, on these occasions, utter the words good spirit, wonderful; but I did not then understand the signification of these terms.

Frankenstein

"My thoughts now became more active, and I longed to discover the motives and feelings of these lovely creatures; I was inquisitive to know why Felix appeared so miserable and Agatha so sad. I thought (foolish wretch!) that it might be in my power to restore happiness to these deserving people. When I slept or was absent, the forms of the venerable blind father, the gentle Agatha, and the excellent Felix flitted before me. I looked upon them as superior beings who would be the arbiters of my future destiny. I formed in my imagination a thousand pictures of presenting myself to them, and their reception of me. I imagined that they would be disgusted, until, by my gentle demeanour and conciliating words, I should first win their favour and afterwards their love.

"These thoughts exhilarated me and led me to apply with fresh ardour to the acquiring the art of language. My organs were indeed harsh, but supple; and although my voice was very unlike the soft music of their tones, yet I pronounced such words as I understood with tolerable ease. It was as the ass and the lap-dog; yet surely the gentle ass whose intentions were affectionate, although his manners were rude, deserved better treatment than blows and execration.

"The pleasant showers and genial warmth of spring greatly altered the aspect of the earth. Men who before this change seemed to have been hid in caves dispersed themselves and were employed in various arts of cultivation. The birds sang in more cheerful notes, and the leaves began to bud forth on the trees. Happy, happy earth! Fit habitation for gods, which, so short a time before, was bleak, damp, and unwholesome. My spirits were elevated by the enchanting appearance of nature; the past was blotted from my memory, the present was tranquil, and the future gilded by bright rays of hope and anticipations of joy."

Chapter 13

"I now hasten to the more moving part of my story. I shall relate events that impressed me with feelings which, from what I had been, have made me what I am.

"Spring advanced rapidly; the weather became fine and the skies cloudless. It surprised me that what before was desert and gloomy should now bloom with the most beautiful flowers and verdure. My senses were gratified and refreshed by a thousand scents of delight and a thousand sights of beauty.

"It was on one of these days, when my cottagers periodically rested from labour—the old man played on his guitar, and the children listened to him—that I observed the countenance of Felix was melancholy beyond expression; he sighed frequently, and once his father paused in his music, and I conjectured by his manner that he inquired the cause of his son's sorrow. Felix replied in a cheerful accent, and the old man was recommencing his music when someone tapped at the door.

"It was a lady on horseback, accompanied by a country-man as a guide. The lady was dressed in a dark suit and covered with a thick black veil. Agatha asked a question, to which the stranger only replied by pronouncing, in a sweet accent, the name of Felix. Her voice was musical but unlike that of either of my friends. On hearing this word, Felix came up hastily to the lady, who, when she saw him, threw up her veil, and I beheld a countenance of angelic beauty and expression. Her hair of a shining raven black, and curiously braided; her eyes were dark, but gentle, although animated; her features of a regular proportion, and her complexion wondrously fair, each cheek tinged with a lovely pink.

"Felix seemed ravished with delight when he saw her, every trait of sorrow vanished from his face, and it instantly expressed a degree of ecstatic joy, of which I could hardly have believed it capable; his eyes sparkled, as his cheek flushed with pleasure; and at that moment I thought him as beautiful as the stranger. She appeared affected by different feelings; wiping a few tears from her lovely eyes, she held out her hand to Felix, who kissed it rapturously and called her, as well as I could distinguish, his sweet Arabian. She did not appear to understand him, but smiled. He assisted her to dismount, and dismissing her guide, conducted her into the cottage. Some conversation took place between him and his father, and the young stranger knelt at the old man's feet and would have kissed his hand, but he raised her and embraced her affectionately.

Frankenstein

"I soon perceived that although the stranger uttered articulate sounds and appeared to have a language of her own, she was neither understood by nor herself understood the cottagers. They made many signs which I did not comprehend, but I saw that her presence diffused gladness through the cottage, dispelling their sorrow as the sun dissipates the morning mists. Felix seemed peculiarly happy and with smiles of delight welcomed his Arabian. Agatha, the ever-gentle Agatha, kissed the hands of the lovely stranger, and pointing to her brother, made signs which appeared to me to mean that he had been sorrowful until she came. Some hours passed thus, while they, by their countenances, expressed joy, the cause of which I did not comprehend. Presently I found, by the frequent recurrence of some sound which the stranger repeated after them, that she was endeavouring to learn their language; and the idea instantly occurred to me that I should make use of the same instructions to the same end. The stranger learned about twenty words at the first lesson; most of them, indeed, were those which I had before understood, but I profited by the others.

"As night came on, Agatha and the Arabian retired early. When they separated Felix kissed the hand of the stranger and said, 'Good night sweet Safie.' He sat up much longer, conversing with his father, and by the frequent repetition of her name I conjectured that their lovely guest was the subject of their conversation. I ardently desired to understand them, and bent every faculty towards that purpose, but found it utterly impossible.

"The next morning Felix went out to his work, and after the usual occupations of Agatha were finished, the Arabian sat at the feet of the old man, and taking his guitar, played some airs so entrancingly beautiful that they at once drew tears of sorrow and delight from my eyes. She sang, and her voice flowed in a rich cadence, swelling or dying away like a nightingale of the woods.

"When she had finished, she gave the guitar to Agatha, who at first declined it. She played a simple air, and her voice accompanied it in sweet accents, but unlike the wondrous strain of the stranger. The old man appeared enraptured and said some words which Agatha endeavoured to explain to Safie, and by which he appeared to wish to express that she bestowed on him the greatest delight by her music.

"The days now passed as peaceably as before, with the sole alteration that joy had taken place of sadness in the countenances of my friends. Safie was always gay and happy; she and I improved rapidly in the knowledge of language, so that in two months I began to comprehend most of the words uttered by my protectors.

"In the meanwhile also the black ground was covered with herbage, and the green banks interspersed with innumerable flowers, sweet to the scent and the eyes, stars of pale radiance among the moonlight woods; the sun became warmer, the nights clear and balmy; and my nocturnal rambles were an extreme pleasure to me, although they were considerably shortened by the late setting and early rising of the sun, for I never ventured abroad during daylight, fearful of meeting with the same treatment I had formerly endured in the first village which I entered.

"My days were spent in close attention, that I might more speedily master the language; and I may boast that I improved more rapidly than the Arabian, who understood very little and conversed in broken accents, whilst I comprehended and could imitate almost every word that was spoken.

"While I improved in speech, I also learned the science of letters as it was taught to the stranger, and this opened before me a wide field for wonder and delight.

"The book from which Felix instructed Safie was Volney's Ruins of Empires. I should not have understood the purport of this book had not Felix, in reading it, given very minute explanations. He had chosen this work, he said, because the declamatory style was framed in imitation of the Eastern authors. Through this work I obtained a cursory knowledge of history and a view of the several empires at present existing in the world; it gave me an insight into the manners, governments, and religions of the different nations of the earth. I heard of the slothful Asiatics, of the stupendous genius and mental activity of the Grecians, of the wars and wonderful virtue of the early Romans — of their subsequent degenerating — of the decline of that mighty empire, of chivalry, Christianity, and kings. I heard of the discovery of the American hemisphere and wept with Safie over the hapless fate of its original inhabitants.

"These wonderful narrations inspired me with strange feelings. Was man, indeed, at once so powerful, so virtuous and magnificent, yet so vicious and base? He appeared at one time a mere scion of the evil principle and at another as all that can be conceived of noble and godlike. To be a great and virtuous man appeared the highest honour that can befall a sensitive being; to

Frankenstein

be base and vicious, as many on record have been, appeared the lowest degradation, a condition more abject than that of the blind mole or harmless worm. For a long time I could not conceive how one man could go forth to murder his fellow, or even why there were laws and governments; but when I heard details of vice and bloodshed, my wonder ceased and I turned away with disgust and loathing.

"Every conversation of the cottagers now opened new wonders to me. While I listened to the instructions which Felix bestowed upon the Arabian, the strange system of human society was explained to me. I heard of the division of property, of immense wealth and squalid poverty, of rank, descent, and noble blood.

"The words induced me to turn towards myself. I learned that the possessions most esteemed by your fellow creatures were high and unsullied descent united with riches. A man might be respected with only one of these advantages, but without either he was considered, except in very rare instances, as a vagabond and a slave, doomed to waste his powers for the profits of the chosen few! And what was I? Of my creation and creator I was absolutely ignorant, but I knew that I possessed no money, no friends, no kind of property. I was, besides, endued with a figure hideously deformed and loathsome; I was not even of the same nature as man. I was more agile than they and could subsist upon coarser diet; I bore the extremes of heat and cold with less injury to my frame; my stature far exceeded theirs. When I looked around I saw and heard of none like me. Was I, then, a monster, a blot upon the earth, from which all men fled and whom all men disowned?

"I cannot describe to you the agony that these reflections inflicted upon me; I tried to dispel them, but sorrow only increased with knowledge. Oh, that I had for ever remained in my native wood, nor known nor felt beyond the sensations of hunger, thirst, and heat!

"Of what a strange nature is knowledge! It clings to the mind when it has once seized on it like a lichen on the rock. I wished sometimes to shake off all thought and feeling, but I learned that there was but one means to overcome the sensation of pain, and that was death—a state which I feared yet did not understand. I admired virtue and good feelings and loved the gentle manners and amiable qualities of my cottagers, but I was shut out from intercourse with them, except through means which I obtained by stealth, when I was unseen and unknown, and which rather increased than satisfied the desire I had of becoming one among my fellows. The gentle words of Agatha and the animated smiles of the charming Arabian were not for me. The mild exhortations of the old man and the lively conversation of the loved Felix were not for me. Miserable, unhappy wretch!

"Other lessons were impressed upon me even more deeply. I heard of the difference of sexes, and the birth and growth of children, how the father doted on the smiles of the infant, and the lively sallies of the older child, how all the life and cares of the mother were wrapped up in the precious charge, how the mind of youth expanded and gained knowledge, of brother, sister, and all the various relationships which bind one human being to another in mutual bonds.

"But where were my friends and relations? No father had watched my infant days, no mother had blessed me with smiles and caresses; or if they had, all my past life was now a blot, a blind vacancy in which I distinguished nothing. From my earliest remembrance I had been as I then was in height and proportion. I had never yet seen a being resembling me or who claimed any intercourse with me. What was I? The question again recurred, to be answered only with groans.

"I will soon explain to what these feelings tended, but allow me now to return to the cottagers, whose story excited in me such various feelings of indignation, delight, and wonder, but which all terminated in additional love and reverence for my protectors (for so I loved, in an innocent, half-painful self-deceit, to call them)."

Chapter 14

"Some time elapsed before I learned the history of my friends. It was one which could not fail to impress itself deeply on my mind, unfolding as it did a number of circumstances, each interesting and wonderful to one so utterly inexperienced as I was.

"The name of the old man was De Lacey. He was descended from a good family in France, where he had lived for many years in affluence, respected by his superiors and beloved by his equals. His son was bred in the service of his country, and Agatha had ranked with ladies of the highest distinction. A few months before my arrival they had lived in a large and luxurious city called Paris, surrounded by friends and possessed of every enjoyment which virtue, refinement of intellect, or taste, accompanied by a moderate fortune, could afford.

"The father of Safie had been the cause of their ruin. He was a Turkish merchant and had inhabited Paris for many years, when, for some reason which I could not learn, he became obnoxious to the government. He was seized and cast into prison the very day that Safie arrived from Constantinople to join him. He was tried and condemned to death. The injustice of his sentence was very flagrant; all Paris was indignant; and it was judged that his religion and wealth rather than the crime alleged against him had been the cause of his condemnation.

"Felix had accidentally been present at the trial; his horror and indignation were uncontrollable when he heard the decision of the court. He made, at that moment, a solemn vow to deliver him and then looked around for the means. After many fruitless attempts to gain admittance to the prison, he found a strongly grated window in an unguarded part of the building, which lighted the dungeon of the unfortunate Muhammadan, who, loaded with chains, waited in despair the execution of the barbarous sentence. Felix visited the grate at night and made known to the prisoner his intentions in his favour. The Turk, amazed and delighted, endeavoured to kindle the zeal of his deliverer by promises of reward and wealth. Felix rejected his offers with contempt, yet when he saw the lovely Safie, who was allowed to visit her father and who by her gestures expressed her lively gratitude, the youth could not help owning to his own mind that the captive possessed a treasure which would fully reward his toil and hazard.

"The Turk quickly perceived the impression that his daughter had made on the heart of Felix and endeavoured to secure him more entirely in his interests by the promise of her hand in marriage so soon as he should be conveyed to a place of safety. Felix was too delicate to accept this offer, yet he looked forward to the probability of the event as to the consummation of his happiness.

"During the ensuing days, while the preparations were going forward for the escape of the merchant, the zeal of Felix was warmed by several letters that he received from this lovely girl, who found means to express her thoughts in the language of her lover by the aid of an old man, a servant of her father who understood French. She thanked him in the most ardent terms for his intended services towards her parent, and at the same time she gently deplored her own fate.

"I have copies of these letters, for I found means, during my residence in the hovel, to procure the implements of writing; and the letters were often in the hands of Felix or Agatha. Before I depart I will give them to you; they will prove the truth of my tale; but at present, as the sun is already far declined, I shall only have time to repeat the substance of them to you.

"Safie related that her mother was a Christian Arab, seized and made a slave by the Turks; recommended by her beauty, she had won the heart of the father of Safie, who married her. The young girl spoke in high and enthusiastic terms of her mother, who, born in freedom, spurned the bondage to which she was now reduced. She instructed her daughter in the tenets of her religion and taught her to aspire to higher powers of intellect and an independence of spirit forbidden to the female followers of Muhammad. This lady died, but her lessons were indelibly impressed on the mind of Safie, who sickened at the prospect of again returning to Asia and being immured within the walls of a harem, allowed only to occupy herself with infantile amusements, ill-suited to the temper of her soul, now accustomed to grand ideas and a noble emulation for virtue. The prospect of marrying a Christian and remaining in a country where women were allowed to take a rank in society was enchanting to her.

"The day for the execution of the Turk was fixed, but on the night previous to it he quitted his prison and before morning was distant many leagues from Paris. Felix had procured passports in the name of his father, sister, and himself. He had previously communicated his plan to the former, who aided the deceit by quitting his house, under the pretence of a journey

Frankenstein

and concealed himself, with his daughter, in an obscure part of Paris.

"Felix conducted the fugitives through France to Lyons and across Mont Cenis to Leghorn, where the merchant had decided to wait a favourable opportunity of passing into some part of the Turkish dominions.

"Safie resolved to remain with her father until the moment of his departure, before which time the Turk renewed his promise that she should be united to his deliverer; and Felix remained with them in expectation of that event; and in the meantime he enjoyed the society of the Arabian, who exhibited towards him the simplest and tenderest affection. They conversed with one another through the means of an interpreter, and sometimes with the interpretation of looks; and Safie sang to him the divine airs of her native country.

"The Turk allowed this intimacy to take place and encouraged the hopes of the youthful lovers, while in his heart he had formed far other plans. He loathed the idea that his daughter should be united to a Christian, but he feared the resentment of Felix if he should appear lukewarm, for he knew that he was still in the power of his deliverer if he should choose to betray him to the Italian state which they inhabited. He revolved a thousand plans by which he should be enabled to prolong the deceit until it might be no longer necessary, and secretly to take his daughter with him when he departed. His plans were facilitated by the news which arrived from Paris.

"The government of France were greatly enraged at the escape of their victim and spared no pains to detect and punish his deliverer. The plot of Felix was quickly discovered, and De Lacey and Agatha were thrown into prison. The news reached Felix and roused him from his dream of pleasure. His blind and aged father and his gentle sister lay in a noisome dungeon while he enjoyed the free air and the society of her whom he loved. This idea was torture to him. He quickly arranged with the Turk that if the latter should find a favourable opportunity for escape before Felix could return to Italy, Safie should remain as a boarder at a convent at Leghorn; and then, quitting the lovely Arabian, he hastened to Paris and delivered himself up to the vengeance of the law, hoping to free De Lacey and Agatha by this proceeding.

"He did not succeed. They remained confined for five months before the trial took place, the result of which deprived them of their fortune and condemned them to a perpetual exile from their native country.

"They found a miserable asylum in the cottage in Germany, where I discovered them. Felix soon learned that the treacherous Turk, for whom he and his family endured such unheard-of oppression, on discovering that his deliverer was thus reduced to poverty and ruin, became a traitor to good feeling and honour and had quitted Italy with his daughter, insultingly sending Felix a pittance of money to aid him, as he said, in some plan of future maintenance.

"Such were the events that preyed on the heart of Felix and rendered him, when I first saw him, the most miserable of his family. He could have endured poverty, and while this distress had been the meed of his virtue, he gloried in it; but the ingratitude of the Turk and the loss of his beloved Safie were misfortunes more bitter and irreparable. The arrival of the Arabian now infused new life into his soul.

"When the news reached Leghorn that Felix was deprived of his wealth and rank, the merchant commanded his daughter to think no more of her lover, but to prepare to return to her native country. The generous nature of Safie was outraged by this command; she attempted to expostulate with her father, but he left her angrily, reiterating his tyrannical mandate.

"A few days after, the Turk entered his daughter's apartment and told her hastily that he had reason to believe that his residence at Leghorn had been divulged and that he should speedily be delivered up to the French government; he had consequently hired a vessel to convey him to Constantinople, for which city he should sail in a few hours. He intended to leave his daughter under the care of a confidential servant, to follow at her leisure with the greater part of his property, which had not yet arrived at Leghorn.

"When alone, Safie resolved in her own mind the plan of conduct that it would become her to pursue in this emergency. A residence in Turkey was abhorrent to her; her religion and her feelings were alike averse to it. By some papers of her father which fell into her hands she heard of the exile of her lover and learnt the name of the spot where he then resided. She hesitated some time, but at length she formed her determination. Taking with her some jewels that belonged to her and a sum of money, she quitted Italy with an attendant, a native of Leghorn, but who understood the common language of Turkey, and departed for Germany.

Frankenstein

"She arrived in safety at a town about twenty leagues from the cottage of De Lacey, when her attendant fell dangerously ill. Safie nursed her with the most devoted affection, but the poor girl died, and the Arabian was left alone, unacquainted with the language of the country and utterly ignorant of the customs of the world. She fell, however, into good hands. The Italian had mentioned the name of the spot for which they were bound, and after her death the woman of the house in which they had lived took care that Safie should arrive in safety at the cottage of her lover."

Chapter 15

"Such was the history of my beloved cottagers. It impressed me deeply. I learned, from the views of social life which it developed, to admire their virtues and to deprecate the vices of mankind.

"As yet I looked upon crime as a distant evil, benevolence and generosity were ever present before me, inciting within me a desire to become an actor in the busy scene where so many admirable qualities were called forth and displayed. But in giving an account of the progress of my intellect, I must not omit a circumstance which occurred in the beginning of the month of August of the same year.

"One night during my accustomed visit to the neighbouring wood where I collected my own food and brought home firing for my protectors, I found on the ground a leathern portmanteau containing several articles of dress and some books. I eagerly seized the prize and returned with it to my hovel. Fortunately the books were written in the language, the elements of which I had acquired at the cottage; they consisted of Paradise Lost, a volume of Plutarch's Lives, and the Sorrows of Werter. The possession of these treasures gave me extreme delight; I now continually studied and exercised my mind upon these histories, whilst my friends were employed in their ordinary occupations.

"I can hardly describe to you the effect of these books. They produced in me an infinity of new images and feelings, that sometimes raised me to ecstasy, but more frequently sunk me into the lowest dejection. In the Sorrows of Werter, besides the interest of its simple and affecting story, so many opinions are canvassed and so many lights thrown upon what had hitherto been to me obscure subjects that I found in it a never-ending source of speculation and astonishment. The gentle and domestic manners it described, combined with lofty sentiments and feelings, which had for their object something out of self, accorded well with my experience among my protectors and with the wants which were for ever alive in my own bosom. But I thought Werter himself a more divine being than I had ever beheld or imagined; his character contained no pretension, but it sank deep. The disquisitions upon death and suicide were calculated to fill me with wonder. I did not pretend to enter into the merits of the case, yet I inclined towards the opinions of the hero, whose extinction I wept, without precisely understanding it.

Frankenstein

"As I read, however, I applied much personally to my own feelings and condition. I found myself similar yet at the same time strangely unlike to the beings concerning whom I read and to whose conversation I was a listener. I sympathised with and partly understood them, but I was unformed in mind; I was dependent on none and related to none. 'The path of my departure was free,' and there was none to lament my annihilation. My person was hideous and my stature gigantic. What did this mean? Who was I? What was I? Whence did I come? What was my destination? These questions continually recurred, but I was unable to solve them.

"The volume of Plutarch's Lives which I possessed contained the histories of the first founders of the ancient republics. This book had a far different effect upon me from the Sorrows of Werter. I learned from Werter's imaginations despondency and gloom, but Plutarch taught me high thoughts; he elevated me above the wretched sphere of my own reflections, to admire and love the heroes of past ages. Many things I read surpassed my understanding and experience. I had a very confused knowledge of kingdoms, wide extents of country, mighty rivers, and boundless seas. But I was perfectly unacquainted with towns and large assemblages of men. The cottage of my protectors had been the only school in which I had studied human nature, but this book developed new and mightier scenes of action. I read of men concerned in public affairs, governing or massacring their species. I felt the greatest ardour for virtue rise within me, and abhorrence for vice, as far as I understood the signification of those terms, relative as they were, as I applied them, to pleasure and pain alone. Induced by these feelings, I was of course led to admire peaceable lawgivers, Numa, Solon, and Lycurgus, in preference to Romulus and Theseus. The patriarchal lives of my protectors caused these impressions to take a firm hold on my mind; perhaps, if my first introduction to humanity had been made by a young soldier, burning for glory and slaughter, I should have been imbued with different sensations.

"But Paradise Lost excited different and far deeper emotions. I read it, as I had read the other volumes which had fallen into my hands, as a true history. It moved every feeling of wonder and awe that the picture of an omnipotent God warring with his creatures was capable of exciting. I often referred the several situations, as their similarity struck me, to my own. Like Adam, I was apparently united by no link to any other being in existence; but his state was far different from mine in every other respect. He had come forth from the hands of God a perfect creature, happy and prosperous, guarded by the especial care of his Creator; he was allowed to converse with and acquire knowledge from beings of a superior nature, but I was wretched, helpless, and alone. Many times I considered Satan as the fitter emblem of my condition, for often, like him, when I viewed the bliss of my protectors, the bitter gall of envy rose within me.

"Another circumstance strengthened and confirmed these feelings. Soon after my arrival in the hovel I discovered some papers in the pocket of the dress which I had taken from your laboratory. At first I had neglected them, but now that I was able to decipher the characters in which they were written, I began to study them with diligence. It was your journal of the four months that preceded my creation. You minutely described in these papers every step you took in the progress of your work; this history was mingled with accounts of domestic occurrences. You doubtless recollect these papers. Here they are. Everything is related in them which bears reference to my accursed origin; the whole detail of that series of disgusting circumstances which produced it is set in view; the minutest description of my odious and loathsome person is given, in language which painted your own horrors and rendered mine indelible. I sickened as I read. 'Hateful day when I received life!' I exclaimed in agony. 'Accursed creator! Why did you form a monster so hideous that even you turned from me in disgust? God, in pity, made man beautiful and alluring, after his own image; but my form is a filthy type of yours, more horrid even from the very resemblance. Satan had his companions, fellow devils, to admire and encourage him, but I am solitary and abhorred.'

"These were the reflections of my hours of despondency and solitude; but when I contemplated the virtues of the cottagers, their amiable and benevolent dispositions, I persuaded myself that when they should become acquainted with my admiration of their virtues they would compassionate me and overlook my personal deformity. Could they turn from their door one, however monstrous, who solicited their compassion and friendship? I resolved, at least, not to despair, but in every way to fit myself for an interview with them which would decide my fate. I postponed this attempt for some months longer, for the importance attached to its success inspired me with a dread lest I should fail. Besides, I found that my understanding improved so much with every day's experience that I was unwilling to commence this undertaking until a few more months should have added to my sagacity.

"Several changes, in the meantime, took place in the cottage.

Frankenstein

The presence of Safie diffused happiness among its inhabitants, and I also found that a greater degree of plenty reigned there. Felix and Agatha spent more time in amusement and conversation, and were assisted in their labours by servants. They did not appear rich, but they were contented and happy; their feelings were serene and peaceful, while mine became every day more tumultuous. Increase of knowledge only discovered to me more clearly what a wretched outcast I was. I cherished hope, it is true, but it vanished when I beheld my person reflected in water or my shadow in the moonshine, even as that frail image and that inconstant shade.

"I endeavoured to crush these fears and to fortify myself for the trial which in a few months I resolved to undergo; and sometimes I allowed my thoughts, unchecked by reason, to ramble in the fields of Paradise, and dared to fancy amiable and lovely creatures sympathising with my feelings and cheering my gloom; their angelic countenances breathed smiles of consolation. But it was all a dream; no Eve soothed my sorrows nor shared my thoughts; I was alone. I remembered Adam's supplication to his Creator. But where was mine? He had abandoned me, and in the bitterness of my heart I cursed him.

"Autumn passed thus. I saw, with surprise and grief, the leaves decay and fall, and nature again assume the barren and bleak appearance it had worn when I first beheld the woods and the lovely moon. Yet I did not heed the bleakness of the weather; I was better fitted by my conformation for the endurance of cold than heat. But my chief delights were the sight of the flowers, the birds, and all the gay apparel of summer; when those deserted me, I turned with more attention towards the cottagers. Their happiness was not decreased by the absence of summer. They loved and sympathised with one another; and their joys, depending on each other, were not interrupted by the casualties that took place around them. The more I saw of them, the greater became my desire to claim their protection and kindness; my heart yearned to be known and loved by these amiable creatures; to see their sweet looks directed towards me with affection was the utmost limit of my ambition. I dared not think that they would turn them from me with disdain and horror. The poor that stopped at their door were never driven away. I asked, it is true, for greater treasures than a little food or rest: I required kindness and sympathy; but I did not believe myself utterly unworthy of it.

"The winter advanced, and an entire revolution of the seasons had taken place since I awoke into life. My attention at this time was solely directed towards my plan of introducing myself into the cottage of my protectors. I revolved many projects, but that on which I finally fixed was to enter the dwelling when the blind old man should be alone. I had sagacity enough to discover that the unnatural hideousness of my person was the chief object of horror with those who had formerly beheld me. My voice, although harsh, had nothing terrible in it; I thought, therefore, that if in the absence of his children I could gain the good will and mediation of the old De Lacey, I might by his means be tolerated by my younger protectors.

"One day, when the sun shone on the red leaves that strewed the ground and diffused cheerfulness, although it denied warmth, Safie, Agatha, and Felix departed on a long country walk, and the old man, at his own desire, was left alone in the cottage. When his children had departed, he took up his guitar and played several mournful but sweet airs, more sweet and mournful than I had ever heard him play before. At first his countenance was illuminated with pleasure, but as he continued, thoughtfulness and sadness succeeded; at length, laying aside the instrument, he sat absorbed in reflection.

"My heart beat quick; this was the hour and moment of trial, which would decide my hopes or realise my fears. The servants were gone to a neighbouring fair. All was silent in and around the cottage; it was an excellent opportunity; yet, when I proceeded to execute my plan, my limbs failed me and I sank to the ground. Again I rose, and exerting all the firmness of which I was master, removed the planks which I had placed before my hovel to conceal my retreat. The fresh air revived me, and with renewed determination I approached the door of their cottage.

"I knocked. 'Who is there?' said the old man. 'Come in.'

"I entered. 'Pardon this intrusion,' said I; 'I am a traveller in want of a little rest; you would greatly oblige me if you would allow me to remain a few minutes before the fire.'

"'Enter,' said De Lacey, 'and I will try in what manner I can to relieve your wants; but, unfortunately, my children are from home, and as I am blind, I am afraid I shall find it difficult to procure food for you.'

"'Do not trouble yourself, my kind host; I have food; it is warmth and rest only that I need.'

"I sat down, and a silence ensued. I knew that every minute was precious to me, yet I remained irresolute in what manner to

Frankenstein

commence the interview, when the old man addressed me.

'By your language, stranger, I suppose you are my countryman; are you French?'

"'No; but I was educated by a French family and understand that language only. I am now going to claim the protection of some friends, whom I sincerely love, and of whose favour I have some hopes.'

"'Are they Germans?'

"'No, they are French. But let us change the subject. I am an unfortunate and deserted creature, I look around and I have no relation or friend upon earth. These amiable people to whom I go have never seen me and know little of me. I am full of fears, for if I fail there, I am an outcast in the world for ever.'

"'Do not despair. To be friendless is indeed to be unfortunate, but the hearts of men, when unprejudiced by any obvious self-interest, are full of brotherly love and charity. Rely, therefore, on your hopes; and if these friends are good and amiable, do not despair.'

"'They are kind — they are the most excellent creatures in the world; but, unfortunately, they are prejudiced against me. I have good dispositions; my life has been hitherto harmless and in some degree beneficial; but a fatal prejudice clouds their eyes, and where they ought to see a feeling and kind friend, they behold only a detestable monster.'

"'That is indeed unfortunate; but if you are really blameless, cannot you undeceive them?'

"'I am about to undertake that task; and it is on that account that I feel so many overwhelming terrors. I tenderly love these friends; I have, unknown to them, been for many months in the habits of daily kindness towards them; but they believe that I wish to injure them, and it is that prejudice which I wish to overcome.'

"'Where do these friends reside?'

"'Near this spot.'

"The old man paused and then continued, 'If you will unreservedly confide to me the particulars of your tale, I perhaps may be of use in undeceiving them. I am blind and cannot judge of your countenance, but there is something in your words which persuades me that you are sincere. I am poor and an exile, but it will afford me true pleasure to be in any way serviceable to a human creature.'

"'Excellent man! I thank you and accept your generous offer. You raise me from the dust by this kindness; and I trust that, by your aid, I shall not be driven from the society and sympathy of your fellow creatures.'

"'Heaven forbid! Even if you were really criminal, for that can only drive you to desperation, and not instigate you to virtue. I also am unfortunate; I and my family have been condemned, although innocent; judge, therefore, if I do not feel for your misfortunes.'

"'How can I thank you, my best and only benefactor? From your lips first have I heard the voice of kindness directed towards me; I shall be for ever grateful; and your present humanity assures me of success with those friends whom I am on the point of meeting.'

"'May I know the names and residence of those friends?'

"I paused. This, I thought, was the moment of decision, which was to rob me of or bestow happiness on me for ever. I struggled vainly for firmness sufficient to answer him, but the effort destroyed all my remaining strength; I sank on the chair and sobbed aloud. At that moment I heard the steps of my younger protectors. I had not a moment to lose, but seizing the hand of the old man, I cried, 'Now is the time! Save and protect me! You and your family are the friends whom I seek. Do not you desert me in the hour of trial!'

"'Great God!' exclaimed the old man. 'Who are you?'

"At that instant the cottage door was opened, and Felix, Safie, and Agatha entered. Who can describe their horror and consternation on beholding me? Agatha fainted, and Safie, unable to attend to her friend, rushed out of the cottage. Felix darted forward, and with supernatural force tore me from his father, to whose knees I clung, in a transport of fury, he dashed me to the ground and struck me violently with a stick. I could have torn him limb from limb, as the lion rends the antelope. But my heart sank within me as with bitter sickness, and I refrained. I saw him on the point of repeating his blow, when, overcome by pain and anguish, I quitted the cottage, and in the general tumult escaped unperceived to my hovel."

Chapter 16

"Cursed, cursed creator! Why did I live? Why, in that instant, did I not extinguish the spark of existence which you had so wantonly bestowed? I know not; despair had not yet taken possession of me; my feelings were those of rage and revenge. I could with pleasure have destroyed the cottage and its inhabitants and have glutted myself with their shrieks and misery.

"When night came I quitted my retreat and wandered in the wood; and now, no longer restrained by the fear of discovery, I gave vent to my anguish in fearful howlings. I was like a wild beast that had broken the toils, destroying the objects that obstructed me and ranging through the wood with a stag-like swiftness. Oh! What a miserable night I passed! The cold stars shone in mockery, and the bare trees waved their branches above me; now and then the sweet voice of a bird burst forth amidst the universal stillness. All, save I, were at rest or in enjoyment; I, like the arch-fiend, bore a hell within me, and finding myself unsympathised with, wished to tear up the trees, spread havoc and destruction around me, and then to have sat down and enjoyed the ruin.

"But this was a luxury of sensation that could not endure; I became fatigued with excess of bodily exertion and sank on the damp grass in the sick impotence of despair. There was none among the myriads of men that existed who would pity or assist me; and should I feel kindness towards my enemies? No: from that moment I declared everlasting war against the species, and more than all, against him who had formed me and sent me forth to this insupportable misery.

"The sun rose; I heard the voices of men and knew that it was impossible to return to my retreat during that day. Accordingly I hid myself in some thick underwood, determining to devote the ensuing hours to reflection on my situation.

"The pleasant sunshine and the pure air of day restored me to some degree of tranquillity; and when I considered what had passed at the cottage, I could not help believing that I had been too hasty in my conclusions. I had certainly acted imprudently. It was apparent that my conversation had interested the father in my behalf, and I was a fool in having exposed my person to the horror of his children. I ought to have familiarised the old De Lacey to me, and by degrees to have discovered myself to the rest of his family, when they should have been prepared for my approach. But I did not believe my errors to be irretrievable, and after much consideration I resolved to return to the cottage, seek the old man, and by my representations win him to my party.

"These thoughts calmed me, and in the afternoon I sank into a profound sleep; but the fever of my blood did not allow me to be visited by peaceful dreams. The horrible scene of the preceding day was for ever acting before my eyes; the females were flying and the enraged Felix tearing me from his father's feet. I awoke exhausted, and finding that it was already night, I crept forth from my hiding-place, and went in search of food.

"When my hunger was appeased, I directed my steps towards the well-known path that conducted to the cottage. All there was at peace. I crept into my hovel and remained in silent expectation of the accustomed hour when the family arose. That hour passed, the sun mounted high in the heavens, but the cottagers did not appear. I trembled violently, apprehending some dreadful misfortune. The inside of the cottage was dark, and I heard no motion; I cannot describe the agony of this suspense.

"Presently two countrymen passed by, but pausing near the cottage, they entered into conversation, using violent gesticulations; but I did not understand what they said, as they spoke the language of the country, which differed from that of my protectors. Soon after, however, Felix approached with another man; I was surprised, as I knew that he had not quitted the cottage that morning, and waited anxiously to discover from his discourse the meaning of these unusual appearances.

"'Do you consider,' said his companion to him, 'that you will be obliged to pay three months' rent and to lose the produce of your garden? I do not wish to take any unfair advantage, and I beg therefore that you will take some days to consider of your determination.'

"'It is utterly useless,' replied Felix; 'we can never again inhabit your cottage. The life of my father is in the greatest danger, owing to the dreadful circumstance that I have related. My wife and my sister will never recover from their horror. I entreat you not to reason with me any more. Take possession of your tenement and let me fly from this place.'

"Felix trembled violently as he said this. He and his companion entered the cottage, in which they remained for a few minutes, and then departed. I never saw any of the family

Frankenstein

of De Lacey more.

"I continued for the remainder of the day in my hovel in a state of utter and stupid despair. My protectors had departed and had broken the only link that held me to the world. For the first time the feelings of revenge and hatred filled my bosom, and I did not strive to control them, but allowing myself to be borne away by the stream, I bent my mind towards injury and death. When I thought of my friends, of the mild voice of De Lacey, the gentle eyes of Agatha, and the exquisite beauty of the Arabian, these thoughts vanished and a gush of tears somewhat soothed me. But again when I reflected that they had spurned and deserted me, anger returned, a rage of anger, and unable to injure anything human, I turned my fury towards inanimate objects. As night advanced, I placed a variety of combustibles around the cottage, and after having destroyed every vestige of cultivation in the garden, I waited with forced impatience until the moon had sunk to commence my operations.

"As the night advanced, a fierce wind arose from the woods and quickly dispersed the clouds that had loitered in the heavens; the blast tore along like a mighty avalanche and produced a kind of insanity in my spirits that burst all bounds of reason and reflection. I lighted the dry branch of a tree and danced with fury around the devoted cottage, my eyes still fixed on the western horizon, the edge of which the moon nearly touched. A part of its orb was at length hid, and I waved my brand; it sank, and with a loud scream I fired the straw, and heath, and bushes, which I had collected. The wind fanned the fire, and the cottage was quickly enveloped by the flames, which clung to it and licked it with their forked and destroying tongues.

"As soon as I was convinced that no assistance could save any part of the habitation, I quitted the scene and sought for refuge in the woods.

"And now, with the world before me, whither should I bend my steps? I resolved to fly far from the scene of my misfortunes; but to me, hated and despised, every country must be equally horrible. At length the thought of you crossed my mind. I learned from your papers that you were my father, my creator; and to whom could I apply with more fitness than to him who had given me life? Among the lessons that Felix had bestowed upon Safie, geography had not been omitted; I had learned from these the relative situations of the different countries of the earth. You had mentioned Geneva as the name of your native town, and towards this place I resolved to proceed.

"But how was I to direct myself? I knew that I must travel in a southwesterly direction to reach my destination, but the sun was my only guide. I did not know the names of the towns that I was to pass through, nor could I ask information from a single human being; but I did not despair. From you only could I hope for succour, although towards you I felt no sentiment but that of hatred. Unfeeling, heartless creator! You had endowed me with perceptions and passions and then cast me abroad an object for the scorn and horror of mankind. But on you only had I any claim for pity and redress, and from you I determined to seek that justice which I vainly attempted to gain from any other being that wore the human form.

"My travels were long and the sufferings I endured intense. It was late in autumn when I quitted the district where I had so long resided. I travelled only at night, fearful of encountering the visage of a human being. Nature decayed around me, and the sun became heatless; rain and snow poured around me; mighty rivers were frozen; the surface of the earth was hard and chill, and bare, and I found no shelter. Oh, earth! How often did I imprecate curses on the cause of my being! The mildness of my nature had fled, and all within me was turned to gall and bitterness. The nearer I approached to your habitation, the more deeply did I feel the spirit of revenge enkindled in my heart. Snow fell, and the waters were hardened, but I rested not. A few incidents now and then directed me, and I possessed a map of the country; but I often wandered wide from my path. The agony of my feelings allowed me no respite; no incident occurred from which my rage and misery could not extract its food; but a circumstance that happened when I arrived on the confines of Switzerland, when the sun had recovered its warmth and the earth again began to look green, confirmed in an especial manner the bitterness and horror of my feelings.

"I generally rested during the day and travelled only when I was secured by night from the view of man. One morning, however, finding that my path lay through a deep wood, I ventured to continue my journey after the sun had risen; the day, which was one of the first of spring, cheered even me by the loveliness of its sunshine and the balminess of the air. I felt emotions of gentleness and pleasure, that had long appeared dead, revive within me. Half surprised by the novelty of these sensations, I allowed myself to be borne away by them, and forgetting my solitude and deformity, dared to be happy. Soft tears again bedewed my cheeks, and I even raised my humid eyes with thankfulness towards the blessed sun, which bestowed such joy upon me.

Frankenstein

"I continued to wind among the paths of the wood, until I came to its boundary, which was skirted by a deep and rapid river, into which many of the trees bent their branches, now budding with the fresh spring. Here I paused, not exactly knowing what path to pursue, when I heard the sound of voices, that induced me to conceal myself under the shade of a cypress. I was scarcely hid when a young girl came running towards the spot where I was concealed, laughing, as if she ran from someone in sport. She continued her course along the precipitous sides of the river, when suddenly her foot slipped, and she fell into the rapid stream. I rushed from my hiding-place and with extreme labour, from the force of the current, saved her and dragged her to shore. She was senseless, and I endeavoured by every means in my power to restore animation, when I was suddenly interrupted by the approach of a rustic, who was probably the person from whom she had playfully fled. On seeing me, he darted towards me, and tearing the girl from my arms, hastened towards the deeper parts of the wood. I followed speedily, I hardly knew why; but when the man saw me draw near, he aimed a gun, which he carried, at my body and fired. I sank to the ground, and my injurer, with increased swiftness, escaped into the wood.

"This was then the reward of my benevolence! I had saved a human being from destruction, and as a recompense I now writhed under the miserable pain of a wound which shattered the flesh and bone. The feelings of kindness and gentleness which I had entertained but a few moments before gave place to hellish rage and gnashing of teeth. Inflamed by pain, I vowed eternal hatred and vengeance to all mankind. But the agony of my wound overcame me; my pulses paused, and I fainted.

"For some weeks I led a miserable life in the woods, endeavouring to cure the wound which I had received. The ball had entered my shoulder, and I knew not whether it had remained there or passed through; at any rate I had no means of extracting it. My sufferings were augmented also by the oppressive sense of the injustice and ingratitude of their infliction. My daily vows rose for revenge—a deep and deadly revenge, such as would alone compensate for the outrages and anguish I had endured.

"After some weeks my wound healed, and I continued my journey. The labours I endured were no longer to be alleviated by the bright sun or gentle breezes of spring; all joy was but a mockery which insulted my desolate state and made me feel more painfully that I was not made for the enjoyment of pleasure.

"But my toils now drew near a close, and in two months from this time I reached the environs of Geneva.

"It was evening when I arrived, and I retired to a hiding-place among the fields that surround it to meditate in what manner I should apply to you. I was oppressed by fatigue and hunger and far too unhappy to enjoy the gentle breezes of evening or the prospect of the sun setting behind the stupendous mountains of Jura.

"At this time a slight sleep relieved me from the pain of reflection, which was disturbed by the approach of a beautiful child, who came running into the recess I had chosen, with all the sportiveness of infancy. Suddenly, as I gazed on him, an idea seized me that this little creature was unprejudiced and had lived too short a time to have imbibed a horror of deformity. If, therefore, I could seize him and educate him as my companion and friend, I should not be so desolate in this peopled earth.

"Urged by this impulse, I seized on the boy as he passed and drew him towards me. As soon as he beheld my form, he placed his hands before his eyes and uttered a shrill scream; I drew his hand forcibly from his face and said, 'Child, what is the meaning of this? I do not intend to hurt you; listen to me.'

"He struggled violently. 'Let me go,' he cried; 'monster! Ugly wretch! You wish to eat me and tear me to pieces. You are an ogre. Let me go, or I will tell my papa.'

"'Boy, you will never see your father again; you must come with me.'

"'Hideous monster! Let me go. My papa is a syndic—he is M. Frankenstein—he will punish you. You dare not keep me.'

"'Frankenstein! you belong then to my enemy—to him towards whom I have sworn eternal revenge; you shall be my first victim.'

"The child still struggled and loaded me with epithets which carried despair to my heart; I grasped his throat to silence him, and in a moment he lay dead at my feet.

"I gazed on my victim, and my heart swelled with exultation and hellish triumph; clapping my hands, I exclaimed, 'I too can create desolation; my enemy is not invulnerable; this death will carry despair to him, and a thousand other miseries shall torment and destroy him.'

"As I fixed my eyes on the child, I saw something glittering on his breast. I took it; it was a portrait of a most lovely woman. In spite of my malignity, it softened and attracted me. For a few moments I gazed with delight on her dark eyes, fringed by deep lashes, and her lovely lips; but presently my rage returned; I remembered that I was for ever deprived of the delights that such beautiful creatures could bestow and that she whose resemblance I contemplated would, in regarding me, have changed that air of divine benignity to one expressive of disgust and affright.

"Can you wonder that such thoughts transported me with rage? I only wonder that at that moment, instead of venting my sensations in exclamations and agony, I did not rush among mankind and perish in the attempt to destroy them.

"While I was overcome by these feelings, I left the spot where I had committed the murder, and seeking a more secluded hiding-place, I entered a barn which had appeared to me to be empty. A woman was sleeping on some straw; she was young, not indeed so beautiful as her whose portrait I held, but of an agreeable aspect and blooming in the loveliness of youth and health. Here, I thought, is one of those whose joy-imparting smiles are bestowed on all but me. And then I bent over her and whispered, 'Awake, fairest, thy lover is near — he who would give his life but to obtain one look of affection from thine eyes; my beloved, awake!'

"The sleeper stirred; a thrill of terror ran through me. Should she indeed awake, and see me, and curse me, and denounce the murderer? Thus would she assuredly act if her darkened eyes opened and she beheld me. The thought was madness; it stirred the fiend within me — not I, but she, shall suffer; the murder I have committed because I am for ever robbed of all that she could give me, she shall atone. The crime had its source in her; be hers the punishment! Thanks to the lessons of Felix and the sanguinary laws of man, I had learned now to work mischief. I bent over her and placed the portrait securely in one of the folds of her dress. She moved again, and I fled.

"For some days I haunted the spot where these scenes had taken place, sometimes wishing to see you, sometimes resolved to quit the world and its miseries for ever. At length I wandered towards these mountains, and have ranged through their immense recesses, consumed by a burning passion which you alone can gratify. We may not part until you have promised to comply with my requisition. I am alone and miserable; man will not associate with me; but one as deformed and horrible as myself would not deny herself to me. My companion must be of the same species and have the same defects. This being you must create."

Chapter 17

The being finished speaking and fixed his looks upon me in the expectation of a reply. But I was bewildered, perplexed, and unable to arrange my ideas sufficiently to understand the full extent of his proposition. He continued,

"You must create a female for me with whom I can live in the interchange of those sympathies necessary for my being. This you alone can do, and I demand it of you as a right which you must not refuse to concede."

The latter part of his tale had kindled anew in me the anger that had died away while he narrated his peaceful life among the cottagers, and as he said this I could no longer suppress the rage that burned within me.

"I do refuse it," I replied; "and no torture shall ever extort a consent from me. You may render me the most miserable of men, but you shall never make me base in my own eyes. Shall I create another like yourself, whose joint wickedness might desolate the world. Begone! I have answered you; you may torture me, but I will never consent."

"You are in the wrong," replied the fiend; "and instead of threatening, I am content to reason with you. I am malicious because I am miserable. Am I not shunned and hated by all mankind? You, my creator, would tear me to pieces and triumph; remember that, and tell me why I should pity man more than he pities me? You would not call it murder if you could precipitate me into one of those ice-rifts and destroy my frame, the work of your own hands. Shall I respect man when he condemns me? Let him live with me in the interchange of kindness, and instead of injury I would bestow every benefit upon him with tears of gratitude at his acceptance. But that cannot be; the human senses are insurmountable barriers to our union. Yet mine shall not be the submission of abject slavery. I will revenge my injuries; if I cannot inspire love, I will cause fear, and chiefly towards you my arch-enemy, because my creator, do I swear inextinguishable hatred. Have a care; I will work at your destruction, nor finish until I desolate your heart, so that you shall curse the hour of your birth."

A fiendish rage animated him as he said this; his face was wrinkled into contortions too horrible for human eyes to behold; but presently he calmed himself and proceeded—

"I intended to reason. This passion is detrimental to me, for you do not reflect that you are the cause of its excess. If any being felt emotions of benevolence towards me, I should return them a hundred and a hundredfold; for that one creature's sake I would make peace with the whole kind! But I now indulge in dreams of bliss that cannot be realised. What I ask of you is reasonable and moderate; I demand a creature of another sex, but as hideous as myself; the gratification is small, but it is all that I can receive, and it shall content me. It is true, we shall be monsters, cut off from all the world; but on that account we shall be more attached to one another. Our lives will not be happy, but they will be harmless and free from the misery I now feel. Oh! My creator, make me happy; let me feel gratitude towards you for one benefit! Let me see that I excite the sympathy of some existing thing; do not deny me my request!"

I was moved. I shuddered when I thought of the possible consequences of my consent, but I felt that there was some justice in his argument. His tale and the feelings he now expressed proved him to be a creature of fine sensations, and did I not as his maker owe him all the portion of happiness that it was in my power to bestow? He saw my change of feeling and continued,

"If you consent, neither you nor any other human being shall ever see us again; I will go to the vast wilds of South America. My food is not that of man; I do not destroy the lamb and the kid to glut my appetite; acorns and berries afford me sufficient nourishment. My companion will be of the same nature as myself and will be content with the same fare. We shall make our bed of dried leaves; the sun will shine on us as on man and will ripen our food. The picture I present to you is peaceful and human, and you must feel that you could deny it only in the wantonness of power and cruelty. Pitiless as you have been towards me, I now see compassion in your eyes; let me seize the favourable moment and persuade you to promise what I so ardently desire."

"You propose," replied I, "to fly from the habitations of man, to dwell in those wilds where the beasts of the field will be your only companions. How can you, who long for the love and sympathy of man, persevere in this exile? You will return and again seek their kindness, and you will meet with their detestation; your evil passions will be renewed, and you will then have a companion to aid you in the task of destruction. This may not be; cease to argue the point, for I cannot consent."

Frankenstein

"How inconstant are your feelings! But a moment ago you were moved by my representations, and why do you again harden yourself to my complaints? I swear to you, by the earth which I inhabit, and by you that made me, that with the companion you bestow, I will quit the neighbourhood of man and dwell, as it may chance, in the most savage of places. My evil passions will have fled, for I shall meet with sympathy! My life will flow quietly away, and in my dying moments I shall not curse my maker."

His words had a strange effect upon me. I compassionated him and sometimes felt a wish to console him, but when I looked upon him, when I saw the filthy mass that moved and talked, my heart sickened and my feelings were altered to those of horror and hatred. I tried to stifle these sensations; I thought that as I could not sympathise with him, I had no right to withhold from him the small portion of happiness which was yet in my power to bestow.

"You swear," I said, "to be harmless; but have you not already shown a degree of malice that should reasonably make me distrust you? May not even this be a feint that will increase your triumph by affording a wider scope for your revenge?"

"How is this? I must not be trifled with, and I demand an answer. If I have no ties and no affections, hatred and vice must be my portion; the love of another will destroy the cause of my crimes, and I shall become a thing of whose existence everyone will be ignorant. My vices are the children of a forced solitude that I abhor, and my virtues will necessarily arise when I live in communion with an equal. I shall feel the affections of a sensitive being and become linked to the chain of existence and events from which I am now excluded."

I paused some time to reflect on all he had related and the various arguments which he had employed. I thought of the promise of virtues which he had displayed on the opening of his existence and the subsequent blight of all kindly feeling by the loathing and scorn which his protectors had manifested towards him. His power and threats were not omitted in my calculations; a creature who could exist in the ice-caves of the glaciers and hide himself from pursuit among the ridges of inaccessible precipices was a being possessing faculties it would be vain to cope with. After a long pause of reflection I concluded that the justice due both to him and my fellow creatures demanded of me that I should comply with his request. Turning to him, therefore, I said,

"I consent to your demand, on your solemn oath to quit Europe for ever, and every other place in the neighbourhood of man, as soon as I shall deliver into your hands a female who will accompany you in your exile."

"I swear," he cried, "by the sun, and by the blue sky of heaven, and by the fire of love that burns my heart, that if you grant my prayer, while they exist you shall never behold me again. Depart to your home and commence your labours; I shall watch their progress with unutterable anxiety; and fear not but that when you are ready I shall appear."

Saying this, he suddenly quitted me, fearful, perhaps, of any change in my sentiments. I saw him descend the mountain with greater speed than the flight of an eagle, and quickly lost among the undulations of the sea of ice.

His tale had occupied the whole day, and the sun was upon the verge of the horizon when he departed. I knew that I ought to hasten my descent towards the valley, as I should soon be encompassed in darkness; but my heart was heavy, and my steps slow. The labour of winding among the little paths of the mountain and fixing my feet firmly as I advanced perplexed me, occupied as I was by the emotions which the occurrences of the day had produced. Night was far advanced when I came to the halfway resting-place and seated myself beside the fountain. The stars shone at intervals as the clouds passed from over them; the dark pines rose before me, and every here and there a broken tree lay on the ground; it was a scene of wonderful solemnity and stirred strange thoughts within me. I wept bitterly, and clasping my hands in agony, I exclaimed, "Oh! stars and clouds and winds, ye are all about to mock me; if ye really pity me, crush sensation and memory; let me become as nought; but if not, depart, depart, and leave me in darkness."

These were wild and miserable thoughts, but I cannot describe to you how the eternal twinkling of the stars weighed upon me and how I listened to every blast of wind as if it were a dull ugly siroc on its way to consume me.

Morning dawned before I arrived at the village of Chamounix; I took no rest, but returned immediately to Geneva. Even in my own heart I could give no expression to my sensations—they weighed on me with a mountain's weight and their excess destroyed my agony beneath them. Thus I returned home, and entering the house, presented myself to the family. My haggard and wild appearance awoke intense alarm, but I answered no question, scarcely did I speak. I felt as if I were placed under a ban—as if I had no right to claim their sympathies—as if never more might I enjoy companionship with them. Yet even thus I loved them to adoration; and to save them, I resolved to dedicate myself to my most abhorred task. The prospect of such an occupation made every other circumstance of existence pass before me like a dream, and that thought only had to me the reality of life.

Chapter 18

Day after day, week after week, passed away on my return to Geneva; and I could not collect the courage to recommence my work. I feared the vengeance of the disappointed fiend, yet I was unable to overcome my repugnance to the task which was enjoined me. I found that I could not compose a female without again devoting several months to profound study and laborious disquisition. I had heard of some discoveries having been made by an English philosopher, the knowledge of which was material to my success, and I sometimes thought of obtaining my father's consent to visit England for this purpose; but I clung to every pretence of delay and shrank from taking the first step in an undertaking whose immediate necessity began to appear less absolute to me. A change indeed had taken place in me; my health, which had hitherto declined, was now much restored; and my spirits, when unchecked by the memory of my unhappy promise, rose proportionably. My father saw this change with pleasure, and he turned his thoughts towards the best method of eradicating the remains of my melancholy, which every now and then would return by fits, and with a devouring blackness overcast the approaching sunshine. At these moments I took refuge in the most perfect solitude. I passed whole days on the lake alone in a little boat, watching the clouds and listening to the rippling of the waves, silent and listless. But the fresh air and bright sun seldom failed to restore me to some degree of composure, and on my return I met the salutations of my friends with a readier smile and a more cheerful heart.

It was after my return from one of these rambles that my father, calling me aside, thus addressed me,

"I am happy to remark, my dear son, that you have resumed your former pleasures and seem to be returning to yourself. And yet you are still unhappy and still avoid our society. For some time I was lost in conjecture as to the cause of this, but yesterday an idea struck me, and if it is well founded, I conjure you to avow it. Reserve on such a point would be not only useless, but draw down treble misery on us all."

I trembled violently at his exordium, and my father continued —

"I confess, my son, that I have always looked forward to your marriage with our dear Elizabeth as the tie of our domestic comfort and the stay of my declining years. You were attached to each other from your earliest infancy; you studied together, and appeared, in dispositions and tastes, entirely suited to one another. But so blind is the experience of man that what I conceived to be the best assistants to my plan may have entirely destroyed it. You, perhaps, regard her as your sister, without any wish that she might become your wife. Nay, you may have met with another whom you may love; and considering yourself as bound in honour to Elizabeth, this struggle may occasion the poignant misery which you appear to feel."

"My dear father, reassure yourself. I love my cousin tenderly and sincerely. I never saw any woman who excited, as Elizabeth does, my warmest admiration and affection. My future hopes and prospects are entirely bound up in the expectation of our union."

"The expression of your sentiments of this subject, my dear Victor, gives me more pleasure than I have for some time experienced. If you feel thus, we shall assuredly be happy, however present events may cast a gloom over us. But it is this gloom which appears to have taken so strong a hold of your mind that I wish to dissipate. Tell me, therefore, whether you object to an immediate solemnisation of the marriage. We have been unfortunate, and recent events have drawn us from that everyday tranquillity befitting my years and infirmities. You are younger; yet I do not suppose, possessed as you are of a competent fortune, that an early marriage would at all interfere with any future plans of honour and utility that you may have formed. Do not suppose, however, that I wish to dictate happiness to you or that a delay on your part would cause me any serious uneasiness. Interpret my words with candour and answer me, I conjure you, with confidence and sincerity."

I listened to my father in silence and remained for some time incapable of offering any reply. I revolved rapidly in my mind a multitude of thoughts and endeavoured to arrive at some conclusion. Alas! To me the idea of an immediate union with my Elizabeth was one of horror and dismay. I was bound by a solemn promise which I had not yet fulfilled and dared not break, or if I did, what manifold miseries might not impend over me and my devoted family! Could I enter into a festival with this deadly weight yet hanging round my neck and bowing me to the ground? I must perform my engagement and let the monster depart with his mate before I allowed myself to enjoy the delight of a union from which I expected peace.

I remembered also the necessity imposed upon me of either journeying to England or entering into a long correspondence with those philosophers of that country whose knowledge and discoveries were of indispensable use to me in my present undertaking. The latter method of obtaining the desired intelligence was dilatory and unsatisfactory; besides, I had an insurmountable aversion to the idea of engaging myself in my loathsome task in my father's house while in habits of familiar intercourse with those I loved. I knew that a thousand fearful accidents might occur, the slightest of which would disclose a tale to thrill all connected with me with horror. I was aware also that I should often lose all self-command, all capacity of hiding the harrowing sensations that would possess me during the progress of my unearthly occupation. I must absent myself from all I loved while thus employed. Once commenced, it would quickly be achieved, and I might be restored to my family in peace and happiness. My promise fulfilled, the monster would depart for ever. Or (so my fond fancy imaged) some accident might meanwhile occur to destroy him and put an end to my slavery for ever.

These feelings dictated my answer to my father. I expressed a wish to visit England, but concealing the true reasons of this request, I clothed my desires under a guise which excited no suspicion, while I urged my desire with an earnestness that easily induced my father to comply. After so long a period of an absorbing melancholy that resembled madness in its intensity and effects, he was glad to find that I was capable of taking pleasure in the idea of such a journey, and he hoped that change of scene and varied amusement would, before my return, have restored me entirely to myself.

The duration of my absence was left to my own choice; a few months, or at most a year, was the period contemplated. One paternal kind precaution he had taken to ensure my having a companion. Without previously communicating with me, he had, in concert with Elizabeth, arranged that Clerval should join me at Strasburgh. This interfered with the solitude I coveted for the prosecution of my task; yet at the commencement of my journey the presence of my friend could in no way be an impediment, and truly I rejoiced that thus I should be saved many hours of lonely, maddening reflection. Nay, Henry might stand between me and the intrusion of my foe. If I were alone, would he not at times force his abhorred presence on me to remind me of my task or to contemplate its progress?

To England, therefore, I was bound, and it was understood that my union with Elizabeth should take place immediately on my return. My father's age rendered him extremely averse to delay. For myself, there was one reward I promised myself from my detested toils—one consolation for my unparalleled sufferings; it was the prospect of that day when, enfranchised

Frankenstein

from my miserable slavery, I might claim Elizabeth and forget the past in my union with her.

I now made arrangements for my journey, but one feeling haunted me which filled me with fear and agitation. During my absence I should leave my friends unconscious of the existence of their enemy and unprotected from his attacks, exasperated as he might be by my departure. But he had promised to follow me wherever I might go, and would he not accompany me to England? This imagination was dreadful in itself, but soothing inasmuch as it supposed the safety of my friends. I was agonised with the idea of the possibility that the reverse of this might happen. But through the whole period during which I was the slave of my creature I allowed myself to be governed by the impulses of the moment; and my present sensations strongly intimated that the fiend would follow me and exempt my family from the danger of his machinations.

It was in the latter end of September that I again quitted my native country. My journey had been my own suggestion, and Elizabeth therefore acquiesced, but she was filled with disquiet at the idea of my suffering, away from her, the inroads of misery and grief. It had been her care which provided me a companion in Clerval — and yet a man is blind to a thousand minute circumstances which call forth a woman's sedulous attention. She longed to bid me hasten my return; a thousand conflicting emotions rendered her mute as she bade me a tearful, silent farewell.

I threw myself into the carriage that was to convey me away, hardly knowing whither I was going, and careless of what was passing around. I remembered only, and it was with a bitter anguish that I reflected on it, to order that my chemical instruments should be packed to go with me. Filled with dreary imaginations, I passed through many beautiful and majestic scenes, but my eyes were fixed and unobserving. I could only think of the bourne of my travels and the work which was to occupy me whilst they endured.

After some days spent in listless indolence, during which I traversed many leagues, I arrived at Strasburgh, where I waited two days for Clerval. He came. Alas, how great was the contrast between us! He was alive to every new scene, joyful when he saw the beauties of the setting sun, and more happy when he beheld it rise and recommence a new day. He pointed out to me the shifting colours of the landscape and the appearances of the sky. "This is what it is to live," he cried; "now I enjoy existence! But you, my dear Frankenstein, wherefore are you desponding and sorrowful!" In truth, I was occupied by gloomy thoughts and neither saw the descent of the evening star nor the golden sunrise reflected in the Rhine. And you, my friend, would be far more amused with the journal of Clerval, who observed the scenery with an eye of feeling and delight, than in listening to my reflections. I, a miserable wretch, haunted by a curse that shut up every avenue to enjoyment.

We had agreed to descend the Rhine in a boat from Strasburgh to Rotterdam, whence we might take shipping for London. During this voyage we passed many willowy islands and saw several beautiful towns. We stayed a day at Mannheim, and on the fifth from our departure from Strasburgh, arrived at Mainz. The course of the Rhine below Mainz becomes much more picturesque. The river descends rapidly and winds between hills, not high, but steep, and of beautiful forms. We saw many ruined castles standing on the edges of precipices, surrounded by black woods, high and inaccessible. This part of the Rhine, indeed, presents a singularly variegated landscape. In one spot you view rugged hills, ruined castles overlooking tremendous precipices, with the dark Rhine rushing beneath; and on the sudden turn of a promontory, flourishing vineyards with green sloping banks and a meandering river and populous towns occupy the scene.

We travelled at the time of the vintage and heard the song of the labourers as we glided down the stream. Even I, depressed in mind, and my spirits continually agitated by gloomy feelings, even I was pleased. I lay at the bottom of the boat, and as I gazed on the cloudless blue sky, I seemed to drink in a tranquillity to which I had long been a stranger. And if these were my sensations, who can describe those of Henry? He felt as if he had been transported to Fairy-land and enjoyed a happiness seldom tasted by man. "I have seen," he said, "the most beautiful scenes of my own country; I have visited the lakes of Lucerne and Uri, where the snowy mountains descend almost perpendicularly to the water, casting black and impenetrable shades, which would cause a gloomy and mournful appearance were it not for the most verdant islands that relieve the eye by their gay appearance; I have seen this lake agitated by a tempest, when the wind tore up whirlwinds of water and gave you an idea of what the water-spout must be on the great ocean; and the waves dash with fury the base of the mountain, where the priest and his mistress were overwhelmed by an avalanche and where their dying voices are still said to be heard amid the pauses of the nightly wind; I have seen the mountains of La Valais, and the Pays de Vaud; but this country, Victor, pleases me more than all those wonders. The mountains

Frankenstein

of Switzerland are more majestic and strange, but there is a charm in the banks of this divine river that I never before saw equalled. Look at that castle which overhangs yon precipice; and that also on the island, almost concealed amongst the foliage of those lovely trees; and now that group of labourers coming from among their vines; and that village half hid in the recess of the mountain. Oh, surely the spirit that inhabits and guards this place has a soul more in harmony with man than those who pile the glacier or retire to the inaccessible peaks of the mountains of our own country."

Clerval! Beloved friend! Even now it delights me to record your words and to dwell on the praise of which you are so eminently deserving. He was a being formed in the "very poetry of nature." His wild and enthusiastic imagination was chastened by the sensibility of his heart. His soul overflowed with ardent affections, and his friendship was of that devoted and wondrous nature that the worldly-minded teach us to look for only in the imagination. But even human sympathies were not sufficient to satisfy his eager mind. The scenery of external nature, which others regard only with admiration, he loved with ardour:—

– –The sounding cataract

Haunted him like a passion: the tall rock,

The mountain, and the deep and gloomy wood,

Their colours and their forms, were then to him

An appetite; a feeling, and a love,

That had no need of a remoter charm,

By thought supplied, or any interest

Unborrow'd from the eye.

[Wordsworth's "Tintern Abbey".]

And where does he now exist? Is this gentle and lovely being lost for ever? Has this mind, so replete with ideas, imaginations fanciful and magnificent, which formed a world, whose existence depended on the life of its creator;—has this mind perished? Does it now only exist in my memory? No, it is not thus; your form so divinely wrought, and beaming with beauty, has decayed, but your spirit still visits and consoles your unhappy friend.

Pardon this gush of sorrow; these ineffectual words are but a slight tribute to the unexampled worth of Henry, but they soothe my heart, overflowing with the anguish which his remembrance creates. I will proceed with my tale.

Beyond Cologne we descended to the plains of Holland; and we resolved to post the remainder of our way, for the wind was contrary and the stream of the river was too gentle to aid us.

Our journey here lost the interest arising from beautiful scenery, but we arrived in a few days at Rotterdam, whence we proceeded by sea to England. It was on a clear morning, in the latter days of December, that I first saw the white cliffs of Britain. The banks of the Thames presented a new scene; they were flat but fertile, and almost every town was marked by the remembrance of some story. We saw Tilbury Fort and remembered the Spanish Armada, Gravesend, Woolwich, and Greenwich—places which I had heard of even in my country.

At length we saw the numerous steeples of London, St. Paul's towering above all, and the Tower famed in English history.

Chapter 19

London was our present point of rest; we determined to remain several months in this wonderful and celebrated city. Clerval desired the intercourse of the men of genius and talent who flourished at this time, but this was with me a secondary object; I was principally occupied with the means of obtaining the information necessary for the completion of my promise and quickly availed myself of the letters of introduction that I had brought with me, addressed to the most distinguished natural philosophers.

If this journey had taken place during my days of study and happiness, it would have afforded me inexpressible pleasure. But a blight had come over my existence, and I only visited these people for the sake of the information they might give me on the subject in which my interest was so terribly profound. Company was irksome to me; when alone, I could fill my mind with the sights of heaven and earth; the voice of Henry soothed me, and I could thus cheat myself into a transitory peace. But busy, uninteresting, joyous faces brought back despair to my heart. I saw an insurmountable barrier placed between me and my fellow men; this barrier was sealed with the blood of William and Justine, and to reflect on the events connected with those names filled my soul with anguish.

But in Clerval I saw the image of my former self; he was inquisitive and anxious to gain experience and instruction. The difference of manners which he observed was to him an inexhaustible source of instruction and amusement. He was also pursuing an object he had long had in view. His design was to visit India, in the belief that he had in his knowledge of its various languages, and in the views he had taken of its society, the means of materially assisting the progress of European colonization and trade. In Britain only could he further the execution of his plan. He was for ever busy, and the only check to his enjoyments was my sorrowful and dejected mind. I tried to conceal this as much as possible, that I might not debar him from the pleasures natural to one who was entering on a new scene of life, undisturbed by any care or bitter recollection. I often refused to accompany him, alleging another engagement, that I might remain alone. I now also began to collect the materials necessary for my new creation, and this was to me like the torture of single drops of water continually falling on the head. Every thought that was devoted to it was an extreme anguish, and every word that I spoke in allusion to it caused my lips to quiver, and my heart to palpitate.

After passing some months in London, we received a letter from a person in Scotland who had formerly been our visitor at Geneva. He mentioned the beauties of his native country and asked us if those were not sufficient allurements to induce us to prolong our journey as far north as Perth, where he resided. Clerval eagerly desired to accept this invitation, and I, although I abhorred society, wished to view again mountains and streams and all the wondrous works with which Nature adorns her chosen dwelling-places.

We had arrived in England at the beginning of October, and it was now February. We accordingly determined to commence our journey towards the north at the expiration of another month. In this expedition we did not intend to follow the great road to Edinburgh, but to visit Windsor, Oxford, Matlock, and the Cumberland lakes, resolving to arrive at the completion of this tour about the end of July. I packed up my chemical instruments and the materials I had collected, resolving to finish my labours in some obscure nook in the northern highlands of Scotland.

We quitted London on the 27th of March and remained a few days at Windsor, rambling in its beautiful forest. This was a new scene to us mountaineers; the majestic oaks, the quantity of game, and the herds of stately deer were all novelties to us.

From thence we proceeded to Oxford. As we entered this city, our minds were filled with the remembrance of the events that had been transacted there more than a century and a half before. It was here that Charles I. had collected his forces. This city had remained faithful to him, after the whole nation had forsaken his cause to join the standard of Parliament and liberty. The memory of that unfortunate king and his companions, the amiable Falkland, the insolent Goring, his queen, and son, gave a peculiar interest to every part of the city which they might be supposed to have inhabited. The spirit of elder days found a dwelling here, and we delighted to trace its footsteps. If these feelings had not found an imaginary gratification, the appearance of the city had yet in itself sufficient beauty to obtain our admiration. The colleges are ancient and picturesque; the streets are almost magnificent; and the lovely Isis, which flows beside it through meadows of exquisite verdure, is spread forth into a placid expanse of waters, which reflects its majestic assemblage of towers, and spires, and domes, embosomed among aged trees.

I enjoyed this scene, and yet my enjoyment was embittered both by the memory of the past and the anticipation of the

Frankenstein

future. I was formed for peaceful happiness. During my youthful days discontent never visited my mind, and if I was ever overcome by ennui, the sight of what is beautiful in nature or the study of what is excellent and sublime in the productions of man could always interest my heart and communicate elasticity to my spirits. But I am a blasted tree; the bolt has entered my soul; and I felt then that I should survive to exhibit what I shall soon cease to be—a miserable spectacle of wrecked humanity, pitiable to others and intolerable to myself.

We passed a considerable period at Oxford, rambling among its environs and endeavouring to identify every spot which might relate to the most animating epoch of English history. Our little voyages of discovery were often prolonged by the successive objects that presented themselves. We visited the tomb of the illustrious Hampden and the field on which that patriot fell. For a moment my soul was elevated from its debasing and miserable fears to contemplate the divine ideas of liberty and self-sacrifice of which these sights were the monuments and the remembrancers. For an instant I dared to shake off my chains and look around me with a free and lofty spirit, but the iron had eaten into my flesh, and I sank again, trembling and hopeless, into my miserable self.

We left Oxford with regret and proceeded to Matlock, which was our next place of rest. The country in the neighbourhood of this village resembled, to a greater degree, the scenery of Switzerland; but everything is on a lower scale, and the green hills want the crown of distant white Alps which always attend on the piny mountains of my native country. We visited the wondrous cave and the little cabinets of natural history, where the curiosities are disposed in the same manner as in the collections at Servox and Chamounix. The latter name made me tremble when pronounced by Henry, and I hastened to quit Matlock, with which that terrible scene was thus associated.

From Derby, still journeying northwards, we passed two months in Cumberland and Westmorland. I could now almost fancy myself among the Swiss mountains. The little patches of snow which yet lingered on the northern sides of the mountains, the lakes, and the dashing of the rocky streams were all familiar and dear sights to me. Here also we made some acquaintances, who almost contrived to cheat me into happiness. The delight of Clerval was proportionably greater than mine; his mind expanded in the company of men of talent, and he found in his own nature greater capacities and resources than he could have imagined himself to have possessed while he associated with his inferiors. "I could pass my life here," said he to me; "and among these mountains I should scarcely regret Switzerland and the Rhine."

But he found that a traveller's life is one that includes much pain amidst its enjoyments. His feelings are for ever on the stretch; and when he begins to sink into repose, he finds himself obliged to quit that on which he rests in pleasure for something new, which again engages his attention, and which also he forsakes for other novelties.

We had scarcely visited the various lakes of Cumberland and Westmorland and conceived an affection for some of the inhabitants when the period of our appointment with our Scotch friend approached, and we left them to travel on. For my own part I was not sorry. I had now neglected my promise for some time, and I feared the effects of the dæmon's disappointment. He might remain in Switzerland and wreak his vengeance on my relatives. This idea pursued me and tormented me at every moment from which I might otherwise have snatched repose and peace. I waited for my letters with feverish impatience; if they were delayed I was miserable and overcome by a thousand fears; and when they arrived and I saw the superscription of Elizabeth or my father, I hardly dared to read and ascertain my fate. Sometimes I thought that the fiend followed me and might expedite my remissness by murdering my companion. When these thoughts possessed me, I would not quit Henry for a moment, but followed him as his shadow, to protect him from the fancied rage of his destroyer. I felt as if I had committed some great crime, the consciousness of which haunted me. I was guiltless, but I had indeed drawn down a horrible curse upon my head, as mortal as that of crime.

I visited Edinburgh with languid eyes and mind; and yet that city might have interested the most unfortunate being. Clerval did not like it so well as Oxford, for the antiquity of the latter city was more pleasing to him. But the beauty and regularity of the new town of Edinburgh, its romantic castle and its environs, the most delightful in the world, Arthur's Seat, St. Bernard's Well, and the Pentland Hills, compensated him for the change and filled him with cheerfulness and admiration. But I was impatient to arrive at the termination of my journey.

We left Edinburgh in a week, passing through Coupar, St. Andrew's, and along the banks of the Tay, to Perth, where our friend expected us. But I was in no mood to laugh and talk with strangers or enter into their feelings or plans with the good humour expected from a guest; and accordingly I told Clerval that I wished to make the tour of Scotland alone. "Do you," said

Frankenstein

I, "enjoy yourself, and let this be our rendezvous. I may be absent a month or two; but do not interfere with my motions, I entreat you; leave me to peace and solitude for a short time; and when I return, I hope it will be with a lighter heart, more congenial to your own temper."

Henry wished to dissuade me, but seeing me bent on this plan, ceased to remonstrate. He entreated me to write often. "I had rather be with you," he said, "in your solitary rambles, than with these Scotch people, whom I do not know; hasten, then, my dear friend, to return, that I may again feel myself somewhat at home, which I cannot do in your absence."

Having parted from my friend, I determined to visit some remote spot of Scotland and finish my work in solitude. I did not doubt but that the monster followed me and would discover himself to me when I should have finished, that he might receive his companion.

With this resolution I traversed the northern highlands and fixed on one of the remotest of the Orkneys as the scene of my labours. It was a place fitted for such a work, being hardly more than a rock whose high sides were continually beaten upon by the waves. The soil was barren, scarcely affording pasture for a few miserable cows, and oatmeal for its inhabitants, which consisted of five persons, whose gaunt and scraggy limbs gave tokens of their miserable fare. Vegetables and bread, when they indulged in such luxuries, and even fresh water, was to be procured from the mainland, which was about five miles distant.

On the whole island there were but three miserable huts, and one of these was vacant when I arrived. This I hired. It contained but two rooms, and these exhibited all the squalidness of the most miserable penury. The thatch had fallen in, the walls were unplastered, and the door was off its hinges. I ordered it to be repaired, bought some furniture, and took possession, an incident which would doubtless have occasioned some surprise had not all the senses of the cottagers been benumbed by want and squalid poverty. As it was, I lived ungazed at and unmolested, hardly thanked for the pittance of food and clothes which I gave, so much does suffering blunt even the coarsest sensations of men.

In this retreat I devoted the morning to labour; but in the evening, when the weather permitted, I walked on the stony beach of the sea to listen to the waves as they roared and dashed at my feet. It was a monotonous yet ever-changing scene. I thought of Switzerland; it was far different from this desolate and appalling landscape. Its hills are covered with vines, and its cottages are scattered thickly in the plains. Its fair lakes reflect a blue and gentle sky, and when troubled by the winds, their tumult is but as the play of a lively infant when compared to the roarings of the giant ocean.

In this manner I distributed my occupations when I first arrived, but as I proceeded in my labour, it became every day more horrible and irksome to me. Sometimes I could not prevail on myself to enter my laboratory for several days, and at other times I toiled day and night in order to complete my work. It was, indeed, a filthy process in which I was engaged. During my first experiment, a kind of enthusiastic frenzy had blinded me to the horror of my employment; my mind was intently fixed on the consummation of my labour, and my eyes were shut to the horror of my proceedings. But now I went to it in cold blood, and my heart often sickened at the work of my hands.

Thus situated, employed in the most detestable occupation, immersed in a solitude where nothing could for an instant call my attention from the actual scene in which I was engaged, my spirits became unequal; I grew restless and nervous. Every moment I feared to meet my persecutor. Sometimes I sat with my eyes fixed on the ground, fearing to raise them lest they should encounter the object which I so much dreaded to behold. I feared to wander from the sight of my fellow creatures lest when alone he should come to claim his companion.

In the mean time I worked on, and my labour was already considerably advanced. I looked towards its completion with a tremulous and eager hope, which I dared not trust myself to question but which was intermixed with obscure forebodings of evil that made my heart sicken in my bosom.

Chapter 20

I sat one evening in my laboratory; the sun had set, and the moon was just rising from the sea; I had not sufficient light for my employment, and I remained idle, in a pause of consideration of whether I should leave my labour for the night or hasten its conclusion by an unremitting attention to it. As I sat, a train of reflection occurred to me which led me to consider the effects of what I was now doing. Three years before, I was engaged in the same manner and had created a fiend whose unparalleled barbarity had desolated my heart and filled it for ever with the bitterest remorse. I was now about to form another being of whose dispositions I was alike ignorant; she might become ten thousand times more malignant than her mate and delight, for its own sake, in murder and wretchedness. He had sworn to quit the neighbourhood of man and hide himself in deserts, but she had not; and she, who in all probability was to become a thinking and reasoning animal, might refuse to comply with a compact made before her creation. They might even hate each other; the creature who already lived loathed his own deformity, and might he not conceive a greater abhorrence for it when it came before his eyes in the female form? She also might turn with disgust from him to the superior beauty of man; she might quit him, and he be again alone, exasperated by the fresh provocation of being deserted by one of his own species.

Even if they were to leave Europe and inhabit the deserts of the new world, yet one of the first results of those sympathies for which the dæmon thirsted would be children, and a race of devils would be propagated upon the earth who might make the very existence of the species of man a condition precarious and full of terror. Had I right, for my own benefit, to inflict this curse upon everlasting generations? I had before been moved by the sophisms of the being I had created; I had been struck senseless by his fiendish threats; but now, for the first time, the wickedness of my promise burst upon me; I shuddered to think that future ages might curse me as their pest, whose selfishness had not hesitated to buy its own peace at the price, perhaps, of the existence of the whole human race.

I trembled and my heart failed within me, when, on looking up, I saw by the light of the moon the dæmon at the casement. A ghastly grin wrinkled his lips as he gazed on me, where I sat fulfilling the task which he had allotted to me. Yes, he had followed me in my travels; he had loitered in forests, hid himself in caves, or taken refuge in wide and desert heaths; and he now came to mark my progress and claim the fulfilment of my promise.

As I looked on him, his countenance expressed the utmost extent of malice and treachery. I thought with a sensation of madness on my promise of creating another like to him, and trembling with passion, tore to pieces the thing on which I was engaged. The wretch saw me destroy the creature on whose future existence he depended for happiness, and with a howl of devilish despair and revenge, withdrew.

I left the room, and locking the door, made a solemn vow in my own heart never to resume my labours; and then, with trembling steps, I sought my own apartment. I was alone; none were near me to dissipate the gloom and relieve me from the sickening oppression of the most terrible reveries.

Several hours passed, and I remained near my window gazing on the sea; it was almost motionless, for the winds were hushed, and all nature reposed under the eye of the quiet moon. A few fishing vessels alone specked the water, and now and then the gentle breeze wafted the sound of voices as the fishermen called to one another. I felt the silence, although I was hardly conscious of its extreme profundity, until my ear was suddenly arrested by the paddling of oars near the shore, and a person landed close to my house.

In a few minutes after, I heard the creaking of my door, as if some one endeavoured to open it softly. I trembled from head to foot; I felt a presentiment of who it was and wished to rouse one of the peasants who dwelt in a cottage not far from mine; but I was overcome by the sensation of helplessness, so often felt in frightful dreams, when you in vain endeavour to fly from an impending danger, and was rooted to the spot.

Presently I heard the sound of footsteps along the passage; the door opened, and the wretch whom I dreaded appeared. Shutting the door, he approached me and said in a smothered voice,

"You have destroyed the work which you began; what is it that you intend? Do you dare to break your promise? I have endured toil and misery; I left Switzerland with you; I crept along the shores of the Rhine, among its willow islands and over the summits of its hills. I have dwelt many months in the heaths of England and among the deserts of Scotland. I have endured incalculable fatigue, and cold, and hunger; do you dare destroy my hopes?"

Frankenstein

"Begone! I do break my promise; never will I create another like yourself, equal in deformity and wickedness."

"Slave, I before reasoned with you, but you have proved yourself unworthy of my condescension. Remember that I have power; you believe yourself miserable, but I can make you so wretched that the light of day will be hateful to you. You are my creator, but I am your master; obey!"

"The hour of my irresolution is past, and the period of your power is arrived. Your threats cannot move me to do an act of wickedness; but they confirm me in a determination of not creating you a companion in vice. Shall I, in cool blood, set loose upon the earth a dæmon whose delight is in death and wretchedness? Begone! I am firm, and your words will only exasperate my rage."

The monster saw my determination in my face and gnashed his teeth in the impotence of anger. "Shall each man," cried he, "find a wife for his bosom, and each beast have his mate, and I be alone? I had feelings of affection, and they were requited by detestation and scorn. Man! You may hate, but beware! Your hours will pass in dread and misery, and soon the bolt will fall which must ravish from you your happiness for ever. Are you to be happy while I grovel in the intensity of my wretchedness? You can blast my other passions, but revenge remains— revenge, henceforth dearer than light or food! I may die, but first you, my tyrant and tormentor, shall curse the sun that gazes on your misery. Beware, for I am fearless and therefore powerful. I will watch with the wiliness of a snake, that I may sting with its venom. Man, you shall repent of the injuries you inflict."

"Devil, cease; and do not poison the air with these sounds of malice. I have declared my resolution to you, and I am no coward to bend beneath words. Leave me; I am inexorable."

"It is well. I go; but remember, I shall be with you on your wedding-night."

I started forward and exclaimed, "Villain! Before you sign my death-warrant, be sure that you are yourself safe."

I would have seized him, but he eluded me and quitted the house with precipitation. In a few moments I saw him in his boat, which shot across the waters with an arrowy swiftness and was soon lost amidst the waves.

All was again silent, but his words rang in my ears. I burned with rage to pursue the murderer of my peace and precipitate him into the ocean. I walked up and down my room hastily and perturbed, while my imagination conjured up a thousand images to torment and sting me. Why had I not followed him and closed with him in mortal strife? But I had suffered him to depart, and he had directed his course towards the mainland. I shuddered to think who might be the next victim sacrificed to his insatiate revenge. And then I thought again of his words—"I will be with you on your wedding-night." That, then, was the period fixed for the fulfilment of my destiny. In that hour I should die and at once satisfy and extinguish his malice. The prospect did not move me to fear; yet when I thought of my beloved Elizabeth, of her tears and endless sorrow, when she should find her lover so barbarously snatched from her, tears, the first I had shed for many months, streamed from my eyes, and I resolved not to fall before my enemy without a bitter struggle.

The night passed away, and the sun rose from the ocean; my feelings became calmer, if it may be called calmness when the violence of rage sinks into the depths of despair. I left the house, the horrid scene of the last night's contention, and walked on the beach of the sea, which I almost regarded as an insuperable barrier between me and my fellow creatures; nay, a wish that such should prove the fact stole across me. I desired that I might pass my life on that barren rock, wearily, it is true, but uninterrupted by any sudden shock of misery. If I returned, it was to be sacrificed or to see those whom I most loved die under the grasp of a dæmon whom I had myself created.

I walked about the isle like a restless spectre, separated from all it loved and miserable in the separation. When it became noon, and the sun rose higher, I lay down on the grass and was overpowered by a deep sleep. I had been awake the whole of the preceding night, my nerves were agitated, and my eyes inflamed by watching and misery. The sleep into which I now sank refreshed me; and when I awoke, I again felt as if I belonged to a race of human beings like myself, and I began to reflect upon what had passed with greater composure; yet still the words of the fiend rang in my ears like a death-knell; they appeared like a dream, yet distinct and oppressive as a reality.

The sun had far descended, and I still sat on the shore, satisfying my appetite, which had become ravenous, with an oaten cake, when I saw a fishing-boat land close to me, and one of the men brought me a packet; it contained letters from Geneva, and one from Clerval entreating me to join him. He said that he was wearing away his time fruitlessly where he was, that letters from the friends he had formed in London desired his return to complete the negotiation they had entered into for his Indian enterprise. He could not any longer delay his departure; but as his journey to London might be followed, even sooner than he now conjectured, by his longer voyage, he entreated me to bestow as much of my society on him as I could spare. He besought me, therefore, to leave my solitary isle and to meet him at Perth, that we might proceed southwards together. This letter in a degree recalled me to life, and I determined to quit my island at the expiration of two days.

Yet, before I departed, there was a task to perform, on which I shuddered to reflect; I must pack up my chemical instruments, and for that purpose I must enter the room which had been the scene of my odious work, and I must handle those utensils the sight of which was sickening to me. The next morning, at daybreak, I summoned sufficient courage and unlocked the door of my laboratory. The remains of the half-finished creature, whom I had destroyed, lay scattered on the floor, and I almost felt as if I had mangled the living flesh of a human being. I paused to collect myself and then entered the chamber. With trembling hand I conveyed the instruments out of the room, but I reflected that I ought not to leave the relics of my work to excite the horror and suspicion of the peasants; and I accordingly put them into a basket, with a great quantity of stones, and laying them up, determined to throw them into the sea that very night; and in the meantime I sat upon the beach, employed in cleaning and arranging my chemical apparatus.

Nothing could be more complete than the alteration that had taken place in my feelings since the night of the appearance of the dæmon. I had before regarded my promise with a gloomy despair as a thing that, with whatever consequences, must be fulfilled; but I now felt as if a film had been taken from before my eyes and that I for the first time saw clearly. The idea of renewing my labours did not for one instant occur to me; the threat I had heard weighed on my thoughts, but I did not reflect that a voluntary act of mine could avert it. I had resolved in my own mind that to create another like the fiend I had first made would be an act of the basest and most atrocious selfishness, and I banished from my mind every thought that could lead to a different conclusion.

Between two and three in the morning the moon rose; and I then, putting my basket aboard a little skiff, sailed out about four miles from the shore. The scene was perfectly solitary; a few boats were returning towards land, but I sailed away from them. I felt as if I was about the commission of a dreadful crime and avoided with shuddering anxiety any encounter with my fellow creatures. At one time the moon, which had before been clear, was suddenly overspread by a thick cloud, and I took advantage of the moment of darkness and cast my basket into the sea; I listened to the gurgling sound as it sank and then sailed away from the spot. The sky became clouded, but the air was pure, although chilled by the northeast breeze that was then rising. But it refreshed me and filled me with such agreeable sensations that I resolved to prolong my stay on the water, and fixing the rudder in a direct position, stretched myself at the bottom of the boat. Clouds hid the moon, everything was obscure, and I heard only the sound of the boat as its keel cut through the waves; the murmur lulled me, and in a short time I slept soundly.

    I do not know how long I remained in this situation, but when I awoke I found that the sun had already mounted considerably. The wind was high, and the waves continually threatened the safety of my little skiff. I found that the wind was northeast and must have driven me far from the coast from which I had embarked. I endeavoured to change my course but quickly found that if I again made the attempt the boat would be instantly filled with water. Thus situated, my only resource was to drive before the wind. I confess that I felt a few sensations of terror. I had no compass with me and was so slenderly acquainted with the geography of this part of the world that the sun was of little benefit to me. I might be driven into the wide Atlantic and feel all the tortures of starvation or be swallowed up in the immeasurable waters that roared and buffeted around me. I had already been out many hours and felt the torment of a burning thirst, a prelude to my other sufferings. I looked on the heavens, which were covered by clouds that flew before the wind, only to be replaced by others; I looked upon the sea; it was to be my grave. "Fiend," I exclaimed, "your task is already fulfilled!" I thought of Elizabeth, of my father, and of Clerval—all left behind, on whom the monster might satisfy his sanguinary and merciless passions. This idea plunged me into a reverie so despairing and frightful that even now, when the scene is on the point of closing before me for ever, I shudder to reflect on it.

    Some hours passed thus; but by degrees, as the sun declined towards the horizon, the wind died away into a gentle breeze and the sea became free from breakers. But these gave place to a heavy swell; I felt sick and hardly able to hold the rudder, when suddenly I saw a line of high land towards the south.

Frankenstein

Almost spent, as I was, by fatigue and the dreadful suspense I endured for several hours, this sudden certainty of life rushed like a flood of warm joy to my heart, and tears gushed from my eyes.

How mutable are our feelings, and how strange is that clinging love we have of life even in the excess of misery! I constructed another sail with a part of my dress and eagerly steered my course towards the land. It had a wild and rocky appearance, but as I approached nearer I easily perceived the traces of cultivation. I saw vessels near the shore and found myself suddenly transported back to the neighbourhood of civilised man. I carefully traced the windings of the land and hailed a steeple which I at length saw issuing from behind a small promontory. As I was in a state of extreme debility, I resolved to sail directly towards the town, as a place where I could most easily procure nourishment. Fortunately I had money with me. As I turned the promontory I perceived a small neat town and a good harbour, which I entered, my heart bounding with joy at my unexpected escape.

As I was occupied in fixing the boat and arranging the sails, several people crowded towards the spot. They seemed much surprised at my appearance, but instead of offering me any assistance, whispered together with gestures that at any other time might have produced in me a slight sensation of alarm. As it was, I merely remarked that they spoke English, and I therefore addressed them in that language. "My good friends," said I, "will you be so kind as to tell me the name of this town and inform me where I am?"

"You will know that soon enough," replied a man with a hoarse voice. "Maybe you are come to a place that will not prove much to your taste, but you will not be consulted as to your quarters, I promise you."

I was exceedingly surprised on receiving so rude an answer from a stranger, and I was also disconcerted on perceiving the frowning and angry countenances of his companions. "Why do you answer me so roughly?" I replied. "Surely it is not the custom of Englishmen to receive strangers so inhospitably."

"I do not know," said the man, "what the custom of the English may be, but it is the custom of the Irish to hate villains."

While this strange dialogue continued, I perceived the crowd rapidly increase. Their faces expressed a mixture of curiosity and anger, which annoyed and in some degree alarmed me. I inquired the way to the inn, but no one replied. I then moved forward, and a murmuring sound arose from the crowd as they followed and surrounded me, when an ill-looking man approaching tapped me on the shoulder and said, "Come, sir, you must follow me to Mr. Kirwin's to give an account of yourself."

"Who is Mr. Kirwin? Why am I to give an account of myself? Is not this a free country?"

"Ay, sir, free enough for honest folks. Mr. Kirwin is a magistrate, and you are to give an account of the death of a gentleman who was found murdered here last night."

This answer startled me, but I presently recovered myself. I was innocent; that could easily be proved; accordingly I followed my conductor in silence and was led to one of the best houses in the town. I was ready to sink from fatigue and hunger, but being surrounded by a crowd, I thought it politic to rouse all my strength, that no physical debility might be construed into apprehension or conscious guilt. Little did I then expect the calamity that was in a few moments to overwhelm me and extinguish in horror and despair all fear of ignominy or death.

I must pause here, for it requires all my fortitude to recall the memory of the frightful events which I am about to relate, in proper detail, to my recollection.

Chapter 21

I was soon introduced into the presence of the magistrate, an old benevolent man with calm and mild manners. He looked upon me, however, with some degree of severity, and then, turning towards my conductors, he asked who appeared as witnesses on this occasion.

About half a dozen men came forward; and, one being selected by the magistrate, he deposed that he had been out fishing the night before with his son and brother-in-law, Daniel Nugent, when, about ten o'clock, they observed a strong northerly blast rising, and they accordingly put in for port. It was a very dark night, as the moon had not yet risen; they did not land at the harbour, but, as they had been accustomed, at a creek about two miles below. He walked on first, carrying a part of the fishing tackle, and his companions followed him at some distance. As he was proceeding along the sands, he struck his foot against something and fell at his length on the ground. His companions came up to assist him, and by the light of their lantern they found that he had fallen on the body of a man, who was to all appearance dead. Their first supposition was that it was the corpse of some person who had been drowned and was thrown on shore by the waves, but on examination they found that the clothes were not wet and even that the body was not then cold. They instantly carried it to the cottage of an old woman near the spot and endeavoured, but in vain, to restore it to life. It appeared to be a handsome young man, about five and twenty years of age. He had apparently been strangled, for there was no sign of any violence except the black mark of fingers on his neck.

The first part of this deposition did not in the least interest me, but when the mark of the fingers was mentioned I remembered the murder of my brother and felt myself extremely agitated; my limbs trembled, and a mist came over my eyes, which obliged me to lean on a chair for support. The magistrate observed me with a keen eye and of course drew an unfavourable augury from my manner.

The son confirmed his father's account, but when Daniel Nugent was called he swore positively that just before the fall of his companion, he saw a boat, with a single man in it, at a short distance from the shore; and as far as he could judge by the light of a few stars, it was the same boat in which I had just landed.

A woman deposed that she lived near the beach and was standing at the door of her cottage, waiting for the return of the fishermen, about an hour before she heard of the discovery of the body, when she saw a boat with only one man in it push off from that part of the shore where the corpse was afterwards found.

Another woman confirmed the account of the fishermen having brought the body into her house; it was not cold. They put it into a bed and rubbed it, and Daniel went to the town for an apothecary, but life was quite gone.

Several other men were examined concerning my landing, and they agreed that, with the strong north wind that had arisen during the night, it was very probable that I had beaten about for many hours and had been obliged to return nearly to the same spot from which I had departed. Besides, they observed that it appeared that I had brought the body from another place, and it was likely that as I did not appear to know the shore, I might have put into the harbour ignorant of the distance of the town of —— from the place where I had deposited the corpse.

Mr. Kirwin, on hearing this evidence, desired that I should be taken into the room where the body lay for interment, that it might be observed what effect the sight of it would produce upon me. This idea was probably suggested by the extreme agitation I had exhibited when the mode of the murder had been described. I was accordingly conducted, by the magistrate and several other persons, to the inn. I could not help being struck by the strange coincidences that had taken place during this eventful night; but, knowing that I had been conversing with several persons in the island I had inhabited about the time that the body had been found, I was perfectly tranquil as to the consequences of the affair.

I entered the room where the corpse lay and was led up to the coffin. How can I describe my sensations on beholding it? I feel yet parched with horror, nor can I reflect on that terrible moment without shuddering and agony. The examination, the presence of the magistrate and witnesses, passed like a dream from my memory when I saw the lifeless form of Henry Clerval stretched before me. I gasped for breath, and throwing myself on the body, I exclaimed, "Have my murderous machinations deprived you also, my dearest Henry, of life? Two I have already destroyed; other victims await their destiny; but you, Clerval, my friend, my benefactor—"

The human frame could no longer support the agonies that I endured, and I was carried out of the room in strong convulsions.

Frankenstein

A fever succeeded to this. I lay for two months on the point of death; my ravings, as I afterwards heard, were frightful; I called myself the murderer of William, of Justine, and of Clerval. Sometimes I entreated my attendants to assist me in the destruction of the fiend by whom I was tormented; and at others I felt the fingers of the monster already grasping my neck, and screamed aloud with agony and terror. Fortunately, as I spoke my native language, Mr. Kirwin alone understood me; but my gestures and bitter cries were sufficient to affright the other witnesses.

Why did I not die? More miserable than man ever was before, why did I not sink into forgetfulness and rest? Death snatches away many blooming children, the only hopes of their doting parents; how many brides and youthful lovers have been one day in the bloom of health and hope, and the next a prey for worms and the decay of the tomb! Of what materials was I made that I could thus resist so many shocks, which, like the turning of the wheel, continually renewed the torture?

But I was doomed to live and in two months found myself as awaking from a dream, in a prison, stretched on a wretched bed, surrounded by gaolers, turnkeys, bolts, and all the miserable apparatus of a dungeon. It was morning, I remember, when I thus awoke to understanding; I had forgotten the particulars of what had happened and only felt as if some great misfortune had suddenly overwhelmed me; but when I looked around and saw the barred windows and the squalidness of the room in which I was, all flashed across my memory and I groaned bitterly.

This sound disturbed an old woman who was sleeping in a chair beside me. She was a hired nurse, the wife of one of the turnkeys, and her countenance expressed all those bad qualities which often characterise that class. The lines of her face were hard and rude, like that of persons accustomed to see without sympathising in sights of misery. Her tone expressed her entire indifference; she addressed me in English, and the voice struck me as one that I had heard during my sufferings.

"Are you better now, sir?" said she.

I replied in the same language, with a feeble voice, "I believe I am; but if it be all true, if indeed I did not dream, I am sorry that I am still alive to feel this misery and horror."

"For that matter," replied the old woman, "if you mean about the gentleman you murdered, I believe that it were better for you if you were dead, for I fancy it will go hard with you! However, that's none of my business; I am sent to nurse you and get you well; I do my duty with a safe conscience; it were well if everybody did the same."

I turned with loathing from the woman who could utter so unfeeling a speech to a person just saved, on the very edge of death; but I felt languid and unable to reflect on all that had passed. The whole series of my life appeared to me as a dream; I sometimes doubted if indeed it were all true, for it never presented itself to my mind with the force of reality.

As the images that floated before me became more distinct, I grew feverish; a darkness pressed around me; no one was near me who soothed me with the gentle voice of love; no dear hand supported me. The physician came and prescribed medicines, and the old woman prepared them for me; but utter carelessness was visible in the first, and the expression of brutality was strongly marked in the visage of the second. Who could be interested in the fate of a murderer but the hangman who would gain his fee?

These were my first reflections, but I soon learned that Mr. Kirwin had shown me extreme kindness. He had caused the best room in the prison to be prepared for me (wretched indeed was the best); and it was he who had provided a physician and a nurse. It is true, he seldom came to see me, for although he ardently desired to relieve the sufferings of every human creature, he did not wish to be present at the agonies and miserable ravings of a murderer. He came, therefore, sometimes to see that I was not neglected, but his visits were short and with long intervals.

One day, while I was gradually recovering, I was seated in a chair, my eyes half open and my cheeks livid like those in death. I was overcome by gloom and misery and often reflected I had better seek death than desire to remain in a world which to me was replete with wretchedness. At one time I considered whether I should not declare myself guilty and suffer the penalty of the law, less innocent than poor Justine had been. Such were my thoughts when the door of my apartment was opened and Mr. Kirwin entered. His countenance expressed sympathy and compassion; he drew a chair close to mine and addressed me in French,

"I fear that this place is very shocking to you; can I do anything to make you more comfortable?"

"I thank you, but all that you mention is nothing to me; on the whole earth there is no comfort which I am capable of receiving."

"I know that the sympathy of a stranger can be but of little relief to one borne down as you are by so strange a misfortune. But you will, I hope, soon quit this melancholy abode, for doubtless evidence can easily be brought to free you from the criminal charge."

"That is my least concern; I am, by a course of strange events, become the most miserable of mortals. Persecuted and tortured as I am and have been, can death be any evil to me?"

"Nothing indeed could be more unfortunate and agonising than the strange chances that have lately occurred. You were thrown, by some surprising accident, on this shore, renowned for its hospitality, seized immediately, and charged with murder. The first sight that was presented to your eyes was the body of your friend, murdered in so unaccountable a manner and placed, as it were, by some fiend across your path."

As Mr. Kirwin said this, notwithstanding the agitation I endured on this retrospect of my sufferings, I also felt considerable surprise at the knowledge he seemed to possess concerning me. I suppose some astonishment was exhibited in my countenance, for Mr. Kirwin hastened to say,

"Immediately upon your being taken ill, all the papers that were on your person were brought me, and I examined them that I might discover some trace by which I could send to your relations an account of your misfortune and illness. I found several letters, and, among others, one which I discovered from its commencement to be from your father. I instantly wrote to Geneva; nearly two months have elapsed since the departure of my letter. But you are ill; even now you tremble; you are unfit for agitation of any kind."

"This suspense is a thousand times worse than the most horrible event; tell me what new scene of death has been acted, and whose murder I am now to lament?"

"Your family is perfectly well," said Mr. Kirwin with gentleness; "and someone, a friend, is come to visit you."

I know not by what chain of thought the idea presented itself, but it instantly darted into my mind that the murderer had come to mock at my misery and taunt me with the death of

Clerval, as a new incitement for me to comply with his hellish desires. I put my hand before my eyes, and cried out in agony,

"Oh! Take him away! I cannot see him; for God's sake, do not let him enter!"

Mr. Kirwin regarded me with a troubled countenance. He could not help regarding my exclamation as a presumption of my guilt and said in rather a severe tone,

"I should have thought, young man, that the presence of your father would have been welcome instead of inspiring such violent repugnance."

"My father!" cried I, while every feature and every muscle was relaxed from anguish to pleasure. "Is my father indeed come? How kind, how very kind! But where is he, why does he not hasten to me?"

My change of manner surprised and pleased the magistrate; perhaps he thought that my former exclamation was a momentary return of delirium, and now he instantly resumed his former benevolence. He rose and quitted the room with my nurse, and in a moment my father entered it.

Nothing, at this moment, could have given me greater pleasure than the arrival of my father. I stretched out my hand to him and cried,

"Are you then safe—and Elizabeth—and Ernest?"

My father calmed me with assurances of their welfare and endeavoured, by dwelling on these subjects so interesting to my heart, to raise my desponding spirits; but he soon felt that a prison cannot be the abode of cheerfulness. "What a place is this that you inhabit, my son!" said he, looking mournfully at the barred windows and wretched appearance of the room. "You travelled to seek happiness, but a fatality seems to pursue you. And poor Clerval—"

The name of my unfortunate and murdered friend was an agitation too great to be endured in my weak state; I shed tears.

"Alas! Yes, my father," replied I; "some destiny of the most horrible kind hangs over me, and I must live to fulfil it, or surely I should have died on the coffin of Henry."

Frankenstein

We were not allowed to converse for any length of time, for the precarious state of my health rendered every precaution necessary that could ensure tranquillity. Mr. Kirwin came in and insisted that my strength should not be exhausted by too much exertion. But the appearance of my father was to me like that of my good angel, and I gradually recovered my health.

As my sickness quitted me, I was absorbed by a gloomy and black melancholy that nothing could dissipate. The image of Clerval was for ever before me, ghastly and murdered. More than once the agitation into which these reflections threw me made my friends dread a dangerous relapse. Alas! Why did they preserve so miserable and detested a life? It was surely that I might fulfil my destiny, which is now drawing to a close. Soon, oh, very soon, will death extinguish these throbbings and relieve me from the mighty weight of anguish that bears me to the dust; and, in executing the award of justice, I shall also sink to rest. Then the appearance of death was distant, although the wish was ever present to my thoughts; and I often sat for hours motionless and speechless, wishing for some mighty revolution that might bury me and my destroyer in its ruins.

The season of the assizes approached. I had already been three months in prison, and although I was still weak and in continual danger of a relapse, I was obliged to travel nearly a hundred miles to the country town where the court was held. Mr. Kirwin charged himself with every care of collecting witnesses and arranging my defence. I was spared the disgrace of appearing publicly as a criminal, as the case was not brought before the court that decides on life and death. The grand jury rejected the bill, on its being proved that I was on the Orkney Islands at the hour the body of my friend was found; and a fortnight after my removal I was liberated from prison.

My father was enraptured on finding me freed from the vexations of a criminal charge, that I was again allowed to breathe the fresh atmosphere and permitted to return to my native country. I did not participate in these feelings, for to me the walls of a dungeon or a palace were alike hateful. The cup of life was poisoned for ever, and although the sun shone upon me, as upon the happy and gay of heart, I saw around me nothing but a dense and frightful darkness, penetrated by no light but the glimmer of two eyes that glared upon me. Sometimes they were the expressive eyes of Henry, languishing in death, the dark orbs nearly covered by the lids and the long black lashes that fringed them; sometimes it was the watery, clouded eyes of the monster, as I first saw them in my chamber at Ingolstadt.

My father tried to awaken in me the feelings of affection. He talked of Geneva, which I should soon visit, of Elizabeth and Ernest; but these words only drew deep groans from me. Sometimes, indeed, I felt a wish for happiness and thought with melancholy delight of my beloved cousin or longed, with a devouring maladie du pays, to see once more the blue lake and rapid Rhone, that had been so dear to me in early childhood; but my general state of feeling was a torpor in which a prison was as welcome a residence as the divinest scene in nature; and these fits were seldom interrupted but by paroxysms of anguish and despair. At these moments I often endeavoured to put an end to the existence I loathed, and it required unceasing attendance and vigilance to restrain me from committing some dreadful act of violence.

Yet one duty remained to me, the recollection of which finally triumphed over my selfish despair. It was necessary that I should return without delay to Geneva, there to watch over the lives of those I so fondly loved and to lie in wait for the murderer, that if any chance led me to the place of his concealment, or if he dared again to blast me by his presence, I might, with unfailing aim, put an end to the existence of the monstrous image which I had endued with the mockery of a soul still more monstrous. My father still desired to delay our departure, fearful that I could not sustain the fatigues of a journey, for I was a shattered wreck—the shadow of a human being. My strength was gone. I was a mere skeleton, and fever night and day preyed upon my wasted frame.

Still, as I urged our leaving Ireland with such inquietude and impatience, my father thought it best to yield. We took our passage on board a vessel bound for Havre-de-Grace and sailed with a fair wind from the Irish shores. It was midnight. I lay on the deck looking at the stars and listening to the dashing of the waves. I hailed the darkness that shut Ireland from my sight, and my pulse beat with a feverish joy when I reflected that I should soon see Geneva. The past appeared to me in the light of a frightful dream; yet the vessel in which I was, the wind that blew me from the detested shore of Ireland, and the sea which surrounded me, told me too forcibly that I was deceived by no vision and that Clerval, my friend and dearest companion, had fallen a victim to me and the monster of my creation. I repassed, in my memory, my whole life; my quiet happiness while residing with my family in Geneva, the death of my mother, and my departure for Ingolstadt. I remembered, shuddering, the mad enthusiasm that hurried me on to the creation of my hideous enemy, and I called to mind the night in which he first lived. I was unable to pursue the train of thought; a thousand feelings pressed upon me, and I wept bitterly.

Ever since my recovery from the fever, I had been in the custom of taking every night a small quantity of laudanum, for it was by means of this drug only that I was enabled to gain the rest necessary for the preservation of life. Oppressed by the recollection of my various misfortunes, I now swallowed double my usual quantity and soon slept profoundly. But sleep did not afford me respite from thought and misery; my dreams presented a thousand objects that scared me. Towards morning I was possessed by a kind of nightmare; I felt the fiend's grasp in my neck and could not free myself from it; groans and cries rang in my ears. My father, who was watching over me, perceiving my restlessness, awoke me; the dashing waves were around, the cloudy sky above, the fiend was not here: a sense of security, a feeling that a truce was established between the present hour and the irresistible, disastrous future imparted to me a kind of calm forgetfulness, of which the human mind is by its structure peculiarly susceptible.

Chapter 22

The voyage came to an end. We landed, and proceeded to Paris. I soon found that I had overtaxed my strength and that I must repose before I could continue my journey. My father's care and attentions were indefatigable, but he did not know the origin of my sufferings and sought erroneous methods to remedy the incurable ill. He wished me to seek amusement in society. I abhorred the face of man. Oh, not abhorred! They were my brethren, my fellow beings, and I felt attracted even to the most repulsive among them, as to creatures of an angelic nature and celestial mechanism. But I felt that I had no right to share their intercourse. I had unchained an enemy among them whose joy it was to shed their blood and to revel in their groans. How they would, each and all, abhor me and hunt me from the world, did they know my unhallowed acts and the crimes which had their source in me!

My father yielded at length to my desire to avoid society and strove by various arguments to banish my despair. Sometimes he thought that I felt deeply the degradation of being obliged to answer a charge of murder, and he endeavoured to prove to me the futility of pride.

"Alas! My father," said I, "how little do you know me. Human beings, their feelings and passions, would indeed be degraded if such a wretch as I felt pride. Justine, poor unhappy Justine, was as innocent as I, and she suffered the same charge; she died for it; and I am the cause of this — I murdered her. William, Justine, and Henry — they all died by my hands."

My father had often, during my imprisonment, heard me make the same assertion; when I thus accused myself, he sometimes seemed to desire an explanation, and at others he appeared to consider it as the offspring of delirium, and that, during my illness, some idea of this kind had presented itself to my imagination, the remembrance of which I preserved in my convalescence. I avoided explanation and maintained a continual silence concerning the wretch I had created. I had a persuasion that I should be supposed mad, and this in itself would for ever have chained my tongue. But, besides, I could not bring myself to disclose a secret which would fill my hearer with consternation and make fear and unnatural horror the inmates of his breast. I checked, therefore, my impatient thirst for sympathy and was silent when I would have given the world to have confided the fatal secret. Yet, still, words like those I have recorded would burst uncontrollably from me. I could offer no explanation of them, but their truth in part relieved the burden of my mysterious woe.

Upon this occasion my father said, with an expression of unbounded wonder, "My dearest Victor, what infatuation is this? My dear son, I entreat you never to make such an assertion again."

"I am not mad," I cried energetically; "the sun and the heavens, who have viewed my operations, can bear witness of my truth. I am the assassin of those most innocent victims; they died by my machinations. A thousand times would I have shed my own blood, drop by drop, to have saved their lives; but I could not, my father, indeed I could not sacrifice the whole human race."

The conclusion of this speech convinced my father that my ideas were deranged, and he instantly changed the subject of our conversation and endeavoured to alter the course of my thoughts. He wished as much as possible to obliterate the memory of the scenes that had taken place in Ireland and never alluded to them or suffered me to speak of my misfortunes.

As time passed away I became more calm; misery had her dwelling in my heart, but I no longer talked in the same incoherent manner of my own crimes; sufficient for me was the consciousness of them. By the utmost self-violence I curbed the imperious voice of wretchedness, which sometimes desired to declare itself to the whole world, and my manners were calmer and more composed than they had ever been since my journey to the sea of ice.

A few days before we left Paris on our way to Switzerland, I received the following letter from Elizabeth:

"My dear Friend,

"It gave me the greatest pleasure to receive a letter from my uncle dated at Paris; you are no longer at a formidable distance, and I may hope to see you in less than a fortnight. My poor cousin, how much you must have suffered! I expect to see you looking even more ill than when you quitted Geneva. This winter has been passed most miserably, tortured as I have been by anxious suspense; yet I hope to see peace in your countenance and to find that your heart is not totally void of comfort and tranquillity.

"Yet I fear that the same feelings now exist that made you so miserable a year ago, even perhaps augmented by time. I would not disturb you at this period, when so many misfortunes weigh upon you, but a conversation that I had with my uncle previous to his departure renders some explanation necessary before we meet.

Explanation! You may possibly say, What can Elizabeth have to explain? If you really say this, my questions are answered and all my doubts satisfied. But you are distant from me, and it is possible that you may dread and yet be pleased with this explanation; and in a probability of this being the case, I dare not any longer postpone writing what, during your absence, I have often wished to express to you but have never had the courage to begin.

"You well know, Victor, that our union had been the favourite plan of your parents ever since our infancy. We were told this when young, and taught to look forward to it as an event that would certainly take place. We were affectionate playfellows during childhood, and, I believe, dear and valued friends to one another as we grew older. But as brother and sister often entertain a lively affection towards each other without desiring a more intimate union, may not such also be our case? Tell me, dearest Victor. Answer me, I conjure you by our mutual happiness, with simple truth—Do you not love another?

"You have travelled; you have spent several years of your life at Ingolstadt; and I confess to you, my friend, that when I saw you last autumn so unhappy, flying to solitude from the society of every creature, I could not help supposing that you might regret our connection and believe yourself bound in honour to fulfil the wishes of your parents, although they opposed themselves to your inclinations. But this is false reasoning. I confess to you, my friend, that I love you and that in my airy dreams of futurity you have been my constant friend and companion. But it is your happiness I desire as well as my own when I declare to you that our marriage would render me eternally miserable unless it were the dictate of your own free choice. Even now I weep to think that, borne down as you are by the cruellest misfortunes, you may stifle, by the word honour, all hope of that love and happiness which would alone restore you to yourself. I, who have so disinterested an affection for you, may increase your miseries tenfold by being an obstacle to your wishes. Ah! Victor, be assured that your cousin and playmate has too sincere a love for you not to be made miserable by this supposition. Be happy, my friend; and if you obey me in this one request, remain satisfied that nothing on earth will have the power to interrupt my tranquillity.

Frankenstein

"Do not let this letter disturb you; do not answer tomorrow, or the next day, or even until you come, if it will give you pain. My uncle will send me news of your health, and if I see but one smile on your lips when we meet, occasioned by this or any other exertion of mine, I shall need no other happiness.

"Elizabeth Lavenza.

"Geneva, May 18th, 17—"

This letter revived in my memory what I had before forgotten, the threat of the fiend—"I will be with you on your wedding-night!" Such was my sentence, and on that night would the dæmon employ every art to destroy me and tear me from the glimpse of happiness which promised partly to console my sufferings. On that night he had determined to consummate his crimes by my death. Well, be it so; a deadly struggle would then assuredly take place, in which if he were victorious I should be at peace and his power over me be at an end. If he were vanquished, I should be a free man. Alas! What freedom? Such as the peasant enjoys when his family have been massacred before his eyes, his cottage burnt, his lands laid waste, and he is turned adrift, homeless, penniless, and alone, but free. Such would be my liberty except that in my Elizabeth I possessed a treasure, alas, balanced by those horrors of remorse and guilt which would pursue me until death.

Sweet and beloved Elizabeth! I read and reread her letter, and some softened feelings stole into my heart and dared to whisper paradisiacal dreams of love and joy; but the apple was already eaten, and the angel's arm bared to drive me from all hope. Yet I would die to make her happy. If the monster executed his threat, death was inevitable; yet, again, I considered whether my marriage would hasten my fate. My destruction might indeed arrive a few months sooner, but if my torturer should suspect that I postponed it, influenced by his menaces, he would surely find other and perhaps more dreadful means of revenge. He had vowed to be with me on my wedding-night, yet he did not consider that threat as binding him to peace in the meantime, for as if to show me that he was not yet satiated with blood, he had murdered Clerval immediately after the enunciation of his threats. I resolved, therefore, that if my immediate union with my cousin would conduce either to hers or my father's happiness, my adversary's designs against my life should not retard it a single hour.

In this state of mind I wrote to Elizabeth. My letter was calm and affectionate. "I fear, my beloved girl," I said, "little happiness remains for us on earth; yet all that I may one day enjoy is centred in you. Chase away your idle fears; to you alone do I consecrate my life and my endeavours for contentment. I have one secret, Elizabeth, a dreadful one; when revealed to you, it will chill your frame with horror, and then, far from being surprised at my misery, you will only wonder that I survive what I have endured. I will confide this tale of misery and terror to you the day after our marriage shall take place, for, my sweet cousin, there must be perfect confidence between us. But until then, I conjure you, do not mention or allude to it. This I most earnestly entreat, and I know you will comply."

In about a week after the arrival of Elizabeth's letter we returned to Geneva. The sweet girl welcomed me with warm affection, yet tears were in her eyes as she beheld my emaciated frame and feverish cheeks. I saw a change in her also. She was thinner and had lost much of that heavenly vivacity that had before charmed me; but her gentleness and soft looks of compassion made her a more fit companion for one blasted and miserable as I was.

The tranquillity which I now enjoyed did not endure. Memory brought madness with it, and when I thought of what had passed, a real insanity possessed me; sometimes I was furious and burnt with rage, sometimes low and despondent. I neither spoke nor looked at anyone, but sat motionless, bewildered by the multitude of miseries that overcame me.

Elizabeth alone had the power to draw me from these fits; her gentle voice would soothe me when transported by passion and inspire me with human feelings when sunk in torpor. She wept with me and for me. When reason returned, she would remonstrate and endeavour to inspire me with resignation. Ah! It is well for the unfortunate to be resigned, but for the guilty there is no peace. The agonies of remorse poison the luxury there is otherwise sometimes found in indulging the excess of grief.

Soon after my arrival my father spoke of my immediate marriage with Elizabeth. I remained silent.

"Have you, then, some other attachment?"

"None on earth. I love Elizabeth and look forward to our union with delight. Let the day therefore be fixed; and on it I will consecrate myself, in life or death, to the happiness of my cousin."

Frankenstein

"My dear Victor, do not speak thus. Heavy misfortunes have befallen us, but let us only cling closer to what remains and transfer our love for those whom we have lost to those who yet live. Our circle will be small but bound close by the ties of affection and mutual misfortune. And when time shall have softened your despair, new and dear objects of care will be born to replace those of whom we have been so cruelly deprived."

Such were the lessons of my father. But to me the remembrance of the threat returned; nor can you wonder that, omnipotent as the fiend had yet been in his deeds of blood, I should almost regard him as invincible, and that when he had pronounced the words "I shall be with you on your wedding-night," I should regard the threatened fate as unavoidable. But death was no evil to me if the loss of Elizabeth were balanced with it, and I therefore, with a contented and even cheerful countenance, agreed with my father that if my cousin would consent, the ceremony should take place in ten days, and thus put, as I imagined, the seal to my fate.

Great God! If for one instant I had thought what might be the hellish intention of my fiendish adversary, I would rather have banished myself for ever from my native country and wandered a friendless outcast over the earth than have consented to this miserable marriage. But, as if possessed of magic powers, the monster had blinded me to his real intentions; and when I thought that I had prepared only my own death, I hastened that of a far dearer victim.

As the period fixed for our marriage drew nearer, whether from cowardice or a prophetic feeling, I felt my heart sink within me. But I concealed my feelings by an appearance of hilarity that brought smiles and joy to the countenance of my father, but hardly deceived the ever-watchful and nicer eye of Elizabeth. She looked forward to our union with placid contentment, not unmingled with a little fear, which past misfortunes had impressed, that what now appeared certain and tangible happiness might soon dissipate into an airy dream and leave no trace but deep and everlasting regret.

Preparations were made for the event, congratulatory visits were received, and all wore a smiling appearance. I shut up, as well as I could, in my own heart the anxiety that preyed there and entered with seeming earnestness into the plans of my father, although they might only serve as the decorations of my tragedy. Through my father's exertions a part of the inheritance of Elizabeth had been restored to her by the Austrian government. A small possession on the shores of Como belonged to her. It was agreed that, immediately after our union, we should proceed to Villa Lavenza and spend our first days of happiness beside the beautiful lake near which it stood.

In the meantime I took every precaution to defend my person in case the fiend should openly attack me. I carried pistols and a dagger constantly about me and was ever on the watch to prevent artifice, and by these means gained a greater degree of tranquillity. Indeed, as the period approached, the threat appeared more as a delusion, not to be regarded as worthy to disturb my peace, while the happiness I hoped for in my marriage wore a greater appearance of certainty as the day fixed for its solemnisation drew nearer and I heard it continually spoken of as an occurrence which no accident could possibly prevent.

Elizabeth seemed happy; my tranquil demeanour contributed greatly to calm her mind. But on the day that was to fulfil my wishes and my destiny, she was melancholy, and a presentiment of evil pervaded her; and perhaps also she thought of the dreadful secret which I had promised to reveal to her on the following day. My father was in the meantime overjoyed, and, in the bustle of preparation, only recognised in the melancholy of his niece the diffidence of a bride.

After the ceremony was performed a large party assembled at my father's, but it was agreed that Elizabeth and I should commence our journey by water, sleeping that night at Evian and continuing our voyage on the following day. The day was fair, the wind favourable; all smiled on our nuptial embarkation.

Those were the last moments of my life during which I enjoyed the feeling of happiness. We passed rapidly along; the sun was hot, but we were sheltered from its rays by a kind of canopy while we enjoyed the beauty of the scene, sometimes on one side of the lake, where we saw Mont Salêve, the pleasant banks of Montalègre, and at a distance, surmounting all, the beautiful Mont Blanc, and the assemblage of snowy mountains that in vain endeavour to emulate her; sometimes coasting the opposite banks, we saw the mighty Jura opposing its dark side to the ambition that would quit its native country, and an almost insurmountable barrier to the invader who should wish to enslave it.

I took the hand of Elizabeth. "You are sorrowful, my love. Ah! If you knew what I have suffered and what I may yet endure, you would endeavour to let me taste the quiet and freedom from despair that this one day at least permits me to enjoy."

"Be happy, my dear Victor," replied Elizabeth; "there is, I hope, nothing to distress you; and be assured that if a lively joy is not painted in my face, my heart is contented. Something whispers to me not to depend too much on the prospect that is opened before us, but I will not listen to such a sinister voice. Observe how fast we move along and how the clouds, which sometimes obscure and sometimes rise above the dome of Mont Blanc, render this scene of beauty still more interesting. Look also at the innumerable fish that are swimming in the clear waters, where we can distinguish every pebble that lies at the bottom. What a divine day! How happy and serene all nature appears!"

Thus Elizabeth endeavoured to divert her thoughts and mine from all reflection upon melancholy subjects. But her temper was fluctuating; joy for a few instants shone in her eyes, but it continually gave place to distraction and reverie.

The sun sank lower in the heavens; we passed the river Drance and observed its path through the chasms of the higher and the glens of the lower hills. The Alps here come closer to the lake, and we approached the amphitheatre of mountains which forms its eastern boundary. The spire of Evian shone under the woods that surrounded it and the range of mountain above mountain by which it was overhung.

The wind, which had hitherto carried us along with amazing rapidity, sank at sunset to a light breeze; the soft air just ruffled the water and caused a pleasant motion among the trees as we approached the shore, from which it wafted the most delightful scent of flowers and hay. The sun sank beneath the horizon as we landed, and as I touched the shore I felt those cares and fears revive which soon were to clasp me and cling to me for ever.

Chapter 23

It was eight o'clock when we landed; we walked for a short time on the shore, enjoying the transitory light, and then retired to the inn and contemplated the lovely scene of waters, woods, and mountains, obscured in darkness, yet still displaying their black outlines.

The wind, which had fallen in the south, now rose with great violence in the west. The moon had reached her summit in the heavens and was beginning to descend; the clouds swept across it swifter than the flight of the vulture and dimmed her rays, while the lake reflected the scene of the busy heavens, rendered still busier by the restless waves that were beginning to rise. Suddenly a heavy storm of rain descended.

I had been calm during the day, but so soon as night obscured the shapes of objects, a thousand fears arose in my mind. I was anxious and watchful, while my right hand grasped a pistol which was hidden in my bosom; every sound terrified me, but I resolved that I would sell my life dearly and not shrink from the conflict until my own life or that of my adversary was extinguished.

Elizabeth observed my agitation for some time in timid and fearful silence, but there was something in my glance which communicated terror to her, and trembling, she asked, "What is it that agitates you, my dear Victor? What is it you fear?"

"Oh! Peace, peace, my love," replied I; "this night, and all will be safe; but this night is dreadful, very dreadful."

I passed an hour in this state of mind, when suddenly I reflected how fearful the combat which I momentarily expected would be to my wife, and I earnestly entreated her to retire, resolving not to join her until I had obtained some knowledge as to the situation of my enemy.

She left me, and I continued some time walking up and down the passages of the house and inspecting every corner that might afford a retreat to my adversary. But I discovered no trace of him and was beginning to conjecture that some fortunate chance had intervened to prevent the execution of his menaces when suddenly I heard a shrill and dreadful scream. It came from the room into which Elizabeth had retired. As I heard it, the whole truth rushed into my mind, my arms dropped, the motion of every muscle and fibre was suspended; I could feel the blood trickling in my veins and tingling in the extremities of my limbs. This state lasted but for an instant; the scream was repeated, and I rushed into the room.

Great God! Why did I not then expire! Why am I here to relate the destruction of the best hope and the purest creature on earth? She was there, lifeless and inanimate, thrown across the bed, her head hanging down and her pale and distorted features half covered by her hair. Everywhere I turn I see the same figure—her bloodless arms and relaxed form flung by the murderer on its bridal bier. Could I behold this and live? Alas! Life is obstinate and clings closest where it is most hated. For a moment only did I lose recollection; I fell senseless on the ground.

When I recovered I found myself surrounded by the people of the inn; their countenances expressed a breathless terror, but the horror of others appeared only as a mockery, a shadow of the feelings that oppressed me. I escaped from them to the room where lay the body of Elizabeth, my love, my wife, so lately living, so dear, so worthy. She had been moved from the posture in which I had first beheld her, and now, as she lay, her head upon her arm and a handkerchief thrown across her face and neck, I might have supposed her asleep. I rushed towards her and embraced her with ardour, but the deadly languor and coldness of the limbs told me that what I now held in my arms had ceased to be the Elizabeth whom I had loved and cherished. The murderous mark of the fiend's grasp was on her neck, and the breath had ceased to issue from her lips.

While I still hung over her in the agony of despair, I happened to look up. The windows of the room had before been darkened, and I felt a kind of panic on seeing the pale yellow light of the moon illuminate the chamber. The shutters had been thrown back, and with a sensation of horror not to be described, I saw at the open window a figure the most hideous and abhorred. A grin was on the face of the monster; he seemed to jeer, as with his fiendish finger he pointed towards the corpse of my wife. I rushed towards the window, and drawing a pistol from my bosom, fired; but he eluded me, leaped from his station, and running with the swiftness of lightning, plunged into the lake.

The report of the pistol brought a crowd into the room. I pointed to the spot where he had disappeared, and we followed the track with boats; nets were cast, but in vain. After passing several hours, we returned hopeless, most of my companions believing it to have been a form conjured up by my fancy. After having landed, they proceeded to search the country, parties going in different directions among the woods and vines.

    I attempted to accompany them and proceeded a short distance from the house, but my head whirled round, my steps were like those of a drunken man, I fell at last in a state of utter exhaustion; a film covered my eyes, and my skin was parched with the heat of fever. In this state I was carried back and placed on a bed, hardly conscious of what had happened; my eyes wandered round the room as if to seek something that I had lost.

    After an interval I arose, and as if by instinct, crawled into the room where the corpse of my beloved lay. There were women weeping around; I hung over it and joined my sad tears to theirs; all this time no distinct idea presented itself to my mind, but my thoughts rambled to various subjects, reflecting confusedly on my misfortunes and their cause. I was bewildered, in a cloud of wonder and horror. The death of William, the execution of Justine, the murder of Clerval, and lastly of my wife; even at that moment I knew not that my only remaining friends were safe from the malignity of the fiend; my father even now might be writhing under his grasp, and Ernest might be dead at his feet. This idea made me shudder and recalled me to action. I started up and resolved to return to Geneva with all possible speed.

    There were no horses to be procured, and I must return by the lake; but the wind was unfavourable, and the rain fell in torrents. However, it was hardly morning, and I might reasonably hope to arrive by night. I hired men to row and took an oar myself, for I had always experienced relief from mental torment in bodily exercise. But the overflowing misery I now felt, and the excess of agitation that I endured rendered me incapable of any exertion. I threw down the oar, and leaning my head upon my hands, gave way to every gloomy idea that arose. If I looked up, I saw scenes which were familiar to me in my happier time and which I had contemplated but the day before in the company of her who was now but a shadow and a recollection. Tears streamed from my eyes. The rain had ceased for a moment, and I saw the fish play in the waters as they had done a few hours before; they had then been observed by Elizabeth. Nothing is so painful to the human mind as a great and sudden change. The sun might shine or the clouds might lower, but nothing could appear to me as it had done the day before. A fiend had snatched from me every hope of future happiness; no creature had ever been so miserable as I was; so frightful an event is single in the history of man.

But why should I dwell upon the incidents that followed this last overwhelming event? Mine has been a tale of horrors; I have reached their acme, and what I must now relate can but be tedious to you. Know that, one by one, my friends were snatched away; I was left desolate. My own strength is exhausted, and I must tell, in a few words, what remains of my hideous narration.

I arrived at Geneva. My father and Ernest yet lived, but the former sunk under the tidings that I bore. I see him now, excellent and venerable old man! His eyes wandered in vacancy, for they had lost their charm and their delight—his Elizabeth, his more than daughter, whom he doted on with all that affection which a man feels, who in the decline of life, having few affections, clings more earnestly to those that remain. Cursed, cursed be the fiend that brought misery on his grey hairs and doomed him to waste in wretchedness! He could not live under the horrors that were accumulated around him; the springs of existence suddenly gave way; he was unable to rise from his bed, and in a few days he died in my arms.

What then became of me? I know not; I lost sensation, and chains and darkness were the only objects that pressed upon me. Sometimes, indeed, I dreamt that I wandered in flowery meadows and pleasant vales with the friends of my youth, but I awoke and found myself in a dungeon. Melancholy followed, but by degrees I gained a clear conception of my miseries and situation and was then released from my prison. For they had called me mad, and during many months, as I understood, a solitary cell had been my habitation.

Liberty, however, had been a useless gift to me, had I not, as I awakened to reason, at the same time awakened to revenge. As the memory of past misfortunes pressed upon me, I began to reflect on their cause—the monster whom I had created, the miserable dæmon whom I had sent abroad into the world for my destruction. I was possessed by a maddening rage when I thought of him, and desired and ardently prayed that I might have him within my grasp to wreak a great and signal revenge on his cursed head.

Nor did my hate long confine itself to useless wishes; I began to reflect on the best means of securing him; and for this purpose, about a month after my release, I repaired to a criminal judge in the town and told him that I had an accusation to make, that I knew the destroyer of my family, and that I required him to exert his whole authority for the apprehension of the murderer.

The magistrate listened to me with attention and kindness. "Be assured, sir," said he, "no pains or exertions on my part shall be spared to discover the villain."

"I thank you," replied I; "listen, therefore, to the deposition that I have to make. It is indeed a tale so strange that I should fear you would not credit it were there not something in truth which, however wonderful, forces conviction. The story is too connected to be mistaken for a dream, and I have no motive for falsehood." My manner as I thus addressed him was impressive but calm; I had formed in my own heart a resolution to pursue my destroyer to death, and this purpose quieted my agony and for an interval reconciled me to life. I now related my history briefly but with firmness and precision, marking the dates with accuracy and never deviating into invective or exclamation.

The magistrate appeared at first perfectly incredulous, but as I continued he became more attentive and interested; I saw him sometimes shudder with horror; at others a lively surprise, unmingled with disbelief, was painted on his countenance.

When I had concluded my narration, I said, "This is the being whom I accuse and for whose seizure and punishment I call upon you to exert your whole power. It is your duty as a magistrate, and I believe and hope that your feelings as a man will not revolt from the execution of those functions on this occasion."

This address caused a considerable change in the physiognomy of my own auditor. He had heard my story with that half kind of belief that is given to a tale of spirits and supernatural events; but when he was called upon to act officially in consequence, the whole tide of his incredulity returned. He, however, answered mildly, "I would willingly afford you every aid in your pursuit, but the creature of whom you speak appears to have powers which would put all my exertions to defiance. Who can follow an animal which can traverse the sea of ice and inhabit caves and dens where no man would venture to intrude? Besides, some months have elapsed since the commission of his crimes, and no one can conjecture to what place he has wandered or what region he may now inhabit."

"I do not doubt that he hovers near the spot which I inhabit, and if he has indeed taken refuge in the Alps, he may be hunted like the chamois and destroyed as a beast of prey. But I perceive your thoughts; you do not credit my narrative and do not intend to pursue my enemy with the punishment which is his desert."

As I spoke, rage sparkled in my eyes; the magistrate was intimidated. "You are mistaken," said he. "I will exert myself, and if it is in my power to seize the monster, be assured that he shall suffer punishment proportionate to his crimes. But I fear, from what you have yourself described to be his properties, that this will prove impracticable; and thus, while every proper measure is pursued, you should make up your mind to disappointment."

"That cannot be; but all that I can say will be of little avail. My revenge is of no moment to you; yet, while I allow it to be a vice, I confess that it is the devouring and only passion of my soul. My rage is unspeakable when I reflect that the murderer, whom I have turned loose upon society, still exists. You refuse my just demand; I have but one resource, and I devote myself, either in my life or death, to his destruction."

I trembled with excess of agitation as I said this; there was a frenzy in my manner, and something, I doubt not, of that haughty fierceness which the martyrs of old are said to have possessed. But to a Genevan magistrate, whose mind was occupied by far other ideas than those of devotion and heroism, this elevation of mind had much the appearance of madness. He endeavoured to soothe me as a nurse does a child and reverted to my tale as the effects of delirium.

"Man," I cried, "how ignorant art thou in thy pride of wisdom! Cease; you know not what it is you say."

I broke from the house angry and disturbed and retired to meditate on some other mode of action.

Chapter 24

My present situation was one in which all voluntary thought was swallowed up and lost. I was hurried away by fury; revenge alone endowed me with strength and composure; it moulded my feelings and allowed me to be calculating and calm at periods when otherwise delirium or death would have been my portion.

My first resolution was to quit Geneva for ever; my country, which, when I was happy and beloved, was dear to me, now, in my adversity, became hateful. I provided myself with a sum of money, together with a few jewels which had belonged to my mother, and departed.

And now my wanderings began which are to cease but with life. I have traversed a vast portion of the earth and have endured all the hardships which travellers in deserts and barbarous countries are wont to meet. How I have lived I hardly know; many times have I stretched my failing limbs upon the sandy plain and prayed for death. But revenge kept me alive; I dared not die and leave my adversary in being.

When I quitted Geneva my first labour was to gain some clue by which I might trace the steps of my fiendish enemy. But my plan was unsettled, and I wandered many hours round the confines of the town, uncertain what path I should pursue. As night approached I found myself at the entrance of the cemetery where William, Elizabeth, and my father reposed. I entered it and approached the tomb which marked their graves. Everything was silent except the leaves of the trees, which were gently agitated by the wind; the night was nearly dark, and the scene would have been solemn and affecting even to an uninterested observer. The spirits of the departed seemed to flit around and to cast a shadow, which was felt but not seen, around the head of the mourner.

The deep grief which this scene had at first excited quickly gave way to rage and despair. They were dead, and I lived; their murderer also lived, and to destroy him I must drag out my weary existence. I knelt on the grass and kissed the earth and with quivering lips exclaimed, "By the sacred earth on which I kneel, by the shades that wander near me, by the deep and eternal grief that I feel, I swear; and by thee, O Night, and the spirits that preside over thee, to pursue the dæmon who caused this misery, until he or I shall perish in mortal conflict. For this purpose I will preserve my life; to execute this dear revenge will I again behold the sun and tread the green herbage of earth,

Frankenstein

which otherwise should vanish from my eyes for ever. And I call on you, spirits of the dead, and on you, wandering ministers of vengeance, to aid and conduct me in my work. Let the cursed and hellish monster drink deep of agony; let him feel the despair that now torments me."

I had begun my adjuration with solemnity and an awe which almost assured me that the shades of my murdered friends heard and approved my devotion, but the furies possessed me as I concluded, and rage choked my utterance.

I was answered through the stillness of night by a loud and fiendish laugh. It rang on my ears long and heavily; the mountains re-echoed it, and I felt as if all hell surrounded me with mockery and laughter. Surely in that moment I should have been possessed by frenzy and have destroyed my miserable existence but that my vow was heard and that I was reserved for vengeance. The laughter died away, when a well-known and abhorred voice, apparently close to my ear, addressed me in an audible whisper, "I am satisfied, miserable wretch! You have determined to live, and I am satisfied."

I darted towards the spot from which the sound proceeded, but the devil eluded my grasp. Suddenly the broad disk of the moon arose and shone full upon his ghastly and distorted shape as he fled with more than mortal speed.

I pursued him, and for many months this has been my task. Guided by a slight clue, I followed the windings of the Rhone, but vainly. The blue Mediterranean appeared, and by a strange chance, I saw the fiend enter by night and hide himself in a vessel bound for the Black Sea. I took my passage in the same ship, but he escaped, I know not how.

Amidst the wilds of Tartary and Russia, although he still evaded me, I have ever followed in his track. Sometimes the peasants, scared by this horrid apparition, informed me of his path; sometimes he himself, who feared that if I lost all trace of him I should despair and die, left some mark to guide me. The snows descended on my head, and I saw the print of his huge step on the white plain. To you first entering on life, to whom care is new and agony unknown, how can you understand what I have felt and still feel? Cold, want, and fatigue were the least pains which I was destined to endure; I was cursed by some devil and carried about with me my eternal hell; yet still a spirit of good followed and directed my steps and when I most murmured would suddenly extricate me from seemingly insurmountable difficulties. Sometimes, when nature, overcome by hunger, sank under the exhaustion, a repast was prepared for me in the desert that restored and inspirited me. The fare was, indeed, coarse, such as the peasants of the country ate, but I will not doubt that it was set there by the spirits that I had invoked to aid me. Often, when all was dry, the heavens cloudless, and I was parched by thirst, a slight cloud would bedim the sky, shed the few drops that revived me, and vanish.

I followed, when I could, the courses of the rivers; but the dæmon generally avoided these, as it was here that the population of the country chiefly collected. In other places human beings were seldom seen, and I generally subsisted on the wild animals that crossed my path. I had money with me and gained the friendship of the villagers by distributing it; or I brought with me some food that I had killed, which, after taking a small part, I always presented to those who had provided me with fire and utensils for cooking.

My life, as it passed thus, was indeed hateful to me, and it was during sleep alone that I could taste joy. O blessed sleep! Often, when most miserable, I sank to repose, and my dreams lulled me even to rapture. The spirits that guarded me had provided these moments, or rather hours, of happiness that I might retain strength to fulfil my pilgrimage. Deprived of this respite, I should have sunk under my hardships. During the day I was sustained and inspirited by the hope of night, for in sleep I saw my friends, my wife, and my beloved country; again I saw the benevolent countenance of my father, heard the silver tones of my Elizabeth's voice, and beheld Clerval enjoying health and youth. Often, when wearied by a toilsome march, I persuaded myself that I was dreaming until night should come and that I should then enjoy reality in the arms of my dearest friends. What agonising fondness did I feel for them! How did I cling to their dear forms, as sometimes they haunted even my waking hours, and persuade myself that they still lived! At such moments vengeance, that burned within me, died in my heart, and I pursued my path towards the destruction of the dæmon more as a task enjoined by heaven, as the mechanical impulse of some power of which I was unconscious, than as the ardent desire of my soul.

What his feelings were whom I pursued I cannot know. Sometimes, indeed, he left marks in writing on the barks of the trees or cut in stone that guided me and instigated my fury. "My reign is not yet over"—these words were legible in one of these inscriptions—"you live, and my power is complete. Follow me; I seek the everlasting ices of the north, where you will feel the misery of cold and frost, to which I am impassive.

Frankenstein

You will find near this place, if you follow not too tardily, a dead hare; eat and be refreshed. Come on, my enemy; we have yet to wrestle for our lives, but many hard and miserable hours must you endure until that period shall arrive."

Scoffing devil! Again do I vow vengeance; again do I devote thee, miserable fiend, to torture and death. Never will I give up my search until he or I perish; and then with what ecstasy shall I join my Elizabeth and my departed friends, who even now prepare for me the reward of my tedious toil and horrible pilgrimage!

As I still pursued my journey to the northward, the snows thickened and the cold increased in a degree almost too severe to support. The peasants were shut up in their hovels, and only a few of the most hardy ventured forth to seize the animals whom starvation had forced from their hiding-places to seek for prey. The rivers were covered with ice, and no fish could be procured; and thus I was cut off from my chief article of maintenance.

The triumph of my enemy increased with the difficulty of my labours. One inscription that he left was in these words: "Prepare! Your toils only begin; wrap yourself in furs and provide food, for we shall soon enter upon a journey where your sufferings will satisfy my everlasting hatred."

My courage and perseverance were invigorated by these scoffing words; I resolved not to fail in my purpose, and calling on Heaven to support me, I continued with unabated fervour to traverse immense deserts, until the ocean appeared at a distance and formed the utmost boundary of the horizon. Oh! How unlike it was to the blue seasons of the south! Covered with ice, it was only to be distinguished from land by its superior wildness and ruggedness. The Greeks wept for joy when they beheld the Mediterranean from the hills of Asia, and hailed with rapture the boundary of their toils. I did not weep, but I knelt down and with a full heart thanked my guiding spirit for conducting me in safety to the place where I hoped, notwithstanding my adversary's gibe, to meet and grapple with him.

Some weeks before this period I had procured a sledge and dogs and thus traversed the snows with inconceivable speed. I know not whether the fiend possessed the same advantages, but I found that, as before I had daily lost ground in the pursuit, I now gained on him, so much so that when I first saw the ocean he was but one day's journey in advance, and I hoped to intercept him before he should reach the beach. With new courage, therefore, I pressed on, and in two days arrived at a wretched hamlet on the seashore. I inquired of the inhabitants concerning the fiend and gained accurate information. A gigantic monster, they said, had arrived the night before, armed with a gun and many pistols, putting to flight the inhabitants of a solitary cottage through fear of his terrific appearance. He had carried off their store of winter food, and placing it in a sledge, to draw which he had seized on a numerous drove of trained dogs, he had harnessed them, and the same night, to the joy of the horror-struck villagers, had pursued his journey across the sea in a direction that led to no land; and they conjectured that he must speedily be destroyed by the breaking of the ice or frozen by the eternal frosts.

On hearing this information I suffered a temporary access of despair. He had escaped me, and I must commence a destructive and almost endless journey across the mountainous ices of the ocean, amidst cold that few of the inhabitants could long endure and which I, the native of a genial and sunny climate, could not hope to survive. Yet at the idea that the fiend should live and be triumphant, my rage and vengeance returned, and like a mighty tide, overwhelmed every other feeling. After a slight repose, during which the spirits of the dead hovered round and instigated me to toil and revenge, I prepared for my journey.

I exchanged my land-sledge for one fashioned for the inequalities of the Frozen Ocean, and purchasing a plentiful stock of provisions, I departed from land.

I cannot guess how many days have passed since then, but I have endured misery which nothing but the eternal sentiment of a just retribution burning within my heart could have enabled me to support. Immense and rugged mountains of ice often barred up my passage, and I often heard the thunder of the ground sea, which threatened my destruction. But again the frost came and made the paths of the sea secure.

By the quantity of provision which I had consumed, I should guess that I had passed three weeks in this journey; and the continual protraction of hope, returning back upon the heart, often wrung bitter drops of despondency and grief from my eyes. Despair had indeed almost secured her prey, and I should soon have sunk beneath this misery. Once, after the poor animals that conveyed me had with incredible toil gained the summit of a sloping ice mountain, and one, sinking under his fatigue, died, I viewed the expanse before me with anguish,

Frankenstein

when suddenly my eye caught a dark speck upon the dusky plain. I strained my sight to discover what it could be and uttered a wild cry of ecstasy when I distinguished a sledge and the distorted proportions of a well-known form within. Oh! With what a burning gush did hope revisit my heart! Warm tears filled my eyes, which I hastily wiped away, that they might not intercept the view I had of the dæmon; but still my sight was dimmed by the burning drops, until, giving way to the emotions that oppressed me, I wept aloud.

But this was not the time for delay; I disencumbered the dogs of their dead companion, gave them a plentiful portion of food, and after an hour's rest, which was absolutely necessary, and yet which was bitterly irksome to me, I continued my route. The sledge was still visible, nor did I again lose sight of it except at the moments when for a short time some ice-rock concealed it with its intervening crags. I indeed perceptibly gained on it, and when, after nearly two days' journey, I beheld my enemy at no more than a mile distant, my heart bounded within me.

But now, when I appeared almost within grasp of my foe, my hopes were suddenly extinguished, and I lost all trace of him more utterly than I had ever done before. A ground sea was heard; the thunder of its progress, as the waters rolled and swelled beneath me, became every moment more ominous and terrific. I pressed on, but in vain. The wind arose; the sea roared; and, as with the mighty shock of an earthquake, it split and cracked with a tremendous and overwhelming sound. The work was soon finished; in a few minutes a tumultuous sea rolled between me and my enemy, and I was left drifting on a scattered piece of ice that was continually lessening and thus preparing for me a hideous death.

In this manner many appalling hours passed; several of my dogs died, and I myself was about to sink under the accumulation of distress when I saw your vessel riding at anchor and holding forth to me hopes of succour and life. I had no conception that vessels ever came so far north and was astounded at the sight. I quickly destroyed part of my sledge to construct oars, and by these means was enabled, with infinite fatigue, to move my ice raft in the direction of your ship. I had determined, if you were going southwards, still to trust myself to the mercy of the seas rather than abandon my purpose. I hoped to induce you to grant me a boat with which I could pursue my enemy. But your direction was northwards. You took me on board when my vigour was exhausted, and I should soon have sunk under my multiplied hardships into a death which I still dread, for my task is unfulfilled.

Oh! When will my guiding spirit, in conducting me to the dæmon, allow me the rest I so much desire; or must I die, and he yet live? If I do, swear to me, Walton, that he shall not escape, that you will seek him and satisfy my vengeance in his death. And do I dare to ask of you to undertake my pilgrimage, to endure the hardships that I have undergone? No; I am not so selfish. Yet, when I am dead, if he should appear, if the ministers of vengeance should conduct him to you, swear that he shall not live—swear that he shall not triumph over my accumulated woes and survive to add to the list of his dark crimes. He is eloquent and persuasive, and once his words had even power over my heart; but trust him not. His soul is as hellish as his form, full of treachery and fiend-like malice. Hear him not; call on the names of William, Justine, Clerval, Elizabeth, my father, and of the wretched Victor, and thrust your sword into his heart. I will hover near and direct the steel aright.

Walton, in continuation.

August 26th, 17—.

You have read this strange and terrific story, Margaret; and do you not feel your blood congeal with horror, like that which even now curdles mine? Sometimes, seized with sudden agony, he could not continue his tale; at others, his voice broken, yet piercing, uttered with difficulty the words so replete with anguish. His fine and lovely eyes were now lighted up with indignation, now subdued to downcast sorrow and quenched in infinite wretchedness. Sometimes he commanded his countenance and tones and related the most horrible incidents with a tranquil voice, suppressing every mark of agitation; then, like a volcano bursting forth, his face would suddenly change to an expression of the wildest rage as he shrieked out imprecations on his persecutor.

His tale is connected and told with an appearance of the simplest truth, yet I own to you that the letters of Felix and Safie, which he showed me, and the apparition of the monster seen from our ship, brought to me a greater conviction of the truth of his narrative than his asseverations, however earnest and connected. Such a monster has, then, really existence! I cannot doubt it, yet I am lost in surprise and admiration. Sometimes I endeavoured to gain from Frankenstein the particulars of his creature's formation, but on this point he was impenetrable.

Frankenstein

"Are you mad, my friend?" said he. "Or whither does your senseless curiosity lead you? Would you also create for yourself and the world a demoniacal enemy? Peace, peace! Learn my miseries and do not seek to increase your own."

Frankenstein discovered that I made notes concerning his history; he asked to see them and then himself corrected and augmented them in many places, but principally in giving the life and spirit to the conversations he held with his enemy. "Since you have preserved my narration," said he, "I would not that a mutilated one should go down to posterity."

Thus has a week passed away, while I have listened to the strangest tale that ever imagination formed. My thoughts and every feeling of my soul have been drunk up by the interest for my guest which this tale and his own elevated and gentle manners have created. I wish to soothe him, yet can I counsel one so infinitely miserable, so destitute of every hope of consolation, to live? Oh, no! The only joy that he can now know will be when he composes his shattered spirit to peace and death. Yet he enjoys one comfort, the offspring of solitude and delirium; he believes that when in dreams he holds converse with his friends and derives from that communion consolation for his miseries or excitements to his vengeance, that they are not the creations of his fancy, but the beings themselves who visit him from the regions of a remote world. This faith gives a solemnity to his reveries that render them to me almost as imposing and interesting as truth.

Our conversations are not always confined to his own history and misfortunes. On every point of general literature he displays unbounded knowledge and a quick and piercing apprehension. His eloquence is forcible and touching; nor can I hear him, when he relates a pathetic incident or endeavours to move the passions of pity or love, without tears. What a glorious creature must he have been in the days of his prosperity, when he is thus noble and godlike in ruin! He seems to feel his own worth and the greatness of his fall.

"When younger," said he, "I believed myself destined for some great enterprise. My feelings are profound, but I possessed a coolness of judgment that fitted me for illustrious achievements. This sentiment of the worth of my nature supported me when others would have been oppressed, for I deemed it criminal to throw away in useless grief those talents that might be useful to my fellow creatures. When I reflected on the work I had completed, no less a one than the creation of a sensitive and rational animal, I could not rank myself with the herd of common projectors. But this thought, which supported me in the commencement of my career, now serves only to plunge me lower in the dust. All my speculations and hopes are as nothing, and like the archangel who aspired to omnipotence, I am chained in an eternal hell. My imagination was vivid, yet my powers of analysis and application were intense; by the union of these qualities I conceived the idea and executed the creation of a man. Even now I cannot recollect without passion my reveries while the work was incomplete. I trod heaven in my thoughts, now exulting in my powers, now burning with the idea of their effects. From my infancy I was imbued with high hopes and a lofty ambition; but how am I sunk! Oh! My friend, if you had known me as I once was, you would not recognise me in this state of degradation. Despondency rarely visited my heart; a high destiny seemed to bear me on, until I fell, never, never again to rise."

Must I then lose this admirable being? I have longed for a friend; I have sought one who would sympathise with and love me. Behold, on these desert seas I have found such a one, but I fear I have gained him only to know his value and lose him. I would reconcile him to life, but he repulses the idea.

"I thank you, Walton," he said, "for your kind intentions towards so miserable a wretch; but when you speak of new ties and fresh affections, think you that any can replace those who are gone? Can any man be to me as Clerval was, or any woman another Elizabeth? Even where the affections are not strongly moved by any superior excellence, the companions of our childhood always possess a certain power over our minds which hardly any later friend can obtain. They know our infantine dispositions, which, however they may be afterwards modified, are never eradicated; and they can judge of our actions with more certain conclusions as to the integrity of our motives. A sister or a brother can never, unless indeed such symptoms have been shown early, suspect the other of fraud or false dealing, when another friend, however strongly he may be attached, may, in spite of himself, be contemplated with suspicion. But I enjoyed friends, dear not only through habit and association, but from their own merits; and wherever I am, the soothing voice of my Elizabeth and the conversation of Clerval will be ever whispered in my ear. They are dead, and but one feeling in such a solitude can persuade me to preserve my life. If I were engaged in any high undertaking or design, fraught with extensive utility to my fellow creatures, then could I live to fulfil it. But such is not my destiny; I must pursue and destroy the being to whom I gave existence; then my lot on earth will be fulfilled and I may die."

Frankenstein

My beloved Sister,

September 2d.

I write to you, encompassed by peril and ignorant whether I am ever doomed to see again dear England and the dearer friends that inhabit it. I am surrounded by mountains of ice which admit of no escape and threaten every moment to crush my vessel. The brave fellows whom I have persuaded to be my companions look towards me for aid, but I have none to bestow. There is something terribly appalling in our situation, yet my courage and hopes do not desert me. Yet it is terrible to reflect that the lives of all these men are endangered through me. If we are lost, my mad schemes are the cause.

And what, Margaret, will be the state of your mind? You will not hear of my destruction, and you will anxiously await my return. Years will pass, and you will have visitings of despair and yet be tortured by hope. Oh! My beloved sister, the sickening failing of your heart-felt expectations is, in prospect, more terrible to me than my own death. But you have a husband and lovely children; you may be happy. Heaven bless you and make you so!

My unfortunate guest regards me with the tenderest compassion. He endeavours to fill me with hope and talks as if life were a possession which he valued. He reminds me how often the same accidents have happened to other navigators who have attempted this sea, and in spite of myself, he fills me with cheerful auguries. Even the sailors feel the power of his eloquence; when he speaks, they no longer despair; he rouses their energies, and while they hear his voice they believe these vast mountains of ice are mole-hills which will vanish before the resolutions of man. These feelings are transitory; each day of expectation delayed fills them with fear, and I almost dread a mutiny caused by this despair.

September 5th.

A scene has just passed of such uncommon interest that, although it is highly probable that these papers may never reach you, yet I cannot forbear recording it.

We are still surrounded by mountains of ice, still in imminent danger of being crushed in their conflict. The cold is excessive, and many of my unfortunate comrades have already found a grave amidst this scene of desolation. Frankenstein has daily declined in health; a feverish fire still glimmers in his eyes, but he is exhausted, and when suddenly roused to any exertion, he speedily sinks again into apparent lifelessness.

I mentioned in my last letter the fears I entertained of a mutiny. This morning, as I sat watching the wan countenance of my friend—his eyes half closed and his limbs hanging listlessly—I was roused by half a dozen of the sailors, who demanded admission into the cabin. They entered, and their leader addressed me. He told me that he and his companions had been chosen by the other sailors to come in deputation to me to make me a requisition which, in justice, I could not refuse. We were immured in ice and should probably never escape, but they feared that if, as was possible, the ice should dissipate and a free passage be opened, I should be rash enough to continue my voyage and lead them into fresh dangers, after they might happily have surmounted this. They insisted, therefore, that I should engage with a solemn promise that if the vessel should be freed I would instantly direct my course southwards.

This speech troubled me. I had not despaired, nor had I yet conceived the idea of returning if set free. Yet could I, in justice, or even in possibility, refuse this demand? I hesitated before I answered, when Frankenstein, who had at first been silent, and indeed appeared hardly to have force enough to attend, now roused himself; his eyes sparkled, and his cheeks flushed with momentary vigour. Turning towards the men, he said,

"What do you mean? What do you demand of your captain? Are you, then, so easily turned from your design? Did you not call this a glorious expedition? "And wherefore was it glorious? Not because the way was smooth and placid as a southern sea, but because it was full of dangers and terror, because at every new incident your fortitude was to be called forth and your courage exhibited, because danger and death surrounded it, and these you were to brave and overcome. For this was it a glorious, for this was it an honourable undertaking. You were hereafter to be hailed as the benefactors of your species, your names adored as belonging to brave men who encountered death for honour and the benefit of mankind. And now, behold, with the first imagination of danger, or, if you will, the first mighty and terrific trial of your courage, you shrink away and are content to be handed down as men who had not strength enough to endure cold and peril; and so, poor souls, they were chilly and returned to their warm firesides. Why, that requires not this preparation; ye need not have come thus far and dragged your captain to the shame of a defeat merely to prove yourselves cowards. Oh! Be men, or be more than men. Be steady to your purposes and firm as a rock. This ice is not made

Frankenstein

of such stuff as your hearts may be; it is mutable and cannot withstand you if you say that it shall not. Do not return to your families with the stigma of disgrace marked on your brows. Return as heroes who have fought and conquered and who know not what it is to turn their backs on the foe."

He spoke this with a voice so modulated to the different feelings expressed in his speech, with an eye so full of lofty design and heroism, that can you wonder that these men were moved? They looked at one another and were unable to reply. I spoke; I told them to retire and consider of what had been said, that I would not lead them farther north if they strenuously desired the contrary, but that I hoped that, with reflection, their courage would return.

They retired and I turned towards my friend, but he was sunk in languor and almost deprived of life.

How all this will terminate, I know not, but I had rather die than return shamefully, my purpose unfulfilled. Yet I fear such will be my fate; the men, unsupported by ideas of glory and honour, can never willingly continue to endure their present hardships.

September 7th.

The die is cast; I have consented to return if we are not destroyed. Thus are my hopes blasted by cowardice and indecision; I come back ignorant and disappointed. It requires more philosophy than I possess to bear this injustice with patience.

September 12th.

It is past; I am returning to England. I have lost my hopes of utility and glory; I have lost my friend. But I will endeavour to detail these bitter circumstances to you, my dear sister; and while I am wafted towards England and towards you, I will not despond.

September 9th, the ice began to move, and roarings like thunder were heard at a distance as the islands split and cracked in every direction. We were in the most imminent peril, but as we could only remain passive, my chief attention was occupied by my unfortunate guest whose illness increased in such a degree that he was entirely confined to his bed. The ice cracked behind us and was driven with force towards the north; a breeze sprang from the west, and on the 11th the passage towards the south became perfectly free. When the sailors saw this and that their return to their native country was apparently assured, a shout of tumultuous joy broke from them, loud and long-continued. Frankenstein, who was dozing, awoke and asked the cause of the tumult. "They shout," I said, "because they will soon return to England."

"Do you, then, really return?"

"Alas! Yes; I cannot withstand their demands. I cannot lead them unwillingly to danger, and I must return."

"Do so, if you will; but I will not. You may give up your purpose, but mine is assigned to me by Heaven, and I dare not. I am weak, but surely the spirits who assist my vengeance will endow me with sufficient strength." Saying this, he endeavoured to spring from the bed, but the exertion was too great for him; he fell back and fainted.

It was long before he was restored, and I often thought that life was entirely extinct. At length he opened his eyes; he breathed with difficulty and was unable to speak. The surgeon gave him a composing draught and ordered us to leave him undisturbed. In the meantime he told me that my friend had certainly not many hours to live.

His sentence was pronounced, and I could only grieve and be patient. I sat by his bed, watching him; his eyes were closed, and I thought he slept; but presently he called to me in a feeble voice, and bidding me come near, said, "Alas! The strength I relied on is gone; I feel that I shall soon die, and he, my enemy and persecutor, may still be in being. Think not, Walton, that in the last moments of my existence I feel that burning hatred and ardent desire of revenge I once expressed; but I feel myself justified in desiring the death of my adversary. During these last days I have been occupied in examining my past conduct; nor do I find it blamable. In a fit of enthusiastic madness I created a rational creature and was bound towards him to assure, as far as was in my power, his happiness and well-being. This was my duty, but there was another still paramount to that. My duties towards the beings of my own species had greater claims to my attention because they included a greater proportion of happiness or misery. Urged by this view, I refused, and I did right in refusing, to create a companion for the first creature. He showed unparalleled malignity and selfishness in evil; he destroyed my friends; he devoted to destruction beings who possessed exquisite sensations, happiness, and wisdom; nor do I know where this thirst for vengeance may end. Miserable

Frankenstein

himself that he may render no other wretched, he ought to die. The task of his destruction was mine, but I have failed. When actuated by selfish and vicious motives, I asked you to undertake my unfinished work, and I renew this request now, when I am only induced by reason and virtue.

"Yet I cannot ask you to renounce your country and friends to fulfil this task; and now that you are returning to England, you will have little chance of meeting with him. But the consideration of these points, and the well balancing of what you may esteem your duties, I leave to you; my judgment and ideas are already disturbed by the near approach of death. I dare not ask you to do what I think right, for I may still be misled by passion.

"That he should live to be an instrument of mischief disturbs me; in other respects, this hour, when I momentarily expect my release, is the only happy one which I have enjoyed for several years. The forms of the beloved dead flit before me, and I hasten to their arms. Farewell, Walton! Seek happiness in tranquillity and avoid ambition, even if it be only the apparently innocent one of distinguishing yourself in science and discoveries. Yet why do I say this? I have myself been blasted in these hopes, yet another may succeed."

His voice became fainter as he spoke, and at length, exhausted by his effort, he sank into silence. About half an hour afterwards he attempted again to speak but was unable; he pressed my hand feebly, and his eyes closed for ever, while the irradiation of a gentle smile passed away from his lips.

Margaret, what comment can I make on the untimely extinction of this glorious spirit? What can I say that will enable you to understand the depth of my sorrow? All that I should express would be inadequate and feeble. My tears flow; my mind is overshadowed by a cloud of disappointment. But I journey towards England, and I may there find consolation.

I am interrupted. What do these sounds portend? It is midnight; the breeze blows fairly, and the watch on deck scarcely stir. Again there is a sound as of a human voice, but hoarser; it comes from the cabin where the remains of Frankenstein still lie. I must arise and examine. Good night, my sister.

Great God! what a scene has just taken place! I am yet dizzy with the remembrance of it. I hardly know whether I shall have the power to detail it; yet the tale which I have recorded would be incomplete without this final and wonderful catastrophe.

I entered the cabin where lay the remains of my ill-fated and admirable friend. Over him hung a form which I cannot find words to describe—gigantic in stature, yet uncouth and distorted in its proportions. As he hung over the coffin, his face was concealed by long locks of ragged hair; but one vast hand was extended, in colour and apparent texture like that of a mummy. When he heard the sound of my approach, he ceased to utter exclamations of grief and horror and sprung towards the window. Never did I behold a vision so horrible as his face, of such loathsome yet appalling hideousness. I shut my eyes involuntarily and endeavoured to recollect what were my duties with regard to this destroyer. I called on him to stay.

He paused, looking on me with wonder, and again turning towards the lifeless form of his creator, he seemed to forget my presence, and every feature and gesture seemed instigated by the wildest rage of some uncontrollable passion.

"That is also my victim!" he exclaimed. "In his murder my crimes are consummated; the miserable series of my being is wound to its close! Oh, Frankenstein! Generous and self-devoted being! What does it avail that I now ask thee to pardon me? I, who irretrievably destroyed thee by destroying all thou lovedst. Alas! He is cold, he cannot answer me."

His voice seemed suffocated, and my first impulses, which had suggested to me the duty of obeying the dying request of my friend in destroying his enemy, were now suspended by a mixture of curiosity and compassion. I approached this tremendous being; I dared not again raise my eyes to his face, there was something so scaring and unearthly in his ugliness. I attempted to speak, but the words died away on my lips. The monster continued to utter wild and incoherent self-reproaches. At length I gathered resolution to address him in a pause of the tempest of his passion.

"Your repentance," I said, "is now superfluous. If you had listened to the voice of conscience and heeded the stings of remorse before you had urged your diabolical vengeance to this extremity, Frankenstein would yet have lived."

"And do you dream?" said the dæmon. "Do you think that I was then dead to agony and remorse? He," he continued, pointing to the corpse, "he suffered not in the consummation of the deed. Oh! Not the ten-thousandth portion of the anguish that was mine during the lingering detail of its execution. A frightful selfishness hurried me on, while my heart was poisoned with remorse. Think you that the groans of Clerval were music to my ears? My heart was fashioned to be susceptible of love and sympathy, and when wrenched by misery to vice and hatred, it did not endure the violence of the change without torture such as you cannot even imagine.

"After the murder of Clerval I returned to Switzerland, heart-broken and overcome. I pitied Frankenstein; my pity amounted to horror; I abhorred myself. But when I discovered that he, the author at once of my existence and of its unspeakable torments, dared to hope for happiness, that while he accumulated wretchedness and despair upon me he sought his own enjoyment in feelings and passions from the indulgence of which I was for ever barred, then impotent envy and bitter indignation filled me with an insatiable thirst for vengeance. I recollected my threat and resolved that it should be accomplished. I knew that I was preparing for myself a deadly torture, but I was the slave, not the master, of an impulse which I detested yet could not disobey. Yet when she died! Nay, then I was not miserable. I had cast off all feeling, subdued all anguish, to riot in the excess of my despair. Evil thenceforth became my good. Urged thus far, I had no choice but to adapt my nature to an element which I had willingly chosen. The completion of my demoniacal design became an insatiable passion. And now it is ended; there is my last victim!"

I was at first touched by the expressions of his misery; yet, when I called to mind what Frankenstein had said of his powers of eloquence and persuasion, and when I again cast my eyes on the lifeless form of my friend, indignation was rekindled within me. "Wretch!" I said. "It is well that you come here to whine over the desolation that you have made. You throw a torch into a pile of buildings, and when they are consumed, you sit among the ruins and lament the fall. Hypocritical fiend! If he whom you mourn still lived, still would he be the object, again would he become the prey, of your accursed vengeance. It is not pity that you feel; you lament only because the victim of your malignity is withdrawn from your power."

"Oh, it is not thus—not thus," interrupted the being. "Yet such must be the impression conveyed to you by what appears to be the purport of my actions. Yet I seek not a fellow feeling in my misery. No sympathy may I ever find. When I first sought it, it was the love of virtue, the feelings of happiness and affection with which my whole being overflowed, that I wished to be participated. But now that virtue has become to me a shadow, and that happiness and affection are turned into bitter and loathing despair, in what should I seek for sympathy? I am content to suffer alone while my sufferings shall endure; when I die, I am well satisfied that abhorrence and opprobrium should load my memory. Once my fancy was soothed with dreams of virtue, of fame, and of enjoyment. Once I falsely hoped to meet with beings who, pardoning my outward form, would love me for the excellent qualities which I was capable of unfolding. I was nourished with high thoughts of honour and devotion. But now crime has degraded me beneath the meanest animal. No guilt, no mischief, no malignity, no misery, can be found comparable to mine. When I run over the frightful catalogue of my sins, I cannot believe that I am the same creature whose thoughts were once filled with sublime and transcendent visions of the beauty and the majesty of goodness. But it is even so; the fallen angel becomes a malignant devil. Yet even that enemy of God and man had friends and associates in his desolation; I am alone.

"You, who call Frankenstein your friend, seem to have a knowledge of my crimes and his misfortunes. But in the detail which he gave you of them he could not sum up the hours and months of misery which I endured wasting in impotent passions. For while I destroyed his hopes, I did not satisfy my own desires. They were for ever ardent and craving; still I desired love and fellowship, and I was still spurned. Was there no injustice in this? Am I to be thought the only criminal, when all humankind sinned against me? Why do you not hate Felix, who drove his friend from his door with contumely? Why do you not execrate the rustic who sought to destroy the saviour of his child? Nay, these are virtuous and immaculate beings! I, the miserable and the abandoned, am an abortion, to be spurned at, and kicked, and trampled on. Even now my blood boils at the recollection of this injustice.

"But it is true that I am a wretch. I have murdered the lovely and the helpless; I have strangled the innocent as they slept and grasped to death his throat who never injured me or any other living thing. I have devoted my creator, the select specimen of all that is worthy of love and admiration among men, to misery; I have pursued him even to that irremediable ruin. There he lies, white and cold in death. You hate me, but your abhorrence cannot equal that with which I regard myself. I look on the hands which executed the deed; I think on the heart in which the imagination of it was conceived and long for the moment when these hands will meet my eyes, when that imagination will haunt my thoughts no more.

Frankenstein

"Fear not that I shall be the instrument of future mischief. My work is nearly complete. Neither yours nor any man's death is needed to consummate the series of my being and accomplish that which must be done, but it requires my own. Do not think that I shall be slow to perform this sacrifice. I shall quit your vessel on the ice raft which brought me thither and shall seek the most northern extremity of the globe; I shall collect my funeral pile and consume to ashes this miserable frame, that its remains may afford no light to any curious and unhallowed wretch who would create such another as I have been. I shall die. I shall no longer feel the agonies which now consume me or be the prey of feelings unsatisfied, yet unquenched. He is dead who called me into being; and when I shall be no more, the very remembrance of us both will speedily vanish. I shall no longer see the sun or stars or feel the winds play on my cheeks. Light, feeling, and sense will pass away; and in this condition must I find my happiness. Some years ago, when the images which this world affords first opened upon me, when I felt the cheering warmth of summer and heard the rustling of the leaves and the warbling of the birds, and these were all to me, I should have wept to die; now it is my only consolation. Polluted by crimes and torn by the bitterest remorse, where can I find rest but in death?

"Farewell! I leave you, and in you the last of humankind whom these eyes will ever behold. Farewell, Frankenstein! If thou wert yet alive and yet cherished a desire of revenge against me, it would be better satiated in my life than in my destruction. But it was not so; thou didst seek my extinction, that I might not cause greater wretchedness; and if yet, in some mode unknown to me, thou hadst not ceased to think and feel, thou wouldst not desire against me a vengeance greater than that which I feel. Blasted as thou wert, my agony was still superior to thine, for the bitter sting of remorse will not cease to rankle in my wounds until death shall close them for ever.

"But soon," he cried with sad and solemn enthusiasm, "I shall die, and what I now feel be no longer felt. Soon these burning miseries will be extinct. I shall ascend my funeral pile triumphantly and exult in the agony of the torturing flames. The light of that conflagration will fade away; my ashes will be swept into the sea by the winds. My spirit will sleep in peace, or if it thinks, it will not surely think thus. Farewell."

He sprang from the cabin-window as he said this, upon the ice raft which lay close to the vessel. He was soon borne away by the waves and lost in darkness and distance.

Presumption; or, The Fate of Frankenstein

By Richard Brinsley Peake

DRAMATIS PERSONAE

English Opera House, 28 July, 1823

Frankenstein: Mr. Wallack

Clerval (his friend, in love with Elizabeth): Mr. Bland

William (brother of Frankenstein): Master Boden

Fritz (servant of Frankenstein): Mr. Keeley

De Lacey (a banished gentleman-blind): Mr. Rowbotham

Felix De Lacey (his son): Mr. Pearman

Tanskin (a gipsy): Mr. Shield

Hammerpan (a tinker): Mr. Salter

First Gipsy

A Guide (an old man): Mr. R. Phillips

********: Mr. T. P. Cooke

Elizabeth (sister of Frankenstein): Mrs. Austin

Agatha (daughter of De Lacey): Miss L. Dance

Safie (an Arabian girl, betrothed to Felix): Miss Povey

Madame Ninon (wife to Fritz): Mrs. T. Weippert

Gipsies, Peasants, Choristers, and Dancers (Male and Female)

Presumption

Scene-Geneva and its vicinity

ACT I, SCENE I

A Gothic Chamber in the house of Frankenstein.

Fritz discovered in a Gothic arm-chair, nodding asleep. During the Symphony of the Song, he starts, rubs his eyes, and comes forward.

AIR — FRITZ

Oh, dear me! what's the matter?

How I shake at each clatter.

  My Marrow

  They harrow.

Oh, dear me! what's the matter?

If Mouse squeaks, or cat sneezes,

Cricket chirps, or cock wheezes,

  Then I fret

  In cold sweat.

Every noise my nerves teazes;

Bless my heart – heaven preserve us!

I declare I'm so nervous.

  Ev'ry Knock

  Is a shock.

I declare I'm so nervous!

I'm so nervous.

FRITZ. Oh, Fritz, Fritz, Fritz! What is it come to! you are frighten'd out of your wits. Why did you ever leave your native village! why couldn't you be happy in your native Village with an innocent cow for your companion (bless its sweet breath!) instead of coming here to the City of Geneva to be hired as a servant! (Starts.) What's that? – nothing. And then how complimentary! Master only hired me because he thought I looked so stupid! Stupid! ha, ha, ha! but am I stupid though? To be sure Mr. Frankenstein is a kind man, and I should respect him, but that I thinks as how he holds converse with somebody below with a long tail, horns and hoofs, who shall be nameless. (Starts again.) What's that! Oh, a gnat on my nose! Ah, anything frightens me now – I'm so nervous! I spill all my bread and milk when I feed myself at breakfast! Lord! Lord! In the country, if a dog bray'd, or a donkey bark'd ever so loud, it had no effect upon me. (Two distinct loud knocks – Fritz jumps.) Oh, mercy! I jump like a maggot out of cheese! How my heart beats!

CLER. (Without.) Fritz, Fritz!

[FRITZ. It's a human being however –]

CLER. (Without.) Open the door, Fritz!

FRITZ. Yes. It's only Mr. Clerval, master's friend, who is going to marry Miss Elizabeth, master's sister. (Opens the door.)

Enter Clerval.

How d'ye do, sir!

CLER. Good morrow, Fritz! Is Mr. Frankenstein to be seen?

FRITZ. I fear not, Sir, he has as usual been fumi – fumi – fumigating all night at his chemistry. I have not dared to disturb him.

CLER. Mr. Frankenstein pursues his studies with too much ardour.

FRITZ. And what can be the use of it, Mr. Clerval? Work, work, work – always at it. Now, putting a case to you. Now, when I was in the country, with my late cow (she's no more now, poor thing!) if I had sat to and milked her for a fortnight together, day and night, without stopping, do you think I should be any the better for it? I ask you as a gentleman and a scholar.

CLER. Ha, ha, ha! Certainly not!

FRITZ. Nor my cow neither, poor creter. (Wipes his eyes.) Excuse my crying – she's defunct, and I always whimper a little

Presumption

when I think on her; and my wife lives away from me, but I don't care so much for that. Oh! Mr. Clerval, between ourselves – hush! didn't you hear a noise! – between ourselves, I want to unbosom my confidence.

CLER. Well?

FRITZ. Between ourselves – there's nobody at the door, is there? – (Crosses to door.) – No! well, between ourselves, Mr. Clerval, I have been so very nervous since I came to this place –

CLER. Pshaw!

FRITZ. "Nay," don't 'Pshaw!' till you've heard me out. – My poor Master – I know you are his friend, but he has dealings with the Gentleman in black!

[CLER. Yes, I know – the Notary who comes to consult him on my marriage contract –

FRITZ. Notary – no – somebody deeper than that – Oh, Mr. Clerval! I'll tell you. One night Mr. Frankenstein did indulge himself by going to bed. He was worn with fatigue and study. I had occasion to go into his chamber. He was asleep, but frightfully troubled; he groaned and ground his teeth, setting mine on edge. 'It is accomplished!' said he. Accomplished! I knew that had nothing to do with me, but I listened. He started up in his sleep, though his eyes were opened and dead as oysters, he cried, 'It is animated – it rises – walks!' Now, my shrewd guess, sir, is that, like Doctor Faustus, my master is raising the Devil.

CLER. Fritz, you are simple; drive such impressions from your mind, you must not misconstrue your Master's words in a dream. Do you never dream?

FRITZ. (Mournfully.) I dream about my Cow sometimes.

CLER. Your master is a studious Chemist – nay, as I sometimes suspect, an alchemist.

FRITZ. Eh! Ah, I think he is. What is an alchemist Mr. Clerval?

CLER. Does he not sometimes speak of the art of making gold?

FRITZ. Lord, sir! do you take Mr. Frankenstein for a coiner?

CLER. Did you never hear him make mention of the grand

Presumption

elixer, which can prolong life to immortality.

FRITZ. Never in all my life!

CLER. Well go – find out if it is possible I can see him. I will not detain him.

FRITZ. Yes, sir. Oh, that laboratory! I've got two loose teeth, and I am afraid I shall loose them, for whenever I go towards that infernal place my head shakes like a dice-box. (Goes to door.) Oh, mercy! what's that? Two shining eyes – how they glisten! Dear, dear, why I declare it's only the cat on the stairs. Puss, puss, pussy! How you frighten'd me, you young dog, when you know I am so very nervous!

CLER. Frankenstein, friend of my youth, how extraordinary and secret are thy pursuits! how art thou altered by study! Strange, what a hold has philosophy taken of thy mind – but thou wert always enthusiastic and of boundless ambition. But "Elizabeth – the fair Elizabeth, his sister – what a difference in disposition! Everyone adores her. Happy Clerval, to be now the possessor of Elizabeth, who, unconscious of her beauty, stole thy heart away!

SONG – CLERVAL

Ere witching love my heart possest,

   And bade my sighs the nymph pursue,

Calm as the infant's smiling rest,

   No anxious hope nor fear it knew.

But doom'd – ah! doom'd at last to mourn,

   What tumults in that heart arose!

An ocean trembling, wild, and torn

   By tempests from its deep repose.

Yet let me not the virgin blame,

   As tho' she wish'd my heart despair,

How could the maid suspect a flame,

   Who never knew that she was fair.

Presumption

– But Frankenstein approaches.

Enter Frankenstein, thoughtfully, shown in by Fritz, who exits.

CLER. My dear friend!

FRANK. Clerval!

CLER. Frankenstein, how ill you appear – So [thin and] pale! You look as if your night-watchings had been long and uninterrupted.

FRANK. [You have guessed rightly! –] I have lately been so deeply engaged in one occupation that I have not allowed myself sufficient rest. But how left you my sister, Elizabeth?

CLER. Well, and very happy, only a little uneasy that she sees you so seldom.

FRANK. Aye, I am engaged heart and soul in the pursuit of a discovery – a grand, unheard of wonder! None but those who have experienced can conceive the enticement of Science; he who looks into the book of nature, finds an inexhaustible source of novelty, of wonder, and delight. What hidden treasures are contained in her mighty volume – what strange, undreamed-of mysteries!

CLER. But some little respite – your health should he considered.

FRANK. (Abstracted.) After so much time spent in painful labour, to arrive at once at the summit of my desires, would be indeed a glorious consummation of my toils.

CLER. How wild and mysterious his abstractions – he heeds me not! (Aside.)

FRANK. (Apart.) This discovery will be so vast, so overwhelming, that all the steps by which I have been progressively led will be obliterated, and I shall behold only the astonishing result.

CLER. Frankenstein!

FRANK. Ha! (To Clerval.) I see by your eagerness that you expect to be informed of the secret with which I am acquainted. That cannot be.

CLER. I do not wish to pry into your secrets, Frankenstein. I am no natural philosopher; my imagination is too vivid for the details of science. If I contemplate, let it be the charms of your fair sister, Elizabeth. My message hither now – I wish to fix the day for our nuptials. But we must be certain on so important and happy an event, that we shall enjoy the society of our Frankenstein.

FRANK. Pardon me, Clerval! My first thoughts should recur to those dear friends whom I most love, and who are so deserving of my love – name the day?

CLER. On the morn after to-morrow, may I lead the charming Elizabeth to the altar?

FRANK. E'en as you will – e'en as you will! (Aside.) My wonderful task will be ere that completed. It will be animated! It will live – will think! (Crosses in deep reflection – afterwards turns up the stage.)

CLER. (Apart.) Again in reverie! this becomes alarming – surely his head is affected. I am bound in duty to counteract this madness, and discover the secret of his deep reflections.

Frankenstein sits down – musing.

Farewell, Frankenstein! He heeds me not – 'tis in vain to claim his notice – but I will seek the cause, and, if possible, effect his cure. No time must be lost. Fritz must assist me, and this way he went.

(Exit Clerval)

FRANK. Every moment lost, fevers me. What time have I devoted? (Rises.) Had I not been heated by an almost supernatural enthusiasm, my application to this study would have been irksome, disgusting, and almost intolerable. To examine the causes of life – I have had recourse to death – I have seen how the fine form of man has been wasted and degraded – have beheld the corruption of death succeed to the blooming cheek of life! I have seen how the worm inherits the wonders of the eye and brain – I paused – analysing all the minutiae of causation as exemplified in the change of life from death-until from the midst of this darkness the sudden light broke in upon me! A light so brilliant and dazzling, some miracle must have produced the flash! The vital principle! The cause of life! – Like Prometheus of old, have I daringly attempted the formation – the animation of a Being! To my task

Presumption

– away with reflection – to my task – to my task!

(Exit)

Enter Clerval and Fritz..

FRITZ. Now he's going to blow up his fire again!

CLER. And thus you say for whole days and nights together, without repose, and almost without food he has immured himself in his study.

FRITZ. Yes – there he is – amongst otamies and phials and crucibles, and retorts, and charcoal, and fire, and the Devil – for I'm sure he's at the bottom of it, and that makes me so nervous.

CLER. Fritz, you love your master, and are, I know, a discreet servant – but his friends and relations are all unhappy on his account. His health is rapidly sinking under the fatigue of his present labours – will you not assist to call him back to life and to his family?

FRITZ. La! I'd call out all day long, if that would do any good.

CLER. I know his mind has been devoted to obstruse and occult sciences – that his brain has been bewildered with the wild fancies of Cornelius Agrippa, Paracelsus, and Albertus Magnus –

FRITZ. Oh! Mr. Clerval! how can you mention such crazy tooth-breaking names? There sounds something wicked in them.

CLER. Wicked? Psha, man! they are the renowned names of the earliest experimental philosophers. The sages who promised to the hopes of the laborious alchymist the transmutation of metals and the elixer of life.

FRITZ. 0! Ah! indeed! Lack a daisy me!

CLER. Do you understand me!

FRITZ. Not particularly –

CLER. Fritz – tho' simple, you are an excellent fellow – have you any idea what is the strange object of which your master is in search?

FRITZ. I have my suspicions truly.

Presumption

CLER. What are they?

FRITZ. (Looks round.) Hush – no – nothing but the wind – To tell you the truth, I suspect that the grand object is –

CLER. What?

FRITZ. A secret – there now the murder's out.

CLER. (Aside.) This fellow is more knave than fool – he wants a bribe. Now, sirrah! answer me with candour. What is it you like best in the world?

FRITZ. Milk!

CLER. Simpleton! I mean what station of Life would you covet?

FRITZ. Station?

CLER. Yes. Would you like to be master of a cottage?

FRITZ. What, and keep a cow? – the very thing. Why, Mr. Clerval, you're a conjuror, and know my thoughts by art.

CLER. Fritz, I want to discover – but you must be prudent – (Takes out purse and gives a florin to Fritz.) Here's an earnest of my future intentions touching the cow and cottage.

FRITZ. Bodikins! a florin! (Examining money.)

CLER. Friend Fritz, you must some time, when Mr. Frankenstein is absent from home, admit me into his study.

FRITZ. Oh, dear, I can't! – don't take your florin back again [sir] (Puts up money.) – for he always locks the door. To be sure, there's a little window – on the gallery – I can see when he puffs up his fire.

CLER. Well, they say the end justifies the means; and in this case I admit the maxim. You can peep through that window, and inform me minutely of what you see.

FRITZ. But what is to become of my nerves?

CLER. Remember your cottage –

FRITZ. And the Cow

Presumption

CLER. Put me in possession of the secret, and both shall be secured to you. Some one approaches.

FRITZ. Mr. Clerval, I'm your man. I'm nervous, and the devil sticks in my gizzard; but the cow will drive it out again. (Starts.) What's that? Oh, nothing – oh, dear, I'm so nervous.

(Exeunt Fritz and Clerval)

SCENE II

    Part of the Villa Residence of Elizabeth at Belrive. – Garden Terrace – Sunset – William discovered sleeping on a garden bench – Enter Elizabeth from the house.

SONG – ELIZABETH

The summer sun shining on tree and on tower,

  And gilding the landscape with radiance divine,

May give joy to the heart o'er which pleasure has power,

  But eve's pensive beauties are dearer to mine.

Through trees gently sighing, the cool breeze of even

  Seems sympathy's voice to the ear of despair;

And the dew-drops (like tears shed by angels of heaven),

  Revive the frail hopes in the bosom of care.

During this scene the stage becomes progressively dark.

MAD. NINON. (Within.) William! little William!

ELIZ. Where can our little favorite have secreted himself?

Enter Madame Ninon, from the house.

NIN. Heaven bless Mont Blanc and all the neighbouring hills! Why, where is the boy? How angry shall I be with him for staying out so late.

ELIZ. Why, Ninon, assuage your friendly wrath – yonder is William.

NIN. (Goes to child.) Fast asleep, I declare, the pretty boy – how like his poor mother, who is gone. La, La, I daresay my Fritz was just such another, only his hair was red. Pretty William – he was the pin basket. Bless the thirteen cantons, I nursed him. William – (Kisses him.) – a pair of gloves, Sir! (William waking.) Fie, you idle urchin, sleeping so early this beautiful evening.

William rises. All come forward.

Presumption

WILL. Indeed, dear Ninon, I know not how I fell asleep; but I rose with the sun, and thinking I would lie down with it, I closed my eyes, and –

NIN. Slumbered like a young dormouse?

ELIZ. But, William, you have not neglected your books?

WILL. Oh, no; for then I should not be such a scholar as my elder brother, Victor Frankenstein.

(Runs to end of terrace.)

ELIZ. Alas, poor Frankenstein! he studies indeed too deeply; but love -- blighted love, drove him to solitude and abstruse research.

NIN. Ah, Madame, may love make you happy! Mr. Clerval was here this morning, and looked as handsome –

ELIZ. Peace, Ninon! And yet, why should I check your Cheerfulness? Ninon, I have given orders to my milliner to make you a handsome new cap. When your husband, Fritz, comes from Geneva, he may call and bring it.

NIN. Thank you, dear madam; but see –

Re-Enter William from terrace, and runs, crossing behind.)

WILL. Oh, sister – oh, Madame Ninon! two travellers are coming up the hill – such a beautiful lady – but her guide, I think, has fallen from his horse. See – here's the lady, helping the poor man.

Melo-Music. Enter Safie, supporting the Guide, from terrace.

ELIZ. Madame, allow me to offer my assistance.

SAFIE. Thanks – thanks, fair Lady; it is not for myself I require rest or help, for I am young. But this aged man, my faithful follower, is completely worn with fatigue.

ELIZ. Ninon, see him conveyed into the house. Give him your support, and assist to welcome our guests.

NIN. (Crossing to guide.) Lean on me, old sir – aye, as heavy as you like; bless you my arm is strong, tho' I am little. Come, gently – gently – there – there –

Ninon leads the guide into house, William following them. By this time the wing lights are turned off.

SAFIE. I can only weep my thanks, of late I have been unused to kindness.

ELIZ. Your garb and manner denote you a stranger here – yet you are acquainted with our language, and you appear to have travelled a great distance.

SAFIE. From Leghorn, – a wearisome journey. How far am I distant from the Valley of the Lake?

ELIZ. But a few leagues.

SAFIE. Then tonight I probably could reach it? (Animated.)

ELIZ. I would not advise the attempt till the morning – the sun is down now; you are distant from any inn; your horses are fatigued; permit me to offer in my house refreshment and repose.

SAFIE. No, no; no repose until my purpose is accomplished. Yet my poor follower needs rest; generous stranger, I gratefully accept your hospitality.

ELIZ. And be assured such comfort as Eliza Frankenstein can offer shall be freely yours.

SAFIE. You – you mention the name of Frankenstein!

ELIZ. I bear that appellation.

SAFIE. How fortunate! happy chance that brought me to your hospitable door. Know you the family of De Lacey?

ELIZ. I knew it well, but years have elapsed since I have heard of them.

SAFIE. I seek their retreat. Exiled from France, they now exist in the Valley of the Lake.

ELIZ. So near, and I not acquainted with their residence! Does the gentle Agatha De Lacey yet live?

SAFIE. Tomorrow's morn I trust will find me locked in her embrace.

Presumption

ELIZ. What rapturous news for my dear brother, Frankenstein – night approaches – let us in and converse further on this subject, which is of deep interest to me – hark! – the sweet nightingale is pouring forth its evening melody.

DUETT – ELIZABETH AND SAFIE

Hark how it floats upon the dewy air!

Oh! what a dying, dying close was there!

'Tis harmony from yon sequester'd bower,

Sweet harmony that soothes the midnight hour!

(Exeunt into house)

SCENE III

The sleeping Apartment of Frankenstein. Dark. The Bed is within a recess between the wings, enclosed by dark green curtains. A Sword (to break) hanging. A Large French Window; between the wings a staircase leading to a Gallery across the stage, on which is the Door of the Laboratory above. A small high Lattice in centre of scene, next the Laboratory Door. A Gothic Table on stage, screwed. A Gothic Chair in centre, and Footstool. Music expressive of the rising of a storm. Enter Frankenstein, with a Lighted Lamp, which he places on the table. Distant thunder heard.

FRANK. This evening – this lowering evening, will, in all probability, complete my task. Years have I laboured, and at length discovered that to which so many men of genius have in vain directed their inquiries. After days and nights of incredible labour and fatigue, I have become master of the secret of bestowing animation upon lifeless matter. With so astonishing a power in my hands, long, long did I hesitate how to employ it. The object of my experiments lies there (Pointing up to the laboratory.) – A huge automaton in human form. Should I succeed in animating it, Life and Death would appear to me as ideal bounds, which I shall break through and pour a torrent of light into our dark world. I have lost all soul or sensation but for this one pursuit. (Storm.) A storm has hastily arisen! – 'Tis a dreary night – the rain patters dismally against the panes – 'tis a night for such a task – I'll in and attempt to infuse the spark of life. –

Music. – Frankenstein takes up lamp, cautiously looks around him, ascends the stairs, crosses the gallery above, and exits into door of laboratory. Enter Fritz, trembling, with a candle.

FRITZ. Master isn't here – dare I peep. Only think of the reward Mr. Clerval promised me, a cow and a cottage, milk and a mansion. Master is certainly not come up yet. My candle burns all manner of colours, and spits like a roasted apple. (Runs against the chair and drops his light, which goes out.) There, now, I'm in the dark. Oh my nerves.

A blue flame appears at the small lattice window above, as from the laboratory.

What's that? 0 lord; there he is, kicking up the devil's own flame! Oh my Cow! I'll venture up – oh my cottage! I'll climb to the window – it will be only one peep to make my fortune.

Presumption

Music. – Fritz takes up footstool, he ascends the stairs, when on the gallery landing place, he stands on the footstool tiptoe to look through the small high lattice window of the laboratory, a sudden combustion is heard within. The blue flame changes to one of a reddish hue.

FRANK. (Within.) It lives! it lives!

FRITZ. (Speaks through music.) Oh, dear! oh, dear! oh, dear!

Fritz, greatly alarmed, jumps down hastily, totters tremblingly down the stairs in vast hurry; when in front of stage, having fallen flat in fright, with difficulty speaks.

FRITZ. There's a hob – hob-goblin, 20 feet high! wrapp'd in a mantle – mercy – mercy –

[Falls down.]

Music. – Frankenstein rushes from the laboratory, without lamp, fastens the door in apparent dread, and hastens down the stairs, watching the entrance of the laboratory.

FRANK. It lives! [It lives.] I saw the dull yellow eye of the creature open, it breathed hard, and a convulsive motion agitated its limbs. What a wretch have I formed, [his legs are in proportion and] I had selected his features as beautiful – beautiful! Ah, horror! his cadaverous skin scarcely covers the work of muscles and arteries beneath, his hair lustrous, black, and flowing – his teeth of pearly whiteness – but these luxuriances only form more horrible contrasts with the deformities of the Demon.

Music. – He listens at the foot of the staircase.

[It is yet quiet –] What have I accomplished? the beauty of my dream has vanished! and breathless horror and disgust fill my heart. For this I have deprived myself of rest and health, have worked my brain to madness; and when I looked to reap my great reward, a flash breaks in upon my darkened soul, and tells me my attempt was impious, and that its fruition will be fatal to my peace for ever. (He listens again.) All is still! The dreadful spectre of a human form – no mortal could withstand the horror of that countenance – a mummy endued with animation could be so hideous as the wretch I have endowed with life! – miserable and impious being that I am! [– lost – lost] Elizabeth! brother! Agatha! – faithful Agatha! never more dare I look upon your virtuous faces. Lost! lost! lost!

Music – Frankenstein sinks on a chair.

[FRITZ. (Looks up once or twice before he speaks.) Oh my nerves; I feel as if I had just come out of strong fits, and nobody to throw water in my face – Master sleeps, so I'll, if my legs won't 1ap up under me – just – make my escape.

Sudden combustion heard, and smoke issues, the door of the laboratory breaks to pieces with a loud crash – red fire within.

FRITZ. Oh – Oh. (Runs out hastily)

Music. The Demon discovered at door entrance in smoke, which evaporates – the red flame continues visible. The Demon advances forward, breaks through the balustrade or railing of gallery immediately facing the door of laboratory, jumps on the table beneath, and from thence leaps on the stage, stands in attitude before Frankenstein, who had started up in terror; they gaze for a moment at each other.

FRANK. The demon corpse to which I have given life!

Music. – The Demon looks at Frankenstein most intently, approaches him with gestures of conciliation. Frankenstein retreats, the Demon pursuing him.

Its unearthly ugliness renders it too horrible for human eyes! [The Demon approaches him.]

Fiend! do not dare approach me – avaunt, or dread the fierce vengeance of my arm wrecked on your miserable head –

Music. – Frankenstein takes the sword from the nail, points with it at the Demon, who snatches the sword, snaps it in two and throws it on stage. The Demon then seizes Frankenstein – loud thunder heard – throws him violently on the floor, ascends the staircase, opens the large window, and disappears through the casement. Frankenstein remains motionless on the ground. – Thunder and lightning until the drop falls. End of Act I

Presumption

ACT II, SCENE I

An apartment in the House of Elizabeth, at Belrive. – Table and chairs. The hurried music from the close of the First Act to play in continuance until this scene is discovered, and Frankenstein enters, hastily, to centre of stage. Music ceases.

FRANK. At length in my sister's house! – and safe! I have paced with quick steps, but at every turn feared to meet the wretch – my heart palpitates with the sickness of fear! [He does not pursue me – dreams that have been my food and pleasant rest for so long a space, are now become a hell to me – the change so rapid, the overthrow so complete –] What have I cast on the world? a creature powerful in form, of supernatural and gigantic strength, but with the mind of an infant. Oh, that I could recall my impious labour, or suddenly extinguish the spark which I have so presumptuously bestowed. – Yet that were murder – murder in its worse and most horrid form – for he is mine – my own formation. Ha! who approaches?

Enter Elizabeth, they embrace.

ELIZ. My dear Victor! my dear brother!

FRANK. Elizabeth! [My love, how sweet is this embrace –]

ELIZ. You [are] come to stay, I hope, until our wedding is over. Clerval will be here presently. Alas! Frankenstein! your cheek is pallid – your eye has lost its wonted lustre. Oh, Victor, what are the secrets that prey upon your mind and form? – The pernicious air of your laboratory will be fatal to you.

FRANK. (Apart.) Fatal indeed!

ELIZ. I pray you, for my sake, cease – I understand upon one subject you have laboured incessantly.

FRANK. One subject! (Aside.) Am I discovered?

ELIZ. You change colour, my dear brother. I will not mention it – I – there is a wildness in your eyes for which I cannot account.

FRANK. (Starts.) See – see – he is there!

ELIZ. Dearest Frankenstein – what is the cause of this?

FRANK. Do not ask me. I – I thought I saw the dreaded spectre glide into the room.

Presumption

ELIZ. Calm your mind, Victor.

FRANK. Pardon me, Elizabeth. I know not what you will think of me.

ELIZ. I have intelligence of one dear to you and for whom, prior to your close attention to study, you had the tenderest regard. – Say, Victor, will you not be glad to hear that I have a clue to lead you to your lost love, Agatha De Lacey!

FRANK. Agatha! dearest Agatha! her name recalls my sinking spirits – where – where is she to be found? Oh, would that I ne'er had been robbed of her! 'Twas her loss that drove me to deep and fatal experiments!

ELIZ. A traveller! a beautiful Arabian girl, was here but last night; she was seeking Felix De Lacey, the brother of Agatha, to whom she had been betrothed – she gave me the information that the family are but a short distance from hence – the Valley of the Lake.

FRANK. And Agatha there? – Agatha! there is yet life and hope for me – Ah no. (Aside.) The dreadful monster I have formed! – away with thought! Elizabeth, I will instantly seek her. Agatha's smiles shall move this heavy pressure – to the Valley of the Lake. – Farewell, sister, farewell!

(Embraces Elizabeth, and Exit hastily)

[ELIZ. Unfortunate Frankenstein! – what can thus agitate him? – he will not hint the mysterious calamity to his affectionate sister – but he flies now to seek her who possessed his first love, and Agatha will sooth his mind to its former peaceful state – Ah love! All potent love! – If care or misfortune prey on my heart, I have only to think of Clerval, and be happy. –

SONG – ELIZABETH

When evening breezes mildly blow,

   And all day's tumults cease;

Where streams in gentle murmurs flow;

   And all around breathes peace –

What shall my pensive mind employ,

Presumption

   From ev'rything free?

I'll turn to life's best dearest joy,

   And think of love and Thee!

When pleasure's smile no longer gleams,

   And sorrow weighs my breast

When hope withdraws its placid beams

   I sink with care opprest –

Ah whither shall my heart then turn,

   To what sweet refuge flee?

With passion's fire then shall burn

   And throb with love and thee. (Exit)

SCENE II

A wood in the neighbourhood of Geneva. A Bush – A Gypsy's fire flaming, over which hangs a cauldron. A group of Gypsies discovered surrounding the fire in various positions. All laugh as the scene discovers them. When Tanskin, Hammerpan, with others (male and female) advance to sing the following

CHORUS

Urge the slow rising smoke,

Give the faggot a poke,

For unroof'd rovers are we;

Whilst our rags flutt'ring fly,

We the brown skin espy,

Our vellum of pedigree.

Behold each tawney face

Of our hard-faring race,

Which the cold blast ne'er can feel;

See our glossy hair wave,

Hear us, loud, as we crave

But dumb only when we steal!

TANS. I tell you it was even so, friend Hammerpan – a giant creature with something of a human shape; but ugly and terrible to behold as you would paint the Devil.

HAM. And does this monster any mischief, or is he a pacific monster?

TANS. I never heard of any being harmed by him!

HAM. Then why are you so frightened, Master Tanskin? For my part, should he come across my path, let who will fly, I'll stand my ground like an anvil!

Presumption

TANS. And get well beat like one for your pains.

(Flute heard.)

What sounds are those?

HAM. (Returning to the fire.) Why, 'tis Felix, the son of old De Lacey. The young fellow is much famed for his excellence upon the flute, as the father for his piety, charities, and twanging on the harp, which, together with the beauty of his daughter, seems to have turned the heads and won the hearts of all the surrounding country. Now my merry wanderers, our meal is smoking. I'faith, I'm in a rare relishing humour for it, so, prithee, Dame, ladle us our porridge, with a whole dead sheep in it. Fegs, it scents rarely! (Sniffs.)

Music. – The gipsies crowd round the fire with their bowls. The Demon rapidly crosses the platform at the back – Disappears.

1ST GYP. Hilliho! – what tall bully's that? the steeple of Ingoldstadt taking a walk. See yonder, comrades!

HAM. See what?

TANS. (Trembling.) As I'm a living rogue, 'tis he!

HAM. One of the Devil's grenadier's, mayhap! Pooh, pooh! Old Tanskin, we all know you are a living rogue, but you won't frighten us with your ten feet. Come, give me a drink, I say.

One of the gipsies gives him a wooden bowl.

Gentlemen Gipsies, here's all your good – ha! ha! ha! –

Music. – The Demon appears on an eminence of the bush, or a projecting rock.

Help! murder! wouns! 'tis the Devil himself! away with the porridge!

Music. Throws bowl away. Hammerpan and all the Gipsies shriek and run off The Demon descends, portrays by action his sensitiveness of light and air, perceives the gipsies's fire, which excites his admiration – thrusts his hand into the flame, withdraws it hastily in pain. Takes out a lighted piece of stick, compares it with another faggot which has not been ignited. Takes the food expressive of surprise and pleasure. A flute is heard, without. The Demon, breathless with delight, eagerly listens. It ceases – he expresses disappointment. Footsteps heard and the Demon retreats behind the rock.

Enter Agatha, followed by Felix, his flute slung at his back.

AGA. Those sweet sounds recall happier days to my memory. – In the midst of [our] poverty, how consoling it is to possess such a brother as you are. Dear, thoughtful Felix, the first little white flower that peeped out from beneath the snowy ground you brought, because you thought it would give pleasure to your poor Agatha.

FELIX. We are the children of misfortune; [Agatha –] poverty's chilling grasp nearly annihilates us. Our poor blind father, now the inmate of yon cottage – he who has been blessed with prosperity to be thus reduced – the noble-minded old De Lacey. Wretched man that I am, to have been the cause of ruin to both father and sister.

AGA. Why, Felix, we suffered in a virtuous cause! Poor Safie, thy beloved –

FELIX. Is, I fear, lost to me for ever. The treacherous Mahometan, her father, whose escape I aided from a dungeon in Paris (where he was confined as a State prisoner), that false father has doubtless arrived at Constantinople, and is triumphing at the fate of his wretched dupes.

AGA. Nay, Felix –

FELIX. Alas, Agatha! for aiding that escape, my family – my beloved family – are suffering exile and total confiscation of fortune.

AGA. But Safie still loves you?

FELIX. That thought is the more maddening! Safie! fairest Safie! – and she was my promised reward for liberating her faithless father – dragged away with him and forced to comply with his obdurate wishes. Oh, she is lost – lost to me for ever!

AGA. Let not hope forsake you, Felix –

FELIX. [Agatha! It requires resignation to bear our heavy woes.] The early passion of each of us has been blighted, our rigorous imprisonment and sudden banishment have driven all trace of thee from thy admirer, young Frankenstein.

Presumption

AGA. Dear Felix, press not more wretched recollections on my mind. I consider Frankenstein lost to me for ever. In abject poverty, dare I hope that the brilliant and animated student could e'er think of the unfortunate Agatha. (Weeps.) Let me dry these unworthy tears and exert a woman's firmest fortitude. My soul is henceforth devoted exclusively to the service of my poor dark father.

FELIX, you shall behold me no longer unhappy.

DUET – FELIX AND AGATHA

Of all the knots which Nature ties,

The secret, sacred sympathies,

That, as with viewless chains of gold,

The heart a happy prisoner hold,

None is more chaste – more bright – more pure,

Stronger, stern trials to endure;

None is more pure of earthly leaven,

More like the love of highest heaven,

Than that which binds, in bonds how blest

A daughter to a father's breast.

(Exeunt)

Music. – The Demon cautiously ventures out – his mantle having been caught by the bush, he disrobes himself leaving the mantle attached to the rock; he watches Felix and Agatha with wonder and rapture, appears irresolute whether he dares to follow them; he hears the flute of Felix, stands amazed and pleased, looks around him, snatches at the empty air, and with clenched hands puts them to each ear – appears vexed at his disappointment in not possessing the sound; rushes forward afterwards, again listens, and, delighted with the sound, steals off catching at it with his hands.

SCENE III

Exterior of the Cottage of Old De Lacey. On right, a hovel, with a low door, near which are two or three large logs of wood and a hatchet; a small basket with violets on a stool at the right side of the cottage door, and a stool also on the left side of the cottage, whereon De Lacey is discovered seated, leaning on his cane, a common harp at his side. – Music.

DEL. Another day is added to the life of banished De Lacey! (Rises and comes forward.) But how will it be passed – like the preceding days – in wretched poverty, hopeless grief, and miserable darkness! (Calls.) Agatha! Felix! Alas! I am alone! Hark – no – I thought I heard footsteps – my children come. They must not suppose me cheerless – my lute is here – 'tis a fair deceit on them – this lute which has so oft been damped with the tears from my sightless eyes – the sound of it is the only indication I can give that I am contented with my lot!

Music. – De Lacey returns to his seat and plays several chords. The Demon enters, attracted by the lute, suddenly perceives De Lacey, and approaches towards him – expresses surprise by action that De Lacey does not avoid him – discovers his loss of sight, which the Demon appears to understand by placing his hand over his own eyes, and feeling his way. At the conclusion of the music on the lute – occasioned, as it were, by the Demon having placed his hand on the instrument – a short pause, and during which the Demon, having lost the sound, appears to he looking for it, when the lute music is again resumed. In the midst of the music (without ceasing) a voice is heard.

FELIX. (Within.) This way, Agatha.

The Demon, alarmed, observes the little door of hovel, which he pushes open, signifies that he wishes for shelter, and retreats into this hovel or wood-house by the ending of the lute music by De Lacey, when Enter Felix and Agatha.

FELIX. (Apart to Agatha.) Observe his countenance, beaming with benevolence and love – behold those silver hairs – and, Agatha, I – I have reduced him to this pitiable state of poverty!

AGA. Cease, Felix – this self reproach? (Goes to De Lacey.) We have returned, dear father. Have you wanted us?

Agatha leads her father forward.

DEL. No, no, Agatha! You anticipate all my wants, and perform

Presumption

every little office of affection with gentleness.

AGA. Is it not my duty, and am I not rewarded by your kind smiles?

DEL. Amiable girl, let thy poor father kiss thee. (They embrace.) Felix, my son, where are you? (Felix comes forward, and takes his hand.) Now I am cheerful – I am happy! – indeed I am, my children. Let me encourage you to cast off your gloom. What – a tear, Agatha!

AGA. Nay, dear sir!

DEL. 'Tis on my hand. (Pressing her hand to his lips, which he had held in his while speaking to Felix.)

The Demon appears watching them with attention and interest.

FELIX. (Apart.) At first my father's countenance was illuminated with pleasure – but thoughtfulness and sadness have again succeeded – (Assuming gaiety.) Now must I to labour again. Our [stock of] fuel is nearly exhausted. My time has been lately so occupied I have omitted my task in the forest.

Music. – Felix takes up a hatchet and chops a log of wood.

AGA. And I, too, have been neglectful – these flowers of which you are so fond, my dear father, have wither'd – they must be replaced –

[Music – she takes them from the basket – Felix is busied cutting the wood –]

SAFIE. (At a distance.) Felix!

AGA. What voice was that?

FELIX. It cannot be – no – it was but fancy!

Music resumed. – Felix chops the log in continuance – at a similar break in the tune the same voice heard again, nearer.

SAFIE. (Without.) Felix!

No music.

FELIX. That magic sound! Alas! no – there is no such happiness in store for me!

SAFIE. (Without, louder.) Felix! Felix!

Music. – Felix drops the hatchet, rushes forward. – At the same instant Safie enters, and falls into the arms of Felix – pronouncing "Felix."

FELIX. 'Tis she! – Safie! Beloved of my soul! – Ah! revive!

DEL. Safie, the traitor's daughter? Impossible!

AGA. 'Tis, indeed, our sweet Safie!

FELIX. We never will part more! Father! father! would that you could behold her! It is my dear, lost Safie.

Music. – Safie revives, and crosses to old De Lacey, kneels, and kisses his hand, during which the Demon appears at the little hovel, watching them, and then retires within again.

DEL. Bless you, my child! where is your father – where the treacherous friend who devoted us to ignominy?

SAFIE. (Rises.) I have fled from him; he would have sacrificed his daughter, loathing the idea that I should be united to one of Christian faith. Sickening at the prospect of again returning to Asia and being immured in a harem – ill suited to the temper of my soul now accustomed to a nobler emulation – I – I have sought the love and protection of my Felix!

FELIX. Faithful girl! Your constancy shall be crowned by eternal love and gratitude.

AGA. But Safie, you are fatigued. Come, dear girl, and on my lowly couch, seek repose.

Music. – Safie affectionately kisses and presses De Lacey's hand, embraces Felix, crosses back to Agatha, and is led into the cottage by Agatha and Felix.

FELIX. (Who returns with a gun from the cottage-door.) Father, I am wild with joy! – no longer the sad, pining Felix. The sun of prosperity again gleams on us – Safie is returned! I am rich! – happy! But hold! I must procure refreshment for our guest. Our larder is not too much encumbered with provision. I'll to the village – I'll cross the forest – I'll hunt, shoot – and all in ecstasy! Farewell, father! I'll soon be back. Farewell!

[Music. – Exit Felix. – The Demon ventures out, and looks with

Presumption

a kind expression on De Lacey.

DEL. Good Felix! Now, by the return of Safie will his hopes be rewarded – yet must he remain in perpetual poverty and unceasing labour. But this instant, did he complain that our store of fuel was consumed – unless he possessed superhuman strength his day's employment must be doubled – where are my favorite violets?

Music. – De Lacey feels for the Basket which contained them – the Demon apppears to comprehend his wish, and rushes off.

DEL. My flower basket not yet replenished. – My dear children amply repay my former anxious care – they have toiled for my support thoughout our misfortunes –

Music. – The Demon re-enters cautiously and tremblingly with a handful of flowers, which he gently places in the basket.

DEL. Thanks dear Agatha! – ever watchful of your poor father's comfort –

Music. – De Lacey turns up the stage, and again seats himself on the cottage stool. – The Demon examines log of wood, takes up hatchet, points to the wood, intimating he understands the use of it – Agatha appearing at the window – The Demon rushes off with the hatchet. – Music ceases.

DEL. Agatha!

Enter Agatha from cottage.

AGA. Did you call, father?

DEL. Sleeps your sweet guest?

AGA. Fatigue will soon lull her to repose. I should not have left her had I not thought I heard you call me. Ah, father, some one has punished my negligence by replenishing your basket of violets.

DEL. Did you not fill it, Agatha?

AGA. No, dear sir. – Ah, Felix has forestalled me.

Exit Agatha into cottage again.

DEL. [No person has been here since the departure of Felix.] (De

Presumption

Lacey rises and takes up the basket of flowers from the stool. Smelling the violets.) How delightful is the perfume! – more exquisite because I am debarred the pleasure of beholding these sweet emblems of spring! The touch and scent elevate my spirits! How ungrateful am I to complain! In the contemplation of thee, oh, Nature, the past will be blotted from my memory! – the present is tranquil, and the future gilded by bright rays of hope and anticipated joy.

Music. – DeLacey replaces the basket of flowers, and returns to his seat, leaning pensively on his cane. – The Demon enters with a pile of green faggots with foliage on his shoulders and throws them loosely on the stage. – Smiles with gratulation at that which he has accomplished. – Approaches De Lacey, falls flat at his feet, then kneels to him, and is about to press his hand. – De Lacey feels around him with his cane and hand, without the knowledge of anyone being near him, and seated all the time – then calls.

DEL. Agatha! Agatha!

Music. – The Demon instantly retreats into hovel, and Agatha enters from cottoge door.

Agatha, child, I pray you lead me in. (Rises from his seat and comes forward.)

AGA. Yes, father. Good Heavens! why, Felix could not have returned from the forest so quickly? What a quantity of wood!

DEL. How?

AGA. Here is fuel to last us for a long time. [– Surely some kind spirit [watches over us – or] how could we have been so bountifully supplied? Come, father, to the cottage – come!

Music. – Agatha leads De Lacy into cottage, afterwards comes forward.

– Frankenstein! vain is the endeavour to drive you from my recollection. Each bird that sings, each note of music that I hear, reminds me of the sweet moments of my former love!

SONG – AGATHA

(Flute accompaniment, behind the scenes.)

In vain I view the landscapes round,

206

Presumption

   Or climb the highest hill;
In vain, in vain, I listen to the sound
   Of ev'ry murmuring rill.
For vain is all I hear or see,
When Victor dear is far from me. (Thrice)
But hark, hark, hark,
My love, my love is near,
His well-known dulcet notes I hear. (Thrice)
Oh, yes, my love is near,
  I hear him in the grove;
Soon will he be here,
  And breathe soft vows of love.
Oh, fly not yet, ye blissful hours,
  Oh, fly not yet away;
While love its soft enchanting pours,
  Prolong, prolong your stay! (Thrice)
Oh, yes, my love is near,
  I hear him in the grove,
Soon will he be here,
  And breathe soft vows of love!
(Exit Agatha into cottage)

SCENE IV

A Wild Forest.

Enter Felix, with his gun.

FELIX. Not a shot yet – and, egad, joy has made my hand so unsteady, that were a fine pheasant to get up, I could not bring it down again. Thy return, sweet Safie, has restored me to existence. When I thought I had lost thee for ever, I was occupied by gloomy thoughts, and neither heeded the descent of the evening star nor the golden sunrise reflected on the lake; but now my love fills my imagination, and all is enjoyment!

SONG – FELIX

Thy youthful charms, bright maid, inspire
  And grace my fav'rite theme,
Whose person kindles soft desire,
  Whose mind secures esteem.
Oh, hear me then my flame avow,
  And fill my heart with joy –
A flame which taught by time to grow,
  No time can e'er destroy.
My tender suit with smiles approve,
  And share the sweets of mutual love.
When autumn yields her ripen'd corn,
  Or winter, darkening, lowers,
With tenderest care I'll soothe thy morn,
  And cheer thy evening hours.
Again, when smiling spring returns,
  We'll breathe the vernal air;

Presumption

And still when summer sultry burns,

  To woodland walks repair –

There seek retirement's sheltered grove,

  And share the sweets of mutual love.

Felix retires up stage. Enter Frankenstein.

FRANK. In vain do I seek a respite from these dreadful thoughts – where'er I turn my eyes, I expect to behold the supernatural Being! – to see him spring from each woody recess – but on, on to Agatha, and repose.

FELIX. A traveller! and surely I know his air and manner. (Comes forward.)

FRANK. Good stranger, can you direct me to the habitation of old De Lacey?

FELIX. Better than most persons, I trust.

FRANK. How! Felix De Lacey!

FELIX. The same! the same! Frankenstein! You know, my friend – 'tis long since we have met.

FRANK. Your strange and sudden disappearance from Paris –

FELIX. Makes as strange a story, with which I shall not now detain you. Come to our humble cottage. [– Ah, Frankenstein, we have been as poor as mice, and our dwelling is not much larger than a trap –] Egad! I'm overjoyed to see you!

FRANK. And Agatha?

FELIX. Is queen of the Castle! – and between ourselves Frankenstein has still a warm corner of her heart for you. Come, we have only to cross the wood. [– I'm in high spirits, my friend – I've this day recover'd my mistress – but that will make another strange story. – This is indeed a lucky day – Safie is restored – and I ramble out to kill a Pheasant, and pop upon a philosopher who is likely to become a brother-in-law –]

HAM. (Without.) Any good Christians in the neighbourhood?

FELIX. What have we here?

Presumption

Enter Hammerpan, with a long pole, tinker's utensils, fire kettle, &c.

HAM. Real Christians! human beings! Oh, good Gentlemen, have you seen it?

FELIX. It! – what?

HAM. Ah! that's it! As I live, I saw it an hour ago in the forest!

FELIX. What do you mean by it?

HAM. My hair stood on end like mustard and cress, and so will yours when you see it!

FELIX. Get you gone! you are tipsy!

HAM. I wish I was. As I take it, you are Master Felix, of the Valley of the Lake; we've done business together before now.

FELIX. I know you not!

HAM. I mended your kettle t'other day. You did me a good turn – one good turn deserves another – I'll put you on your guard – the very devil is abroad.

FRANK. (Aside.) How!

FELIX. (Laughs.) Ha! ha! ha! You romancing tinker! [– and pray how was his worship dressed?

HAM. [Dress'd – why it was stark undressed all but a cloak.] You may laugh, but the other gentleman don't laugh. You may perceive he believes it . (To Frankenstein.) I saw it – I saw with this one eye.

FELIX. One eye!

HAM. Yes, I'm blind of the other – a little boy threw a pebble at it, so I've been stone blind ever since, gentlemen. He was ten foot six long, (Holds his pole high up.) with a head of black lanky locks down to his very elbows.

FRANK. 'Tis the Demon! (Apart to himself)

HAM. I lifted up my hammer to strike it but I was so tremulous that I knock'd my own head instead.

210

Presumption

FRANK. What did this strange object? (To Hammerpan.)

HAM. It didn't speak to me, nor I to it. I saw it at first in the forest picking acorns and berries – and then, after it had dispersed our tribe, like a ferret among the rats – it took a drink at our broth, and burnt its fingers in our fire.

FRANK. And what became of this creature?

HAM. I wasn't curious enough to inquire. My wife was in fits at the sight of the devil – so I was obliged to keep my one eye upon her.

FELIX. Your one eye has been pretty well employed. Come, come, gipsy, we'll cross the wood and see if this man mountain is to be met.

HAM. The good genius of wandering tinkers forbid!

FELIX. (To Frankenstein.) And now, my friend, we'll on to the cottage.

FRANK. So, so! (Apart.) I will follow ye!

(Exeunt Felix and Hammerpan)

So! the peasants have already been terrified by the ungainly form! Ambitious experimentalist! The consciousness of the crime I have committed eternally haunts me! I have indeed drawn a horrible curse on my head! He may be malignant, and delight [for its own sake] in murder and wretchedness! a whole country may execrate me as their pest! Every thought that bears towards my baneful project causes my lips to quiver and [my] heart to palpitate. [But, away with these wretched reflections –] I must now to the cottage of Felix. Agatha, fairest Agatha, [fairest Agatha,] instead of smiles, your lover will meet you with dark and hopeless despondency! (Exit Frankenstein)

SCENE V Evening. – Interior of the cottage of De Lacey. – The thatched roof in sight. A woodfire. – Through an open rustic porch are visible a rivulet, and small wooden bridge – a wooden couch – Music. – De Lacey discovered seated thereon, with Agatha next him in attendance. The Demon appears through the portico, watching them, and regards Agatha with rapture. – Agatha kisses her father's hand, takes a small pail or hand bucket, and trips through the portico on to the bridge to procure water. The Demon having retreated on Agatha's approach, pursues her on the bridge. Agatha, turning suddenly perceives the Demon, screams loudly, and swoons, falling into the rivulet.

DEL. Gracious Heaven – that cry of horror! Agatha!

The Demon leaps from the bridge and rescues her.

DEL. Gracious Heaven – that cry of Horror! – Agatha! My sweet child, where art thou? – Agatha, Agatha!

Music – The Demon places Agatha, insensible, on a bench near De Lacey.

DEL. This silence – this suspense is dreadful!

The Demon tenderly guides the hand of De Lacey and places it on Agatha.

DEL. My child – cold, cold, and insensible! – this mystery – cruel fate – Dead? – no, no, no, her heart still beats. – Kind Heaven has saved me that pang! – Felix, Felix, where art thou? My dear daughter, for your poor father's sake revive!

Music. – Agatha recovers. – The Demon hangs over them, with fondness. Felix and Frankenstein suddenly enter.

FRANK. Misery! The Demon!

FELIX. What horrid monster is this? – Agatha, my father is in danger? The Demon retreats.

Music. – Felix discharges his gun and wounds the Demon, who writhes under the wound. – In desperation pulls a burning branch from the fire – rushes at them – beholds Frankenstein – in agony of feeling dashes through the portico. Safie Enters to Agatha. – Hurried Music.

FINALE

Tell us – tell us – what form was there?

(With anxious fear enquiring)

Saw you its Eye – the hideous glare

Terrific dread inspiring!

The Demon is seen climbing the outside of the Portico. He bursts through the thatch with burning brand.

Presumption

The fiend of Sin

With ghastly grin!

Behold the Cottage firing!

The Demon hangs to the Rafters, setting light to the thatch and Rafters, with malignant joy – as parts of the building fall – groups of gypsies appear on the bridge, and through the burning apertures – who join in the Chorus.

FULL CHORUS OF GYPSIES

Beware! Beware!

The hideous glare,

The fiend of Sin

With ghastly grin –

Behold the cottage firing.

Felix forces his way through the flames with his father and Safie – Frankenstein rushes out with Agatha.

END OF ACT II

ACT III, SCENE I

The Garden of Elizabeth, at Belrive. – Morning. (Same as Act I, Scene II.)

Enter Clerval from terrace entrance.

CLER. What a delightful morning! It is an auspicious commencement of the day which is to make me happy in the possession of my love! Elizabeth yet sleeps, peaceful be her slumbers! [Love has awakened me – the freshness of the air, and the beauty of the scenery animate me to the height of cheerfulness –] Soft, she approaches.

Enter Elizabeth from the house.

Elizabeth, my love, why that look of anxiety?

ELIZ. Oh, Clerval! We have had strange occurrences since you quitted me yesternight, our house is full of guests, my brother has brought here the family of De Lacey of whom you have heard me so often speak –

CLER. The family of De Lacey, the relatives of Agatha.

ELIZ. By some extraordinary mystery, which is yet unexplained to me, the Cottage in which Frankenstein discovered his mistress and her family was destroyed by fire; they arrived late last night and all appear overcome with fatigue and terror; some dreadful calamity hangs about my dear brother.

CLER. How astonishing is his conduct. Alas! my sweet Elizabeth, in the midst of all this misery I am selfish – I trust these singular occurrences will not postpone our marriage. Consider, our friends are invited, the church is prepared.

ELIZ.. A few hours may explain all. See now (Looks towards house.) Frankenstein approaches – observe his agitated countenance and restless step; he has not slept since his return – he has armed himself with pistols and appears continually watching.

CLER. We will retire and avoid him for the present. This way, love.(Exeunt)

Presumption

Music – Enter Frankenstein from house.

FRANK. How am I to avoid the powerful vengeance of the monster formed by my cursed ambition. I gave him energy and strength, to crush my own guilty head! My hours pass in dread, and soon the bolt may fall which will deprive me of existence! [The diabolical act I have committed in raising a being, recurs each moment and conscience stricken – I shudder to think -- Agatha! Agatha! gladly would I sacrifice my own life to preserve yours –] Yet the Demon preserved the life of Agatha – he had some feeling of affection – [and] how were those feelings requited! – by detestation, scorn, and wounds! – his look of everlasting malice! He will watch with the wiliness of a serpent, that he may sting with its venom! There is no hope but in the destruction of the Demon. (Takes out his pistol.) I must not cease to guard and protect my friends. (Going to the door.) Agatha has arisen. (Conceals pistol.)

Enter Agatha, a locket round her neck, from the house.

AGA. Frankenstein, I behold you unhappy – fleeing to solitude – and I cannot help supposing that you might regret the renewal of our connexion. [Do you love another?

FRANK. Agatha! Can you forgive my cold neglect? At the sight of you, my long smothered passion bursts out anew – but I thought you lost – receive me once again with smiles and bring me back to life and hope.

AGA. These transports ill accord with the heavy gloom which pervades you –] Dear Frankenstein, I still love you, and confess that in my airy dreams of futurity you have been my constant friend and companion.

FRANK. [Blessed sounds –] Agatha, you shall be mine! I will then divulge to you the secret which disturbs – nay, distracts me.

Music, the Harmonica. – Distant church bells.

Those cheerful chimes announce the wedding day of Elizabeth and Clerval! [This way – Agatha –] My care-worn looks will but damp their merriment.

(Music. – Exeunt Frankenstein and Agatha)

Enter Felix and Safie from house.

FELIX. Listen, Safie, to those merry village bells; they ring a rare contrast to our last night's misery. Soon, my eastern Rose, will they chime for us; and then away with care. This kiss – (Embracing her.)

SAFIE. Fie, Felix! In open daylight. You will deepen the blush of you Eastern rose.

DUET – SAFIE AND FELIX

Come with me, dear, to my mountain home,

And Hymen shall hallow the peaceful dome.

Leave all the world for love and for me,

And I will be all the world to thee.

Our life shall be all holiday –

Shall be all holiday.

Come o'er the dew-bespangled vale,

Where the violet blue and primrose pale

Peep from the verdant shade.

Come o'er the dew-bespangled vale,

Where the violet blue and primrose pale,

Where the violet blue and primrose pale

Peep from the verdant shade.

Come o'er the dew, &c., &c.

We'll fly to the shady grove,

And sign and whisper, love,

Till day begins to fade,

Till day begins, &c., &c.

We'll roam, and I will woo thee, love,

Presumption

Where birds sing sweetly through the grove –

Where birds sing sweetly thro' the grove

Till day begins to fade.

We'll roam, and I will woo thee, love,

Where birds sing sweetly thro' the grove –

While birds sing, &c., &c., &c.

Music, with the bells. – Enter Madame Ninon, leading a group of Dancing Villagers, from the terrace entrance, and Elizabeth, with Clerval, re-enter.

NIN. Now, Madame Elizabeth – now, Mr. Clerval – we are all ready, and the priest is in waiting.

Music resumed. – Elizabeth and Clerval, as also Safie and Felix, join the procession, and all the villagers dance off to music along the terrace, except Madame Ninon.

NIN. There they go to be coupled, pretty dears! (Calls.) Fritz! Fritz! Where is my stupid husband? I've stretched my neck out of joint looking for him. I expect him from the market at Geneva with a cargo of eatables and my new-fashioned beehive cap – all for our wedding festival of Mr. Frankenstein, who has brought his bride and family here in consequence, as I am told, of their cottage being accidentally destroyed by fire last night. Oh! here the fellow comes, with a basket on his back, creeping like a snail.

Enter Fritz, from the terrace entrance, with hamper at his back containing various articles, a lady's cap, and a live duck.

FRITZ. Here I am, spousy. I've brought your list of articles.

Ninon assists him in putting down his basket.

There's the trout, and the sugar-loaf, and the melons, and the nutmegs.

NIN. But dear Fritz, where's my new beehive [cap] you were to bring from the milliner's at Geneva?

FRITZ. Somewhere, I know. (Looking and examining the contents of the hamper, cautiously opening the top.) The three

Presumption

live ducks are lying a top of the maccaroni, squeezed up under the large Gruyere cheese.

NIN. I hope to goodness my cap is not squeezed up!

FRITZ. It's quite safe, I tell you. I put it at the very bottom of the basket.

NIN. It will be in a nice state for my head, then!

FRITZ. lord, here's a rummaging fuss for the cap. I was so nervous about it – you cautioned me so, you know. (Still kneeling and searching the hamper.) Oh, dear, where is it now? Oh, la, to be sure, spousy – here it is at last; la, I knew it was safe. (He pulls the cap out, with a live duck in it.)

NIN. (Takes her cap from him.) Oh, Fritz, it's spoiled! That duck has been laying in it.

FRITZ. Not an egg, I hope, Ninon!

NIN. Alas! see how it is rumpled. (She takes from the cap two or three of the duck's small feathers, which fall on the stage.)

FRITZ. (Aside.) Ha! – he! he! Cap and feathers!

NIN. You careless, good-for-nothing dog!

FRITZ. (Aside.) Dog and Duck!

NIN. Take the basket in, you sinner! (Having first replaced her cap in the hamper.)

FRITZ. Oh! (To the duck.) You look very jolly, my fine fellow, considering you are going to be killed for dinner. Wait till the peas are ready! I never seen such a piece of quackery as that cap in all my life!

Draws the basket after him into the house, and comes forward during the duet.

NIN. My finery destroyed by that varlet! But even that shall not disconcert me. My sweet mistress is united to-day to the man of her heart, and in spite of my cap I will be merry, and dance till [I'm so old] I can dance no longer.

218

Presumption

DUET- NINON AND FRITZ

(Welsh air.)

NIN. Oh! I'll hail the wedding day,

And be the gayest of the gay,

Till age has tripp'd my steps away.

FRITZ. (Re-entering from house.) Away!

NIN. Your manners were not taught in France.

FRITZ. La, wife! when you're too old to Dance –

A horse at sixty – (Aside.) – cannot prance –

Ah, nay!

NIN. While pipes and tabors playing sweetly,

With all my soul I'll foot it featly,

FRITZ.. Yes, I guess you'll hobble neatly.

Wife!

NIN. Don't wife me, you saucy fellow!

Sure you're tipsy –

FRITZ. Only mellow.

We'll all be so, for that is fun and life!

TOGETHER. Don't wife me, you saucy fellow.

I won't wife you, I'm only mellow.

NIN. I ne'er was tipsy.

FRITZ. You ne'er was tipsy, only mellow.

Wife!

Fritz dances her up to the house, Ninon turns, boxes his ear, and they exeunt into house.

Presumption

Music. – The Demon appears from terrace entrance, watching about, and retreats as Fritz re-enters from house.

FRITZ. Oh! (Rubbing his cheek.) What's the use of a fine cap to her? she's so short, unless she stood upon a chair, in the crowd – no one would see her, or her new-fashioned bee-hive either.

During the above speech, William comes from the house, behind Fritz on tiptoe, and gives Fritz a smart smack on the back, who being fearfully alarmed, cries out lustily.

Oh, bless my soul! There now, that's just the way to make me nervous again. What do you want, Master William?

WILL. I can't get a soul to speak to me in the house – some are busy – some are going to be married – will you play with me, Fritz?

FRITZ. I like a game of play – it's so relaxing. When work was over I used to play with my cow.

WILL. (Throwing a ball.) Run and fetch that ball –

FRITZ. Lord, my dear, that's very fatiguing. – What a way you've thrown it – right among the cauliflowers.

Music – Goes off. Demon suddenly appears at the railing – watches the Child – Fritz returns.

FRITZ. Here it is, Master Willy! There's your ball, William Frankenstein.

WILL. Now again.

FRITZ. La – no – you give me more trouble than your brother used in his laboratory – when he –

William throws the ball behind the balustrade.

I won't fetch it – you may find it yourself –

Demon points to William – intimating that the boy must be dear to Frankenstein.

WILL. If you are too idle to go – I'm not –

FRITZ. I shan't look –

220

Presumption

William goes to the balustrade. – The Demon suddenly seizes him.

WILL. Help! help! help!

FRITZ. Ah – that won't do – that won't do, young master – I'm not to be had –

WILL. Help! help!

Music. The Demon stops the boy's mouth – and throws him across his shoulder – Fritz turns – sees them – utters a cry of horror – the Demon rushes off.

FRITZ. Help! help! murder – wife! wife! the devil – oh my nerves!

(Runs off)

SCENE II

A Country View. Rustic Church in the distance. A large Yew Thee, spread plentifully with boughs. Music. – A Foreground with pathway behind it. The procession, as before, returning from the marriage ceremony. The corps de ballet, Villagers, preceding, dancing, followed by Felix, Safie, Clerval, and Elizabeth.

[CONGRATULATORY SESTETTO

[Agatha – Safie – Elizabeth – Felix – Clerval and Bass

[Since all to beauty's rip'ning bloom

[Their cheerful homage pay,

[Be not displeas'd that we presume

[To hail thy bridal day.

[But if, by Time's all conquering hand,

[Thy bloom must wear away,

[The roses of thy mind shall stand

[And never more decay.]

Presumption

NIN. (heard without.) Oh, mistress! Oh!

FRITZ. I couldn't help it – murder!

Ninon and Fritz enter.

NIN. But where did you leave him?

FRITZ. He left me – Oh dear – (Cries.) Murder!

NIN. Oh wretched fate!

ELIZ. What is the matter, good Ninon?

NIN. William, your brother William is the matter; the boy is lost. I sent him to that Fritz, that he might be out of the way.

FRITZ. Yes; and now he's out of everybody's way.

ELIZ. This is most extraordinary – a frolic of the little rogue.

FRITZ. No, no, it isn't; I saw – my nerves! Oh, dear! I saw – a great something snatch him up. (Cries.) I – oh dear – oh dear. Oh! murder!

CLER. Here's Frankenstein.

Enter Frankenstein, with a pistol.

ELIZ. My dear Victor, know you aught of William? The child has been missed in a most unaccountable manner.

FRANK. My brother missing!

NIN. Fritz was with him.

FRITZ. Oh, master! a great creature – [wrapped in a mantle] oh! oh! oh! [(Cries.) murder!]

FRANK. [(Aside.) No sooner has the idea crossed my imagination than I am convinced of its truth – the horrible Demon!]

CLER. Hasten, my friends, one and all – all search. Our pastime is marr'd till the boy is found.

Music. – All exeunt in consternation at different entrances, excepting Frankenstein, who appears lost in desponding

222

Presumption

reverie. – He turns; the boughs of the yew tree are pulled apart, and the Demon is discovered behind it, with William in his grasp. – Frankenstein draws a pistol, and points it – the Demon holds forth the child, when Frankenstein lowers his pistol, and kneels. – The Demon again shoulders the child, and rushes off within the path. – Frankenstein rises, and pursues them in despair.

SCENE III

An Apartment in the Villa Belrive. – A wide folding window opening to the Garden, closed. A table with red baize covering.

Enter Agatha and Ninon.

NIN. The most unaccountable disappearance of my dear little boy, at such a moment – on such a day – when we should have been so merry!

AGA. It is indeed strange and fearful; let us hope that William will soon be discovered, and brought home. (Aside.) The wild phantom that fired our cottage, surely, is not concerned.

NIN. I can do nothing but think of William – that is your room, ma'am – (Pointing to the door.) – you will find it well furnished – with such sweet blue eyes – everything is comfortable – unhappy little boy! There's a fire grate in the room – with two little dimples on each cheek! There's a cabinet in the corner – curly locks! Forgive me, ma'am; I fostered the pretty child, and I cannot get him out of my head.

AGA. Pray leave me, Ninon, and give me the earliest intelligence of Mr. Frankenstein's return.

NIN. All the festivities of the wedding-day destroyed, till this dear unlucky urchin is found. [Bless me the large looking glass, with the curtain undrawn – well, it may e'en remain so – for we cannot be gay till the truant comes back.] (Sobbing.) The sweet little, naughty, rosy-cheek'd rogue! how I will whip him when he comes home. (Exit Ninon)

During the above the Demon is seen at the window watching, and disappears.

AGA. Frankenstein! what a singular fatality is attached to you – with wealth and friends, doomed to be miserable! – This mystery! – I feel a heavy foreboding of mischance! a presentiment of evil pervades my mind. I may regret the day that I have again met Frankenstein – I may rue the hour that I left our humble hut.

(Exit Agatha to Room)

Afterwards, enter Frankenstein, reflecting – two pistols in his belt.

Presumption

FRANK. One sudden and desolating change has taken place – the fangs of remorse tear my bosom and will not forgo their hold! – pursue the Demon! One might as well attempt to overtake the winds, or confine a mountain torrent. My poor Brother – I – I am thy murderer – the author of unalterable evils. [I live in momentary fear lest the monster I have created should still commit some signal crime which by its enormity will almost efface the recollection of the past.] There is scope for fear, so long as anything I love remains. (Goes to door.) Agatha! she reclines sleeping on yon sofa [– yesternight's fatigue.]

Music. – The Demon during the above soliloquy reappears on the balcony of the window – and while Frankenstein is looking in at the door, the Demon creeps in at the window, crouching beneath the table, unseen.

Sleep on, sweet innocence! I dare not leave you; I will stay and guard your slumber, or the remorseless Demon will snatch your breath away.

Music. – Frankenstein takes out a pistol and primes it – lays it on the table.

The wretch ev'n now may be haunting the room – let me search around.

[Searches – The Demon eludes him – Frankenstein goes to the curtain which covers the glass.

This Drapery which covers the glass may conceal the monster.

Frankenstein feels the drapery fearfully with the point of the sword – while Frankenstein is thus employed – Demon creeps along the floor into Agatha's room – Frankenstein draws the curtain – Agatha's door is reflected in the glass.]

Oh, Agatha! would that I had banished myself for ever from my native country, and wandered a friendless outcast over the earth, rather than I had again met you – perhaps to bring you in the grasp of my fiendish adversary – perhaps to – (A piercing scream.) – My blood curdles! that shriek! Ah! What do I behold!

In the large glass – Agatha appears on her knees with a veil over her head. – The Demon with his hand on her throat – she falls – the Demon disappears after tearing a locket from Agatha's neck.

My last, last hope! (Rushes into room.)

The figure of Frankenstein appears in the glass, kneeling over the body of Agatha. The Demon crosses by the window in a boat with great swiftness – exulting.

Presumption

SCENE IV

An Ante-chamber in Belrive.

Enter Elizabeth, hastily, meeting Ninon. – Music ceases.

ELIZ. Whence is this fresh alarm?

NIN. I know not madam. Oh, wretched day for poor Ninon! Mr. Frankenstein is stark mad; he ran but out this instant, jumped into his boat, and rowed off rapidly.

Enter Fritz, alarmed.

FRITZ. Oh, oh, oh! – I've seen it – seen it again! The great monster, it got out of one of our windows and scudded off in a boat, and there's Mr. Frankenstein got another boat, and is going after the great creature like lightning.

ELIZ. Where – where are our friends?

FRITZ. Mr. Clerval and Mr. Felix have followed Mr. Frankenstein.

SAFIE. (Without.) Help! ah, help!

Enter Safie hastily, throws herself into the arms of Elizabeth.

SAFIE. Ah Madam! Agatha, my sister – the gentle Agatha – I fear, is no more!

OMNES. Agatha!

ELIZ. Gracious Heaven! what horrible destiny hangs over us?

SAFIE. Stretched on the ground she lies! [a livid mark on her neck!) Ah! Elizabeth, the spark of life may yet not be extinct.

ELIZ. Hasten – hasten to the room. (Exeunt hastily)

Hurried Music.

SCENE V

Wild Border of the Lake. At the extremity of the stage, a lofty over-hanging mountain of snow.

Music. – All the Gipsies discovered in various groups. A pistol shot is heard. The Gipsies start up alarmed. A second pistol is fired nearer. The Demon rushes on with the locket worn by Agatha, during the piece. The Gipsies scream out and fly in all directions. Hammerpan is on the point of escaping, when the Demon seizes him, and Hammerpan falls down on being dragged back. The Demon points off to intimate that Frankenstein is approaching, throws down the locket, commands the gipsy, Hammerpan, to show it to Frankenstein – the Demon threatens him, and rushing up the mountain, climbs, and disappears. Enter Frankenstein, with two loaded pistols and a musket unloaded. – At the same time Hammerpan rises and gets near first wing.

FRANK. In vain do I pursue the wretch, in vain have I fired on him. (Throws his gun from him.) He eludes the bullet. Say, fellow, have you seen aught pass here?

HAM. The giant creature, who aroused us in the forest, rushed upon me but this instant, and pointing to the path by which you came, intimated that I should give you this. (Presents locket to Frankenstein.)

FRANK. 'Tis Agatha's – the murdered Agatha! Malicious fiend! it will joy you to know that my lacerated heart bleeds afresh. Revenge shall henceforth be the devouring and only passion of my soul. I have but one resource – I devote myself either in my life or death to the destruction of the Demon. Agatha! William! you shall be avenged!

HAM. See yonder (Points.) the monster climbs the snow.

FRANK. Then this rencontre shall terminate his detested life or mine.

Music. – Frankenstein draws his pistol – rushes off at back of stage. – The gipsies return at various entrances. – At the same time, enter Felix and Clerval with pistols, and Safie, Elizabeth, and Ninon following. – The Demon appears at the base of the mountain, Frankenstein pursuing.

CLER. Behold our friend and his mysterious enemy.

Presumption

FELIX. See – Frankenstein aims his musket at him – let us follow and assist him.(Is going up stage with Clerval.)

HAM. Hold master! if the gun is fired, it will bring down a mountain of snow [on their heads.] Many an avalanche has fallen there.

[FELIX. He fires –]

Music. – Frankenstein discharges his musket. – The Demon and Frankenstein meet at the very extremity of the stage. – Frankenstein fires – the avalanche falls and annihilates the Demon and Frankenstein. – A heavy fall of snow succeeds. – Loud thunder heard, and all the characters form a picture as the curtain falls.

The Private Memoire and Confessions of a Justified Sinner

By Himself

WITH A DETAIL OF CURIOUS TRADITIONARY FACTS, AND OTHER EVIDENCE, BY THE EDITOR

By

James Hogg

THE EDITOR'S NARRATIVE

It appears from tradition, as well as some parish registers still extant, that the lands of Dalcastle (or Dalchastel, as it is often spelled) were possessed by a family of the name of Colwan, about one hundred and fifty years ago, and for at least a century previous to that period. That family was supposed to have been a branch of the ancient family of Colquhoun, and it is certain that from it spring the Cowans that spread towards the Border. I find that, in the year 1687, George Colwan succeeded his uncle of the same name, in the lands of Dalchastel and Balgrennan; and, this being all I can gather of the family from history, to tradition I must appeal for the remainder of the motley adventures of that house. But, of the matter furnished by the latter of these powerful monitors, I have no reason to complain: It has been handed down to the world in unlimited abundance; and I am certain that, in recording the hideous events which follow, I am only relating to the greater part of the inhabitants of at least four counties of Scotland matters of which they were before perfectly well informed.

This George was a rich man, or supposed to be so, and was married, when considerably advanced in life, to the sole heiress and reputed daughter of a Baillie Orde, of Glasgow. This proved a conjunction anything but agreeable to the parties contracting. It is well known that the Reformation principles had long before that time taken a powerful hold of the hearts and affections of the people of Scotland, although the feeling was by no means general, or in equal degrees; and it so happened that this married couple felt completely at variance on the subject. Granting it to have been so, one would have thought that the laird, owing to his retiring situation, would have been the one that inclined to the stern doctrines of the reformers; and that the young and gay dame from the city would have adhered to the free principles cherished by the court party, and indulged in rather to extremity, in opposition to their severe and carping contemporaries.

The contrary, however, happened to be the case. The laird was what his country neighbours called "a droll, careless chap", with a very limited proportion of the fear of God in his heart, and very nearly as little of the fear of man. The laird had not intentionally wronged or offended either of the parties, and perceived not the necessity of deprecating their vengeance. He had hitherto believed that he was living in most cordial terms with the greater part of the inhabitants of the earth, and with the powers above in particular: but woe be unto him if he was not soon convinced of the fallacy of such damning security! for his lady was the most severe and gloomy of all bigots to the principles of the Reformation. Hers were not the tenets of the great reformers, but theirs mightily overstrained and deformed. Theirs was an unguent hard to be swallowed; but hers was that unguent embittered and overheated until nature could not longer bear it. She had imbibed her ideas from the doctrines of one flaming predestinarian divine alone; and these were so rigid that they became a stumbling block to many of his brethren, and a mighty handle for the enemies of his party to turn the machine of the state against them.

The wedding festivities at Dalcastle partook of all the gaiety, not of that stern age, but of one previous to it. There was feasting, dancing, piping, and singing: the liquors were handed, around in great fulness, the ale in large wooden bickers, and the brandy in capacious horns of oxen. The laird gave full scope to his homely glee. He danced — he snapped his fingers to the music — clapped his hands and shouted at the turn of the tune. He saluted every girl in the hall whose appearance was anything tolerable, and requested of their sweethearts to take the same freedom with his bride, by way of retaliation. But there she sat at the head of the hall in still and blooming beauty, absolutely refusing to tread a single measure with any gentleman there. The only enjoyment in which she appeared to partake was in now and then stealing a word of sweet conversation with her favourite pastor about divine things; for he had accompanied her home after marrying her to her husband, to see her fairly settled in her new dwelling. He addressed her several times by her new name, Mrs. Colwan; but she turned away her head disgusted, and looked with pity and contempt towards the old inadvertent sinner, capering away in the height of his unregenerated mirth. The minister perceived the workings of her pious mind, and thenceforward addressed her by the courteous title of Lady Dalcastle, which sounded somewhat better, as not coupling her name with one of the wicked: and there is too great reason to believe that, for all the solemn vows she had come under, and these were of no ordinary binding, particularly on the laird's part, she at that time despised, if not abhorred him, in her heart.

The good parson again blessed her, and went away. She took leave of him with tears in her eyes, entreating him often to visit her in that heathen land of the Amorite, the Hittite, and the Girgashite: to which he assented, on many solemn and qualifying conditions—and then the comely bride retired to her chamber to pray.

It was customary, in those days, for the bride's-man and maiden, and a few select friends, to visit the new-married couple after they had retired to rest, and drink a cup to their healths, their happiness, and a numerous posterity. But the laird delighted not in this: he wished to have his jewel to himself; and, slipping away quietly from his jovial party, he retired to his chamber to his beloved, and bolted the door. He found her engaged with the writings of the Evangelists, and terribly demure. The laird went up to caress her; but she turned away her head, and spoke of the follies of aged men, and something of the broad way that leadeth to destruction. The laird did not thoroughly comprehend this allusion; but being considerably flustered by drinking, and disposed to take all in good part, he only remarked, as he took off his shoes and stockings, that, "whether the way was broad or narrow, it was time that they were in their bed."

"Sure, Mr. Colwan, you won't go to bed to-night, at such an important period of your life, without first saying prayers for yourself and me."

When she said this, the laird had his head down almost to the ground, loosing his shoe-buckle; but when he heard of prayers, on such a night, he raised his face suddenly up, which was all over as flushed and red as a rose, and answered:

The Private Memoirs and Confessions of a Justified Sinner

"Prayers, Mistress! Lord help your crazed head, is this a night for prayers?"

He had better have held his peace. There was such a torrent of profound divinity poured out upon him that the laird became ashamed, both of himself and his new-made spouse, and wist not what to say: but the brandy helped him out.

"It strikes me, my dear, that religious devotion would be somewhat out of place to-night," said he. "Allowing that it is ever so beautiful, and ever so beneficial, were we to ride on the rigging of it at all times, would we not be constantly making a farce of it: It would be like reading the Bible and the jestbook, verse about, and would render the life of man a medley of absurdity and confusion."

But, against the cant of the bigot or the hypocrite, no reasoning can aught avail. If you would argue until the end of life, the infallible creature must alone be right. So it proved with the laird. One Scripture text followed another, not in the least connected, and one sentence of the profound Mr. Wringhim's sermons after another, proving the duty of family worship, till the laird lost patience, and tossing himself into bed, said carelessly that he would leave that duty upon her shoulders for one night.

The meek mind of Lady Dalcastle was somewhat disarranged by this sudden evolution. She felt that she was left rather in an awkward situation. However, to show her unconscionable spouse that she was resolved to hold fast her integrity, she kneeled down and prayed in terms so potent that she deemed she was sure of making an impression on him. She did so; for in a short time the laird began to utter a response so fervent that she was utterly astounded, and fairly driven from the chain of her orisons. He began, in truth, to sound a nasal bugle of no ordinary calibre—the notes being little inferior to those of a military trumpet. The lady tried to proceed, but every returning note from the bed burst on her ear with a louder twang, and a longer peal, till the concord of sweet sounds became so truly pathetic that the meek spirit of the dame was quite overcome; and, after shedding a flood of tears, she arose from her knees, and retired to the chimney-corner with her Bible in her lap, there to spend the hours in holy meditation till such time as the inebriated trumpeter should awaken to a sense of propriety.

The laird did not awake in any reasonable time; for, he being overcome with fatigue and wassail, his sleep became sounder, and his Morphean measures more intense. These varied a little in their structure; but the general run of the bars sounded something in this way: "Hic-hoc-wheew!" It was most profoundly ludicrous; and could not have missed exciting risibility in anyone save a pious, a disappointed, and humbled bride.

The good dame wept bitterly. She could not for her life go and awaken the monster, and request him to make room for her: but she retired somewhere, for the laird, on awaking next morning, found that he was still lying alone. His sleep had been of the deepest and most genuine sort; and, all the time that it lasted, he had never once thought of either wives, children, or sweethearts, save in the way of dreaming about them; but, as his spirit began again by slow degrees to verge towards the boundaries of reason, it became lighter and more buoyant from the effects of deep repose, and his dreams partook of that buoyancy, yea, to a degree hardly expressible. He dreamed of the reel, the jig, the strathspey, and the corant; and the elasticity of his frame was such that he was bounding over the heads of maidens, and making his feet skimmer against the ceiling, enjoying, the while, the most ecstatic emotions. These grew too fervent for the shackles of the drowsy god to restrain. The nasal bugle ceased its prolonged sounds in one moment, and a sort of hectic laugh took its place. "Keep it going — play up, you devils!" cried the laird, without changing his position on the pillow. But this exertion to hold the fiddlers at their work fairly awakened the delighted dreamer, and, though he could not refrain from continuing, his laugh, beat length, by tracing out a regular chain of facts, came to be sensible of his real situation. "Rabina, where are you? What's become of you, my dear?" cried the laird. But there was no voice nor anyone that answered or regarded. He flung open the curtains, thinking to find her still on her knees, as he had seen her, but she was not there, either sleeping or waking. "Rabina! Mrs. Colwan!" shouted he, as loud as he could call, and then added in the same breath, "God save the king — I have lost my wife!"

He sprung up and opened the casement: the day-light was beginning to streak the east, for it was spring, and the nights were short, and the mornings very long. The laird half dressed himself in an instant, and strode through every room in the house, opening the windows as he went, and scrutinizing every bed and every corner. He came into the hall where the wedding festival had been held; and as he opened the various windowboards, loving couples flew off like hares surprised too late in the morning among the early braird. "Hoo-boo! Fie, be frightened!" cried the laird. "Fie, rin like fools, as if ye were caught in an ill-turn!" His bride was not among them; so he was obliged to betake himself to further search. "She will be praying in some corner, poor woman," said he to himself. "It is an unlucky thing this praying. But, for my part, I fear I have behaved very ill; and I must endeavour to make amends."

The laird continued his search, and at length found his beloved in the same bed with her Glasgow cousin who had acted as bridesmaid. "You sly and malevolent imp," said the laird; "you have played me such a trick when I was fast asleep! I have not known a frolic so clever, and, at the same time, so severe. Come along, you baggage you!"

"Sir, I will let you know that I detest your principles and your person alike," said she. "It shall never be said, Sir, that my person was at the control of a heathenish man of Belial—a dangler among the daughters of women—a promiscuous dancer—and a player of unlawful games. Forgo your rudeness, Sir, I say, and depart away from my presence and that of my kinswoman."

"Come along, I say, my charming Rab. If you were the pink of all puritans, and the saint of all saints, you are my wife, and must do as I command you."

"Sir, I will sooner lay down my life than be subjected to your godless will; therefore I say, desist, and begone with you."

But the laird regarded none of these testy sayings: he rolled her in a blanket, and bore her triumphantly away to his chamber, taking care to keep a fold or two of the blanket always rather near to her mouth, in case of any outrageous forthcoming of noise.

The next day at breakfast the bride was long in making her appearance. Her maid asked to see her; but George did not choose that anybody should see her but himself. He paid her several visits, and always turned the key as he came out. At length breakfast was served; and during the time of refreshment the laird tried to break several jokes; but it was remarked that they wanted their accustomed brilliancy, and that his nose was particularly red at the top.

Matters, without all doubt, had been very bad between the new-married couple; for in the course of the day the lady deserted her quarters, and returned to her father's house in Glasgow, after having been a night on the road; stage-coaches and steam-boats having then no existence in that quarter.

The Private Memoirs and Confessions of a Justified Sinner

Though Baillie Orde had acquiesced in his wife's asseveration regarding the likeness of their only daughter to her father, he never loved or admired her greatly; therefore this behaviour nothing astounded him. He questioned her strictly as to the grievous offence committed against her, and could discover nothing that warranted a procedure so fraught with disagreeable consequences. So, after mature deliberation, the baillie addressed her as follows:

"Aye, aye, Raby! An' sae I find that Dalcastle has actually refused to say prayers with you when you ordered him; an' has guidit you in a rude indelicate manner, outstepping the respect due to my daughter—as my daughter. But, wi' regard to what is due to his own wife, of that he's a better judge nor me. However, since he has behaved in that manner to MY DAUGHTER, I shall be revenged on him for aince; for I shall return the obligation to ane nearer to him: that is, I shall take pennyworths of his wife—an' let him lick at that."

"What do you mean, Sir?" said the astonished damsel.

"I mean to be revenged on that villain Dalcastle," said he, "for what he has done to my daughter. Come hither, Mrs. Colwan, you shall pay for this."

So saying, the baillie began to inflict corporal punishment on the runaway wife. His strokes were not indeed very deadly, but he made a mighty flourish in the infliction, pretending to be in a great rage only at the Laird of Dalcastle. "Villain that he is!" exclaimed he, "I shall teach him to behave in such a manner to a child of mine, be she as she may; since I cannot get at himself, I shall lounder her that is nearest to him in life. Take you that, and that, Mrs. Colwan, for your husband's impertinence!"

The poor afflicted woman wept and prayed, but the baillie would not abate aught of his severity. After fuming and beating her with many stripes, far drawn, and lightly laid down, he took her up to her chamber, five stories high, locked her in, and there he fed her on bread and water, all to be revenged on the presumptuous Laird of Dalcastle; but ever and anon, as the baillie came down the stair from carrying his daughter's meal, he said to himself: "I shall make the sight of the laird the blithest she ever saw in her life."

Lady Dalcastle got plenty of time to read, and pray, and meditate; but she was at a great loss for one to dispute with about religious tenets; for she found that, without this advantage, about which there was a perfect rage at that time, the reading and learning of Scripture texts, and sentences of intricate doctrine, availed her naught; so she was often driven to sit at her casement and look out for the approach of the heathenish Laird of Dalcastle.

That hero, after a considerable lapse of time, at length made his appearance. Matters were not hard to adjust; for his lady found that there was no refuge for her in her father's house; and so, after some sighs and tears, she accompanied her husband home. For all that had passed, things went on no better. She WOULD convert the laird in spite of his teeth: the laird would not be converted. She WOULD have the laird to say family prayers, both morning and evening: the laird would neither pray morning nor evening. He would not even sing psalms, and kneel beside her while she performed the exercise; neither would he converse at all times, and in all places, about the sacred mysteries of religion, although his lady took occasion to contradict flatly every assertion that he made, in order that she might spiritualize him by drawing him into argument.

The laird kept his temper a long while, but at length his patience wore out; he cut her short in all her futile attempts at spiritualization, and mocked at her wire-drawn degrees of faith, hope, and repentance. He also dared to doubt of the great standard doctrine of absolute predestination, which put the crown on the lady's Christian resentment. She declared her helpmate to be a limb of Antichrist, and one with whom no regenerated person could associate. She therefore bespoke a separate establishment, and, before the expiry of the first six months, the arrangements of the separation were amicably adjusted. The upper, or third, story of the old mansion-house was awarded to the lady for her residence. She had a separate door, a separate stair, a separate garden, and walks that in no instance intersected the laird's; so that one would have thought the separation complete. They had each their own parties, selected from their own sort of people; and, though the laird never once chafed himself about the lady's companies, it was not long before she began to intermeddle about some of his.

"Who is that fat bouncing dame that visits the laird so often, and always by herself?" said she to her maid Martha one day.

"Oh dear, mem, how can I ken? We're banished frae our acquaintances here, as weel as frae the sweet gospel ordinances."

"Find me out who that jolly dame is, Martha. You, who hold communion with the household of this ungodly man, can be at no loss to attain this information. I observe that she always casts her eye up toward our windows, both in coming and going; and I suspect that she seldom departs from the house emptyhanded."

That same evening Martha came with the information that this august visitor was a Miss Logan, an old and intimate acquaintance of the laird's, and a very worthy respectable lady, of good connections, whose parents had lost their patrimony in the civil wars.

"Ha! very well!" said the lady; "very well, Martha! But, nevertheless, go thou and watch this respectable lady's motions and behaviour the next time she comes to visit the laird—and the next after that. You will not, I see, lack opportunities."

Martha's information turned out of that nature that prayers were said in the uppermost story of Dalcastle house against the Canaanitish woman, every night and every morning; and great discontent prevailed there, even to anathemas and tears. Letter after letter was dispatched to Glasgow; and at length, to the lady's great consolation, the Rev. Mr. Wringhim arrived safely and devoutly in her elevated sanctuary. Marvellous was the conversation between these gifted people. Wringhim had held in his doctrines that there were eight different kinds of FAITH, all perfectly distinct in their operations and effects. But the lady, in her secluded state, had discovered another five, making twelve [sic] in all: the adjusting of the existence or fallacy of these five faiths served for a most enlightened discussion of nearly seventeen hours; in the course of which the two got warm in their arguments, always in proportion as they receded from nature, utility, and common sense. Wringhim at length got into unwonted fervour about some disputed point between one of these faiths and TRUST: when the lady, fearing that zeal was getting beyond its wonted barrier, broke in on his vehement asseverations with the following abrupt discomfiture: "But, Sir, as long as I remember, what is to be done with this case of open and avowed iniquity?"

The minister was struck dumb. He leaned him back on his chair, stroked his beard, hemmed—considered, and hemmed again, and then said, in an altered and softened tone: "Why, that is a secondary consideration; you mean the case between your husband and Miss Logan?"

"The same, Sir. I am scandalized at such intimacies going on under my nose. The sufferance of it is a great and crying evil."

The Private Memoirs and Confessions of a Justified Sinner

"Evil, madam, may be either operative, or passive. To them it is an evil, but to us none. We have no more to do with the sins of the wicked and unconverted here than with those of an infidel Turk; for all earthly bonds and fellowships are absorbed and swallowed up in the holy community of the Reformed Church. However, if it is your wish, I shall take him to task, and reprimand and humble him in such a manner that he shall be ashamed of his doings, and renounce such deeds for ever, out of mere self-respect, though all unsanctified the heart, as well as the deed, may be. To the wicked, all things are wicked; but to the just, all things are just and right."

"Ah, that is a sweet and comfortable saying, Mr. Wringhim! How delightful to think that a justified person can do no wrong! Who would not envy the liberty wherewith we are made free? Go to my husband, that poor unfortunate, blindfolded person, and open his eyes to his degenerate and sinful state; for well are you fitted to the task."

"Yea, I will go in unto him, and confound him. I will lay the strong holds of sin and Satan as flat before my face as the dung that is spread out to fatten the land."

"Master, there's a gentleman at the fore-door wants a private word o' ye."

"Tell him I'm engaged: I can't see any gentleman to-night. But I shall attend on him to-morrow as soon as he pleases."

"'He's coming straight in, Sir. Stop a wee bit, Sir, my master is engaged. He cannot see you at present, Sir."

"Stand aside, thou Moabite! My mission admits of no delay. I come to save him from the jaws of destruction!"

"An that be the case, Sir, it maks a wide difference; an', as the danger may threaten us a', I fancy I may as weel let ye gang by as fight wi' ye, sin' ye seem sae intent on 't. — The man says he's comin' to save ye, an' canna stop, Sir. Here he is."

The laird was going to break out into a volley of wrath against Waters, his servant; but, before he got a word pronounced, the Rev. Mr. Wringhim had stepped inside the room, and Waters had retired, shutting the door behind him.

No introduction could be more mal-a-propos: it was impossible; for at that very moment the laird and Arabella Logan were both sitting on one seat, and both looking on one book, when the door opened. "What is it, Sir?" said the laird fiercely.

"A message of the greatest importance, Sir," said the divine, striding unceremoniously up to the chimney, turning his back to the fire, and his face to the culprits. "I think you should know me, Sir?" continued he, looking displeasedly at the laird, with his face half turned round.

"I think I should," returned the laird. "You are a Mr. How's—tey—ca'—him, of Glasgow, who did me the worst turn ever I got done to me in my life. You gentry are always ready to do a man such a turn. Pray, Sir, did you ever do a good job for anyone to counterbalance that? For, if you have not, you ought to be—"

"Hold, Sir, I say! None of your profanity before me. If I do evil to anyone on such occasions, it is because he will have it so; therefore, the evil is not of my doing. I ask you, Sir, before God and this witness, I ask you, have you kept solemnly and inviolate the vows which I laid upon you that day? Answer me!"

"Has the partner whom you bound me to kept hers inviolate? Answer me that, Sir! None can better do so than you, Mr. How's—tey—ca'—you."

"So, then, you confess your backslidings, and avow the profligacy of your life. And this person here is, I suppose, the partner of your iniquity—she whose beauty hath caused you to err! Stand up, both of you, till I rebuke you, and show you what you are in the eyes of God and man."

"In the first place, stand you still there, till I tell you what you are in the eyes of God and man. You are, Sir, a presumptuous, self-conceited pedagogue, a stirrer up of strife and commotion in church, in state, in families, and communities. You are one, Sir, whose righteousness consists in splitting the doctrines of Calvin into thousands of undistinguishable films, and in setting up a system of justifying-grace against all breaches of all laws, moral or divine. In short, Sir, you are a mildew—a canker-worm in the bosom of the Reformed Church, generating a disease of which she will never be purged, but by the shedding of blood. Go thou in peace, and do these abominations no more; but humble thyself, lest a worse reproof come upon thee."

Wringhim heard all this without flinching. He now and then

twisted his mouth in disdain, treasuring up, meantime, his vengeance against the two aggressors; for he felt that he had them on the hip, and resolved to pour out his vengeance and indignation upon them. Sorry am I that the shackles of modern decorum restrain me from penning that famous rebuke; fragments of which have been attributed to every divine of old notoriety throughout Scotland. But I have it by heart; and a glorious morsel it is to put into the hands of certain incendiaries. The metaphors are so strong and so appalling that Miss Logan could only stand them a very short time; she was obliged to withdraw in confusion. The laird stood his ground with much ado, though his face was often crimsoned over with the hues of shame and anger. Several times he was on the point of turning the officious sycophant to the door; but good manners, and an inherent respect that he entertained for the clergy, as the immediate servants of the Supreme Being, restrained him.

Wringhim, perceiving these symptoms of resentment, took them for marks of shame and contrition, and pushed his reproaches farther than ever divine ventured to do in a similar case. When he had finished, to prevent further discussion, he walked slowly and majestically out of the apartment, making his robes to swing behind him in a most magisterial manner; he being, without doubt, elated with his high conquest. He went to the upper story, and related to his metaphysical associate his wonderful success; how he had driven the dame from the house in tears and deep confusion, and left the backsliding laird in such a quandary of shame and repentance that he could neither articulate a word nor lift up his countenance. The dame thanked him most cordially, lauding his friendly zeal and powerful eloquence; and then the two again set keenly to the splitting of hairs, and making distinctions in religion where none existed.

They being both children of adoption, and secured from falling into snares, or anyway under the power of the wicked one, it was their custom, on each visit, to sit up a night in the same apartment, for the sake of sweet spiritual converse; but that time, in the course of the night, they differed so materially on a small point somewhere between justification and final election that the minister, in the heat of his zeal, sprung from his seat, paced the floor, and maintained his point with such ardour that Martha was alarmed, and, thinking they were going to fight, and that the minister would be a hard match for her mistress, she put on some clothes, and twice left her bed and stood listening at the back of the door, ready to burst in should need require it. Should anyone think this picture over-strained, I can assure him that it is taken from nature and from truth; but I will not likewise aver that the theologist was neither crazed nor inebriated. If the listener's words were to be relied on, there was no love, no accommodating principle manifested between the two, but a fiery burning zeal, relating to points of such minor importance that a true Christian would blush to hear them mentioned, and the infidel and profane make a handle of them to turn our religion to scorn.

Great was the dame's exultation at the triumph of her beloved pastor over her sinful neighbours in the lower parts of the house; and she boasted of it to Martha in high-sounding terms. But it was of short duration; for, in five weeks after that, Arabella Logan came to reside with the laird as his housekeeper, sitting at his table and carrying the keys as mistress-substitute of the mansion. The lady's grief and indignation were now raised to a higher pitch than ever; and she set every agent to work, with whom she had any power, to effect a separation between these two suspected ones. Remonstrance was of no avail: George laughed at them who tried such a course, and retained his housekeeper, while the lady gave herself up to utter despair; for, though she would not consort with her husband herself, she could not endure that any other should do so.

But, to countervail this grievous offence, our saintly and afflicted dame, in due time, was safely delivered of a fine boy whom the laird acknowledged as his son and heir, and had him christened by his own name, and nursed in his own premises. He gave the nurse permission to take the boy to his mother's presence if ever she should desire to see him; but, strange as it may appear, she never once desired to see him from the day that he was born. The boy grew up, and was a healthful and happy child; and, in the course of another year, the lady presented him with a brother. A brother he certainly was, in the eye of the law, and it is more than probable that he was his brother in reality. But the laird thought otherwise; and, though he knew and acknowledged that he was obliged to support and provide for him, he refused to acknowledge him in other respects. He neither would countenance the banquet nor take the baptismal vows on him in the child's name; of course, the poor boy had to live and remain an alien from the visible church for a year and a day; at which time, Mr. Wringhim out of pity and kindness, took the lady herself as sponsor for the boy, and baptized him by the name of Robert Wringhim—that being the noted divine's own name.

George was brought up with his father, and educated partly at the parish school, and partly at home, by a tutor hired for the purpose. He was a generous and kind-hearted youth; always ready to oblige, and hardly ever dissatisfied with anybody. Robert was brought up with Mr. Wringhim, the laird paying a certain allowance for him yearly; and there the boy was early inured to all the sternness and severity of his pastor's arbitrary and unyielding creed. He was taught to pray twice every day, and seven times on Sabbath days; but he was only to pray for the elect, and, like Devil of old, doom all that were aliens from God to destruction. He had never, in that family into which he had been as it were adopted, heard aught but evil spoken of his reputed father and brother; consequently he held them in utter abhorrence, and prayed against them every day, often "that the old hoary sinner might be cut off in the full flush of his iniquity, and be carried quick into hell; and that the young stem of the corrupt trunk might also be taken from a world that he disgraced, but that his sins might be pardoned, because he knew no better."

Such were the tenets in which it would appear young Robert was bred. He was an acute boy, an excellent learner, had ardent and ungovernable passions, and, withal, a sternness of demeanour from which other boys shrunk. He was the best grammarian, the best reader, writer, and accountant in the various classes that he attended, and was fond of writing essays on controverted points of theology, for which he got prizes, and great praise from his guardian and mother. George was much behind him in scholastic acquirements, but greatly his superior in personal prowess, form, feature, and all that constitutes gentility in the deportment and appearance. The laird had often manifested to Miss Logan an earnest wish that the two young men should never meet, or at all events that they should be as little conversant as possible; and Miss Logan, who was as much attached to George as if he had been her own son, took every precaution, while he was a boy, that he should never meet with his brother; but, as they advanced towards manhood, this became impracticable. The lady was removed from her apartments in her husband's house to Glasgow, to her great content; and all to prevent the young laird being tainted with the company of her and her second son; for the laird had felt the effects of the principles they professed, and dreaded them more than persecution, fire, and sword. During all the dreadful times that had overpast, though the laird had been a moderate man, he had still leaned to the side of kingly prerogative, and had escaped confiscation and fines, without ever taking any active hand in suppressing the Covenanters. But, after experiencing a specimen of their tenets and manner in his wife, from a secret favourer of them and their doctrines, he grew alarmed at the prevalence of such stern and factious principles, now that there was no check or restraint upon them; and from that time he began to set himself against them, joining with the Cavalier party of that day in all their proceedings.

It so happened that, under the influence of the Earls of Seafield and Tullibardine, he was returned for a Member of Parliament in the famous session that sat at Edinburgh when the Duke of Queensberry was commissioner, and in which party spirit ran to such an extremity. The young laird went with his father to the court, and remained in town all the time that the session lasted; and, as all interested people of both factions flocked to the town at that period, so the important Mr. Wringhim was there among the rest, during the greater part of the time, blowing the coal of revolutionary principles with all his might, in every society to which he could obtain admission. He was a great favourite with some of the west country gentlemen of that faction, by reason of his unbending impudence. No opposition could for a moment cause him either to blush, or retract one item that he had advanced. Therefore the Duke of Argyle and his friends made such use of him as sportsmen often do of terriers, to start the game, and make a great yelping noise to let them know whither the chase is proceeding. They often did this out of sport, in order to tease their opponent; for of all pesterers that ever fastened on man he was the most insufferable: knowing that his coat protected him from manual chastisement, he spared no acrimony, and delighted in the chagrin and anger of those with whom he contended. But he was sometimes likewise of real use to the heads of the Presbyterian faction, and therefore was admitted to their tables, and of course conceived himself a very great man.

His ward accompanied him; and, very shortly after their arrival in Edinburgh, Robert, for the first time, met with the young laird his brother, in a match at tennis. The prowess and agility of the young squire drew forth the loudest plaudits of approval from his associates, and his own exertion alone carried the game every time on the one side, and that so far as all I along to count three for their one. The hero's name soon ran round the circle, and when his brother Robert, who was an onlooker, learned who it was that was gaining so much applause, he came and stood close beside him all the time that the game lasted, always now and then putting in a cutting remark by way of mockery.

George could not help perceiving him, not only on account of his impertinent remarks, but he, moreover, stood so near him that he several times impeded him in his rapid evolutions, and of course got himself shoved aside in no very ceremonious way. Instead of making him keep his distance, these rude shocks and pushes, accompanied sometimes with hasty curses, only made him cling the closer to this king of the game. He seemed determined to maintain his right to his place as an onlooker, as well as any of those engaged in the game, and, if they had tried him at an argument, he would have carried his point; or perhaps he wished to quarrel with this spark of his jealousy and aversion, and draw the attention of the gay crowd to himself by these means; for, like his guardian, he knew no other pleasure but what consisted in opposition. George took him for some impertinent student of divinity, rather set upon a joke than anything else. He perceived a lad with black clothes, and a methodistical face, whose countenance and eye he disliked exceedingly, several times in his way, and that was all the notice he took of him the first time they two met. But the next day, and every succeeding one, the same devilish-looking youth attended him as constantly as his shadow; was always in his way as with intention to impede him and ever and anon his deep and malignant eye met those of his elder brother with a glance so fierce that it sometimes startled him.

The very next time that George was engaged at tennis, he had not struck the ball above twice till the same intrusive being was again in his way. The party played for considerable stakes that day, namely, a dinner and wine at the Black Bull tavern; and George, as the hero and head of his party, was much interested in its honour; consequently the sight of this moody and hellish-looking student affected him in no very pleasant manner. "Pray Sir, be so good as keep without the range of the ball," said he.

"Is there any law or enactment that can compel me to do so?" said the other, biting his lip with scorn.

"If there is not, they are here that shall compel you," returned George. "So, friend, I rede you to be on your guard."

As he said this, a flush of anger glowed in his handsome face and flashed from his sparkling blue eye; but it was a stranger to both, and momently took its departure. The black-coated youth set up his cap before, brought his heavy brows over his deep dark eyes, put his hands in the pockets of his black plush breeches, and stepped a little farther into the semicircle, immediately on his brother's right hand, than he had ever ventured to do before. There he set himself firm on his legs, and, with a face as demure as death, seemed determined to keep his ground. He pretended to be following the ball with his eyes; but every moment they were glancing aside at George. One of the competitors chanced to say rashly, in the moment of exultation,

The Private Memoirs and Confessions of a Justified Sinner

"That's a d—d fine blow, George!" On which the intruder took up the word, as characteristic of the competitors, and repeated it every stroke that was given, making such a ludicrous use of it that several of the onlookers were compelled to laugh immoderately; but the players were terribly nettled at it, as he really contrived, by dint of sliding in some canonical terms, to render the competitors and their game ridiculous.

But matters at length came to a crisis that put them beyond sport. George, in flying backward to gain the point at which the ball was going to light, came inadvertently so rudely in contact with this obstreperous interloper that he not only overthrew him, but also got a grievous fall over his legs; and, as he arose, the other made a spurn at him with his foot, which, if it had hit to its aim, would undoubtedly have finished the course of the young laird of Dalcastle and Balgrennan. George, being irritated beyond measure, as may well be conceived, especially at the deadly stroke aimed at him, struck the assailant with his racket, rather slightly, but so that his mouth and nose gushed out blood; and, at the same time, he said, turning to his cronies: "Does any of you know who the infernal puppy is?"

"Do you know, Sir?" said one of the onlookers, a stranger, "the gentleman is your own brother, Sir—Mr. Robert Wringhim Colwan!"

"No, not Colwan, Sir," said Robert, putting his hands in his pockets, and setting himself still farther forward than before, "not a Colwan, Sir; henceforth I disclaim the name."

"No, certainly not," repeated George. "My mother's son you may be—but not a Colwan! There you are right." Then, turning around to his informer, he said: "Mercy be about us, Sir! Is this the crazy minister's son from Glasgow?"

This question was put in the irritation of the moment, but it was too rude, and far too out of place, and no one deigned any answer to it. He felt the reproof, and felt it deeply; seeming anxious for some opportunity to make an acknowledgment, or some reparation.

In the meantime, young Wringhim was an object to all of the uttermost disgust. The blood flowing from his mouth and nose he took no pains to stem, neither did he so much as wipe it away; so that it spread over all his cheeks, and breast, even off at his toes. In that state did he take up his station in the middle of the competitors; and he did not now keep his place, but ran about, impeding everyone who attempted to make at the ball.

They loaded him with execrations, but it availed nothing; he seemed courting persecution and buffetings, keeping steadfastly to his old joke of damnation, and marring the game so completely that, in spite of every effort on the part of the players, he forced them to stop their game and give it up. He was such a rueful-looking object, covered with blood, that none of them had the heart to kick him, although it appeared the only thing he wanted; and, as for George, he said not another word to him, either in anger or reproof.

When the game was fairly given up, and the party were washing their hands in the stone fount, some of them besought Robert Wringhim to wash himself; but he mocked at them, and said he was much better as he was. George, at length, came forward abashedly towards him, and said: "I have been greatly to blame, Robert, and am very sorry for what I have done. But, in the first instance, I erred through ignorance, not knowing you were my brother, which you certainly are; and, in the second, through a momentary irritation, for which I am ashamed. I pray you, therefore, to pardon me, and give me your hand."

As he said this, he held out his hand towards his polluted brother; but the froward predestinarian took not his from his breeches pocket, but lifting his foot, he gave his brother's hand a kick. "I'll give you what will suit such a hand better than mine," said he, with a sneer. And then, turning lightly about, he added: "Are there to be no more of these d—-d fine blows, gentlemen? For shame, to give up such a profitable and edifying game!"

"This is too bad," said George. "But, since it is thus, I have the less to regret." And, having made this general remark, he took no more note of the uncouth aggressor. But the persecution of the latter terminated not on the play-ground: he ranked up among them, bloody and disgusting as he was, and, keeping close by his brother's side, he marched along with the party all the way to the Black Bull. Before they got there, a great number of boys and idle people had surrounded them, hooting and incommoding them exceedingly, so that they were glad to get into the inn; and the unaccountable monster actually tried to get in alongst with them, to make one of the party at dinner. But the innkeeper and his men, getting the hint, by force prevented him from entering, although he attempted it again and again, both by telling lies and offering a bribe. Finding he could not prevail, he set to exciting the mob at the door to acts of violence; in which he had like to have succeeded. The landlord had no other shift, at last, but to send privately for two officers, and have him carried to the guard-house; and the hilarity and joy of the party of young gentlemen, for the evening, was quite spoiled by the inauspicious termination of their game.

The Rev. Robert Wringhim was now to send for, to release his beloved ward. The messenger found him at table, with a number of the leaders of the Whig faction, the Marquis of Annandale being in the chair; and, the prisoner's note being produced, Wringhim read it aloud, accompanying it with some explanatory remarks. The circumstances of the case being thus magnified and distorted, it excited the utmost abhorrence, both of the deed and the perpetrators, among the assembled faction. They declaimed against the act as an unnatural attempt on the character, and even the life, of an unfortunate brother, who had been expelled from his father's house. And, as party spirit was the order of the day, an attempt was made to lay the burden of it to that account. In short, the young culprit got some of the best blood of the land to enter as his securities, and was set at liberty. But, when Wringhim perceived the plight that he was in, he took him, as he was, and presented him to his honourable patrons. This raised the indignation against the young laird and his associates a thousand-fold, which actually roused the party to temporary madness. They were, perhaps, a little excited by the wine and spirits they had swallowed; else a casual quarrel between two young men, at tennis, could not have driven them to such extremes. But certain it is that, from one at first arising to address the party on the atrocity of the offence, both in a moral and political point of view, on a sudden there were six on their feet, at the same time, expatiating on it; and, in a very short time thereafter, everyone in the room was up talking with the utmost vociferation, all on the same subject, and all taking the same side in the debate.

In the midst of this confusion, someone or other issued from the house, which was at the back of the Canongate, calling out: "A plot, a plot! Treason, treason! Down with the bloody incendiaries at the Black Bull!"

The concourse of people that were assembled in Edinburgh at that time was prodigious; and, as they were all actuated by political motives, they wanted only a ready-blown coal to set the mountain on fire. The evening being fine, and the streets thronged, the cry ran from mouth to mouth through the whole city. More than that, the mob that had of late been gathered to the door of the Black Bull had, by degrees, dispersed; but, they being young men, and idle vagrants, they had only spread themselves over the rest of the street to lounge in search of further amusement: consequently, a word was sufficient to send them back to their late rendezvous, where they had previously witnessed something they did not much approve of.

The Private Memoirs and Confessions of a Justified Sinner

The master of the tavern was astonished at seeing the mob again assembling; and that with such hurry and noise. But, his inmates being all of the highest respectability, he judged himself sure of protection, or at least of indemnity. He had two large parties in his house at the time; the largest of which was of the Revolutionist faction. The other consisted of our young Tennis-players, and their associates, who were all of the Jacobite order; or, at all events, leaned to the Episcopal side. The largest party were in a front room; and the attack of the mob fell first on their windows, though rather with fear and caution. Jingle went one pane; then a loud hurrah; and that again was followed by a number of voices, endeavouring to restrain the indignation from venting itself in destroying the windows, and to turn it on the inmates. The Whigs, calling the landlord, inquired what the assault meant: he cunningly answered that he suspected it was some of the youths of the Cavalier, or High-Church party, exciting the mob against them. The party consisted mostly of young gentlemen, by that time in a key to engage in any row; and, at all events, to suffer nothing from the other party, against whom their passions were mightily inflamed.

The landlord, therefore, had no sooner given them the spirit-rousing intelligence than everyone, as by instinct, swore his own natural oath, and grasped his own natural weapon. A few of those of the highest rank were armed with swords, which they boldly drew; those of the subordinate orders immediately flew to such weapons as the room, kitchen, and scullery afforded — such as tongs, pokers, spits, racks, and shovels; and breathing vengeance on the prelatic party, the children of Antichrist and the heirs of d—n—t—n! the barterers of the liberties of their country, and betrayers of the most sacred trust — thus elevated, and thus armed, in the cause of right, justice, and liberty, our heroes rushed to the street, and attacked the mob with such violence that they broke the mass in a moment, and dispersed their thousands like chaff before the wind. The other party of young Jacobites, who sat in a room farther from the front, and were those against whom the fury of the mob was meant to have been directed, knew nothing of this second uproar, till the noise of the sally made by the Whigs assailed their ears; being then informed that the mob had attacked the house on account of the treatment they themselves had given to a young gentleman of the adverse faction, and that another jovial party had issued from the house in their defence, and was now engaged in an unequal combat, the sparks likewise flew, to the field to back their defenders with all their prowess, without troubling their heads about who they were.

A mob is like a spring tide in an eastern storm, that retires only to return with more overwhelming fury. The crowd was taken by surprise when such a strong and well-armed party issued from the house with so great fury, laying all prostrate that came in their way. Those who were next to the door, and were, of course, the first whom the imminent danger assailed, rushed backwards among the crowd with their whole force. The Black Bull standing in a small square half-way between the High Street and the Cowgate, and the entrance to it being by two closes, into these the pressure outwards was simultaneous, and thousands were moved to an involuntary flight, they knew not why.

But the High Street of Edinburgh, which they soon reached, is a dangerous place in which to make an open attack upon a mob. And it appears that the entrances to the tavern had been somewhere near to the Cross, on the south side of the street; for the crowd fled with great expedition, both to the east and west, and the conquerors, separating themselves as chance directed, pursued impetuously, wounding and maiming as they flew. But it so chanced that, before either of the wings had followed the flying squadrons of their enemies for the space of a hundred yards each way, the devil an enemy they had to pursue! the multitude had vanished like so many thousands of phantoms! What could our heroes do? Why, they faced about to return towards their citadel, the Black Bull. But that feat was not so easily, nor so readily accomplished as they divined. The unnumbered alleys on each side of the street had swallowed up the multitude in a few seconds; but from these they were busy reconnoitring; and perceiving the deficiency in the number of their assailants, the rush from both sides of the street was as rapid, and as wonderful, as the disappearance of the crowd had been a few minutes before. Each close vomited out its levies, and these better armed with missiles than when they sought it for a temporary retreat. Woe then to our two columns of victorious Whigs! The mob actually closed around them as they would have swallowed them up; and, in the meanwhile, shower after shower of the most abominable weapons of offence were rained in upon them. If the gentlemen were irritated before, this inflamed them still further; but their danger was now so apparent they could not shut their eyes on it; therefore, both parties, as if actuated by the same spirit, made a desperate effort to join, and the greater part effected it; but some were knocked down, and others were separated from their friends, and blithe to become silent members of the mob.

The Private Memoirs and Confessions of a Justified Sinner

The battle now raged immediately in front of the closes leading to the Black Bull; the small body of Whig gentlemen was hardly bested, and it is likely would have been overcome and trampled down every man, had they not been then and there joined by the young Cavaliers; who, fresh to arms, broke from the wynd, opened the head of the passage, laid about them manfully, and thus kept up the spirits of the exasperated Whigs, who were the men in fact that wrought the most deray among the populace.

The town-guard was now on the alert; and two companies of the Cameronian Regiment, with the Hon. Captain Douglas, rushed down from the Castle to the scene of action; but, for all the noise and hubbub that these caused in the street, the combat had become so close and inveterate that numbers of both sides were taken prisoners fighting hand to hand, and could scarcely be separated when the guardsmen and soldiers had them by the necks.

Great was the alarm and confusion that night in Edinburgh; for everyone concluded that it was a party scuffle, and, the two parties being so equal in power, the most serious consequences were anticipated. The agitation was so prevailing that every party in town, great and small, was broken up; and the lord-commissioner thought proper to go to the Council Chamber himself, even at that late hour, accompanied by the sheriffs of Edinburgh and Linlithgow, with sundry noblemen besides, in order to learn something of the origin of the affray.

For a long time the court was completely puzzled. Every gentleman brought in exclaimed against the treatment he had received, in most bitter terms, blaming a mob set on him and his friends by the adverse party, and matters looked extremely ill until at length they began to perceive that they were examining gentlemen of both parties, and that they had been doing so from the beginning, almost alternately, so equally had the prisoners been taken from both parties. Finally, it turned out that a few gentlemen, two-thirds of whom were strenuous Whigs themselves, had joined in mauling the whole Whig population of Edinburgh. The investigation disclosed nothing the effect of which was not ludicrous; and the Duke of Queensberry, whose aim was at that time to conciliate the two factions, tried all that he could to turn the whole fracas into a joke—an unlucky frolic, where no ill was meant on either side, and which yet had been productive of a great deal.

The greater part of the people went home satisfied; but not so the Rev. Robert Wringhim. He did all that he could to

The Private Memoirs and Confessions of a Justified Sinner

inflame both judges and populace against the young Cavaliers, especially against the young Laird of Dalcastle, whom he represented as an incendiary, set on by an unnatural parent to slander his mother, and make away with a hapless and only brother; and, in truth, that declaimer against all human merit had that sort of powerful, homely, and bitter eloquence which seldom missed affecting his hearers: the consequence at that time was that he made the unfortunate affair between the two brothers appear in extremely bad colours, and the populace retired to their homes impressed with no very favourable opinion of either the Laird of Dalcastle or his son George, neither of whom were there present to speak for themselves.

As for Wringhim himself, he went home to his lodgings, filled with gall and with spite against the young laird, whom he was made to believe the aggressor, and that intentionally. But most of all he was filled with indignation against the father, whom he held in abhorrence at all times, and blamed solely for this unmannerly attack made on his favourite ward, namesake, and adopted son; and for the public imputation of a crime to his own reverence in calling the lad his son, and thus charging him with a sin against which he was well known to have levelled all the arrows of church censure with unsparing might.

But, filled as his heart was with some portion of these bad feelings, to which all flesh is subject, he kept, nevertheless, the fear of the Lord always before his eyes so far as never to omit any of the external duties of religion, and farther than that man hath no power to pry. He lodged with the family of a Mr. Miller, whose lady was originally from Glasgow, and had been a hearer and, of course, a great admirer of Mr. Wringhim. In that family he made public worship every evening; and that night, in his petitions at a throne of grace, he prayed for so many vials of wrath to be poured on the head of some particular sinner that the hearers trembled, and stopped their ears. But that he might not proceed with so violent a measure, amounting to excommunication, without due scripture warrant, he began the exercise of the evening by singing the following verses, which it is a pity should ever have been admitted into a Christian psalmody, being so adverse to all its mild and benevolent principles:

Set thou the wicked over him,

And upon his right hand

Give thou his greatest enemy,

Even Satan, leave to stand.

> And, when by thee he shall be judged,
> Let him remembered be;
> And let his prayer be turned to sin
> When he shall call on thee.
> Few be his days; and in his room
> His charge another take;
> His children let be fatherless;
> His wife a widow make:
> Let God his father's wickedness
> Still to remembrance call;
> And never let his mother's sin
> Be blotted out at all.
> As he in cursing pleasure took
> So let it to him fall;
> As he delighted not to bless,
> So bless him not at all.
> As cursing he like clothes put on,
> Into his bowels so,
> Like water, and into his bones
> Like oil, down let it go.

Young Wringhim only knew the full purport of this spiritual song; and went to his bed better satisfied than ever that his father and brother were castaways, reprobates, aliens from the Church and the true faith, and cursed in time and eternity.

The next day George and his companions met as usual—all who were not seriously wounded of them. But, as they strolled about the city, the rancorous eye and the finger of scorn was pointed against them. None of them was at first aware of the reason; but it threw a damp over their spirits and enjoyments, which they could not master. They went to take a forenoon game at their old play of tennis, not on a match, but by way of improving themselves; but they had not well taken their places till young Wringhim appeared in his old station, at his brother's right hand, with looks more demure and determined than ever. His lips were primmed so close that his mouth was hardly discernible, and his dark deep eye flashed gleams of holy indignation on the godless set, but particularly on his brother. His presence acted as a mildew on all social intercourse or enjoyment; the game was marred, and ended ere ever it was well begun. There were whisperings apart—the party separated, and, in order to shake off the blighting influence of this dogged persecutor, they entered sundry houses of their acquaintances, with an understanding that they were to meet on the Links for a game at cricket.

They did so; and, stripping off part of their clothes, they began that violent and spirited game. They had not played five minutes till Wringhim was stalking in the midst of them, and totally impeding the play. A cry arose from all corners of: "Oh, this will never do. Kick him out of the play-ground! Knock down the scoundrel; or bind him, and let him lie in peace."

"By no means," cried George. "It is evident he wants nothing else. Pray do not humour him so much as to touch him with either foot or finger." Then, turning to a friend, he said in a whisper: "Speak to him, Gordon; he surely will not refuse to let us have the ground to ourselves, if you request it of him."

Gordon went up to him, and requested of him, civilly, but ardently, "to retire to a certain distance, else none of them could or would be answerable, however sore he might be hurt."

He turned disdainfully on his heel, uttered a kind of pulpit hem! and then added, "I will take my chance of that; hurt me, any of you, at your peril."

The young gentlemen smiled, through spite and disdain of the dogged animal. Gordon followed him up, and tried to remonstrate with him; but he let him know that "it was his pleasure to be there at that time; and, unless he could demonstrate to him what superior right he and his party had to that ground, in preference to him, and to the exclusion of all others, he was determined to assert his right, and the rights of his fellow-citizens, by keeping possession of whatsoever part of that common field he chose."

"You are no gentleman, Sir," said Gordon.

"Are you one, Sir?" said the other.

"Yes, Sir. I will let you know that I am, by G—!"

The Private Memoirs and Confessions of a Justified Sinner

"Then, thanks be to Him whose name you have profaned, I am none. If one of the party be a gentleman, I do hope in God am not!"

It was now apparent to them all that he was courting obloquy and manual chastisement from their hands, if by any means he could provoke them to the deed; and, apprehensive that he had some sinister and deep-laid design in hunting after such a singular favour, they wisely restrained one another from inflicting the punishment that each of them yearned to bestow, personally, and which he so well deserved.

But the unpopularity of the younger George Colwan could no longer be concealed from his associates. It was manifested wherever the populace were assembled; and his young and intimate friend, Adam Gordon, was obliged to warn him of the circumstance that he might not be surprised at the gentlemen of their acquaintance withdrawing themselves from his society, as they could not be seen with him without being insulted. George thanked him; and it was agreed between them that the former should keep himself retired during the daytime while he remained in Edinburgh, and that at night they should meet together, along with such of their companions as were disengaged.

George found it every day more and more necessary to adhere to this system of seclusion; for it was not alone the hisses of the boys and populace that pursued him—a fiend of more malignant aspect was ever at his elbow, in the form of his brother. To whatever place of amusement he betook himself, and however well he concealed his intentions of going there from all flesh living, there was his brother Wringhim also, and always within a few yards of him, generally about the same distance, and ever and anon darting looks at him that chilled his very soul. They were looks that cannot be described; but they were felt piercing to the bosom's deepest core. They affected even the onlookers in a very particular manner, for all whose eyes caught a glimpse of these hideous glances followed them to the object towards which they were darted: the gentlemanly and mild demeanour of that object generally calmed their startled apprehensions; for no one ever yet noted the glances of the young man's eye, in the black coat, at the face of his brother, who did not at first manifest strong symptoms of alarm.

George became utterly confounded; not only at the import of this persecution, but how in the world it came to pass that this unaccountable being knew all his motions, and every intention of his heart, as it were intuitively. On consulting his own

255

previous feelings and resolutions, he found that the circumstances of his going to such and such a place were often the most casual incidents in nature—the caprice of a moment had carried him there, and yet he had never sat or stood many minutes till there was the selfsame being, always in the same position with regard to himself, as regularly as the shadow is cast from the substance, or the ray of light from the opposing denser medium.

    For instance, he remembered one day of setting out with the intention of going to attend divine worship in the High Church, and when, within a short space of its door, he was overtaken by young Kilpatrick of Closeburn, who was bound to the Grey-Friars to see his sweetheart, as he said: "and if you will go with me, Colwan," said he, "I will let you see her too, and then you will be just as far forward as I am."

    George assented at once, and went; and, after taking his seat, he leaned his head forwards on the pew to repeat over to himself a short ejaculatory prayer, as had always been his custom on entering the house of God. When he had done, he lifted his eye naturally towards that point on his right hand where the fierce apparition of his brother had been wont to meet his view: there he was, in the same habit, form, demeanour, and precise point of distance, as usual! George again laid down his head, and his mind was so astounded that he had nearly fallen into a swoon. He tried shortly after to muster up courage to look at the speaker, at the congregation, and at Captain Kilpatrick's sweetheart in particular; but the fiendish glances of the young man in the black clothes were too appalling to be withstood—his eye caught them whether he was looking that way or not: at length his courage was fairly mastered, and he was obliged to look down during the remainder of the service.

    By night or by day it was the same. In the gallery of the Parliament House, in the boxes of the play-house, in the church, in the assembly, in the streets, suburbs, and the fields; and every day, and every hour, from the first rencounter of the two, the attendance became more and more constant, more inexplicable, and altogether more alarming and insufferable, until at last George was fairly driven from society, and forced to spend his days in his and his father's lodgings with closed doors. Even there, he was constantly harassed with the idea that, the next time he lifted his eyes, he would to a certainty see that face, the most repulsive to all his feelings of aught the earth contained. The attendance of that brother was now become like the attendance of a demon on some devoted being that had sold himself to destruction; his approaches as undiscerned, and his looks as fraught with hideous malignity. It was seldom that he saw him either following him in the streets, or entering any house or church after him; he only appeared in his place, George wist not how, or whence; and, having sped so ill in his first friendly approaches, he had never spoken to his equivocal attendant a second time.

It came at length into George's head, as he was pondering, by himself, on the circumstances of this extraordinary attendance, that perhaps his brother had relented, and, though of so sullen and unaccommodating a temper that he would not acknowledge it, or beg a reconciliation, it might be for that very purpose that he followed his steps night and day in that extraordinary manner. "I cannot for my life see for what other purpose it can be," thought he. "He never offers to attempt my life; nor dares he, if he had the inclination; therefore, although his manner is peculiarly repulsive to me, I shall not have my mind burdened with the reflection that my own mother's son yearned for a reconciliation with me and was repulsed by my haughty and insolent behaviour. The next time he comes to my hand, I am resolved that I will accost him as one brother ought to address another, whatever it may cost me; and, if I am still flouted with disdain, then shall the blame rest with him."

After this generous resolution, it was a good while before his gratuitous attendant appeared at his side again; and George began to think that his visits were discontinued. The hope was a relief that could not be calculated; but still George had a feeling that it was too supreme to last. His enemy had been too pertinacious to abandon his design, whatever it was. He, however, began to indulge in a little more liberty, and for several days he enjoyed it with impunity.

George was, from infancy, of a stirring active disposition and could not endure confinement; and, having been of late much restrained in his youthful exercises by this singular persecutor, he grew uneasy under such restraint, and, one morning, chancing to awaken very early, he arose to make an excursion to the top of Arthur's Seat, to breathe the breeze of the dawning, and see the sun arise out of the eastern ocean. The morning was calm and serene; and as he walked down the south back of the Canongate, towards the Palace, the haze was so close around him that he could not see the houses on the opposite side of the way. As he passed the Lord-Commissioner's house, the guards were in attendance, who cautioned him not to go by the Palace, as all the gates would be shut and guarded for an hour to come, on which he went by the back of St. Anthony's gardens, and found his way into that little romantic glade adjoining to the saint's chapel and well. He was still involved in a blue haze, like a dense smoke, but yet in the midst of it the respiration was the most refreshing and delicious. The grass and the flowers were loaden with dew; and, on taking off his hat to wipe his forehead, he perceived that the black glossy fur of which his chaperon was wrought was all covered with a tissue of the most delicate silver—a fairy web, composed of little spheres, so minute that no eye could discern any of them; yet there they were shining in lovely millions. Afraid of defacing so beautiful and so delicate a garnish, he replaced his hat with the greatest caution, and went on his way light of heart.

As he approached the swire at the head of the dell—that little delightful verge from which in one moment the eastern limits and shores of Lothian arise on the view—as he approached it, I say, and a little space from the height, he beheld, to his astonishment, a bright halo in the cloud of haze, that rose in a semicircle over his head like a pale rainbow. He was struck motionless at the view of the lovely vision; for it so chanced that he had never seen the same appearance before, though common at early morn. But he soon perceived the cause of the phenomenon, and that it proceeded from the rays of the sun from a pure unclouded morning sky striking upon this dense vapour which refracted them. But, the better all the works of nature are understood, the more they will be ever admired. That was a scene that would have entranced the man of science with delight, but which the uninitiated and sordid man would have regarded less than the mole rearing up his hill in silence and in darkness.

George did admire this halo of glory, which still grew wider, and less defined, as he approached the surface, of the cloud. But, to his utter amazement and supreme delight, he found, on reaching the top of Arthur's Seat, that this sublunary rainbow, this terrestrial glory, was spread in its most vivid hues beneath his feet. Still he could not perceive the body of the sun, although the light behind him was dazzling; but the cloud of haze lying dense in that deep dell that separates the hill from the rocks of Salisbury, and the dull shadow of the hill mingling with that cloud made the dell a pit of darkness. On that shadowy cloud was the lovely rainbow formed, spreading itself on a horizontal plain, and having a slight and brilliant shade of all the colours of the heavenly bow, but all of them paler and less defined. But this terrestrial phenomenon of the early morn cannot be better delineated than by the name given of it by the shepherd boys, "The little wee ghost of the rainbow."

Such was the description of the morning, and the wild shades of the hill, that George gave to his father and Mr. Adam Gordon that same day on which he had witnessed them; and it is necessary that the reader should comprehend something of their nature to understand what follows.

He seated himself on the pinnacle of the rocky precipice, a little within the top of the hill to the westward, and, with a light and buoyant heart, viewed the beauties of the morning, and inhaled its salubrious breeze. "Here," thought he, "I can converse with nature without disturbance, and without being intruded on by any appalling or obnoxious visitor." The idea of his brother's dark and malevolent looks coming at that moment across his mind, he turned his eyes instinctively to the right, to the point where that unwelcome guest was wont to make his appearance. Gracious Heaven! What an apparition was there presented to his view! He saw, delineated in the cloud, the shoulders, arms, and features of a human being of the most dreadful aspect. The face was the face of his brother, but dilated to twenty times the natural size. Its dark eyes gleamed on him through the mist, while every furrow of its hideous brow frowned deep as the ravines on the brow of the hill. George started, and his hair stood up in bristles as he gazed on this horrible monster. He saw every feature and every line of the face distinctly as it gazed on him with an intensity that was hardly brookable. Its eyes were fixed on him, in the same manner as those of some carnivorous animal fixed on its prey; and yet there was fear and trembling in these unearthly features, as plainly depicted as murderous malice. The giant apparition seemed sometimes to be cowering down as in terror, so that nothing but his brow and eyes were seen; still these never turned one moment from their object—again it rose imperceptively up, and began to approach with great caution; and, as it neared, the dimensions of its form lessened, still continuing, however, far above the natural size.

George conceived it to be a spirit. He could conceive it to be nothing else; and he took it for some horrid demon by which he was haunted, that had assumed the features of his brother in every lineament, but, in taking on itself the human form, had miscalculated dreadfully on the size, and presented itself thus to him in a blown-up, dilated frame of embodied air, exhaled from the caverns of death or the regions of devouring fire. He was further confirmed in the belief that it was a malignant spirit on perceiving that it approached him across the front of a precipice, where there was not footing for thing of mortal frame. Still, what with terror and astonishment, he continued riveted to the spot, till it approached, as he deemed, to within two yards of him; and then, perceiving that it was setting itself to make a violent spring on him, he started to his feet and fled distractedly in the opposite direction, keeping his eye cast behind him lest he had been seized in that dangerous place. But the very first bolt that he made in his flight he came in contact with a real body of flesh and blood, and that with such violence that both went down among some scragged rocks, and George rolled over the other. The being called out "Murder"; and, rising, fled precipitately. George then perceived that it was his brother; and being confounded between the shadow and the substance, he knew not what he was doing or what he had done; and, there being only one natural way of retreat from the brink of the rock, he likewise arose and pursued the affrighted culprit with all his speed towards the top of the hill. Wringhim was braying out, "Murder! murder!" at which George, being disgusted, and his spirits all in a ferment from some hurried idea of intended harm, the moment he came up with the craven he seized him rudely by the shoulder, and clapped his hand on his mouth. "Murder, you beast!" said he; "what do you mean by roaring out murder in that way? Who the devil is murdering you, or offering to murder you?"

Wringhim forced his mouth from under his brother's hand, and roared with redoubled energy: "Eh! Egh! Murder! murder!" etc. George had felt resolute to put down this shocking alarm, lest someone might hear it and fly to the spot, or draw inferences widely different from the truth; and, perceiving the terror of this elect youth to be so great that expostulation was vain, he seized him by the mouth and nose with his left hand so strenuously that he sank his fingers into his cheeks. But, the poltroon still attempting to bray out, George gave him such a stunning blow with his fist on the left temple that he crumbled, as it were, to the ground, but more from the effects of terror than those of the blow. His nose, however, again gushed out blood, a system of defence which seemed as natural to him as that resorted to by the race of stinkards. He then raised himself on his knees and hams, and raising up his ghastly face, while the blood streamed over both ears, he besought his life of his brother, in the most abject whining manner, gaping and blubbering most piteously.

"Tell me then, Sir," said George, resolved to make the most of the wretch's terror—"tell me for what purpose it is that you haunt my steps? Tell me plainly, and instantly, else I will throw you from the verge of that precipice."

"Oh, I will never do it again! I will never do it again! Spare my life, dear, good brother! Spare my life! Sure I never did you any hurt."

"Swear to me, then, by the God that made you, that you will never henceforth follow after me to torment me with your hellish threatening looks; swear that you will never again come into my presence without being invited. Will you take an oath to this effect?"

"Oh yes! I will, I will!"

"But this is not all: you must tell me for what purpose you sought me out here this morning?"

"Oh, brother! For nothing but your good. I had nothing at heart but your unspeakable profit, and great and endless good."

"So, then, you indeed knew that I was here?"

"I was told so by a friend, but I did not believe him; a—a—at least I did not know that it was true till I saw you."

"Tell me this one thing, then, Robert, and all shall be forgotten and forgiven. Who was that friend?"

"You do not know him."

"How then does he know me?"

"I cannot tell."

"Was he here present with you to-day?"

"Yes; he was not far distant. He came to this hill with me."

"Where then is he now?"

"I canot tell."

"Then, wretch, confess that the devil was that friend who told you I was here, and who came here with you. None else could possibly know of my being here."

"Ah! how little you know of him! Would you argue that there is neither man nor spirit endowed with so much foresight as to deduce natural conclusions from previous actions and incidents but the devil? Alas, brother! But why should I wonder at such abandoned notions and principles? It was fore-ordained that you should cherish them, and that they should be the ruin of your soul and body, before the world was framed. Be assured of this, however, that I had no aim of seeking you but your good!"

"Well, Robert, I will believe it. I am disposed to be hasty and passionate: it is a fault in my nature; but I never meant, or wished you evil; and God is my witness that I would as soon stretch out my hand to my own life, or my father's, as to yours." At these words, Wringhim uttered a hollow exulting laugh, put his hands in his pockets, and withdrew a space to his accustomed distance. George continued: "And now, once for all, I request that we may exchange forgiveness, and that we may part and remain friends."

"Would such a thing be expedient, think you? Or consistent with the glory of God? I doubt it."

"I can think of nothing that would be more so. Is it not consistent with every precept of the Gospel? Come, brother, say that our reconciliation is complete."

"Oh yes, certainly! I tell you, brother, according to the flesh: it is just as complete as the lark's is with the adder, no more so, nor ever can. Reconciled, forsooth! To what would I be reconciled?"

As he said this, he strode indignantly away. From the moment that he heard his life was safe, he assumed his former insolence and revengeful looks—and never were they more dreadful than on parting with his brother that morning on the top of the hill. "Well, go thy way," said George; "some would despise, but I pity thee. If thou art not a limb of Satan, I never saw one."

The sun had now dispelled the vapours; and, the morning being lovely beyond description, George sat himself down on the top of the hill, and pondered deeply on the unaccountable incident that had befallen to him that morning. He could in nowise comprehend it; but, taking it with other previous circumstances, he could not get quit of a conviction that he was haunted by some evil genius in the shape of his brother, as well as by that dark and mysterious wretch himself. In no other way could he account for the apparition he saw that morning on the face of the rock, nor for several sudden appearances of the same being, in places where there was no possibility of any foreknowledge that he himself was to be there, and as little that the same being, if he were flesh and blood like other men, could always start up in the same position with regard to him. He

The Private Memoirs and Confessions of a Justified Sinner

determined, therefore, on reaching home, to relate all that had happened, from beginning to end, to his father, asking his counsel and his assistance, although he knew full well that his father was not the fittest man in the world to solve such a problem. He was now involved in party politics, over head and ears; and, moreover, he could never hear the names of either of the Wringhims mentioned without getting into a quandary of disgust and anger; and all that he would deign to say of them was, to call them by all the opprobrious names he could invent.

It turned out as the young man from the first suggested: old Dalcastle would listen to nothing concerning them with any patience. George complained that his brother harassed him with his presence at all times, and in all places. Old Dal asked why he did not kick the dog out of his presence whenever he felt him disagreeable? George said he seemed to have some demon for a familiar. Dal answered that he did not wonder a bit at that, for the young spark was the third in a direct line who had all been children of adultery; and it was well known that all such were born half-deils themselves, and nothing was more likely than that they should hold intercourse with their fellows. In the same style did he sympathize with all his son's late sufferings and perplexities.

In Mr. Adam Gordon, however, George found a friend who entered into all his feelings, and had seen and known everything about the matter. He tried to convince him that at all events there could be nothing supernatural in the circumstances; and that the vision he had seen on the rock, among the thick mist, was the shadow of his brother approaching behind him. George could not swallow this, for he had seen his own shadow on the cloud, and, instead of approaching to aught like his own figure, he perceived nothing but a halo of glory round a point of the cloud that was whiter and purer than the rest. Gordon said, if he would go with him to a mountain of his father's, which he named, in Aberdeenshire, he would show him a giant spirit of the same dimensions, any morning at the rising of the sun, provided he shone on that spot. This statement excited George's curiosity exceedingly; and, being disgusted with some things about Edinburgh, and glad to get out of the way, he consented to go with Gordon to the Highlands for a space. The day was accordingly set for their departure, the old laird's assent obtained, and the two young sparks parted in a state of great impatience for their excursion.

One of them found out another engagement, however, the instant after this last was determined on. Young Wringhim went off the hill that morning, and home to his upright guardian again without washing the blood from his face and neck; and there he told a most woeful story indeed: how he had gone out to take a morning's walk on the hill, where he had encountered with his reprobate brother among the mist, who had knocked him down and very near murdered him; threatening dreadfully, and with horrid oaths, to throw him from the top of the cliff.

The wrath of the great divine was kindled beyond measure. He cursed the aggressor in the name of the Most High; and bound himself, by an oath, to cause that wicked one's transgressions return upon his own head sevenfold. But, before he engaged further in the business of vengeance, he kneeled with his adopted son, and committed the whole cause unto the Lord, whom he addressed as one coming breathing burning coals of juniper, and casting his lightnings before him, to destroy and root out all who had moved hand or tongue against the children of the promise. Thus did he arise confirmed, and go forth to certain conquest.

We cannot enter into the detail of the events that now occurred without forestalling a part of the narrative of one who knew all the circumstances — was deeply interested in them, and whose relation is of higher value than anything that can be retailed out of the stores of tradition and old registers; but, his narrative being different from these, it was judged expedient to give the account as thus publicly handed down to us. Suffice it that, before evening, George was apprehended, and lodged in jail, on a criminal charge of an assault and battery, to the shedding of blood, with the intent of committing fratricide. Then was the old laird in great consternation, and blamed himself for treating the thing so lightly, which seemed to have been gone about, from the beginning, so systematically, and with an intent which the villains were now going to realize, namely, to get the young laird disposed of; and then his brother, in spite of the old gentleman's teeth, would be laird himself.

Old Dal now set his whole interest to work among the noblemen and lawyers of his party. His son's case looked exceedingly ill, owing to the former assault before witnesses, and the unbecoming expressions made use of by him on that occasion, as well as from the present assault, which George did not deny, and for which no moving cause or motive could be made to appear.

On his first declaration before the sheriff, matters looked no better: but then the sheriff was a Whig. It is well known how differently the people of the present day, in Scotland, view the cases of their own party-men and those of opposite political principles. But this day is nothing to that in such matters, although, God knows, they are still sometimes barefaced enough. It appeared, from all the witnesses in the first case, that the complainant was the first aggressor—that he refused to stand out of the way, though apprised of his danger; and, when his brother came against him inadvertently, he had aimed a blow at him with his foot, which, if it had taken effect, would have killed him. But as to the story of the apparition in fair daylight—the flying from the face of it—the running foul of his brother pursuing him, and knocking him down, why the judge smiled at the relation, and saying: "It was a very extraordinary story," he remanded George to prison, leaving the matter to the High Court of Justiciary.

When the case came before that court, matters took a different turn. The constant and sullen attendance of the one brother upon the other excited suspicions; and these were in some manner confirmed when the guards at Queensberry House deported that the prisoner went by them on his way to the hill that morning, about twenty minutes before the complainant, and, when the latter passed, he asked if such a young man had passed before him, describing the prisoner's appearance to them; and that, on being answered in the affirmative, he mended his pace and fell a-running.

The Lord Justice, on hearing this, asked the prisoner if he had any suspicions that his brother had a design on his life.

He answered that all along, from the time of their first unfortunate meeting, his brother had dogged his steps so constantly, and so unaccountably, that he was convinced it was with some intent out of the ordinary course of events; and that if, as his lordship supposed, it was indeed his shadow that he had seen approaching him through the mist, then, from the cowering and cautious manner that it advanced, there was no little doubt that his brother's design had been to push him headlong from the cliff that morning.

A conversation then took place between the judge and the Lord Advocate; and, in the meantime, a bustle was seen in the hall; on which the doors were ordered to be guarded, and, behold, the precious Mr. R. Wringhim was taken into custody, trying to make his escape out of court. Finally it turned out that George was honourably acquitted, and young Wringhim bound over to keep the peace, with heavy penalties and securities.

The Private Memoirs and Confessions of a Justified Sinner

That was a day of high exultation to George and his youthful associates, all of whom abhorred Wringhim; and, the evening being spent in great glee, it was agreed between Mr. Adam Gordon and George that their visit to the Highlands, though thus long delayed, was not to be abandoned; and though they had, through the machinations of an incendiary, lost the season of delight, they would still find plenty of sport in deer-shooting. Accordingly, the day was set a second time for their departure; and, on the day preceding that, all the party were invited by George to dine with him once more at the sign of the Black Bull of Norway. Everyone promised to attend, anticipating nothing but festivity and joy. Alas, what short-sighted improvident creatures we are, all of us; and how often does the evening cup of joy lead to sorrow in the morning!

The day arrived — the party of young noblemen and gentlemen met, and were as happy and jovial as men could be. George was never seen so brilliant, or so full of spirits; and exulting to see so many gallant young chiefs and gentlemen about him, who all gloried in the same principles of loyalty (perhaps this word should have been written disloyalty), he made speeches, gave toasts, and sung songs, all leaning slyly to the same side, until a very late hour. By that time he had pushed the bottle so long and so freely that its fumes had taken possession of every brain to such a degree that they held Dame Reason rather at the staff's end, overbearing all her counsels and expostulations; and it was imprudently proposed by a wild inebriated spark, and carried by a majority of voices, that the whole party should adjourn to a bagnio for the remainder of the night.

They did so; and it appears from what follows that the house, to which they retired must have been somewhere on the opposite side of the street to the Black Bull Inn, a little farther to the eastward. They had not been an hour in that house till some altercation chanced to arise between George Colwan and a Mr. Drummond, the younger son of a nobleman of distinction. It was perfectly casual, and no one thenceforward, to this day, could ever tell what it was about, if it was not about the misunderstanding of some word or term that the one had uttered. However it was, some high words passed between them; these were followed by threats, and, in less than two minutes from the commencement of the quarrel, Drummond left the house in apparent displeasure, hinting to the other that they two should settle that in a more convenient place.

The company looked at one another, for all was over before any of them knew such a thing was begun. "What the devil is

The Private Memoirs and Confessions of a Justified Sinner

the matter?" cried one. "What ails Drummond?" cried another. "Who has he quarrelled with?" asked a third.

"Don't know." — "Can't tell, on my life." — "He has quarrelled with his wine, I suppose, and is going to send it a challenge."

Such were the questions, and such the answers that passed in the jovial party, and the matter was no more thought of.

But in the course of a very short space, about the length which the ideas of the company were the next day at great variance, a sharp rap came to the door. It was opened by a female; but, there being a chain inside, she only saw one side of the person at the door. He appeared to be a young gentleman, in appearance like him who had lately left the house, and asked, in a low whispering voice, "if young Dalcastle was still in the house?" The woman did not know. "If he is," added he, "pray tell him to speak with me for a few minutes." The woman delivered the message before all the party, among whom there were then sundry courteous ladies of notable distinction, and George, on receiving it, instantly rose from the side of one of them, and said, in the hearing of them all, "I will bet a hundred merks that is Drummond." — "Don't go to quarrel with him, George," said one. — "Bring him in with you," said another. George stepped out; the door was again bolted, the chain drawn across, and the inadvertent party, left within, thought no more of the circumstance till the morning, that the report had spread over the city that a young gentleman had been slain, on a little washing-green at the side of the North Loch, and at the very bottom of the close where this thoughtless party had been assembled.

Several of them, on first hearing the report, basted to the dead-room in the Guard-house, where the corpse had been deposited, and soon discovered the body to be that of their friend and late entertainer, George Colwan. Great were the consternation and grief of all concerned, and, in particular, of his old father and Miss Logan; for George had always been the sole hope and darling of both, and the news of the event paralysed them so as to render them incapable of all thought or exertion. The spirit of the old laird was broken by the blow, and he descended at once from a jolly, good-natured and active man to a mere driveller, weeping over the body of his son, kissing his wound, his lips, and his cold brow alternately; denouncing vengeance on his murderers, and lamenting that he himself had not met the cruel doom, so that the hope of his race might have been preserved. In short, finding that all further motive of action and object of concern or of love, here below, were for ever removed from him, he abandoned himself to despair, and threatened to go down to the grave with his son.

But, although he made no attempt to discover the murderers, the arm of justice was not idle; and, it being evident to all that the crime must infallibly be brought home to young Drummond, some of his friends sought him out, and compelled him, sorely against his will, to retire into concealment till the issue of the proof that should be led was made known. At the same time, he denied all knowledge of the incident with a resolution that astonished his intimate friends and relations, who to a man suspected him guilty. His father was not in Scotland, for I think it was said to me that this young man was second son to a John, Duke of Melfort, who lived abroad with the royal family of the Stuarts; but this young gentleman lived with the relations of his mother, one of whom, an uncle, was a Lord of Session: these, having thoroughly effected his concealment, went away, and listened to the evidence; and the examination of every new witness convinced them that their noble young relative was the slayer of his friend.

All the young gentlemen of the party were examined, save Drummond, who, when sent for, could not be found, which circumstance sorely confirmed the suspicions against him in the minds of judges and jurors, friends and enemies; and there is little doubt that the care of his relations in concealing him injured his character and his cause. The young gentlemen of whom the party was composed varied considerably with respect to the quarrel between him and the deceased. Some of them had neither heard nor noted it; others had, but not one of them could tell how it began. Some of them had heard the threat uttered by Drummond on leaving the house, and one only had noted him lay his hand on his sword. Not one of them could swear that it was Drummond who came to the door and desired to speak with the deceased, but the general impression on the minds of them all was to that effect; and one of the women swore that she heard the voice distinctly at the door, and every word that voice pronounced, and at the same time heard the deceased say that it was Drummond's.

On the other hand, there were some evidences on Drummond's part, which Lord Craigie, his uncle, had taken care to collect. He produced the sword which his nephew had worn that night, on which there was neither blood nor blemish; and, above all, he insisted on the evidence of a number of surgeons, who declared that both the wounds which the deceased had received had been given behind. One of these was below the left arm, and a slight one; the other was quite through the body, and both evidently inflicted with the same weapon, a two-edged sword, of the same dimensions as that worn by Drummond.

Upon the whole, there was a division in the court, but a majority decided it. Drummond was pronounced guilty of the murder; outlawed for not appearing, and a high reward offered for his apprehension. It was with the greatest difficulty that he escaped on board of a small trading vessel, which landed him in Holland, and from thence, flying into Germany, he entered into the service of the Emperor Charles VI. Many regretted that he was not taken, and made to suffer the penalty due for such a crime, and the melancholy incident became a pulpit theme over a great part of Scotland, being held up as a proper warning to youth to beware of such haunts of vice and depravity, the nurses of all that is precipitate, immoral, and base, among mankind.

After the funeral of this promising and excellent young man, his father never more held up his head. Miss Logan, with all her art, could not get him to attend to any worldly thing, or to make any settlement whatsoever of his affairs, save making her over a present of what disposable funds he had about him. As to his estates, when they were mentioned to him, he wished them all in the bottom of the sea, and himself along with them. But, whenever she mentioned the circumstance of Thomas Drummond having been the murderer of his son, he shook his head, and once made the remark that "It was all a mistake, a gross and fatal error; but that God, who had permitted such a flagrant deed, would bring it to light in his own time and way." In a few weeks he followed his son to the grave, and the notorious Robert Wringhim took possession of his estates as the lawful son of the late laird, born in wedlock, and under his father's roof. The investiture was celebrated by prayer, singing of psalms, and religious disputation. The late guardian and adopted father, and the mother of the new laird, presided on the grand occasion, making a conspicuous figure in all the work of the day; and, though the youth himself indulged rather more freely in the bottle than he had ever been seen to do before, it was agreed by all present that there had never been a festivity so sanctified within the great hall of Dalcastle. Then, after due thanks returned, they parted rejoicing in spirit; which thanks, by the by, consisted wholly in telling the Almighty what he was; and informing, with very particular precision, what they were who addressed him; for Wringhim's whole system of popular declamation consisted, it seems, in this—to denounce all men and women to destruction, and then hold out hopes to his adherents that they were the chosen few, included in the promises, and who could never fall away. It would appear that this pharisaical doctrine is a very delicious one, and the most grateful of all others to the worst characters.

But the ways of heaven are altogether inscrutable, and soar as far above and beyond the works and the comprehensions of man as the sun, flaming in majesty, is above the tiny boy's evening rocket. It is the controller of Nature alone that can bring light out of darkness, and order out of confusion. Who is he that causeth the mole, from his secret path of darkness, to throw up the gem, the gold, and the precious ore? The same that from the mouths of babes and sucklings can extract the perfection of praise, and who can make the most abject of his creatures instrumental in bringing the most hidden truths to light.

Miss Logan had never lost the thought of her late master's prediction that Heaven would bring to light the truth concerning the untimely death of his son. She perceived that some strange conviction, too horrible for expression, preyed on his mind from the moment that the fatal news reached him to the last of his existence; and, in his last ravings, he uttered some incoherent words about justification by faith alone and absolute and eternal predestination having been the ruin of his house. These, to be sure, were the words of superannuation, and of the last and severest kind of it; but, for all that, they sunk deep into Miss Logan's soul, and at last she began to think with herself: "Is it possible the Wringhims, and the sophisticating wretch who is in conjunction with them, the mother of my late beautiful and amiable young master, can have effected his destruction? If so, I will spend my days, and my little patrimony, in endeavours to rake up and expose the unnatural deed."

In all her outgoings and incomings Mrs. Logan (as she was now styled) never lost sight of this one object. Every new disappointment only whetted her desire to fish up some particulars, concerning it; for she thought so long and so ardently upon it that by degrees it became settled in her mind as a sealed truth. And, as woman is always most jealous of her own sex in such matters, her suspicions were fixed on her greatest enemy, Mrs. Colwan, now the Lady Dowager of Dalcastle. All was wrapt in a chaos of confusion and darkness; but at last, by dint of a thousand sly and secret inquiries, Mrs. Logan found out where Lady Dalcastle had been on the night that the murder happened, and likewise what company she had kept, as well as some of the comers and goers; and she had hopes of having discovered a clue, which, if she could keep hold of the thread, would lead her through darkness to the light of truth.

The Private Memoirs and Confessions of a Justified Sinner

Returning very late one evening from a convocation of family servants, which she had drawn together in order to fish something out of them, her maid having been in attendance on her all the evening, they found, on going home, that the house had been broken and a number of valuable articles stolen therefrom. Mrs. Logan had grown quite heartless before this stroke, having been altogether unsuccessful in her inquiries, and now she began to entertain some resolutions of giving up the fruitless search.

In a few days thereafter, she received intelligence that her clothes and plate were mostly recovered, and that she for one was bound over to prosecute the depredator, provided the articles turned out to be hers, as libelled in the indictment, and as a king's evidence had given out. She was likewise summoned, or requested, I know not which, being ignorant of these matters, to go as far as the town of Peebles in Tweedside, in order to survey these articles on such a day, and make affidavit to their identity before the Sheriff. She went accordingly; but, on entering the town by the North Gate, she was accosted by a poor girl in tattered apparel, who with great earnestness inquired if her name was not Mrs. Logan? On being answered in the affirmative, she said that the unfortunate prisoner in the Tolbooth requested her, as she valued all that was dear to her in life, to go and see her before she appeared in court at the hour of cause, as she (the prisoner) had something of the greatest moment to impart to her. Mrs. Logan's curiosity was excited, and she followed the girl straight to the Tolbooth, who by the way said to her that she would find in the prisoner a woman of superior mind, who had gone through all the vicissitudes of life. "She has been very unfortunate, and I fear very wicked," added the poor thing, "but she is my mother, and God knows, with all her faults and failings, she has never been unkind to me. You, madam, have it in your power to save her; but she has wronged you, and therefore, if you will not do it for her sake, do it for mine, and the God of the fatherless will reward you."

Mrs. Logan answered her with a cast of the head, and a hem! and only remarked, that "the guilty must not always be suffered to escape, or what a world must we be doomed to live in!"

She was admitted to the prison, and found a tall emaciated figure, who appeared to have once possessed a sort of masculine beauty in no ordinary degree, but was now considerably advanced in years. She viewed Mrs. Logan with a stern, steady gaze, as if reading her features as a margin to her intellect; and when she addressed her it was not with that humility, and agonized fervour, which are natural for one in such circumstances to address to another who has the power of her life and death in her hands.

"I am deeply indebted to you for this timely visit, Mrs. Logan," said she. "It is not that I value life, or because I fear death, that I have sent for you so expressly. But the manner of the death that awaits me has something peculiarly revolting in it to a female mind. Good God! when I think of being hung up, a spectacle to a gazing, gaping multitude, with numbers of which I have had intimacies and connections, that would render the moment of parting so hideous, that, believe me, it rends to flinders a soul born for another sphere than that in which it has moved, had not the vile selfishness of a lordly fiend ruined all my prospects and all my hopes. Hear me then; for I do not ask your pity: I only ask of you to look to yourself, and behave with womanly prudence; if you deny this day that these goods are yours, there is no other evidence whatever against my life, and it is safe for the present. For, as for the word of the wretch who has betrayed me, it is of no avail; he has prevaricated so notoriously to save himself. If you deny them, you shall have them all again to the value of a mite, and more to the bargain. If you swear to the identity of them, the process will, one way and another, cost you the half of what they are worth."

"And what security have I for that?" said Mrs. Logan.

"You have none but my word," said the other proudly, "and that never yet was violated. If you cannot take that, I know the worst you can do. But I had forgot—I have a poor helpless child without, waiting and starving about the prison door. Surely it was of her that I wished to speak. This shameful death of mine will leave her in a deplorable state."

"The girl seems to have candour and strong affections," said Mrs. Logan. "I grievously mistake if such a child would not be a thousand times better without such a guardian and director."

"Then will you be so kind as to come to the Grass Market and see me put down?" said the prisoner. "I thought a woman would estimate a woman's and a mother's feelings, when such a dreadful throw was at stake, at least in part. But you are callous, and have never known any feelings but those of subordination to your old unnatural master. Alas, I have no cause of offence! I have wronged you; and justice must take its course. Will you forgive me before we part?"

Mrs. Logan hesitated, for her mind ran on something else.

On which the other subjoined: "No, you will not forgive me, I see. But you will pray to God to forgive me? I know you will do that."

Mrs. Logan heard not this jeer, but, looking at the prisoner with an absent and stupid stare, she said: "Did you know my late master?"

"Ay, that I did, and never for any good," said she. "I knew the old and the young spark both, and was by when the latter was slain."

This careless sentence affected Mrs. Logan in a most peculiar manner. A shower of tears burst from her eyes ere it was done, and, when it was, she appeared like one bereaved of her mind. She first turned one way and then another, as if looking for something she had dropped. She seemed to think she had lost her eyes, instead of her tears, and at length, as by instinct, she tottered close up to the prisoner's face, and, looking wistfully and joyfully in it, said, with breathless earnestness: "Pray, mistress, what is your name?"

"My name is Arabella Calvert," said the other. "Miss, mistress, or widow, as you choose, for I have been all the three, and that not once nor twice only. Ay, and something beyond all these. But, as for you, you have never been anything!"

"Ay, ay! and so you are Bell Calvert? Well, I thought so—I thought so," said Mrs. Logan; and, helping herself to a seat, she came and sat down close by the prisoner's knee. "So you are indeed Bell Calvert, so called once. Well, of all the world you are the woman whom I have longed and travailed the most to see. But you were invisible; a being to be heard of, not seen."

"There have been days, madam," returned she, "when I was to be seen, and when there were few to be seen like me. But since that time there have indeed been days on which I was not to be seen. My crimes have been great, but my sufferings have been greater. So great that neither you nor the world can ever either know or conceive them. I hope they will be taken into account by the Most High. Mine have been crimes of utter desperation. But whom am I speaking to? You had better leave me to myself, mistress."

"Leave you to yourself? That I will be loth to do till you tell me where you were that night my young master was murdered."

"Where the devil would, I was! Will that suffice you? Ah, it was a vile action! A night to be remembered that was! Won't you be going? I want to trust my daughter with a commission."

"No, Mrs. Calvert, you and I part not till you have divulged that mystery to me."

"You must accompany me to the other world, then, for you shall not have it in this."

"If you refuse to answer me, I can have you before a tribunal, where you shall be sifted to the soul."

"Such miserable inanity! What care I for your threatenings of a tribunal? I who must soon stand before my last earthly one? What could the word of such a culprit avail? Or, if it could, where is the judge that could enforce it?"

"Did you not say that there was some mode of accommodating matters on that score?"

"Yes, I prayed you to grant me my life, which is in your power. The saving of it would not have cost you a plack, yet you refused to do it. The taking of it will cost you a great deal, and yet to that purpose you adhere. I can have no parley with such a spirit. I would not have my life in a present from its motions, nor would I exchange courtesies with its possessor."

"Indeed, Mrs. Calvert, since ever we met, I have been so busy thinking about who you might be that I know not what you have been proposing. I believe I meant to do what I could to save you. But, once for all, tell me everything that you know concerning that amiable young gentleman's death, and here is my hand there shall be nothing wanting that I can effect for you."

"No I despise all barter with such mean and selfish curiosity; and, as I believe that passion is stronger with you, than fear with me, we part on equal terms. Do your worst; and my secret shall go to the gallows and the grave with me."

Mrs. Logan was now greatly confounded, and after proffering in vain to concede everything she could ask in exchange, for the particulars relating to the murder, she became the suppliant in her turn. But the unaccountable culprit, exulting in her advantage, laughed her to scorn; and finally, in a paroxysm of pride and impatience, called in the jailor and had her expelled, ordering him in her hearing not to grant her

274

The Private Memoirs and Confessions of a Justified Sinner

admittance a second time, on any pretence.

Mrs. Logan was now hard put to it, and again driven almost to despair. She might have succeeded in the attainment of that she thirsted for most in life so easily had she known the character with which she had to deal. Had she known to have soothed her high and afflicted spirit: but that opportunity was past, and the hour of examination at hand. She once thought of going and claiming her articles, as she at first intended; but then, when she thought again of the Wringhims swaying it at Dalcastle, where she had been wont to hear them held in such contempt, if not abhorrence, and perhaps of holding it by the most diabolical means, she was withheld from marring the only chance that remained of having a glimpse into that mysterious affair.

Finally, she resolved not to answer to her name in the court, rather than to appear and assert a falsehood, which she might be called on to certify by oath. She did so; and heard the Sheriff give orders to the officers to make inquiry for Miss Logan from Edinburgh, at the various places of entertainment in town, and to expedite her arrival in court, as things of great value were in dependence. She also heard the man who had turned king's evidence against the prisoner examined for the second time, and sifted most cunningly. His answers gave anything but satisfaction to the Sheriff, though Mrs. Logan believed them to be mainly truth. But there were a few questions and answers that struck her above all others.

"How long is it since Mrs. Calvert and you became acquainted?"

"About a year and a half."

"State the precise time, if you please; the day, or night, according to your remembrance."

"It was on the morning of the 28th of February, 1705."

"What time of the morning?"

"Perhaps about one."

"So early as that? At what place did you meet then?"

"It was at the foot of one of the north wynds of Edinburgh."

"Was it by appointment that you met?"

"No, it was not."

"For what purpose was it then?"

"For no purpose."

"How is it that you chance to remember the day and hour so minutely, if you met that woman, whom you have accused, merely by chance, and for no manner of purpose, as you must have met others that night, perhaps to the amount of hundreds, in the same way?"

"I have good cause to remember it, my lord."

"What was that cause? — No answer? — You don't choose to say what that cause was?"

"I am not at liberty to tell."

The Sheriff then descended to other particulars, all of which tended to prove that the fellow was an accomplished villain, and that the principal share of the atrocities had been committed by him. Indeed the Sheriff hinted that he suspected the only share Mrs. Calvert had in them was in being too much in his company, and too true to him. The case was remitted to the Court of Justiciary; but Mrs. Logan had heard enough to convince her that the culprits first met at the very spot, and the very hour, on which George Colwan was slain; and she had no doubt that they were incendiaries set on by his mother, to forward her own and her darling son's way to opulence. Mrs. Logan was wrong, as will appear in the sequel; but her antipathy to Mrs. Colwan made her watch the event with all care. She never quitted Peebles as long as Bell Calvert remained there, and, when she was removed to Edinburgh, the other followed. When the trial came on, Mrs. Logan and her maid were again summoned as witnesses before the jury, and compelled by the prosecutor for the Crown to appear.

The maid was first called; and, when she came into the witness box, the anxious and hopeless looks of the prisoner were manifest to all. But the girl, whose name, she said, was Bessy Gillies, answered in so flippant and fearless a way that the auditors were much amused. After a number of routine questions, the depute-advocate asked her if she was at home on the morning of the fifth of September last, when her mistress's house was robbed.

"Was I at hame, say ye? Na, faith-ye, lad! An' I had been at hame, there had been mair to dee. I wad hae raised sic a yelloch!"

"Where were you that morning?"

"Where was I, say you? I was in the house where my mistress was, sitting dozing an' half sleeping in the kitchen. I thought aye she would be setting out every minute, for twa hours."

"And, when you went home, what did you find?"

"What found we? Be my sooth, we found a broken lock, an' toom kists."

"Relate some of the particulars, if you please."

"Sir, the thieves didna stand upon particulars: they were halesale dealers in a' our best wares."

"I mean, what passed between your mistress and you on the occasion?"

"What passed, say ye? O, there wasna muckle: I was in a great passion, but she was dung doitrified a wee. When she gaed to put the key i' the door, up it flew to the fer wa'. 'Bless ye, jaud, what's the meaning o' this?' quo she. 'Ye hae left the door open, ye tawpie!' quo she. 'The ne'er o' that I did,' quo I, 'or may my shakel bane never turn another key.' When we got the candle lightit, a' the house was in a hoad-road. 'Bessy, my woman,' quo she, 'we are baith ruined and undone creatures.' 'The deil a bit,' quo I; 'that I deny positively.' H'mh! to speak o' a lass o' my age being ruined and undone! I never had muckle except what was within a good jerkin, an' let the thief ruin me there wha can."

"Do you remember aught else that your mistress said on the occasion? Did you hear her blame any person?"

"O, she made a gread deal o' grumphing an' groaning about the misfortune, as she ca'd it, an' I think she said it was a part o' the ruin, wrought by the Ringans, or some sic name. 'They'll hae't a'! They'll hae't a'!' cried she, wringing her hands; 'a'! they'll hae' a', an' hell wi't, an' they'll get them baith.' 'Aweel, that's aye some satisfaction,' quo I."

"Whom did she mean by the Ringans, do you know?"

"I fancy they are some creatures that she has dreamed about, for I think there canna be as ill folks living as she ca's them."

"Did you never hear say that the prisoner at the bar there, Mrs. Calvert, or Bell Calvert, was the robber of her house; or that she was one of the Ringans?"

"Never. Somebody tauld her lately that ane Bell Calvert robbed her house, but she disna believe it. Neither do I."

"What reasons have you for doubting it?"

"Because it was nae woman's fingers that broke up the bolts an' the locks that were torn open that night."

"Very pertinent, Bessy. Come then within the bar, and look, at these articles on the table. Did you ever see these silver spoons before?"

"I hae seen some very like them, and whaever has seen siller spoons has done the same."

"Can you swear you never saw them before?"

"Na, na, I wadna swear to ony siller spoons that ever war made, unless I had put a private mark on them wi' my ain hand, an' that's what I never did to ane."

"See, they are all marked with a C."

"Sae are a' the spoons in Argyle, an' the half o' them in Edinburgh I think. A C is a very common letter, an' so are a' the names that begin wi't. Lay them by, lay them by, an' gie the poor woman her spoons again. They are marked wi' her ain name, an' I hae little doubt they are hers, an' that she has seen better days."

"Ah, God bless her heart!" sighed the prisoner; and that blessing was echoed in the breathings of many a feeling breast.

"Did you ever see this gown before, think you?"

"I hae seen ane very like it."

"Could you not swear that gown was your mistress's once?"

"No, unless I saw her hae't on, an' kend that she had paid for't. I am very scrupulous about an oath. Like is an ill mark. Sae ill indeed that I wad hardly swear to anything."

"But you say that gown is very like one your mistress used to wear."

"I never said sic a thing. It is like one I hae seen her hae out airing on the hay raip i' the back green. It is very like ane I hae seen Mrs. Butler in the Grass Market wearing too: I rather think it is the same. Bless you, sir, I wadna swear to my ain forefinger, if it had been as lang out o' my sight an', brought in an' laid on that table."

"Perhaps you are not aware, girl, that this scrupulousness of yours is likely to thwart the purposes of justice, and bereave your mistress of property to the amount of a thousand merks." (From the Judge.)

"I canna help that, my lord: that's her look-out. For my part, I am resolved to keep a clear conscience, till I be married, at any rate."

"Look over these things and see if there is any one article among them which you can fix on as the property of your mistress."

"No ane o' them, sir, no ane o' them. An oath is an awfu' thing, especially when it is for life or death. Gie the poor woman her things again, an' let my mistress pick up the next she finds: that's my advice."

When Mrs. Logan came into the box, the prisoner groaned and laid down her head. But how she was astonished when she heard her deliver herself something to the following purport— That, whatever penalties she was doomed to abide, she was determined she would not bear witness against a woman's life, from a certain conviction that it could not be a woman who broke her house. "I have no doubt that I may find some of my own things there," added she, "but, if they were found in her possession, she has been made a tool, or the dupe, of an infernal set, who shall be nameless here. I believe she did not rob me, and for that reason I will have no hand in her condemnation."

The judge: "This is the most singular perversion I have ever witnessed. Mrs. Logan, I entertain strong suspicions that the prisoner, or her agents, have made some agreement with you on this matter to prevent the course of justice."

"So far from that, my lord, I went into the jail at Peebles to this woman, whom I had never seen before, and proffered to withdraw my part in the prosecution, as well as my evidence, provided she would tell me a few simple facts; but she spurned at my offer, and had me turned insolently out of the prison, with orders to the jailor never to admit me again on any pretence."

The prisoner's counsel, taking hold of this evidence, addressed the jury with great fluency; and, finally, the prosecution was withdrawn, and the prisoner dismissed from the bar, with a severe reprimand for her past conduct, and an exhortation to keep better company.

It was not many days till a caddy came with a large parcel to Mrs. Logan's house, which parcel he delivered into her hands, accompanied with a sealed note, containing an inventory of the articles, and a request to know if the unfortunate Arabella Calvert would be admitted to converse with Mrs. Logan.

Never was there a woman so much overjoyed as Mrs. Logan was at this message. She returned compliments. Would be most happy to see her; and no article of the parcel should be looked at, or touched, till her arrival. It was not long till she made her appearance, dressed in somewhat better style than she had yet seen her; delivered her over the greater part of the stolen property, besides many things that either never had belonged to Mrs. Logan or that she thought proper to deny in order that the other might retain them.

The tale that she told of her misfortunes was of the most distressing nature, and was enough to stir up all the tender, as well as abhorrent feelings in the bosom of humanity. She had suffered every deprivation in fame, fortune, and person. She had been imprisoned; she had been scourged, and branded as an impostor; and all on account of her resolute and unmoving fidelity and truth to several of the very worst of men, every one of whom had abandoned her to utter destitution and shame. But this story we cannot enter on at present, as it would perhaps mar the thread of our story, as much as it did the anxious anticipations of Mrs. Logan, who sat pining and longing for the relation that follows.

"Now I know, Mrs. Logan, that you are expecting a detail of the circumstances relating to the death of Mr. George Colwan; and, in gratitude for your unbounded generosity and disinterestedness, I will tell you all that I know, although, for causes that will appear obvious to you, I had determined never

The Private Memoirs and Confessions of a Justified Sinner

in life to divulge one circumstance of it. I can tell you, however, that you will be disappointed, for it was not the gentleman who was accused, found guilty, and would have suffered the utmost penalty of the law had he not made his escape. It was not he, I say, who slew your young master, nor had he any hand in it."

"I never thought he had. But, pray, how do you come to know this?"

"You shall hear. I had been abandoned in York by an artful and consummate fiend; and found guilty of being art and part concerned in the most heinous atrocities, and, in his place, suffered what I yet shudder to think of I was banished the county, begged my way with my poor outcast child up to Edinburgh, and was there obliged, for the second time in my life, to betake myself to the most degrading of all means to support two wretched lives. I hired a dress, and betook me, shivering, to the High Street, too well aware that my form and appearance would soon draw me suitors enow at that throng and intemperate time of the Parliament. On my very first stepping out to the street, a party of young gentlemen was passing. I heard by the noise they made, and the tenor of their speech, that they were more then mellow, and so I resolved to keep near them, in order, if possible, to make some of them my prey. But, just as one of them began to eye me, I was rudely thrust into a narrow close by one of the guardsmen. I had heard to what house the party was bound, for the men were talking exceedingly loud, and making no secret of it: so I hasted down the close, and round below to the one where their rendezvous was to be; but I was too late, they were all housed and the door bolted. I resolved to wait, thinking they could not all stay long; but I was perishing with famine, and was like to fall down. The moon shone as bright as day, and I perceived, by a sign at the bottom of the close, that there was a small tavern of a certain description up two stairs there. I went up and called, telling the mistress of the house my plan. She approved of it mainly, and offered me her best apartment, provided I could get one of these noble mates to accompany me. She abused Lucky Sudds, as she called her, at the inn where the party was, envying her huge profits, no doubt, and giving me afterwards something to drink for which I really felt exceedingly grateful in my need. I stepped downstairs in order to be on the alert. The moment that I reached the ground, the door of Lucky Sudds' house opened and shut, and down came the Honourable Thomas Drummond, with hasty and impassioned strides, his sword rattling at his heel. I accosted him in a soft and soothing tone. He was taken with my address; for he instantly stood still and gazed intently at me, then at the place, and then at me again. I beckoned him to follow me, which he did without further ceremony, and we soon found ourselves together in the best room of a house where everything was wretched. He still looked about him, and at me; but all this while he had never spoken a word. At length, I asked if he would take any refreshment? 'If you please,' said he. I asked what he would have, but he only answered, 'Whatever you choose, madam.' If he was taken with my address, I was much more taken with his; for he was a complete gentleman, and a gentleman will ever act as one. At length, he began as follows:

"'I am utterly at a loss to account for this adventure, madam. It seems to me like enchantment, and I can hardly believe my senses. An English lady, I judge, and one, who from her manner and address should belong to the first class of society, in such a place as this, is indeed matter of wonder to me. At the foot of a close in Edinburgh! and at this time of the night! Surely it must have been no common reverse of fortune that reduced you to this?' I wept, or pretended to do so; on which he added, 'Pray, madam, take heart. Tell me what has befallen you; and if I can do anything for you, in restoring you to your country or your friends, you shall command my interest.'

"I had great need of a friend then, and I thought now was the time to secure one. So I began and told him the moving tale I have told you. But I soon perceived that I had kept by the naked truth too unvarnishedly, and thereby quite overshot my mark. When he learned that he was sitting in a wretched corner of an irregular house, with a felon, who had so lately been scourged and banished as a swindler and impostor, his modest nature took the alarm, and he was shocked, instead of being moved with pity. His eye fixed on some of the casual stripes on my arm, and from that moment he became restless and impatient to be gone. I tried some gentle arts to retain him, but in vain; so, after paying both the landlady and me for pleasures he had neither tasted nor asked, he took his leave.

"I showed him downstairs; and, just as he turned the corner of the next land, a man came rushing violently by him; exchanged looks with him, and came running up to me. He appeared in great agitation, and was quite out of breath; and, taking my hand in his, we ran upstairs together without speaking, and were instantly in the apartment I had left, where a stoup of wine still stood untasted. 'Ah, this is fortunate!' said my new spark, and helped himself. In the meanwhile, as our apartment was a corner one, and looked both east and north, I ran to the eastern casement to look after Drummond. Now, note me well: I saw him going eastward in his tartans and bonnet,

The Private Memoirs and Confessions of a Justified Sinner

and the gilded hilt of his claymore glittering in the moon; and, at the very same time, I saw two men, the one in black, and the other likewise in tartans, coming towards the steps from the opposite bank, by the foot of the loch; and I saw Drummond and they eyeing each other as they passed. I kept view of him till he vanished towards Leith Wynd, and by that time the two strangers had come close up under our window. This is what I wish you to pay particular attention to. I had only lost sight of Drummond (who had given me his name and address) for the short space of time that we took in running up one pair of short stairs; and during that space he had halted a moment, for, when I got my eye on him again, he had not crossed the mouth of the next entry, nor proceeded above ten or twelve paces, and, at the same time, I saw the two men coming down the bank on the opposite side of the loch, at about three hundred paces' distance. Both he and they were distinctly in my view, and never within speech of each other, until he vanished into one of the wynds leading towards the bottom of the High Street, at which precise time the two strangers came below my window; so that it was quite clear he neither could be one of them nor have any communication with them.

"Yet, mark me again; for, of all things I have ever seen, this was the most singular. When I looked down at the two strangers, one of them was extremely like Drummond. So like was he that there was not one item in dress, form, feature, nor voice, by which I could distinguish the one from the other. I was certain it was not he, because I had seen the one going and the other approaching at the same time, and my impression at the moment was that I looked upon some spirit, or demon, in his likeness. I felt a chillness creep all round my heart, my knees tottered, and, withdrawing my head from the open casement that lay in the dark shade, I said to the man who was with me, 'Good God, what is this?'

"'What is it, my dear?' said he, as much alarmed as I was.

"'As I live, there stands an apparition!' said I.

"He was not so much afraid when he heard me say so, and, peeping cautiously out, he looked and listened awhile, and then, drawing back, he said in a whisper, 'They are both living men, and one of them is he I passed at the corner.'

"'That he is not,' said I, emphatically. 'To that I will make oath.'

"He smiled and shook his head, and then added, 'I never

then saw a man before, whom I could not know again, particularly if he was the very last I had seen. But what matters it whether it be or not? As it is no concern of ours, let us sit down and enjoy ourselves.'

'But it does matter a very great deal with me, sir,' said I. 'Bless me, my head is giddy—my breath quite gone, and I feel as if I were surrounded with fiends. Who are you, sir?'

'You shall know that ere we two part, my love,' said he. 'I cannot conceive why the return of this young gentleman to the spot he so lately left should discompose you. I suppose he got a glance of you as he passed, and has returned to look after you, and that is the whole secret of the matter.'

"'If you will be so civil as to walk out and join him then, it will oblige me hugely,' said I, 'for I never in my life experienced such boding apprehensions of evil company. I cannot conceive how you should come up here without asking my permission. Will it please you to be gone, sir?' I was within an ace of prevailing. He took out his purse—I need not say more—I was bribed to let him remain. Ah, had I kept my frail resolution of dismissing him at that moment, what a world of shame and misery had been evited! But that, though uppermost still in my mind, has nothing ado here.

"When I peeped over again, the two men were disputing in a whisper, the one of them in violent agitation and terror, and the other upbraiding him, and urging him on to some desperate act. At length I heard the young man in the Highland garb say indignantly, 'Hush, recreant! It is God's work which you are commissioned to execute, and it must be done. But, if you positively decline it, I will do it myself, and do you beware of the consequences.'

"'Oh, I will, I will!' cried the other in black clothes, in a wretched beseeching tone. 'You shall instruct me in this, as in all things else.'

"I thought all this while I was closely concealed from them, and wondered not a little when he in tartans gave me a sly nod, as much as to say, 'What do you think of this?' or, 'Take note of what you see,' or something to that effect; from which I perceived that, whatever he was about, he did not wish it to be kept a secret. For all that, I was impressed with a terror and anxiety that I could not overcome, but it only made me mark every event with the more intense curiosity. The Highlander, whom I still could not help regarding as the evil genius of

The Private Memoirs and Confessions of a Justified Sinner

Thomas Drummond, performed every action as with the quickness of thought. He concealed the youth in black in a narrow entry, a little to the westward of my windows, and, as he was leading him across the moonlight green by the shoulder, I perceived, for the first time, that both of them were armed with rapiers. He pushed him without resistance into the dark shaded close, made another signal to me, and hasted up the close to Lucky Sudds' door. The city and the morning were so still that I heard every word that was uttered, on putting my head out a little. He knocked at the door sharply, and, after waiting a considerable space, the bolt was drawn, and the door, as I conceived, edged up as far as the massy chain would let it. 'Is young Dalcastle still in the house?' said he sharply.

"I did not hear the answer, but I heard him say, shortly after, 'If he is, pray tell him to speak with me for a few minutes.' He then withdrew from the door, and came slowly down the close, in a lingering manner, looking oft behind him. Dalcastle came out; advanced a few steps after him, and then stood still, as if hesitating whether or not he should call out a friend to accompany him; and that instant the door behind him was closed, chained, and the iron bolt drawn; on hearing of which, he followed his adversary without further hesitation. As he passed below my window, I heard him say, 'I beseech you, Tom, let us do nothing in this matter rashly'; but I could not hear the answer of the other, who had turned the corner.

"I roused up my drowsy companion, who was leaning on the bed, and we both looked together from the north window. We were in the shade, but the moon shone full on the two young gentlemen. Young Dalcastle was visibly the worse of liquor, and, his back being turned towards us, he said something to the other which I could not make out, although he spoke a considerable time, and, from his tones and gestures, appeared to be reasoning.

"When he had done, the tall young man in the tartans drew his sword, and, his face being straight to us, we heard him say distinctly, 'No more words about it, George, if you please; but if you be a man, as I take you to be, draw your sword, and let us settle it here.'

"Dalcastle drew his sword, without changing his attitude; but he spoke with more warmth, for we heard his words, 'Think you that I fear you, Tom? Be assured, Sir, I would not fear ten of the best of your name, at each other's backs: all that I want is to have friends with us to see fair play, for, if you close with me, you are a dead man.'

The Private Memoirs and Confessions of a Justified Sinner

"The other stormed at these words. 'You are a braggart, Sir,' cried he, 'a wretch—a blot on the cheek of nature—a blight on the Christian world—a reprobate—I'll have your soul, Sir. You must play at tennis, and put down elect brethren in another world to-morrow.' As he said this, he brandished his rapier, exciting Dalcastle to offence. He gained his point. The latter, who had previously drawn, advanced upon his vapouring and licentious antagonist, and a fierce combat ensued. My companion was delighted beyond measure, and I could not keep him from exclaiming, loud enough to have been heard, 'That's grand! That's excellent!' For me, my heart quaked like an aspen. Young Dalcastle either had a decided advantage over his adversary, or else the other thought proper to let him have it; for he shifted, and swore, and flitted from Dalcastle's thrusts like a shadow, uttering ofttimes a sarcastic laugh, that seemed to provoke the other beyond all bearing. At one time, he would spring away to a great distance, then advance again on young Dalcastle with the swiftness of lightning. But that young hero always stood his ground, and repelled the attack: he never gave way, although they fought nearly twice round the bleaching green, which you know is not a very small one. At length they fought close up to the mouth of the dark entry, where the fellow in black stood all this while concealed, and then the combatant in tartans closed with his antagonist, or pretended to do so; but, the moment they began to grapple, he wheeled about, turning Colwan's back towards the entry, and then cried out, 'Ah, hell has it! My friend, my friend!'

"That moment the fellow in black rushed from his cover with his drawn rapier, and gave the brave young Dalcastle two deadly wounds in the back, as quick as arm could thrust, both of which I thought pierced through his body. He fell, and, rolling himself on his back, he perceived who it was that had slain him thus foully, and said, with a dying emphasis, which I never heard equalled, 'oh, dog of hell, it is you who has done this!'

"He articulated some more, which I could not hear for other sounds; for, the moment that the man in black inflicted the deadly wound, my companion called out, 'That's unfair, you rip! That's damnable! to strike a brave fellow behind! One at a time, you cowards!' etc., to all which the unnatural fiend in the tartans answered with a loud exulting laugh; and then, taking the poor paralysed murderer by the bow of the arm, he hurried him in the dark entry once more, where I lost sight of them for ever."

Before this time Mrs. Logan had risen up; and, when the

The Private Memoirs and Confessions of a Justified Sinner

narrator had finished, she was standing with her arms stretched upwards at their full length, and her visage turned down, on which were portrayed the lines of the most absolute horror. "The dark suspicions of my late benefactor have been just, and his last prediction is fulfilled," cried she. "The murderer of the accomplished George Colwan has been his own brother, set on, there is little doubt, by her who bare them both, and her directing angel, the self-justified bigot. Aye, and yonder they sit, enjoying the luxuries so dearly purchased, with perfect impunity! If the Almighty do not hurl them down, blasted with shame and confusion, there is no hope of retribution in this life. And, by His might, I will be the agent to accomplish it! Why did the man not pursue the foul murderers? Why did he not raise the alarm, and call the watch?"

"He? The wretch! He durst not move from the shelter he had obtained. No, not for the soul of him. He was pursued for his life, at the moment when he first flew into my arms. But I did not know it; no, I did not then know him. May the curse of heaven, and the blight of hell, settle on the detestable wretch! He pursue for the sake of justice! No; his efforts have all been for evil, but never for good. But I raised the alarm; miserable and degraded as I was, I pursued and raised the watch myself. Have you not heard the name of Bell Calvert coupled with that hideous and mysterious affair?"

"Yes, I have. In secret often I have heard it. But how came it that you could never be found? How came it that you never appeared in defence of the Honourable Thomas Drummond; you, the only person who could have justified him?"

"I could not, for I then fell under the power and guidance of a wretch who durst not for the soul of him be brought forward in the affair. And, what was worse, his evidence would have overborne mine, for he would have sworn that the man who called out and fought Colwan was the same he met leaving my apartment, and there was an end of it. And, moreover, it is well known that this same man—this wretch of whom I speak, never mistook one man for another in his life, which makes the mystery of the likeness between this incendiary and Drummond the more extraordinary."

"If it was Drummond, after all that you have asserted, then are my surmises still wrong."

"There is nothing of which I can be more certain than that it was not Drummond. We have nothing on earth but our senses to depend upon. If these deceive us, what are we to do? I own I cannot account for it; nor ever shall be able to account for it as long as I live."

"Could you know the man in black, if you saw him again?"

"I think I could, if I saw him walk or run: his gait was very particular. He walked as if he had been flat-soled, and his legs made of steel, without any joints in his feet or ankles."

"The very same! The very same! The very same! Pray will you take a few days' journey into the country with me, to look at such a man?"

"You have preserved my life, and for you I will do anything. I will accompany you with pleasure: and I think I can say that I will know him, for his form left an impression on my heart not soon to be effaced. But of this I am sure, that my unworthy companion will recognize him, and that he will be able to swear to his identity every day as long as he lives."

"Where is he? Where is he? Oh! Mrs. Calvert, where is he?"

"Where is he? He is the wretch whom you heard giving me up to the death; who, after experiencing every mark of affection that a poor ruined being could confer, and after committing a thousand atrocities of which she was ignorant, became an informer to save his diabolical life, and attempted to offer up mine as a sacrifice for all. We will go by ourselves first, and I will tell you if it is necessary to send any farther."

The two dames, the very next morning, dressed themselves like country goodwives, and, hiring two stout ponies furnished with pillions, they took their journey westward, and the second evening after leaving Edinburgh they arrived at the village about two miles below Dalcastle, where they alighted. But Mrs. Logan, being anxious to have Mrs. Calvert's judgment, without either hint or preparation, took care not to mention that they were so near to the end of their journey. In conformity with this plan, she said, after they had sat a while: "Heigh-ho, but I am weary! What, suppose we should rest a day here before we proceed farther on our journey?"

Mrs. Calvert was leaning on the casement and looking out when her companion addressed these words to her, and by far too much engaged to return any answer, for her eyes were riveted on two young men who approached from the farther end of the village; and at length, turning round her head, she said, with the most intense interest, "Proceed farther on our

288

journey, did you say? That we need not do; for, as I live, here comes the very man!"

Mrs. Logan ran to the window, and, behold, there was indeed Robert Wringhim Colwan (now the Laird of Dalcastle) coming forward almost below their window, walking arm in arm with another young man; and, as the two passed, the latter looked up and made a sly signal to the two dames, biting his lip, winking with his left eye, and nodding his head. Mrs. Calvert was astonished at this recognizance, the young man's former companion having made exactly such another signal on the night of the duel, by the light of the moon; and it struck her, moreover, that she had somewhere seen this young man's face before. She looked after him, and he winked over his shoulder to her; but she was prevented from returning his salute by her companion, who uttered a loud cry, between a groan and shriek, and fell down on the floor with a rumble like a wall that had suddenly been undermined. She had fainted quite away, and required all her companion's attention during the remainder of the evening, for she had scarcely ever well recovered out of one fit before she fell into another, and in the short intervals she raved like one distracted or in a dream. After falling into a sound sleep by night, she recovered her equanimity, and the two began to converse seriously on what they had seen. Mrs. Calvert averred that the young man who passed next to the window was the very man who stabbed George Colwan in the back, and she said she was willing to take her oath on it at any time when required, and was certain, if the wretch Ridsley saw him, that he would make oath to the same purport, for that his walk was so peculiar no one of common discernment could mistake it.

Mrs. Logan was in great agitation, and said: "It is what I have suspected all along, and what I am sure my late master and benefactor was persuaded of, and the horror of such an idea cut short his days. That wretch, Mrs. Calvert, is the born brother of him he murdered, sons of the same mother they were, whether or not of the same father, the Lord only knows. But, Oh, Mrs. Calvert, that is not the main thing that has discomposed me, and shaken my nerves to pieces at this time. Who do you think the young man was who walked in his company to-night?"

"I cannot for my life recollect, but am convinced I have seen the same fine form and face before."

"And did not he seem to know us, Mrs. Calvert? You who are able to recollect things as they happened, did he not seem to recollect us, and make signs to that effect?"

"He did, indeed, and apparently with great good humour."

"Oh, Mrs Calvert, hold me, else I shall fall into hysterics again! Who is he? Who is he? Tell me who you suppose he is, for I cannot say my own thought."

"On my life, I cannot remember."

"Did you note the appearance of the young gentleman you saw slain that night? Do you recollect aught of the appearance of my young master, George Colwan?"

Mrs. Calvert sat silent, and stared the other mildly in the face. Their looks encountered, and there was an unearthly amazement that gleamed from each, which, meeting together, caught real fire, and returned the flame to their heated imaginations, till the two associates became like two statues, with their hands spread, their eyes fixed, and their chops fallen down upon their bosoms. An old woman who kept the lodging-house, having been called in before when Mrs. Logan was faintish, chanced to enter at this crisis with some cordial; and, seeing the state of her lodgers, she caught the infection, and fell into the same rigid and statue-like appearance. No scene more striking was ever exhibited; and if Mrs. Calvert had not resumed strength of mind to speak, and break the spell, it is impossible to say how long it might have continued. "It is he, I believe," said she, uttering the words as it were inwardly. "It can be none other but he. But, no, it is impossible! I saw him stabbed through and through the heart; I saw him roll backward on the green in his own blood, utter his last words, and groan away his soul. Yet, if it is not he, who can it be?"

"It is he!" cried Mrs. Logan, hysterically.

"Yes, yes, it is he!" cried the landlady, in unison.

"It is who?" said Mrs. Calvert. "Whom do you mean, mistress?"

"Oh, I don't know! I don't know! I was affrighted."

"Hold your peace then till you recover your senses, and tell me, if you can, who that young gentleman is who keeps company with the new Laird of Dalcastle?"

"Oh, it is he! It is he!" screamed Mrs. Logan, wringing her

hands.

"Oh, it is he! It is he!" cried the landlady, wringing hers.

Mrs. Calvert turned the latter gently and civilly out of the apartment, observing that there seemed to be some infection in the air of the room, and she would be wise for herself to keep out of it.

The two dames had a restless and hideous night. Sleep came not to their relief, for their conversation was wholly about the dead, who seemed to be alive, and their minds were wandering and groping in a chaos of mystery. "Did you attend to his corpse, and know that he positively died and was buried?" said Mrs. Calvert.

"Oh, yes, from the moment that his fair but mangled corpse was brought home, I attended it till that when it was screwed in the coffin. I washed the long stripes of blood from his lifeless form, on both sides of the body. I bathed the livid wound that passed through his generous and gentle heart. There was one through the flesh of his left side too, which had bled most outwardly of them all. I bathed them, and bandaged them up with wax and perfumed ointment, but still the blood oozed through all, so that when he was laid in the coffin he was like one newly murdered. My brave, my generous young master. He was always as a son to me, and no son was ever more kind or more respectful to a mother. But he was butchered—he was cut off from the earth ere he had well reached to manhood—most barbarously and unfairly slain. And how is it, how can it be, that we again see him here, walking arm in arm with his murderer?"

"The thing cannot be, Mrs. Logan. It is a phantasy of our disturbed imaginations, therefore let us compose ourselves till we investigate this matter farther."

"It cannot be in nature, that is quite clear," said Mrs. Logan. "Yet how it should be that I should think so—I who knew and nursed him from his infancy—there lies the paradox. As you said once before, we have nothing but our senses to depend on, and, if you and I believe that we see a person, why, we do see him. Whose word, or whose reasoning can convince us against our own senses? We will disguise ourselves as poor women selling a few country wares, and we will go up to the Hall, and see what is to see, and hear what we can hear, for this is a weighty business in which we are engaged, namely, to turn the vengeance of the law upon an unnatural monster; and we will further learn, if we can, who this is that accompanies him."

Mrs. Calvert acquiesced, and the two dames took their way to Dalcastle, with baskets well furnished with trifles. They did not take the common path from the village, but went about, and approached the mansion by a different way. But it seemed as if some overruling power ordered it that they should miss no chance of attaining the information they wanted. For ere ever they came within half a mile of Dalcastle they perceived the two youths coming as to meet them, on the same path. The road leading from Dalcastle towards the north-east, as all the country knows, goes along a dark bank of brush-wood called the Bogle-heuch. It was by this track that the two women were going, and, when they perceived the two gentlemen meeting them, they turned back, and, the moment they were out of their sight, they concealed themselves in a thicket close by the road. They did this because Mrs. Logan was terrified for being discovered, and because they wished to reconnoitre without being seen. Mrs. Calvert now charged her, whatever she saw, or whatever she heard, to put on a resolution, and support it, for if she fainted there and was discovered, what was to become of her!

The two young men came on, in earnest and vehement conversation; but the subject they were on was a terrible one, and hardly fit to be repeated in the face of a Christian community. Wringhim was disputing the boundlessness of the true Christian's freedom, and expressing doubts that, chosen as he knew he was from all eternity, still it might be possible for him to commit acts that would exclude him from the limits of the covenant. The other argued, with mighty fluency, that the thing was utterly impossible, and altogether inconsistent with eternal predestination. The arguments of the latter prevailed, and the laird was driven to sullen silence. But, to the women's utter surprise, as the conquering disputant passed, he made a signal of recognizance through the brambles to them, as formerly, and, that he might expose his associate fully, and in his true colours, he led him backwards and forwards by the women more than twenty times, making him to confess both the crimes that he had done and those he had in contemplation. At length he said to him: "Assuredly I saw some strolling vagrant women on this walk, my dear friend: I wish we could find them, for there is little doubt that they are concealed here in your woods."

"I wish we could find them," answered Wringhim. "We would have fine sport maltreating and abusing them."

"That we should, that we should! Now tell me, Robert, if you found a malevolent woman, the latent enemy of your prosperity, lurking in these woods to betray you, what would you inflict on her?"

"I would tear her to pieces with my dogs, and feed them with her flesh. Oh, my dear friend, there is an old strumpet who lived with my unnatural father, whom I hold in such utter detestation that I stand constantly in dread of her, and would sacrifice the half of my estate to shed her blood!"

"What will you give me if I will put her in your power, and give you a fair and genuine excuse for making away with her; one for which you shall answer at the bar, here or hereafter?"

"I should like to see the vile hag put down. She is in possession of the family plate, that is mine by right, as well as a thousand valuable relics, and great riches besides, all of which the old profligate gifted shamefully away. And it is said, besides all these, that she has sworn my destruction."

"She has, she has. But I see not how she can accomplish that, seeing the deed was done so suddenly, and in the silence of the night."

"It was said there were some onlookers. But where shall we find that disgraceful Miss Logan?"

"I will show you her by and by. But will you then consent to the other meritorious deed? Come, be a man, and throw away scruples."

"If you can convince me that the promise is binding I will."

"Then step this way, till I give you a piece of information."

They walked a little way out of hearing, but went not out of sight; therefore, though the women were in a terrible quandary, they durst not stir, for they had some hopes that this extraordinary person was on a mission of the same sort with themselves, knew of them, and was going to make use of their testimony. Mrs. Logan was several times on the point of falling into a swoon, so much did the appearance of the young man impress her, until her associate covered her face that she might listen without embarrassment. But this latter dialogue roused different feelings within them; namely, those arising from imminent personal danger. They saw his waggish associate point out the place of their concealment to Wringhim, who came towards them, out of curiosity to see what his friend meant by what he believed to be a joke, manifestly without crediting it in the least degree. When he came running away, the other called after him: "If she is too hard for you, call to me." As he said this, he hasted out of sight, in the contrary direction, apparently much delighted with the joke.

Wringhim came rushing through the thicket impetuously, to the very spot where Mrs. Logan lay squatted. She held the wrapping close about her head, but he tore it off and discovered her. "The curse of God be on thee!" said he. "What fiend has brought thee here, and for what purpose art thou come? But, whatever has brought thee, I have thee!" and with that he seized her by the throat. The two women, when they heard what jeopardy they were in from such a wretch, had squatted among the underwood at a small distance from each other, so that he had never observed Mrs. Calvert; but, no sooner had he seized her benefactor, than, like a wild cat, she sprung out of the thicket, and had both hands fixed at his throat, one of them twisted in his stock, in a twinkling. She brought him back-over among the brushwood, and the two, fixing on him like two harpies, mastered him with ease. Then indeed was he woefully beset. He deemed for a while that his friend was at his back, and, turning his bloodshot eyes towards the path, he attempted to call; but there was no friend there, and the women cut short his cries by another twist of his stock. "Now, gallant and rightful Laird of Dalcastle," said Mrs. Logan, "what hast thou to say for thyself? Lay thy account to dree the weird thou hast so well earned. Now shalt thou suffer due penance for murdering thy brave and only brother."

"Thou liest, thou hag of the pit! I touched not my brother's life."

"I saw thee do it with these eyes that now look thee in the face; ay, when his back was to thee, too, and while he was hotly engaged with thy friend," said Mrs. Calvert.

"I heard thee confess it again and again this same hour," said Mrs. Logan.

"Ay, and so did I," said her companion. "Murder will out, though the Almighty should lend hearing to the ears of the willow, and speech to the seven tongues of the woodriff."

"You are liars and witches!" said he, foaming with rage, "and creatures fitted from the beginning for eternal destruction. I'll have your bones and your blood sacrificed on your cursed altars! O Gil-Martin! Gil-Martin! Where art thou now? Here,

The Private Memoirs and Confessions of a Justified Sinner

here is the proper food for blessed vengeance! Hilloa!"

There was no friend, no Gil-Martin there to hear or assist him: he was in the two women's mercy, but they used it with moderation. They mocked, they tormented, and they threatened him; but, finally, after putting him in great terror, they bound his hands behind his back, and his feet fast with long straps of garters which they chanced to have in their baskets, to prevent him from pursuing them till they were out of his reach. As they left him, which they did in the middle of the path, Mrs. Calvert said: "We could easily put an end to thy sinful life, but our hands shall be free of thy blood. Nevertheless thou art still in our power, and the vengeance of thy country shall overtake thee, thou mean and cowardly murderer, ay, and that more suddenly than thou art aware!"

The women posted to Edinburgh; and as they put themselves under the protection of an English merchant, who was journeying thither with twenty horses laden, and armed servants, so they had scarcely any conversation on the road. When they arrived at Mrs. Logan's house, then they spoke of what they had seen and heard, and agreed that they had sufficient proof to condemn young Wringhim, who they thought richly deserved the severest doom of the law.

"I never in my life saw any human being," said Mrs. Calvert, "whom I thought so like a fiend. If a demon could inherit flesh and blood, that youth is precisely such a being as I could conceive that demon to be. The depth and the malignity of his eye is hideous. His breath is like the airs from a charnel house, and his flesh seems fading from his bones, as if the worm that never dies were gnawing it away already."

"He was always repulsive, and every way repulsive," said the other, "but he is now indeed altered greatly to the worse. While we were hand-fasting him, I felt his body to be feeble and emaciated; but yet I know him to be so puffed up with spiritual pride that I believe he weens every one of his actions justified before God, and, instead of having stings of conscience for these, he takes great merit to himself in having effected them. Still my thoughts are less about him than the extraordinary being who accompanies him. He does everything with so much ease and indifference, so much velocity and effect, that all bespeak him an adept in wickedness. The likeness to my late hapless young master is so striking that I can hardly believe it to be a chance model; and I think he imitates him in everything, for some purpose or some effect on his sinful associate. Do you know that he is so like in every lineament, look, and gesture,

The Private Memoirs and Confessions of a Justified Sinner

that, against the clearest light of reason, I cannot in my mind separate the one from the other, and have a certain indefinable expression on my mind that they are one and the same being, or that the one was a prototype of the other."

"If there is an earthly crime," said Mrs. Calvert, "for the due punishment of which the Almighty may be supposed to subvert the order of nature, it is fratricide. But tell me, dear friend, did you remark to what the subtile and hellish villain was endeavouring to prompt the assassin?"

"No, I could not comprehend it. My senses were altogether so bewildered that I thought they had combined to deceive me, and I gave them no credit."

"Then hear me: I am almost certain he was using every persuasion to induce him to make away with his mother; and I likewise conceive that I heard the incendiary give his consent!"

"This is dreadful. Let us speak and think no more about it, till we see the issue. In the meantime, let us do that which is our bounden duty — go and divulge all that we know relating to this foul murder."

Accordingly the two women went to Sir Thomas Wallace of Craigie, the Lord justice Clerk (who was, I think, either uncle or grandfather to young Drummond, who was outlawed and obliged to fly his country on account of Colwan's death), and to that gentleman they related every circumstance of what they had seen and heard. He examined Calvert very minutely, and seemed deeply interested in her evidence — said he knew she was relating the truth, and, in testimony of it, brought a letter of young Drummond's from his desk, wherein that young gentleman, after protesting his innocence in the most forcible terms, confessed having been with such a woman in such a house, after leaving the company of his friends; and that, on going home, Sir Thomas's servant had let him in, in the dark, and from these circumstances he found it impossible to prove an alibi. He begged of his relative, if ever an opportunity offered, to do his endeavour to clear up that mystery, and remove the horrid stigma from his name in his country, and among his kin, of having stabbed a friend behind his back.

Lord Craigie, therefore, directed the two women to the proper authorities, and, after hearing their evidence there, it was judged proper to apprehend the present Laird of Dalcastle, and bring him to his trial. But, before that, they sent the prisoner in the Tolbooth, he who had seen the whole transaction along with Mrs. Calvert, to take a view of Wringhim privately; and, his discrimination being so well known as to be proverbial all over the land, they determined secretly to be ruled by his report. They accordingly sent him on a pretended mission of legality to Dalcastle, with orders to see and speak with the proprietor, without giving him a hint what was wanted. On his return, they examined him, and he told them that he found all things at the place in utter confusion and dismay; that the lady of the place was missing, and could not be found, dead or alive. On being asked if he had ever seen the proprietor before, he looked astounded and unwilling to answer. But it came out that he had; and that he had once seen him kill a man on such a spot at such an hour.

Officers were then dispatched, without delay, to apprehend the monster, and bring him to justice. On these going to the mansion, and inquiring for him, they were told he was at home; on which they stationed guards, and searched all the premises, but he was not to be found. It was in vain that they overturned beds, raised floors, and broke open closets: Robert Wringhim Colwan was lost once and for ever. His mother also was lost; and strong suspicions attached to some of the farmers and house servants to whom she was obnoxious, relating to her disappearance.

The Honourable Thomas Drummond became a distinguished officer in the Austrian service, and died in the memorable year for Scotland, 1715; and this is all with which history, justiciary records, and tradition, furnish me relating to these matters.

I have now the pleasure of presenting my readers with an original document of a most singular nature, and preserved for their perusal in a still more singular manner. I offer no remarks on it, and make as few additions to it, leaving everyone to judge for himself. We have heard much of the rage of fanaticism in former days, but nothing to this.

PRIVATE MEMOIRS AND CONFESSIONS OF A SINNER

My life has been a life of trouble and turmoil; of change and vicissitude; of anger and exultation; of sorrow and of vengeance. My sorrows have all been for a slighted gospel, and my vengeance has been wreaked on its adversaries. Therefore, in the might of Heaven, I will sit down and write: I will let the wicked of this world know what I have done in the faith of the promises, and justification by grace, that they may read and tremble, and bless their gods of silver and gold that the minister of Heaven was removed from their sphere before their blood was mingled with their sacrifices.

I was born an outcast in the world, in which I was destined to act so conspicuous a part. My mother was a burning and a shining light, in the community of Scottish worthies, and in the days of her virginity had suffered much in the persecution of the saints. But it so pleased Heaven that, as a trial of her faith, she was married to one of the wicked; a man all over spotted with the leprosy of sin. As well might they have conjoined fire and water together, in hopes that they would consort and amalgamate, as purity and corruption: She fled from his embraces the first night after their marriage, and from that time forth his iniquities so galled her upright heart that she quitted his society altogether, keeping her own apartments in the same house with him.

I was the second son of this unhappy marriage, and, ere ever I was born, my father according to the flesh disclaimed all relation or connection with me, and all interest in me, save what the law compelled him to take, which was to grant me a scanty maintenance; and had it not been for a faithful minister of the gospel, my mother's early instructor, I should have remained an outcast from the church visible. He took pity on me, admitting me not only into that, but into the bosom of his own household and ministry also, and to him am I indebted, under Heaven, for the high conceptions and glorious discernment between good and evil, right and wrong, which I attained even at an early age. It was he who directed my studies aright, both in the learning of the ancient fathers and the doctrines of the reformed church, and designed me for his assistant and successor in the holy office. I missed no opportunity of perfecting myself particularly in all the minute points of theology in which my reverend father and mother took great delight; but at length I acquired so much skill that I astonished my teachers, and made them gaze at one another. I remember that it was the custom, in my patron's house, to ask questions of the Single Catechism round every Sabbath night. He asked the first, my mother the second, and so on, everyone saying the question asked and then asking the next. It fell to my mother to ask Effectual Calling at me. I said the answer with propriety and emphasis. "Now, madam," added I, "my question to you is: What is Ineffectual Calling?"

"Ineffectual Calling? There is no such thing, Robert," said she.

"But there is, madam," said I, and that answer proves how much you say these fundamental precepts by rote, and without any consideration. Ineffectual Calling is the outward call of the gospel without any effect on the hearts of unregenerated and impenitent sinners. Have not all these the same calls, warnings, doctrines, and reproofs, that we have? And is not this ineffectual Calling? Has not Ardinferry the same? Has not Patrick M'Lure the same? Has not the Laird of Dalcastle and his reprobate heir the same? And will any tell me that this is not Ineffectual Calling?"

"What a wonderful boy he is!" said my mother.

"I'm feared he turn out to be a conceited gowk," said old Barnet, the minister's man.

"No," said my pastor, and father (as I shall henceforth denominate him). "No, Barnet, he is a wonderful boy; and no marvel, for I have prayed for these talents to be bestowed on him from his infancy: and do you think that Heaven would refuse a prayer so disinterested? No, it is impossible. But my dread is, madam," continued he, turning to my mother, "that he is yet in the bond of iniquity."

"God forbid!" said my mother.

"I have struggled with the Almighty long and hard," continued he; "but have as yet no certain token of acceptance in his behalf, I have indeed fought a hard fight, but have been repulsed by him who hath seldom refused my request; although I cited his own words against him, and endeavoured to hold him at his promise, he hath so many turnings in the supremacy of his power, that I have been rejected. How dreadful is it to think of our darling being still without the pale of the covenant! But I have vowed a vow, and in that there is hope."

The Private Memoirs and Confessions of a Justified Sinner

My heart quaked with terror when I thought of being still living in a state of reprobation, subjected to the awful issues of death, judgment, and eternal misery, by the slightest accident or casualty; and I set about the duty of prayer myself with the utmost earnestness. I prayed three times every day, and seven times on the Sabbath; but, the more frequently and fervently that I prayed, I sinned still the more. About this time, and for a long period afterwards, amounting to several years, I lived in a hopeless and deplorable state of mind; for I said to myself, "If my name is not written in the book of life from all eternity, it is in vain for me to presume that either vows or prayers of mine, or those of all mankind combined, can ever procure its insertion now." I had come under many vows, most solemnly taken, every one of which I had broken; and I saw with the intensity of juvenile grief that there was no hope for me. I went on sinning every hour, and all the while most strenuously warring against sin, and repenting of every one transgression as soon after the commission of it as I got leisure to think. But, oh, what a wretched state this unregenerated state is, in which every effort after righteousness only aggravates our offences! I found it vanity to contend; for, after communing with my heart, the conclusion was as follows: "If I could repent me of all my sins, and shed tears of blood for them, still have I not a load of original transgression pressing on me that is enough to crush me to the lowest hell. I may be angry with my first parents for having sinned, but how I shall repent me of their sin is beyond what I am able to comprehend."

Still, in those days of depravity and corruption, I had some of those principles implanted in my mind which were afterwards to spring up with such amazing fertility among the heroes of the faith and the promises. In particular, I felt great indignation against all the wicked of this world, and often wished for the means of ridding it of such a noxious burden. I liked John Barnet, my reverend father's serving-man, extremely ill; but, from a supposition that he might be one of the justified, I refrained from doing him any injury. He gave always his word against me, and when we were by ourselves, in the barn or the fields, he rated me with such severity for my faults that my heart could brook it no longer. He discovered some notorious lies that I had framed, and taxed me with them in such a manner that I could in no wise get off. My cheek burnt, with offence, rather than shame; and he, thinking he had got the mastery of me, exulted over me most unmercifully, telling me I was a selfish and conceited blackguard, who made great pretences towards religious devotion to cloak a disposition tainted with deceit, and that it would not much astonish him if I brought myself to the gallows.

The Private Memoirs and Confessions of a Justified Sinner

I gathered some courage from his over-severity, and answered him as follows: "Who made thee a judge of the actions or dispositions of the Almighty's creatures—thou who art a worm and no man in his sight? How it befits thee to deal out judgments and anathemas! Hath he not made one vessel to honour, and another to dishonour, as in the case with myself and thee? Hath he not built his stories in the heavens, and laid the foundations thereof in the earth, and how can a being like thee judge between good and evil, that are both subjected to the workings of his hand; or of the opposing principles in the soul of man, correcting, modifying, and refining one another?"

I said this with that strong display of fervour for which I was remarkable at my years, and expected old Barnet to be utterly confounded; but he only shook his head, and, with the most provoking grin, said: "There he goes! Sickan sublime and ridiculous sophistry I never heard come out of another mouth but ane. There needs nae aiths to be sworn afore the session wha is your father, young goodman. I ne'er, for my part, saw a son sac like a dad, sin' my een first opened." With that he went away, saying with an ill-natured wince: "You made to honour and me to dishonour! Dirty bow-kail thing that thou be'st!"

"I will have the old rascal on the hip for this, if I live," thought I. So I went and asked my mother if John was a righteous man. She could not tell, but supposed he was, and therefore I got no encouragement from her. I went next to my reverend father, and inquired his opinion, expecting as little from that quarter. He knew the elect as it were by instinct, and could have told you of all those in his own, and some neighbouring parishes, who were born within the boundaries of the covenant of promise, and who were not.

"I keep a good deal in company with your servant, old Barnet, father," said I.

"You do, boy, you do, I see," said he.

"I wish I may not keep too much in his company," said I, "not knowing what kind of society I am in. Is John a good man, father?"

"Why, boy, he is but so so. A morally good man John is, but very little of the leaven of true righteousness, which is faith, within. I am afraid old Barnet, with all his stock of morality, will be a castaway."

The Private Memoirs and Confessions of a Justified Sinner

My heart was greatly cheered by this remark; and I sighed very deeply, and hung my head to one side. The worthy father observed me, and inquired the cause, when I answered as follows: "How dreadful the thought, that I have been going daily in company and fellowship with one whose name is written on the red-letter side of the book of life; whose body and soul have been, from all eternity, consigned over to everlasting destruction, and to whom the blood of the atonement can never, never reach! Father, this is an awful thing, and beyond my comprehension."

"While we are in the world, we must mix with the inhabitants thereof," said he; "and the stains which adhere to us by reason of this mixture, which is unavoidable, shall all be washed away. It is our duty, however, to shun the society of wicked men as much as possible, lest we partake of their sins, and become sharers with them in punishment. John, however, is morally a good man, and may yet get a cast of grace."

"I always thought him a good man till to-day," said I, "when he threw out some reflections on your character, so horrible that I quake to think of the wickedness and malevolence of his heart. He was rating me very impertinently for some supposed fault, which had no being save in his own jealous brain, when I attempted to reason him out of his belief in the spirit of calm Christian argument. But how do you think he answered me? He did so, sir, by twisting his mouth at me, and remarking that such sublime and ridiculous sophistry never came out of another mouth but one (meaning yours) and that no oath before a kirk session was necessary to prove who was my dad, for that he had never seen a son so like a father as I was like mine."

"He durst not for his soul's salvation, and for his daily bread, which he values much more, say such a word, boy; therefore, take care what you assert," said my reverend father.

"He said these very words, and will not deny them, sir," said I.

My reverend father turned about in great wrath and indignation, and went away in search of John, but I kept out of the way, and listened at a back window; for John was dressing the plot of ground behind the house; and I hope it was no sin in me that I did rejoice in the dialogue which took place, it being the victory of righteousness over error.

"Well, John, this is a fine day for your delving work."

"Ay, it's a tolerable day, sir."

"Are you thankful in heart, John, for such temporal mercies as these?"

"Aw doubt we're a' ower little thankfu', sir, baith for temporal an' speeritual mercies; but it isna aye the maist thankfu' heart that maks the greatest fraze wi' the tongue."

"I hope there is nothing personal under that remark, John?"

"Gin the bannet fits ony body's head, they're unco welcome to it, sir, for me."

"John, I do not approve of these innuendoes. You have an arch malicious manner of vending your aphorisms, which the men of the world are too apt to read the wrong way, for your dark hints are sure to have one very bad meaning."

"Hout na, sir, it's only bad folks that think sac. They find ma bits o' gibes come hame to their hearts wi' a kind o' yerk, an' that gars them wince."

"That saying is ten times worse than the other, John; it is a manifest insult: it is just telling me to my face that you think me a bad man."

"A body canna help his thoughts, sir."

"No, but a man's thoughts are generally formed from observation. Now I should like to know, even from the mouth of a misbeliever, what part of my conduct warrants such a conclusion."

"Nae particular pairt, sir; I draw a' my conclusions frae the haill o' a man's character, an' I'm no that aften far wrong."

"Well, John, and what sort of general character do you suppose mine to be?"

"Yours is a Scripture character, sir, an' I'll prove it."

"I hope so, John. Well, which of the Scripture characters do you think approximates nearest to my own?"

"Guess, sir, guess; I wish to lead a proof."

The Private Memoirs and Confessions of a Justified Sinner

"Why, if it be an Old Testament character, I hope it is Melchizedek, for at all events you cannot deny there is one point of resemblance: I, like him, am a preacher of righteousness. If it be a New Testament character, I suppose you mean the Apostle of the Gentiles, of whom I am an unworthy representative."

"Na, na, sir, better nor that still, an' fer closer is the resemblance. When ye bring me to the point, I maun speak. Ye are the just Pharisee, sir, that gaed up wi' the poor publican to pray in the Temple; an' ye're acting the very same pairt at this time, an' saying i' your heart, 'God, I thank thee that I am not as other men are, an' in nae way like this poor misbelieving unregenerate sinner, John Barnet.'"

"I hope I may say so indeed."

"There now! I tauld you how it was! But, d'ye hear, maister. Here stands the poor sinner, John Barnet, your beadle an' servantman, wha wadna change chances wi' you in the neist world, nor consciences in this, for ten times a' that you possess—your justification by faith an' awthegither."

"You are extremely audacious and impertinent, John; but the language of reprobation cannot affect me: I came only to ask you one question, which I desire you to answer candidly. Did you ever say to anyone that I was the boy Robert's natural father?"

"Hout na, sir! Ha-ha-ha! Aih, fie, na, sir! I durst-na say that for my life. I doubt the black stool, an' the sack gown, or maybe the juggs wad hae been my portion had I said sic a thing as that. Hout, hout! Fie, fie! Unco-like doings thae for a Melchizedek or a Saint Paul!"

"John, you are a profane old man, and I desire that you will not presume to break your jests on me. Tell me, dare you say, or dare you think, that I am the natural father of that boy?"

"Ye canna hinder me to think whatever I like, sir, nor can I hinder mysel."

"But did you ever say to anyone that he resembled me, and fathered himself well enough?"

"I hae said mony a time that he resembled you, sir. Naebody can mistake that."

"But, John, there are many natural reasons for such likenesses, besides that of consanguinity. They depend much on the thoughts and affections of the mother; and it is probable that the mother of this boy, being deserted by her worthless husband, having turned her thoughts on me, as likely to be her protector, may have caused this striking resemblance."

"Ay, it may be, sir. I coudna say."

"I have known a lady, John, who was delivered of a blackamoor child, merely from the circumstance of having got a start by the sudden entrance of her negro servant, and not being able to forget him for several hours."

"It may be, sir; but I ken this—an' I had been the laird, I wadna hae ta'en that story in."

"So, then, John, you positively think, from a casual likeness, that this boy is my son?"

"Man's thoughts are vanity, sir; they come unasked, an' gang away without a dismissal, an' he canna' help them. I'm neither gaun to say that I think he's your son, nor that I think he's no your son: sae ye needna pose me nae mair about it."

"Hear then my determination, John. If you do not promise to me, in faith and honour, that you never will say, or insinuate such a thing again in your life, as that that boy is my natural son, I will take the keys of the church from you, and dismiss you from my service."

John pulled out the keys, and dashed them on the gravel at the reverend minister's feet. "There are the keys o' your kirk, sir! I hae never had muckle mense o' them sin' ye entered the door o't. I hae carried them this three and thretty year, but they hae aye been like to burn a hole i' my pouch sin' ever they were turned for your admittance. Tak them again, an' gie them to wha you will, and muckle gude may he get o' them. Auld John may dee a beggar in a hay barn, or at the back of a dike, but he sall aye be master o' his ain thoughts an' gie them vent or no, as he likes."

He left the manse that day, and I rejoiced in the riddance; for I disdained to be kept so much under by one who was in bond of iniquity, and of whom there seemed no hope, as he rejoiced in his frowardness, and refused to submit to that faithful teacher, his master.

The Private Memoirs and Confessions of a Justified Sinner

It was about this time that my reverend father preached a sermon, one sentence of which affected me most disagreeably. It was to the purport that every unrepented sin was productive of a new sin with each breath that a man drew; and every one of these new sins added to the catalogue in the same manner. I was utterly confounded at the multitude of my transgressions; for I was sensible that there were great numbers of sins of which I had never been able thoroughly to repent, and these momentary ones, by moderate calculation, had, I saw, long ago, amounted to a hundred and fifty thousand in the minute, and I saw no end to the series of repentances to which I had subjected myself. A life-time was nothing to enable me to accomplish the sum, and then being, for anything I was certain of, in my state of nature, and the grace of repentance withheld from me—what was I to do, or what was to become of me? In the meantime, I went on sinning without measure; but I was still more troubled about the multitude than the magnitude of my transgressions, and the small minute ones puzzled me more than those that were more heinous, as the latter had generally some good effects in the way of punishing wicked men, froward boys, and deceitful women; and I rejoiced, even then in my early youth, at being used as a scourge in the hand of the Lord; another Jehu, a Cyrus, or a Nebuchadnezzar.

On the whole, I remember that I got into great confusion relating to my sins and repentances, and knew neither where to begin nor how to proceed, and often had great fears that I was wholly without Christ, and that I would find God a consuming fire to me. I could not help running into new sins continually; but then I was mercifully dealt with, for I was often made to repent of them most heartily, by reason of bodily chastisements received on these delinquencies being discovered. I was particularly prone to lying, and I cannot but admire the mercy that has freely forgiven me all these juvenile sins. Now that I know them all to be blotted out, and that I am an accepted person, I may the more freely confess them: the truth is, that one lie always paved the way for another, from hour to hour, from day to day, and from year to year; so that I found myself constantly involved in a labyrinth of deceit, from which it was impossible to extricate myself. If I knew a person to be a godly one, I could almost have kissed his feet; but, against the carnal portion of mankind, I set my face continually. I esteemed the true ministers of the gospel; but the prelatic party, and the preachers up of good works I abhorred, and to this hour I account them the worst and most heinous of all transgressors.

There was only one boy at Mr. Witch's class who kept always the upper hand of me in every part of education. I strove against him from year to year, but it was all in vain; for he was a very wicked boy, and I was convinced he had dealings with the Devil. Indeed, it was believed all over the country that his mother was a witch; and I was at length convinced, that it was no human ingenuity that beat me with so much ease in the Latin, after I had often sat up a whole night with my reverend father, studying my lesson in all its bearings. I often read as well and sometimes better than he; but, the moment Mr. Wilson began to examine us, my opponent popped up above me. I determined (as I knew him for a wicked person, and one of the Devil's handfasted children) to be revenged on him, and to humble him by some means or other. Accordingly I lost no opportunity of setting the master against him, and succeeded several times in getting him severely beaten for faults of which he was innocent. I can hardly describe the joy that it gave to my heart to see a wicked creature suffering, for, though he deserved it not for one thing, he richly deserved it for others. This may be by some people accounted a great sin in me; but I deny it, for I did it as a duty, and what a man or boy does for the right will never be put into the sum of his transgressions.

This boy, whose name was M'Gill, was, at all his leisure hours, engaged in drawing profane pictures of beasts, men, women, houses, and trees, and, in short, of all things that his eye encountered. These profane things the master often smiled at, and admired; therefore I began privately to try my hand likewise. I had scarcely tried above once to draw the figure of a man, ere I conceived that I had hit the very features of Mr. Wilson. They were so particular that they could not be easily mistaken, and I was so tickled and pleased with the droll likeness that I had drawn that I laughed immoderately at it. I tried no other figure but this; and I tried it in every situation in which a man and a schoolmaster could be placed. I often wrought for hours together at this likeness, nor was it long before I made myself so much master of the outline that I could have drawn it in any situation whatever, almost off hand. I then took M'Gill's account book of algebra home with me, and at my leisure put down a number of gross caricatures of Mr. Wilson here and there, several of them in situations notoriously ludicrous. I waited the discovery of this treasure with great impatience; but the book, chancing to be one that M'Gill was not using, I saw it might be long enough before I enjoyed the consummation of my grand scheme: therefore, with all the ingenuity I was master of, I brought it before our dominie's eye. But never shall I forget the rage that gleamed in the tyrant's phiz! I was actually terrified to look at him, and trembled at his voice. M'Gill was called upon, and examined relating to the obnoxious figures. He denied flatly that any of them were of his doing. But the master inquiring at him whose they were, he could not tell, but affirmed it to be some trick. Mr. Wilson at one time began, as I thought, to hesitate; but the evidence was so strong against M'Gill that at length his solemn asseverations of innocence only proved an aggravation of his crime. There was not one in the school who had ever been known to draw a figure but himself, and on him fell the whole weight of the tyrant's vengeance. It was dreadful; and I was once in hopes that he would not leave life in the culprit. He, however, left the school for several months, refusing to return to be subjected to punishment for the faults of others, and I stood king of the class.

Matters, were at last made up between M'Gill's parents and the schoolmaster, but by that time I had got the start of him, and never in my life did I exert myself so much as to keep the mastery. It was in vain; the powers of enchantment prevailed, and I was again turned down with the tear in my eye. I could think of no amends but one, and, being driven to desperation, I put it in practice. I told a lie of him. I came boldly up to the master, and told him that M'Gill had in my hearing cursed him in a most shocking manner, and called him vile names. He called M'Gill, and charged him with the crime, and the proud young coxcomb was so stunned at the atrocity of the charge that his face grew as red as crimson, and the words stuck in his throat as he feebly denied it. His guilt was manifest, and he was again flogged most nobly and dismissed the school for ever in disgrace, as a most incorrigible vagabond.

This was a great victory gained, and I rejoiced and exulted exceedingly in it. It had, however, very nigh cost me my life; for not long thereafter I encountered M'Gill in the fields, on which he came up and challenged me for a liar, daring me to fight him. I refused, and said that I looked on him as quite below my notice; but he would not quit me, and finally told me that he should either lick me, or I should lick him, as he had no other means of being revenged on such a scoundrel. I tried to intimidate him, but it would not do; and I believe I would have given all that I had in the world to be quit of him. He at length went so far as first to kick me, and then strike me on the face; and, being both older and stronger than he, I thought it scarcely became me to take such insults patiently. I was, nevertheless, well aware that the devilish powers of his mother would finally prevail; and either the dread of this, or the inward consciousness of having wronged him, certainly unnerved my arm, for I fought wretchedly, and was soon wholly overcome. I was so sore defeated that I kneeled and was going to beg his pardon; but another thought struck me momentarily, and I threw myself on my face, and inwardly begged aid from

The Private Memoirs and Confessions of a Justified Sinner

heaven; at the same time I felt as if assured that my prayer was heard, and would be answered. While I was in this humble attitude, the villain kicked me with his foot and cursed me; and I, being newly encouraged, arose and encountered him once more. We had not fought long at this second turn before I saw a man hastening towards us; on which I uttered a shout of joy, and laid on valiantly; but my very next look assured me that the man was old John Barnet, whom I had likewise wronged all that was in my power, and between these two wicked persons I expected anything but justice. My arm was again enfeebled, and that of my adversary prevailed. I was knocked down and mauled most grievously, and, while the ruffian was kicking and cuffing me at his will and pleasure, up came old John Barnet, breathless with running, and, at one blow with his open hand, levelled my opponent with the earth. "Tak ye that, maister!" said John, "to learn ye better breeding. Hout awa, man! An ye will fight, fight fair. Gude sauf us, ir ye a gentleman's brood, that ye will kick an' cuff a lad when he's down?"

When I heard this kind and unexpected interference, I began once more to value myself on my courage, and, springing up, I made at my adversary; but John, without saying a word, bit his lip, and seizing me by the neck threw me down. M'Gill begged of him to stand and see fair play, and suffer us to finish the battle; for, added he, "he is a liar, and a scoundrel, and deserves ten times more than I can give him."

"I ken he's a' that ye say, an' mair, my man," quoth John. "But am I sure that ye're no as bad, an' waur? It says nae muckle for ony o' ye to be tearing like tikes at one anither here."

John cocked his cudgel and stood between us, threatening to knock the one dead who first offered to lift his hand against the other; but, perceiving no disposition in any of us to separate, he drove me home before him like a bullock, and keeping close guard behind me, lest M'Gill had followed. I felt greatly indebted to John, yet I complained of his interference to my mother, and the old officious sinner got no thanks for his pains.

As I am writing only from recollection, so I remember of nothing farther in these early days, in the least worthy of being recorded. That I was a great, a transcendent sinner, I confess. But still I had hopes of forgiveness, because I never sinned from principle, but accident; and then I always tried to repent of these sins by the slump, for individually it was impossible; and, though not always successful in my endeavours, I could not help that, the grace of repentance being withheld from me, I regarded myself as in no degree accountable for the failure.

Moreover, there were many of the most deadly sins into which I never fell, for I dreaded those mentioned in the Revelations as excluding sins, so that I guarded against them continually. In particular, I brought myself to despise, if not to abhor, the beauty of women, looking on it as the greatest snare to which mankind was subjected, and though young men and maidens, and even old women (my mother among the rest), taxed me with being an unnatural wretch, I gloried in my acquisition; and, to this day, am thankful for having escaped the most dangerous of all snares.

I kept myself also free of the sins of idolatry and misbelief, both of a deadly nature; and, upon the whole, I think I had not then broken, that is, absolutely broken, above four out of the ten commandments; but, for all that, I had more sense than to regard either my good works, or my evil deeds, as in the smallest degree influencing the eternal decrees of God concerning me, either with regard to my acceptance or reprobation. I depended entirely on the bounty of free grace, holding all the righteousness of man as filthy rags, and believing in the momentous and magnificent truth that, the more heavily loaden with transgressions, the more welcome was the believer at the throne of grace. And I have reason to believe that it was this dependence and this belief that at last ensured my acceptance there.

I come now to the most important period of my existence — the period that has modelled my character, and influenced every action of my life — without which, this detail of my actions would have been as a tale that hath been told — a monotonous farrago — an uninteresting harangue — in short, a thing of nothing. Whereas, lo! it must now be a relation of great and terrible actions, done in the might, and by the commission of heaven. Amen.

Like the sinful king of Israel, I had been walking softly before the Lord for a season. I had been humbled for my transgressions, and, as far as I recollect, sorry on account of their numbers and heinousness. My reverend father had been, moreover, examining me every day regarding the state of my soul, and my answers sometimes appeared to give him satisfaction, and sometimes not. As for my mother, she would harp on the subject of my faith for ever; yet, though I knew her to be a Christian, I confess that I always despised her motley instructions, nor had I any great regard for her person. If this was a crime in me, I never could help it. I confess it freely, and believe it was a judgment from heaven inflicted on her for some sin of former days, and that I had no power to have acted

The Private Memoirs and Confessions of a Justified Sinner

otherwise towards her than I did.

In this frame of mind was I when my reverend father one morning arose from his seat, and, meeting me as I entered the room, he embraced me, and welcomed me into the community of the just upon earth. I was struck speechless, and could make no answer save by looks of surprise. My mother also came to me, kissed, and wept over me; and, after showering unnumbered blessings on my head, she also welcomed me into the society of the just made perfect. Then each of them took me by a hand, and my reverend father explained to me how he had wrestled with God, as the patriarch of old had done, not for a night, but for days and years, and that in bitterness and anguish of spirit, on my account; but, that he had at last prevailed, and had now gained the long and earnestly desired assurance of my acceptance with the Almighty, in and through the merits and sufferings of his Son. That I was now a justified person, adopted among the number of God's children—my name written in the Lamb's book of life, and that no by-past transgression, nor any future act of my own, or of other men, could be instrumental in altering the decree. "All the powers of darkness," added he, "shall never be able to pluck you again out of your Redeemer's hand. And now, my son, be strong and steadfast in the truth. Set your face against sin, and sinful men, and resist even to blood, as many of the faithful of this land have done, and your reward shall be double. I am assured of your acceptance by the word and spirit of Him who cannot err, and your sanctification and repentance unto life will follow in due course. Rejoice and be thankful, for you are plucked as a brand out of the burning, and now your redemption is sealed and sure."

I wept for joy to be thus assured of my freedom from all sin, and of the impossibility of my ever again falling away from my new state. I bounded away into the fields and the woods, to pour out my spirit in prayer before the Almighty for his kindness to me: my whole frame seemed to be renewed; every nerve was buoyant with new life; I felt as if I could have flown in the air, or leaped over the tops of the trees. An exaltation of spirit lifted me, as it were, far above the earth and the sinful creatures crawling on its surface; and I deemed myself as an eagle among the children of men, soaring on high, and looking down with pity and contempt on the grovelling creatures below.

As I thus wended my way, I beheld a young man of a mysterious appearance coming towards me. I tried to shun him, being bent on my own contemplations; but he cast himself in my way, so that I could not well avoid him; and, more than that,

The Private Memoirs and Confessions of a Justified Sinner

I felt a sort of invisible power that drew me towards him, something like the force of enchantment, which I could not resist. As we approached each other, our eyes met and I can never describe the strange sensations that thrilled through my whole frame at that impressive moment; a moment to me fraught with the most tremendous consequences; the beginning of a series of adventures which has puzzled myself, and will puzzle the world when I am no more in it. That time will now soon arrive, sooner than anyone can devise who knows not the tumult of my thoughts and the labour of my spirit; and when it hath come and passed over, when my flesh and my bones are decayed, and my soul has passed to its everlasting home, then shall the sons of men ponder on the events of my life; wonder and tremble, and tremble and wonder how such things should be.

That strange youth and I approached each other in silence, and slowly, with our eyes fixed on each other's eyes. We approached till not more than a yard intervened between us, and then stood still and gazed, measuring each other from head to foot. What was my astonishment on perceiving that he was the same being as myself! The clothes were the same to the smallest item. The form was the same; the apparent age; the colour of the hair; the eyes; and, as far as recollection could serve me from viewing my own features in a glass, the features too were the very same. I conceived at first that I saw a vision, and that my guardian angel had appeared to me at this important era of my life; but this singular being read my thoughts in my looks, anticipating the very words that I was going to utter.

"You think I am your brother," said he; "or that I am your second self. I am indeed your brother, not according to the flesh, but in my belief of the same truths, and my assurance in the same mode of redemption, than which I hold nothing so great or so glorious on earth."

"Then you are an associate well adapted to my present state," said I. "For this time is a time of great rejoicing in spirit to me. I am on my way to return thanks to the Most High for my redemption from the bonds of sin and misery. If you will join with me heart and hand in youthful thanksgiving, then shall we two go and worship together; but, if not, go your way, and I shall go mine."

"Ah, you little know with how much pleasure I will accompany you, and join with you in your elevated devotions," said he fervently. "Your state is a state to be envied indeed; but I have been advised of it, and am come to be a humble disciple of yours; to be initiated into the true way of salvation by conversing with you, and perhaps of being assisted by your prayers."

My spiritual pride being greatly elevated by this address, I began to assume the preceptor, and questioned this extraordinary youth with regard to his religious principles, telling him plainly, if he was one who expected acceptance with God at all, on account of good works, that I would hold no communion with him. He renounced these at once, with the greatest vehemence, and declared his acquiescence in my faith. I asked if he believed in the eternal and irrevocable decrees of God, regarding the salvation and condemnation of all mankind? He answered that he did so: aye, what would signify all things else that he believed, if he did not believe in that? We then went on to commune about all our points of belief; and in everything that I suggested he acquiesced, and, as I thought that day, often carried them to extremes, so that I had a secret dread he was advancing blasphemies. He had such a way with him, and paid such a deference to all my opinions, that I was quite captivated, and, at the same time, I stood in a sort of awe of him, which I could not account for, and several times was seized with an involuntary inclination to escape from his presence by making a sudden retreat. But he seemed constantly to anticipate my thoughts, and was sure to divert my purpose by some turn in the conversation that particularly interested me. He took care to dwell much on the theme of the impossibility of those ever falling away who were once accepted and received into covenant with God, for he seemed to know that in that confidence, and that trust, my whole hopes were centred.

We moved about from one place to another, until the day was wholly spent. My mind had all the while been kept in a state of agitation resembling the motion of a whirlpool, and, when we came to separate, I then discovered that the purpose for which I had sought the fields had been neglected, and that I had been diverted from the worship of God by attending to the quibbles and dogmas of this singular and unaccountable being, who seemed to have more knowledge and information than all the persons I had ever known put together.

We parted with expressions of mutual regret, and when I left him I felt a deliverance, but at the same time a certain consciousness that I was not thus to get free of him, but that he was like to be an acquaintance that was to stick to me for good or for evil. I was astonished at his acuteness and knowledge about everything; but, as for his likeness to me, that was quite unaccountable. He was the same person in every respect, but yet he was not always so; for I observed several times, when we were speaking of certain divines and their tenets, that his face assumed something of the appearance of theirs; and it struck me that, by setting his features to the mould of other people's, he entered at once into their conceptions and feelings. I had been greatly flattered, and greatly interested by his conversation; whether I had been the better for it or the worse, I could not tell. I had been diverted from returning thanks to my gracious Maker for his great kindness to me, and came home as I went away, but not with the same buoyancy and lightness of heart. Well may I remember the day in which I was first received into the number, and made an heir to all the privileges of the children of God, and on which I first met this mysterious associate, who from that day forth contrived to wind himself into all my affairs, both spiritual and temporal, to this day on which I am writing the account of it. It was on the 25th day of March, 1704, when I had just entered the eighteenth year of my age. Whether it behoves me to bless God for the events of that day, or to deplore them, has been hid from my discernment, though I have inquired into it with fear and trembling; and I have now lost all hopes of ever discovering the true import of these events until that day when my accounts are to make up and reckon for in another world.

When I came home, I went straight into the parlour, where my mother was sitting by herself. She started to her feet, and uttered a smothered scream. "What ails you, Robert?" cried she. "My dear son, what is the matter with you?"

"Do you see anything the matter with me?" said I. "It appears that the ailment is with yourself and either in your crazed head or your dim eyes, for there is nothing the matter with me."

"Ah, Robert, you are ill!" cried she. "You are very ill, my dear boy; you are quite changed; your very voice and manner are changed. Ah, Jane, haste you up to the study, and tell Mr. Wringhim to come here on the instant and speak to Robert."

"I beseech you, woman, to restrain yourself," said I. "If you suffer your frenzy to run away with your judgment in this manner, I will leave the house. What do you mean? I tell you, there is nothing ails me: I never was better."

She screamed, and ran between me and the door, to bar my retreat: in the meantime my reverend father entered, and I have not forgot how he gazed, through his glasses, first at my mother, and then at me. I imagined that his eyes burnt like candles, and was afraid of him, which I suppose made my looks more unstable than they would otherwise have been.

"What is all this for?" said he. "Mistress! Robert! What is the matter here?"

"Oh, sir, our boy!" cried my mother; "our dear boy, Mr. Wringhim! Look at him, and speak to him: he is either dying or translated, sir!"

He looked at me with a countenance of great alarm; mumbling some sentences to himself, and then taking me by the arm, as if to feel my pulse, he said, with a faltering voice: "Something has indeed befallen you, either in body or mind, boy, for you are transformed, since the morning, that I could not have known you for the same person. Have you met with any accident?"

"No."

"Have you seen anything out of the ordinary course of nature?"

"No."

"Then, Satan, I fear, has been busy with you, tempting you in no ordinary degree at this momentous crisis of your life?"

My mind turned on my associate for the day, and the idea that he might be an agent of the Devil had such an effect on me that I could make no answer.

"I see how it is," said he; "you are troubled in spirit, and I have no doubt that the enemy of our salvation has been busy with you. Tell me this, has he overcome you, or has he not?"

"He has not, my dear father," said I. "In the strength of the Lord, I hope I have withstood him. But indeed, if he has been busy with me, I knew it not. I have been conversant this day with one stranger only, whom I took rather for an angel of light."

"It is one of the Devil's most profound wiles to appear like one," said my mother.

"Woman, hold thy peace!" said my reverend father. "Thou pretendest to teach what thou knowest not. Tell me this, boy: did this stranger, with whom you met, adhere to the religious principles in which I have educated you?"

"Yes, to every one of them in their fullest latitude," said I.

"Then he was no agent of the Wicked One with whom you held converse," said he: "for that is the doctrine that was made to overturn the principalities and powers, the might and dominion of the kingdom of darkness. Let us pray."

After spending about a quarter of an hour in solemn and sublime thanksgiving, this saintly man and minister of Christ Jesus, gave out that the day following should be kept by the family as a day of solemn thanksgiving, and spent in prayer and praise, on account of the calling and election of one of its members; or rather for the election of that individual being revealed on earth, as well as confirmed in Heaven.

The next day was with me a day of holy exultation. It was begun by my reverend father laying his hands upon my head and blessing me, and then dedicating me to the Lord in the most awful and impressive manner. It was in no common way that he exercised this profound rite, for it was done with all the zeal and enthusiasm of a devotee to the true cause, and a champion on the side he had espoused. He used these remarkable words, which I have still treasured up in my heart: "I give him unto Thee only, to Thee wholly, and to Thee for ever. I dedicate him unto Thee, soul, body, and spirit. Not as the wicked of this world, or the hirelings of a Church profanely called by Thy name, do I dedicate this Thy servant to Thee: Not in words and form, learned by rote, and dictated by the limbs of Antichrist, but, Lord, I give him into Thy hand, as a captain putteth a sword into the hand of his sovereign, wherewith to lay waste his enemies. May he be a two-edged weapon in Thy hand and a spear coming out of Thy mouth, to destroy, and overcome, and pass over; and may the enemies of Thy Church fall down before him, and be as dung to fat the land!"

From the moment, I conceived it decreed, not that I should be a minister of the gospel, but a champion of it, to cut off the enemies of the Lord from the face of the earth; and I rejoiced in the commission, finding it more congenial to my nature to be cutting sinners off with the sword than to be haranguing them from the pulpit, striving to produce an effect which God, by his act of absolute predestination, had for ever rendered impracticable. The more I pondered on these things the more I saw of the folly and inconsistency of ministers in spending their lives striving and remonstrating with sinners in order to induce them to do that which they had it not in their power to do.

The Private Memoirs and Confessions of a Justified Sinner

Seeing that God had from all eternity decided the fate of every individual that was to be born of woman, how vain was it in man to endeavour to save those whom their Maker had, by an unchangeable decree, doomed to destruction. I could not disbelieve the doctrine which the best of men had taught me, and towards which he made the whole of the Scriptures to bear, and yet it made the economy of the Christian world appear to me as an absolute contradiction. How much more wise would it be, thought I, to begin and cut sinners off with the sword! For till that is effected, the saints can never inherit the earth in peace. Should I be honoured as an instrument to begin this great work of purification, I should rejoice in it. But, then, where had I the means, or under what direction was I to begin? There was one thing clear, I was now the Lord's and it behoved me to bestir myself in His service. Oh that I had an host at my command, then would I be as a devouring fire among the workers of iniquity!

Full of these great ideas, I hurried through the city, and sought again the private path through the field and wood of Finnieston, in which my reverend preceptor had the privilege of walking for study, and to which he had a key that was always at my command. Near one of the stiles, I perceived a young man sitting in a devout posture, reading a Bible. He rose, lifted his hat, and made an obeisance to me, which I returned and walked on. I had not well crossed the stile till it struck me I knew the face of the youth and that he was some intimate acquaintance, to whom I ought to have spoken. I walked on, and returned, and walked on again, trying to recollect who he was; but for my life I could not. There was, however, a fascination in his look and manner that drew me back towards him in spite of myself, and I resolved to go to him, if it were merely to speak and see who he was.

I came up to him and addressed him, but he was so intent on his book that, though I spoke, he lifted not his eyes. I looked on the book also, and still it seemed a Bible, having columns, chapters, and verses; but it was in a language of which I was wholly ignorant, and all intersected with red lines and verses. A sensation resembling a stroke of electricity came over me, on first casting my eyes on that mysterious book, and I stood motionless. He looked up, smiled, closed his book, and put it in his bosom. "You seem strangely affected, dear sir, by looking at my book," said he mildly.

"In the name of God, what book is that?" said I. "Is it a Bible?"

"It is my Bible, sir," said he, "but I will cease reading it, for I am glad to see you. Pray, is not this a day for holy festivity with you?"

I stared in his face, but made no answer, for my senses were bewildered.

"Do you not know me?" said he. "You appear to be somehow at a loss. Had not you and I some sweet communion and fellowship yesterday?"

"I beg your pardon, sir," said I. "But, surely, if you are the young gentleman with whom I spent the hours yesterday, you have the chameleon art of changing your appearance; I never could have recognized you."

"My countenance changes with my studies and sensations," said he. "It is a natural peculiarity in me, over which I have not full control. If I contemplate a man's features seriously, mine own gradually assume the very same appearance and character. And what is more, by contemplating a face minutely, I not only attain the same likeness but, with the likeness, I attain the very same ideas as well as the same mode of arranging them, so that, you see, by looking at a person attentively, I by degrees assume his likeness, and by assuming his likeness I attain to the possession of his most secret thoughts. This, I say, is a peculiarity in my nature, a gift of the God that made me; but, whether or not given me for a blessing, He knows Himself, and so do I. At all events, I have this privilege, I can never be mistaken of a character in whom I am interested."

"It is a rare qualification," replied I, "and I would give worlds to possess it. Then, it appears that it is needless to dissemble with you, since you can at any time extract our most secret thoughts from our bosoms. You already know my natural character?"

"Yes," said he, "and it is that which attaches me to you. By assuming your likeness yesterday, I became acquainted with your character, and was no less astonished at the profundity and range of your thoughts than at the heroic magnanimity with which these were combined. And now, in addition to these, you are dedicated to the great work of the Lord; for which reasons I have resolved to attach myself as closely to you as possible, and to render you all the service of which my poor abilities are capable."

The Private Memoirs and Confessions of a Justified Sinner

I confess that I was greatly flattered by these compliments paid to my abilities by a youth of such superior qualifications; by one who, with a modesty and affability rare at his age, combined a height of genius and knowledge almost above human comprehension. Nevertheless, I began to assume a certain superiority of demeanour towards him, as judging it incumbent on me to do so, in order to keep up his idea of my exalted character. We conversed again till the day was near a close; and the things that he strove most to inculcate on my mind were the infallibility of the elect, and the preordination of all things that come to pass. I pretended to controvert the first of these, for the purpose of showing him the extent of my argumentative powers, and said that "indubitably there were degrees of sinning which would induce the Almighty to throw off the very elect." But behold my hitherto humble and modest companion took up the argument with such warmth that he put me not only to silence but to absolute shame.

"Why, sir," said he, "by vending such an insinuation, you put discredit on the great atonement, in which you trust. Is there not enough of merit in the blood of Jesus to save thousands of worlds, if it was for these worlds that he died? Now, when you know, as you do (and as every one of the elect may know of himself) that this Saviour died for you, namely and particularly, dare you say that there is not enough of merit in His great atonement to annihilate all your sins, let them be as heinous and atrocious as they may? And, moreover, do you not acknowledge that God hath pre-ordained and decreed whatsoever comes to pass? Then, how is it that you should deem it in your power to eschew one action of your life, whether good or evil? Depend on it, the advice of the great preacher is genuine: 'What thine hand findeth to do, do it with all thy might, for none of us knows what a day may bring forth.' That is, none of us knows what is pre-ordained, but whatever it is pre-ordained we must do, and none of these things will be laid to our charge."

I could hardly believe that these sayings were genuine or orthodox; but I soon felt that, instead of being a humble disciple of mine, this new acquaintance was to be my guide and director, and all under the humble guise of one stooping at my feet to learn the right. He said that he saw I was ordained to perform some great action for the cause of Jesus and His Church, and he earnestly coveted being a partaker with me; but he besought of me never to think it possible for me to fall from the truth, or the favour of Him who had chosen me, else that misbelief would baulk every good work to which I set my face.

The Private Memoirs and Confessions of a Justified Sinner

There was something so flattering in all this that I could not resist it. Still, when he took leave of me, I felt it as a great relief; and yet, before the morrow, I wearied and was impatient to see him again. We carried on our fellowship from day to day, and all the while I knew not who he was, and still my mother and reverend father kept insisting that I was an altered youth, changed in my appearance, my manners, and my whole conduct; yet something always prevented me from telling them more about my new acquaintance than I had done on the first day we met. I rejoiced in him, was proud of him, and soon could not live without him; yet, though resolved every day to disclose the whole story of my connection with him, I had it not in my power. Something always prevented me, till at length I thought no more of it, but resolved to enjoy his fascinating company in private, and by all means to keep my own with him. The resolution was vain: I set a bold face to it, but my powers were inadequate to the task; my adherent, with all the suavity imaginable, was sure to carry his point. I sometimes fumed, and sometimes shed tears at being obliged to yield to proposals against which I had at first felt every reasoning power of my soul rise in opposition; but for all that he never faded in carrying conviction along with him in effect, for he either forced me to acquiesce in his measures, and assent to the truth of his positions, or he put me so completely down that I had not a word left to advance against them.

After weeks, and I may say months of intimacy, I observed, somewhat to my amazement, that we had never once prayed together; and, more than that, that he had constantly led my attentions away from that duty, causing me to neglect it wholly. I thought this a bad mark of a man seemingly so much set on inculcating certain important points of religion, and resolved next day to put him to the test, and request him to perform that sacred duty in name of us both. He objected boldly; saying there were very few people indeed with whom he could join in prayer, and he made a point of never doing it, as he was sure they were to ask many things of which he disapproved, and that, if he were to officiate himself, he was as certain to allude to many things that came not within the range of their faith. He disapproved of prayer altogether in the manner it was generally gone about, he said. Man made it merely a selfish concern, and was constantly employed asking, asking, for everything. Whereas it became all God's creatures to be content with their lot, and only to kneel before him in order to thank him for such benefits as he saw meet to bestow. In short, he argued with such energy that before we parted I acquiesced, as usual, in his position, and never mentioned prayer to him any more.

The Private Memoirs and Confessions of a Justified Sinner

Having been so frequently seen in his company, several people happened to mention the circumstance to my mother and reverend father; but at the same time had all described him differently. At length, they began to examine me with respect to the company I kept, as I absented myself from home day after day. I told them I kept company only with one young gentleman, whose whole manner of thinking on religious subjects I found so congenial with my own that I could not live out of his society. My mother began to lay down some of her old hackneyed rules of faith, but I turned from hearing her with disgust; for, after the energy of my new friend's reasoning, hers appeared so tame I could not endure it. And I confess with shame that my reverend preceptor's religious dissertations began, about this time, to lose their relish very much, and by degrees became exceedingly tiresome to my ear. They were so inferior, in strength and sublimity, to the most common observations of my young friend that in drawing a comparison the former appeared as nothing. He, however, examined me about many things relating to my companion, in all of which I satisfied him, save in one: I could neither tell him who my friend was, what was his name, nor of whom he was descended; and I wondered at myself how I had never once adverted to such a thing for all the time we had been intimate.

I inquired the next day what his name was; as I said I was often at a loss for it, when talking with him. He replied that there was no occasion for any one friend ever naming another, when their society was held in private, as ours was; for his part he had never once named me since we first met, and never intended to do so, unless by my own request. "But if you cannot converse without naming me, you may call me Gil for the present," added he, "and if I think proper to take another name at any future period, it shall be with your approbation."

"Gil!" said I. "Have you no name but Gil? Or which of your names is it? Your Christian or surname?"

"Oh, you must have a surname too, must you!" replied he. "Very well, you may call me Gil-Martin. It is not my Christian name; but it is a name which may serve your turn."

"This is very strange!" said I. "Are you ashamed of your parents that you refuse to give your real name?"

"I have no parents save one, whom I do not acknowledge," said he proudly. "Therefore, pray drop that subject, for it is a disagreeable one. I am a being of a very peculiar temper, for, though I have servants and subjects more than I can number, yet, to gratify a certain whim, I have left them, and retired to this city, and, for all the society it contains, you see I have attached myself only to you. This is a secret, and I tell you only in friendship, therefore pray let it remain one, and say not another word about the matter."

I assented, and said no more concerning it; for it instantly struck me that this was no other than the Czar Peter of Russia, having heard that he had been travelling through Europe in disguise, and I cannot say that I had not thenceforward great and mighty hopes of high preferment, as a defender and avenger of the oppressed Christian Church, under the influence of this great potentate. He had hinted as much already, as that it was more honourable, and of more avail to put down the wicked with the sword than try to reform them, and I thought myself quite justified in supposing that he intended me for some great employment, that he had thus selected me for his companion out of all the rest in Scotland, and even pretended to learn the great truths of religion from my mouth. From that time I felt disposed to yield to such a great prince's suggestions without hesitation.

Nothing ever astonished me so much as the uncommon powers with which he seemed invested. In our walk one day, we met with a Mr. Blanchard, who was reckoned a worthy, pious divine, but quite of the moral cast, who joined us; and we three walked on, and rested together in the fields. My companion did not seem to like him, but, nevertheless, regarded him frequently with deep attention, and there were several times, while he seemed contemplating him, and trying to find out his thoughts, that his face became so like Mr. Blanchard's that it was impossible to have distinguished the one from the other. The antipathy between the two was mutual, and discovered itself quite palpably in a short time. When my companion the prince was gone, Mr. Blanchard asked me anent him, and I told him that he was a stranger in the city, but a very uncommon and great personage. Mr. Blanchard's answer to me was as follows: "I never saw anybody I disliked so much in my life, Mr. Robert; and if it be true that he is a stranger here, which I doubt, believe me he is come for no good."

"Do you not perceive what mighty powers of mind he is possessed of?" said I, "and also how clear and unhesitating he is on some of the most interesting points of divinity?"

"It is for his great mental faculties that I dread him," said he. "It is incalculable what evil such a person as he may do, if so disposed. There is a sublimity in his ideas, with which there is

The Private Memoirs and Confessions of a Justified Sinner

to me a mixture of terror; and, when he talks of religion, he does it as one that rather dreads its truths than reverences them. He, indeed, pretends great strictness of orthodoxy regarding some of the points of doctrine embraced by the reformed church; but you do not seem to perceive that both you and he are carrying these points to a dangerous extremity. Religion is a sublime and glorious thing, the bonds of society on earth, and the connector of humanity with the Divine nature; but there is nothing so dangerous to man as the wresting of any of its principles, or forcing them beyond their due bounds: this is of all others the readiest way to destruction. Neither is there anything so easily done. There is not an error into which a man can fall which he may not press Scripture into his service as proof of the probity of, and though your boasted theologian shunned the full discussion of the subject before me, while you pressed it, I can easily see that both you and he are carrying your ideas of absolute predestination, and its concomitant appendages, to an extent that overthrows all religion and revelation together; or, at least, jumbles them into a chaos, out of which human capacity can never select what is good. Believe me, Mr. Robert, the less you associate with that illustrious stranger the better, for it appears to me that your creed and his carries damnation on the very front of it."

I was rather stunned at this; but pretended to smile with disdain, and said it did not become youth to control age; and, as I knew our principles differed fundamentally, it behoved us to drop the subject. He, however, would not drop it, but took both my principles and me fearfully to task, for Blanchard was an eloquent and powerful-minded old man; and, before we parted, I believe I promised to drop my new acquaintance, and was all but resolved to do it.

As well might I have laid my account with shunning the light of day. He was constant to me as my shadow, and by degrees he acquired such an ascendency over me that I never was happy out of his company, nor greatly so in it. When I repeated to him all that Mr. Blanchard had said, his countenance kindled with indignation and rage; and then by degrees his eyes sunk inward, his brow lowered, so that I was awed, and withdrew my eyes from looking at him. A while afterwards as I was addressing him, I chanced to look him again in the face, and the sight of him made me start violently. He had made himself so like Mr. Blanchard that I actually believed I had been addressing that gentleman, and that I had done so in some absence of mind that I could not account for. Instead of being amused at the quandary I was in, he seemed offended: indeed, he never was truly amused with anything. And he then

The Private Memoirs and Confessions of a Justified Sinner

asked me sullenly, if I conceived such personages as he to have no other endowments than common mortals?

I said I never conceived that princes or potentates had any greater share of endowments than other men, and frequently not so much. He shook his head, and bade me think over the subject again; and there was an end of it. I certainly felt every day the more disposed to acknowledge such a superiority in him; and, from all that I could gather, I had now no doubt that he was Peter of Russia. Everything combined to warrant the supposition, and, of course, I resolved to act in conformity with the discovery I had made.

For several days the subject of Mr. Blanchard's doubts and doctrines formed the theme of our discourse. My friend deprecated them most devoutly; and then again he would deplore them, and lament the great evil that such a man might do among the human race. I joined with him in allowing the evil in its fullest latitude; and, at length, after he thought he had fully prepared my nature for such a trial of its powers and abilities, he proposed calmly that we two should make away with Mr. Blanchard. I was so shocked that my bosom became as it were a void, and the beatings of my heart sounded loud and hollow in it; my breath cut, and my tongue and palate became dry and speechless. He mocked at my cowardice, and began a-reasoning on the matter with such powerful eloquence that, before we parted, I felt fully convinced that it was my bounden duty to slay Mr. Blanchard; but my will was far, very far from consenting to the deed.

I spent the following night without sleep, or nearly so; and the next morning, by the time the sun arose, I was again abroad, and in the company of my illustrious friend. The same subject was resumed, and again he reasoned to the following purport: That supposing me placed at the head of any army of Christian soldiers, all bent on putting down the enemies of the Church, would I have any hesitation in destroying and rooting out these enemies? None, surely. Well then, when I saw and was convinced that here was an individual who was doing more detriment to the Church of Christ on earth than tens of thousands of such warriors were capable of doing, was it not my duty to cut him off, and save the elect? "He who would be a champion in the cause of Christ and His Church, my brave young friend," added he, "must begin early, and no man can calculate to what an illustrious eminence small beginnings may lead. If the man Blanchard is worthy, he is only changing his situation for a better one; and, if unworthy, it is better that one fall than that a thousand souls perish. Let us be up and doing in

The Private Memoirs and Confessions of a Justified Sinner

our vocations. For me, my resolution is taken; I have but one great aim in this world, and I never for a moment lose sight of it."

I was obliged to admit the force of his reasoning; for, though I cannot from memory repeat his words, his eloquence was of that overpowering nature that the subtilty of other men sunk before it; and there is also little doubt that the assurance I had that these words were spoken by a great potentate who could raise me to the highest eminence (provided that I entered into his extensive and decisive measures) assisted mightily in dispelling my youthful scruples and qualms of conscience; and I thought moreover that, having such a powerful back friend to support me, I hardly needed to be afraid of the consequences. I consented! But begged a little time to think of it. He said the less one thought of a duty the better; and we parted.

But the most singular instance of this wonderful man's power over my mind was that he had as complete influence over me by night as by day. All my dreams corresponded exactly with his suggestions; and, when he was absent from me, still his arguments sunk deeper in my heart than even when he was present. I dreamed that night of a great triumph obtained, and, though the whole scene was but dimly and confusedly defined in my vision, yet the overthrow and death of Mr. Blanchard was the first step by which I attained the eminent station I occupied. Thus, by dreaming of the event by night, and discoursing of it by day, it soon became so familiar to my mind that I almost conceived it as done. It was resolved on: which was the first and greatest victory gained; for there was no difficulty in finding opportunities enow of cutting off a man who, every good day, was to be found walking by himself in private grounds. I went and heard him preach for two days, and in fact I held his tenets scarcely short of blasphemy; they were such as I had never heard before, and his congregation, which was numerous, were turning up their ears and drinking in his doctrines with the utmost delight; for Oh they suited their carnal natures and self-sufficiency to a hair! He was actually holding it forth, as a fact, that "it was every man's own blame if he was not saved!" What horrible misconstruction! And then he was alleging, and trying to prove from nature and reason, that no man ever was guilty of a sinful action who might not have declined it had he so chosen! "Wretched controvertist!" thought I to myself an hundred times, "shall not the sword of the Lord be moved from its place of peace for such presumptuous, absurd testimonies as these!"

When I began to tell the prince about these false doctrines, to my astonishment I found that he had been in the church himself, and had every argument that the old divine had used verbatim; and he remarked on them with great concern that these were not the tenets that corresponded with his views in society, and that he had agents in every city, and every land, exerting their powers to put them down. I asked, with great simplicity: "Are all your subjects Christians, prince?"

"All my European subjects are, or deem themselves so," returned he; "and they are the most faithful and true subjects I have."

Who could doubt, after this, that he was the Czar of Russia? I have nevertheless had reasons to doubt of his identity since that period, and which of my conjectures is right I believe the God of Heaven only knows, for I do not. I shall go on to write such things as I remember, and, if anyone shall ever take the trouble to read over these confessions, such a one will judge for himself. It will be observed that, since ever I fell in with this extraordinary person, I have written about him only, and I must continue to do so to the end of this memoir, as I have performed no great or interesting action in which he had not a principal share.

He came to me one day and said: "We must not linger thus in executing what we have resolved on. We have much before our hands to perform for the benefit of mankind, both civil as well as religious. Let us do what we have to do here, and then we must wend our way to other cities, and perhaps to other countries. Mr. Blanchard is to hold forth in the high church of Paisley on Sunday next, on some particularly great occasion: this must be defeated; he must not go there. As he will be busy arranging his discourses, we may expect him to be walking by himself in Finnieston Dell the greater part of Friday and Saturday. Let us go and cut him off. What is the life of a man more than the life of a lamb, or any guiltless animal? It is not half so much, especially when we consider the immensity of the mischief this old fellow is working among our fellow-creatures. Can there be any doubt that it is the duty of one consecrated to God to cut off such a mildew?"

"I fear me, great sovereign," said I, "that your ideas of retribution are too sanguine, and too arbitrary for the laws of this country. I dispute not that your motives are great and high; but have you debated the consequences, and settled the result?"

"I have," returned be, "and hold myself amenable for the action to the laws of God and of equity; as to the enactments of men, I despise them. Fain would I see the weapon of the Lord of Hosts begin the work of vengeance that awaits it to do!"

I could not help thinking that I perceived a little derision of countenance on his face as he said this, nevertheless I sunk dumb before such a man, aroused myself to the task, seeing he would not have it deferred. I approved of it in theory, but my spirit stood aloof from the practice. I saw and was convinced that the elect of God would be happier, and purer, were the wicked and unbelievers all cut off from troubling and misleading them, but if it had not been the instigations of this illustrious stranger, I should never have presumed to begin so great a work myself. Yet, though he often aroused my zeal to the highest pitch, still my heart at times shrunk from the shedding of life-blood, and it was only at the earnest and unceasing instigations of my enlightened and voluntary patron that I at length put my hand to the conclusive work. After I said all that I could say, and all had been overborne (I remember my actions and words as well as it had been yesterday), I turned round hesitatingly, and looked up to Heaven for direction; but there was a dimness come over my eyes that I could not see. The appearance was as if there had been a veil drawn over me, so nigh that I put up my hand to feel it; and then Gil-Martin (as this great sovereign was pleased to have himself called) frowned, and asked me what I was grasping at. I knew not what to say, but answered, with fear and shame: "I have no weapons, not one; nor know I where any are to be found."

"The God whom thou servest will provide these," said he, "if thou provest worthy of the trust committed to thee."

I looked again up into the cloudy veil that covered us and thought I beheld golden weapons of every description let down in it, but all with their points towards me. I kneeled, and was going to stretch out my hand to take one, when my patron seized me, as I thought, by the clothes, and dragged me away with as much ease as I had been a lamb, saying, with a joyful and elevated voice: "Come, my friend, let us depart: thou art dreaming—thou art dreaming. Rouse up all the energies of thy exalted mind, for thou art an highly favoured one; and doubt thou not that He whom thou servest, will be ever at thy right and left hand, to direct and assist thee."

These words, but particularly the vision I had seen, of the golden weapons descending out of Heaven, inflamed my zeal to that height that I was as one beside himself; which my parents perceived that night, and made some motions towards confining me to my room. I joined in the family prayers, and then I afterwards sung a psalm and prayed by myself; and I had good reasons for believing that that small oblation of praise and prayer was not turned to sin. But there are strange things, and unaccountable agencies in nature: He only who dwells between the Cherubim can unriddle them, and to Him the honour must redound for ever. Amen.

I felt greatly strengthened and encouraged that night, and the next morning I ran to meet my companion, out of whose eye I had now no life. He rejoiced at seeing me so forward in the great work of reformation by blood, and said many things to raise my hopes of future fame and glory; and then producing two pistols of pure beaten gold, he held them out and proffered me the choice of one, saying: "See what thy master hath provided thee!" I took one of them eagerly, for I perceived at once that they were two of the very weapons that were let down from Heaven in the cloudy veil, the dim tapestry of the firmament; and I said to myself. "Surely this is the will of the Lord."

The little splendid and enchanting piece was so perfect, so complete, and so ready for executing the will of the donor, that I now longed to use it in his service. I loaded it with my own hand, as Gil-Martin did the other, and we took our stations behind a bush of hawthorn and bramble on the verge of the wood, and almost close to the walk. My patron was so acute in all his calculations that he never mistook an event. We had not taken our stand above a minute and a half till old Mr. Blanchard appeared, coming slowly on the path. When we saw this, we cowered down and leaned each of us a knee upon the ground, pointing the pistols through the bush, with an aim so steady that it was impossible to miss our victim.

He came deliberately on, pausing at times so long that we dreaded he was going to turn. Gil-Martin dreaded it, and I said I did, but wished in my heart that he might. He, however, came onward, and I will never forget the manner in which he came! No, I don't believe I ever can forget it, either in the narrow bounds of time or the ages of eternity! He was a broadly, ill-shaped man, of a rude exterior, and a little bent with age; his hands were clasped behind his back and below his coat, and he walked with a slow swinging air that was very peculiar. When he paused and looked abroad on nature, the act was highly impressive: he seemed conscious of being all alone, and conversant only with God and the elements of his creation. Never was there such a picture of human inadvertency! a man approaching step by step to the one that was to hurl him out of one existence into another with as much ease and indifference

The Private Memoirs and Confessions of a Justified Sinner

as the ox goeth to the stall. Hideous vision, wilt thou not be gone from my mental sight! if not, let me bear with thee as I can!

When he came straight opposite to the muzzles of our pieces, Gil-Martin called out "Eh!" with a short quick sound. The old man, without starting, turned his face and breast towards us, and looked into the wood, but looked over our heads.

"Now!" whispered my companion, and fired. But my hand refused the office, for I was not at that moment sure about becoming an assassin in the cause of Christ and His Church. I thought I heard a sweet voice behind me, whispering to me to beware, and I was going to look round, when my companion exclaimed: "Coward, we are ruined!"

I had no time for an alternative: Gil-Martin's ball had not taken effect, which was altogether wonderful, as the old man's breast was within a few yards of him. "Hilloa!" cried Blanchard, "what is that for, you dog!" and with that he came forward to look over the bush. I hesitated, as I said, and attempted to look behind me; but there was no time: the next step discovered two assassins lying in covert, waiting for blood. "Coward, we are ruined!" cried my indignant friend; and that moment my piece was discharged. The effect was as might have been expected: the old man first stumbled to one side, and then fell on his back. We kept our places, and I perceived my companion's eyes gleaming with an unnatural joy. The wounded man raised himself from the bank to a sitting posture, and I beheld his eyes swimming; he however appeared sensible, for we heard him saying in a low and rattling voice: "Alas, alas! whom have I offended, that they should have been driven to an act like this! Come forth and shew yourselves, that I may either forgive you before I die, or curse you in the name of the Lord." He then fell a-groping with both hands on the ground, as if feeling for something he had lost manifestly in the agonies of death; and, with a solemn and interrupted prayer for forgiveness, he breathed his last.

I had become rigid as a statue, whereas my associate appeared to be elevated above measure. "Arise, thou faint-hearted one, and let us be going," said he. "Thou hast done well for once; but wherefore hesitate in such a cause? This is but a small beginning of so great a work as that of purging the Christian world. But the first victim is a worthy one, and more of such lights must be extinguished immediately."

We touched not our victim, nor anything pertaining to him, for fear of staining our hands with his blood; and the firing having brought three men within view, who were hasting towards the spot, my undaunted companion took both the pistols, and went forward as with intent to meet them, bidding me shift for myself. I ran off in a contrary direction, till I came to the foot of the Pearman Sike, and then, running up the hollow of that, I appeared on the top of the bank as if I had been another man brought in view by hearing the shots in such a place. I had a full view of a part of what passed, though not of all. I saw my companion going straight to meet the men, apparently with a pistol in every hand, waving in a careless manner. They seemed not quite clear of meeting with him, and so he went straight on, and passed between them. They looked after him, and came onwards; but, when they came to the old man lying stretched in his blood, then they turned and pursued my companion, though not so quickly as they might have done; and I understand that from the first they saw no more of him.

Great was the confusion that day in Glasgow. The most popular of all their preachers of morality was (what they called) murdered in cold blood, and a strict and extensive search was made for the assassin. Neither of the accomplices was found, however, that is certain, nor was either of them so much as suspected; but another man was apprehended under circumstances that warranted suspicion. This was one of the things that I witnessed in my life, which I never understood, and it surely was one of my patron's most dexterous tricks, for I must still say, what I have thought from the beginning, that like him there never was a man created. The young man who was taken up was a preacher; and it was proved that he had purchased fire-arms in town, and gone out with them that morning. But the far greatest mystery of the whole was that two of the men, out of the three who met my companion, swore that that unfortunate preacher was the man whom they met with a pistol in each hand, fresh from the death of the old divine. The poor fellow made a confused speech himself, which there is not the least doubt was quite true; but it was laughed to scorn, and an expression of horror ran through both the hearers and jury. I heard the whole trial, and so did Gil-Martin; but we left the journeyman preacher to his fate, and from that time forth I have had no faith in the justice of criminal trials. If once a man is prejudiced on one side, he will swear anything in support of such prejudice. I tried to expostulate with my mysterious friend on the horrid injustice of suffering this young man to die for our act, but the prince exulted in it more than the other, and said the latter was the most dangerous man of the two.

The alarm in and about Glasgow was prodigious. The country being divided into two political parties, the court and

The Private Memoirs and Confessions of a Justified Sinner

the country party, the former held meetings, issued proclamations, and offered rewards, ascribing all to the violence of party spirit, and deprecating the infernal measures of their opponents. I did not understand their political differences; but it was easy to see that the true Gospel preachers joined all on one side, and the upholders of pure morality and a blameless life on the other, so that this division proved a test to us, and it was forthwith resolved that we two should pick out some of the leading men of this unsaintly and heterodox cabal, and cut them off one by one, as occasion should suit.

Now, the ice being broke, I felt considerable zeal in our great work, but pretended much more; and we might soon have kidnapped them all through the ingenuity of my patron, had not our next attempt miscarried, by some awkwardness or mistake of mine. The consequence was that he was discovered fairly, and very nigh seized. I also was seen, and suspected so far that my reverend father, my mother, and myself were examined privately. I denied all knowledge of the matter; and they held it in such a ridiculous light, and their conviction of the complete groundlessness of the suspicion was so perfect, that their testimony prevailed, and the affair was hushed. I was obliged, however, to walk circumspectly, and saw my companion the prince very seldom, who was prowling about every day, quite unconcerned about his safety. He was every day a new man, however, and needed not to be alarmed at any danger; for such a facility had he in disguising himself that, if it had not been for a password which we had between us, for the purposes of recognition, I never could have known him myself.

It so happened that my reverend father was called to Edinburgh about this time, to assist with his counsel in settling the national affairs. At my earnest request I was permitted to accompany him, at which both my associate and I rejoiced, as we were now about to move in a new and extensive field. All this time I never knew where my illustrious friend resided. He never once invited me to call on him at his lodgings, nor did he ever come to our house, which made me sometimes to suspect that, if any of our great efforts in the cause of true religion were discovered, he intended leaving me in the lurch. Consequently, when we met in Edinburgh (for we travelled not in company), I proposed to go with him to look for lodgings, telling him at the same time what a blessed religious family my reverend instructor and I were settled in. He said he rejoiced at it, but he made a rule of never lodging in any particular house, but took these daily, or hourly, as he found it convenient, and that he never was at a loss in any circumstance.

"What a mighty trouble you put yourself to, great sovereign!" said I, "and all, it would appear, for the purpose of seeing and knowing more and more of the human race."

"I never go but where I have some great purpose to serve," returned he, "either in the advancement of my own power and dominion or in thwarting my enemies."

"With all due deference to your great comprehension, my illustrious friend," said I, "it strikes me that you can accomplish very little either the one way or the other here, in the humble and private capacity you are pleased to occupy."

"It is your own innate modesty that prompts such a remark," said he. "Do you think the gaining of you to my service is not an attainment worthy of being envied by the greatest potentate in Christendom? Before I had missed such a prize as the attainment of your services, I would have travelled over one half of the habitable globe."—I bowed with great humility, but at the same time how could I but feel proud and highly flattered? He continued: "Believe me, my dear friend, for such a prize I account no effort too high. For a man who is not only dedicated to the King of Heaven in the most solemn manner, soul, body, and spirit, but also chosen of him from the beginning, justified, sanctified, and received into a communion that never shall be broken, and from which no act of his shall ever remove him—the possession of such a man, I tell you, is worth kingdoms; because, every deed that he performs, he does it with perfect safety to himself and honour to me."—I bowed again, lifting my hat, and he went on.—"I am now going to put his courage in the cause he has espoused to a severe test—to a trial at which common nature would revolt, but he who is dedicated to be the sword of the Lord must raise himself above common humanity. You have a father and a brother according to the flesh: what do you know of them?"

"I am sorry to say I know nothing good," said I. "They are reprobates, castaways, beings devoted to the Wicked One, and, like him, workers of every species of iniquity with greediness."

"They must both fall!" said he, with a sigh and melancholy look. "It is decreed in the councils above that they must both fall by your hand."

"The God of Heaven forbid it!" said I. "They are enemies to Christ and His Church, that I know and believe; but they shall live and die in their iniquity for me, and reap their guerdon when their time cometh. There my hand shall not strike."

"The feeling is natural, and amiable," said he. "But you must think again. Whether are the bonds of carnal nature or the bonds and vows of the Lord strongest?"

"I will not reason with you on this head, mighty potentate," said I, "for whenever I do so it is but to be put down. I shall only, express my determination not to take vengeance out of the Lord's hand in this instance. It availeth not. These are men that have the mark of the beast in their foreheads and right hands; they are lost beings themselves, but have no influence over others. Let them perish in their sins; for they shall not be meddled with by me."

"How preposterously you talk, my dear friend!" said he. "These people are your greatest enemies; they would rejoice to see you annihilated. And, now that you have taken up the Lord's cause of being avenged on His enemies, wherefore spare those that are your own as well as His? Besides, you ought to consider what great advantages would be derived to the cause of righteousness and truth were the estate and riches of that opulent house in your possession, rather than in that of such as oppose the truth and all manner of holiness."

This was a portion of the consequence of following my illustrious adviser's summary mode of procedure that had never entered into my calculation. I disclaimed all idea of being influenced by it; however, I cannot but say that the desire of being enabled to do so much good, by the possession of these bad men's riches, made some impression on my heart, and I said I would consider of the matter. I did consider it, and that right seriously as well as frequently; and there was scarcely an hour in the day on which my resolves were not animated by my great friend, till at length I began to have a longing desire to kill my brother, in particular. Should any man ever read this scroll, he will wonder at this confession, and deem it savage and unnatural. So it appeared to me at first, but a constant thinking of an event changes every one of its features. I have done all for the best, and as I was prompted, by one who knew right and wrong much better than I did. I had a desire to slay him, it is true, and such a desire too as a thirsty man has to drink; but, at the same time, this longing desire was mingled with a certain terror, as if I had dreaded that the drink for which I longed was mixed with deadly poison. My mind was so much weakened, or rather softened about this time, that my faith began a little to give way, and I doubted most presumptuously of the least tangible of all Christian tenets, namely, of the infallibility of the elect. I hardly comprehended the great work I had begun, and doubted of my own infallibility, or that of any created being.

But I was brought over again by the unwearied diligence of my friend to repent of my backsliding, and view once more the superiority of the Almighty's counsels in its fullest latitude. Amen.

I prayed very much in secret about this time, and that with great fervour of spirit, as well as humility; and my satisfaction at finding all my requests granted is not to be expressed.

My illustrious friend still continuing to sound in my ears the imperious duty to which I was called, of making away with my sinful relations, and quoting many parallel actions out of the Scriptures, and the writings of the holy fathers, of the pleasure the Lord took in such as executed his vengeance on the wicked, I was obliged to acquiesce in his measures, though with certain limitations. It was not easy to answer his arguments, and yet I was afraid that he soon perceived a leaning to his will on my part. "If the acts of Jehu, in rooting out the whole house of his master, were ordered and approved-of by the Lord," said he, "would it not have been more praiseworthy if one of Ahab's own sons had stood up for the cause of the God of Israel, and rooted out the sinners and their idols out of the land?"

"It would certainly," said I. "To our duty to God all other duties must yield."

"Go thou then and do likewise," said he. "Thou are called to a high vocation; to cleanse the sanctuary of thy God in this thy native land by the shedding of blood; go thou then like a ruling energy, a master spirit of desolation in the dwellings of the wicked, and high shall be your reward both here and hereafter."

My heart now panted with eagerness to look my brother in the face. On which my companion, who was never out of the way, conducted me to a small square in the suburbs of the city, where there were a number of young noblemen and gentlemen playing at a vain, idle, and sinful game, at which there was much of the language of the accursed going on; and among these blasphemers he instantly pointed out my brother to me. I was fired with indignation at seeing him in such company, and so employed; and I placed myself close beside him to watch all his motions, listen to his words, and draw inferences from what I saw and heard. In what a sink of sin was he wallowing! I resolved to take him to task, and, if he refused to be admonished, to inflict on him some condign punishment; and, knowing that my illustrious friend and director was looking on, I resolved to show some spirit. Accordingly, I waited until I heard him profane his Maker's name three times, and then, my

The Private Memoirs and Confessions of a Justified Sinner

spiritual indignation being roused above all restraint, I went up and kicked him. Yes, I went boldly up and struck him with my foot, and meant to have given him a more severe blow than it was my fortune to inflict. It had, however, the effect of rousing up his corrupt nature to quarrelling and strife, instead of taking the chastisement of the Lord in humility and meekness. He ran furiously against me in the choler that is always inspired by the wicked one; but I overthrew him, by reason of impeding the natural and rapid progress of his unholy feet running to destruction. I also fell slightly; but his fall proved a severe one, he arose in wrath, and struck me with the mall which he held in his hand, until my blood flowed copiously; and from that moment I vowed his destruction in my heart. But I chanced to have no weapon at that time, nor any means of inflicting due punishment on the caitiff, which would not have been returned double on my head by him and his graceless associates. I mixed among them at the suggestion of my friend, and, following them to their den of voluptuousness and sin, I strove to be admitted among them, in hopes of finding some means of accomplishing my great purpose, while I found myself moved by the spirit within me so to do. But I was not only debarred, but, by the machinations of my wicked brother and his associates, cast into prison.

I was not sorry at being thus honoured to suffer in the cause of righteousness, and at the hands of sinful men; and, as soon as I was alone, I betook myself to prayer, deprecating the long-suffering of God towards such horrid sinners. My jailer came to me, and insulted me. He was a rude unprincipled fellow, partaking of the loose and carnal manners of the age; but I remembered of having read, in the Cloud of Witnesses, of such men formerly having been converted by the imprisoned saints; so I set myself, with all my heart, to bring about this man's repentance and reformation.

"Fat the deil are ye yoolling an' praying that gate for, man?" said he, coming angrily in. "I thought the days o' praying prisoners had been a' ower. We hath rowth o' them aince; an' they were the poorest an' the blackest bargains that ever poor jailers saw. Gie up your crooning, or I'll pit you to an in-by place, where ye sall get plenty o't."

"Friend," said I, "I am making my appeal at the bar where all human actions are seen and judged, and where you shall not be forgot, sinful as you are. Go in peace, and let me be."

"Hae ye naebody nearer-hand hame to mak your appeal to, man?" said he. "Because an ye hae-na, I dread you an' me may be unco weel acquaintit by an' by."

I then opened up the mysteries of religion to him in a clear and perspicuous manner, but particularly the great doctrine of the election of grace; and then I added: "Now, friend, you must tell me if you pertain to this chosen number. It is in every man's power to ascertain this, and it is every man's duty to do it."

"An' fat the better wad you be for the kenning o' this, man?" said he.

"Because, if you are one of my brethren, I will take you into sweet communion and fellowship," returned I. "But, if you belong to the unregenerate, I have a commission to slay you."

"The deil you hae, callant!" said he, gaping and laughing. "An', pray now, fa was it, that gae you siccan a braw commission?"

"My commission is sealed by the signet above," said I, "and that I will let you and all sinners know. I am dedicated to it by the most solemn vows and engagements. I am the sword of the Lord, and Famine and Pestilence are my sisters. Woe then to the wicked of this land, for they must fall down dead together, that the Church may be purified!"

"Oo, foo, foo! I see how it is," said he. "Yours is a very braw commission, but you will have the small opportunity of carrying it through here. Take my advising, and write a bit of a letter to your friends, and I will send it, for this is no place for such a great man. If you cannot steady your hand to write, as I see you have been at your great work, a word of a mouth may do; for I do assure you this is not the place at all, of any in the world, for your operations."

The man apparently thought I was deranged in my intellect. He could not swallow such great truths at the first morsel. So I took his advice, and sent a line to my reverend father, who was not long in coming, and great was the jailer's wonderment when he saw all the great Christian noblemen of the land sign my bond of freedom.

My reverend father took this matter greatly to heart, and bestirred himself in the good cause till the transgressors were ashamed to shew their faces. My illustrious companion was not idle: I wondered that he came not to me in prison, nor at my release; but he was better employed, in stirring up the just to the execution of God's decrees; and he succeeded so well that my brother and all his associates had nearly fallen victims to their wrath. But many were wounded, bruised, and imprisoned, and much commotion prevailed in the city. For my part, I was greatly strengthened in my resolution by the anathemas of my reverend father, who, privately (that is in a family capacity) in his prayers, gave up my father and brother, according to the flesh, to Satan, making it plain to all my senses of perception that they were being given up of God, to be devoured by fiends of men, at their will and pleasure, and that whosoever should slay them would do God good service.

The next morning my illustrious friend met me at an early hour, and he was greatly overjoyed at hearing my sentiments now chime so much in unison with his own. I said: "I longed for the day and the hour that I might look my brother in the face at Gilgal, and visit on him the iniquity of his father and himself, for that I was now strengthened and prepared for the deed."

"I have been watching the steps and movements of the profligate one," said he, "and, lo, I will take you straight to his presence. Let your heart be as the heart of the lion, and your arms strong as the shekels of brass, and swift to avenge as the bolt that descendeth from heaven, for the blood of the just and the good hath long flowed in Scotland. But already is the day of their avengement begun; the hero is at length arisen who shall send all such as bear enmity to the true Church, or trust in works of their own, to Tophet!"

Thus encouraged, I followed my friend, who led me directly to the same court in which I had chastised the miscreant on the foregoing day; and, behold, there was the same group again assembled. They eyed me with terror in their looks, as I walked among them and eyed them with looks of disapprobation and rebuke; and I saw that the very eye of a chosen one lifted on these children of Belial was sufficient to dismay and put them to flight. I walked aside to my friend, who stood at a distance looking on, and he said to me: "What thinkest thou now?" and I answered in the words of the venal prophet, "Lo, now, if I had a sword into mine hand I would even kill him."

"Wherefore lackest thou it?" said he. "Dost thou not see that they tremble at thy presence, knowing that the avenger of blood is among them."

My heart was lifted up on hearing this, and again I strode into the midst of them, and, eyeing them with threatening looks, they were so much confounded that they abandoned their sinful pastime, and fled everyone to his house!

The Private Memoirs and Confessions of a Justified Sinner

This was a palpable victory gained over the wicked, and I thereby knew that the hand of the Lord was with me. My companion also exulted, and said: "Did not I tell thee? Behold thou dost not know one half of thy might, or of the great things thou art destined to do. Come with me and I will show thee more than this, for these young men cannot subsist without the exercises of sin. I listened to their councils, and I know where they will meet again."

Accordingly he led me a little farther to the south, and we walked aside till by degrees we saw some people begin to assemble; and in a short time we perceived the same group stripping off their clothes to make them more expert in the practice of madness and folly. Their game was begun before we approached, and so also were the oaths and cursing. I put my hands in my pockets, and walked with dignity and energy into the midst of them. It was enough. Terror and astonishment seized them. A few of them cried out against me, but their voices were soon hushed amid the murmurs of fear. One of them, in the name of the rest, then came and besought of me to grant them liberty to amuse themselves; but I refused peremptorily, dared the whole multitude so much as to touch me with one of their fingers, and dismissed them in the name of the Lord.

Again they all fled and dispersed at my eye, and I went home in triumph, escorted by my friend, and some well-meaning young Christians, who, however, had not learned to deport themselves with soberness and humility. But my ascendancy over my enemies was great indeed; for wherever I appeared I was hailed with approbation, and, wherever my guilty brother made his appearance, he was hooted and held in derision, till he was forced to hide his disgraceful head, and appear no more in public.

Immediately after this I was seized with a strange distemper, which neither my friends nor physicians could comprehend, and it confined me to my chamber for many days; but I knew, myself, that I was bewitched, and suspected my father's reputed concubine of the deed. I told my fears to my reverend protector, who hesitated concerning them, but I knew by his words and looks that he was conscious I was right. I generally conceived myself to be two people. When I lay in bed, I deemed there were two of us in it; when I sat up I always beheld another person, and always in the same position from the place where I sat or stood, which was about three paces off me towards my left side. It mattered not how many or how few were present: this my second self was sure to be present in his place, and this occasioned a confusion in all my words and ideas that utterly astounded my friends, who all declared that, instead of being deranged in my intellect, they had never heard my conversation manifest so much energy or sublimity of conception; but, for all that, over the singular delusion that I was two persons my reasoning faculties had no power. The most perverse part of it was that I rarely conceived myself to be any of the two persons. I thought for the most part that my companion was one of them, and my brother the other; and I found that, to be obliged to speak and answer in the character of another man, was a most awkward business at the long run.

Who can doubt, from this statement, that I was bewitched, and that my relatives were at the ground of it? The constant and unnatural persuasion that I was my brother proved it to my own satisfaction, and must, I think, do so to every unprejudiced person. This victory of the Wicked One over me kept me confined in my chamber at Mr. Millar's house for nearly a month, until the prayers of the faithful prevailed, and I was restored. I knew it was a chastisement for my pride, because my heart was lifted up at my superiority over the enemies of the Church; nevertheless I determined to make short work with the aggressor, that the righteous might not be subjected to the effect of his diabolical arts again.

I say I was confined a month. I beg he that readeth to take note of this, that he may estimate how much the word, or even the oath, of a wicked man is to depend on. For a month I saw no one but such as came into my room, and, for all that, it will be seen that there were plenty of the same set to attest upon oath that I saw my brother every day during this period; that I persecuted him, with my presence day and night, while all the time I never saw his face save in a delusive dream. I cannot comprehend what manoeuvres my illustrious friend was playing off with them about this time; for he, having the art of personating whom he chose, had peradventure deceived them, else many of them had never all attested the same thing. I never saw any man so steady in his friendships and attentions as he; but as he made a rule of never calling at private houses, for fear of some discovery being made of his person, so I never saw him while my malady lasted; but, as soon as I grew better, I knew I had nothing ado but to attend at some of our places of meeting to see him again. He was punctual, as usual, and I had not to wait.

My reception was precisely as I apprehended. There was no flaring, no flummery, nor bombastical pretensions, but a dignified return to my obeisance, and an immediate recurrence, in converse, to the important duties incumbent on us, in our stations, as reformers and purifiers of the Church.

"I have marked out a number of most dangerous characters in this city," said he, "all of whom must be cut off from cumbering the true vineyard before we leave this land. And, if you bestir not yourself in the work to which you are called, I must raise up others who shall have the honour of it!"

"I am, most illustrious prince, wholly at your service," said I. "Show but what ought to be done, and here is the heart to dare and the hand to execute. You pointed out my relations, according to the flesh, as brands fitted to be thrown into the burning. I approve peremptorily of the award; nay, I thirst to accomplish it; for I myself have suffered severely from their diabolical arts. When once that trial of my devotion to the faith is accomplished, then be your future operations disclosed."

"You are free of your words and promises," said he.

"So will I be of my deeds in the service of my master, and that shalt thou see," said I. "I lack not the spirit, nor the will, but I lack experience woefully; and, because of that shortcoming, must bow to your suggestions!"

"Meet me here to-morrow betimes," said he, "and perhaps you may hear of some opportunity of displaying your zeal in the cause of righteousness."

I met him as he desired me; and he addressed me with a hurried and joyful expression, telling me that my brother was astir, and that a few minutes ago he had seen him pass on his way to the mountain. "The hill is wrapped in a cloud," added he, "and never was there such an opportunity of executing divine justice on a guilty sinner. You may trace him in the dew, and shall infallibly find him on the top of some precipice; for it is only in secret that he dares show his debased head to the sun."

"I have no arms, else assuredly I would pursue him and discomfit him," said I.

"Here is a small dagger," said he; "I have nothing of weaponkind about me save that, but it is a potent one; and, should you require it, there is nothing more ready or sure."

"Will not you accompany me?" said I. "Sure you will?"

340

"I will be with you, or near you," said he. "Go you on before."

I hurried away as he directed me, and imprudently asked some of Queensberry's guards if such and such a young man passed by them going out from the city. I was answered in the affirmative, and till then had doubted of my friend's intelligence, it was so inconsistent with a profligate's life to be so early astir. When I got the certain intelligence that my brother was before me, I fell a-running, scarcely knowing what I did; and, looking several times behind me, I perceived nothing of my zealous and arbitrary friend. The consequence of this was that, by the time I reached St. Anthony's well, my resolution began to give way. It was not my courage, for, now that I had once shed blood in the cause of the true faith, I was exceedingly bold and ardent, but, whenever I was left to myself, I was subject to sinful doubtings. These always hankered on one point. I doubted if the elect were infallible, and if the Scripture promises to them were binding in all situations and relations. I confess this, and that it was a sinful and shameful weakness in me, but my nature was subject to it, and I could not eschew it. I never doubted that I was one of the elect myself; for, besides the strong inward and spiritual conviction that I possessed, I had my kind father's assurance; and these had been revealed to him in that way and measure that they could not be doubted.

In this desponding state, I sat myself down on a stone, and bethought me of the rashness of my undertaking. I tried to ascertain, to my own satisfaction, whether or not I really had been commissioned of God to perpetrate these crimes in His behalf, for, in the eyes and by the laws of men, they were great and crying transgressions. While I sat pondering on these things, I was involved in a veil of white misty vapour, and, looking up to heaven, I was just about to ask direction from above, when I heard as it were a still small voice close by me, which uttered some words of derision and chiding. I looked intensely in the direction whence it seemed to come, and perceived a lady robed in white, who hastened towards me. She regarded me with a severity of look and gesture that appalled me so much I could not address her; but she waited not for that, but coming close to my side said, without stopping: "Preposterous wretch! How dare you lift your eyes to Heaven with such purposes in your heart? Escape homewards, and save your Soul, or farewell for ever!"

These were all the words that she uttered, as far as I could ever recollect, but my spirits were kept in such a tumult that morning that something might have escaped me. I followed her eagerly with my eyes, but in a moment she glided over the rocks above the holy well, and vanished. I persuaded myself that I had seen a vision, and that the radiant being that had addressed me was one of the good angels, or guardian spirits, commissioned by the Almighty to watch over the steps of the just. My first impulse was to follow her advice, and make my escape home; for I thought to myself. "How is this interested and mysterious foreigner a proper judge of the actions of a free Christian?"

The thought was hardly framed, nor had I moved in a retrograde direction six steps, when I saw my illustrious friend and great adviser descending the ridge towards me with hasty and impassioned strides. My heart fainted within me; and, when he came up and addressed me, I looked as one caught in a trespass. "What hath detained thee, thou desponding trifler?" said he. "Verily now shall the golden opportunity be lost which may never be recalled. I have traced the reprobate to his sanctuary in the cloud, and lo he is perched on the pinnacle of a precipice an hundred fathoms high. One ketch with thy foot, or toss with thy finger, shall throw him from thy sight into the foldings of the cloud, and he shall be no more seen till found at the bottom of the cliff dashed to pieces. Make haste, therefore, thou loiterer, if thou wouldst ever prosper and rise to eminence in the work of thy Lord and Master."

"I go no farther in this work," said I, "for I have seen a vision that has reprimanded the deed!"

"A vision?" said he. "Was it that wench who descended from the hill?"

"The being that spake to me, and warned me of my danger, was indeed in the form of a lady," said I.

"She also approached me and said a few words," returned he, "and I thought there was something mysterious in her manner. Pray, what did she say? for the words of such a singular message, and from such a messenger, ought to be attended to. If I understood her aright, she was chiding us for our misbelief and preposterous delay."

I recited her words, but he answered that I had been in a state of sinful doubting at the time, and it was to these doubtings she had adverted. In short, this wonderful and clear-sighted stranger soon banished all my doubts and despondency, making me utterly ashamed of them, and again I set out with him in the pursuit of my brother. He showed me the traces of his footsteps in the dew, and pointed out the spot where I should find him. "You have nothing more to do than go softly down behind him," said he, "which you can do to within an ell of him, without being seen; then rush upon him, and throw him from his seat, where there is neither footing nor hold. I will go, meanwhile, and amuse his sight by some exhibition in the contrary direction, and he shall neither know nor perceive who had done him this kind office: for, exclusive of more weighty concerns, be assured of this that, the sooner he falls, the fewer crimes will he have to answer for, and his estate in the other world will be proportionally more tolerable than if he spent a long unregenerate life steeped in iniquity to the loathing of the soul."

"Nothing can be more plain or more pertinent," said I. "Therefore, I fly to perform that which is both a duty towards God and towards man!"

"You shall yet rise to great honour and preferment," said he.

"I value it not, provided I do honour and justice to the cause of my master here," said I.

"You shall be lord of your father's riches and demesnes," added he.

"I disclaim and deride every selfish motive thereto relating," said I, "further than as it enables me to do good."

"Aye, but that is a great and a heavenly consideration, that longing for ability to do good," said he—and, as he said so, I could not help remarking a certain derisive exultation of expression which I could not comprehend; and indeed I have noted this very often in my illustrious friend, and sometimes mentioned it civilly to him, but he has never failed to disclaim it. On this occasion I said nothing, but, concealing his poniard in my clothes, I hasted up the mountain, determined to execute my purpose before any misgivings should again visit me; and I never had more ado than in keeping firm my resolution. I could not help my thoughts, and there are certain trains and classes of thoughts that have great power in enervating the mind. I thought of the awful thing of plunging a fellow creature from the top of a cliff into the dark and misty void below—of his being dashed to pieces on the protruding rocks, and of hearing his shrieks as he descended the cloud, and beheld the shagged points on which he was to alight. Then I thought of plunging a soul so abruptly into Hell, or, at the best, sending it to hover on the confines of that burning abyss—of its appearance at the bar of the Almighty to receive its sentence. And then I thought:

The Private Memoirs and Confessions of a Justified Sinner

"Will there not be a sentence pronounced against me there, by a jury of the just made perfect, and written down in the registers of Heaven?"

These thoughts, I say, came upon me unasked, and, instead of being able to dispel them, they mustered upon the summit of my imagination in thicker and stronger array: and there was another that impressed me in a very particular manner, though I have reason to believe not so strongly as those above written. It was this: "What if I should fail in my first effort? Will the consequence not be that I am tumbled from the top of the rock myself?" and then all the feelings anticipated, with regard to both body and soul, must happen to me! This was a spinebreaking reflection; and yet, though the probability was rather on that side, my zeal in the cause of godliness was such that it carried me on, maugre all danger and dismay.

I soon came close upon my brother, sitting on the dizzy pinnacle, with his eyes fixed steadfastly in the direction opposite to me. I descended the little green ravine behind him with my feet foremost, and every now and then raised my head, and watched his motions. His posture continued the same, until at last I came so near him I could have heard him breathe if his face had been towards me. I laid my cap aside, and made me ready to spring upon him and push him over. I could not for my life accomplish it! I do not think it was that I durst not, I have always felt my courage equal to anything in a good cause. But I had not the heart, or something that I ought to have had. In short, it was not done in time, as it easily might have been. These THOUGHTS are hard enemies wherewith to combat! And I was so grieved that I could not effect my righteous purpose that I laid me down on my face and shed tears. Then, again, I thought of what my great enlightened friend and patron would say to me, and again my resolution rose indignant and indissoluble save by blood. I arose on my right knee and left foot, and had just begun to advance the latter forward: the next step my great purpose had been accomplished, and the culprit had suffered the punishment due to his crimes. But what moved him I knew not: in the critical moment he sprung to his feet, and, dashing himself furiously against me, he overthrew me, at the imminent peril of my life. I disencumbered myself by main force and fled, but he overhied me, knocked me down, and threatened, with dreadful oaths, to throw me from the cliff. After I was a little recovered from the stunning blow, I aroused myself to the combat; and, though I do not recollect the circumstances of that deadly scuffle very minutely, I know that I vanquished him so far as to force him to ask my pardon, and crave a reconciliation. I spurned at both and left him to the

The Private Memoirs and Confessions of a Justified Sinner

chastisements of his own wicked and corrupt heart.

My friend met me again on the hill and derided me in a haughty and stern manner for my imbecility and want of decision. I told him how nearly I had effected my purpose, and excused myself as well as I was able. On this, seeing me bleeding, he advised me to swear the peace against my brother, and have him punished in the meantime, he being the first aggressor. I promised compliance and we parted, for I was somewhat ashamed of my failure, and was glad to be quit for the present of one of whom I stood so much in awe.

When my reverend father beheld me bleeding a second time by the hand of a brother, he was moved to the highest point of displeasure; and, relying on his high interest and the justice of his cause, he brought the matter at once before the courts. My brother and I were first examined face to face. His declaration was a mere romance: mine was not the truth; but as it was by the advice of my reverend father, and that of my illustrious friend, both of whom I knew to be sincere Christians and true believers, that I gave it, I conceived myself completely justified on that score. I said I had gone up into the mountain early on the morning to pray, and had withdrawn myself, for entire privacy, into a little sequestered dell—had laid aside my cap, and was in the act of kneeling when I was rudely attacked by my brother, knocked over, and nearly slain. They asked my brother if this was true. He acknowledged that it was; that I was bare-headed and in the act of kneeling when he ran foul of me without any intent of doing so. But the judge took him to task on the improbability of this, and put the profligate sore out of countenance. The rest of his tale told still worse, insomuch that he was laughed at by all present, for the judge remarked to him that, granting it was true that he had at first run against me on an open mountain and overthrown me by accident, how was it that, after I had extricated myself and fled, that he had pursued, overtaken, and knocked me down a second time? Would he pretend that all that was likewise by chance? The culprit had nothing to say for himself on this head, and I shall not forget my exultation and that of my reverend father when the sentence of the judge was delivered. It was that my wicked brother should be thrown into prison and tried on a criminal charge of assault and battery, with the intent of committing murder. This was a just and righteous judge, and saw things in their proper bearings, that is, he could discern between a righteous and a wicked man, and then there could be no doubt as to which of the two were acting right and which wrong.

The Private Memoirs and Confessions of a Justified Sinner

Had I not been sensible that a justified person could do nothing wrong, I should not have been at my ease concerning the statement I had been induced to give on this occasion. I could easily perceive that, by rooting out the weeds from the garden of the Church, I heightened the growth of righteousness; but, as to the tardy way of giving false evidence on matters of such doubtful issue, I confess I saw no great propriety in it from the beginning. But I now only moved by the will and mandate of my illustrious friend. I had no peace or comfort when out of his Sight, nor have I ever been able to boast of much in his presence; so true is it that a Christian's life is one of suffering.

My time was now much occupied, along with my reverend preceptor, in making ready for the approaching trial, as the prosecutors. Our counsel assured us of a complete victory, and that banishment would be the mildest award of the law on the offender. Mark how different was the result! From the shifts and ambiguities of a wicked Bench, who had a fellow-feeling of iniquity with the defenders, my suit was lost, the graceless libertine was absolved, and I was incarcerated, and bound over to keep the peace, with heavy penalties, before I was set at liberty.

I was exceedingly disgusted at this issue, and blamed the counsel of my friend to his face. He expressed great grief, and expatiated on the wickedness of our judicatories, adding: "I see I cannot depend on you for quick and summary measures, but for your sake I shall be revenged on that wicked judge, and that you shall see in a few days." The Lord Justice Clerk died that same week! But he died in his own house and his own bed, and by what means my friend effected it I do not know. He would not tell me a single word of the matter, but the judge's sudden death made a great noise, and I made so many curious inquiries regarding the particulars of it that some suspicions were like to attach to our family of some unfair means used. For my part I know nothing, and rather think he died by the visitation of Heaven, and that my friend had foreseen it, by symptoms, and soothed me by promises of complete revenge.

It was some days before he mentioned my brother's meditated death to me again, and certainly he then found me exasperated against him personally to the highest degree. But I told him that I could not now think any more of it owing to the late judgment of the court, by which, if my brother were missing or found dead, I would not only forfeit my life but my friends would be ruined by the penalties.

The Private Memoirs and Confessions of a Justified Sinner

"I suppose you know and believe in the perfect safety of your soul," said he, "and that that is a matter settled from the beginning of time, and now sealed and ratified both in Heaven and earth?"

"I believe in it thoroughly and perfectly," said I; "and, whenever I entertain doubts of it, I am sensible of sin and weakness."

"Very well, so then am I," said he. "I think I can now divine, with all manner of certainty, what will be the high and merited guerdon of your immortal part. Hear me then further: I give you my solemn assurance, and bond of blood, that no human hand shall ever henceforth be able to injure your life, or shed one drop of your precious blood; but it is on the condition that you walk always by my directions."

"I will do so with cheerfulness," said I, "for, without your enlightened counsel, I feel that I can do nothing. But, as to your power of protecting my life, you must excuse me for doubting of it. Nay, were we in your proper dominions, you could not ensure that."

"In whatever dominion or land I am, my power accompanies me," said he, "and it is only against human might and human weapon that I ensure your life; on that will I keep an eye, and on that you may depend. I have never broken word or promise with you. Do you credit me?"

"Yes, I do," said I, "for I see you are in earnest. I believe, though I do not comprehend you."

"Then why do you not at once challenge your brother to the field of honour? Seeing you now act without danger, cannot you also act without fear?"

"It is not fear," returned I, "believe me. I hardly know what fear is. It is a doubt that, on all these emergencies, constantly haunts my mind that, in performing such and such actions, I may fall from my upright state. This makes fratricide a fearful task!"

"This is imbecility itself," said he. "We have settled and agreed on that point an hundred times. I would therefore advise that you challenge your brother to single combat. I shall ensure your safety, and he cannot refuse giving you satisfaction."

"But then the penalties?" said I.

"We will try to evade these," said he, "and, supposing you should be caught, if once you are Laird of Dalcastle and Balgrennan, what are the penalties to you?"

"Might we not rather pop him off in private and quietness, as we did the deistical divine?" said I.

"The deed would be alike meritorious, either way," said he. "But may we not wait for years before we find an opportunity? My advice is to challenge him, as privately as you will, and there cut him off."

"So be it then," said I. "When the moon is at the full, I will send for him forth to speak with one, and there will I smite him and slay him, and he shall trouble the righteous no more."

"Then this is the very night," said he, "The moon is nigh to the full, and this night your brother and his sinful mates hold carousal; for there is an intended journey to-morrow. The exulting profligate leaves town, where we must remain till the time of my departure hence; and then is he safe, and must live to dishonour God, and not only destroy his own soul but those of many others. Alack, and woe is me! The sins that he and his friends will commit this very night will cry to Heaven against us for our shameful delay! When shall our great work of cleansing the sanctuary be finished, if we proceed at this puny rate?"

"I see the deed must be done, then," said I, "and, since it is so, it shall be done. I will arm myself forthwith, and from the midst of his wine and debauchery you shall call him forth to me, and there will I smite him with the edge of the sword, that our great work be not retarded."

"If thy execution were equal to thy intent, how great a man you soon might be!" said he. "We shall make the attempt once more; and, if it fail again, why, I must use other means to bring about my high purposes relating to mankind. Home and make ready. I will go and procure what information I can regarding their motions, and will meet you in disguise twenty minutes hence, at the first turn of Hewie's Lane beyond the loch."

"I have nothing to make ready," said I, "for I do not choose to go home. Bring me a sword, and we may consecrate it with prayer and vows, and, if I use it not to the bringing down of the wicked and profane, then may the Lord do so to me, and more also!"

The Private Memoirs and Confessions of a Justified Sinner

We parted, and there was I left again to the multiplicity of my own thoughts for the space of twenty minutes, a thing my friend never failed in subjecting me to, and these were worse to contend with than hosts of sinful men. I prayed inwardly that these deeds of mine might never be brought to the knowledge of men who were incapable of appreciating the high motives that led to them; and then I sung part of the 10th Psalm, likewise in spirit; but, for all these efforts, my sinful doubts returned, so that when my illustrious friend joined me, and proffered me the choice of two gilded rapiers, I declined accepting any of them, and began, in a very bold and energetic manner, to express my doubts regarding the justification of all the deeds of perfect men. He chided me severely and branded me with cowardice, a thing that my nature never was subject to; and then he branded me with falsehood and breach of the most solemn engagements both to God and man.

I was compelled to take the rapier, much against my inclination; but, for all the arguments, threats, and promises that he could use, I would not consent to send a challenge to my brother by his mouth. There was one argument only that he made use of which had some weight with me, but yet it would not preponderate. He told me my brother was gone to a notorious and scandalous habitation of women, and that, if I left him to himself for ever so short a space longer, it might embitter his state through ages to come. This was a trying concern to me; but I resisted it, and reverted to my doubts. On this he said that he had meant to do me honour, but, since I put it out of his power, he would do the deed, and take the responsibility on himself. "I have with sore travail procured a guardship of your life," added he. "For my own, I have not; but, be that as it will, I shall not be baffled in my attempts to benefit my friends without a trial. You will at all events accompany me, and see that I get justice?"

"Certes, I will do thus much," said I, "and woe be to him if his arm prevail against my friend and patron!"

His lip curled with a smile of contempt, which I could hardly brook; and I began to be afraid that the eminence to which I had been destined by him was already fading from my view. And I thought what I should then do to ingratiate myself again with him, for without his countenance I had no life. "I will be a man in act," thought I, "but in sentiment I will not yield, and for this he must surely admire me the more."

As we emerged from the shadowy lane into the fair moonshine, I started so that my whole frame underwent the most chilling vibrations of surprise. I again thought I had been taken at unawares and was conversing with another person. My friend was equipped in the Highland garb, and so completely translated into another being that, save by his speech, all the senses of mankind could not have recognized him. I blessed myself, and asked whom it was his pleasure to personify tonight? He answered me carelessly that it was a spark whom he meant should bear the blame of whatever might fall out tonight; and that was all that passed on the subject.

We proceeded by some stone steps at the foot of the North Loch, in hot argument all the way. I was afraid that our conversation might be overheard, for the night was calm and almost as light as day, and we saw sundry people crossing us as we advanced. But the zeal of my friend was so high that he disregarded all danger, and continued to argue fiercely and loudly on my delinquency, as he was pleased to call it. I stood on one argument alone, which was that "I did not think the Scripture promises to the elect, taken in their utmost latitude, warranted the assurance that they could do no wrong; and that, therefore, it behoved every man to look well to his steps."

There was no religious scruple that irritated my enlightened friend and master so much as this. He could not endure it. And, the sentiments of our great covenanted reformers being on his side, there is not a doubt that I was wrong. He lost all patience on hearing what I advanced on this matter, and, taking hold of me, he led me into a darksome booth in a confined entry; and, after a friendly but cutting reproach, he bade me remain there in secret and watch the event. "And, if I fall," said he, "you will not fail to avenge my death?"

I was so entirely overcome with vexation that I could make no answer, on which he left me abruptly, a prey to despair; and I saw or heard no more till he came down to the moonlight green followed by my brother. They had quarrelled before they came within my hearing, for the first words I heard were those of my brother, who was in a state of intoxication, and he was urging a reconciliation, as was his wont on such occasions. My friend spurned at the suggestion, and dared him to the combat; and after a good deal of boastful altercation, which the turmoil of my spirits prevented me from remembering, my brother was compelled to draw his sword and stand on the defensive. It was a desperate and terrible engagement. I at first thought that the royal stranger and great champion of the faith would overcome his opponent with ease, for I considered Heaven as on his side, and nothing but the arm of sinful flesh against him. But I was deceived. The sinner stood firm as a rock, while the assailant

The Private Memoirs and Confessions of a Justified Sinner

flitted about like a shadow, or rather like a spirit. I smiled inwardly, conceiving that these lightsome manoeuvres were all a sham to show off his art and mastership in the exercise, and that, whenever they came to close fairly, that instant my brother would be overcome. Still I was deceived. My brother's arm seemed invincible, so that the closer they fought the more palpably did it prevail. They fought round the green to the very edge of the water, and so round till they came close up to the covert where I stood. There being no more room to shift ground, my brother then forced him to come to close quarters, on which, the former still having the decided advantage, my friend quitted his sword and called out. I could resist no longer; so, springing from my concealment, I rushed between them with my sword drawn, and parted them as if they had been two schoolboys: then, turning to my brother, I addressed him as follows: "Wretch! miscreant! knowest thou what thou art attempting? Wouldest thou lay thine hand on the Lord's anointed, or shed his precious blood? Turn thee to me, that I may chastise thee for all thy wickedness, and not for the many injuries thou hast done to me!" To it we went, with full thirst of vengeance on every side. The duel was fierce; but the might of Heaven prevailed, and not my might. The ungodly and reprobate young man fell covered with wounds, and with curses and blasphemy in his mouth, while I escaped uninjured. Thereto his power extended not.

I will not deny that my own immediate impressions of this affair in some degree differed from this statement. But this is precisely as my illustrious friend described it to be afterwards, and I can rely implicitly on his information, as he was at that time a looker-on, and my senses all in a state of agitation, and he could have no motive for saying what was not the positive truth.

Never till my brother was down did we perceive that there had been witnesses to the whole business. Our ears were then astounded by rude challenges of unfair play, which were quite appalling to me; but my friend laughed at them and conducted me off in perfect safety. As to the unfairness of the transaction, I can say thus much, that my royal friend's sword was down ere ever mine was presented. But if it still be accounted unfair to take up a conqueror, and punish him in his own way, I answer: That if a man is sent on a positive mission by his master, and hath laid himself under vows to do his work, he ought not to be too nice in the means of accomplishing it; and, further, I appeal to holy writ, wherein many instances are recorded of the pleasure the Lord takes in the final extinction of the wicked and profane; and this position I take to be unanswerable.

really so absurd, so far from my principles, so from the purity of nature and frame to which I was born and consecrated, that I hold it as an insult, and regard it with contempt."

I would have said more in reprobation of such an idea, had not my servant entered, and said that a gentleman wanted to see me on business. Being glad of an opportunity of getting quit of my lady visitor, I ordered the servant to show him in; and forthwith a little lean gentleman, with a long aquiline nose, and a bald head, daubed all over with powder and pomatum, entered. I thought I recollected having seen him too, but could not remember his name, though he spoke to me with the greatest familiarity; at least, that sort of familiarity that an official person generally assumes. He bustled about and about, speaking to everyone, but declined listening for a single moment to any. The lady offered to withdraw, but he stopped her.

"No, no, Mrs. Keeler, you need not go; you need not go; you must not go, madam. The business I came about concerns you—yes, that it does. Bad business yon of Walker's? Eh? Could not help it—did all I could, Mr. Wringhim. Done your business. Have it all cut and dry here, sir. No, this is not it—Have it among them, though.—I'm at a little loss for your name, sir (addressing my friend)—seen you very often, though—exceedingly often—quite well acquainted with you."

"No, sir, you are not," said my friend, sternly. The intruder never regarded him; never so much as lifted his eyes from his bundle of law papers, among which he was bustling with great hurry and importance, but went on:

"Impossible! Have seen a face very like it, then—what did you say your name was, sir?—very like it indeed. Is it not the young laird who was murdered whom you resemble so much?"

Here Mrs. Keeler uttered a scream, which so much startled me that it seems I grew pale, and, on looking at my friend's face, there was something struck me so forcibly in the likeness between him and my late brother that I had very nearly fainted. The woman exclaimed that it was my brother's spirit that stood beside me.

"Impossible!" exclaimed the attorney. "At least, I hope not, else his signature is not worth a pin. There is some balance due on yon business, madam. Do you wish your account? because I have it here, ready discharged, and it does not suit letting such things lie over. This business of Mr. Colwan's will be a severe one on you, madam—rather a severe one."

"What business of mine, if it be your will, sir," said I. "For my part I never engaged you in business of any sort less or more." He never regarded me, but went on: "You may appeal, though. Yes, yes, there are such things as appeals for the refractory. Here it is, gentlemen. Here they are all together. Here is, in the first place, sir, your power of attorney, regularly warranted, sealed, and signed with your own hand."

"I declare solemnly that I never signed that document," said I.

"Aye, aye, the system of denial is not a bad one in general," said my attorney. "But at present there is no occasion for it. You do not deny your own hand?"

"I deny everything connected with the business," cried I. "I disclaim it in toto, and declare that I know no more about it than the child unborn."

"That is exceedingly good!" exclaimed he. "I like your pertinacity vastly! I have three of your letters, and three of your signatures; that part is all settled, and I hope so is the whole affair; for here is the original grant to your father, which he has never thought proper to put in requisition. Simple gentleman! But here have I, Lawyer Linkum, in one hundredth part of the time that any other notary, writer, attorney, or writer of the signet in Britain would have done it, procured the signature of His Majesty's commissioner, and thereby confirmed the charter to you and your house, sir, for ever and ever—Begging your pardon, madam." The lady, as well as myself, tried several times to interrupt the loquacity of Linkum, but in vain: he only raised his hand with a quick flourish, and went on:

"Here it is:

JAMES, by the grace of God, King of Great Britain, France, and Ireland, to his right trusty cousin, sendeth greeting: And whereas his right leal and trust-worthy cousin, George Colwan, of Dalcastle and Balgrennan, hath suffered great losses, and undergone much hardship, on behalf of his Majesty's rights and titles; he therefore, for himself, and as prince and steward of Scotland, and by the consent of his right trusty cousins and councillors hereby grants to the said George Colwan, his heirs and assignees whatsomever, heritably and irrevocably, all and haill the lands and others underwritten: To wit, All and haill, the five merk land of Kipplerig; the five pound land of Easter

The Private Memoirs and Confessions of a Justified Sinner

Knockward, with all the towers, fortalices, manor-places, houses, biggings, yards, orchards, tofts, crofts, mills, woods, fishings, mosses, muirs, meadows, commonties, pasturages, coals, coal-heughs, tennants, tenantries, services of free tenants, annexes, connexes, dependencies, parts, pendicles, and pertinents of the same whatsomever; to be peaceably brooked, joysed, set, used, and disposed of by him and his aboves, as specified, heritably and irrevocably, in all time coming: And, in testimony thereof, his Majesty, for himself, and as prince steward of Scotland, with the advice and consent of his foresaids, knowledge, proper motive, and kingly power, makes, erects, creates, unites, annexes, and incorporates, the whole lands above mentioned in a haill and free barony, by all the rights, miethes, and marches thereof, old and divided, as the same lies, in length and breadth, in houses, biggings, mills, multures, hawking, bunting, fishing; with court, plaint, herezeld, fock, fork, sack, sock, thole, thame, vert, wraik, waith, wair, venison, outfang thief, infang thief, pit and gallows, and all and sundry other commodities. Given at our Court of Whitehall, &c., &c. God save the King.

Compositio 5 lib. 13.8.

Registrate 26th September 1687.

"See, madam, here are ten signatures of privy councillors of that year, and here are other ten of the present year, with His Grace the Duke of Queensberry at the head. All right. See here it is, sir — all right — done your work. So you see, madam, this gentleman is the true and sole heritor of all the land that your father possesses, with all the rents thereof for the last twenty years, and upwards. Fine job for my employers! Sorry on your account, madam — can't help it."

I was again going to disclaim all interest or connection in the matter but my friend stopped me; and the plaints and lamentations of the dame became so overpowering that they put an end to all further colloquy; but Lawyer Linkum followed me, and stated his great outlay, and the important services he had rendered me, until I was obliged to subscribe an order to him for L100 on my banker.

I was now glad to retire with my friend, and ask seriously for some explanation of all this. It was in the highest degree unsatisfactory. He confirmed all that had been stated to me; assuring me that I had not only been assiduous in my endeavours to seduce a young lady of great beauty, which it seemed I had effected, but that I had taken counsel, and got this

358

The Private Memoirs and Confessions of a Justified Sinner

supposed, old, false, and forged grant raked up and now signed, to ruin the young lady's family quite, so as to throw her entirely on myself for protection, and be wholly at my will.

This was to me wholly incomprehensible. I could have freely made oath to the contrary of every particular. Yet the evidences were against me, and of a nature not to be denied. Here I must confess that, highly as I disapproved of the love of women, and all intimacies and connections with the sex, I felt a sort of indefinite pleasure, an ungracious delight in having a beautiful woman solely at my disposal. But I thought of her spiritual good in the meantime. My friend spoke of my backslidings with concern; requesting me to make sure of my forgiveness, and to forsake them; and then he added some words of sweet comfort. But from this time forth I began to be sick at times of my existence. I had heart-burnings, longings, and, yearnings that would not be satisfied; and I seemed hardly to be an accountable creature; being thus in the habit of executing transactions of the utmost moment without being sensible that I did them. I was a being incomprehensible to myself. Either I had a second self, who transacted business in my likeness, or else my body was at times possessed by a spirit over which it had no control, and of whose actions my own soul was wholly unconscious. This was an anomaly not to be accounted for by any philosophy of mine, and I was many times, in contemplating it, excited to terrors and mental torments hardly describable. To be in a state of consciousness and unconsciousness, at the same time, in the same body and same spirit, was impossible. I was under the greatest anxiety, dreading some change would take place momently in my nature; for of dates I could make nothing: one-half, or two-thirds of my time, seemed to me totally lost. I often, about this time, prayed with great fervour, and lamented my hopeless condition, especially in being liable to the commission of crimes which I was not sensible of and could not eschew. And I confess, notwithstanding the promises on which I had been taught to rely, I began to have secret terrors that the great enemy of man's salvation was exercising powers over me that might eventually lead to my ruin. These were but temporary and sinful fears, but they added greatly to my unhappiness.

The worst thing of all was what hitherto I had never felt, and, as yet, durst not confess to myself, that the presence of my illustrious and devoted friend was becoming irksome to me. When I was by myself, I breathed freer, and my step was lighter; but, when he approached, a pang went to my heart, and, in his company, I moved and acted as if under a load that I could hardly endure. What a state to be in! And yet to shake him off was impossible—we were incorporated together—identified with one another, as it were, and the power was not in me to separate myself from him. I still knew nothing who he was, further than that he was a potentate of some foreign land, bent on establishing some pure and genuine doctrines of Christianity, hitherto only half understood, and less than half exercised. Of this I could have no doubts after all that he had said, done and suffered in the cause. But, alongst with this, I was also certain that he was possessed of some supernatural power, of the source of which I was wholly ignorant. That a man could be a Christian and at the same time a powerful necromancer, appeared inconsistent, and adverse to every principle taught in our Church and from this I was led to believe that he inherited his powers from on high, for I could not doubt either of the soundness of his principles or that he accomplished things impossible to account for. Thus was I sojourning in the midst of a chaos of confusion. I looked back on my by-past life with pain, as one looks back on a perilous journey, in which he has attained his end, without gaining any advantage either to himself or others; and I looked forward, as on a darksome waste, full of repulsive and terrific shapes, pitfalls, and precipices, to which there was no definite bourn, and from which I turned with disgust. With my riches, my unhappiness was increased tenfold; and here, with another great acquisition of property, for which I had pleaded, and which I had gained in a dream, my miseries and difficulties were increasing. My principal feeling, about this time, was an insatiable longing for something that I cannot describe or denominate properly, unless I say it was for utter oblivion that I longed. I desired to sleep; but it was for a deeper and longer sleep than that in which the senses were nightly steeped. I longed to be at rest and quiet, and close my eyes on the past and the future alike, as far as this frail life was concerned. But what had been formerly and finally settled in the councils above, I presumed not to call in question.

In this state of irritation and misery was I dragging on an existence, disgusted with all around me, and in particular with my mother, who, with all her love and anxiety, had such an insufferable mode of manifesting them that she had by this time rendered herself exceedingly obnoxious to me. The very sound of her voice at a distance went to my heart like an arrow, and made all my nerves to shrink; and, as for the beautiful young lady for whom they told me I had been so much enamoured, I shunned all intercourse with her or hers, as I would have done with the Devil. I read some of their letters and burnt them, but refused to see either the young lady or her mother on any account.

The Private Memoirs and Confessions of a Justified Sinner

About this time it was that my worthy and reverend parent came with one of his elders to see my mother and myself. His presence always brought joy with it into our family, for my mother was uplifted, and I had so few who cared for me, or for whom I cared, that I felt rather gratified at seeing him. My illustrious friend was also much more attached to him than any other person (except myself) for their religious principles tallied in every point, and their conversation was interesting, serious, and sublime. Being anxious to entertain well and highly the man to whom I had been so much indebted, and knowing that, with all his integrity and righteousness, he disdained not the good things of this life, I brought from the late laird's well-stored cellars various fragrant and salubrious wines, and we drank, and became merry, and I found that my miseries and overpowering calamities passed away over my head like a shower that is driven by the wind. I became elevated and happy, and welcomed my guests an hundred times; and then I joined them in religious conversation, with a zeal and enthusiasm which I had not often experienced, and which made all their hearts rejoice, so that I said to myself. "Surely every gift of God is a blessing, and ought to be used with liberality and thankfulness."

The next day I waked from a profound and feverish sleep, and called for something to drink. There was a servant answered whom I had never seen before, and he was clad in my servant's clothes and livery. I asked for Andrew Handyside, the servant who had waited at table the night before; but the man answered with a stare and a smile:

"What do you mean, sirrah," said I. "Pray what do you here? Or what are you pleased to laugh at? I desire you to go about your business, and send me up Handyside. I want him to bring me something to drink."

"Ye sanna want a drink, maister," said the fellow. "Tak a hearty ane, and see if it will wauken ye up something, sae that ye dinna ca' for ghaists through your sleep. Surely ye haena forgotten that Andrew Handyside has been in his grave these six months?"

This was a stunning blow to me. I could not answer further, but sunk back on my pillow as if I had been a lump of lead, refusing to take a drink or anything else at the fellow's hand, who seemed thus mocking me with so grave a face. The man seemed sorry, and grieved at my being offended, but I ordered him away, and continued sullen and thoughtful. Could I have again been for a season in utter oblivion to myself, and transacting business which I neither approved of nor had any connection with! I tried to recollect something in which I might have been engaged, but nothing was portrayed on my mind subsequent to the parting with my friends at a late hour the evening before. The evening before it certainly was: but, if so, how came it that Andrew Handyside, who served at table that evening, should have been in his grave six months! This was a circumstance somewhat equivocal; therefore, being afraid to arise lest accusations of I know not what might come against me, I was obliged to call once more in order to come at what intelligence I could. The same fellow appeared to receive my orders as before, and I set about examining him with regard to particulars. He told me his name was Scrape; that I hired him myself; of whom I hired him; and at whose recommendation. I smiled, and nodded so as to let the knave see I understood he was telling me a chain of falsehoods, but did not choose to begin with any violent asseverations to the contrary.

"And where is my noble friend and companion?" said I. "How has he been engaged in the interim?"

"I dinna ken him, sir," said Scrape, "but have heard it said that the strange mysterious person that attended you, him that the maist part of folks countit uncanny, had gane awa wi' a Mr. Ringan o' Glasko last year, and had never returned."

I thanked the Lord in my heart for this intelligence, hoping that the illustrious stranger had returned to his own land and people, and that I should thenceforth be rid of his controlling and appalling presence. "And where is my mother?" said, I. The man's breath cut short, and he looked at me without returning any answer.—"I ask you where my mother is?" said I.

"God only knows, and not I, where she is," returned he. "He knows where her soul is, and, as for her body, if you dinna ken something o' it, I suppose nae man alive does."

"What do you mean, you knave?" said I. "What dark hints are these you are throwing out? Tell me precisely and distinctly what you know of my mother?"

"It is unco queer o' ye to forget, or pretend to forget everything that gate the day, sir," said he. "I'm sure you heard enough about it yestreen; an' I can tell you there are some gayan ill-faurd stories gaun about that business. But, as the thing is to be tried afore the circuit lords, it wad be far wrang to say either this or that to influence the public mind; it is best just to let justice tak its swee. I hae naething to say, sir. Ye hae been a good enough maister to me, and paid my wages regularly, but ye hae muckle need to be innocent, for there are some heavy accusations rising against you."

"I fear no accusations of man," said I, "as long as I can justify my cause in the sight of Heaven; and that I can do this I am well aware. Go you and bring me some wine and water, and some other clothes than these gaudy and glaring ones."

I took a cup of wine and water; put on my black clothes and walked out. For all the perplexity that surrounded me, I felt my spirits considerably buoyant. It appeared that I was rid of the two greatest bars to my happiness, by what agency I knew not. My mother, it seemed, was gone, who had become a grievous thorn in my side of late; and my great companion and counsellor, who tyrannized over every spontaneous movement of my heart, had likewise taken himself off. This last was an unspeakable relief; for I found that for a long season I had only been able to act by the motions of his mysterious mind and spirit. I therefore thanked God for my deliverance, and strode through my woods with a daring and heroic step; with independence in my eye, and freedom swinging in my right hand.

At the extremity of the Colwan wood, I perceived a figure approaching me with slow and dignified motion. The moment that I beheld it, my whole frame received a shock as if the ground on which I walked had sunk suddenly below me. Yet, at that moment, I knew not who it was; it was the air and motion of someone that I dreaded, and from whom I would gladly have escaped; but this I even had not power to attempt. It came slowly onward, and I advanced as slowly to meet it; yet, when we came within speech, I still knew not who it was. It bore the figure, air, and features of my late brother, I thought, exactly; yet in all these there were traits so forbidding, so mixed with an appearance of misery, chagrin and despair, that I still shrunk from the view, not knowing in whose face I looked. But, when the being spoke, both my mental and bodily frame received another shock more terrible than the first, for it was the voice of the great personage I had so long denominated my friend, of whom I had deemed myself for ever freed, and whose presence and counsels I now dreaded more than Hell. It was his voice, but so altered—I shall never forget it till my dying day. Nay, I can scarce conceive it possible that any earthly sounds could be so discordant, so repulsive to every feeling of a human soul, as the tones of the voice that grated on my ear at that moment. They were the sounds of the pit, wheezed through a grated cranny, or seemed so to my distempered imagination.

"So! Thou shudderest at my approach now, dost thou?" said he. "Is this all the gratitude that you deign for an attachment of which the annals of the world furnish no parallel? An attachment which has caused me to forego power and dominion, might, homage, conquest and adulation: all that I might gain one highly valued and sanctified spirit to my great and true, principles of reformation among mankind. Wherein have I offended? What have I done for evil, or what have I not done for your good; that you would thus shun my presence?"

"Great and magnificent prince," said I humbly; "let me request of you to abandon a poor worthless wight to his own wayward fortune, and return to the dominion of your people. I am unworthy of the sacrifices you have made for my sake; and, after all your efforts, I do not feel that you have rendered either more virtuous or more happy. For the sake of that which is estimable in human nature, depart from me to your own home, before you render me a being either altogether above or below the rest of my fellow creatures. Let me plod on towards Heaven and happiness in my own way, like those that have gone before me, and I promise to stick fast by the great principles which you have so strenuously inculcated, on condition that you depart and leave me for ever."

"Sooner shall you make the mother abandon the child of her bosom; nay, sooner cause the shadow to relinquish the substance, than separate me from your side. Our beings are amalgamated, as it were, and consociated in one, and never shall I depart from this country until I can carry you in triumph with me."

I can in nowise describe the effect this appalling speech had on me. It was like the announcement of death to one who had of late deemed himself free, if not of something worse than death, and of longer continuance. There was I doomed to remain in misery, subjugated, soul and body, to one whose presence was become more intolerable to me than aught on earth could compensate. And at that moment, when he beheld the anguish of my soul, he could not conceal that he enjoyed it. I was troubled for an answer, for which he was waiting: it became incumbent on me to say something after such a protestation of attachment; and, in some degree to shake the validity of it, I asked, with great simplicity, where he had been all this while?

"Your crimes and your extravagances forced me from your side for a season," said he, "but now that I hope the day of grace is returned, I am again drawn towards you by an affection that has neither bounds nor interest; an affection for which I receive not even the poor return of gratitude, and which seems to have its radical sources in fascination. I have been far, far abroad, and have seen much, and transacted much, since I last spoke with you. During that space, I grievously suspect that you have been guilty of great crimes and misdemeanours, crimes that would have sunk an unregenerated person to perdition; but as I knew it to be only a temporary falling off, a specimen of that liberty by which the chosen and elected ones are made free, I closed my eyes on the wilful debasement of our principles, knowing that the transgressions could never be accounted to your charge, and that in good time you would come to your senses, and throw the whole weight of your crimes on the shoulders that had voluntarily stooped to receive the load."

"Certainly I will," said I, "as I and all the justified have a good right to do. But what crimes? What misdemeanours and transgressions do you talk about? For my part, I am conscious of none, and am utterly amazed at insinuations which I do not comprehend."

"You have certainly been left to yourself for a season," returned he, "having gone on rather like a person in a delirium than a Christian in his sober sense. You are accused of having made away with your mother privately; as also of the death of a beautiful young lady, whose affections you had seduced."

"It is an intolerable and monstrous falsehood!" cried I, interrupting, him. "I never laid a hand on a woman to take away her life, and have even shunned their society from my childhood. I know nothing of my mother's exit; nor of that young lady's whom you mention. Nothing whatever."

"I hope it is so," said he. "But it seems there are some strong presumptuous proofs against you, and I came to warn you this day that a precognition is in progress, and that unless you are perfectly convinced, not only of your innocence but of your ability to prove it, it will be the safest course for you to abscond, and let the trial go on without you."

"Never shall it be said that I shrunk from such a trial as this," said I. "It would give grounds for suspicions of guilt that never had existence, even in thought. I will go and show myself in every public place, that no slanderous tongue may wag against me. I have shed the blood of sinners, but of these deaths I am guiltless; therefore I will face every tribunal, and put all my accusers down."

"Asseveration will avail you but little," answered he, composedly. "It is, however, justifiable in its place, although to me it signifies nothing, who know too well that you did commit both crimes, in your own person, and with your own hands. Far be it from me to betray you; indeed, I would rather endeavour to palliate the offences; for, though adverse to nature, I can prove them not to be so to the cause of pure Christianity, by the mode of which we have approved of it, and which we wish to promulgate."

"If this that you tell me be true," said I, "then is it as true that I have two souls, which take possession of my bodily frame by turns, the one being all unconscious of what the other performs; for as sure as I have at this moment a spirit within me, fashioned and destined to eternal felicity, as sure am I utterly ignorant of the crimes you now lay to my charge."

"Your supposition may be true in effect," said he. "We are all subjected to two distinct natures in the same person. I myself have suffered grievously in that way. The spirit that now directs my energies is not that with which I was endowed at my creation. It is changed within me, and so is my whole nature. My former days were those of grandeur and felicity. But, would you believe it? I was not then a Christian. Now I am. I have been converted to its truths by passing through the fire, and, since my final conversion, my misery has been extreme. You complain that I have not been able to render you more happy than you were. Alas! do you expect it in the difficult and exterminating career which you have begun? I, however, promise you this—a portion of the only happiness which I enjoy, sublime in its motions, and splendid in its attainments—I will place you on the right hand of my throne, and show you the grandeur of my domains, and the felicity of my millions of true professors."

I was once more humbled before this mighty potentate, and promised to be ruled wholly by his directions, although at that moment my nature shrunk from the concessions, and my soul longed rather to be inclosed in the deeps of the sea, or involved once more in utter oblivion. I was like Daniel in the den of lions, without his faith in Divine support, and wholly at their mercy. I felt as one round whose body a deadly snake is twisted, which continues to hold him in its fangs, without injuring him, further than in moving its scaly infernal folds with exulting delight, to let its victim feel to whose power he has subjected himself; and thus did I for a space drag an existence from day to day, in utter weariness and helplessness; at one time worshipping with great fervour of spirit, and at other times so wholly left to myself as to

The Private Memoirs and Confessions of a Justified Sinner

work all manner of vices and follies with greediness. In these my enlightened friend never accompanied me, but I always observed that he was the first to lead me to every one of them, and then leave me in the lurch. The next day, after these my fallings off, he never failed to reprove me gently, blaming me for my venial transgressions; but then he had the art of reconciling all, by reverting to my justified and infallible state, which I found to prove a delightful healing salve for every sore.

But, of all my troubles, this was the chief. I was every day and every hour assailed with accusations of deeds of which I was wholly ignorant; of acts of cruelty, injustice, defamation, and deceit; of pieces of business which I could not be made to comprehend; with lawsuits, details, arrestments of judgment, and a thousand interminable quibbles from the mouth of my loquacious and conceited attorney. So miserable was my life rendered by these continued attacks that I was often obliged to lock myself up for days together, never seeing any person save my man Samuel Scrape, who was a very honest blunt fellow, a staunch Cameronian, but withal very little conversant in religious matters. He said he came from a place called Penpunt, which I thought a name so ludicrous that I called him by the name of his native village, an appellation of which he was very proud, and answered everything with more civility and perspicuity when I denominated him Penpunt, than Samuel, his own Christian name. Of this peasant was I obliged to make a companion on sundry occasions, and strange indeed were the details which he gave me concerning myself, and the ideas of the country people concerning me. I took down a few of these in writing, to put off the time, and here leave them on record to show how the best and greatest actions are misconstrued among sinful and ignorant men:

"You say, Samuel, that I hired you myself—that I have been a good enough master to you, and have paid you your weekly wages punctually. Now, how is it that you say this, knowing, as you do, that I never hired you, and never paid you a sixpence of wages in the whole course of my life, excepting this last month?"

"Ye may as weel say, master, that water's no water, or that, stanes are no stanes. But that's just your gate, an' it's a great pity, aye to do a thing an profess the clean contrair. Weel then, since you havena paid me ony wages, an' I can prove day and date when I was hired, an' came hame to your service, will you be sae kind as to pay me now? That's the best way o' curing a man o' the mortal disease o' leasing-making that I ken o'."

"I should think that Penpunt and Cameronian principles would not admit of a man taking twice payment for the same article."

"In sic a case as this, sir, it disna hinge upon principles, but a piece o' good manners; an' I can tell you that, at sic a crisis, a Cameronian is a gay-an weel-bred man. He's driven to this, and he maun either make a breach in his friend's good name, or in his purse; an' oh, sir, whilk o' thae, think you, is the most precious? For instance, an a Galloway drover had comed to the town o' Penpunt, an' said to a Cameronian (the folk's a' Cameronians there), 'Sir, I want to buy your cow,' 'Vera weel,' says the Cameronian, 'I just want to sell the cow, sae gie me twanty punds Scots, an' take her w' ye.' It's a bargain. The drover takes away the cow, an' gies the Cameronian his twanty pund Scots. But after that, he meets him again on the white sands, amang a' the drovers an' dealers o' the land, an' the Gallowayman, he says to the Cameronian, afore a' thae witnesses, 'Come, Master Whiggam, I hae never paid you for yon bit useless cow that I bought. I'll pay her the day, but you maun mind the luck-penny; there's muckle need for 't'—or something to that purpose. The Cameronian then turns out to be a civil man, an' canna bide to make the man baith a feele an' liar at the same time, afore a' his associates; an' therefore he pits his principles aff at the side, to be kind o' sleepin' partner, as it war, an' brings up his good breeding to stand at the counter: he pockets the money, gies the Galloway drover time o' day, an' comes his way. An' wha's to blame? Man mind yoursel is the first commandment. A Cameronian's principles never came atween him an' his purse, nor sanna in the present case; for, as I canna bide to make you out a leear, I'll thank you for my wages."

"Well, you shall have them, Samuel, if you declare to me that I hired you myself in this same person, and bargained with you with this same tongue and voice with which I speak to you just now."

"That I do declare, unless ye hae twa persons o' the same appearance, and twa tongues to the same voice. But, 'od saif us, sir, do you ken what the auld wives o' the clachan say about you?"

"How should I, when no one repeats it to me?"

"Oo, I trow it's a' stuff—folk shouldna heed what's said by auld crazy kimmers. But there are some o' them weel kend for witches, too; an' they say, 'Lord have a care o' us!' They say the deil's often seen gaun sidie for sidie w' ye, whiles in ae shape, an' whiles in another. An' they say that he whiles takes your ain shape, or else enters into you, and then you turn a deil yoursel."

I was so astounded at this terrible idea that had gone abroad, regarding my fellowship with the Prince of Darkness, that I could make no answer to the fellow's information, but sat like one in a stupor; and if it had not been for my well-founded faith, and conviction that I was a chosen and elected one before the world was made, I should at that moment have given in to the popular belief, and fallen into the sin of despondency; but I was preserved from such a fatal error by an inward and unseen supporter. Still the insinuation was so like what I felt myself that I was greatly awed and confounded.

The poor fellow observed this, and tried to do away the impression by some further sage remarks of his own.

"Hout, dear sir, it is balderdash, there's nae doubt o't. It is the crownhead o' absurdity to tak in the havers o' auld wives for gospel. I told them that my master was a peeous man, an' a sensible man; an', for praying, that he could ding auld Macmillan himsel. 'Sae could the deil,' they said, 'when he liket, either at preaching or praying, if these war to answer his ain ends.' 'Na, na,' says I, 'but he's a strick believer in a' the truths o' Christianity, my master.' They said, sae was Satan, for that he was the firmest believer in a' the truths of Christianity that was out o' Heaven; an' that, sin' the Revolution that the Gospel had turned sae rife, he had been often driven to the shift o' preaching it himsel, for the purpose o' getting some wrang tenets introduced into it, and thereby turning it into blasphemy and ridicule."

I confess, to my shame, that I was so overcome by this jumble of nonsense that a chillness came over me, and, in spite of all my efforts to shake off the impression it had made, I fell into a faint. Samuel soon brought me to myself, and, after a deep draught of wine and water, I was greatly revived, and felt my spirit rise above the sphere of vulgar conceptions and the restrained views of unregenerate men. The shrewd but loquacious fellow, perceiving this, tried to make some amends for the pain he had occasioned to me by the following story, which I noted down, and which was brought on by a conversation to the following purport:

"Now, Penpunt, you may tell me all that passed between you and the wives of the clachan. I am better of that stomach qualm, with which I am sometimes seized, and shall be much amused by hearing the sentiments of noted witches regarding myself and my connections."

"Weel, you see, sir, I says to them, 'It will be lang afore the deil intermeddle wi' as serious a professor, and as fervent a prayer as my master, for, gin he gets the upper hand o' sickan men, wha's to be safe?' An', what think ye they said, sir? There was ane Lucky Shaw set up her lang lantern chafts, an' answered me, an' a' the rest shanned and noddit in assent an' approbation: 'Ye silly, sauchless, Cameronian cuif!' quo she, 'is that a' that ye ken about the wiles and doings o' the Prince o' the Air, that rules an' works in the bairns of disobedience? Gin ever he observes a proud professor, wha has mae than ordinary pretensions to a divine calling, and that reards and prays till the very howlets learn his preambles, that's the man Auld Simmie fixes on to mak a dishclout o'. He canna get rest in Hell, if he sees a man, or a set of men o' this stamp, an, when he sets fairly to work, it is seldom that he disna bring them round till his ain measures by hook or by crook. Then, Oh! it is a grand prize for him, an' a proud Deil he is, when he gangs hame to his ain ha', wi' a batch o' the souls o' sic strenuous professors on his back. Aye, I trow, auld Ingleby, the Liverpool packman, never came up Glasco street wi' prouder pomp when he had ten horse-laids afore him o' Flanders lace, an' Hollin lawn, an' silks an' satins frae the eastern Indians, than Satan wad strodge into Hell with a packlaid o' the souls o' proud professors on his braid shoulders. Ha, ha, ha! I think I see how the auld thief wad be gaun through his gizened dominions, crying his wares, in derision, "Wha will buy a fresh, cauler divine, a bouzy bishop, a fasting zealot, or a piping priest?" For a' their prayers an' their praises, their aumuses, an' their penances, their whinings, their howlings, their rantings, an' their ravings, here they come at last! Behold the end! Here go the rare and precious wares! A fat professor for a bodle, an' a lean ane for half a merk!' I declare I trembled at the auld hag's ravings, but the lave o' the kimmers applauded the sayings as sacred truths. An' then Lucky went on: 'There are many wolves in sheep's claithing, among us, my man; mony deils aneath the masks o' zealous professors, roaming about in kirks and meetinghouses o' the land. It was but the year afore the last that the people o' the town o' Auchtermuchty grew so rigidly righteous that the meanest hind among them became a shining light in ither towns an' parishes. There was naught to be heard, neither night nor day, but preaching, praying, argumentation, an' catechising in a' the famous town o' Auchtermuchty. The young men wooed their sweethearts out o' the Song o' Solomon, an' the girls returned answers in strings o' verses out o' the Psalms. At the lint-swinglings, they said questions round; and read chapters, and sang hymns at bridals;

The Private Memoirs and Confessions of a Justified Sinner

auld and young prayed in their dreams, an' prophesied in their sleep, till the deils in the farrest nooks o' Hell were alarmed, and moved to commotion. Gin it hadna been an auld carl, Robin Ruthven, Auchtermuchty wad at that time hae been ruined and lost for ever. But Robin was a cunning man, an' had rather mae wits than his ain, for he had been in the hands o' the fairies when he was young, an' a' kinds o' spirits were visible to his een, an' their language as familiar to him as his ain mother tongue. Robin was sitting on the side o' the West Lowmond, ae still gloomy night in September, when he saw a bridal o' corbie craws coming east the lift, just on the edge o' the gloaming. The moment that Robin saw them, he kenned, by their movements, that they were craws o' some ither warld than this; so he signed himself, and crap into the middle o' his bourock. The corbie craws came a' an' sat down round about him, an' they poukit their black sooty wings, an' spread them out to the breeze to cool; and Robin heard ae corbie speaking, an' another answering him; and the tane said to the tither: "Where will the ravens find a prey the night?" "On the lean crazy souls o' Auchtermuchty," quo the tither. "I fear they will be o'er weel wrappit up in the warm flannens o' faith, an clouted wi' the dirty duds o' repentance, for us to mak a meal o'," quo the first. "Whaten vile sounds are these that I hear coming bumming up the hill?" "Oh, these are the hymns and praises o' the auld wives and creeshy louns o' Auchtermuchty, wha are gaun crooning their way to Heaven; an', gin it warna for the shame o' being beat, we might let our great enemy tak them. For sic a prize as he will hae! Heaven, forsooth! What shall we think o' Heaven, if it is to be filled wi' vermin like thae, amang whom there is mair poverty and pollution than I can name." "No matter for that," said the first, "we cannot have our power set at defiance; though we should put them on the thief's hole, we must catch them, and catch them with their own bait, too. Come all to church to-morrow, and I'll let you hear how I'll gull the saints of Auchtermuchty. In the meantime, there is a feast on the Sidlaw hills tonight, below the hill of Macbeth—Mount, Diabolus, and fly." Then, with loud croaking and crowing, the bridal of corbies again scaled the dusky air, and left Robin Ruthven in the middle of his cairn.

"'The next day the congregation met in the kirk of Auchtermuchty, but the minister made not his appearance. The elder ran out and in making inquiries; but they could learn nothing, save that the minister was missing. They ordered the clerk to sing a part of the 119th Psalm, until they saw if the minister would cast up. The clerk did as he was ordered, and, by the time he reached the 77th verse, a strange divine entered the church, by the western door, and advanced solemnly up to the pulpit. The eyes of all the congregation were riveted on the sublime stranger, who was clothed in a robe of black sackcloth, that flowed all around him, and trailed far behind, and they weened him an angel, come to exhort them, in disguise. He read out his text from the Prophecies of Ezekiel, which consisted of these singular words: "I will overturn, overturn, overturn it; and it shall be no more, until he come, whose right it is, and I will give it him."

"'From these words he preached such a sermon as never was heard by human ears, at least never by ears of Auchtermuchty. It was a true, sterling, gospel sermon—it was striking, sublime, and awful in the extreme. He finally made out the IT, mentioned in the text, to mean, properly and positively, the notable town of Auchtermuchty. He proved all the people in it, to their perfect satisfaction, to be in the gall of bitterness and bond of iniquity, and he assured them that God would overturn them, their principles, and professions; and that they should be no more, until the Devil, the town's greatest enemy, came, and then it should be given unto him for a prey, for it was his right, and to him it belonged, if there was not forthwith a radical change made in all their opinions and modes of worship.

"'The inhabitants of Auchtermuchty were electrified—they were charmed; they were actually raving mad about the grand and sublime truths delivered to them by this eloquent and impressive preacher of Christianity. "He is a prophet of the Lord," said one, "sent to warn us, as Jonah was sent to the Ninevites." "Oh, he is an angel sent from Heaven, to instruct this great city," said another, "for no man ever uttered truths so sublime before." The good people of Auchtermuchty were in perfect raptures with the preacher, who had thus sent them to Hell by the slump, tag-rag, and bobtail! Nothing in the world delights a truly religious people so much as consigning them to eternal damnation. They wandered after the preacher—they crowded together, and spoke of his sermon with admiration, and still, as they conversed, the wonder and the admiration increased; so that honest Robin Ruthven's words would not be listened to. It was in vain that he told them he heard a raven speaking, and another raven answering him: the people laughed him to scorn, and kicked him out of their assemblies, as a one who spoke evil of dignities; and they called him a warlock, an' a daft body, to think to mak language out o' the crouping o' craws.

"'The sublime preacher could not be heard of, although all the country was sought for him, even to the minutest corner of St. Johnston and Dundee; but as he had announced another

The Private Memoirs and Confessions of a Justified Sinner

sermon on the same text, on a certain day, all the inhabitants of that populous country, far and near, flocked to Auchtermuchty. Cupar, Newburgh, and Strathmiglo, turned out men, women and children. Perth and Dundee gave their thousands; and, from the East Nook of Fife to the foot of the Grampian hills, there was nothing but running and riding that morning to Auchtermuchty. The kirk would not hold the thousandth part of them. A splendid tent was erected on the brae north of the town, and round that the countless congregation assembled. When they were all waiting anxiously for the great preacher, behold, Robin Ruthven set up his head in the tent, and warned his countrymen to beware of the doctrines they were about to hear, for he could prove, to their satisfaction, that they were all false, and tended to their destruction!

"'The whole multitude raised a cry of indignation against Robin, and dragged him from the tent, the elders rebuking him, and the multitude threatening to resort to stronger measures; and, though he told them a plain and unsophisticated tale of the black corbies, he was only derided. The great preacher appeared once more, and went through his two discourses with increased energy and approbation. All who heard him were amazed, and many of them went into fits, writhing and foaming in a state of the most horrid agitation. Robin Ruthven sat on the outskirts of the great assembly, listening with the rest, and perceived what they, in the height of their enthusiasm, perceived not the ruinous tendency of the tenets so sublimely inculcated. Robin kenned the voice of his friend the corby-craw again, and was sure he could not be wrong: sae, when public worship was finished, a' the elders an' a' the gentry flocked about the great preacher, as he stood on the green brae in the sight of the hale congregation, an' a' war alike anxious to pay him some mark o' respect. Robin Ruthven came in amang the thrang, to try to effect what he had promised; and, with the greatest readiness and simplicity, just took baud o' the side o' the wide gown, and, in sight of a' present, held it aside as high as the preacher's knee, and, behold, there was a pair o' cloven feet! The auld thief was fairly catched in the very height o' his proud conquest, an' put down by an auld carl. He could feign nae mair, but, gnashing on Robin wi' his teeth, he dartit into the air like a fiery dragon, an' keust a reid rainbow o'er the taps o' the Lowmonds.

"'A' the auld wives an weavers o' Auchtermuchty fell down flat wi' affright, an' betook them to their prayers aince again, for they saw the dreadfu' danger they had escapit, an' frae that day to this it is a hard matter to gar an Auchtermuchty man listen to a sermon at a', an' a harder ane still to gar him applaud ane, for he thinks aye that he sees the cloven foot peeping out frae

373

aneath ilka sentence.

"'Now, this is a true story, my man,' quo the auld wife, 'an', whenever you are doubtfu' of a man, take auld Robin Ruthven's plan, an' look for the cloven foot, for it's a thing that winna weel hide; an' it appears whiles where ane wadna think o't. It will keek out frae aneath the parson's gown, the lawyer's wig, and the Cameronian's blue bannet; but still there is a gouden rule whereby to detect it, an' that never, never fails.' The auld witch didna gie me the rule, an' though I hae heard tell o't often an' often, shame fa' me an I ken what it is! But ye will ken it well, an' it wad be nae the waur of a trial on some o' your friends, maybe; for they say there's a certain gentleman seen walking wi' you whiles, that, wherever he sets his foot, the grass withers as gin it war scoudered wi' a het ern. His presence be about us! What's the matter wi' you, master. Are ye gaun to take the calm o' the stamock again?'"

The truth is, that the clown's absurd story, with the still more ridiculous application, made me sick at heart a second time. It was not because I thought my illustrious friend was the Devil, or that I took a fool's idle tale as a counterbalance to Divine revelation that had assured me of my justification in the sight of God before the existence of time. But, in short, it gave me a view of my own state, at which I shuddered, as indeed I now always did when the image of my devoted friend and ruler presented itself to my mind. I often communed, with my heart on this, and wondered how a connection, that had the well-being of mankind solely in view, could be productive of fruits so bitter. I then went to try my works by the Saviour's golden rule, as my servant had put it into my head to do; and, behold, not one of them could stand the test. I had shed blood on a ground on which I could not admit that any man had a right to shed mine; and I began to doubt the motives of my adviser once more, not that they were intentionally bad, but that his was some great mind led astray by enthusiasm or some overpowering passion.

He seemed to comprehend every one of these motions of my heart, for his manner towards me altered every day. It first became anything but agreeable, then supercilious, and, finally, intolerable; so that I resolved to shake him off, cost what it would, even though I should be reduced to beg my bread in a foreign land. To do it at home was impossible, as he held my life in his hands, to sell it whenever he had a mind; and, besides, his ascendancy over me was as complete as that of a huntsman over his dogs: I was even so weak as, the next time I met with him, to look steadfastly at his foot, to see if it was not cloven into two hoofs. It was the foot of a gentleman in every respect, so far as appearances went, but the form of his counsels was somewhat equivocal, and, if not double, they were amazingly crooked.

But, if I had taken my measures to abscond and fly from my native place, in order to free myself of this tormenting, intolerant, and bloody reformer, he had likewise taken his to expel me, or throw me into the hands of justice. It seems that, about this time, I was haunted by some spies connected with my late father and brother, of whom the mistress of the former was one. My brother's death had been witnessed by two individuals; indeed, I always had an impression that it was witnessed by more than one, having some faint recollection of hearing voices and challenges close beside me; and this woman had searched about until she found these people; but, as I shrewdly suspected, not without the assistance of the only person in my secret—my own warm and devoted friend. I say this, because I found that he had them concealed in the neighbourhood, and then took me again and again where I was fully exposed to their view, without being aware. One time in particular, on pretence of gratifying my revenge on that base woman, he knew so well where she lay concealed that he led me to her, and left me to the mercy of two viragos who had very nigh taken my life. My time of residence at Dalcastle was wearing to a crisis. I could no longer live with my tyrant, who haunted me like my shadow; and, besides, it seems there were proofs of murder leading against me from all quarters. Of part of these I deemed myself quite free, but the world deemed otherwise; and how the matter would have gone God only knows, for, the case never having undergone a judicial trial, I do not. It perhaps, however, behoves me here to relate all that I know of it, and it is simply this:

On the first of June, 1712 (well may I remember the day), I was sitting locked in my secret chamber, in a state of the utmost despondency, revolving in my mind what I ought to do to be free of my persecutors, and wishing myself a worm, or a moth, that I might be crushed and at rest, when behold Samuel entered, with eyes like to start out of his head, exclaiming: "For God's sake, master, fly and hide yourself, for your mother's found, an' as sure as you're a living soul, the blame is gaun to fa' on you!"

"My mother found!" said I. "And, pray, where has she been all this while?" In the meantime, I was terribly discomposed at the thoughts of her return.

The Private Memoirs and Confessions of a Justified Sinner

"Been, sir! Been? Why, she has been where ye pat her, it seems—lying buried in the sands o' the linn. I can tell you, ye will see her a frightsome figure, sic as I never wish to see again. An' the young lady is found too, sir: an' it is said the Devil—I beg pardon, sir, your friend, I mean—it is said your friend has made the discovery, an' the folk are away to raise officers, an' they will be here in an hour or two at the farthest, sir; an' sae you hae not a minute to lose, for there's proof, sir, strong proof, an' sworn proof, that ye were last seen wi' them baith; sae, unless ye can gie a' the better an account o' baith yoursel an' them either hide or flee for your bare life."

"I will neither hide nor fly," said I, "for I am as guiltless of the blood of these women as the child unborn."

"The country disna think sae, master; an' I can assure you that, should evidence fail, you run a risk o' being torn limb frae limb. They are bringing the corpse here, to gar ye touch them baith afore witnesses, an' plenty o' witnesses there will be!"

"They shall not bring them here," cried I, shocked beyond measure at the experiment about to be made. "Go, instantly and debar them from entering my gate with their bloated and mangled carcases!"

"The body of your own mother, sir!" said the fellow emphatically. I was in terrible agitation; and, being driven to my wits' end, I got up and strode furiously round and round the room. Samuel wist not what to do, but I saw by his staring he deemed me doubly guilty. A tap came to the chamber door: we both started like guilty creatures; and as for Samuel, his hairs stood all on end with alarm, so that, when I motioned to him, he could scarcely advance to open the door. He did so at length, and who should enter but my illustrious friend, manifestly in the utmost state of alarm. The moment that Samuel admitted him, the former made his escape by the prince's side as he entered, seemingly in a state of distraction. I was little better, when I saw this dreaded personage enter my chamber, which he had never before attempted; and, being unable to ask his errand, I suppose I stood and gazed on him like a statue.

"I come with sad and tormenting tidings to you, my beloved and ungrateful friend," said he, "but, having only a minute left to save your life, I have come to attempt it. There is a mob coming towards you with two dead bodies, which will place you in circumstances disagreeable enough: but that is not the worst, for of that you may be able to clear yourself. At this moment there is a party of officers, with a justiciary warrant from Edinburgh, surrounding the house, and about to begin the search of it for you. If you fall into their hands, you are inevitably lost; for I have been making earnest inquiries, and find that everything is in train for your ruin."

"Aye, and who has been the cause of all this?" said I, with great bitterness. But he stopped me short, adding, "There is no time for such reflections at present; I gave my word of honour, that your life should be safe from the hand of man. So it shall, if the power remain with me to save it. I am come to redeem my pledge, and to save your life by the sacrifice of my own. Here—not one word of expostulation, change habits with me, and you may then pass by the officers, and guards, and even through the approaching mob, with the most perfect temerity. There is a virtue in this garb, and, instead of offering to detain you, they shall pay you obeisance. Make haste, and leave this place for the present, flying where you best may, and, if I escape from these dangers that surround me, I will endeavour to find you out, and bring you what intelligence I am able."

I put on his green frock coat, buff belt, and a sort of a turban that he always wore on his head, somewhat resembling a bishop's mitre: he drew his hand thrice across my face, and I withdrew as he continued to urge me. My hall door and postern gate were both strongly guarded, and there were sundry armed people within, searching the closets; but all of them made way for me, and lifted their caps as I passed by them. Only one superior officer accosted me, asking if I had seen the culprit. I knew not what answer to make, but chanced to say, with great truth and propriety: "He is safe enough." The man beckoned with a smile, as much as to say: "Thank you, sir, that is quite sufficient," and I walked deliberately away.

I had not well left the gate till, hearing a great noise coming from the deep glen towards the east, I turned that way, deeming myself quite secure in this my new disguise, to see what it was, and if matters were as had been described to me. There I met a great mob, sure enough, coming with two dead bodies stretched on boards, and decently covered with white sheets. I would fain have examined their appearance, had I not perceived the apparent fury in the looks of the men, and judged from that how much more safe it was for me not to intermeddle in the affray. I cannot tell how it was, but I felt a strange and unwonted delight in viewing this scene, and a certain pride of heart in being supposed the perpetrator of the unnatural crimes laid to my charge. This was a feeling quite new to me; and if there were virtues in the robes of the illustrious foreigner, who had without all dispute preserved my life at this time: I say, if there was any inherent virtue in these robes of his, as he had suggested, this was one of their effects' that they turned my heart towards that which was evil, horrible, and disgustful.

I mixed with the mob to hear what they were saying. Every tongue was engaged in loading me with the most opprobrious epithets! One called me a monster of nature; another an incarnate devil; and another a creature made to be cursed in time and eternity. I retired from them and, winded my way southwards, comforting myself with the assurance that so mankind had used and persecuted the greatest fathers and apostles of the Christian Church, and that their vile opprobrium could not alter the counsels of Heaven concerning me.

On going over that rising ground called Dorington Moor, I could not help turning round and taking a look of Dalcastle. I had little doubt that it would be my last look, and nearly as little ambition that it should not. I thought how high my hopes of happiness and advancement had been on entering that mansion, and taking possession of its rich and extensive domains, and how miserably I had been disappointed. On the contrary, I had experienced nothing but chagrin, disgust, and terror; and I now consoled myself with the hope that I should henceforth shake myself free of the chains of my great tormentor, and for that privilege was I willing to encounter any earthly distress. I could not help perceiving that I was now on a path which was likely to lead me into a species of distress hitherto unknown, and hardly dreamed of by me, and that was total destitution. For all the riches I had been possessed of a few hours previous to this, I found that here I was turned out of my lordly possessions without a single merk, or the power of lifting and commanding the smallest sum, without being thereby discovered and seized. Had it been possible for me to have escaped in my own clothes, I had a considerable sum secreted in these, but, by the sudden change, I was left without a coin for present necessity. But I had hope in Heaven, knowing that the just man would not be left destitute and that, though many troubles surrounded him, he would at last be set free from them all. I was possessed of strong and brilliant parts, and a liberal education; and, though I had somehow unaccountably suffered my theological qualifications to fall into desuetude, since my acquaintance with the ablest and most rigid of all theologians, I had nevertheless hopes that, by preaching up redemption by grace, preordination, and eternal purpose, I should yet be enabled to benefit mankind in some country, and rise to high distinction.

The Private Memoirs and Confessions of a Justified Sinner

These were some of the thoughts by which I consoled myself as I posted on my way southwards, avoiding the towns and villages, and falling into the cross ways that led from each of the great roads passing east and west to another. I lodged the first night in the house of a country weaver, into which I stepped at a late hour, quite overcome with hunger and fatigue, having travelled not less than thirty miles from my late home. The man received me ungraciously, telling me of a gentleman's house at no great distance, and of an inn a little farther away; but I said I delighted more in the society of a man like him than that of any gentleman of the land, for my concerns were with the poor of this world, it being easier for a camel to go through the eye of a needle than for a rich man to enter into the kingdom of heaven.

The weaver's wife, who sat with a child on her knee, and had not hitherto opened her mouth, hearing me speak in that serious and religious style, stirred up the fire with her one hand; then, drawing a chair near it, she said: "Come awa, honest lad, in by here; sin' it be sae that you belang to Him wha gies us a' that we hae, it is but right that you should share a part. You are a stranger, it is true, but them that winna entertain a stranger will never entertain an angel unawares."

I never was apt to be taken with the simplicity of nature; in general I despised it; but, owing to my circumstances at the time, I was deeply affected by the manner of this poor woman's welcome. The weaver continued in a churlish mood throughout the evening, apparently dissatisfied with what his wife had done in entertaining me, and spoke to her in a manner so crusty that I thought proper to rebuke him, for the woman was comely in her person, and virtuous in her conversation; but the weaver, her husband, was large of make, ill-favoured, and pestilent; therefore did I take him severely to task for the tenor of his conduct; but the man was froward, and answered me rudely with sneering and derision and, in the height of his caprice, he said to his wife: "Whan focks are sae keen of a chance o' entertaining angels, gude-wife, it wad maybe be worth their while to tak tent what kind o' angels they are. It wadna wonder me vera muckle an ye had entertained your friend the Deil the night, for aw thought aw fand a saur o' reek an' brimstane about him. He's nane o' the best o' angels, an focks winna hae muckle credit by entertaining him."

Certainly, in the assured state I was in, I had as little reason to be alarmed at mention being made of the Devil as any person on earth: of late, however, I felt that the reverse was the case, and that any allusion to my great enemy moved me exceedingly. The weaver's speech had such an effect on me that both he and his wife were alarmed at my looks. The latter thought I was angry, and chided her husband gently for his rudeness; but the weaver himself rather seemed to be confirmed in his opinion that I was the Devil, for he looked round like a startled roe-buck, and immediately betook him to the family Bible.

I know not whether it was on purpose to prove my identity or not, but I think he was going to desire me either to read a certain portion of Scripture that he had sought out, or to make family worship, had not the conversation at that instant taken another turn; for the weaver, not knowing how to address me, abruptly asked my name, as he was about to put the Bible into my hands. Never having considered myself in the light of a male-factor, but rather as a champion in the cause of truth, and finding myself perfectly safe under my disguise, I had never once thought of the utility of changing my name, and, when the man asked me, I hesitated; but, being compelled to say something, I said my name was Cowan. The man stared at me, and then at his wife, with a look that spoke a knowledge of something alarming or mysterious.

"Ha! Cowan?" said he. "That's most extraordinar! Not Colwan, I hope?"

"No: Cowan is my sirname," said I. "But why not Colwan, there being so little difference in the sound?"

"I was feared ye might be that waratch that the Deil has taen the possession o', an' eggit him on to kill baith his father an' his mother, his only brother, an' his sweetheart," said he; "an', to say the truth, I'm no that sure about you yet, for I see you're gaun wi' arms on ye."

"Not I, honest man," said I. "I carry no arms; a man conscious of his innocence and uprightness of heart needs not to carry arms in his defence now."

"Aye, aye, maister," said he; "an' pray what div ye ca' this bit windlestrae that's appearing here?" With that he pointed to something on the inside of the breast of my frock-coat. I looked at it, and there certainly was the gilded haft of a poniard, the same weapon I had seen and handled before, and which I knew my illustrious companion carried about with him; but till that moment I knew not that I was in possession of it. I drew it out: a more dangerous or insidious-looking weapon could not be conceived. The weaver and his wife were both frightened, the latter in particular; and she being my friend, and I dependent on their hospitality for that night, I said: "I declare I knew not that I carried this small rapier, which has been in my coat by chance, and not by any design of mine. But, lest you should think that I meditate any mischief to any under this roof I give it into your hands, requesting of you to lock it by till tomorrow, or when I shall next want it."

The woman seemed rather glad to get hold of it; and taking it from me, she went into a kind of pantry out of my sight, and locked the weapon up; and then the discourse went on.

"There cannot be such a thing in reality," said I, "as the story you were mentioning just now, of a man whose name resembles mine."

"It's likely that you ken a wee better about the story than I do, maister," said he, "suppose you do leave the L out of your name. An' yet I think sic a waratch, an' a murderer, wad hae taen a name wi' some gritter difference in the sound. But the story is just that true that there were twa o' the Queen's officers here nae mair than an hour ago, in pursuit o' the vagabond, for they gat some intelligence that he had fled this gate; yet they said he had been last seen wi' black claes on, an' they supposed he was clad in black. His ain servant is wi' them, for the purpose o' kennin the scoundrel, an' they're galloping through the country like madmen. I hope in God they'll get him, an' rack his neck for him!"

I could not say Amen to the weaver's prayer, and therefore tried to compose myself as well as I could, and made some religious comment on the causes of the nation's depravity. But suspecting that my potent friend had betrayed my flight and disguise, to save his life, I was very uneasy, and gave myself up for lost. I said prayers in the family, with the tenor of which the wife was delighted, but the weaver still dissatisfied; and, after a supper of the most homely fare, he tried to start an argument with me, proving that everything for which I had interceded in my prayer was irrelevant to man's present state. But I, being weary and distressed in mind, shunned the contest, and requested a couch whereon to repose.

I was conducted into the other end of the house, among looms, treadles, pirns, and confusion without end; and there, in a sort of box, was I shut up for my night's repose, for the weaver, as he left me, cautiously turned the key of my apartment, and left me to shift for myself among the looms, determined that I should escape from the house with nothing. After he and his wife and children were crowded into their den,

The Private Memoirs and Confessions of a Justified Sinner

I heard the two mates contending furiously about me in suppressed voices, the one maintaining the probability that I was the murderer, and the other proving the impossibility of it. The husband, however, said as much as let me understand that he had locked me up on purpose to bring the military, or officers of justice, to seize me. I was in the utmost perplexity, yet for all that, and the imminent danger I was in, I fell asleep, and a more troubled and tormenting sleep never enchained a mortal frame. I had such dreams that they will not bear repetition, and early in the morning I awaked, feverish, and parched with thirst.

I went to call mine host, that he might let me out to the open air, but, before doing so, I thought it necessary to put on some clothes. In attempting to do this, a circumstance arrested my attention (for which I could in nowise account, which to this day I cannot unriddle, nor shall I ever be able to comprehend it while I live): the frock and turban, which had furnished my disguise on the preceding day, were both removed, and my own black coat and cocked hat laid down in their place. At first I thought I was in a dream, and felt the weaver's beam, web, and treadle-strings with my hands, to convince myself that I was awake. I was certainly awake; and there was the door locked firm and fast as it was the evening before. I carried my own black coat to the small window and examined it. It was my own in verity; and the sums of money that I had concealed in case of any emergency, remained untouched. I trembled with astonishment; and on my return from the small window went doiting in amongst the weaver's looms, till I entangled myself, and could not get out again without working great deray amongst the coarse linen threads that stood in warp from one end of the apartment unto the other. I had no knife whereby to cut the cords of this wicked man, and therefore was obliged to call out lustily for assistance. The weaver came half naked, unlocked the door, and, setting in his head and long neck, accosted me thus:

"What now, Mr. Satan? What for art ye roaring that gate? Are you fawn inna little hell, instead o' the big muckil ane? Deil be in your reistit trams! What for have ye abscondit yoursel into ma leddy's wab for?"

"Friend, I beg your pardon," said I. "I wanted to be at the light, and have somehow unfortunately involved myself in the intricacies of your web, from which I cannot get clear without doing you a great injury. Pray do lend your experienced hand to extricate me."

The Private Memoirs and Confessions of a Justified Sinner

"May aw the pearls o' damnation light on your silly snout, an I dinna estricat ye weel enough! Ye ditit donnart, deil's burd that ye be! What made ye gang howkin in there to be a poor man's ruin? Come out, ye vile rag-of-a-muffin, or I gar ye come out wi' mair shame and disgrace, an' fewer haill banes in your body."

My feet had slipped down through the double warpings of a web, and not being able to reach the ground with them (there being a small pit below) I rode upon a number of yielding threads, and, there being nothing else that I could reach, to extricate myself was impossible. I was utterly powerless; and, besides, the yarn and cords hurt me very much. For all that, the destructive weaver seized a loom-spoke, and began a-beating me most unmercifully, while, entangled as I was, I could do nothing but shout aloud for mercy, or assistance, whichever chanced to be within hearing. The latter at length made its appearance in the form of the weaver's wife, in the same state of dishabille with himself, who instantly interfered, and that most strenuously, on my behalf. Before her arrival, however, I had made a desperate effort to throw myself out of the entanglement I was in; for the weaver continued repeating his blows and cursing me so that I determined to get out of his meshes at any risk. The effect made my case worse; for, my feet being wrapt among the nether threads, as I threw myself from my saddle on the upper ones, my feet brought the others up through these, and I hung with my head down and my feet as firm as they had been in a vice. The predicament of the web being thereby increased, the weaver's wrath was doubled in proportion, and he laid on without mercy.

At this critical juncture the wife arrived, and without hesitation rushed before her offended lord, withholding his hand from injuring me further, although then it was uplifted along with the loom-spoke in overbearing ire. "Dear Johnny! I think ye be gaen dementit this morning. Be quiet, my dear, an' dinna begin a Boddel Brigg business in your ain house. What for ir ye persecutin' a servant o' the Lord's that gate, an' pitting the life out o' him wi' his head down an' his heels up?"

"Had ye said a servant o' the Deil's, Nans, ye wad hae been nearer the nail, for gin he binna the Auld Ane himsel, he's gayan sib till him. There, didna I lock him in on purpose to bring the military on him; an' in the place o' that, hasna he keepit me in a sleep a' this while as deep as death? An' here do I find him abscondit like a speeder i' the mids o' my leddy's wab, an' me dreamin' a' the night that I had the Deil i' my house, an' that he was clapper-clawin me ayont the loom. Have at you, ye brunstane thief!" and, in spite of the good woman's struggles, he lent me another severe blow.

"Now, Johnny Dods, my man! oh, Johnny Dods, think if that be like a Christian, and ane o' the heroes o' Boddel Brigg, to entertain a stranger, an' then bind him in a web wi' his head down, an' mell him to death! oh, Johnny Dods, think what you are about! Slack a pin, an' let the good honest religious lad out."

The weaver was rather overcome, but still stood to his point that I was the Deil, though in better temper; and, as he slackened the web to release me, he remarked, half laughing: "Wha wad hae thought that John Dods should hae escapit a' the snares an' dangers that circumfauldit him, an' at last should hae weaved a net to catch the Deil."

The wife released me soon, and carefully whispered me, at the same time, that it would be as well for me to dress and be going. I was not long in obeying, and dressed myself in my black clothes, hardly knowing what I did, what to think, or whither to betake myself. I was sore hurt by the blows of the desperate ruffian; and, what was worse, my ankle was so much strained that I could hardly set my foot to the ground. I was obliged to apply to the weaver once more, to see if I could learn anything about my clothes, or how the change was effected. "Sir," said I, "how comes it that you have robbed me of my clothes, and put these down in their place over night?"

"Ha! thae claes? Me pit down the claes!" said he, gaping with astonishment, and touching the clothes with the point of his forefinger. "I never saw them afore, as I have death to meet wi', so help me God!"

He strode into the work-house where I slept, to satisfy himself that my clothes were not there, and returned perfectly aghast with consternation. "The doors were baith fast lockit," said he. "I could hae defied a rat either to hae gotten out or in. My dream has been true! My dream has been true! The Lord judge between thee and me; but in His name, I charge you to depart out o' this house; an', gin it be your will, dinna tak the braidside o't w'ye, but gang quietly out at the door wi' your face foremost. Wife, let naught o' this enchanter's remain i' the house, to be a curse, an' a snare to us; gang an' bring him his gildit weapon, an' may the Lord protect a' his ain against its hellish an' deadly point!"

The wife went to seek my poniard, trembling so excessively that she could hardly walk, and, shortly after, we heard a feeble scream from the pantry. The weapon had disappeared with the clothes, though under double lock and key; and, the terror of the good people having now reached a disgusting extremity, I thought proper to make a sudden retreat, followed by the weaver's anathemas.

My state both of body and mind was now truly deplorable. I was hungry, wounded, and lame, an outcast and a vagabond in society; my life sought after with avidity, and all for doing that to which I was predestined by Him who fore-ordains whatever comes to pass. I knew not whither to betake me. I had purposed going into England and there making some use of the classical education I had received, but my lameness rendered this impracticable for the present. I was therefore obliged to turn my face towards Edinburgh, where I was little known — where concealment was more practicable than by skulking in the country, and where I might turn my mind to something that was great and good. I had a little money, both Scotch and English, now in my possession, but not one friend in the whole world on whom I could rely. One devoted friend, it is true, I had, but he was become my greatest terror. To escape from him, I now felt that I would willingly travel to the farthest corners of the world, and be subjected to every deprivation; but after the certainty of what had taken place last night, after I had travelled thirty miles by secret and by-ways, I saw not how escape from him was possible.

Miserable, forlorn, and dreading every person that I saw, either behind or before me, I hasted on towards Edinburgh, taking all the by and unfrequented paths; and, the third night after I left the weaver's house, I reached the West Port, without meeting with anything remarkable. Being exceedingly fatigued and lame, I took lodgings in the first house I entered, and for these I was to pay two groats a week, and to board and sleep with a young man who wanted a companion to make his rent easier. I liked this; having found from experience that the great personage who had attached himself to me, and was now become my greatest terror among many surrounding evils, generally haunted me when I was alone keeping aloof from all other society.

My fellow lodger came home in the evening, and was glad at my coming. His name was Linton, and I changed mine to Elliot. He was a flippant unstable being, one on whom nothing appeared a difficulty, in his own estimation, but who could effect very little after all. He was what is called by some a compositor, in the Queen's printing house, then conducted by a Mr. James Watson. In the course of our conversation that night,

I told him I was a first-rate classical scholar, and would gladly turn my attention to some business wherein my education might avail me something; and that there was nothing would delight me so much as an engagement in the Queen's printing office. Linton made no difficulty in bringing about that arrangement. His answer was: "Oo, gud sir, you are the very man we want. Gud bless your breast and your buttons, sir! Aye, that's neither here nor there. That's all very well. Ha, ha, ha. A by-word in the house, sir. But, as I was saying, you are the very man we want. You will get any money you like to ask, sir. Any money you like, sir. God bless your buttons! — That's settled — All done — Settled, settled — I'll do it, I'll do it — No more about it; no more about it. Settled, settled."

The next day I went with him to the office, and he presented me to Mr. Watson as the most wonderful genius and scholar ever known. His recommendation had little sway with Mr. Watson, who only smiled at Linton's extravagances, as one does at the prattle of an infant. I sauntered about the printing office for the space of two or three hours, during which time Watson bustled about with green spectacles on his nose, and took no heed of me. But, seeing that I still lingered, he addressed me at length, in a civil gentlemanly way, and inquired concerning my views. I satisfied him with all my answers, in particular those to his questions about the Latin and Greek languages; but when he came to ask testimonials of my character and acquirements, and found that I could produce none, he viewed me with a jealous eye, and said he dreaded I was some n'er-do-weel, run from my parents or guardians, and he did not choose to employ any such. I said my parents were both dead; and that, being thereby deprived of the means of following out my education, it behoved me to apply to some business in which my education might be of some use to me. He said he would take me into the office, and pay me according to the business I performed and the manner in which I deported myself; but he could take no man into Her Majesty's printing office upon a regular engagement who could not produce the most respectable references with regard to morals.

I could not but despise the man in my heart who laid such a stress upon morals, leaving grace out of the question; and viewed it as a deplorable instance of human depravity and self-conceit; but, for all that, I was obliged to accept of his terms, for I had an inward thirst and longing to distinguish myself in the great cause of religion, and I thought, if once I could print my own works, how I would astonish mankind, and confound their self-wisdom and their esteemed morality — blow up the idea of any dependence on good works, and morality, forsooth! And I

The Private Memoirs and Confessions of a Justified Sinner

weened that I might thus get me a name even higher than if I had been made a general of the Czar Peter's troops against the infidels.

I attended the office some hours every day, but got not much encouragement, though I was eager to learn everything, and could soon have set types considerably well. It was here that I first conceived the idea of writing this journal, and having it printed, and applied to Mr. Watson to print it for me, telling him it was a religious parable such as the Pilgrim's Progress. He advised me to print it close, and make it a pamphlet, and then, if it did not sell, it would not cost me much; but that religious pamphlets, especially if they had a shade of allegory in them, were the very rage of the day. I put my work to the press, and wrote early and late; and encouraging my companion to work at odd hours and on Sundays, before the press-work of the second sheet was begun, we had the work all in types, corrected, and a clean copy thrown off for further revisal. The first sheet was wrought off; and I never shall forget how my heart exulted when at the printing house this day I saw what numbers of my works were to go abroad among mankind, and I determined with myself that I would not put the Border name of Elliot, which I had assumed, to the work.

Thus far have my History and Confessions been carried.

I must now furnish my Christian readers with a key to the process, management, and winding up of the whole matter; which I propose, by the assistance of God, to limit to a very few pages.

Chesters, July 27, 1712.—My hopes and prospects are a wreck. My precious journal is lost! consigned to the flames! My enemy hath found me out, and there is no hope of peace or rest for me on this side the grave.

In the beginning of last week, my fellow lodger came home, running in a great panic, and told me a story of the Devil having appeared twice in the printing house, assisting the workmen at the printing of my book, and that some of them had been frightened out of their wits. That the story was told to Mr. Watson, who till that time had never paid any attention to the treatise, but who, out of curiosity, began and read a part of it, and thereupon flew into a great rage, called my work a medley of lies and blasphemy, and ordered the whole to be consigned to the flames, blaming his foreman, and all connected with the press, for letting a work go so far that was enough to bring down the vengeance of Heaven on the concern.

The Private Memoirs and Confessions of a Justified Sinner

If ever I shed tears through perfect bitterness of spirit it was at that time, but I hope it was more for the ignorance and folly of my countrymen than the overthrow of my own hopes. But my attention was suddenly aroused to other matters, by Linton mentioning that it was said by some in the office the Devil had inquired for me.

"Surely you are not such a fool," said I, "as to believe that the Devil really was in the printing office?"

"Oo, Gud bless you, sir! Saw him myself, gave him a nod, and good-day. Rather a gentlemanly personage—Green Circassian hunting coat and turban—Like a foreigner—Has the power of vanishing in one moment though—Rather a suspicious circumstance that. Otherwise, his appearance not much against him."

If the former intelligence thrilled me with grief, this did so with terror. I perceived who the personage was that had visited the printing house in order to further the progress of my work; and, at the approach of every person to our lodgings, I from that instant trembled every bone, lest it should be my elevated and dreaded friend. I could not say I had ever received an office at his hand that was not friendly, yet these offices had been of a strange tendency; and the horror with which I now regarded him was unaccountable to myself. It was beyond description, conception, or the soul of man to bear. I took my printed sheets, the only copy of my unfinished work existing; and, on pretence of going straight to Mr. Watson's office, decamped from my lodgings at Portsburgh a little before the fall of evening, and took the road towards England.

As soon as I got clear of the city, I ran with a velocity I knew not before I had been capable of. I flew out the way towards Dalkeith so swiftly that I often lost sight of the ground, and I said to myself, "Oh, that I had the wings of a dove, that I might fly to the farthest corners of the earth, to hide me from those against whom I have no power to stand!"

I travelled all that night and the next morning, exerting myself beyond my power; and about noon the following day I went into a yeoman's house, the name of which was Ellanshaws, and requested of the people a couch of any sort to lie down on, for I was ill, and could not proceed on my journey. They showed me to a stable-loft where there were two beds, on one of which I laid me down; and, falling into a sound sleep, I did not awake till the evening, that other three men came from the fields to sleep in the same place, one of whom lay down beside me, at which I was exceedingly glad. They fell all sound asleep, and I was terribly alarmed at a conversation I overheard somewhere outside the stable. I could not make out a sentence, but trembled to think I knew one of the voices at least, and, rather than not be mistaken, I would that any man had run me through with a sword. I fell into a cold sweat, and once thought of instantly putting hand to my own life, as my only means of relief (may the rash and sinful thought be in mercy forgiven!) when I heard as it were two persons at the door, contending, as I thought, about their right and interest in me. That the one was forcibly preventing the admission of the other, I could hear distinctly, and their language was mixed with something dreadful and mysterious. In an agony of terror, I awakened my snoring companion with great difficulty, and asked him, in a low whisper, who these were at the door. The man lay silent and listening till fairly awake, and then asked if I heard anything. I said I had heard strange voices contending at the door.

"Then I can tell you, lad, it has been something neither good nor canny," said he. "It's no for naething that our horses are snorking that gate."

For the first time, I remarked that the animals were snorting and rearing as if they wished to break through the house. The man called to them by their names, and ordered them to be quiet; but they raged still the more furiously. He then roused his drowsy companions, who were alike alarmed at the panic of the horses, all of them declaring that they had never seen either Mause or Jolly start in their lives before. My bed-fellow and another then ventured down the ladder, and I heard one of them then saying: "Lord be wi' us! What can be i' the house? The sweat's rinning off the poor beasts like water."

They agreed to sally out together, and if possible to reach the kitchen and bring a light. I was glad at this, but not so much so when I heard the one man saying to the other, in a whisper: "I wish that stranger man may be canny enough."

"God kens!" said the other. "It does nae look unco weel."

The lad in the other bed, hearing this, set up his head in manifest affright as the other two departed for the kitchen; and, I believed he would have been glad to have been in their company. This lad was next the ladder, at which I was extremely glad, for, had he not been there, the world should not have induced me to wait the return of these two men. They were not well gone before I heard another distinctly enter the stable, and come towards the ladder. The lad who was sitting up in his bed, intent on the watch, called out: "Wha's that there? Walker, is that you? Purdie, I say is it you?"

The darkling intruder paused for a few moments, and then came towards the foot of the ladder. The horses broke loose, and, snorting and neighing for terror, raged through the house. In all my life I never heard so frightful a commotion. The being that occasioned it all now began to mount the ladder towards our loft, on which the lad in the bed next the ladder sprung from his couch, crying out: "The L—d A—y preserve us! What can it be?" With that he sped across the loft and by my bed, praying lustily all the way; and, throwing himself from the other end of the loft into a manger, he darted, naked as he was, through among the furious horses, and, making the door that stood open, in a moment he vanished and left me in the lurch. Powerless with terror, and calling out fearfully, I tried to follow his example; but, not knowing the situation of the places with regard to one another, I missed the manger, and fell on the pavement in one of the stalls. I was both stunned and lamed on the knee; but, terror prevailing, I got up and tried to escape. It was out of my power; for there were divisions and cross divisions in the house, and mad horses smashing everything before them, so that I knew not so much as on what side of the house the door was. Two or three times was I knocked down by the animals, but all the while I never stinted crying out with all my power. At length, I was seized by the throat and hair of the head, and dragged away, I wist not whither. My voice was now laid, and all my powers, both mental and bodily, totally overcome; and I remember no more till I found myself lying naked on the kitchen table of the farm-house, and something like a horse's rug thrown over me. The only hint that I got from the people of the house on coming to myself was that my absence would be good company; and that they had got me in a woeful state, one which they did not choose to describe, or hear described.

As soon as day-light appeared, I was packed about my business, with the hisses and execrations of the yeoman's family, who viewed me as a being to be shunned, ascribing to me the visitations of that unholy night. Again was I on my way southwards, as lonely, hopeless, and degraded a being as was to be found on life's weary round. As I limped out the way, I wept, thinking of what I might have been, and what I really had become: of my high and flourishing hopes when I set out as the avenger of God on the sinful children of men; of all that I had dared for the exaltation and progress of the truth; and it was with great difficulty that my faith remained unshaken, yet was I preserved from that sin, and comforted myself with the certainty that the believer's progress through life is one of warfare and suffering.

My case was indeed a pitiable one. I was lame, hungry, fatigued, and my resources on the very eve of being exhausted. Yet these were but secondary miseries, and hardly worthy of a thought compared with those I suffered inwardly. I not only looked around me with terror at every one that approached, but I was become a terror to myself, or, rather, my body and soul were become terrors to each other; and, had it been possible, I felt as if they would have gone to war. I dared not look at my face in a glass, for I shuddered at my own image and likeness. I dreaded the dawning, and trembled at the approach of night, nor was there one thing in nature that afforded me the least delight.

In this deplorable state of body and mind, was I jogging on towards the Tweed, by the side of the small river called Ellan, when, just at the narrowest part of the glen, whom should I meet full in the face but the very being in all the universe of God would the most gladly have shunned. I had no power to fly fro him, neither durst I, for the spirit within me, accuse him of falsehood and renounce his fellowship. I stood before him like a condemned criminal, staring him in the face, ready to be winded, twisted, and tormented as he pleased. He regarded me with a sad and solemn look. How changed was now that majestic countenance to one of haggard despair—changed in all save the extraordinary likeness to my late brother, a resemblance which misfortune and despair tended only to heighten. There were no kind greetings passed between us at meeting, like those which pass between the men of the world; he looked on me with eyes that froze the currents of my blood, but spoke not till I assumed as much courage as to articulate: "You here! I hope you have brought me tidings of comfort?"

"Tidings of despair!" said he. "But such tidings as the timid and the ungrateful deserve, and have reason to expect. You are an outlaw, and a vagabond in your country, and a high reward is offered for your apprehension. The enraged populace have burnt your house, and all that is within it; and the farmers on the land bless themselves at being rid of you. So fare it with everyone who puts his hand to the great work of man's restoration to freedom, and draweth back, contemning the light that is within him! Your enormities caused me to leave you to yourself for a season, and you see what the issue has been. You have given some evil ones power over you, who long to devour you, both soul and body, and it has required all my power and

The Private Memoirs and Confessions of a Justified Sinner

influence to save you. Had it not been for my hand, you had been torn in pieces last night; but for once I prevailed. We must leave this land forthwith, for here there is neither peace, safety, nor comfort for us. Do you now and here pledge yourself to one who has so often saved your life and has put his own at stake to do so? Do you pledge yourself that you will henceforth be guided by my counsel, and follow me whithersoever I choose to lead?"

"I have always been swayed by your counsel," said I, "and for your sake, principally, am I sorry that all our measures have proved abortive. But I hope still to be useful in my native isle, therefore let me plead that your highness will abandon a poor despised and outcast wretch to his fate, and betake you to your realms, where your presence cannot but be greatly wanted."

"Would that I could do so!" said he woefully. "But to talk of that is to talk of an impossibility. I am wedded to you so closely that I feel as if I were the same person. Our essences are one, our bodies and spirits being united, so that I am drawn towards you as by magnetism, and, wherever you are, there must my presence be with you."

Perceiving how this assurance affected me, he began to chide me most bitterly for my ingratitude; and then he assumed such looks that it was impossible for me longer to bear them; therefore I staggered out of the way, begging and beseeching of him to give me up to my fate, and hardly knowing what I said; for it struck me that, with all his assumed appearance of misery and wretchedness, there were traits of exultation in his hideous countenance, manifesting a secret and inward joy at my utter despair.

It was long before I durst look over my shoulder, but, when I did so, I perceived this ruined and debased potentate coming slowly on the same path, and I prayed that the Lord would hide me in the bowels of the earth or depths of the sea. When I crossed the Tweed, I perceived him still a little behind me; and, my despair being then at its height, I cursed the time I first met with such a tormentor; though on a little recollection it occurred that it was at that blessed time when I was solemnly dedicated to the Lord, and assured of my final election, and confirmation, by an eternal decree never to be annulled. This being my sole and only comfort, I recalled my curse upon the time, and repented me o my rashness.

After crossing the Tweed, I saw no more of my persecutor that day, and had hopes that he had left me for a season; but,

The Private Memoirs and Confessions of a Justified Sinner

alas, what hope was there of my relief after the declaration I had so lately heard! I took up my lodgings that night in a small miserable inn in the village of Ancrum, of which the people seemed alike poor and ignorant. Before going to bed, I asked if it was customary with them to have family worship of evenings. The man answered that they were so hard set with the world they often could not get time, but if I would be so kind as to officiate they would be much obliged to me. I accepted the invitation, being afraid to go to rest lest the commotions of the foregoing night might be renewed, and continued the worship as long as in decency I could. The poor people thanked me, hoped my prayers would be heard both on their account and my own, seemed much taken with my abilities, and wondered how a man of my powerful eloquence chanced to be wandering about in a condition so forlorn. I said I was a poor student of theology, on my way to Oxford. They stared at one another with expressions of wonder, disappointment, and fear. I afterwards came to learn that the term theology was by them quite misunderstood, and that they had some crude conceptions that nothing was taught at Oxford but the black arts, which ridiculous idea prevailed over all the south of Scotland. For the present I could not understand what the people meant, and less so when the man asked me, with deep concern: "If I was serious in my intentions of going to Oxford? He hoped not, and that I would be better guided."

I said my education wanted finishing; but he remarked that the Oxford arts were a bad finish for a religious man's education. Finally, I requested him to sleep with me, or in my room all the night, as I wanted some serious and religious conversation with him, and likewise to convince him that the study of the fine arts, though not absolutely necessary, were not incompatible with the character of a Christian divine. He shook his head, and wondered how I could call them fine arts—hoped I did not mean to convince him by any ocular demonstration, and at length reluctantly condescended to sleep with me, and let the lass and wife sleep together for one night. I believe he would have declined it had it not been some hints from his wife, stating that it was a good arrangement, by which I understood there were only two beds in the house, and that when I was preferred to the lass's bed, she had one to shift for.

The landlord and I accordingly retired to our homely bed, and conversed for some time about indifferent matters, till he fell sound asleep. Not so with me: I had that within which would not suffer me to close my eyes; and, about the dead of night, I again heard the same noises and contention begin outside the house as I had heard the night before; and again I heard it was about a sovereign and peculiar right in me. At one time the noise was on the top of the house, straight above our bed, as if the one party were breaking through the roof, and the other forcibly preventing it; at another it was at the door, and at a third time at the window; but still mine host lay sound by my side, and did not waken. I was seized with terrors indefinable, and prayed fervently, but did not attempt rousing my sleeping companion until I saw if no better could be done. The women, however, were alarmed, and, rushing into our apartment, exclaimed that all the devils in hell were besieging the house. Then, indeed, the landlord awoke, and it was time for him, for the tumult had increased to such a degree that it shook the house to its foundations, being louder and more furious than I could have conceived the heat of battle to be when the volleys of artillery are mixed with groans, shouts, and blasphemous cursing. It thundered and lightened; and there were screams, groans, laughter, and execrations, all intermingled.

I lay trembling and bathed in a cold perspiration, but was soon obliged to bestir myself, the inmates attacking me one after the other.

"Oh, Tam Douglas! Tam Douglas! haste ye an' rise out frayont that incarnal devil!" cried the wife. "Ye are in ayont the auld ane himsel, for our lass Tibbie saw his cloven cloots last night."

"Lord forbid!" roared Tam Douglas, and darted over the bed like a flying fish. Then, hearing the unearthly tumult with which he was surrounded, he turned to the side of the bed, and addressed me thus, with long and fearful intervals:

"If ye be the Deil, rise up, an' depart in peace out o' this house—afore the bedstrae take kindling about ye, an' than it'll maybe be the waur for ye. Get up—an' gang awa out amang your cronies, like a good lad. There's nae body here wishes you ony ill. D'ye hear me?"

"Friend," said I, "no Christian would turn out a fellow creature on such a night as this and in the midst of such a commotion of the villagers."

"Na, if ye be a mortal man," said he, "which I rather think, from the use you made of the holy book. Nane o' your practical jokes on strangers an' honest foks. These are some o' your Oxford tricks, an' I'll thank you to be ower wi' them. Gracious heaven, they are brikkin through the house at a' the four corners at the same time!"

The Private Memoirs and Confessions of a Justified Sinner

The lass Tibby, seeing the innkeeper was not going to prevail with me to rise, flew towards the bed in desperation, and, seizing me by the waist, soon landed me on the floor, saying: "Be ye deil, be ye chiel, ye's no lie there till baith the house an' us be swallowed up!"

Her master and mistress applauding the deed, I was obliged to attempt dressing myself, a task to which my powers were quite inadequate in the state I was in, but I was readily assisted by every one of the three; and, as soon as they got my clothes thrust on in a loose way, they shut their eyes lest they should see what might drive them distracted, and thrust me out to the street, cursing me, and calling on the fiends to take their prey and be gone.

The scene that ensued is neither to be described nor believed if it were. I was momently surrounded by a number of hideous fiends, who gnashed on me with their teeth, and clenched their crimson paws in my face; and at the same instant I was seized by the collar of my coat behind, by my dreaded and devoted friend, who pushed me on and, with his gilded rapier waving and brandishing around me, defended me against all their united attacks. Horrible as my assailants were in appearance (and they all had monstrous shapes) I felt that I would rather have fallen into their hands than be thus led away captive by my defender at his will and pleasure without having the right or power to say my life, or any part of my will, was my own. I could not even thank him for his potent guardianship, but hung down my head, and moved on I knew not whither, like a criminal led to execution and still the infernal combat continued till about the dawning, at which time I looked up, and all the fiends were expelled but one, who kept at a distance; and still my persecutor and defender pushed me by the neck before him.

At length he desired me to sit down and take some rest, with which I complied, for I had great need of it, and wanted the power to withstand what he desired. There, for a whole morning did he detain me, tormenting me with reflections on the past, and pointing out the horrors of the future, until a thousand times I wished myself non-existent. "I have attached myself to your wayward fortune," said he, "and it has been my ruin as well as thine. Ungrateful as you are, I cannot give you up to be devoured; but this is a life that it is impossible to brook longer. Since our hopes are blasted in this world, and all our schemes of grandeur overthrown; and since our everlasting destiny is settled by a decree which no act of ours can invalidate, let us fall by our own hands, or by the hands of each other; die like heroes; and, throwing off this frame of dross and corruption, mingle with the pure ethereal essence of existence, from which we derived our being."

I shuddered at a view of the dreadful alternative, yet was obliged to confess that in my present circumstances existence was not to be borne. It was in vain that I reasoned on the sinfulness of the deed, and on its damning nature; he made me condemn myself out of my own mouth, by allowing the absolute nature of justifying grace and the impossibility of the elect ever falling from the faith, or the glorious end to which they were called; and then he said, this granted, self-destruction was the act of a hero, and none but a coward would shrink from it, to suffer a hundred times more every day and night that passed over his head.

I said I was still contented to be that coward; and all that I begged of him was to leave me to my fortune for a season, and to the just judgement of my Creator; but he said his word and honour were engaged on my behalf, and these, in such a case, were not to be violated. "If you will not pity yourself, have pity on me," added he. "Turn your eyes on me, and behold to what I am reduced."

Involuntarily did I turn at the request, and caught a half glance of his features. May no eye destined to reflect the beauties of the New Jerusalem inward upon the beatific soul behold such a sight as mine then beheld! My immortal spirit, blood and bones, were all withered at the blasting sight; and I arose and withdrew, with groanings which the pangs of death shall never wring from me.

Not daring to look behind me, I crept on my way, and that night reached this hamlet on the Scottish border; and being grown reckless of danger, and hardened to scenes of horror, I took up my lodging with a poor hind, who is a widower, and who could only accommodate me with a bed of rushes at his fireside. At midnight I heard some strange sounds, too much resembling those to which I had of late been inured; but they kept at a distance, and I was soon persuaded that there was a power protected that house superior to those that contended for or had the mastery over me. Overjoyed at finding such an asylum, I remained in the humble cot. This is the third day I have lived under the roof, freed of my hellish assailants, spending my time in prayer, and writing out this my journal, which I have fashioned to stick in with my printed work, and to which I intend to add portions while I remain in this pilgrimage state, which, I find too well, cannot be long.

The Private Memoirs and Confessions of a Justified Sinner

August 3, 1712.—This morning the hind has brought me word from Redesdale, whither he had been for coals, that a stranger gentleman had been traversing that country, making the most earnest inquiries after me, or one of the same appearance; and, from the description that he brought of this stranger, I could easily perceive who it was. Rejoicing that my tormentor has lost traces of me for once, I am making haste to leave my asylum, on pretence of following this stranger, but in reality to conceal myself still more completely from his search. Perhaps this may be the last sentence ever I am destined to write. If so, farewell, Christian reader! May God grant to thee a happier destiny than has been allotted to me here on earth, and the same assurance of acceptance above! Amen.

Ault-Righ, August 24, 1712.—Here am I, set down on the open moor to add one sentence more to my woeful journal; and, then, farewell, all beneath the sun!

On leaving the hind's cottage on the Border, I hasted to the north-west, because in that quarter I perceived the highest and wildest hills before me. As I crossed the mountains above Hawick, I exchanged clothes with a poor homely shepherd, whom I found lying on a hill-side, singing to himself some woeful love ditty. He was glad of the change, and proud of his saintly apparel; and I was no less delighted with mine, by which I now supposed myself completely disguised; and I found moreover that in this garb of a common shepherd I was made welcome in every house. I slept the first night in a farm-house nigh to the church of Roberton, without hearing or seeing aught extraordinary; yet I observed next morning that all the servants kept aloof from me, and regarded me with looks of aversion. The next night I came to this house, where the farmer engaged me as a shepherd; and, finding him a kind, worthy, and religious man, I accepted of his terms with great gladness. I had not, however, gone many times to the sheep, before all the rest of the shepherds told my master that I knew nothing about herding, and begged of him to dismiss me. He perceived too well the truth of their intelligence; but, being much taken with my learning and religious conversation, he would not put me away, but set me to herd his cattle.

It was lucky for me that before I came here a report had prevailed, perhaps for an age, that this farm-house was haunted at certain seasons by a ghost. I say it was lucky for me for I had not been in it many days before the same appalling noises began to prevail around me about midnight, often continuing till near the dawning. Still they kept aloof, and without doors; for this gentleman's house, like the cottage I was in formerly, seemed to

397

be a sanctuary from all demoniacal power. He appears to be a good man and a just, and mocks at the idea of supernatural agency, and he either does not hear these persecuting spirits or will not acknowledge it, though of late he appears much perturbed.

The consternation of the menials has been extreme. They ascribe all to the ghost, and tell frightful stories of murders having been committed there long ago. Of late, however, they are beginning to suspect that it is I that am haunted; and, as I have never given them any satisfactory account of myself, they are whispering that I am a murderer, and haunted by the spirits of those I have slain.

August 30. — This day I have been informed that I am to be banished the dwelling-house by night, and to sleep in an outhouse by myself, to try if the family can get any rest when freed of my presence. I have peremptorily refused acquiescence, on which my master's brother struck me, and kicked me with his foot. My body being quite exhausted by suffering, I am grown weak and feeble both in mind and bodily frame, and actually unable to resent any insult or injury. I am the child of earthly misery and despair, if ever there was one existent. My master is still my friend; but there are so many masters here, and everyone of them alike harsh to me, that I wish myself in my grave every hour of the day. If I am driven from the family sanctuary by night, I know I shall be torn in pieces before morning; and then who will deign or dare to gather up my mangled limbs, and give me honoured burial?

My last hour is arrived: I see my tormentor once more approaching me in this wild. Oh, that the earth would swallow me up, or the hill fall and cover me! Farewell for ever!

September 7, 1712. — My devoted, princely, but sanguine friend has been with me again and again. My time is expired and I find a relief beyond measure, for he has fully convinced me that no act of mine can mar the eternal counsel, or in the smallest degree alter or extenuate one event which was decreed before the foundations of the world were laid. He said he had watched over me with the greatest anxiety, but, perceiving my rooted aversion towards him, he had forborne troubling me with his presence. But now, seeing that I was certainly to be driven from my sanctuary that night, and that there would be a number of infernals watching to make a prey of my body, he came to caution me not to despair, for that he would protect me at all risks, if the power remained with him. He then repeated an ejaculatory prayer, which I was to pronounce, if in great extremity. I objected to the words as equivocal, and susceptible of being rendered in a meaning perfectly dreadful; but he reasoned against this, and all reasoning with him is to no purpose. He said he did not ask me to repeat the words unless greatly straitened; and that I saw his strength and power giving way, and when perhaps nothing else could save me.

The dreaded hour of night arrived; and, as he said, I was expelled from the family residence, and ordered to a byre, or cow-house, that stood parallel with the dwelling-house behind, where, on a divot loft, my humble bedstead stood, and the cattle grunted and puffed below me. How unlike the splendid halls of Dalcastle! And to what I am now reduced, let the reflecting reader judge. Lord, thou knowest all that I have done for Thy cause on earth! Why then art Thou laying Thy hand so sore upon me? Why hast Thou set me as a butt of Thy malice? But Thy will must be done! Thou wilt repay me in a better world. Amen.

September 8. — My first night of trial in this place is overpast! Would that it were the last that I should ever see in this detested world! If the horrors of hell are equal to those I have suffered, eternity will be of short duration there, for no created energy can support them for one single month, or week. I have been buffeted as never living creature was. My vitals have all been torn, and every faculty and feeling of my soul racked, and tormented into callous insensibility. I was even hung by the locks over a yawning chasm, to which I could perceive no bottom, and then — not till then, did I repeat the tremendous prayer! — I was instantly at liberty; and what I now am, the Almighty knows! Amen.

September 18, 1712. — Still am I living, though liker to a vision than a human being; but this is my last day of mortal existence. Unable to resist any longer, I pledged myself to my devoted friend that on this day we should die together, and trust to the charity of the children of men for a grave. I am solemnly pledged; and, though I dared to repent, I am aware he will not be gainsaid, for he is raging with despair at his fallen and decayed majesty, and there is some miserable comfort in the idea that my tormentor shall fall with me. Farewell, world, with all thy miseries; for comforts or enjoyments hast thou none! Farewell, woman, whom I have despised and shunned; and man, whom I have hated; whom, nevertheless, I desire to leave in charity! And thou, sun, bright emblem of a far brighter effulgence, I bid farewell to thee also! I do not now take my last look of thee, for to thy glorious orb shall a poor suicide's last earthly look be raised. But, ah! who is yon that I see approaching furiously, his stern face blackened with horrid despair! My hour is at hand. Almighty God, what is this that I am about to do! The hour of repentance is past, and now my fate is inevitable. Amen, for ever! I will now seal up my little book, and conceal it; and cursed be he who trieth to alter or amend.

END OF THE MEMOIR

WHAT can this work be? Sure, you will say, it must be an allegory; or (as the writer calls it) a religious PARABLE, showing the dreadful danger of self-righteousness? I cannot tell. Attend to the sequel: which is a thing so extraordinary, so unprecedented, and so far out of the common course of human events that, if there were not hundreds of living witnesses to attest the truth of it, I would not bid any rational being believe it.

In the first place, take the following extract from an authentic letter, published in Blackwood's Magazine for August, 1823.

"On the top of a wild height called Cowan's-Croft, where the lands of three proprietors meet all at one point, there has been for long and many years the grave of a suicide marked out by a stone standing at the head and another at the feet. Often have I stood musing over it myself, when a shepherd on one of the farms, of which it formed the extreme boundary, and thinking what could induce a young man, who had scarcely reached the prime of life, to brave his Maker, and rush into His presence by an act of his own erring hand, and one so unnatural and preposterous. But it never once occurred to me, as an object of curiosity, to dig up the mouldering bones of the Culprit, which I considered as the most revolting of all objects. The thing was, however, done last month, and a discovery made of one of the greatest natural phenomena that I have heard of in this country.

"The little traditionary history that remains of this unfortunate youth is altogether a singular one. He was not a native of the place, nor would he ever tell from what place he came; but he was remarkable for a deep, thoughtful, and sullen disposition. There was nothing against his character that anybody knew of here, and he had been a considerable time in the place. The last service he was in was with a Mr. Anderson, of Eltrive (Ault-Righ, the King's Burn), who died about 100 years ago, and who had hired him during the summer to herd a stock of young cattle in Eltrive Hope. It happened one day in the month of September that James Anderson, his master's son, went with this young man to the Hope to divert himself. The herd had his dinner along with him, and about one o'clock, when the boy proposed going home, the former pressed him very hard to stay and take share of his dinner; but the boy refused for fear his parents might be alarmed about him, and said he would go home: on which the herd said to him, 'Then, if ye winna stay with me, James, ye may depend on't I'll cut my throat afore ye come back again.'

"I have heard it likewise reported, but only by one person, that there had been some things stolen out of his master's house a good while before, and that the boy had discovered a silver knife and fork that was a part of the stolen property, in the herd's possession that day, and that it was this discovery that drove him to despair.

"The boy did not return to the Hope that afternoon; and, before evening, a man coming in at the pass called The Hart Loup, with a drove of lambs, on the way for Edinburgh, perceived something like a man standing in a strange frightful position at the side of one of Eldinhope hay-ricks. The driver's attention was riveted on this strange uncouth figure, and, as the drove-road passed at no great distance from the spot, he first called, but, receiving no answer, he went up to the spot, and behold it was the above-mentioned young man, who had hung himself in the hay rope that was tying down the rick.

"This was accounted a great wonder; and everyone said, if the Devil had not assisted him, it was impossible the thing could have been done; for, in general, these ropes are so brittle, being made of green hay, that they will scarcely bear to be bound over the rick. And, the more to horrify the good people of this neighbourhood, the driver said, when he first came in view, he could almost give his oath that he saw two people busily engaged at the hay-rick going round it and round it, and he thought they were dressing it.

"If this asseveration approximated at all to truth, it makes this evident at least, that the unfortunate young man had hanged himself after the man with the lambs came in view. He was, however, quite dead when he cut him down. He had fastened two of the old hay-ropes at the bottom of the rick on one side (indeed, they are all fastened so when first laid on) so that he had nothing to do but to loosen two of the ends on the other side. These he had tied in a knot round his neck, and then slackening his knees, and letting himself down gradually, till the hay-rope bore all his weight, he had contrived to put an end to his existence in that way. Now the fact is, that, if you try all the ropes that are thrown over all the out-field hay-ricks in Scotland, there is not one among a thousand of them will hang a colley dog; so that the manner of this wretch's death was rather a singular circumstance.

"Early next morning, Mr. Anderson's servants went reluctantly away, and, taking an old blanket with them for a winding sheet, they rolled up the body of the deceased, first in his own plaid, letting the hay-rope still remain about his neck, and then, rolling the old blanket over all, they bore the loathed remains away to the distance of three miles or so, on spokes, to the top of Cowan's-Croft, at the very point where the Duke of Buccleuch's land, the Laird of Drummelzier's, and Lord Napier's meet, and there they buried him, with all that he had on and about him, silver knife and fork and altogether. Thus far went tradition, and no one ever disputed one jot of the disgusting oral tale.

"A nephew of that Mr. Anderson's who was with the hapless youth that day he died says that, as far as he can gather from the relations of friends that he remembers, and of that same uncle in particular, it is one hundred and five years next month (that is September, 1823) since that event happened; and I think it likely that this gentleman's information is correct. But sundry other people, much older than he, whom I have consulted, pretend that it is six or seven years more. They say they have heard that Mr. James Anderson was then a boy ten years of age; that he lived to an old age, upwards of fourscore, and it is two and forty years since he died. Whichever way it may be, it was about that period some way: of that there is no doubt.

"It so happened that two young men, William Shiel and W. Sword, were out on an adjoining height this summer, casting peats, and it came into their heads to open this grave in the wilderness, and see if there were any of the bones of the suicide of former ages and centuries remaining. They did so, but opened only one half of the grave, beginning at the head and about the middle at the same time. It was not long till they came upon the old blanket—I think, they said not much more than a foot from the surface. They tore that open, and there was the hay-rope lying stretched down alongst his breast, so fresh that they saw at first sight that it was made of risp, a sort of long sword-grass that grows about marshes and the sides of lakes. One of the young men seized the rope and pulled by it, but the old enchantment of the Devil remained—it would not break; and so he pulled and pulled at it, till behold the body came up into a sitting posture, with a broad blue bonnet on its head, and its plaid around it, all as fresh as that day it was laid in! I never heard of a preservation so wonderful, if it be true as was related to me, for still I have not had the curiosity to go and view the body myself. The features were all so plain that an acquaintance might easily have known him. One of the lads gripped the face of the corpse with his finger and thumb, and the cheeks felt quite soft and fleshy, but the dimples remained and did not spring out again. He had fine yellow hair, about nine inches long; but not a hair of it could they pull out till they cut part of it off with a knife. They also cut off some portions of his clothes, which were all quite fresh, and distributed them among their acquaintances, sending a portion to me, among the rest, to keep as natural curiosities. Several gentlemen have in a manner forced me to give them fragments of these enchanted garments: I have, however, retained a small portion for you, which I send along with this, being a piece of his plaid, and another of his waistcoat breast, which you will see are still as fresh as that day they were laid in the grave.

"His broad blue bonnet was sent to Edinburgh several weeks ago, to the great regret of some gentlemen connected with the land, who wished to have it for a keep-sake. For my part, fond as I am of blue bonnets, and broad ones in particular, I declare I durst not have worn that one. There was nothing of the silver knife and fork discovered, that I heard of, nor was it very likely it should; but it would appear he had been very near run out of cash, which I daresay had been the cause of his utter despair; for, on searching his pockets, nothing was found but three old Scotch halfpennies. These young men meeting with another shepherd afterwards, his curiosity was so much excited that they went and digged up the curious remains a second time, which was a pity, as it is likely that by these exposures to the air, and the impossibility of burying it up again as closely as it was before, the flesh will now fall to dust."

The letter from which the above is an extract, is signed JAMES HOGG, and dated from Altrive Lake, August 1st, 1823. It bears the stamp of authenticity in every line; yet so often had I been hoaxed by the ingenious fancies displayed in that Magazine, that when this relation met my eye I did not believe it; but, from the moment that I perused it, I half formed the resolution of investigating these wonderful remains personally, if any such existed; for, in the immediate vicinity of the scene, as I supposed, I knew of more attractive metal than the dilapidated remains of mouldering suicides.

Accordingly, having some business in Edinburgh in September last, and being obliged to wait a few days for the arrival of a friend from London, I took that opportunity to pay a visit to my townsman and fellow collegian, Mr. L—t of C—d, advocate. I mentioned to him Hogg's letter, asking him if the statement was founded at all on truth. His answer was: "I suppose so. For my part I never doubted the thing, having been told that there has been a deal of talking about it up in the Forest for some time past. But God knows! Hogg has imposed as ingenious lies on the public ere now."

I said, if it was within reach, I should like exceedingly to visit both the Shepherd and the Scotch mummy he had described. Mr. L—t assented on the first proposal, saying he had no objections to take a ride that length with me, and make the fellow produce his credentials. That we would have a delightful jaunt through a romantic and now classical country, and some good sport into the bargain, provided he could procure a horse for me, from his father-in-law, next day. He sent up to a Mr. L—w to inquire, who returned for answer that there was an excellent pony at my service, and that he himself would accompany us, being obliged to attend a great sheep-fair at Thirlestane; and that he was certain the Shepherd would be there likewise.

Mr. L—t said that was the very man we wanted to make our party complete; and at an early hour next morning we started for the ewe-fair of Thirlestane, taking Blackwood's Magazine for August along with us. We rode through the ancient royal burgh of Selkirk, halted and corned our horses at a romantic village, nigh to some deep linns on the Ettrick, and reached the market ground at Thirlestane-green a little before mid-day. We soon found Hogg, standing near the foot of the market, as he called it, beside a great drove of paulies, a species of stock that I never heard of before. They were small sheep, striped on the backs with red chalk. Mr. L—t introduced me to him as a great wool-stapler, come to raise the price of that article; but he eyed me with distrust, and, turning his back on us, answered: "I hae sell'd mine."

I followed, and, shewing him the above-quoted letter, said I was exceedingly curious to have a look of these singular remains he had so ingeniously described; but he only answered me with the remark that "It was a queer fancy for a wool-stapler to tak."

His two friends then requested him to accompany us to the spot, and to take some of his shepherds with us to assist in raising the body; but he spurned at the idea, saying: "Od bless ye, lad! I hae ither matters to mind. I hae a' thae paulies to sell, an', a' yon Highland stotts down on the green, every ane; an' then I hae ten scores o' yowes to buy after, an', If I canna first sell my ain stock, I canna buy nae ither body's. I hae mair ado than I can manage the day, foreby ganging to houk up hunder-year-auld-banes."

Finding that we could make nothing of him, we left him with his paulies, Highland stotts, grey jacket, and broad blue bonnet, to go in search of some other guide. L—w soon found one, for he seemed acquainted with every person in the fair. We got a fine old shepherd, named W—m B—e, a great original, and a very obliging and civil man, who asked no conditions but that we should not speak of it, because he did not wish it to come to his master's ears that he had been engaged in sic a profane thing. We promised strict secrecy; and accompanied by another farmer, Mr. S—t, and old B—e, we proceeded to the grave, which B—e described as about a mile and a half distant from the market ground.

We went into the shepherd's cot to get a drink of milk, when I read to our guide Mr. Hogg's description, asking him if he thought it correct. He said there was hardly a bit o't correct, for the grave was not on the hill of Cowan's-Croft nor yet on the point where three lairds' lands met, but on the top of a hill called the Faw-Law, where there was no land that was not the Duke of Buccleuch's within a quarter of a mile. He added that it was a wonder how the poet could be mistaken there, who once herded the very ground where the grave is, and saw both hills from his own window. Mr. L—w testified great surprise at such a singular blunder, as also how the body came not to be buried at the meeting of three or four lairds' lands, which had always been customary in the south of Scotland. Our guide said he had always heard it reported that the Eltrive men, with Mr. David Anderson at their head, had risen before day on the Monday morning, it having been on the Sabbath day that the man put down himself; and that they set out with the intention of burying him on Cowan's-Croft, where the three marches met at a point. But, it having been an invariable rule to bury such lost sinners before the rising of the sun, these five men were overtaken by day-light, as they passed the house of Berry-Knowe; and, by the time they reached the top of the Faw-Law, the sun was beginning to skair the east. On this they laid down the body, and digged a deep grave with all expedition; but, when they had done, it was too short, and, the body being stiff, it would not go down; on which Mr. David Anderson, looking to the east and perceiving that the sun would be up on them in a few minutes, set his foot on the suicide's brow, and tramped down his head into the grave with his iron-heeled shoe, until the nose and skull crashed again, and at the same time uttered a terrible curse on the wretch who had disgraced the family and given them all this trouble. This anecdote, our guide said, he had heard when a boy, from the mouth of Robert Laidlaw, one of the five men who buried the body.

We soon reached the spot, and I confess I felt a singular sensation when I saw the grey stone standing at the head, and another at the feet, and the one half of the grave manifestly new-digged, and closed up again as had been described. I could still scarcely deem the thing to be a reality, for the ground did not appear to be wet, but a kind of dry rotten moss. On looking around, we found some fragments of clothes, some teeth, and part of a pocket-book, which had not been returned into the grave when the body had been last raised, for it had been twice raised before this, but only from the loins upward.

To work we fell with two spades, and soon cleared away the whole of the covering. The part of the grave that had been opened before was filled with mossy mortar, which impeded us exceedingly, and entirely prevented a proper investigation of the fore parts of the body. I will describe everything as I saw it before our respectable witnesses, whose names I shall publish at large if permitted. A number of the bones came up separately; for, with the constant flow of liquid stuff into the deep grave, we could not see to preserve them in their places. At length great loads of coarse clothes, blanketing, plaiding, etc. appeared; we tried to lift these regularly up, and, on doing so, part of a skeleton came up, but no flesh, save a little that was hanging in dark flitters about the spine, but which had no consistence; it was merely the appearance of flesh without the substance. The head was wanting, and, I being very anxious to possess the skull, the search was renewed among the mortar and rags. We first found a part of the scalp, with the long hair firm on it; which, on being cleaned, is neither black nor fair, but a darkish dusk, the most common of any other colour. Soon afterwards we found the skull, but it was not complete. A spade had damaged it, and one of the temple quarters was wanting. I am no phrenologist, not knowing one organ from another, but I thought the skull of that wretched man no study. If it was particular for anything, it was for a smooth, almost perfect rotundity, with only a little protuberance above the vent of the ear.

When we came to that part of the grave that had never been opened before, the appearance of everything was quite different. There the remains lay under a close vault of moss, and within a vacant space; and I suppose, by the digging in the

The Private Memoirs and Confessions of a Justified Sinner

former part of the grave, the part had been deepened, and drawn the moisture away from this part, for here all was perfect. The breeches still suited the thigh, the stocking the leg, and the garters were wrapt as neatly and as firm below the knee as if they had been newly tied. The shoes were all open in the seams, the hemp having decayed, but the soles, upper leathers and wooden heels, which were made of birch, were all as fresh as any of those we wore. There was one thing I could not help remarking, that in the inside of one of the shoes there was a layer of cow's dung, about one-eighth of an inch thick, and in the hollow of the sole fully one-fourth of an inch. It was firm, green, and fresh; and proved that he had been working in a byre. His clothes were all of a singular ancient cut, and no less singular in their texture. Their durability certainly would have been prodigious; for in thickness, coarseness, and strength, I never saw any cloth in the smallest degree to equal them. His coat was a frock coat, of a yellowish drab colour, with wide sleeves. It is tweeled, milled, and thicker than a carpet. I cut off two of the skirts and brought them with me. His vest was of striped serge, such as I have often seen worn by country people. It was lined and backed with white stuff. The breeches were a sort of striped plaiding, which I never saw worn, but which our guide assured us was very common in the country once, though, from the old clothes which he had seen remaining of it, he judged that it could not be less than 200 years since it was in fashion. His garters were of worsted, and striped with black or blue; his stockings grey, and wanting the feet. I brought samples of all along with me. I have likewise now got possession of the bonnet, which puzzles me most of all. It is not conformable with the rest of the dress. It is neither a broad bonnet nor a Border bonnet; for there is an open behind, for tying, which no genuine Border bonnet I am told ever had. It seems to have been a Highland bonnet, worn in a flat way, like a scone on the crown, such as is sometimes still seen in the West of Scotland. All the limbs, from the loins to the toes, seemed perfect and entire, but they could not bear handling. Before we got them returned again into the grave they were shaken to pieces, except the thighs, which continued to retain a kind of flabby form.

All his clothes that were sewed with linen yarn were lying in separate portions, the thread having rotten; but such as were sewed with worsted remained perfectly firm and sound. Among such a confusion, we had hard work to find out all his pockets, and our guide supposed that, after all, we did not find above the half of them. In his vest pocket was a long clasp-knife, very sharp; the haft was thin, and the scales shone as if there had been silver inside. Mr. Sc—t took it with him, and presented it to his neighbour, Mr. R—n, of W—n L—e, who still has it in

The Private Memoirs and Confessions of a Justified Sinner

his possession. We found a comb, a gimblet, a vial, a small neat square board, a pair of plated knee-buckles, and several samples of cloth of different kinds, rolled neatly up within one another. At length, while we were busy on the search, Mr. L—t picked up a leathern case, which seemed to have been wrapped round and round by some ribbon, or cord, that had been rotten from it, for the swaddling marks still remained. Both L—w and B—e called out that "it was the tobacco spleuchan, and a well-filled ane too"; but, on opening it out, we found, to our great astonishment, that it contained a printed pamphlet. We were all curious to see what sort of a pamphlet such a person would read; what it could contain that he seemed to have had such a care about. For the slough in which it was rolled was fine chamois leather; what colour it had been could not be known. But the pamphlet was wrapped so close together, and so damp, rotten, and yellow that it seemed one solid piece. We all concluded from some words that we could make out that it was a religious tract, but that it would be impossible to make anything of it. Mr. L—w remarked marked that it was a great pity if a few sentences could not be made out, for that it was a question what might be contained in that little book; and then he requested Mr. L—t to give it to me, as he had so many things of literature and law to attend to that he would never think more of it. He replied that either of us were heartily welcome to it, for that he had thought of returning it into the grave, if he could have made out but a line or two, to have seen what was its tendency.

"Grave, man!" exclaimed L—w, who speaks excellent strong broad Scotch. "My truly, but ye grave weel! I wad esteem the contents o' that spleuchan as the most precious treasure. I'll tell you what it is, sir: I hae often wondered how it was that this man's corpse has been miraculously preserved frae decay, a hunder times langer than any other body's, or than ever a tanner's. But now I could wager a guinea it has been for the preservation o' that little book. And Lord kens what may be in't! It will maybe reveal some mystery that mankind disna ken naething about yet."

"If there be any mysteries in it," returned the other, "it is not for your handling, my dear friend, who are too much taken up about mysteries already." And with these words he presented the mysterious pamphlet to me. With very little trouble, save that of a thorough drying, I unrolled it all with ease, and found the very tract which I have here ventured to lay before the public, part of it in small bad print, and the remainder in manuscript. The title page is written and is as follows:

THE PRIVATE MEMOIRS
AND CONFESSIONS
OF A JUSTIFIED SINNER:

WRITTEN BY HIMSELF

Fideli certa merces.

And, alongst the head, it is the same as given in the present edition of the work. I altered the title to A Self-justified Sinner, but my booksellers did not approve of it; and, there being a curse pronounced by the writer on him that should dare to alter or amend, I have let it stand as it is. Should it be thought to attach discredit to any received principle of our Church, I am blameless. The printed part ends at page 201 and the rest is in a fine old hand, extremely small and close. I have ordered the printer to procure a facsimile of it, to be bound in with the volume. [v. Frontispiece.]

With regard to the work itself, I dare not venture a judgment, for I do not understand it. I believe no person, man or woman, will ever peruse it with the same attention that I have done, and yet I confess that I do not comprehend the writer's drift. It is certainly impossible that these scenes could ever have occurred that he describes as having himself transacted. I think it may be possible that he had some hand in the death of his brother, and yet I am disposed greatly to doubt it; and the numerous traditions, etc. which remain of that event may be attributable to the work having been printed and burnt, and of course the story known to all the printers, with their families and gossips. That the young Laird of Dalcastle came by a violent death, there remains no doubt; but that this wretch slew him, there is to me a good deal. However, allowing this to have been the case, I account all the rest either dreaming or madness; or, as he says to Mr. Watson, a religious parable, on purpose to illustrate something scarcely tangible, but to which he seems to have attached great weight. Were the relation at all consistent with reason, it corresponds so minutely with traditionary facts that it could scarcely have missed to have been received as authentic; but in this day, and with the present generation, it will not go down that a man should be daily tempted by the Devil, in the semblance of a fellow-creature; and at length lured to self-destruction, in the hopes that this same fiend and tormentor was to suffer and fall along with him. It was a bold theme for an allegory, and would have suited that age well had it been taken up by one fully qualified for the task, which this writer was not. In short, we must either conceive him not only the greatest fool, but the greatest wretch, on whom was ever stamped the form of humanity; or, that he was a religious maniac, who wrote and wrote about a deluded creature, till he arrived at that height of madness that he believed himself the very object whom he had been all along describing. And, in order to escape from an ideal tormentor, committed that act for which, according to the tenets he embraced, there was no remission, and which consigned his memory and his name to everlasting detestation.

The Legend of Sleepy Hollow

By Washington Irving

(Found Among the Papers of the Late Diedrich Knickerbocker.)

>   A pleasing land of drowsy head it was,
>
>   Of dreams that wave before the half-shut eye;
>
>   And of gay castles in the clouds that pass,
>
>   Forever flushing round a summer sky.
>
>   —CASTLE OF INDOLENCE.

In the bosom of one of those spacious coves which indent the eastern shore of the Hudson, at that broad expansion of the river denominated by the ancient Dutch navigators the Tappan Zee, and where they always prudently shortened sail and implored the protection of St. Nicholas when they crossed, there lies a small market town or rural port, which by some is called Greensburgh, but which is more generally and properly known by the name of Tarry Town. This name was given, we are told, in former days, by the good housewives of the adjacent country, from the inveterate propensity of their husbands to linger about the village tavern on market days. Be that as it may, I do not vouch for the fact, but merely advert to it, for the sake of being precise and authentic. Not far from this village, perhaps about two miles, there is a little valley or rather lap of land among high hills, which is one of the quietest places in the whole world. A small brook glides through it, with just murmur enough to lull one to repose; and the occasional whistle of a quail or tapping of a woodpecker is almost the only sound that ever breaks in upon the uniform tranquillity.

I recollect that, when a stripling, my first exploit in squirrel-shooting was in a grove of tall walnut-trees that shades one side of the valley. I had wandered into it at noontime, when all nature is peculiarly quiet, and was startled by the roar of my own gun, as it broke the Sabbath stillness around and was prolonged and reverberated by the angry echoes. If ever I should wish for a retreat whither I might steal from the world and its distractions, and dream quietly away the remnant of a troubled life, I know of none more promising than this little valley.

From the listless repose of the place, and the peculiar character of its inhabitants, who are descendants from the original Dutch settlers, this sequestered glen has long been known by the name of SLEEPY HOLLOW, and its rustic lads are called the Sleepy Hollow Boys throughout all the neighboring country. A drowsy, dreamy influence seems to hang over the land, and to pervade the very atmosphere. Some say that the place was bewitched by a High German doctor, during the early days of the settlement; others, that an old Indian chief, the prophet or wizard of his tribe, held his powwows there before the country was discovered by Master Hendrick Hudson. Certain it is, the place still continues under the sway of some witching power, that holds a spell over the minds of the good people, causing them to walk in a continual reverie. They are given to all kinds of marvellous beliefs, are subject to trances and visions, and frequently see strange sights, and hear music and voices in the air. The whole neighborhood abounds with local tales, haunted spots, and twilight superstitions; stars shoot and meteors glare oftener across the valley than in any other part of the country, and the nightmare, with her whole ninefold, seems to make it the favorite scene of her gambols.

The dominant spirit, however, that haunts this enchanted region, and seems to be commander-in-chief of all the powers of the air, is the apparition of a figure on horseback, without a head. It is said by some to be the ghost of a Hessian trooper, whose head had been carried away by a cannon-ball, in some nameless battle during the Revolutionary War, and who is ever and anon seen by the country folk hurrying along in the gloom of night, as if on the wings of the wind. His haunts are not confined to the valley, but extend at times to the adjacent roads, and especially to the vicinity of a church at no great distance. Indeed, certain of the most authentic historians of those parts, who have been careful in collecting and collating the floating facts concerning this spectre, allege that the body of the trooper having been buried in the churchyard, the ghost rides forth to

The Legend of Sleepy Hollow

the scene of battle in nightly quest of his head, and that the rushing speed with which he sometimes passes along the Hollow, like a midnight blast, is owing to his being belated, and in a hurry to get back to the churchyard before daybreak.

Such is the general purport of this legendary superstition, which has furnished materials for many a wild story in that region of shadows; and the spectre is known at all the country firesides, by the name of the Headless Horseman of Sleepy Hollow.

It is remarkable that the visionary propensity I have mentioned is not confined to the native inhabitants of the valley, but is unconsciously imbibed by every one who resides there for a time. However wide awake they may have been before they entered that sleepy region, they are sure, in a little time, to inhale the witching influence of the air, and begin to grow imaginative, to dream dreams, and see apparitions.

I mention this peaceful spot with all possible laud, for it is in such little retired Dutch valleys, found here and there embosomed in the great State of New York, that population, manners, and customs remain fixed, while the great torrent of migration and improvement, which is making such incessant changes in other parts of this restless country, sweeps by them unobserved. They are like those little nooks of still water, which border a rapid stream, where we may see the straw and bubble riding quietly at anchor, or slowly revolving in their mimic harbor, undisturbed by the rush of the passing current. Though many years have elapsed since I trod the drowsy shades of Sleepy Hollow, yet I question whether I should not still find the same trees and the same families vegetating in its sheltered bosom.

In this by-place of nature there abode, in a remote period of American history, that is to say, some thirty years since, a worthy wight of the name of Ichabod Crane, who sojourned, or, as he expressed it, "tarried," in Sleepy Hollow, for the purpose of instructing the children of the vicinity. He was a native of Connecticut, a State which supplies the Union with pioneers for the mind as well as for the forest, and sends forth yearly its legions of frontier woodmen and country schoolmasters. The cognomen of Crane was not inapplicable to his person. He was tall, but exceedingly lank, with narrow shoulders, long arms and legs, hands that dangled a mile out of his sleeves, feet that might have served for shovels, and his whole frame most loosely hung together. His head was small, and flat at top, with huge ears, large green glassy eyes, and a long snipe nose, so that it looked like a weather-cock perched upon his spindle neck to tell which way the wind blew. To see him striding along the profile of a hill on a windy day, with his clothes bagging and fluttering about him, one might have mistaken him for the genius of famine descending upon the earth, or some scarecrow eloped from a cornfield.

His schoolhouse was a low building of one large room, rudely constructed of logs; the windows partly glazed, and partly patched with leaves of old copybooks. It was most ingeniously secured at vacant hours, by a withe twisted in the handle of the door, and stakes set against the window shutters; so that though a thief might get in with perfect ease, he would find some embarrassment in getting out,--an idea most probably borrowed by the architect, Yost Van Houten, from the mystery of an eelpot. The schoolhouse stood in a rather lonely but pleasant situation, just at the foot of a woody hill, with a brook running close by, and a formidable birch-tree growing at one end of it. From hence the low murmur of his pupils' voices, conning over their lessons, might be heard in a drowsy summer's day, like the hum of a beehive; interrupted now and then by the authoritative voice of the master, in the tone of menace or command, or, peradventure, by the appalling sound of the birch, as he urged some tardy loiterer along the flowery path of knowledge. Truth to say, he was a conscientious man, and ever bore in mind the golden maxim, "Spare the rod and spoil the child." Ichabod Crane's scholars certainly were not spoiled.

I would not have it imagined, however, that he was one of those cruel potentates of the school who joy in the smart of their subjects; on the contrary, he administered justice with discrimination rather than severity; taking the burden off the backs of the weak, and laying it on those of the strong. Your mere puny stripling, that winced at the least flourish of the rod, was passed by with indulgence; but the claims of justice were satisfied by inflicting a double portion on some little tough wrong-headed, broad-skirted Dutch urchin, who sulked and swelled and grew dogged and sullen beneath the birch. All this he called "doing his duty by their parents;" and he never inflicted a chastisement without following it by the assurance, so consolatory to the smarting urchin, that "he would remember it and thank him for it the longest day he had to live."

When school hours were over, he was even the companion and playmate of the larger boys; and on holiday afternoons would convoy some of the smaller ones home, who happened to have pretty sisters, or good housewives for mothers, noted

The Legend of Sleepy Hollow

for the comforts of the cupboard. Indeed, it behooved him to keep on good terms with his pupils. The revenue arising from his school was small, and would have been scarcely sufficient to furnish him with daily bread, for he was a huge feeder, and, though lank, had the dilating powers of an anaconda; but to help out his maintenance, he was, according to country custom in those parts, boarded and lodged at the houses of the farmers whose children he instructed. With these he lived successively a week at a time, thus going the rounds of the neighborhood, with all his worldly effects tied up in a cotton handkerchief.

That all this might not be too onerous on the purses of his rustic patrons, who are apt to consider the costs of schooling a grievous burden, and schoolmasters as mere drones, he had various ways of rendering himself both useful and agreeable. He assisted the farmers occasionally in the lighter labors of their farms, helped to make hay, mended the fences, took the horses to water, drove the cows from pasture, and cut wood for the winter fire. He laid aside, too, all the dominant dignity and absolute sway with which he lorded it in his little empire, the school, and became wonderfully gentle and ingratiating. He found favor in the eyes of the mothers by petting the children, particularly the youngest; and like the lion bold, which whilom so magnanimously the lamb did hold, he would sit with a child on one knee, and rock a cradle with his foot for whole hours together.

In addition to his other vocations, he was the singing-master of the neighborhood, and picked up many bright shillings by instructing the young folks in psalmody. It was a matter of no little vanity to him on Sundays, to take his station in front of the church gallery, with a band of chosen singers; where, in his own mind, he completely carried away the palm from the parson. Certain it is, his voice resounded far above all the rest of the congregation; and there are peculiar quavers still to be heard in that church, and which may even be heard half a mile off, quite to the opposite side of the millpond, on a still Sunday morning, which are said to be legitimately descended from the nose of Ichabod Crane. Thus, by divers little makeshifts, in that ingenious way which is commonly denominated "by hook and by crook," the worthy pedagogue got on tolerably enough, and was thought, by all who understood nothing of the labor of headwork, to have a wonderfully easy life of it.

The schoolmaster is generally a man of some importance in the female circle of a rural neighborhood; being considered a kind of idle, gentlemanlike personage, of vastly superior taste and accomplishments to the rough country swains, and, indeed, inferior in learning only to the parson. His appearance, therefore, is apt to occasion some little stir at the tea-table of a farmhouse, and the addition of a supernumerary dish of cakes or sweetmeats, or, peradventure, the parade of a silver teapot. Our man of letters, therefore, was peculiarly happy in the smiles of all the country damsels. How he would figure among them in the churchyard, between services on Sundays; gathering grapes for them from the wild vines that overran the surrounding trees; reciting for their amusement all the epitaphs on the tombstones; or sauntering, with a whole bevy of them, along the banks of the adjacent millpond; while the more bashful country bumpkins hung sheepishly back, envying his superior elegance and address.

From his half-itinerant life, also, he was a kind of travelling gazette, carrying the whole budget of local gossip from house to house, so that his appearance was always greeted with satisfaction. He was, moreover, esteemed by the women as a man of great erudition, for he had read several books quite through, and was a perfect master of Cotton Mather's "History of New England Witchcraft," in which, by the way, he most firmly and potently believed.

He was, in fact, an odd mixture of small shrewdness and simple credulity. His appetite for the marvellous, and his powers of digesting it, were equally extraordinary; and both had been increased by his residence in this spell-bound region. No tale was too gross or monstrous for his capacious swallow. It was often his delight, after his school was dismissed in the afternoon, to stretch himself on the rich bed of clover bordering the little brook that whimpered by his schoolhouse, and there con over old Mather's direful tales, until the gathering dusk of evening made the printed page a mere mist before his eyes. Then, as he wended his way by swamp and stream and awful woodland, to the farmhouse where he happened to be quartered, every sound of nature, at that witching hour, fluttered his excited imagination,--the moan of the whip-poor-will from the hillside, the boding cry of the tree toad, that harbinger of storm, the dreary hooting of the screech owl, or the sudden rustling in the thicket of birds frightened from their roost. The fireflies, too, which sparkled most vividly in the darkest places, now and then startled him, as one of uncommon brightness would stream across his path; and if, by chance, a huge blockhead of a beetle came winging his blundering flight against him, the poor varlet was ready to give up the ghost, with the idea that he was struck with a witch's token. His only resource on such occasions, either to drown thought or drive away evil spirits, was to sing psalm tunes and the good people

The Legend of Sleepy Hollow

of Sleepy Hollow, as they sat by their doors of an evening, were often filled with awe at hearing his nasal melody, "in linked sweetness long drawn out," floating from the distant hill, or along the dusky road.

Another of his sources of fearful pleasure was to pass long winter evenings with the old Dutch wives, as they sat spinning by the fire, with a row of apples roasting and spluttering along the hearth, and listen to their marvellous tales of ghosts and goblins, and haunted fields, and haunted brooks, and haunted bridges, and haunted houses, and particularly of the headless horseman, or Galloping Hessian of the Hollow, as they sometimes called him. He would delight them equally by his anecdotes of witchcraft, and of the direful omens and portentous sights and sounds in the air, which prevailed in the earlier times of Connecticut; and would frighten them woefully with speculations upon comets and shooting stars; and with the alarming fact that the world did absolutely turn round, and that they were half the time topsy-turvy!

But if there was a pleasure in all this, while snugly cuddling in the chimney corner of a chamber that was all of a ruddy glow from the crackling wood fire, and where, of course, no spectre dared to show its face, it was dearly purchased by the terrors of his subsequent walk homewards. What fearful shapes and shadows beset his path, amidst the dim and ghastly glare of a snowy night! With what wistful look did he eye every trembling ray of light streaming across the waste fields from some distant window! How often was he appalled by some shrub covered with snow, which, like a sheeted spectre, beset his very path! How often did he shrink with curdling awe at the sound of his own steps on the frosty crust beneath his feet; and dread to look over his shoulder, lest he should behold some uncouth being tramping close behind him! And how often was he thrown into complete dismay by some rushing blast, howling among the trees, in the idea that it was the Galloping Hessian on one of his nightly scourings!

All these, however, were mere terrors of the night, phantoms of the mind that walk in darkness; and though he had seen many spectres in his time, and been more than once beset by Satan in divers shapes, in his lonely perambulations, yet daylight put an end to all these evils; and he would have passed a pleasant life of it, in despite of the Devil and all his works, if his path had not been crossed by a being that causes more perplexity to mortal man than ghosts, goblins, and the whole race of witches put together, and that was--a woman.

Among the musical disciples who assembled, one evening in each week, to receive his instructions in psalmody, was Katrina Van Tassel, the daughter and only child of a substantial Dutch farmer. She was a blooming lass of fresh eighteen; plump as a partridge; ripe and melting and rosy-cheeked as one of her father's peaches, and universally famed, not merely for her beauty, but her vast expectations. She was withal a little of a coquette, as might be perceived even in her dress, which was a mixture of ancient and modern fashions, as most suited to set off her charms. She wore the ornaments of pure yellow gold, which her great-great-grandmother had brought over from Saardam; the tempting stomacher of the olden time, and withal a provokingly short petticoat, to display the prettiest foot and ankle in the country round.

Ichabod Crane had a soft and foolish heart towards the sex; and it is not to be wondered at that so tempting a morsel soon found favor in his eyes, more especially after he had visited her in her paternal mansion. Old Baltus Van Tassel was a perfect picture of a thriving, contented, liberal-hearted farmer. He seldom, it is true, sent either his eyes or his thoughts beyond the boundaries of his own farm; but within those everything was snug, happy and well-conditioned. He was satisfied with his wealth, but not proud of it; and piqued himself upon the hearty abundance, rather than the style in which he lived. His stronghold was situated on the banks of the Hudson, in one of those green, sheltered, fertile nooks in which the Dutch farmers are so fond of nestling. A great elm tree spread its broad branches over it, at the foot of which bubbled up a spring of the softest and sweetest water, in a little well formed of a barrel; and then stole sparkling away through the grass, to a neighboring brook, that babbled along among alders and dwarf willows. Hard by the farmhouse was a vast barn, that might have served for a church; every window and crevice of which seemed bursting forth with the treasures of the farm; the flail was busily resounding within it from morning to night; swallows and martins skimmed twittering about the eaves; and rows of pigeons, some with one eye turned up, as if watching the weather, some with their heads under their wings or buried in their bosoms, and others swelling, and cooing, and bowing about their dames, were enjoying the sunshine on the roof. Sleek unwieldy porkers were grunting in the repose and abundance of their pens, from whence sallied forth, now and then, troops of sucking pigs, as if to snuff the air. A stately squadron of snowy geese were riding in an adjoining pond, convoying whole fleets of ducks; regiments of turkeys were gobbling through the farmyard, and Guinea fowls fretting about it, like ill-tempered housewives, with their peevish,

The Legend of Sleepy Hollow

discontented cry. Before the barn door strutted the gallant cock, that pattern of a husband, a warrior and a fine gentleman, clapping his burnished wings and crowing in the pride and gladness of his heart,--sometimes tearing up the earth with his feet, and then generously calling his ever-hungry family of wives and children to enjoy the rich morsel which he had discovered.

The pedagogue's mouth watered as he looked upon this sumptuous promise of luxurious winter fare. In his devouring mind's eye, he pictured to himself every roasting-pig running about with a pudding in his belly, and an apple in his mouth; the pigeons were snugly put to bed in a comfortable pie, and tucked in with a coverlet of crust; the geese were swimming in their own gravy; and the ducks pairing cosily in dishes, like snug married couples, with a decent competency of onion sauce. In the porkers he saw carved out the future sleek side of bacon, and juicy relishing ham; not a turkey but he beheld daintily trussed up, with its gizzard under its wing, and, peradventure, a necklace of savory sausages; and even bright chanticleer himself lay sprawling on his back, in a side dish, with uplifted claws, as if craving that quarter which his chivalrous spirit disdained to ask while living.

As the enraptured Ichabod fancied all this, and as he rolled his great green eyes over the fat meadow lands, the rich fields of wheat, of rye, of buckwheat, and Indian corn, and the orchards burdened with ruddy fruit, which surrounded the warm tenement of Van Tassel, his heart yearned after the damsel who was to inherit these domains, and his imagination expanded with the idea, how they might be readily turned into cash, and the money invested in immense tracts of wild land, and shingle palaces in the wilderness. Nay, his busy fancy already realized his hopes, and presented to him the blooming Katrina, with a whole family of children, mounted on the top of a wagon loaded with household trumpery, with pots and kettles dangling beneath; and he beheld himself bestriding a pacing mare, with a colt at her heels, setting out for Kentucky, Tennessee,--or the Lord knows where!

When he entered the house, the conquest of his heart was complete. It was one of those spacious farmhouses, with high-ridged but lowly sloping roofs, built in the style handed down from the first Dutch settlers; the low projecting eaves forming a piazza along the front, capable of being closed up in bad weather. Under this were hung flails, harness, various utensils of husbandry, and nets for fishing in the neighboring river. Benches were built along the sides for summer use; and a great spinning-wheel at one end, and a churn at the other, showed the various uses to which this important porch might be devoted. From this piazza the wondering Ichabod entered the hall, which formed the centre of the mansion, and the place of usual residence. Here rows of resplendent pewter, ranged on a long dresser, dazzled his eyes. In one corner stood a huge bag of wool, ready to be spun; in another, a quantity of linsey-woolsey just from the loom; ears of Indian corn, and strings of dried apples and peaches, hung in gay festoons along the walls, mingled with the gaud of red peppers; and a door left ajar gave him a peep into the best parlor, where the claw-footed chairs and dark mahogany tables shone like mirrors; andirons, with their accompanying shovel and tongs, glistened from their covert of asparagus tops; mock- oranges and conch-shells decorated the mantelpiece; strings of various-colored birds eggs were suspended above it; a great ostrich egg was hung from the centre of the room, and a corner cupboard, knowingly left open, displayed immense treasures of old silver and well-mended china.

From the moment Ichabod laid his eyes upon these regions of delight, the peace of his mind was at an end, and his only study was how to gain the affections of the peerless daughter of Van Tassel. In this enterprise, however, he had more real difficulties than generally fell to the lot of a knight-errant of yore, who seldom had anything but giants, enchanters, fiery dragons, and such like easily conquered adversaries, to contend with and had to make his way merely through gates of iron and brass, and walls of adamant to the castle keep, where the lady of his heart was confined; all which he achieved as easily as a man would carve his way to the centre of a Christmas pie; and then the lady gave him her hand as a matter of course. Ichabod, on the contrary, had to win his way to the heart of a country coquette, beset with a labyrinth of whims and caprices, which were forever presenting new difficulties and impediments; and he had to encounter a host of fearful adversaries of real flesh and blood, the numerous rustic admirers, who beset every portal to her heart, keeping a watchful and angry eye upon each other, but ready to fly out in the common cause against any new competitor.

Among these, the most formidable was a burly, roaring, roystering blade, of the name of Abraham, or, according to the Dutch abbreviation, Brom Van Brunt, the hero of the country round, which rang with his feats of strength and hardihood. He was broad-shouldered and double-jointed, with short curly black hair, and a bluff but not unpleasant countenance, having a mingled air of fun and arrogance. From his Herculean frame

The Legend of Sleepy Hollow

and great powers of limb he had received the nickname of BROM BONES, by which he was universally known. He was famed for great knowledge and skill in horsemanship, being as dexterous on horseback as a Tartar. He was foremost at all races and cock fights; and, with the ascendancy which bodily strength always acquires in rustic life, was the umpire in all disputes, setting his hat on one side, and giving his decisions with an air and tone that admitted of no gainsay or appeal. He was always ready for either a fight or a frolic; but had more mischief than ill-will in his composition; and with all his overbearing roughness, there was a strong dash of waggish good humor at bottom. He had three or four boon companions, who regarded him as their model, and at the head of whom he scoured the country, attending every scene of feud or merriment for miles round. In cold weather he was distinguished by a fur cap, surmounted with a flaunting fox's tail; and when the folks at a country gathering descried this well-known crest at a distance, whisking about among a squad of hard riders, they always stood by for a squall. Sometimes his crew would be heard dashing along past the farmhouses at midnight, with whoop and halloo, like a troop of Don Cossacks; and the old dames, startled out of their sleep, would listen for a moment till the hurry-scurry had clattered by, and then exclaim, "Ay, there goes Brom Bones and his gang!" The neighbors looked upon him with a mixture of awe, admiration, and good-will; and, when any madcap prank or rustic brawl occurred in the vicinity, always shook their heads, and warranted Brom Bones was at the bottom of it.

This rantipole hero had for some time singled out the blooming Katrina for the object of his uncouth gallantries, and though his amorous toyings were something like the gentle caresses and endearments of a bear, yet it was whispered that she did not altogether discourage his hopes. Certain it is, his advances were signals for rival candidates to retire, who felt no inclination to cross a lion in his amours; insomuch, that when his horse was seen tied to Van Tassel's paling, on a Sunday night, a sure sign that his master was courting, or, as it is termed, "sparking," within, all other suitors passed by in despair, and carried the war into other quarters.

Such was the formidable rival with whom Ichabod Crane had to contend, and, considering all things, a stouter man than he would have shrunk from the competition, and a wiser man would have despaired. He had, however, a happy mixture of pliability and perseverance in his nature; he was in form and spirit like a supple-jack--yielding, but tough; though he bent, he never broke; and though he bowed beneath the slightest pressure, yet, the moment it was away--jerk!--he was as erect, and carried his head as high as ever.

To have taken the field openly against his rival would have been madness; for he was not a man to be thwarted in his amours, any more than that stormy lover, Achilles. Ichabod, therefore, made his advances in a quiet and gently insinuating manner. Under cover of his character of singing-master, he made frequent visits at the farmhouse; not that he had anything to apprehend from the meddlesome interference of parents, which is so often a stumbling-block in the path of lovers. Balt Van Tassel was an easy indulgent soul; he loved his daughter better even than his pipe, and, like a reasonable man and an excellent father, let her have her way in everything. His notable little wife, too, had enough to do to attend to her housekeeping and manage her poultry; for, as she sagely observed, ducks and geese are foolish things, and must be looked after, but girls can take care of themselves. Thus, while the busy dame bustled about the house, or plied her spinning-wheel at one end of the piazza, honest Balt would sit smoking his evening pipe at the other, watching the achievements of a little wooden warrior, who, armed with a sword in each hand, was most valiantly fighting the wind on the pinnacle of the barn. In the mean time, Ichabod would carry on his suit with the daughter by the side of the spring under the great elm, or sauntering along in the twilight, that hour so favorable to the lover's eloquence.

I profess not to know how women's hearts are wooed and won. To me they have always been matters of riddle and admiration. Some seem to have but one vulnerable point, or door of access; while others have a thousand avenues, and may be captured in a thousand different ways. It is a great triumph of skill to gain the former, but a still greater proof of generalship to maintain possession of the latter, for man must battle for his fortress at every door and window. He who wins a thousand common hearts is therefore entitled to some renown; but he who keeps undisputed sway over the heart of a coquette is indeed a hero. Certain it is, this was not the case with the redoubtable Brom Bones; and from the moment Ichabod Crane made his advances, the interests of the former evidently declined: his horse was no longer seen tied to the palings on Sunday nights, and a deadly feud gradually arose between him and the preceptor of Sleepy Hollow.

Brom, who had a degree of rough chivalry in his nature, would fain have carried matters to open warfare and have settled their pretensions to the lady, according to the mode of those most concise and simple reasoners, the knights-errant of

The Legend of Sleepy Hollow

yore,-- by single combat; but Ichabod was too conscious of the superior might of his adversary to enter the lists against him; he had overheard a boast of Bones, that he would "double the schoolmaster up, and lay him on a shelf of his own schoolhouse;" and he was too wary to give him an opportunity. There was something extremely provoking in this obstinately pacific system; it left Brom no alternative but to draw upon the funds of rustic waggery in his disposition, and to play off boorish practical jokes upon his rival. Ichabod became the object of whimsical persecution to Bones and his gang of rough riders. They harried his hitherto peaceful domains; smoked out his singing school by stopping up the chimney; broke into the schoolhouse at night, in spite of its formidable fastenings of withe and window stakes, and turned everything topsy-turvy, so that the poor schoolmaster began to think all the witches in the country held their meetings there. But what was still more annoying, Brom took all opportunities of turning him into ridicule in presence of his mistress, and had a scoundrel dog whom he taught to whine in the most ludicrous manner, and introduced as a rival of Ichabod's, to instruct her in psalmody.

In this way matters went on for some time, without producing any material effect on the relative situations of the contending powers. On a fine autumnal afternoon, Ichabod, in pensive mood, sat enthroned on the lofty stool from whence he usually watched all the concerns of his little literary realm. In his hand he swayed a ferule, that sceptre of despotic power; the birch of justice reposed on three nails behind the throne, a constant terror to evil doers, while on the desk before him might be seen sundry contraband articles and prohibited weapons, detected upon the persons of idle urchins, such as half-munched apples, popguns, whirligigs, fly-cages, and whole legions of rampant little paper gamecocks. Apparently there had been some appalling act of justice recently inflicted, for his scholars were all busily intent upon their books, or slyly whispering behind them with one eye kept upon the master; and a kind of buzzing stillness reigned throughout the schoolroom. It was suddenly interrupted by the appearance of a negro in tow-cloth jacket and trowsers, a round-crowned fragment of a hat, like the cap of Mercury, and mounted on the back of a ragged, wild, half-broken colt, which he managed with a rope by way of halter. He came clattering up to the school door with an invitation to Ichabod to attend a merry-making or "quilting frolic," to be held that evening at Mynheer Van Tassel's; and having delivered his message with that air of importance, and effort at fine language, which a negro is apt to display on petty embassies of the kind, he dashed over the brook, and was seen scampering away up the hollow, full of the importance and hurry of his mission.

All was now bustle and hubbub in the late quiet schoolroom. The scholars were hurried through their lessons without stopping at trifles; those who were nimble skipped over half with impunity, and those who were tardy had a smart application now and then in the rear, to quicken their speed or help them over a tall word. Books were flung aside without being put away on the shelves, inkstands were overturned, benches thrown down, and the whole school was turned loose an hour before the usual time, bursting forth like a legion of young imps, yelping and racketing about the green in joy at their early emancipation.

The gallant Ichabod now spent at least an extra half hour at his toilet, brushing and furbishing up his best, and indeed only suit of rusty black, and arranging his locks by a bit of broken looking-glass that hung up in the schoolhouse. That he might make his appearance before his mistress in the true style of a cavalier, he borrowed a horse from the farmer with whom he was domiciliated, a choleric old Dutchman of the name of Hans Van Ripper, and, thus gallantly mounted, issued forth like a knight- errant in quest of adventures. But it is meet I should, in the true spirit of romantic story, give some account of the looks and equipments of my hero and his steed. The animal he bestrode was a broken-down plow-horse, that had outlived almost everything but its viciousness. He was gaunt and shagged, with a ewe neck, and a head like a hammer; his rusty mane and tail were tangled and knotted with burs; one eye had lost its pupil, and was glaring and spectral, but the other had the gleam of a genuine devil in it. Still he must have had fire and mettle in his day, if we may judge from the name he bore of Gunpowder. He had, in fact, been a favorite steed of his master's, the choleric Van Ripper, who was a furious rider, and had infused, very probably, some of his own spirit into the animal; for, old and broken-down as he looked, there was more of the lurking devil in him than in any young filly in the country.

Ichabod was a suitable figure for such a steed. He rode with short stirrups, which brought his knees nearly up to the pommel of the saddle; his sharp elbows stuck out like grasshoppers'; he carried his whip perpendicularly in his hand, like a sceptre, and as his horse jogged on, the motion of his arms was not unlike the flapping of a pair of wings. A small wool hat rested on the top of his nose, for so his scanty strip of forehead might be called, and the skirts of his black coat fluttered out almost to the horses tail. Such was the appearance of Ichabod and his steed as they shambled out of the gate of Hans Van Ripper, and it was altogether such an apparition as is seldom to be met with in broad daylight.

It was, as I have said, a fine autumnal day; the sky was clear and serene, and nature wore that rich and golden livery which we always associate with the idea of abundance. The forests had put on their sober brown and yellow, while some trees of the tenderer kind had been nipped by the frosts into brilliant dyes of orange, purple, and scarlet. Streaming files of wild ducks began to make their appearance high in the air; the bark of the squirrel might be heard from the groves of beech and hickory-nuts, and the pensive whistle of the quail at intervals from the neighboring stubble field.

The small birds were taking their farewell banquets. In the fullness of their revelry, they fluttered, chirping and frolicking from bush to bush, and tree to tree, capricious from the very profusion and variety around them. There was the honest cock robin, the favorite game of stripling sportsmen, with its loud querulous note; and the twittering blackbirds flying in sable clouds; and the golden-winged woodpecker with his crimson crest, his broad black gorget, and splendid plumage; and the cedar bird, with its red-tipt wings and yellow-tipt tail and its little monteiro cap of feathers; and the blue jay, that noisy coxcomb, in his gay light blue coat and white underclothes, screaming and chattering, nodding and bobbing and bowing, and pretending to be on good terms with every songster of the grove.

As Ichabod jogged slowly on his way, his eye, ever open to every symptom of culinary abundance, ranged with delight over the treasures of jolly autumn. On all sides he beheld vast store of apples; some hanging in oppressive opulence on the trees; some gathered into baskets and barrels for the market; others heaped up in rich piles for the cider-press. Farther on he beheld great fields of Indian corn, with its golden ears peeping from their leafy coverts, and holding out the promise of cakes and hasty- pudding; and the yellow pumpkins lying beneath them, turning up their fair round bellies to the sun, and giving ample prospects of the most luxurious of pies; and anon he passed the fragrant buckwheat fields breathing the odor of the beehive, and as he beheld them, soft anticipations stole over his mind of dainty slapjacks, well buttered, and garnished with honey or treacle, by the delicate little dimpled hand of Katrina Van Tassel.

Thus feeding his mind with many sweet thoughts and "sugared suppositions," he journeyed along the sides of a range of hills which look out upon some of the goodliest scenes of the mighty Hudson. The sun gradually wheeled his broad disk down in the west. The wide bosom of the Tappan Zee lay motionless and glassy, excepting that here and there a gentle undulation waved and prolonged the blue shadow of the distant mountain. A few amber clouds floated in the sky, without a breath of air to move them. The horizon was of a fine golden tint, changing gradually into a pure apple green, and from that into the deep blue of the mid-heaven. A slanting ray lingered on the woody crests of the precipices that overhung some parts of the river, giving greater depth to the dark gray and purple of their rocky sides. A sloop was loitering in the distance, dropping slowly down with the tide, her sail hanging uselessly against the mast; and as the reflection of the sky gleamed along the still water, it seemed as if the vessel was suspended in the air.

It was toward evening that Ichabod arrived at the castle of the Heer Van Tassel, which he found thronged with the pride and flower of the adjacent country. Old farmers, a spare leathern-faced race, in homespun coats and breeches, blue stockings, huge shoes, and magnificent pewter buckles. Their brisk, withered little dames, in close-crimped caps, long-waisted short gowns, homespun petticoats, with scissors and pincushions, and gay calico pockets hanging on the outside. Buxom lasses, almost as antiquated as their mothers, excepting where a straw hat, a fine ribbon, or perhaps a white frock, gave symptoms of city innovation. The sons, in short square-skirted coats, with rows of stupendous brass buttons, and their hair generally queued in the fashion of the times, especially if they could procure an eel-skin for the purpose, it being esteemed throughout the country as a potent nourisher and strengthener of the hair.

Brom Bones, however, was the hero of the scene, having come to the gathering on his favorite steed Daredevil, a creature, like himself, full of mettle and mischief, and which no one but himself could manage. He was, in fact, noted for preferring vicious animals, given to all kinds of tricks which kept the rider in constant risk of his neck, for he held a tractable, well-broken horse as unworthy of a lad of spirit.

Fain would I pause to dwell upon the world of charms that burst upon the enraptured gaze of my hero, as he entered the state parlor of Van Tassel's mansion. Not those of the bevy of buxom lasses, with their luxurious display of red and white; but

The Legend of Sleepy Hollow

the ample charms of a genuine Dutch country tea-table, in the sumptuous time of autumn. Such heaped up platters of cakes of various and almost indescribable kinds, known only to experienced Dutch housewives! There was the doughty doughnut, the tender oly koek, and the crisp and crumbling cruller; sweet cakes and short cakes, ginger cakes and honey cakes, and the whole family of cakes. And then there were apple pies, and peach pies, and pumpkin pies; besides slices of ham and smoked beef; and moreover delectable dishes of preserved plums, and peaches, and pears, and quinces; not to mention broiled shad and roasted chickens; together with bowls of milk and cream, all mingled higgledy- piggledy, pretty much as I have enumerated them, with the motherly teapot sending up its clouds of vapor from the midst-- Heaven bless the mark! I want breath and time to discuss this banquet as it deserves, and am too eager to get on with my story. Happily, Ichabod Crane was not in so great a hurry as his historian, but did ample justice to every dainty.

He was a kind and thankful creature, whose heart dilated in proportion as his skin was filled with good cheer, and whose spirits rose with eating, as some men's do with drink. He could not help, too, rolling his large eyes round him as he ate, and chuckling with the possibility that he might one day be lord of all this scene of almost unimaginable luxury and splendor. Then, he thought, how soon he'd turn his back upon the old schoolhouse; snap his fingers in the face of Hans Van Ripper, and every other niggardly patron, and kick any itinerant pedagogue out of doors that should dare to call him comrade!

Old Baltus Van Tassel moved about among his guests with a face dilated with content and good humor, round and jolly as the harvest moon. His hospitable attentions were brief, but expressive, being confined to a shake of the hand, a slap on the shoulder, a loud laugh, and a pressing invitation to "fall to, and help themselves."

And now the sound of the music from the common room, or hall, summoned to the dance. The musician was an old gray-headed negro, who had been the itinerant orchestra of the neighborhood for more than half a century. His instrument was as old and battered as himself. The greater part of the time he scraped on two or three strings, accompanying every movement of the bow with a motion of the head; bowing almost to the ground, and stamping with his foot whenever a fresh couple were to start.

The Legend of Sleepy Hollow

Ichabod prided himself upon his dancing as much as upon his vocal powers. Not a limb, not a fibre about him was idle; and to have seen his loosely hung frame in full motion, and clattering about the room, you would have thought St. Vitus himself, that blessed patron of the dance, was figuring before you in person. He was the admiration of all the negroes; who, having gathered, of all ages and sizes, from the farm and the neighborhood, stood forming a pyramid of shining black faces at every door and window, gazing with delight at the scene, rolling their white eyeballs, and showing grinning rows of ivory from ear to ear. How could the flogger of urchins be otherwise than animated and joyous? The lady of his heart was his partner in the dance, and smiling graciously in reply to all his amorous oglings; while Brom Bones, sorely smitten with love and jealousy, sat brooding by himself in one corner.

When the dance was at an end, Ichabod was attracted to a knot of the sager folks, who, with Old Van Tassel, sat smoking at one end of the piazza, gossiping over former times, and drawing out long stories about the war.

This neighborhood, at the time of which I am speaking, was one of those highly favored places which abound with chronicle and great men. The British and American line had run near it during the war; it had, therefore, been the scene of marauding and infested with refugees, cowboys, and all kinds of border chivalry. Just sufficient time had elapsed to enable each storyteller to dress up his tale with a little becoming fiction, and, in the indistinctness of his recollection, to make himself the hero of every exploit.

There was the story of Doffue Martling, a large blue-bearded Dutchman, who had nearly taken a British frigate with an old iron nine-pounder from a mud breastwork, only that his gun burst at the sixth discharge. And there was an old gentleman who shall be nameless, being too rich a mynheer to be lightly mentioned, who, in the battle of White Plains, being an excellent master of defence, parried a musket-ball with a small sword, insomuch that he absolutely felt it whiz round the blade, and glance off at the hilt; in proof of which he was ready at any time to show the sword, with the hilt a little bent. There were several more that had been equally great in the field, not one of whom but was persuaded that he had a considerable hand in bringing the war to a happy termination.

But all these were nothing to the tales of ghosts and apparitions that succeeded. The neighborhood is rich in legendary treasures of the kind. Local tales and superstitions

The Legend of Sleepy Hollow

thrive best in these sheltered, long-settled retreats; but are trampled under foot by the shifting throng that forms the population of most of our country places. Besides, there is no encouragement for ghosts in most of our villages, for they have scarcely had time to finish their first nap and turn themselves in their graves, before their surviving friends have travelled away from the neighborhood; so that when they turn out at night to walk their rounds, they have no acquaintance left to call upon. This is perhaps the reason why we so seldom hear of ghosts except in our long-established Dutch communities.

The immediate cause, however, of the prevalence of supernatural stories in these parts, was doubtless owing to the vicinity of Sleepy Hollow. There was a contagion in the very air that blew from that haunted region; it breathed forth an atmosphere of dreams and fancies infecting all the land. Several of the Sleepy Hollow people were present at Van Tassel's, and, as usual, were doling out their wild and wonderful legends. Many dismal tales were told about funeral trains, and mourning cries and wailings heard and seen about the great tree where the unfortunate Major André was taken, and which stood in the neighborhood. Some mention was made also of the woman in white, that haunted the dark glen at Raven Rock, and was often heard to shriek on winter nights before a storm, having perished there in the snow. The chief part of the stories, however, turned upon the favorite spectre of Sleepy Hollow, the Headless Horseman, who had been heard several times of late, patrolling the country; and, it was said, tethered his horse nightly among the graves in the churchyard.

The sequestered situation of this church seems always to have made it a favorite haunt of troubled spirits. It stands on a knoll, surrounded by locust-trees and lofty elms, from among which its decent, whitewashed walls shine modestly forth, like Christian purity beaming through the shades of retirement. A gentle slope descends from it to a silver sheet of water, bordered by high trees, between which, peeps may be caught at the blue hills of the Hudson. To look upon its grass-grown yard, where the sunbeams seem to sleep so quietly, one would think that there at least the dead might rest in peace. On one side of the church extends a wide woody dell, along which raves a large brook among broken rocks and trunks of fallen trees. Over a deep black part of the stream, not far from the church, was formerly thrown a wooden bridge; the road that led to it, and the bridge itself, were thickly shaded by overhanging trees, which cast a gloom about it, even in the daytime; but occasioned a fearful darkness at night. Such was one of the favorite haunts of the Headless Horseman, and the place where he was most frequently encountered. The tale was told of old Brouwer, a most heretical disbeliever in ghosts, how he met the Horseman returning from his foray into Sleepy Hollow, and was obliged to get up behind him; how they galloped over bush and brake, over hill and swamp, until they reached the bridge; when the Horseman suddenly turned into a skeleton, threw old Brouwer into the brook, and sprang away over the tree-tops with a clap of thunder.

This story was immediately matched by a thrice marvellous adventure of Brom Bones, who made light of the Galloping Hessian as an arrant jockey. He affirmed that on returning one night from the neighboring village of Sing Sing, he had been overtaken by this midnight trooper; that he had offered to race with him for a bowl of punch, and should have won it too, for Daredevil beat the goblin horse all hollow, but just as they came to the church bridge, the Hessian bolted, and vanished in a flash of fire.

All these tales, told in that drowsy undertone with which men talk in the dark, the countenances of the listeners only now and then receiving a casual gleam from the glare of a pipe, sank deep in the mind of Ichabod. He repaid them in kind with large extracts from his invaluable author, Cotton Mather, and added many marvellous events that had taken place in his native State of Connecticut, and fearful sights which he had seen in his nightly walks about Sleepy Hollow.

The revel now gradually broke up. The old farmers gathered together their families in their wagons, and were heard for some time rattling along the hollow roads, and over the distant hills. Some of the damsels mounted on pillions behind their favorite swains, and their light-hearted laughter, mingling with the clatter of hoofs, echoed along the silent woodlands, sounding fainter and fainter, until they gradually died away,--and the late scene of noise and frolic was all silent and deserted. Ichabod only lingered behind, according to the custom of country lovers, to have a tête-à-tête with the heiress; fully convinced that he was now on the high road to success. What passed at this interview I will not pretend to say, for in fact I do not know. Something, however, I fear me, must have gone wrong, for he certainly sallied forth, after no very great interval, with an air quite desolate and chapfallen. Oh, these women! these women! Could that girl have been playing off any of her coquettish tricks? Was her encouragement of the poor pedagogue all a mere sham to secure her conquest of his rival? Heaven only knows, not I! Let it suffice to say, Ichabod stole forth with the air of one who had been sacking a henroost, rather than a fair lady's

The Legend of Sleepy Hollow

heart. Without looking to the right or left to notice the scene of rural wealth, on which he had so often gloated, he went straight to the stable, and with several hearty cuffs and kicks roused his steed most uncourteously from the comfortable quarters in which he was soundly sleeping, dreaming of mountains of corn and oats, and whole valleys of timothy and clover.

It was the very witching time of night that Ichabod, heavy-hearted and crestfallen, pursued his travels homewards, along the sides of the lofty hills which rise above Tarry Town, and which he had traversed so cheerily in the afternoon. The hour was as dismal as himself. Far below him the Tappan Zee spread its dusky and indistinct waste of waters, with here and there the tall mast of a sloop, riding quietly at anchor under the land. In the dead hush of midnight, he could even hear the barking of the watchdog from the opposite shore of the Hudson; but it was so vague and faint as only to give an idea of his distance from this faithful companion of man. Now and then, too, the long-drawn crowing of a cock, accidentally awakened, would sound far, far off, from some farmhouse away among the hills--but it was like a dreaming sound in his ear. No signs of life occurred near him, but occasionally the melancholy chirp of a cricket, or perhaps the guttural twang of a bullfrog from a neighboring marsh, as if sleeping uncomfortably and turning suddenly in his bed.

All the stories of ghosts and goblins that he had heard in the afternoon now came crowding upon his recollection. The night grew darker and darker; the stars seemed to sink deeper in the sky, and driving clouds occasionally hid them from his sight. He had never felt so lonely and dismal. He was, moreover, approaching the very place where many of the scenes of the ghost stories had been laid. In the centre of the road stood an enormous tulip-tree, which towered like a giant above all the other trees of the neighborhood, and formed a kind of landmark. Its limbs were gnarled and fantastic, large enough to form trunks for ordinary trees, twisting down almost to the earth, and rising again into the air. It was connected with the tragical story of the unfortunate André, who had been taken prisoner hard by; and was universally known by the name of Major André's tree. The common people regarded it with a mixture of respect and superstition, partly out of sympathy for the fate of its ill- starred namesake, and partly from the tales of strange sights, and doleful lamentations, told concerning it.

As Ichabod approached this fearful tree, he began to whistle; he thought his whistle was answered; it was but a blast sweeping sharply through the dry branches. As he approached

The Legend of Sleepy Hollow

a little nearer, he thought he saw something white, hanging in the midst of the tree: he paused and ceased whistling but, on looking more narrowly, perceived that it was a place where the tree had been scathed by lightning, and the white wood laid bare. Suddenly he heard a groan--his teeth chattered, and his knees smote against the saddle: it was but the rubbing of one huge bough upon another, as they were swayed about by the breeze. He passed the tree in safety, but new perils lay before him.

About two hundred yards from the tree, a small brook crossed the road, and ran into a marshy and thickly-wooded glen, known by the name of Wiley's Swamp. A few rough logs, laid side by side, served for a bridge over this stream. On that side of the road where the brook entered the wood, a group of oaks and chestnuts, matted thick with wild grape-vines, threw a cavernous gloom over it. To pass this bridge was the severest trial. It was at this identical spot that the unfortunate André was captured, and under the covert of those chestnuts and vines were the sturdy yeomen concealed who surprised him. This has ever since been considered a haunted stream, and fearful are the feelings of the schoolboy who has to pass it alone after dark.

As he approached the stream, his heart began to thump; he summoned up, however, all his resolution, gave his horse half a score of kicks in the ribs, and attempted to dash briskly across the bridge; but instead of starting forward, the perverse old animal made a lateral movement, and ran broadside against the fence. Ichabod, whose fears increased with the delay, jerked the reins on the other side, and kicked lustily with the contrary foot: it was all in vain; his steed started, it is true, but it was only to plunge to the opposite side of the road into a thicket of brambles and alder bushes. The schoolmaster now bestowed both whip and heel upon the starveling ribs of old Gunpowder, who dashed forward, snuffling and snorting, but came to a stand just by the bridge, with a suddenness that had nearly sent his rider sprawling over his head. Just at this moment a plashy tramp by the side of the bridge caught the sensitive ear of Ichabod. In the dark shadow of the grove, on the margin of the brook, he beheld something huge, misshapen and towering. It stirred not, but seemed gathered up in the gloom, like some gigantic monster ready to spring upon the traveller.

The hair of the affrighted pedagogue rose upon his head with terror. What was to be done? To turn and fly was now too late; and besides, what chance was there of escaping ghost or goblin, if such it was, which could ride upon the wings of the wind? Summoning up, therefore, a show of courage, he

The Legend of Sleepy Hollow

demanded in stammering accents, "Who are you?" He received no reply. He repeated his demand in a still more agitated voice. Still there was no answer. Once more he cudgelled the sides of the inflexible Gunpowder, and, shutting his eyes, broke forth with involuntary fervor into a psalm tune. Just then the shadowy object of alarm put itself in motion, and with a scramble and a bound stood at once in the middle of the road. Though the night was dark and dismal, yet the form of the unknown might now in some degree be ascertained. He appeared to be a horseman of large dimensions, and mounted on a black horse of powerful frame. He made no offer of molestation or sociability, but kept aloof on one side of the road, jogging along on the blind side of old Gunpowder, who had now got over his fright and waywardness.

Ichabod, who had no relish for this strange midnight companion, and bethought himself of the adventure of Brom Bones with the Galloping Hessian, now quickened his steed in hopes of leaving him behind. The stranger, however, quickened his horse to an equal pace. Ichabod pulled up, and fell into a walk, thinking to lag behind,--the other did the same. His heart began to sink within him; he endeavored to resume his psalm tune, but his parched tongue clove to the roof of his mouth, and he could not utter a stave. There was something in the moody and dogged silence of this pertinacious companion that was mysterious and appalling. It was soon fearfully accounted for. On mounting a rising ground, which brought the figure of his fellow-traveller in relief against the sky, gigantic in height, and muffled in a cloak, Ichabod was horror-struck on perceiving that he was headless!--but his horror was still more increased on observing that the head, which should have rested on his shoulders, was carried before him on the pommel of his saddle! His terror rose to desperation; he rained a shower of kicks and blows upon Gunpowder, hoping by a sudden movement to give his companion the slip; but the spectre started full jump with him. Away, then, they dashed through thick and thin; stones flying and sparks flashing at every bound. Ichabod's flimsy garments fluttered in the air, as he stretched his long lank body away over his horse's head, in the eagerness of his flight.

They had now reached the road which turns off to Sleepy Hollow; but Gunpowder, who seemed possessed with a demon, instead of keeping up it, made an opposite turn, and plunged headlong downhill to the left. This road leads through a sandy hollow shaded by trees for about a quarter of a mile, where it crosses the bridge famous in goblin story; and just beyond swells the green knoll on which stands the whitewashed church.

The Legend of Sleepy Hollow

As yet the panic of the steed had given his unskilful rider an apparent advantage in the chase, but just as he had got half way through the hollow, the girths of the saddle gave way, and he felt it slipping from under him. He seized it by the pommel, and endeavored to hold it firm, but in vain; and had just time to save himself by clasping old Gunpowder round the neck, when the saddle fell to the earth, and he heard it trampled under foot by his pursuer. For a moment the terror of Hans Van Ripper's wrath passed across his mind,--for it was his Sunday saddle; but this was no time for petty fears; the goblin was hard on his haunches; and (unskilful rider that he was!) he had much ado to maintain his seat; sometimes slipping on one side, sometimes on another, and sometimes jolted on the high ridge of his horse's backbone, with a violence that he verily feared would cleave him asunder.

An opening in the trees now cheered him with the hopes that the church bridge was at hand. The wavering reflection of a silver star in the bosom of the brook told him that he was not mistaken. He saw the walls of the church dimly glaring under the trees beyond. He recollected the place where Brom Bones's ghostly competitor had disappeared. "If I can but reach that bridge," thought Ichabod, "I am safe." Just then he heard the black steed panting and blowing close behind him; he even fancied that he felt his hot breath. Another convulsive kick in the ribs, and old Gunpowder sprang upon the bridge; he thundered over the resounding planks; he gained the opposite side; and now Ichabod cast a look behind to see if his pursuer should vanish, according to rule, in a flash of fire and brimstone. Just then he saw the goblin rising in his stirrups, and in the very act of hurling his head at him. Ichabod endeavored to dodge the horrible missile, but too late. It encountered his cranium with a tremendous crash,--he was tumbled headlong into the dust, and Gunpowder, the black steed, and the goblin rider, passed by like a whirlwind.

The next morning the old horse was found without his saddle, and with the bridle under his feet, soberly cropping the grass at his master's gate. Ichabod did not make his appearance at breakfast; dinner-hour came, but no Ichabod. The boys assembled at the schoolhouse, and strolled idly about the banks of the brook; but no schoolmaster. Hans Van Ripper now began to feel some uneasiness about the fate of poor Ichabod, and his saddle. An inquiry was set on foot, and after diligent investigation they came upon his traces. In one part of the road leading to the church was found the saddle trampled in the dirt; the tracks of horses' hoofs deeply dented in the road, and evidently at furious speed, were traced to the bridge, beyond

The Legend of Sleepy Hollow

which, on the bank of a broad part of the brook, where the water ran deep and black, was found the hat of the unfortunate Ichabod, and close beside it a shattered pumpkin.

The brook was searched, but the body of the schoolmaster was not to be discovered. Hans Van Ripper as executor of his estate, examined the bundle which contained all his worldly effects. They consisted of two shirts and a half; two stocks for the neck; a pair or two of worsted stockings; an old pair of corduroy small-clothes; a rusty razor; a book of psalm tunes full of dog's-ears; and a broken pitch-pipe. As to the books and furniture of the schoolhouse, they belonged to the community, excepting Cotton Mather's "History of Witchcraft," a "New England Almanac," and a book of dreams and fortune-telling; in which last was a sheet of foolscap much scribbled and blotted in several fruitless attempts to make a copy of verses in honor of the heiress of Van Tassel. These magic books and the poetic scrawl were forthwith consigned to the flames by Hans Van Ripper; who, from that time forward, determined to send his children no more to school, observing that he never knew any good come of this same reading and writing. Whatever money the schoolmaster possessed, and he had received his quarter's pay but a day or two before, he must have had about his person at the time of his disappearance.

The mysterious event caused much speculation at the church on the following Sunday. Knots of gazers and gossips were collected in the churchyard, at the bridge, and at the spot where the hat and pumpkin had been found. The stories of Brouwer, of Bones, and a whole budget of others were called to mind; and when they had diligently considered them all, and compared them with the symptoms of the present case, they shook their heads, and came to the conclusion that Ichabod had been carried off by the Galloping Hessian. As he was a bachelor, and in nobody's debt, nobody troubled his head any more about him; the school was removed to a different quarter of the hollow, and another pedagogue reigned in his stead.

It is true, an old farmer, who had been down to New York on a visit several years after, and from whom this account of the ghostly adventure was received, brought home the intelligence that Ichabod Crane was still alive; that he had left the neighborhood partly through fear of the goblin and Hans Van Ripper, and partly in mortification at having been suddenly dismissed by the heiress; that he had changed his quarters to a distant part of the country; had kept school and studied law at the same time; had been admitted to the bar; turned politician; electioneered; written for the newspapers; and finally had been made a justice of the Ten Pound Court. Brom Bones, too, who, shortly after his rival's disappearance conducted the blooming Katrina in triumph to the altar, was observed to look exceedingly knowing whenever the story of Ichabod was related, and always burst into a hearty laugh at the mention of the pumpkin; which led some to suspect that he knew more about the matter than he chose to tell.

    The old country wives, however, who are the best judges of these matters, maintain to this day that Ichabod was spirited away by supernatural means; and it is a favorite story often told about the neighborhood round the winter evening fire. The bridge became more than ever an object of superstitious awe; and that may be the reason why the road has been altered of late years, so as to approach the church by the border of the millpond. The schoolhouse being deserted soon fell to decay, and was reported to be haunted by the ghost of the unfortunate pedagogue and the plowboy, loitering homeward of a still summer evening, has often fancied his voice at a distance, chanting a melancholy psalm tune among the tranquil solitudes of Sleepy Hollow.

POSTSCRIPT.

FOUND IN THE HANDWRITING OF MR. KNICKERBOCKER.

    The preceding tale is given almost in the precise words in which I heard it related at a Corporation meeting at the ancient city of Manhattoes, at which were present many of its sagest and most illustrious burghers. The narrator was a pleasant, shabby, gentlemanly old fellow, in pepper-and-salt clothes, with a sadly humourous face, and one whom I strongly suspected of being poor--he made such efforts to be entertaining. When his story was concluded, there was much laughter and approbation, particularly from two or three deputy aldermen, who had been asleep the greater part of the time. There was, however, one tall, dry-looking old gentleman, with beetling eyebrows, who maintained a grave and rather severe face throughout, now and then folding his arms, inclining his head, and looking down upon the floor, as if turning a doubt over in his mind. He was one of your wary men, who never laugh but upon good grounds--when they have reason and law on their side. When the mirth of the rest of the company had subsided, and silence was restored, he leaned one arm on the elbow of his chair, and sticking the other akimbo, demanded, with a slight, but exceedingly sage motion of the head, and contraction of the

The Legend of Sleepy Hollow

brow, what was the moral of the story, and what it went to prove?

The story-teller, who was just putting a glass of wine to his lips, as a refreshment after his toils, paused for a moment, looked at his inquirer with an air of infinite deference, and, lowering the glass slowly to the table, observed that the story was intended most logically to prove--

"That there is no situation in life but has its advantages and pleasures--provided we will but take a joke as we find it:

"That, therefore, he that runs races with goblin troopers is likely to have rough riding of it.

"Ergo, for a country schoolmaster to be refused the hand of a Dutch heiress is a certain step to high preferment in the state."

The cautious old gentleman knit his brows tenfold closer after this explanation, being sorely puzzled by the ratiocination of the syllogism, while, methought, the one in pepper-and-salt eyed him with something of a triumphant leer. At length he observed that all this was very well, but still he thought the story a little on the extravagant--there were one or two points on which he had his doubts.

"Faith, sir," replied the story-teller, "as to that matter, I don't believe one-half of it myself." D. K.

Berenice

By Edgar Allan Poe

> Dicebant mihi sodales, si sepulchrum amicae visitarem,
>
> curas meas aliquantulum fore levatas.
>
> --Ebn Zaiat.

MISERY is manifold. The wretchedness of earth is multiform. Overreaching the wide horizon as the rainbow, its hues are as various as the hues of that arch, --as distinct too, yet as intimately blended. Overreaching the wide horizon as the rainbow! How is it that from beauty I have derived a type of unloveliness? --from the covenant of peace a simile of sorrow? But as, in ethics, evil is a consequence of good, so, in fact, out of joy is sorrow born. Either the memory of past bliss is the anguish of to-day, or the agonies which are have their origin in the ecstasies which might have been.

My baptismal name is Egaeus; that of my family I will not mention. Yet there are no towers in the land more time-honored than my gloomy, gray, hereditary halls. Our line has been called a race of visionaries; and in many striking particulars --in the character of the family mansion --in the frescos of the chief saloon --in the tapestries of the dormitories --in the chiselling of some buttresses in the armory --but more especially in the gallery of antique paintings --in the fashion of the library chamber --and, lastly, in the very peculiar nature of the library's contents, there is more than sufficient evidence to warrant the belief.

The recollections of my earliest years are connected with that chamber, and with its volumes --of which latter I will say no more. Here died my mother. Herein was I born. But it is mere idleness to say that I had not lived before --that the soul has no previous existence. You deny it? --let us not argue the matter. Convinced myself, I seek not to convince. There is, however, a remembrance of aerial forms --of spiritual and meaning eyes --of sounds, musical yet sad --a remembrance which will not be

Berenice

excluded; a memory like a shadow, vague, variable, indefinite, unsteady; and like a shadow, too, in the impossibility of my getting rid of it while the sunlight of my reason shall exist.

In that chamber was I born. Thus awaking from the long night of what seemed, but was not, nonentity, at once into the very regions of fairy-land --into a palace of imagination --into the wild dominions of monastic thought and erudition --it is not singular that I gazed around me with a startled and ardent eye --that I loitered away my boyhood in books, and dissipated my youth in reverie; but it is singular that as years rolled away, and the noon of manhood found me still in the mansion of my fathers --it is wonderful what stagnation there fell upon the springs of my life --wonderful how total an inversion took place in the character of my commonest thought. The realities of the world affected me as visions, and as visions only, while the wild ideas of the land of dreams became, in turn, --not the material of my every-day existence-but in very deed that existence utterly and solely in itself.

Berenice and I were cousins, and we grew up together in my paternal halls. Yet differently we grew --I ill of health, and buried in gloom --she agile, graceful, and overflowing with energy; hers the ramble on the hill-side --mine the studies of the cloister --I living within my own heart, and addicted body and soul to the most intense and painful meditation --she roaming carelessly through life with no thought of the shadows in her path, or the silent flight of the raven-winged hours. Berenice! --I call upon her name --Berenice! --and from the gray ruins of memory a thousand tumultuous recollections are startled at the sound! Ah! vividly is her image before me now, as in the early days of her light-heartedness and joy! Oh! gorgeous yet fantastic beauty! Oh! sylph amid the shrubberies of Arnheim! --Oh! Naiad among its fountains! --and then --then all is mystery and terror, and a tale which should not be told. Disease --a fatal disease --fell like the simoom upon her frame, and, even while I gazed upon her, the spirit of change swept, over her, pervading her mind, her habits, and her character, and, in a manner the most subtle and terrible, disturbing even the identity of her person! Alas! the destroyer came and went, and the victim --where was she, I knew her not --or knew her no longer as Berenice.

Among the numerous train of maladies superinduced by that fatal and primary one which effected a revolution of so horrible a kind in the moral and physical being of my cousin, may be mentioned as the most distressing and obstinate in its nature, a species of epilepsy not unfrequently terminating in trance itself --trance very nearly resembling positive dissolution, and from which her manner of recovery was in most instances, startlingly abrupt. In the mean time my own disease --for I have been told that I should call it by no other appelation --my own disease, then, grew rapidly upon me, and assumed finally a monomaniac character of a novel and extraordinary form -- hourly and momently gaining vigor --and at length obtaining over me the most incomprehensible ascendancy. This monomania, if I must so term it, consisted in a morbid irritability of those properties of the mind in metaphysical science termed the attentive. It is more than probable that I am not understood; but I fear, indeed, that it is in no manner possible to convey to the mind of the merely general reader, an adequate idea of that nervous intensity of interest with which, in my case, the powers of meditation (not to speak technically) busied and buried themselves, in the contemplation of even the most ordinary objects of the universe.

To muse for long unwearied hours with my attention riveted to some frivolous device on the margin, or in the topography of a book; to become absorbed for the better part of a summer's day, in a quaint shadow falling aslant upon the tapestry, or upon the door; to lose myself for an entire night in watching the steady flame of a lamp, or the embers of a fire; to dream away whole days over the perfume of a flower; to repeat monotonously some common word, until the sound, by dint of frequent repetition, ceased to convey any idea whatever to the mind; to lose all sense of motion or physical existence, by means of absolute bodily quiescence long and obstinately persevered in; --such were a few of the most common and least pernicious vagaries induced by a condition of the mental faculties, not, indeed, altogether unparalleled, but certainly bidding defiance to anything like analysis or explanation.

Yet let me not be misapprehended. --The undue, earnest, and morbid attention thus excited by objects in their own nature frivolous, must not be confounded in character with that ruminating propensity common to all mankind, and more especially indulged in by persons of ardent imagination. It was not even, as might be at first supposed, an extreme condition or exaggeration of such propensity, but primarily and essentially distinct and different. In the one instance, the dreamer, or enthusiast, being interested by an object usually not frivolous, imperceptibly loses sight of this object in a wilderness of deductions and suggestions issuing therefrom, until, at the conclusion of a day dream often replete with luxury, he finds the incitamentum or first cause of his musings entirely vanished and forgotten. In my case the primary object was invariably

Berenice

frivolous, although assuming, through the medium of my distempered vision, a refracted and unreal importance. Few deductions, if any, were made; and those few pertinaciously returning in upon the original object as a centre. The meditations were never pleasurable; and, at the termination of the reverie, the first cause, so far from being out of sight, had attained that supernaturally exaggerated interest which was the prevailing feature of the disease. In a word, the powers of mind more particularly exercised were, with me, as I have said before, the attentive, and are, with the day-dreamer, the speculative.

My books, at this epoch, if they did not actually serve to irritate the disorder, partook, it will be perceived, largely, in their imaginative and inconsequential nature, of the characteristic qualities of the disorder itself. I well remember, among others, the treatise of the noble Italian Coelius Secundus Curio "de Amplitudine Beati Regni dei"; St. Austin's great work, the "City of God"; and Tertullian "de Carne Christi," in which the paradoxical sentence "Mortuus est Dei filius; credible est quia ineptum est: et sepultus resurrexit; certum est quia impossibile est" occupied my undivided time, for many weeks of laborious and fruitless investigation.

Thus it will appear that, shaken from its balance only by trivial things, my reason bore resemblance to that ocean-crag spoken of by Ptolemy Hephestion, which steadily resisting the attacks of human violence, and the fiercer fury of the waters and the winds, trembled only to the touch of the flower called Asphodel. And although, to a careless thinker, it might appear a matter beyond doubt, that the alteration produced by her unhappy malady, in the moral condition of Berenice, would afford me many objects for the exercise of that intense and abnormal meditation whose nature I have been at some trouble in explaining, yet such was not in any degree the case. In the lucid intervals of my infirmity, her calamity, indeed, gave me pain, and, taking deeply to heart that total wreck of her fair and gentle life, I did not fall to ponder frequently and bitterly upon the wonder-working means by which so strange a revolution had been so suddenly brought to pass. But these reflections partook not of the idiosyncrasy of my disease, and were such as would have occurred, under similar circumstances, to the ordinary mass of mankind. True to its own character, my disorder revelled in the less important but more startling changes wrought in the physical frame of Berenice --in the singular and most appalling distortion of her personal identity.

Berenice

During the brightest days of her unparalleled beauty, most surely I had never loved her. In the strange anomaly of my existence, feelings with me, had never been of the heart, and my passions always were of the mind. Through the gray of the early morning --among the trellised shadows of the forest at noonday --and in the silence of my library at night, she had flitted by my eyes, and I had seen her --not as the living and breathing Berenice, but as the Berenice of a dream --not as a being of the earth, earthy, but as the abstraction of such a being-not as a thing to admire, but to analyze --not as an object of love, but as the theme of the most abstruse although desultory speculation. And now --now I shuddered in her presence, and grew pale at her approach; yet bitterly lamenting her fallen and desolate condition, I called to mind that she had loved me long, and, in an evil moment, I spoke to her of marriage.

And at length the period of our nuptials was approaching, when, upon an afternoon in the winter of the year, --one of those unseasonably warm, calm, and misty days which are the nurse of the beautiful Halcyon*, --I sat, (and sat, as I thought, alone,) in the inner apartment of the library. But uplifting my eyes I saw that Berenice stood before me.

*For as Jove, during the winter season, gives twice seven days of warmth, men have called this clement and temperate time the nurse of the beautiful Halcyon --Simonides.

Was it my own excited imagination --or the misty influence of the atmosphere --or the uncertain twilight of the chamber --or the gray draperies which fell around her figure --that caused in it so vacillating and indistinct an outline? I could not tell. She spoke no word, I --not for worlds could I have uttered a syllable. An icy chill ran through my frame; a sense of insufferable anxiety oppressed me; a consuming curiosity pervaded my soul; and sinking back upon the chair, I remained for some time breathless and motionless, with my eyes riveted upon her person. Alas! its emaciation was excessive, and not one vestige of the former being, lurked in any single line of the contour. My burning glances at length fell upon the face.

The forehead was high, and very pale, and singularly placid; and the once jetty hair fell partially over it, and overshadowed the hollow temples with innumerable ringlets now of a vivid yellow, and Jarring discordantly, in their fantastic character, with the reigning melancholy of the countenance. The eyes were lifeless, and lustreless, and seemingly pupil-less, and I shrank involuntarily from their glassy stare to the contemplation of the thin and shrunken lips. They parted; and in a smile of peculiar

Berenice

meaning, the teeth of the changed Berenice disclosed themselves slowly to my view. Would to God that I had never beheld them, or that, having done so, I had died!

The shutting of a door disturbed me, and, looking up, I found that my cousin had departed from the chamber. But from the disordered chamber of my brain, had not, alas! departed, and would not be driven away, the white and ghastly spectrum of the teeth. Not a speck on their surface --not a shade on their enamel --not an indenture in their edges --but what that period of her smile had sufficed to brand in upon my memory. I saw them now even more unequivocally than I beheld them then. The teeth! --the teeth! --they were here, and there, and everywhere, and visibly and palpably before me; long, narrow, and excessively white, with the pale lips writhing about them, as in the very moment of their first terrible development. Then came the full fury of my monomania, and I struggled in vain against its strange and irresistible influence. In the multiplied objects of the external world I had no thoughts but for the teeth. For these I longed with a phrenzied desire. All other matters and all different interests became absorbed in their single contemplation. They --they alone were present to the mental eye, and they, in their sole individuality, became the essence of my mental life. I held them in every light. I turned them in every attitude. I surveyed their characteristics. I dwelt upon their peculiarities. I pondered upon their conformation. I mused upon the alteration in their nature. I shuddered as I assigned to them in imagination a sensitive and sentient power, and even when unassisted by the lips, a capability of moral expression. Of Mad'selle Salle it has been well said, "que tous ses pas etaient des sentiments," and of Berenice I more seriously believed que toutes ses dents etaient des idees. Des idees! --ah here was the idiotic thought that destroyed me! Des idees! --ah therefore it was that I coveted them so madly! I felt that their possession could alone ever restore me to peace, in giving me back to reason.

And the evening closed in upon me thus-and then the darkness came, and tarried, and went --and the day again dawned --and the mists of a second night were now gathering around --and still I sat motionless in that solitary room; and still I sat buried in meditation, and still the phantasma of the teeth maintained its terrible ascendancy as, with the most vivid hideous distinctness, it floated about amid the changing lights and shadows of the chamber. At length there broke in upon my dreams a cry as of horror and dismay; and thereunto, after a pause, succeeded the sound of troubled voices, intermingled with many low moanings of sorrow, or of pain. I arose from my

Berenice

seat and, throwing open one of the doors of the library, saw standing out in the antechamber a servant maiden, all in tears, who told me that Berenice was --no more. She had been seized with epilepsy in the early morning, and now, at the closing in of the night, the grave was ready for its tenant, and all the preparations for the burial were completed.

I found myself sitting in the library, and again sitting there alone. It seemed that I had newly awakened from a confused and exciting dream. I knew that it was now midnight, and I was well aware that since the setting of the sun Berenice had been interred. But of that dreary period which intervened I had no positive --at least no definite comprehension. Yet its memory was replete with horror --horror more horrible from being vague, and terror more terrible from ambiguity. It was a fearful page in the record my existence, written all over with dim, and hideous, and unintelligible recollections. I strived to decypher them, but in vain; while ever and anon, like the spirit of a departed sound, the shrill and piercing shriek of a female voice seemed to be ringing in my ears. I had done a deed --what was it? I asked myself the question aloud, and the whispering echoes of the chamber answered me, "what was it?"

On the table beside me burned a lamp, and near it lay a little box. It was of no remarkable character, and I had seen it frequently before, for it was the property of the family physician; but how came it there, upon my table, and why did I shudder in regarding it? These things were in no manner to be accounted for, and my eyes at length dropped to the open pages of a book, and to a sentence underscored therein. The words were the singular but simple ones of the poet Ebn Zaiat, "Dicebant mihi sodales si sepulchrum amicae visitarem, curas meas aliquantulum fore levatas." Why then, as I perused them, did the hairs of my head erect themselves on end, and the blood of my body become congealed within my veins?

There came a light tap at the library door, and pale as the tenant of a tomb, a menial entered upon tiptoe. His looks were wild with terror, and he spoke to me in a voice tremulous, husky, and very low. What said he? --some broken sentences I heard. He told of a wild cry disturbing the silence of the night -- of the gathering together of the household-of a search in the direction of the sound; --and then his tones grew thrillingly distinct as he whispered me of a violated grave --of a disfigured body enshrouded, yet still breathing, still palpitating, still alive!

He pointed to garments;-they were muddy and clotted with gore. I spoke not, and he took me gently by the hand; --it was

Ligeia

indented with the impress of human nails. He directed my attention to some object against the wall; --I looked at it for some minutes; --it was a spade. With a shriek I bounded to the table, and grasped the box that lay upon it. But I could not force it open; and in my tremor it slipped from my hands, and fell heavily, and burst into pieces; and from it, with a rattling sound, there rolled out some instruments of dental surgery, intermingled with thirty-two small, white and ivory-looking substances that were scattered to and fro about the floor.

Ligeia

By Edgar Allan Poe

And the will therein lieth, which dieth not. Who knoweth the mysteries of the will, with its vigor? For God is but a great will pervading all things by nature of its intentness. Man doth not yield himself to the angels, nor unto death utterly, save only through the weakness of his feeble will.

- Joseph Glanvill

I CANNOT, for my soul, remember how, when, or even precisely where, I first became acquainted with the lady Ligeia. Long years have since elapsed, and my memory is feeble through much suffering. Or, perhaps, I cannot now bring these points to mind, because, in truth, the character of my beloved, her rare learning, her singular yet placid cast of beauty, and the thrilling and enthralling eloquence of her low musical language, made their way into my heart by paces so steadily and stealthily progressive that they have been unnoticed and unknown. Yet I believe that I met her first and most frequently in some large, old, decaying city near the Rhine. Of her family --I have surely heard her speak. That it is of a remotely ancient date cannot be doubted. Ligeia! Ligeia! in studies of a nature more than all else adapted to deaden impressions of the outward world, it is by that sweet word alone --by Ligeia --that I bring before mine eyes in fancy the image of her who is no more. And now, while I write, a recollection flashes upon me that I have never known the paternal name of her who was my friend and my betrothed, and who became the partner of my studies, and finally the wife of my bosom. Was it a playful charge on the part of my Ligeia? or was it a test of my strength of affection, that I should institute no inquiries upon this point? or was it rather a caprice of my own --a wildly romantic offering on the shrine of the most passionate devotion? I but indistinctly recall the fact itself -- what wonder that I have utterly forgotten the circumstances which originated or attended it? And, indeed, if ever she, the wan and the misty-winged Ashtophet of idolatrous Egypt, presided, as they tell, over marriages ill-omened, then most surely she presided over mine.

Ligeia

There is one dear topic, however, on which my memory fails me not. It is the person of Ligeia. In stature she was tall, somewhat slender, and, in her latter days, even emaciated. I would in vain attempt to portray the majesty, the quiet ease, of her demeanor, or the incomprehensible lightness and elasticity of her footfall. She came and departed as a shadow. I was never made aware of her entrance into my closed study save by the dear music of her low sweet voice, as she placed her marble hand upon my shoulder. In beauty of face no maiden ever equalled her. It was the radiance of an opium-dream --an airy and spirit-lifting vision more wildly divine than the phantasies which hovered vision about the slumbering souls of the daughters of Delos. Yet her features were not of that regular mould which we have been falsely taught to worship in the classical labors of the heathen. "There is no exquisite beauty," says Bacon, Lord Verulam, speaking truly of all the forms and genera of beauty, without some strangeness in the proportion." Yet, although I saw that the features of Ligeia were not of a classic regularity --although I perceived that her loveliness was indeed "exquisite," and felt that there was much of "strangeness" pervading it, yet I have tried in vain to detect the irregularity and to trace home my own perception of "the strange." I examined the contour of the lofty and pale forehead --it was faultless --how cold indeed that word when applied to a majesty so divine! --the skin rivalling the purest ivory, the commanding extent and repose, the gentle prominence of the regions above the temples; and then the raven-black, the glossy, the luxuriant and naturally-curling tresses, setting forth the full force of the Homeric epithet, "hyacinthine!" I looked at the delicate outlines of the nose --and nowhere but in the graceful medallions of the Hebrews had I beheld a similar perfection. There were the same luxurious smoothness of surface, the same scarcely perceptible tendency to the aquiline, the same harmoniously curved nostrils speaking the free spirit. I regarded the sweet mouth. Here was indeed the triumph of all things heavenly --the magnificent turn of the short upper lip --the soft, voluptuous slumber of the under --the dimples which sported, and the color which spoke -- the teeth glancing back, with a brilliancy almost startling, every ray of the holy light which fell upon them in her serene and placid, yet most exultingly radiant of all smiles. I scrutinized the formation of the chin --and here, too, I found the gentleness of breadth, the softness and the majesty, the fullness and the spirituality, of the Greek --the contour which the god Apollo revealed but in a dream, to Cleomenes, the son of the Athenian. And then I peered into the large eyes of Ligeia.

For eyes we have no models in the remotely antique. It might have been, too, that in these eves of my beloved lay the secret to which Lord Verulam alludes. They were, I must believe, far larger than the ordinary eyes of our own race. They were even fuller than the fullest of the gazelle eyes of the tribe of the valley of Nourjahad. Yet it was only at intervals --in moments of intense excitement --that this peculiarity became more than slightly noticeable in Ligeia. And at such moments was her beauty --in my heated fancy thus it appeared perhaps -- the beauty of beings either above or apart from the earth --the beauty of the fabulous Houri of the Turk. The hue of the orbs was the most brilliant of black, and, far over them, hung jetty lashes of great length. The brows, slightly irregular in outline, had the same tint. The "strangeness," however, which I found in the eyes, was of a nature distinct from the formation, or the color, or the brilliancy of the features, and must, after all, be referred to the expression. Ah, word of no meaning! behind whose vast latitude of mere sound we intrench our ignorance of so much of the spiritual. The expression of the eyes of Ligeia! How for long hours have I pondered upon it! How have I, through the whole of a midsummer night, struggled to fathom it! What was it --that something more profound than the well of Democritus --which lay far within the pupils of my beloved? What was it? I was possessed with a passion to discover. Those eyes! those large, those shining, those divine orbs! they became to me twin stars of Leda, and I to them devoutest of astrologers.

There is no point, among the many incomprehensible anomalies of the science of mind, more thrillingly exciting than the fact --never, I believe, noticed in the schools --that, in our endeavors to recall to memory something long forgotten, we often find ourselves upon the very verge of remembrance, without being able, in the end, to remember. And thus how frequently, in my intense scrutiny of Ligeia's eyes, have I felt approaching the full knowledge of their expression --felt it approaching --yet not quite be mine --and so at length entirely depart! And (strange, oh strangest mystery of all!) I found, in the commonest objects of the universe, a circle of analogies to theat expression. I mean to say that, subsequently to the period when Ligeia's beauty passed into my spirit, there dwelling as in a shrine, I derived, from many existences in the material world, a sentiment such as I felt always aroused within me by her large and luminous orbs. Yet not the more could I define that sentiment, or analyze, or even steadily view it. I recognized it, let me repeat, sometimes in the survey of a rapidly-growing vine --in the contemplation of a moth, a butterfly, a chrysalis, a stream of running water. I have felt it in the ocean; in the falling of a meteor. I have felt it in the glances of unusually aged people. And there are one or two stars in heaven --(one especially, a star of the sixth magnitude, double and changeable, to be found near the large star in Lyra) in a telescopic scrutiny of which I have been made aware of the feeling. I have been filled with it by certain sounds from stringed instruments, and not unfrequently by passages from books. Among innumerable other instances, I well remember something in a volume of Joseph Glanvill, which (perhaps merely from its quaintness -- who shall say?) never failed to inspire me with the sentiment; --"And the will therein lieth, which dieth not. Who knoweth the mysteries of the will, with its vigor? For God is but a great will pervading all things by nature of its intentness. Man doth not yield him to the angels, nor unto death utterly, save only through the weakness of his feeble will."

Length of years, and subsequent reflection, have enabled me to trace, indeed, some remote connection between this passage in the English moralist and a portion of the character of Ligeia. An intensity in thought, action, or speech, was possibly, in her, a result, or at least an index, of that gigantic volition which, during our long intercourse, failed to give other and more immediate evidence of its existence. Of all the women whom I have ever known, she, the outwardly calm, the ever-placid Ligeia, was the most violently a prey to the tumultuous vultures of stern passion. And of such passion I could form no estimate, save by the miraculous expansion of those eyes which at once so delighted and appalled me --by the almost magical melody, modulation, distinctness and placidity of her very low voice -- and by the fierce energy (rendered doubly effective by contrast with her manner of utterance) of the wild words which she habitually uttered.

I have spoken of the learning of Ligeia: it was immense -- such as I have never known in woman. In the classical tongues was she deeply proficient, and as far as my own acquaintance extended in regard to the modern dialects of Europe, I have never known her at fault. Indeed upon any theme of the most admired, because simply the most abstruse of the boasted erudition of the academy, have I ever found Ligeia at fault? How singularly --how thrillingly, this one point in the nature of my wife has forced itself, at this late period only, upon my attention! I said her knowledge was such as I have never known in woman --but where breathes the man who has traversed, and successfully, all the wide areas of moral, physical, and mathematical science? I saw not then what I now clearly perceive, that the acquisitions of Ligeia were gigantic, were astounding; yet I was sufficiently aware of her infinite supremacy to resign myself, with a child-like confidence, to her guidance through the chaotic world of metaphysical investigation at which I was most busily occupied during the earlier years of our marriage. With how vast a triumph --with how vivid a delight --with how much of all that is ethereal in hope --did I feel, as she bent over me in studies but little sought --but less known --that delicious vista by slow degrees expanding before me, down whose long, gorgeous, and all untrodden path, I might at length pass onward to the goal of a wisdom too divinely precious not to be forbidden!

How poignant, then, must have been the grief with which, after some years, I beheld my well-grounded expectations take wings to themselves and fly away! Without Ligeia I was but as a child groping benighted. Her presence, her readings alone, rendered vividly luminous the many mysteries of the transcendentalism in which we were immersed. Wanting the radiant lustre of her eyes, letters, lambent and golden, grew duller than Saturnian lead. And now those eyes shone less and less frequently upon the pages over which I pored. Ligeia grew ill. The wild eyes blazed with a too --too glorious effulgence; the pale fingers became of the transparent waxen hue of the grave, and the blue veins upon the lofty forehead swelled and sank impetuously with the tides of the gentle emotion. I saw that she must die --and I struggled desperately in spirit with the grim Azrael. And the struggles of the passionate wife were, to my astonishment, even more energetic than my own. There had been much in her stern nature to impress me with the belief that, to her, death would have come without its terrors; --but not so. Words are impotent to convey any just idea of the fierceness of resistance with which she wrestled with the Shadow. I groaned in anguish at the pitiable spectacle. would have soothed --I would have reasoned; but, in the intensity of her wild desire for life, --for life --but for life --solace and reason were the uttermost folly. Yet not until the last instance, amid the most convulsive writhings of her fierce spirit, was shaken the external placidity of her demeanor. Her voice grew more gentle --grew more low --yet I would not wish to dwell upon the wild meaning of the quietly uttered words. My brain reeled as I hearkened entranced, to a melody more than mortal --to assumptions and aspirations which mortality had never before known.

That she loved me I should not have doubted; and I might have been easily aware that, in a bosom such as hers, love would have reigned no ordinary passion. But in death only, was I fully impressed with the strength of her affection. For long hours, detaining my hand, would she pour out before me the overflowing of a heart whose more than passionate devotion amounted to idolatry. How had I deserved to be so blessed by such confessions? --how had I deserved to be so cursed with the

Ligeia

removal of my beloved in the hour of her making them. But upon this subject I cannot bear to dilate. Let me say only, that in Ligeia's more than womanly abandonment to a love, alas! all unmerited, all unworthily bestowed, I at length recognized the principle of her longing with so wildly earnest a desire for the life which was now fleeing so rapidly away. It is this wild longing --it is this eager vehemence of desire for life --but for life --that I have no power to portray --no utterance capable of expressing.

At high noon of the night in which she departed, beckoning me, peremptorily, to her side, she bade me repeat certain verses composed by herself not many days before. I obeyed her. --They were these:

> Lo! 'tis a gala night
> Within the lonesome latter years!
> An angel throng, bewinged, bedight
> In veils, and drowned in tears,
> Sit in a theatre, to see
> A play of hopes and fears,
> While the orchestra breathes fitfully
> The music of the spheres.
>
> Mimes, in the form of God on high,
> Mutter and mumble low,
> And hither and thither fly --
> Mere puppets they, who come and go
> At bidding of vast formless things
> That shift the scenery to and fro,
> Flapping from out their Condor wings
> Invisible Wo!

That motley drama! --oh, be sure
It shall not be forgot!
With its Phantom chased forever more,
By a crowd that seize it not,
Through a circle that ever returneth in
To the self-same spot,
And much of Madness and more of Sin
And Horror the soul of the plot.

But see, amid the mimic rout,
A crawling shape intrude!
A blood-red thing that writhes from out
The scenic solitude!
It writhes! --it writhes! --with mortal pangs
The mimes become its food,
And the seraphs sob at vermin fangs
In human gore imbued.

Out --out are the lights --out all!
And over each quivering form,
The curtain, a funeral pall,
Comes down with the rush of a storm,
And the angels, all pallid and wan,
Uprising, unveiling, affirm
That the play is the tragedy, "Man,"
And its hero the Conqueror Worm.

"O God!" half shrieked Ligeia, leaping to her feet and extending her arms aloft with a spasmodic movement, as I

Ligeia

made an end of these lines --"O God! O Divine Father! --shall these things be undeviatingly so? --shall this Conqueror be not once conquered? Are we not part and parcel in Thee? Who -- who knoweth the mysteries of the will with its vigor? Man doth not yield him to the angels, nor unto death utterly, save only through the weakness of his feeble will."

And now, as if exhausted with emotion, she suffered her white arms to fall, and returned solemnly to her bed of death. And as she breathed her last sighs, there came mingled with them a low murmur from her lips. I bent to them my ear and distinguished, again, the concluding words of the passage in Glanvill --"Man doth not yield him to the angels, nor unto death utterly, save only through the weakness of his feeble will."

She died; --and I, crushed into the very dust with sorrow, could no longer endure the lonely desolation of my dwelling in the dim and decaying city by the Rhine. I had no lack of what the world calls wealth. Ligeia had brought me far more, very far more than ordinarily falls to the lot of mortals. After a few months, therefore, of weary and aimless wandering, I purchased, and put in some repair, an abbey, which I shall not name, in one of the wildest and least frequented portions of fair England. The gloomy and dreary grandeur of the building, the almost savage aspect of the domain, the many melancholy and time-honored memories connected with both, had much in unison with the feelings of utter abandonment which had driven me into that remote and unsocial region of the country. Yet although the external abbey, with its verdant decay hanging about it, suffered but little alteration, I gave way, with a child-like perversity, and perchance with a faint hope of alleviating my sorrows, to a display of more than regal magnificence within. --For such follies, even in childhood, I had imbibed a taste and now they came back to me as if in the dotage of grief. Alas, I feel how much even of incipient madness might have been discovered in the gorgeous and fantastic draperies, in the solemn carvings of Egypt, in the wild cornices and furniture, in the Bedlam patterns of the carpets of tufted gold! I had become a bounden slave in the trammels of opium, and my labors and my orders had taken a coloring from my dreams. But these absurdities must not pause to detail. Let me speak only of that one chamber, ever accursed, whither in a moment of mental alienation, I led from the altar as my bride --as the successor of the unforgotten Ligeia --the fair-haired and blue-eyed Lady Rowena Trevanion, of Tremaine.

There is no individual portion of the architecture and decoration of that bridal chamber which is not now visibly before me. Where were the souls of the haughty family of the bride, when, through thirst of gold, they permitted to pass the threshold of an apartment so bedecked, a maiden and a daughter so beloved? I have said that I minutely remember the details of the chamber --yet I am sadly forgetful on topics of deep moment --and here there was no system, no keeping, in the fantastic display, to take hold upon the memory. The room lay in a high turret of the castellated abbey, was pentagonal in shape, and of capacious size. Occupying the whole southern face of the pentagon was the sole window --an immense sheet of unbroken glass from Venice --a single pane, and tinted of a leaden hue, so that the rays of either the sun or moon, passing through it, fell with a ghastly lustre on the objects within. Over the upper portion of this huge window, extended the trellice-work of an aged vine, which clambered up the massy walls of the turret. The ceiling, of gloomy-looking oak, was excessively lofty, vaulted, and elaborately fretted with the wildest and most grotesque specimens of a semi-Gothic, semi-Druidical device. From out the most central recess of this melancholy vaulting, depended, by a single chain of gold with long links, a huge censer of the same metal, Saracenic in pattern, and with many perforations so contrived that there writhed in and out of them, as if endued with a serpent vitality, a continual succession of parti-colored fires.

Some few ottomans and golden candelabra, of Eastern figure, were in various stations about --and there was the couch, too --bridal couch --of an Indian model, and low, and sculptured of solid ebony, with a pall-like canopy above. In each of the angles of the chamber stood on end a gigantic sarcophagus of black granite, from the tombs of the kings over against Luxor, with their aged lids full of immemorial sculpture. But in the draping of the apartment lay, alas! the chief phantasy of all. The lofty walls, gigantic in height --even unproportionably so --were hung from summit to foot, in vast folds, with a heavy and massive-looking tapestry --tapestry of a material which was found alike as a carpet on the floor, as a covering for the ottomans and the ebony bed, as a canopy for the bed, and as the gorgeous volutes of the curtains which partially shaded the window. The material was the richest cloth of gold. It was spotted all over, at irregular intervals, with arabesque figures, about a foot in diameter, and wrought upon the cloth in patterns of the most jetty black. But these figures partook of the true character of the arabesque only when regarded from a single point of view. By a contrivance now common, and indeed traceable to a very remote period of

Ligeia

antiquity, they were made changeable in aspect. To one entering the room, they bore the appearance of simple monstrosities; but upon a farther advance, this appearance gradually departed; and step by step, as the visitor moved his station in the chamber, he saw himself surrounded by an endless succession of the ghastly forms which belong to the superstition of the Norman, or arise in the guilty slumbers of the monk. The phantasmagoric effect was vastly heightened by the artificial introduction of a strong continual current of wind behind the draperies --giving a hideous and uneasy animation to the whole.

In halls such as these --in a bridal chamber such as this --I passed, with the Lady of Tremaine, the unhallowed hours of the first month of our marriage --passed them with but little disquietude. That my wife dreaded the fierce moodiness of my temper --that she shunned me and loved me but little --I could not help perceiving; but it gave me rather pleasure than otherwise. I loathed her with a hatred belonging more to demon than to man. My memory flew back, (oh, with what intensity of regret!) to Ligeia, the beloved, the august, the beautiful, the entombed. I revelled in recollections of her purity, of her wisdom, of her lofty, her ethereal nature, of her passionate, her idolatrous love. Now, then, did my spirit fully and freely burn with more than all the fires of her own. In the excitement of my opium dreams (for I was habitually fettered in the shackles of the drug) I would call aloud upon her name, during the silence of the night, or among the sheltered recesses of the glens by day, as if, through the wild eagerness, the solemn passion, the consuming ardor of my longing for the departed, I could restore her to the pathway she had abandoned --ah, could it be forever? --upon the earth.

About the commencement of the second month of the marriage, the Lady Rowena was attacked with sudden illness, from which her recovery was slow. The fever which consumed her rendered her nights uneasy; and in her perturbed state of half-slumber, she spoke of sounds, and of motions, in and about the chamber of the turret, which I concluded had no origin save in the distemper of her fancy, or perhaps in the phantasmagoric influences of the chamber itself. She became at length convalescent --finally well. Yet but a brief period elapsed, ere a second more violent disorder again threw her upon a bed of suffering; and from this attack her frame, at all times feeble, never altogether recovered. Her illnesses were, after this epoch, of alarming character, and of more alarming recurrence, defying alike the knowledge and the great exertions of her physicians. With the increase of the chronic disease which had thus, apparently, taken too sure hold upon her constitution to be eradicated by human means, I could not fail to observe a similar increase in the nervous irritation of her temperament, and in her excitability by trivial causes of fear. She spoke again, and now more frequently and pertinaciously, of the sounds --of the slight sounds --and of the unusual motions among the tapestries, to which she had formerly alluded.

One night, near the closing in of September, she pressed this distressing subject with more than usual emphasis upon my attention. She had just awakened from an unquiet slumber, and I had been watching, with feelings half of anxiety, half of vague terror, the workings of her emaciated countenance. I sat by the side of her ebony bed, upon one of the ottomans of India. She partly arose, and spoke, in an earnest low whisper, of sounds which she then heard, but which I could not hear --of motions which she then saw, but which I could not perceive. The wind was rushing hurriedly behind the tapestries, and I wished to show her (what, let me confess it, I could not all believe) that those almost inarticulate breathings, and those very gentle variations of the figures upon the wall, were but the natural effects of that customary rushing of the wind. But a deadly pallor, overspreading her face, had proved to me that my exertions to reassure her would be fruitless. She appeared to be fainting, and no attendants were within call. I remembered where was deposited a decanter of light wine which had been ordered by her physicians, and hastened across the chamber to procure it. But, as I stepped beneath the light of the censer, two circumstances of a startling nature attracted my attention. I had felt that some palpable although invisible object had passed lightly by my person; and I saw that there lay upon the golden carpet, in the very middle of the rich lustre thrown from the censer, a shadow --a faint, indefinite shadow of angelic aspect -- such as might be fancied for the shadow of a shade. But I was wild with the excitement of an immoderate dose of opium, and heeded these things but little, nor spoke of them to Rowena. Having found the wine, I recrossed the chamber, and poured out a gobletful, which I held to the lips of the fainting lady. She had now partially recovered, however, and took the vessel herself, while I sank upon an ottoman near me, with my eyes fastened upon her person. It was then that I became distinctly aware of a gentle footfall upon the carpet, and near the couch; and in a second thereafter, as Rowena was in the act of raising the wine to her lips, I saw, or may have dreamed that I saw, fall within the goblet, as if from some invisible spring in the atmosphere of the room, three or four large drops of a brilliant and ruby colored fluid. If this I saw --not so Rowena. She swallowed the wine unhesitatingly, and I forbore to speak to her of a circumstance which must, after all, I considered, have been but the suggestion of a vivid imagination, rendered morbidly active by the terror of the lady, by the opium, and by the hour.

Yet I cannot conceal it from my own perception that, immediately subsequent to the fall of the ruby-drops, a rapid change for the worse took place in the disorder of my wife; so that, on the third subsequent night, the hands of her menials prepared her for the tomb, and on the fourth, I sat alone, with her shrouded body, in that fantastic chamber which had received her as my bride. --Wild visions, opium-engendered, flitted, shadow-like, before me. I gazed with unquiet eye upon the sarcophagi in the angles of the room, upon the varying figures of the drapery, and upon the writhing of the parti-colored fires in the censer overhead. My eyes then fell, as I called to mind the circumstances of a former night, to the spot beneath the glare of the censer where I had seen the faint traces of the shadow. It was there, however, no longer; and breathing with greater freedom, I turned my glances to the pallid and rigid figure upon the bed. Then rushed upon me a thousand memories of Ligeia --and then came back upon my heart, with the turbulent violence of a flood, the whole of that unutterable wo with which I had regarded her thus enshrouded. The night waned; and still, with a bosom full of bitter thoughts of the one only and supremely beloved, I remained gazing upon the body of Rowena.

It might have been midnight, or perhaps earlier, or later, for I had taken no note of time, when a sob, low, gentle, but very distinct, startled me from my revery. --I felt that it came from the bed of ebony --the bed of death. I listened in an agony of superstitious terror --but there was no repetition of the sound. I strained my vision to detect any motion in the corpse --but there was not the slightest perceptible. Yet I could not have been deceived. I had heard the noise, however faint, and my soul was awakened within me. I resolutely and perseveringly kept my attention riveted upon the body. Many minutes elapsed before any circumstance occurred tending to throw light upon the mystery. At length it became evident that a slight, a very feeble, and barely noticeable tinge of color had flushed up within the cheeks, and along the sunken small veins of the eyelids. Through a species of unutterable horror and awe, for which the language of mortality has no sufficiently energetic expression, I felt my heart cease to beat, my limbs grow rigid where I sat. Yet a sense of duty finally operated to restore my self-possession. I could no longer doubt that we had been precipitate in our preparations --that Rowena still lived. It was necessary that some immediate exertion be made; yet the turret was altogether apart from the portion of the abbey tenanted by the servants -- there were none within call --I had no means of summoning them to my aid without leaving the room for many minutes -- and this I could not venture to do. I therefore struggled alone in my endeavors to call back the spirit ill hovering. In a short period it was certain, however, that a relapse had taken place; the color disappeared from both eyelid and cheek, leaving a wanness even more than that of marble; the lips became doubly shrivelled and pinched up in the ghastly expression of death; a repulsive clamminess and coldness overspread rapidly the surface of the body; and all the usual rigorous illness immediately supervened. I fell back with a shudder upon the couch from which I had been so startlingly aroused, and again gave myself up to passionate waking visions of Ligeia.

An hour thus elapsed when (could it be possible?) I was a second time aware of some vague sound issuing from the region of the bed. I listened --in extremity of horror. The sound came again --it was a sigh. Rushing to the corpse, I saw -- distinctly saw --a tremor upon the lips. In a minute afterward they relaxed, disclosing a bright line of the pearly teeth. Amazement now struggled in my bosom with the profound awe which had hitherto reigned there alone. I felt that my vision grew dim, that my reason wandered; and it was only by a violent effort that I at length succeeded in nerving myself to the task which duty thus once more had pointed out. There was now a partial glow upon the forehead and upon the cheek and throat; a perceptible warmth pervaded the whole frame; there was even a slight pulsation at the heart. The lady lived; and with redoubled ardor I betook myself to the task of restoration. I chafed and bathed the temples and the hands, and used every exertion which experience, and no little medical reading, could suggest. But in vain. Suddenly, the color fled, the pulsation ceased, the lips resumed the expression of the dead, and, in an instant afterward, the whole body took upon itself the icy chilliness, the livid hue, the intense rigidity, the sunken outline, and all the loathsome peculiarities of that which has been, for many days, a tenant of the tomb.

And again I sunk into visions of Ligeia --and again, (what marvel that I shudder while I write,) again there reached my ears a low sob from the region of the ebony bed. But why shall I minutely detail the unspeakable horrors of that night? Why shall I pause to relate how, time after time, until near the period of the gray dawn, this hideous drama of revivification was repeated; how each terrific relapse was only into a sterner and apparently more irredeemable death; how each agony wore the aspect of a struggle with some invisible foe; and how each struggle was succeeded by I know not what of wild change in the personal appearance of the corpse? Let me hurry to a conclusion.

The greater part of the fearful night had worn away, and she who had been dead, once again stirred --and now more vigorously than hitherto, although arousing from a dissolution more appalling in its utter hopelessness than any. I had long ceased to struggle or to move, and remained sitting rigidly upon the ottoman, a helpless prey to a whirl of violent emotions, of which extreme awe was perhaps the least terrible, the least consuming. The corpse, I repeat, stirred, and now more vigorously than before. The hues of life flushed up with unwonted energy into the countenance --the limbs relaxed -- and, save that the eyelids were yet pressed heavily together, and that the bandages and draperies of the grave still imparted their charnel character to the figure, I might have dreamed that Rowena had indeed shaken off, utterly, the fetters of Death. But if this idea was not, even then, altogether adopted, I could at least doubt no longer, when, arising from the bed, tottering, with feeble steps, with closed eyes, and with the manner of one bewildered in a dream, the thing that was enshrouded advanced boldly and palpably into the middle of the apartment.

I trembled not --I stirred not --for a crowd of unutterable fancies connected with the air, the stature, the demeanor of the figure, rushing hurriedly through my brain, had paralyzed -- had chilled me into stone. I stirred not --but gazed upon the apparition. There was a mad disorder in my thoughts --a tumult unappeasable. Could it, indeed, be the living Rowena who confronted me? Could it indeed be Rowena at all --the fair-haired, the blue-eyed Lady Rowena Trevanion of Tremaine? Why, why should I doubt it? The bandage lay heavily about the mouth --but then might it not be the mouth of the breathing Lady of Tremaine? And the cheeks-there were the roses as in her noon of life --yes, these might indeed be the fair cheeks of the living Lady of Tremaine. And the chin, with its dimples, as in health, might it not be hers? --but had she then grown taller since her malady? What inexpressible madness seized me with that thought? One bound, and I had reached her feet! Shrinking from my touch, she let fall from her head, unloosened, the ghastly cerements which had confined it, and there streamed forth, into the rushing atmosphere of the chamber, huge masses of long and dishevelled hair; it was blacker than the raven wings of the midnight! And now slowly opened the eyes of the figure which stood before me. "Here then, at least," I shrieked aloud, "can I never --can I never be mistaken --these are the full, and the black, and the wild eyes --of my lost love --of the lady --of the LADY LIGEIA."

The Fall of the House of Usher

By Edgar Allan Poe

Son coeur est un luth suspendu;

Sitot qu'on le touche il resonne.

-De Beranger.

DURING the whole of a dull, dark, and soundless day in the autumn of the year, when the clouds hung oppressively low in the heavens, I had been passing alone, on horseback, through a singularly dreary tract of country; and at length found myself, as the shades of the evening drew on, within view of the melancholy House of Usher. I know not how it was --but, with the first glimpse of the building, a sense of insufferable gloom pervaded my spirit. I say insufferable; for the feeling was unrelieved by any of that half-pleasurable, because poetic, sentiment, with which the mind usually receives even the sternest natural images of the desolate or terrible. I looked upon the scene before me --upon the mere house, and the simple landscape features of the domain --upon the bleak walls --upon the vacant eye-like windows --upon a few rank sedges --and upon a few white trunks of decayed trees --with an utter depression of soul which I can compare to no earthly sensation more properly than to the after-dream of the reveller upon opium --the bitter lapse into everyday life --the hideous dropping off of the veil. There was an iciness, a sinking, a sickening of the heart --an unredeemed dreariness of thought which no goading of the imagination could torture into aught of the sublime. What was it --I paused to think --what was it that so unnerved me in the contemplation of the House of Usher? It was a mystery all insoluble; nor could I grapple with the shadowy fancies that crowded upon me as I pondered. I was forced to fall back upon the unsatisfactory conclusion, that while, beyond doubt, there are combinations of very simple natural objects which have the power of thus affecting us, still the analysis of this power lies among considerations beyond our depth. It was possible, I reflected, that a mere different arrangement of the particulars of the scene, of the details of the picture, would be sufficient to modify, or perhaps to annihilate its capacity for sorrowful impression; and, acting upon this idea, I reined my horse to the precipitous brink of a black and lurid tarn that lay in unruffled lustre by the dwelling, and gazed down --but with a shudder even more thrilling than before -- upon the remodelled and inverted images of the gray sedge, and the ghastly tree-stems, and the vacant and eye-like windows.

Nevertheless, in this mansion of gloom I now proposed to myself a sojourn of some weeks. Its proprietor, Roderick Usher, had been one of my boon companions in boyhood; but many years had elapsed since our last meeting. A letter, however, had lately reached me in a distant part of the country --a letter from him --which, in its wildly importunate nature, had admitted of no other than a personal reply. The MS. gave evidence of nervous agitation. The writer spoke of acute bodily illness --of a mental disorder which oppressed him --and of an earnest desire to see me, as his best, and indeed his only personal friend, with a view of attempting, by the cheerfulness of my society, some alleviation of his malady. It was the manner in which all this, and much more, was said --it the apparent heart that went with his request --which allowed me no room for hesitation; and I accordingly obeyed forthwith what I still considered a very singular summons.

Although, as boys, we had been even intimate associates, yet I really knew little of my friend. His reserve had been always excessive and habitual. I was aware, however, that his very ancient family had been noted, time out of mind, for a peculiar sensibility of temperament, displaying itself, through long ages, in many works of exalted art, and manifested, of late, in repeated deeds of munificent yet unobtrusive charity, as well as in a passionate devotion to the intricacies, perhaps even more than to the orthodox and easily recognisable beauties, of musical science. I had learned, too, the very remarkable fact, that the stem of the Usher race, all time-honoured as it was, had put forth, at no period, any enduring branch; in other words, that the entire family lay in the direct line of descent, and had always, with very trifling and very temporary variation, so lain. It was this deficiency, I considered, while running over in thought the perfect keeping of the character of the premises with the accredited character of the people, and while speculating upon the possible influence which the one, in the long lapse of centuries, might have exercised upon the other --it

The Fall of the House of Usher

was this deficiency, perhaps, of collateral issue, and the consequent undeviating transmission, from sire to son, of the patrimony with the name, which had, at length, so identified the two as to merge the original title of the estate in the quaint and equivocal appellation of the "House of Usher" --an appellation which seemed to include, in the minds of the peasantry who used it, both the family and the family mansion.

I have said that the sole effect of my somewhat childish experiment --that of looking down within the tarn --had been to deepen the first singular impression. There can be no doubt that the consciousness of the rapid increase of my superstition --for why should I not so term it? --served mainly to accelerate the increase itself. Such, I have long known, is the paradoxical law of all sentiments having terror as a basis. And it might have been for this reason only, that, when I again uplifted my eyes to the house itself, from its image in the pool, there grew in my mind a strange fancy --a fancy so ridiculous, indeed, that I but mention it to show the vivid force of the sensations which oppressed me. I had so worked upon my imagination as really to believe that about the whole mansion and domain there hung an atmosphere peculiar to themselves and their immediate vicinity-an atmosphere which had no affinity with the air of heaven, but which had reeked up from the decayed trees, and the gray wall, and the silent tarn --a pestilent and mystic vapour, dull, sluggish, faintly discernible, and leaden-hued.

Shaking off from my spirit what must have been a dream, I scanned more narrowly the real aspect of the building. Its principal feature seemed to be that of an excessive antiquity. The discoloration of ages had been great. Minute fungi overspread the whole exterior, hanging in a fine tangled web-work from the eaves. Yet all this was apart from any extraordinary dilapidation. No portion of the masonry had fallen; and there appeared to be a wild inconsistency between its still perfect adaptation of parts, and the crumbling condition of the individual stones. In this there was much that reminded me of the specious totality of old wood-work which has rotted for long years in some neglected vault, with no disturbance from the breath of the external air. Beyond this indication of extensive decay, however, the fabric gave little token of instability. Perhaps the eye of a scrutinising observer might have discovered a barely perceptible fissure, which, extending from the roof of the building in front, made its way down the wall in a zigzag direction, until it became lost in the sullen waters of the tarn.

The Fall of the House of Usher

Noticing these things, I rode over a short causeway to the house. A servant in waiting took my horse, and I entered the Gothic archway of the hall. A valet, of stealthy step, thence conducted me, in silence, through many dark and intricate passages in my progress to the studio of his master. Much that I encountered on the way contributed, I know not how, to heighten the vague sentiments of which I have already spoken. While the objects around me --while the carvings of the ceilings, the sombre tapestries of the walls, the ebon blackness of the floors, and the phantasmagoric armorial trophies which rattled as I strode, were but matters to which, or to such as which, I had been accustomed from my infancy --while I hesitated not to acknowledge how familiar was all this --I still wondered to find how unfamiliar were the fancies which ordinary images were stirring up. On one of the staircases, I met the physician of the family. His countenance, I thought, wore a mingled expression of low cunning and perplexity. He accosted me with trepidation and passed on. The valet now threw open a door and ushered me into the presence of his master.

The room in which I found myself was very large and lofty. The windows were long, narrow, and pointed, and at so vast a distance from the black oaken floor as to be altogether inaccessible from within. Feeble gleams of encrimsoned light made their way through the trellised panes, and served to render sufficiently distinct the more prominent objects around; the eye, however, struggled in vain to reach the remoter angles of the chamber, or the recesses of the vaulted and fretted ceiling. Dark draperies hung upon the walls. The general furniture was profuse, comfortless, antique, and tattered. Many books and musical instruments lay scattered about, but failed to give any vitality to the scene. I felt that I breathed an atmosphere of sorrow. An air of stern, deep, and irredeemable gloom hung over and pervaded all.

Upon my entrance, Usher arose from a sofa on which he had been lying at full length, and greeted me with a vivacious warmth which had much in it, I at first thought, of an overdone cordiality --of the constrained effort of the ennuye man of the world. A glance, however, at his countenance, convinced me of his perfect sincerity. We sat down; and for some moments, while he spoke not, I gazed upon him with a feeling half of pity, half of awe. Surely, man had never before so terribly altered, in so brief a period, as had Roderick Usher! It was with difficulty that I could bring myself to admit the identity of the wan being before me with the companion of my early boyhood. Yet the character of his face had been at all times remarkable. A cadaverousness of complexion; an eye large, liquid, and

The Fall of the House of Usher

luminous beyond comparison; lips somewhat thin and very pallid, but of a surpassingly beautiful curve; a nose of a delicate Hebrew model, but with a breadth of nostril unusual in similar formations; a finely moulded chin, speaking, in its want of prominence, of a want of moral energy; hair of a more than web-like softness and tenuity; these features, with an inordinate expansion above the regions of the temple, made up altogether a countenance not easily to be forgotten. And now in the mere exaggeration of the prevailing character of these features, and of the expression they were wont to convey, lay so much of change that I doubted to whom I spoke. The now ghastly pallor of the skin, and the now miraculous lustre of the eye, above all things startled and even awed me. The silken hair, too, had been suffered to grow all unheeded, and as, in its wild gossamer texture, it floated rather than fell about the face, I could not, even with effort, connect its Arabesque expression with any idea of simple humanity.

In the manner of my friend I was at once struck with an incoherence --an inconsistency; and I soon found this to arise from a series of feeble and futile struggles to overcome an habitual trepidancy --an excessive nervous agitation. For something of this nature I had indeed been prepared, no less by his letter, than by reminiscences of certain boyish traits, and by conclusions deduced from his peculiar physical conformation and temperament. His action was alternately vivacious and sullen. His voice varied rapidly from a tremulous indecision (when the animal spirits seemed utterly in abeyance) to that species of energetic concision --that abrupt, weighty, unhurried, and hollow-sounding enunciation --that leaden, self-balanced and perfectly modulated guttural utterance, which may be observed in the lost drunkard, or the irreclaimable eater of opium, during the periods of his most intense excitement.

It was thus that he spoke of the object of my visit, of his earnest desire to see me, and of the solace he expected me to afford him. He entered, at some length, into what he conceived to be the nature of his malady. It was, he said, a constitutional and a family evil, and one for which he despaired to find a remedy --a mere nervous affection, he immediately added, which would undoubtedly soon pass off. It displayed itself in a host of unnatural sensations. Some of these, as he detailed them, interested and bewildered me; although, perhaps, the terms, and the general manner of the narration had their weight. He suffered much from a morbid acuteness of the senses; the most insipid food was alone endurable; he could wear only garments of certain texture; the odours of all flowers were oppressive; his eyes were tortured by even a faint light; and there were but peculiar sounds, and these from stringed instruments, which did not inspire him with horror.

To an anomalous species of terror I found him a bounden slave. "I shall perish," said he, "I must perish in this deplorable folly. Thus, thus, and not otherwise, shall I be lost. I dread the events of the future, not in themselves, but in their results. I shudder at the thought of any, even the most trivial, incident, which may operate upon this intolerable agitation of soul. I have, indeed, no abhorrence of danger, except in its absolute effect --in terror. In this unnerved-in this pitiable condition --I feel that the period will sooner or later arrive when I must abandon life and reason together, in some struggle with the grim phantasm, FEAR."

I learned, moreover, at intervals, and through broken and equivocal hints, another singular feature of his mental condition. He was enchained by certain superstitious impressions in regard to the dwelling which he tenanted, and whence, for many years, he had never ventured forth --in regard to an influence whose supposititious force was conveyed in terms too shadowy here to be re-stated --an influence which some peculiarities in the mere form and substance of his family mansion, had, by dint of long sufferance, he said, obtained over his spirit-an effect which the physique of the gray walls and turrets, and of the dim tarn into which they all looked down, had, at length, brought about upon the morale of his existence.

He admitted, however, although with hesitation, that much of the peculiar gloom which thus afflicted him could be traced to a more natural and far more palpable origin --to the severe and long-continued illness --indeed to the evidently approaching dissolution-of a tenderly beloved sister --his sole companion for long years --his last and only relative on earth. "Her decease," he said, with a bitterness which I can never forget, "would leave him (him the hopeless and the frail) the last of the ancient race of the Ushers." While he spoke, the lady Madeline (for so was she called) passed slowly through a remote portion of the apartment, and, without having noticed my presence, disappeared. I regarded her with an utter astonishment not unmingled with dread --and yet I found it impossible to account for such feelings. A sensation of stupor oppressed me, as my eyes followed her retreating steps. When a door, at length, closed upon her, my glance sought instinctively and eagerly the countenance of the brother --but he had buried his face in his hands, and I could only perceive that a far more than ordinary wanness had overspread the emaciated fingers through which trickled many passionate tears.

The Fall of the House of Usher

The disease of the lady Madeline had long baffled the skill of her physicians. A settled apathy, a gradual wasting away of the person, and frequent although transient affections of a partially cataleptical character, were the unusual diagnosis. Hitherto she had steadily borne up against the pressure of her malady, and had not betaken herself finally to bed; but, on the closing in of the evening of my arrival at the house, she succumbed (as her brother told me at night with inexpressible agitation) to the prostrating power of the destroyer; and I learned that the glimpse I had obtained of her person would thus probably be the last I should obtain --that the lady, at least while living, would be seen by me no more.

For several days ensuing, her name was unmentioned by either Usher or myself: and during this period I was busied in earnest endeavours to alleviate the melancholy of my friend. We painted and read together; or I listened, as if in a dream, to the wild improvisations of his speaking guitar. And thus, as a closer and still intimacy admitted me more unreservedly into the recesses of his spirit, the more bitterly did I perceive the futility of all attempt at cheering a mind from which darkness, as if an inherent positive quality, poured forth upon all objects of the moral and physical universe, in one unceasing radiation of gloom.

I shall ever bear about me a memory of the many solemn hours I thus spent alone with the master of the House of Usher. Yet I should fail in any attempt to convey an idea of the exact character of the studies, or of the occupations, in which he involved me, or led me the way. An excited and highly distempered ideality threw a sulphureous lustre over all. His long improvised dirges will ring forever in my ears. Among other things, I hold painfully in mind a certain singular perversion and amplification of the wild air of the last waltz of Von Weber. From the paintings over which his elaborate fancy brooded, and which grew, touch by touch, into vaguenesses at which I shuddered the more thrillingly, because I shuddered knowing not why; --from these paintings (vivid as their images now are before me) I would in vain endeavour to educe more than a small portion which should lie within the compass of merely written words. By the utter simplicity, by the nakedness of his designs, he arrested and overawed attention. If ever mortal painted an idea, that mortal was Roderick Usher. For me at least --in the circumstances then surrounding me --there arose out of the pure abstractions which the hypochondriac contrived to throw upon his canvas, an intensity of intolerable awe, no shadow of which felt I ever yet in the contemplation of the certainly glowing yet too concrete reveries of Fuseli.

The Fall of the House of Usher

One of the phantasmagoric conceptions of my friend, partaking not so rigidly of the spirit of abstraction, may be shadowed forth, although feebly, in words. A small picture presented the interior of an immensely long and rectangular vault or tunnel, with low walls, smooth, white, and without interruption or device. Certain accessory points of the design served well to convey the idea that this excavation lay at an exceeding depth below the surface of the earth. No outlet was observed in any portion of its vast extent, and no torch, or other artificial source of light was discernible; yet a flood of intense rays rolled throughout, and bathed the whole in a ghastly and inappropriate splendour.

I have just spoken of that morbid condition of the auditory nerve which rendered all music intolerable to the sufferer, with the exception of certain effects of stringed instruments. It was, perhaps, the narrow limits to which he thus confined himself upon the guitar, which gave birth, in great measure, to the fantastic character of his performances. But the fervid facility of his impromptus could not be so accounted for. They must have been, and were, in the notes, as well as in the words of his wild fantasias (for he not unfrequently accompanied himself with rhymed verbal improvisations), the result of that intense mental collectedness and concentration to which I have previously alluded as observable only in particular moments of the highest artificial excitement. The words of one of these rhapsodies I have easily remembered. I was, perhaps, the more forcibly impressed with it, as he gave it, because, in the under or mystic current of its meaning, I fancied that I perceived, and for the first time, a full consciousness on the part of Usher, of the tottering of his lofty reason upon her throne. The verses, which were entitled "The Haunted Palace," ran very nearly, if not accurately, thus:

I.

In the greenest of our valleys,

By good angels tenanted,

Once fair and stately palace --

Radiant palace --reared its head.

In the monarch Thought's dominion --

The Fall of the House of Usher

It stood there!
Never seraph spread a pinion
Over fabric half so fair.

II.

Banners yellow, glorious, golden,
On its roof did float and flow;
(This --all this --was in the olden
Time long ago)
And every gentle air that dallied,
In that sweet day,
Along the ramparts plumed and pallid,
A winged odour went away.

III.

Wanderers in that happy valley
Through two luminous windows saw
Spirits moving musically
To a lute's well-tuned law,
Round about a throne, where sitting
(Porphyrogene!)
In state his glory well befitting,
The ruler of the realm was seen.

IV.

And all with pearl and ruby glowing

Was the fair palace door,
Through which came flowing, flowing, flowing
And sparkling evermore,
A troop of Echoes whose sweet duty
Was but to sing,
In voices of surpassing beauty,
The wit and wisdom of their king.

V.

But evil things, in robes of sorrow,
Assailed the monarch's high estate;
(Ah, let us mourn, for never morrow
Shall dawn upon him, desolate!)
And, round about his home, the glory
That blushed and bloomed
Is but a dim-remembered story
Of the old time entombed.

VI.

And travellers now within that valley,
Through the red-litten windows, see
Vast forms that move fantastically
To a discordant melody;
While, like a rapid ghastly river,
Through the pale door,
A hideous throng rush out forever,
And laugh --but smile no more.

The Fall of the House of Usher

I well remember that suggestions arising from this ballad led us into a train of thought wherein there became manifest an opinion of Usher's which I mention not so much on account of its novelty, (for other men have thought thus,) as on account of the pertinacity with which he maintained it. This opinion, in its general form, was that of the sentience of all vegetable things. But, in his disordered fancy, the idea had assumed a more daring character, and trespassed, under certain conditions, upon the kingdom of inorganization. I lack words to express the full extent, or the earnest abandon of his persuasion. The belief, however, was connected (as I have previously hinted) with the gray stones of the home of his forefathers. The conditions of the sentience had been here, he imagined, fulfilled in the method of collocation of these stones --in the order of their arrangement, as well as in that of the many fungi which overspread them, and of the decayed trees which stood around --above all, in the long undisturbed endurance of this arrangement, and in its reduplication in the still waters of the tarn. Its evidence --the evidence of the sentience --was to be seen, he said, (and I here started as he spoke,) in the gradual yet certain condensation of an atmosphere of their own about the waters and the walls. The result was discoverable, he added, in that silent, yet importunate and terrible influence which for centuries had moulded the destinies of his family, and which made him what I now saw him --what he was. Such opinions need no comment, and I will make none.

Our books --the books which, for years, had formed no small portion of the mental existence of the invalid --were, as might be supposed, in strict keeping with this character of phantasm. We pored together over such works as the Ververt et Chartreuse of Gresset; the Belphegor of Machiavelli; the Heaven and Hell of Swedenborg; the Subterranean Voyage of Nicholas Klimm by Holberg; the Chiromancy of Robert Flud, of Jean D'Indagine, and of De la Chambre; the Journey into the Blue Distance of Tieck; and the City of the Sun of Campanella. One favourite volume was a small octavo edition of the Directorium Inquisitorum, by the Dominican Eymeric de Gironne; and there were passages in Pomponius Mela, about the old African Satyrs and AEgipans, over which Usher would sit dreaming for hours. His chief delight, however, was found in the perusal of an exceedingly rare and curious book in quarto Gothic --the manual of a forgotten church --the Vigilae Mortuorum secundum Chorum Ecclesiae Maguntinae.

I could not help thinking of the wild ritual of this work, and of its probable influence upon the hypochondriac, when, one evening, having informed me abruptly that the lady Madeline was no more, he stated his intention of preserving her corpse for a fortnight, (previously to its final interment,) in one of the numerous vaults within the main walls of the building. The worldly reason, however, assigned for this singular proceeding, was one which I did not feel at liberty to dispute. The brother had been led to his resolution (so he told me) by consideration of the unusual character of the malady of the deceased, of certain obtrusive and eager inquiries on the part of her medical men, and of the remote and exposed situation of the burial-ground of the family. I will not deny that when I called to mind the sinister countenance of the person whom I met upon the stair case, on the day of my arrival at the house, I had no desire to oppose what I regarded as at best but a harmless, and by no means an unnatural, precaution.

At the request of Usher, I personally aided him in the arrangements for the temporary entombment. The body having been encoffined, we two alone bore it to its rest. The vault in which we placed it (and which had been so long unopened that our torches, half smothered in its oppressive atmosphere, gave us little opportunity for investigation) was small, damp, and entirely without means of admission for light; lying, at great depth, immediately beneath that portion of the building in which was my own sleeping apartment. It had been used, apparently, in remote feudal times, for the worst purposes of a donjon-keep, and, in later days, as a place of deposit for powder, or some other highly combustible substance, as a portion of its floor, and the whole interior of a long archway through which we reached it, were carefully sheathed with copper. The door, of massive iron, had been, also, similarly protected. Its immense weight caused an unusually sharp grating sound, as it moved upon its hinges.

Having deposited our mournful burden upon tressels within this region of horror, we partially turned aside the yet unscrewed lid of the coffin, and looked upon the face of the tenant. A striking similitude between the brother and sister now first arrested my attention; and Usher, divining, perhaps, my thoughts, murmured out some few words from which I learned that the deceased and himself had been twins, and that sympathies of a scarcely intelligible nature had always existed between them. Our glances, however, rested not long upon the dead --for we could not regard her unawed. The disease which had thus entombed the lady in the maturity of youth, had left, as usual in all maladies of a strictly cataleptical character, the mockery of a faint blush upon the bosom and the face, and that suspiciously lingering smile upon the lip which is so terrible in death. We replaced and screwed down the lid, and, having

The Fall of the House of Usher

secured the door of iron, made our way, with toll, into the scarcely less gloomy apartments of the upper portion of the house.

And now, some days of bitter grief having elapsed, an observable change came over the features of the mental disorder of my friend. His ordinary manner had vanished. His ordinary occupations were neglected or forgotten. He roamed from chamber to chamber with hurried, unequal, and objectless step. The pallor of his countenance had assumed, if possible, a more ghastly hue --but the luminousness of his eye had utterly gone out. The once occasional huskiness of his tone was heard no more; and a tremulous quaver, as if of extreme terror, habitually characterized his utterance. There were times, indeed, when I thought his unceasingly agitated mind was labouring with some oppressive secret, to divulge which he struggled for the necessary courage. At times, again, I was obliged to resolve all into the mere inexplicable vagaries of madness, for I beheld him gazing upon vacancy for long hours, in an attitude of the profoundest attention, as if listening to some imaginary sound. It was no wonder that his condition terrified-that it infected me. I felt creeping upon me, by slow yet certain degrees, the wild influences of his own fantastic yet impressive superstitions.

It was, especially, upon retiring to bed late in the night of the seventh or eighth day after the placing of the lady Madeline within the donjon, that I experienced the full power of such feelings. Sleep came not near my couch --while the hours waned and waned away. I struggled to reason off the nervousness which had dominion over me. I endeavoured to believe that much, if not all of what I felt, was due to the bewildering influence of the gloomy furniture of the room --of the dark and tattered draperies, which, tortured into motion by the breath of a rising tempest, swayed fitfully to and fro upon the walls, and rustled uneasily about the decorations of the bed. But my efforts were fruitless. An irrepressible tremour gradually pervaded my frame; and, at length, there sat upon my very heart an incubus of utterly causeless alarm. Shaking this off with a gasp and a struggle, I uplifted myself upon the pillows, and, peering earnestly within the intense darkness of the chamber, hearkened --I know not why, except that an instinctive spirit prompted me --to certain low and indefinite sounds which came, through the pauses of the storm, at long intervals, I knew not whence. Overpowered by an intense sentiment of horror, unaccountable yet unendurable, I threw on my clothes with haste (for I felt that I should sleep no more during the night), and endeavoured to arouse myself from the pitiable condition into which I had fallen, by pacing rapidly to and fro through the apartment.

I had taken but few turns in this manner, when a light step on an adjoining staircase arrested my attention. I presently recognised it as that of Usher. In an instant afterward he rapped, with a gentle touch, at my door, and entered, bearing a lamp. His countenance was, as usual, cadaverously wan --but, moreover, there was a species of mad hilarity in his eyes --an evidently restrained hysteria in his whole demeanour. His air appalled me --but anything was preferable to the solitude which I had so long endured, and I even welcomed his presence as a relief.

"And you have not seen it?" he said abruptly, after having stared about him for some moments in silence --"you have not then seen it? --but, stay! you shall." Thus speaking, and having carefully shaded his lamp, he hurried to one of the casements, and threw it freely open to the storm.

The impetuous fury of the entering gust nearly lifted us from our feet. It was, indeed, a tempestuous yet sternly beautiful night, and one wildly singular in its terror and its beauty. A whirlwind had apparently collected its force in our vicinity; for there were frequent and violent alterations in the direction of the wind; and the exceeding density of the clouds (which hung so low as to press upon the turrets of the house) did not prevent our perceiving the life-like velocity with which they flew careering from all points against each other, without passing away into the distance. I say that even their exceeding density did not prevent our perceiving this --yet we had no glimpse of the moon or stars --nor was there any flashing forth of the lightning. But the under surfaces of the huge masses of agitated vapour, as well as all terrestrial objects immediately around us, were glowing in the unnatural light of a faintly luminous and distinctly visible gaseous exhalation which hung about and enshrouded the mansion.

"You must not --you shall not behold this!" said I, shudderingly, to Usher, as I led him, with a gentle violence, from the window to a seat. "These appearances, which bewilder you, are merely electrical phenomena not uncommon --or it may be that they have their ghastly origin in the rank miasma of the tarn. Let us close this casement; --the air is chilling and dangerous to your frame. Here is one of your favourite romances. I will read, and you shall listen; --and so we will pass away this terrible night together."

The antique volume which I had taken up was the "Mad Trist" of Sir Launcelot Canning; but I had called it a favourite of Usher's more in sad jest than in earnest; for, in truth, there is

The Fall of the House of Usher

little in its uncouth and unimaginative prolixity which could have had interest for the lofty and spiritual ideality of my friend. It was, however, the only book immediately at hand; and I indulged a vague hope that the excitement which now agitated the hypochondriac, might find relief (for the history of mental disorder is full of similar anomalies) even in the extremeness of the folly which I should read. Could I have judged, indeed, by the wild over-strained air of vivacity with which he hearkened, or apparently hearkened, to the words of the tale, I might well have congratulated myself upon the success of my design.

I had arrived at that well-known portion of the story where Ethelred, the hero of the Trist, having sought in vain for peaceable admission into the dwelling of the hermit, proceeds to make good an entrance by force. Here, it will be remembered, the words of the narrative run thus:

"And Ethelred, who was by nature of a doughty heart, and who was now mighty withal, on account of the powerfulness of the wine which he had drunken, waited no longer to hold parley with the hermit, who, in sooth, was of an obstinate and maliceful turn, but, feeling the rain upon his shoulders, and fearing the rising of the tempest, uplifted his mace outright, and, with blows, made quickly room in the plankings of the door for his gauntleted hand; and now pulling there-with sturdily, he so cracked, and ripped, and tore all asunder, that the noise of the dry and hollow-sounding wood alarumed and reverberated throughout the forest.

At the termination of this sentence I started, and for a moment, paused; for it appeared to me (although I at once concluded that my excited fancy had deceived me) --it appeared to me that, from some very remote portion of the mansion, there came, indistinctly, to my ears, what might have been, in its exact similarity of character, the echo (but a stifled and dull one certainly) of the very cracking and ripping sound which Sir Launcelot had so particularly described. It was, beyond doubt, the coincidence alone which had arrested my attention; for, amid the rattling of the sashes of the casements, and the ordinary commingled noises of the still increasing storm, the sound, in itself, had nothing, surely, which should have interested or disturbed me. I continued the story:

"But the good champion Ethelred, now entering within the door, was sore enraged and amazed to perceive no signal of the maliceful hermit; but, in the stead thereof, a dragon of a scaly and prodigious demeanour, and of a fiery tongue, which sate in guard before a palace of gold, with a floor of silver; and upon the wall there hung a shield of shining brass with this legend enwritten --

Who entereth herein, a conqueror hath bin;

Who slayeth the dragon, the shield he shall win.

And Ethelred uplifted his mace, and struck upon the head of the dragon, which fell before him, and gave up his pesty breath, with a shriek so horrid and harsh, and withal so piercing, that Ethelred had fain to close his ears with his hands against the dreadful noise of it, the like whereof was never before heard."

Here again I paused abruptly, and now with a feeling of wild amazement --for there could be no doubt whatever that, in this instance, I did actually hear (although from what direction it proceeded I found it impossible to say) a low and apparently distant, but harsh, protracted, and most unusual screaming or grating sound --the exact counterpart of what my fancy had already conjured up for the dragon's unnatural shriek as described by the romancer.

Oppressed, as I certainly was, upon the occurrence of the second and most extraordinary coincidence, by a thousand conflicting sensations, in which wonder and extreme terror were predominant, I still retained sufficient presence of mind to avoid exciting, by any observation, the sensitive nervousness of my companion. I was by no means certain that he had noticed the sounds in question; although, assuredly, a strange alteration had, during the last few minutes, taken place in his demeanour. From a position fronting my own, he had gradually brought round his chair, so as to sit with his face to the door of the chamber; and thus I could but partially perceive his features, although I saw that his lips trembled as if he were murmuring inaudibly. His head had dropped upon his breast --yet I knew that he was not asleep, from the wide and rigid opening of the eye as I caught a glance of it in profile. The motion of his body, too, was at variance with this idea --for he rocked from side to side with a gentle yet constant and uniform sway. Having rapidly taken notice of all this, I resumed the narrative of Sir Launcelot, which thus proceeded:

"And now, the champion, having escaped from the terrible fury of the dragon, bethinking himself of the brazen shield, and of the breaking up of the enchantment which was upon it, removed the carcass from out of the way before him, and approached valorously over the silver pavement of the castle to where the shield was upon the wall; which in sooth tarried not

The Fall of the House of Usher

for his full coming, but fell down at his feet upon the silver floor, with a mighty great and terrible ringing sound."

No sooner had these syllables passed my lips, than --as if a shield of brass had indeed, at the moment, fallen heavily upon a floor of silver, became aware of a distinct, hollow, metallic, and clangorous, yet apparently muffled reverberation. Completely unnerved, I leaped to my feet; but the measured rocking movement of Usher was undisturbed. I rushed to the chair in which he sat. His eyes were bent fixedly before him, and throughout his whole countenance there reigned a stony rigidity. But, as I placed my hand upon his shoulder, there came a strong shudder over his whole person; a sickly smile quivered about his lips; and I saw that he spoke in a low, hurried, and gibbering murmur, as if unconscious of my presence. Bending closely over him, I at length drank in the hideous import of his words.

"Not hear it? --yes, I hear it, and have heard it. Long --long --long --many minutes, many hours, many days, have I heard it --yet I dared not --oh, pity me, miserable wretch that I am! --I dared not --I dared not speak! We have put her living in the tomb! Said I not that my senses were acute? I now tell you that I heard her first feeble movements in the hollow coffin. I heard them --many, many days ago --yet I dared not --I dared not speak! And now --to-night --Ethelred --ha! ha! --the breaking of the hermit's door, and the death-cry of the dragon, and the clangour of the shield! --say, rather, the rending of her coffin, and the grating of the iron hinges of her prison, and her struggles within the coppered archway of the vault! Oh whither shall I fly? Will she not be here anon? Is she not hurrying to upbraid me for my haste? Have I not heard her footstep on the stair? Do I not distinguish that heavy and horrible beating of her heart? MADMAN!" here he sprang furiously to his feet, and shrieked out his syllables, as if in the effort he were giving up his soul --"MADMAN! I TELL YOU THAT SHE NOW STANDS WITHOUT THE DOOR!"

As if in the superhuman energy of his utterance there had been found the potency of a spell --the huge antique panels to which the speaker pointed, threw slowly back, upon the instant, ponderous and ebony jaws. It was the work of the rushing gust --but then without those doors there DID stand the lofty and enshrouded figure of the lady Madeline of Usher. There was blood upon her white robes, and the evidence of some bitter struggle upon every portion of her emaciated frame. For a moment she remained trembling and reeling to and fro upon the threshold, then, with a low moaning cry, fell heavily inward upon the person of her brother, and in her violent and now final death-agonies, bore him to the floor a corpse, and a victim to the terrors he had anticipated.

From that chamber, and from that mansion, I fled aghast. The storm was still abroad in all its wrath as I found myself crossing the old causeway. Suddenly there shot along the path a wild light, and I turned to see whence a gleam so unusual could have issued; for the vast house and its shadows were alone behind me. The radiance was that of the full, setting, and blood-red moon which now shone vividly through that once barely-discernible fissure of which I have before spoken as extending from the roof of the building, in a zig-zag direction, to the base. While I gazed, this fissure rapidly widened --there came a fierce breath of the whirlwind --the entire orb of the satellite burst at once upon my sight --my brain reeled as I saw the mighty walls rushing asunder --there was a long tumultuous shouting sound like the voice of a thousand waters --and the deep and dank tarn at my feet closed sullenly and silently over the fragments of the "HOUSE OF USHER."

The Masque of the Red Death

By Edgar Allan Poe

THE "Red Death" had long devastated the country. No pestilence had ever been so fatal, or so hideous. Blood was its Avator and its seal -- the redness and the horror of blood. There were sharp pains, and sudden dizziness, and then profuse bleeding at the pores, with dissolution. The scarlet stains upon the body and especially upon the face of the victim, were the pest ban which shut him out from the aid and from the sympathy of his fellow-men. And the whole seizure, progress and termination of the disease, were the incidents of half an hour.

But the Prince Prospero was happy and dauntless and sagacious. When his dominions were half depopulated, he summoned to his presence a thousand hale and light-hearted friends from among the knights and dames of his court, and with these retired to the deep seclusion of one of his castellated abbeys. This was an extensive and magnificent structure, the creation of the prince's own eccentric yet august taste. A strong and lofty wall girdled it in. This wall had gates of iron. The courtiers, having entered, brought furnaces and massy hammers and welded the bolts. They resolved to leave means neither of ingress or egress to the sudden impulses of despair or of frenzy from within. The abbey was amply provisioned. With such precautions the courtiers might bid defiance to contagion. The external world could take care of itself. In the meantime it was folly to grieve, or to think. The prince had provided all the appliances of pleasure. There were buffoons, there were improvisatori, there were ballet-dancers, there were musicians, there was Beauty, there was wine. All these and security were within. Without was the "Red Death."

It was toward the close of the fifth or sixth month of his seclusion, and while the pestilence raged most furiously abroad, that the Prince Prospero entertained his thousand friends at a masked ball of the most unusual magnificence.

It was a voluptuous scene, that masquerade. But first let me tell of the rooms in which it was held. There were seven -- an imperial suite. In many palaces, however, such suites form a long and straight vista, while the folding doors slide back nearly to the walls on either hand, so that the view of the whole extent is scarcely impeded. Here the case was very different; as might have been expected from the duke's love of the bizarre. The apartments were so irregularly disposed that the vision embraced but little more than one at a time. There was a sharp turn at every twenty or thirty yards, and at each turn a novel effect. To the right and left, in the middle of each wall, a tall and narrow Gothic window looked out upon a closed corridor which pursued the windings of the suite. These windows were of stained glass whose color varied in accordance with the prevailing hue of the decorations of the chamber into which it opened. That at the eastern extremity was hung, for example, in blue -- and vividly blue were its windows. The second chamber was purple in its ornaments and tapestries, and here the panes were purple. The third was green throughout, and so were the casements. The fourth was furnished and lighted with orange -- the fifth with white -- the sixth with violet. The seventh apartment was closely shrouded in black velvet tapestries that hung all over the ceiling and down the walls, falling in heavy folds upon a carpet of the same material and hue. But in this chamber only, the color of the windows failed to correspond with the decorations. The panes here were scarlet -- a deep blood color. Now in no one of the seven apartments was there any lamp or candelabrum, amid the profusion of golden ornaments that lay scattered to and fro or depended from the roof. There was no light of any kind emanating from lamp or candle within the suite of chambers. But in the corridors that followed the suite, there stood, opposite to each window, a heavy tripod, bearing a brazier of fire, that projected its rays through the tinted glass and so glaringly illumined the room. And thus were produced a multitude of gaudy and fantastic appearances. But in the western or black chamber the effect of the fire-light that streamed upon the dark hangings through the blood-tinted panes, was ghastly in the extreme, and produced so wild a look upon the countenances of those who entered, that there were few of the company bold enough to set foot within its precincts at all.

It was in this apartment, also, that there stood against the western wall, a gigantic clock of ebony. Its pendulum swung to and fro with a dull, heavy, monotonous clang; and when the minute-hand made the circuit of the face, and the hour was to be stricken, there came from the brazen lungs of the clock a sound which was clear and loud and deep and exceedingly musical, but of so peculiar a note and emphasis that, at each

Masque of the Red Death

lapse of an hour, the musicians of the orchestra were constrained to pause, momentarily, in their performance, to harken to the sound; and thus the waltzers perforce ceased their evolutions; and there was a brief disconcert of the whole gay company; and, while the chimes of the clock yet rang, it was observed that the giddiest grew pale, and the more aged and sedate passed their hands over their brows as if in confused revery or meditation. But when the echoes had fully ceased, a light laughter at once pervaded the assembly; the musicians looked at each other and smiled as if at their own nervousness and folly, and made whispering vows, each to the other, that the next chiming of the clock should produce in them no similar emotion; and then, after the lapse of sixty minutes, (which embrace three thousand and six hundred seconds of the Time that flies,) there came yet another chiming of the clock, and then were the same disconcert and tremulousness and meditation as before.

But, in spite of these things, it was a gay and magnificent revel. The tastes of the duke were peculiar. He had a fine eye for colors and effects. He disregarded the decora of mere fashion. His plans were bold and fiery, and his conceptions glowed with barbaric lustre. There are some who would have thought him mad. His followers felt that he was not. It was necessary to hear and see and touch him to be sure that he was not.

He had directed, in great part, the moveable embellishments of the seven chambers, upon occasion of this great fête; and it was his own guiding taste which had given character to the masqueraders. Be sure they were grotesque. There were much glare and glitter and piquancy and phantasm -- much of what has been since seen in "Hernani." There were arabesque figures with unsuited limbs and appointments. There were delirious fancies such as the madman fashions. There were much of the beautiful, much of the wanton, much of the bizarre, something of the terrible, and not a little of that which might have excited disgust. To and fro in the seven chambers there stalked, in fact, a multitude of dreams. And these -- the dreams -- writhed in and about, taking hue from the rooms, and causing the wild music of the orchestra to seem as the echo of their steps. And, anon, there strikes the ebony clock which stands in the hall of the velvet. And then, for a moment, all is still, and all is silent save the voice of the clock. The dreams are stiff-frozen as they stand. But the echoes of the chime die away -- they have endured but an instant -- and a light, half-subdued laughter floats after them as they depart. And now again the music swells, and the dreams live, and writhe to and fro more merrily than ever, taking hue from the many tinted windows through which stream the rays from the tripods. But to the chamber which lies most westwardly of the seven, there are now none of the maskers who venture; for the night is waning away; and there flows a ruddier light through the blood-colored panes; and the blackness of the sable drapery appals; and to him whose foot falls upon the sable carpet, there comes from the near clock of ebony a muffled peal more solemnly emphatic than any which reaches their ears who indulge in the more remote gaieties of the other apartments.

But these other apartments were densely crowded, and in them beat feverishly the heart of life. And the revel went whirlingly on, until at length there commenced the sounding of midnight upon the clock. And then the music ceased, as I have told; and the evolutions of the waltzers were quieted; and there was an uneasy cessation of all things as before. But now there were twelve strokes to be sounded by the bell of the clock; and thus it happened, perhaps that more of thought crept, with more of time, into the meditations of the thoughtful among those who revelled. And thus too, it happened, perhaps, that before the last echoes of the last chime had utterly sunk into silence, there were many individuals in the crowd who had found leisure to become aware of the presence of a masked figure which had arrested the attention of no single individual before. And the rumor of this new presence having spread itself whisperingly around, there arose at length from the whole company a buzz, or murmur, expressive of disapprobation and surprise -- then, finally, of terror, of horror, and of disgust.

In an assembly of phantasms such as I have painted, it may well be supposed that no ordinary appearance could have excited such sensation. In truth the masquerade license of the night was nearly unlimited; but the figure in question had out-Heroded Herod, and gone beyond the bounds of even the prince's indefinite decorum. There are chords in the hearts of the most reckless which cannot be touched without emotion. Even with the utterly lost, to whom life and death are equally jests, there are matters of which no jest can be made. The whole company, indeed, seemed now deeply to feel that in the costume and bearing of the stranger neither wit nor propriety existed. The figure was tall and gaunt, and shrouded from head to foot in the habiliments of the grave. The mask which concealed the visage was made so nearly to resemble the countenance of a stiffened corpse that the closest scrutiny must have had difficulty in detecting the cheat. And yet all this might have been endured, if not approved, by the mad revellers around. But the mummer had gone so far as to assume the type of the Red Death. His vesture was dabbled in blood -- and his

Masque of the Red Death

broad brow, with all the features of the face, was besprinkled with the scarlet horror.

When the eyes of Prince Prospero fell upon this spectral image (which with a slow and solemn movement, as if more fully to sustain its role, stalked to and fro among the waltzers) he was seen to be convulsed, in the first moment with a strong shudder either of terror or distaste; but, in the next, his brow reddened with rage.

"Who dares?" he demanded hoarsely of the courtiers who stood near him -- "who dares insult us with this blasphemous mockery? Seize him and unmask him -- that we may know whom we have to hang at sunrise, from the battlements!"

It was in the eastern or blue chamber in which stood the Prince Prospero as he uttered these words. They rang throughout the seven rooms loudly and clearly -- for the prince was a bold and robust man, and the music had become hushed at the waving of his hand.

It was in the blue room where stood the prince, with a group of pale courtiers by his side. At first, as he spoke, there was a slight rushing movement of this group in the direction of the intruder, who, at the moment was also near at hand, and now, with deliberate and stately step, made closer approach to the speaker. But from a certain nameless awe with which the mad assumptions of the mummer had inspired the whole party, there were found none who put forth hand to seize him; so that, unimpeded, he passed within a yard of the prince's person; and, while the vast assembly, as if with one impulse, shrank from the centres of the rooms to the walls, he made his way uninterruptedly, but with the same solemn and measured step which had distinguished him from the first, through the blue chamber to the purple -- through the purple to the green -- through the green to the orange -- through this again to the white -- and even thence to the violet, ere a decided movement had been made to arrest him. It was then, however, that the Prince Prospero, maddening with rage and the shame of his own momentary cowardice, rushed hurriedly through the six chambers, while none followed him on account of a deadly terror that had seized upon all. He bore aloft a drawn dagger, and had approached, in rapid impetuosity, to within three or four feet of the retreating figure, when the latter, having attained the extremity of the velvet apartment, turned suddenly and confronted his pursuer. There was a sharp cry -- and the dagger dropped gleaming upon the sable carpet, upon which, instantly afterwards, fell prostrate in death the Prince Prospero.

Then, summoning the wild courage of despair, a throng of the revellers at once threw themselves into the black apartment, and, seizing the mummer, whose tall figure stood erect and motionless within the shadow of the ebony clock, gasped in unutterable horror at finding the grave cerements and corpse-like mask which they handled with so violent a rudeness, untenanted by any tangible form.

And now was acknowledged the presence of the Red Death. He had come like a thief in the night. And one by one dropped the revellers in the blood-bedewed halls of their revel, and died each in the despairing posture of his fall. And the life of the ebony clock went out with that of the last of the gay. And the flames of the tripods expired. And Darkness and Decay and the Red Death held illimitable dominion over all.

The Oval Portrait

By Edgar Allan Poe

THE chateau into which my valet had ventured to make forcible entrance, rather than permit me, in my desperately wounded condition, to pass a night in the open air, was one of those piles of commingled gloom and grandeur which have so long frowned among the Appennines, not less in fact than in the fancy of Mrs. Radcliffe. To all appearance it had been temporarily and very lately abandoned. We established ourselves in one of the smallest and least sumptuously furnished apartments. It lay in a remote turret of the building. Its decorations were rich, yet tattered and antique. Its walls were hung with tapestry and bedecked with manifold and multiform armorial trophies, together with an unusually great number of very spirited modern paintings in frames of rich golden arabesque. In these paintings, which depended from the walls not only in their main surfaces, but in very many nooks which the bizarre architecture of the chateau rendered necessary -- in these paintings my incipient delirium, perhaps, had caused me to take deep interest; so that I bade Pedro to close the heavy shutters of the room -- since it was already night -- to light the tongues of a tall candelabrum which stood by the head of my bed -- and to throw open far and wide the fringed curtains of black velvet which enveloped the bed itself. I wished all this done that I might resign myself, if not to sleep, at least alternately to the contemplation of these pictures, and the perusal of a small volume which had been found upon the pillow, and which purported to criticise and describe them.

Long -- long I read -- and devoutly, devotedly I gazed. Rapidly and gloriously the hours flew by and the deep midnight came. The position of the candelabrum displeased me, and outreaching my hand with difficulty, rather than disturb my slumbering valet, I placed it so as to throw its rays more fully upon the book.

But the action produced an effect altogether unanticipated. The rays of the numerous candles (for there were many) now fell within a niche of the room which had hitherto been thrown into deep shade by one of the bed-posts. I thus saw in vivid light a picture all unnoticed before. It was the portrait of a young girl just ripening into womanhood. I glanced at the

The Oval Portrait

painting hurriedly, and then closed my eyes. Why I did this was not at first apparent even to my own perception. But while my lids remained thus shut, I ran over in my mind my reason for so shutting them. It was an impulsive movement to gain time for thought -- to make sure that my vision had not deceived me -- to calm and subdue my fancy for a more sober and more certain gaze. In a very few moments I again looked fixedly at the painting.

That I now saw aright I could not and would not doubt; for the first flashing of the candles upon that canvas had seemed to dissipate the dreamy stupor which was stealing over my senses, and to startle me at once into waking life.

The portrait, I have already said, was that of a young girl. It was a mere head and shoulders, done in what is technically termed a vignette manner; much in the style of the favorite heads of Sully. The arms, the bosom, and even the ends of the radiant hair melted imperceptibly into the vague yet deep shadow which formed the back-ground of the whole. The frame was oval, richly gilded and filigreed in Moresque. As a thing of art nothing could be more admirable than the painting itself. But it could have been neither the execution of the work, nor the immortal beauty of the countenance, which had so suddenly and so vehemently moved me. Least of all, could it have been that my fancy, shaken from its half slumber, had mistaken the head for that of a living person. I saw at once that the peculiarities of the design, of the vignetting, and of the frame, must have instantly dispelled such idea -- must have prevented even its momentary entertainment. Thinking earnestly upon these points, I remained, for an hour perhaps, half sitting, half reclining, with my vision riveted upon the portrait. At length, satisfied with the true secret of its effect, I fell back within the bed. I had found the spell of the picture in an absolute life-likeliness of expression, which, at first startling, finally confounded, subdued, and appalled me. With deep and reverent awe I replaced the candelabrum in its former position. The cause of my deep agitation being thus shut from view, I sought eagerly the volume which discussed the paintings and their histories. Turning to the number which designated the oval portrait, I there read the vague and quaint words which follow:

"She was a maiden of rarest beauty, and not more lovely than full of glee. And evil was the hour when she saw, and loved, and wedded the painter. He, passionate, studious, austere, and having already a bride in his Art; she a maiden of rarest beauty, and not more lovely than full of glee; all light and

The Oval Portrait

smiles, and frolicsome as the young fawn; loving and cherishing all things; hating only the Art which was her rival; dreading only the pallet and brushes and other untoward instruments which deprived her of the countenance of her lover. It was thus a terrible thing for this lady to hear the painter speak of his desire to pourtray even his young bride. But she was humble and obedient, and sat meekly for many weeks in the dark, high turret-chamber where the light dripped upon the pale canvas only from overhead. But he, the painter, took glory in his work, which went on from hour to hour, and from day to day. And he was a passionate, and wild, and moody man, who became lost in reveries; so that he would not see that the light which fell so ghastly in that lone turret withered the health and the spirits of his bride, who pined visibly to all but him. Yet she smiled on and still on, uncomplainingly, because she saw that the painter (who had high renown) took a fervid and burning pleasure in his task, and wrought day and night to depict her who so loved him, yet who grew daily more dispirited and weak. And in sooth some who beheld the portrait spoke of its resemblance in low words, as of a mighty marvel, and a proof not less of the power of the painter than of his deep love for her whom he depicted so surpassingly well. But at length, as the labor drew nearer to its conclusion, there were admitted none into the turret; for the painter had grown wild with the ardor of his work, and turned his eyes from canvas merely, even to regard the countenance of his wife. And he would not see that the tints which he spread upon the canvas were drawn from the cheeks of her who sate beside him. And when many weeks bad passed, and but little remained to do, save one brush upon the mouth and one tint upon the eye, the spirit of the lady again flickered up as the flame within the socket of the lamp. And then the brush was given, and then the tint was placed; and, for one moment, the painter stood entranced before the work which he had wrought; but in the next, while he yet gazed, he grew tremulous and very pallid, and aghast, and crying with a loud voice, 'This is indeed Life itself!' turned suddenly to regard his beloved: -- She was dead!

The Pit and the Pendulum

By Edgar Allan Poe

Impia tortorum longos hic turba furores

Sanguinis innocui, non satiata, aluit.

Sospite nunc patria, fracto nunc funeris antro,

Mors ubi dira fuit vita salusque patent.

[Quatrain composed for the gates of a market to be erected upon the site of the Jacobin Club House at Paris.]

I WAS sick -- sick unto death with that long agony; and when they at length unbound me, and I was permitted to sit, I felt that my senses were leaving me. The sentence -- the dread sentence of death -- was the last of distinct accentuation which reached my ears. After that, the sound of the inquisitorial voices seemed merged in one dreamy indeterminate hum. It conveyed to my soul the idea of revolution -- perhaps from its association in fancy with the burr of a mill wheel. This only for a brief period; for presently I heard no more. Yet, for a while, I saw; but with how terrible an exaggeration! I saw the lips of the black-robed judges. They appeared to me white -- whiter than the sheet upon which I trace these words -- and thin even to grotesqueness; thin with the intensity of their expression of firmness -- of immoveable resolution -- of stern contempt of human torture. I saw that the decrees of what to me was Fate, were still issuing from those lips. I saw them writhe with a deadly locution. I saw them fashion the syllables of my name; and I shuddered because no sound succeeded. I saw, too, for a few moments of delirious horror, the soft and nearly imperceptible waving of the sable draperies which enwrapped the walls of the apartment. And then my vision fell upon the seven tall candles upon the table. At first they wore the aspect of charity, and seemed white and slender angels who would save me; but then, all at once, there came a most deadly nausea over my spirit, and I felt every fibre in my frame thrill as if I had

The Pit and the Pendulum

touched the wire of a galvanic battery, while the angel forms became meaningless spectres, with heads of flame, and I saw that from them there would be no help. And then there stole into my fancy, like a rich musical note, the thought of what sweet rest there must be in the grave. The thought came gently and stealthily, and it seemed long before it attained full appreciation; but just as my spirit came at length properly to feel and entertain it, the figures of the judges vanished, as if magically, from before me; the tall candles sank into nothingness; their flames went out utterly; the blackness of darkness supervened; all sensations appeared swallowed up in a mad rushing descent as of the soul into Hades. Then silence, and stillness, night were the universe.

I had swooned; but still will not say that all of consciousness was lost. What of it there remained I will not attempt to define, or even to describe; yet all was not lost. In the deepest slumber -- no! In delirium -- no! In a swoon -- no! In death -- no! even in the grave all is not lost. Else there is no immortality for man. Arousing from the most profound of slumbers, we break the gossamer web of some dream. Yet in a second afterward, (so frail may that web have been) we remember not that we have dreamed. In the return to life from the swoon there are two stages; first, that of the sense of mental or spiritual; secondly, that of the sense of physical, existence. It seems probable that if, upon reaching the second stage, we could recall the impressions of the first, we should find these impressions eloquent in memories of the gulf beyond. And that gulf is -- what? How at least shall we distinguish its shadows from those of the tomb? But if the impressions of what I have termed the first stage, are not, at will, recalled, yet, after long interval, do they not come unbidden, while we marvel whence they come? He who has never swooned, is not he who finds strange palaces and wildly familiar faces in coals that glow; is not he who beholds floating in mid-air the sad visions that the many may not view; is not he who ponders over the perfume of some novel flower -- is not he whose brain grows bewildered with the meaning of some musical cadence which has never before arrested his attention.

Amid frequent and thoughtful endeavors to remember; amid earnest struggles to regather some token of the state of seeming nothingness into which my soul had lapsed, there have been moments when I have dreamed of success; there have been brief, very brief periods when I have conjured up remembrances which the lucid reason of a later epoch assures me could have had reference only to that condition of seeming unconsciousness. These shadows of memory tell, indistinctly, of tall figures that lifted and bore me in silence down -- down --

still down -- till a hideous dizziness oppressed me at the mere idea of the interminableness of the descent. They tell also of a vague horror at my heart, on account of that heart's unnatural stillness. Then comes a sense of sudden motionlessness throughout all things; as if those who bore me (a ghastly train!) had outrun, in their descent, the limits of the limitless, and paused from the wearisomeness of their toil. After this I call to mind flatness and dampness; and then all is madness -- the madness of a memory which busies itself among forbidden things.

Very suddenly there came back to my soul motion and sound -- the tumultuous motion of the heart, and, in my ears, the sound of its beating. Then a pause in which all is blank. Then again sound, and motion, and touch -- a tingling sensation pervading my frame. Then the mere consciousness of existence, without thought -- a condition which lasted long. Then, very suddenly, thought, and shuddering terror, and earnest endeavor to comprehend my true state. Then a strong desire to lapse into insensibility. Then a rushing revival of soul and a successful effort to move. And now a full memory of the trial, of the judges, of the sable draperies, of the sentence, of the sickness, of the swoon. Then entire forgetfulness of all that followed; of all that a later day and much earnestness of endeavor have enabled me vaguely to recall.

So far, I had not opened my eyes. I felt that I lay upon my back, unbound. I reached out my hand, and it fell heavily upon something damp and hard. There I suffered it to remain for many minutes, while I strove to imagine where and what I could be. I longed, yet dared not to employ my vision. I dreaded the first glance at objects around me. It was not that I feared to look upon things horrible, but that I grew aghast lest there should be nothing to see. At length, with a wild desperation at heart, I quickly unclosed my eyes. My worst thoughts, then, were confirmed. The blackness of eternal night encompassed me. I struggled for breath. The intensity of the darkness seemed to oppress and stifle me. The atmosphere was intolerably close. I still lay quietly, and made effort to exercise my reason. I brought to mind the inquisitorial proceedings, and attempted from that point to deduce my real condition. The sentence had passed; and it appeared to me that a very long interval of time had since elapsed. Yet not for a moment did I suppose myself actually dead. Such a supposition, notwithstanding what we read in fiction, is altogether inconsistent with real existence; -- but where and in what state was I? The condemned to death, I knew, perished usually at the autos-da-fe, and one of these had been held on the very night of the day of my trial. Had I been

The Pit and the Pendulum

remanded to my dungeon, to await the next sacrifice, which would not take place for many months? This I at once saw could not be. Victims had been in immediate demand. Moreover, my dungeon, as well as all the condemned cells at Toledo, had stone floors, and light was not altogether excluded.

A fearful idea now suddenly drove the blood in torrents upon my heart, and for a brief period, I once more relapsed into insensibility. Upon recovering, I at once started to my feet, trembling convulsively in every fibre. I thrust my arms wildly above and around me in all directions. I felt nothing; yet dreaded to move a step, lest I should be impeded by the walls of a tomb. Perspiration burst from every pore, and stood in cold big beads upon my forehead. The agony of suspense grew at length intolerable, and I cautiously moved forward, with my arms extended, and my eyes straining from their sockets, in the hope of catching some faint ray of light. I proceeded for many paces; but still all was blackness and vacancy. I breathed more freely. It seemed evident that mine was not, at least, the most hideous of fates.

And now, as I still continued to step cautiously onward, there came thronging upon my recollection a thousand vague rumors of the horrors of Toledo. Of the dungeons there had been strange things narrated -- fables I had always deemed them -- but yet strange, and too ghastly to repeat, save in a whisper. Was I left to perish of starvation in this subterranean world of darkness; or what fate, perhaps even more fearful, awaited me? That the result would be death, and a death of more than customary bitterness, I knew too well the character of my judges to doubt. The mode and the hour were all that occupied or distracted me.

My outstretched hands at length encountered some solid obstruction. It was a wall, seemingly of stone masonry -- very smooth, slimy, and cold. I followed it up; stepping with all the careful distrust with which certain antique narratives had inspired me. This process, however, afforded me no means of ascertaining the dimensions of my dungeon; as I might make its circuit, and return to the point whence I set out, without being aware of the fact; so perfectly uniform seemed the wall. I therefore sought the knife which had been in my pocket, when led into the inquisitorial chamber; but it was gone; my clothes had been exchanged for a wrapper of coarse serge. I had thought of forcing the blade in some minute crevice of the masonry, so as to identify my point of departure. The difficulty, nevertheless, was but trivial; although, in the disorder of my fancy, it seemed at first insuperable. I tore a part of the hem

The Pit and the Pendulum

from the robe and placed the fragment at full length, and at right angles to the wall. In groping my way around the prison, I could not fail to encounter this rag upon completing the circuit. So, at least I thought: but I had not counted upon the extent of the dungeon, or upon my own weakness. The ground was moist and slippery. I staggered onward for some time, when I stumbled and fell. My excessive fatigue induced me to remain prostrate; and sleep soon overtook me as I lay.

Upon awaking, and stretching forth an arm, I found beside me a loaf and a pitcher with water. I was too much exhausted to reflect upon this circumstance, but ate and drank with avidity. Shortly afterward, I resumed my tour around the prison, and with much toil came at last upon the fragment of the serge. Up to the period when I fell I had counted fifty-two paces, and upon resuming my walk, I had counted forty-eight more; -- when I arrived at the rag. There were in all, then, a hundred paces; and, admitting two paces to the yard, I presumed the dungeon to be fifty yards in circuit. I had met, however, with many angles in the wall, and thus I could form no guess at the shape of the vault; for vault I could not help supposing it to be.

I had little object -- certainly no hope these researches; but a vague curiosity prompted me to continue them. Quitting the wall, I resolved to cross the area of the enclosure. At first I proceeded with extreme caution, for the floor, although seemingly of solid material, was treacherous with slime. At length, however, I took courage, and did not hesitate to step firmly; endeavoring to cross in as direct a line as possible. I had advanced some ten or twelve paces in this manner, when the remnant of the torn hem of my robe became entangled between my legs. I stepped on it, and fell violently on my face.

In the confusion attending my fall, I did not immediately apprehend a somewhat startling circumstance, which yet, in a few seconds afterward, and while I still lay prostrate, arrested my attention. It was this -- my chin rested upon the floor of the prison, but my lips and the upper portion of my head, although seemingly at a less elevation than the chin, touched nothing. At the same time my forehead seemed bathed in a clammy vapor, and the peculiar smell of decayed fungus arose to my nostrils. I put forward my arm, and shuddered to find that I had fallen at the very brink of a circular pit, whose extent, of course, I had no means of ascertaining at the moment. Groping about the masonry just below the margin, I succeeded in dislodging a small fragment, and let it fall into the abyss. For many seconds I hearkened to its reverberations as it dashed against the sides of the chasm in its descent; at length there was a sullen plunge into

The Pit and the Pendulum

water, succeeded by loud echoes. At the same moment there came a sound resembling the quick opening, and as rapid closing of a door overhead, while a faint gleam of light flashed suddenly through the gloom, and as suddenly faded away.

I saw clearly the doom which had been prepared for me, and congratulated myself upon the timely accident by which I had escaped. Another step before my fall, and the world had seen me no more. And the death just avoided, was of that very character which I had regarded as fabulous and frivolous in the tales respecting the Inquisition. To the victims of its tyranny, there was the choice of death with its direst physical agonies, or death with its most hideous moral horrors. I had been reserved for the latter. By long suffering my nerves had been unstrung, until I trembled at the sound of my own voice, and had become in every respect a fitting subject for the species of torture which awaited me.

Shaking in every limb, I groped my way back to the wall; resolving there to perish rather than risk the terrors of the wells, of which my imagination now pictured many in various positions about the dungeon. In other conditions of mind I might have had courage to end my misery at once by a plunge into one of these abysses; but now I was the veriest of cowards. Neither could I forget what I had read of these pits -- that the sudden extinction of life formed no part of their most horrible plan.

Agitation of spirit kept me awake for many long hours; but at length I again slumbered. Upon arousing, I found by my side, as before, a loaf and a pitcher of water. A burning thirst consumed me, and I emptied the vessel at a draught. It must have been drugged; for scarcely had I drunk, before I became irresistibly drowsy. A deep sleep fell upon me -- a sleep like that of death. How long it lasted of course, I know not; but when, once again, I unclosed my eyes, the objects around me were visible. By a wild sulphurous lustre, the origin of which I could not at first determine, I was enabled to see the extent and aspect of the prison.

In its size I had been greatly mistaken. The whole circuit of its walls did not exceed twenty-five yards. For some minutes this fact occasioned me a world of vain trouble; vain indeed! for what could be of less importance, under the terrible circumstances which environed me, then the mere dimensions of my dungeon? But my soul took a wild interest in trifles, and I busied myself in endeavors to account for the error I had committed in my measurement. The truth at length flashed upon me. In my first attempt at exploration I had counted fifty-two paces, up to the period when I fell; I must then have been within a pace or two of the fragment of serge; in fact, I had nearly performed the circuit of the vault. I then slept, and upon awaking, I must have returned upon my steps -- thus supposing the circuit nearly double what it actually was. My confusion of mind prevented me from observing that I began my tour with the wall to the left, and ended it with the wall to the right.

    I had been deceived, too, in respect to the shape of the enclosure. In feeling my way I had found many angles, and thus deduced an idea of great irregularity; so potent is the effect of total darkness upon one arousing from lethargy or sleep! The angles were simply those of a few slight depressions, or niches, at odd intervals. The general shape of the prison was square. What I had taken for masonry seemed now to be iron, or some other metal, in huge plates, whose sutures or joints occasioned the depression. The entire surface of this metallic enclosure was rudely daubed in all the hideous and repulsive devices to which the charnel superstition of the monks has given rise. The figures of fiends in aspects of menace, with skeleton forms, and other more really fearful images, overspread and disfigured the walls. I observed that the outlines of these monstrosities were sufficiently distinct, but that the colors seemed faded and blurred, as if from the effects of a damp atmosphere. I now noticed the floor, too, which was of stone. In the centre yawned the circular pit from whose jaws I had escaped; but it was the only one in the dungeon.

    All this I saw indistinctly and by much effort: for my personal condition had been greatly changed during slumber. I now lay upon my back, and at full length, on a species of low framework of wood. To this I was securely bound by a long strap resembling a surcingle. It passed in many convolutions about my limbs and body, leaving at liberty only my head, and my left arm to such extent that I could, by dint of much exertion, supply myself with food from an earthen dish which lay by my side on the floor. I saw, to my horror, that the pitcher had been removed. I say to my horror; for I was consumed with intolerable thirst. This thirst it appeared to be the design of my persecutors to stimulate: for the food in the dish was meat pungently seasoned.

    Looking upward, I surveyed the ceiling of my prison. It was some thirty or forty feet overhead, and constructed much as the side walls. In one of its panels a very singular figure riveted my whole attention. It was the painted figure of Time as he is commonly represented, save that, in lieu of a scythe, he held

The Pit and the Pendulum

what, at a casual glance, I supposed to be the pictured image of a huge pendulum such as we see on antique clocks. There was something, however, in the appearance of this machine which caused me to regard it more attentively. While I gazed directly upward at it (for its position was immediately over my own) I fancied that I saw it in motion. In an instant afterward the fancy was confirmed. Its sweep was brief, and of course slow. I watched it for some minutes, somewhat in fear, but more in wonder. Wearied at length with observing its dull movement, I turned my eyes upon the other objects in the cell.

A slight noise attracted my notice, and, looking to the floor, I saw several enormous rats traversing it. They had issued from the well, which lay just within view to my right. Even then, while I gazed, they came up in troops, hurriedly, with ravenous eyes, allured by the scent of the meat. From this it required much effort and attention to scare them away.

It might have been half an hour, perhaps even an hour, (for I could take but imperfect note of time) before I again cast my eyes upward. What I then saw confounded and amazed me. The sweep of the pendulum had increased in extent by nearly a yard. As a natural consequence, its velocity was also much greater. But what mainly disturbed me was the idea that had perceptibly descended. I now observed -- with what horror it is needless to say -- that its nether extremity was formed of a crescent of glittering steel, about a foot in length from horn to horn; the horns upward, and the under edge evidently as keen as that of a razor. Like a razor also, it seemed massy and heavy, tapering from the edge into a solid and broad structure above. It was appended to a weighty rod of brass, and the whole hissed as it swung through the air.

I could no longer doubt the doom prepared for me by monkish ingenuity in torture. My cognizance of the pit had become known to the inquisitorial agents -- the pit whose horrors had been destined for so bold a recusant as myself -- the pit, typical of hell, and regarded by rumor as the Ultima Thule of all their punishments. The plunge into this pit I had avoided by the merest of accidents, I knew that surprise, or entrapment into torment, formed an important portion of all the grotesquerie of these dungeon deaths. Having failed to fall, it was no part of the demon plan to hurl me into the abyss; and thus (there being no alternative) a different and a milder destruction awaited me. Milder! I half smiled in my agony as I thought of such application of such a term.

The Pit and the Pendulum

What boots it to tell of the long, long hours of horror more than mortal, during which I counted the rushing vibrations of the steel! Inch by inch -- line by line -- with a descent only appreciable at intervals that seemed ages -- down and still down it came! Days passed -- it might have been that many days passed -- ere it swept so closely over me as to fan me with its acrid breath. The odor of the sharp steel forced itself into my nostrils. I prayed -- I wearied heaven with my prayer for its more speedy descent. I grew frantically mad, and struggled to force myself upward against the sweep of the fearful scimitar. And then I fell suddenly calm, and lay smiling at the glittering death, as a child at some rare bauble.

There was another interval of utter insensibility; it was brief; for, upon again lapsing into life there had been no perceptible descent in the pendulum. But it might have been long; for I knew there were demons who took note of my swoon, and who could have arrested the vibration at pleasure. Upon my recovery, too, I felt very -- oh, inexpressibly sick and weak, as if through long inanition. Even amid the agonies of that period, the human nature craved food. With painful effort I outstretched my left arm as far as my bonds permitted, and took possession of the small remnant which had been spared me by the rats. As I put a portion of it within my lips, there rushed to my mind a half formed thought of joy -- of hope. Yet what business had I with hope? It was, as I say, a half formed thought -- man has many such which are never completed. I felt that it was of joy -- of hope; but felt also that it had perished in its formation. In vain I struggled to perfect -- to regain it. Long suffering had nearly annihilated all my ordinary powers of mind. I was an imbecile -- an idiot.

The vibration of the pendulum was at right angles to my length. I saw that the crescent was designed to cross the region of the heart. It would fray the serge of my robe -- it would return and repeat its operations -- again -- and again. Notwithstanding terrifically wide sweep (some thirty feet or more) and the hissing vigor of its descent, sufficient to sunder these very walls of iron, still the fraying of my robe would be all that, for several minutes, it would accomplish. And at this thought I paused. I dared not go farther than this reflection. I dwelt upon it with a pertinacity of attention -- as if, in so dwelling, I could arrest here the descent of the steel. I forced myself to ponder upon the sound of the crescent as it should pass across the garment -- upon the peculiar thrilling sensation which the friction of cloth produces on the nerves. I pondered upon all this frivolity until my teeth were on edge.

The Pit and the Pendulum

Down -- steadily down it crept. I took a frenzied pleasure in contrasting its downward with its lateral velocity. To the right -- to the left -- far and wide -- with the shriek of a damned spirit; to my heart with the stealthy pace of the tiger! I alternately laughed and howled as the one or the other idea grew predominant.

Down -- certainly, relentlessly down! It vibrated within three inches of my bosom! I struggled violently, furiously, to free my left arm. This was free only from the elbow to the hand. I could reach the latter, from the platter beside me, to my mouth, with great effort, but no farther. Could I have broken the fastenings above the elbow, I would have seized and attempted to arrest the pendulum. I might as well have attempted to arrest an avalanche!

Down -- still unceasingly -- still inevitably down! I gasped and struggled at each vibration. I shrunk convulsively at its every sweep. My eyes followed its outward or upward whirls with the eagerness of the most unmeaning despair; they closed themselves spasmodically at the descent, although death would have been a relief, oh! how unspeakable! Still I quivered in every nerve to think how slight a sinking of the machinery would precipitate that keen, glistening axe upon my bosom. It was hope that prompted the nerve to quiver -- the frame to shrink. It was hope -- the hope that triumphs on the rack -- that whispers to the death-condemned even in the dungeons of the Inquisition.

I saw that some ten or twelve vibrations would bring the steel in actual contact with my robe, and with this observation there suddenly came over my spirit all the keen, collected calmness of despair. For the first time during many hours -- or perhaps days -- I thought. It now occurred to me that the bandage, or surcingle, which enveloped me, was unique. I was tied by no separate cord. The first stroke of the razorlike crescent athwart any portion of the band, would so detach it that it might be unwound from my person by means of my left hand. But how fearful, in that case, the proximity of the steel! The result of the slightest struggle how deadly! Was it likely, moreover, that the minions of the torturer had not foreseen and provided for this possibility! Was it probable that the bandage crossed my bosom in the track of the pendulum? Dreading to find my faint, and, as it seemed, in last hope frustrated, I so far elevated my head as to obtain a distinct view of my breast. The surcingle enveloped my limbs and body close in all directions -- save in the path of the destroying crescent.

Scarcely had I dropped my head back into its original position, when there flashed upon my mind what I cannot better describe than as the unformed half of that idea of deliverance to which I have previously alluded, and of which a moiety only floated indeterminately through my brain when I raised food to my burning lips. The whole thought was now present -- feeble, scarcely sane, scarcely definite, -- but still entire. I proceeded at once, with the nervous energy of despair, to attempt its execution.

For many hours the immediate vicinity of the low framework upon which I lay, had been literally swarming with rats. They were wild, bold, ravenous; their red eyes glaring upon me as if they waited but for motionlessness on my part to make me their prey. "To what food," I thought, "have they been accustomed in the well?"

They had devoured, in spite of all my efforts to prevent them, all but a small remnant of the contents of the dish. I had fallen into an habitual see-saw, or wave of the hand about the platter: and, at length, the unconscious uniformity of the movement deprived it of effect. In their voracity the vermin frequently fastened their sharp fangs in my fingers. With the particles of the oily and spicy viand which now remained, I thoroughly rubbed the bandage wherever I could reach it; then, raising my hand from the floor, I lay breathlessly still.

At first the ravenous animals were startled and terrified at the change -- at the cessation of movement. They shrank alarmedly back; many sought the well. But this was only for a moment. I had not counted in vain upon their voracity. Observing that I remained without motion, one or two of the boldest leaped upon the frame-work, and smelt at the surcingle. This seemed the signal for a general rush. Forth from the well they hurried in fresh troops. They clung to the wood -- they overran it, and leaped in hundreds upon my person. The measured movement of the pendulum disturbed them not at all. Avoiding its strokes they busied themselves with the anointed bandage. They pressed -- they swarmed upon me in ever accumulating heaps. They writhed upon my throat; their cold lips sought my own; I was half stifled by their thronging pressure; disgust, for which the world has no name, swelled my bosom, and chilled, with a heavy clamminess, my heart. Yet one minute, and I felt that the struggle would be over. Plainly I perceived the loosening of the bandage. I knew that in more than one place it must be already severed. With a more than human resolution I lay still.

The Pit and the Pendulum

Nor had I erred in my calculations -- nor had I endured in vain. I at length felt that I was free. The surcingle hung in ribands from my body. But the stroke of the pendulum already pressed upon my bosom. It had divided the serge of the robe. It had cut through the linen beneath. Twice again it swung, and a sharp sense of pain shot through every nerve. But the moment of escape had arrived. At a wave of my hand my deliverers hurried tumultuously away. With a steady movement -- cautious, sidelong, shrinking, and slow -- I slid from the embrace of the bandage and beyond the reach of the scimitar. For the moment, at least, I was free.

Free! -- and in the grasp of the Inquisition! I had scarcely stepped from my wooden bed of horror upon the stone floor of the prison, when the motion of the hellish machine ceased and I beheld it drawn up, by some invisible force, through the ceiling. This was a lesson which I took desperately to heart. My every motion was undoubtedly watched. Free! -- I had but escaped death in one form of agony, to be delivered unto worse than death in some other. With that thought I rolled my eyes nervously around on the barriers of iron that hemmed me in. Something unusual -- some change which, at first, I could not appreciate distinctly -- it was obvious, had taken place in the apartment. For many minutes of a dreamy and trembling abstraction, I busied myself in vain, unconnected conjecture. During this period, I became aware, for the first time, of the origin of the sulphurous light which illumined the cell. It proceeded from a fissure, about half an inch in width, extending entirely around the prison at the base of the walls, which thus appeared, and were, completely separated from the floor. I endeavored, but of course in vain, to look through the aperture.

As I arose from the attempt, the mystery of the alteration in the chamber broke at once upon my understanding. I have observed that, although the outlines of the figures upon the walls were sufficiently distinct, yet the colors seemed blurred and indefinite. These colors had now assumed, and were momentarily assuming, a startling and most intense brilliancy, that gave to the spectral and fiendish portraitures an aspect that might have thrilled even firmer nerves than my own. Demon eyes, of a wild and ghastly vivacity, glared upon me in a thousand directions, where none had been visible before, and gleamed with the lurid lustre of a fire that I could not force my imagination to regard as unreal.

Unreal! -- Even while I breathed there came to my nostrils the breath of the vapour of heated iron! A suffocating odour pervaded the prison! A deeper glow settled each moment in the eyes that glared at my agonies! A richer tint of crimson diffused itself over the pictured horrors of blood. I panted! I gasped for breath! There could be no doubt of the design of my tormentors -- oh! most unrelenting! oh! most demoniac of men! I shrank from the glowing metal to the centre of the cell. Amid the thought of the fiery destruction that impended, the idea of the coolness of the well came over my soul like balm. I rushed to its deadly brink. I threw my straining vision below. The glare from the enkindled roof illumined its inmost recesses. Yet, for a wild moment, did my spirit refuse to comprehend the meaning of what I saw. At length it forced -- it wrestled its way into my soul -- it burned itself in upon my shuddering reason. -- Oh! for a voice to speak! -- oh! horror! -- oh! any horror but this! With a shriek, I rushed from the margin, and buried my face in my hands -- weeping bitterly.

The heat rapidly increased, and once again I looked up, shuddering as with a fit of the ague. There had been a second change in the cell -- and now the change was obviously in the form. As before, it was in vain that I, at first, endeavoured to appreciate or understand what was taking place. But not long was I left in doubt. The Inquisitorial vengeance had been hurried by my two-fold escape, and there was to be no more dallying with the King of Terrors. The room had been square. I saw that two of its iron angles were now acute -- two, consequently, obtuse. The fearful difference quickly increased with a low rumbling or moaning sound. In an instant the apartment had shifted its form into that of a lozenge. But the alteration stopped not here-I neither hoped nor desired it to stop. I could have clasped the red walls to my bosom as a garment of eternal peace. "Death," I said, "any death but that of the pit!" Fool! might I have not known that into the pit it was the object of the burning iron to urge me? Could I resist its glow? or, if even that, could I withstand its pressure And now, flatter and flatter grew the lozenge, with a rapidity that left me no time for contemplation. Its centre, and of course, its greatest width, came just over the yawning gulf. I shrank back -- but the closing walls pressed me resistlessly onward. At length for my seared and writhing body there was no longer an inch of foothold on the firm floor of the prison. I struggled no more, but the agony of my soul found vent in one loud, long, and final scream of despair. I felt that I tottered upon the brink -- I averted my eyes --

There was a discordant hum of human voices! There was a loud blast as of many trumpets! There was a harsh grating as of a thousand thunders! The fiery walls rushed back! An outstretched arm caught my own as I fell, fainting, into the abyss. It was that of General Lasalle. The French army had entered Toledo. The Inquisition was in the hands of its enemies.

The Black Cat

By Edgar Allan Poe

FOR the most wild, yet most homely narrative which I am about to pen, I neither expect nor solicit belief. Mad indeed would I be to expect it, in a case where my very senses reject their own evidence. Yet, mad am I not -- and very surely do I not dream. But to-morrow I die, and to-day I would unburthen my soul. My immediate purpose is to place before the world, plainly, succinctly, and without comment, a series of mere household events. In their consequences, these events have terrified -- have tortured -- have destroyed me. Yet I will not attempt to expound them. To me, they have presented little but Horror -- to many they will seem less terrible than barroques. Hereafter, perhaps, some intellect may be found which will reduce my phantasm to the common-place -- some intellect more calm, more logical, and far less excitable than my own, which will perceive, in the circumstances I detail with awe, nothing more than an ordinary succession of very natural causes and effects.

From my infancy I was noted for the docility and humanity of my disposition. My tenderness of heart was even so conspicuous as to make me the jest of my companions. I was especially fond of animals, and was indulged by my parents with a great variety of pets. With these I spent most of my time, and never was so happy as when feeding and caressing them. This peculiarity of character grew with my growth, and, in my manhood, I derived from it one of my principal sources of pleasure. To those who have cherished an affection for a faithful and sagacious dog, I need hardly be at the trouble of explaining the nature or the intensity of the gratification thus derivable. There is something in the unselfish and self-sacrificing love of a brute, which goes directly to the heart of him who has had frequent occasion to test the paltry friendship and gossamer fidelity of mere Man.

I married early, and was happy to find in my wife a disposition not uncongenial with my own. Observing my partiality for domestic pets, she lost no opportunity of procuring those of the most agreeable kind. We had birds, gold-fish, a fine dog, rabbits, a small monkey, and a cat.

The Black Cat

This latter was a remarkably large and beautiful animal, entirely black, and sagacious to an astonishing degree. In speaking of his intelligence, my wife, who at heart was not a little tinctured with superstition, made frequent allusion to the ancient popular notion, which regarded all black cats as witches in disguise. Not that she was ever serious upon this point -- and I mention the matter at all for no better reason than that it happens, just now, to be remembered.

Pluto -- this was the cat's name -- was my favorite pet and playmate. I alone fed him, and he attended me wherever I went about the house. It was even with difficulty that I could prevent him from following me through the streets.

Our friendship lasted, in this manner, for several years, during which my general temperament and character -- through the instrumentality of the Fiend Intemperance -- had (I blush to confess it) experienced a radical alteration for the worse. I grew, day by day, more moody, more irritable, more regardless of the feelings of others. I suffered myself to use intemperate language to my wife. At length, I even offered her personal violence. My pets, of course, were made to feel the change in my disposition. I not only neglected, but ill-used them. For Pluto, however, I still retained sufficient regard to restrain me from maltreating him, as I made no scruple of maltreating the rabbits, the monkey, or even the dog, when by accident, or through affection, they came in my way. But my disease grew upon me -- for what disease is like Alcohol ! -- and at length even Pluto, who was now becoming old, and consequently somewhat peevish -- even Pluto began to experience the effects of my ill temper.

One night, returning home, much intoxicated, from one of my haunts about town, I fancied that the cat avoided my presence. I seized him; when, in his fright at my violence, he inflicted a slight wound upon my hand with his teeth. The fury of a demon instantly possessed me. I knew myself no longer. My original soul seemed, at once, to take its flight from my body; and a more than fiendish malevolence, gin-nurtured, thrilled every fibre of my frame. I took from my waistcoat-pocket a pen-knife, opened it, grasped the poor beast by the throat, and deliberately cut one of its eyes from the socket ! I blush, I burn, I shudder, while I pen the damnable atrocity.

When reason returned with the morning -- when I had slept off the fumes of the night's debauch -- I experienced a sentiment half of horror, half of remorse, for the crime of which I had been guilty; but it was, at best, a feeble and equivocal feeling, and the

The Black Cat

soul remained untouched. I again plunged into excess, and soon drowned in wine all memory of the deed.

In the meantime the cat slowly recovered. The socket of the lost eye presented, it is true, a frightful appearance, but he no longer appeared to suffer any pain. He went about the house as usual, but, as might be expected, fled in extreme terror at my approach. I had so much of my old heart left, as to be at first grieved by this evident dislike on the part of a creature which had once so loved me. But this feeling soon gave place to irritation. And then came, as if to my final and irrevocable overthrow, the spirit of PERVERSENESS. Of this spirit philosophy takes no account. Yet I am not more sure that my soul lives, than I am that perverseness is one of the primitive impulses of the human heart -- one of the indivisible primary faculties, or sentiments, which give direction to the character of Man. Who has not, a hundred times, found himself committing a vile or a silly action, for no other reason than because he knows he should not? Have we not a perpetual inclination, in the teeth of our best judgment, to violate that which is Law, merely because we understand it to be such? This spirit of perverseness, I say, came to my final overthrow. It was this unfathomable longing of the soul to vex itself -- to offer violence to its own nature -- to do wrong for the wrong's sake only -- that urged me to continue and finally to consummate the injury I had inflicted upon the unoffending brute. One morning, in cool blood, I slipped a noose about its neck and hung it to the limb of a tree; -- hung it with the tears streaming from my eyes, and with the bitterest remorse at my heart; -- hung it because I knew that it had loved me, and because I felt it had given me no reason of offence; -- hung it because I knew that in so doing I was committing a sin -- a deadly sin that would so jeopardize my immortal soul as to place it -- if such a thing were possible -- even beyond the reach of the infinite mercy of the Most Merciful and Most Terrible God.

On the night of the day on which this cruel deed was done, I was aroused from sleep by the cry of fire. The curtains of my bed were in flames. The whole house was blazing. It was with great difficulty that my wife, a servant, and myself, made our escape from the conflagration. The destruction was complete. My entire worldly wealth was swallowed up, and I resigned myself thenceforward to despair.

I am above the weakness of seeking to establish a sequence of cause and effect, between the disaster and the atrocity. But I am detailing a chain of facts -- and wish not to leave even a possible link imperfect. On the day succeeding the fire, I visited the ruins. The walls, with one exception, had fallen in. This exception was found in a compartment wall, not very thick, which stood about the middle of the house, and against which had rested the head of my bed. The plastering had here, in great measure, resisted the action of the fire -- a fact which I attributed to its having been recently spread. About this wall a dense crowd were collected, and many persons seemed to be examining a particular portion of it with very minute and eager attention. The words "strange!" "singular!" and other similar expressions, excited my curiosity. I approached and saw, as if graven in bas relief upon the white surface, the figure of a gigantic cat. The impression was given with an accuracy truly marvellous. There was a rope about the animal's neck.

When I first beheld this apparition -- for I could scarcely regard it as less -- my wonder and my terror were extreme. But at length reflection came to my aid. The cat, I remembered, had been hung in a garden adjacent to the house. Upon the alarm of fire, this garden had been immediately filled by the crowd -- by some one of whom the animal must have been cut from the tree and thrown, through an open window, into my chamber. This had probably been done with the view of arousing me from sleep. The falling of other walls had compressed the victim of my cruelty into the substance of the freshly-spread plaster; the lime of which, with the flames, and the ammonia from the carcass, had then accomplished the portraiture as I saw it.

Although I thus readily accounted to my reason, if not altogether to my conscience, for the startling fact just detailed, it did not the less fail to make a deep impression upon my fancy. For months I could not rid myself of the phantasm of the cat; and, during this period, there came back into my spirit a half-sentiment that seemed, but was not, remorse. I went so far as to regret the loss of the animal, and to look about me, among the vile haunts which I now habitually frequented, for another pet of the same species, and of somewhat similar appearance, with which to supply its place.

One night as I sat, half stupified, in a den of more than infamy, my attention was suddenly drawn to some black object, reposing upon the head of one of the immense hogsheads of Gin, or of Rum, which constituted the chief furniture of the apartment. I had been looking steadily at the top of this hogshead for some minutes, and what now caused me surprise was the fact that I had not sooner perceived the object thereupon. I approached it, and touched it with my hand. It was a black cat -- a very large one -- fully as large as Pluto, and closely resembling him in every respect but one. Pluto had not a

The Black Cat

white hair upon any portion of his body; but this cat had a large, although indefinite splotch of white, covering nearly the whole region of the breast.

Upon my touching him, he immediately arose, purred loudly, rubbed against my hand, and appeared delighted with my notice. This, then, was the very creature of which I was in search. I at once offered to purchase it of the landlord; but this person made no claim to it -- knew nothing of it -- had never seen it before.

I continued my caresses, and, when I prepared to go home, the animal evinced a disposition to accompany me. I permitted it to do so; occasionally stooping and patting it as I proceeded. When it reached the house it domesticated itself at once, and became immediately a great favorite with my wife.

For my own part, I soon found a dislike to it arising within me. This was just the reverse of what I had anticipated; but -- I know not how or why it was -- its evident fondness for myself rather disgusted and annoyed. By slow degrees, these feelings of disgust and annoyance rose into the bitterness of hatred. I avoided the creature; a certain sense of shame, and the remembrance of my former deed of cruelty, preventing me from physically abusing it. I did not, for some weeks, strike, or otherwise violently ill use it; but gradually -- very gradually -- I came to look upon it with unutterable loathing, and to flee silently from its odious presence, as from the breath of a pestilence.

What added, no doubt, to my hatred of the beast, was the discovery, on the morning after I brought it home, that, like Pluto, it also had been deprived of one of its eyes. This circumstance, however, only endeared it to my wife, who, as I have already said, possessed, in a high degree, that humanity of feeling which had once been my distinguishing trait, and the source of many of my simplest and purest pleasures.

With my aversion to this cat, however, its partiality for myself seemed to increase. It followed my footsteps with a pertinacity which it would be difficult to make the reader comprehend. Whenever I sat, it would crouch beneath my chair, or spring upon my knees, covering me with its loathsome caresses. If I arose to walk it would get between my feet and thus nearly throw me down, or, fastening its long and sharp claws in my dress, clamber, in this manner, to my breast. At such times, although I longed to destroy it with a blow, I was yet withheld from so doing, partly by a memory of my former crime, but chiefly -- let me confess it at once -- by absolute dread of the beast.

This dread was not exactly a dread of physical evil -- and yet I should be at a loss how otherwise to define it. I am almost ashamed to own -- yes, even in this felon's cell, I am almost ashamed to own -- that the terror and horror with which the animal inspired me, had been heightened by one of the merest chimæras it would be possible to conceive. My wife had called my attention, more than once, to the character of the mark of white hair, of which I have spoken, and which constituted the sole visible difference between the strange beast and the one I had destroyed. The reader will remember that this mark, although large, had been originally very indefinite; but, by slow degrees -- degrees nearly imperceptible, and which for a long time my Reason struggled to reject as fanciful -- it had, at length, assumed a rigorous distinctness of outline. It was now the representation of an object that I shudder to name -- and for this, above all, I loathed, and dreaded, and would have rid myself of the monster had I dared -- it was now, I say, the image of a hideous -- of a ghastly thing -- of the GALLOWS ! -- oh, mournful and terrible engine of Horror and of Crime -- of Agony and of Death !

And now was I indeed wretched beyond the wretchedness of mere Humanity. And a brute beast -- whose fellow I had contemptuously destroyed -- a brute beast to work out for me -- for me a man, fashioned in the image of the High God -- so much of insufferable wo! Alas! neither by day nor by night knew I the blessing of Rest any more! During the former the creature left me no moment alone; and, in the latter, I started, hourly, from dreams of unutterable fear, to find the hot breath of the thing upon my face, and its vast weight -- an incarnate Night-Mare that I had no power to shake off -- incumbent eternally upon my heart !

Beneath the pressure of torments such as these, the feeble remnant of the good within me succumbed. Evil thoughts became my sole intimates -- the darkest and most evil of thoughts. The moodiness of my usual temper increased to hatred of all things and of all mankind; while, from the sudden, frequent, and ungovernable outbursts of a fury to which I now blindly abandoned myself, my uncomplaining wife, alas! was the most usual and the most patient of sufferers.

One day she accompanied me, upon some household errand, into the cellar of the old building which our poverty compelled us to inhabit. The cat followed me down the steep

The Black Cat

stairs, and, nearly throwing me headlong, exasperated me to madness. Uplifting an axe, and forgetting, in my wrath, the childish dread which had hitherto stayed my hand, I aimed a blow at the animal which, of course, would have proved instantly fatal had it descended as I wished. But this blow was arrested by the hand of my wife. Goaded, by the interference, into a rage more than demoniacal, I withdrew my arm from her grasp and buried the axe in her brain. She fell dead upon the spot, without a groan.

This hideous murder accomplished, I set myself forthwith, and with entire deliberation, to the task of concealing the body. I knew that I could not remove it from the house, either by day or by night, without the risk of being observed by the neighbors. Many projects entered my mind. At one period I thought of cutting the corpse into minute fragments, and destroying them by fire. At another, I resolved to dig a grave for it in the floor of the cellar. Again, I deliberated about casting it in the well in the yard -- about packing it in a box, as if merchandize, with the usual arrangements, and so getting a porter to take it from the house. Finally I hit upon what I considered a far better expedient than either of these. I determined to wall it up in the cellar -- as the monks of the middle ages are recorded to have walled up their victims.

For a purpose such as this the cellar was well adapted. Its walls were loosely constructed, and had lately been plastered throughout with a rough plaster, which the dampness of the atmosphere had prevented from hardening. Moreover, in one of the walls was a projection, caused by a false chimney, or fireplace, that had been filled up, and made to resemble the rest of the cellar. I made no doubt that I could readily displace the bricks at this point, insert the corpse, and wall the whole up as before, so that no eye could detect any thing suspicious.

And in this calculation I was not deceived. By means of a crow-bar I easily dislodged the bricks, and, having carefully deposited the body against the inner wall, I propped it in that position, while, with little trouble, I re-laid the whole structure as it originally stood. Having procured mortar, sand, and hair, with every possible precaution, I prepared a plaster which could not be distinguished from the old, and with this I very carefully went over the new brick-work. When I had finished, I felt satisfied that all was right. The wall did not present the slightest appearance of having been disturbed. The rubbish on the floor was picked up with the minutest care. I looked around triumphantly, and said to myself -- "Here at least, then, my labor has not been in vain."

My next step was to look for the beast which had been the cause of so much wretchedness; for I had, at length, firmly resolved to put it to death. Had I been able to meet with it, at the moment, there could have been no doubt of its fate; but it appeared that the crafty animal had been alarmed at the violence of my previous anger, and forebore to present itself in my present mood. It is impossible to describe, or to imagine, the deep, the blissful sense of relief which the absence of the detested creature occasioned in my bosom. It did not make its appearance during the night -- and thus for one night at least, since its introduction into the house, I soundly and tranquilly slept; aye, slept even with the burden of murder upon my soul!

The second and the third day passed, and still my tormentor came not. Once again I breathed as a freeman. The monster, in terror, had fled the premises forever! I should behold it no more! My happiness was supreme! The guilt of my dark deed disturbed me but little. Some few inquiries had been made, but these had been readily answered. Even a search had been instituted -- but of course nothing was to be discovered. I looked upon my future felicity as secured.

Upon the fourth day of the assassination, a party of the police came, very unexpectedly, into the house, and proceeded again to make rigorous investigation of the premises. Secure, however, in the inscrutability of my place of concealment, I felt no embarrassment whatever. The officers bade me accompany them in their search. They left no nook or corner unexplored. At length, for the third or fourth time, they descended into the cellar. I quivered not in a muscle. My heart beat calmly as that of one who slumbers in innocence. I walked the cellar from end to end. I folded my arms upon my bosom, and roamed easily to and fro. The police were thoroughly satisfied and prepared to depart. The glee at my heart was too strong to be restrained. I burned to say if but one word, by way of triumph, and to render doubly sure their assurance of my guiltlessness.

"Gentlemen," I said at last, as the party ascended the steps, "I delight to have allayed your suspicions. I wish you all health, and a little more courtesy. By the bye, gentlemen, this -- this is a very well constructed house." (In the rabid desire to say something easily, I scarcely knew what I uttered at all.) -- "I may say an excellently well constructed house. These walls -- are you going, gentlemen? -- these walls are solidly put together;" and here, through the mere phrenzy of bravado, I rapped heavily, with a cane which I held in my hand, upon that very portion of the brick-work behind which stood the corpse of the wife of my bosom.

The Black Cat

But may God shield and deliver me from the fangs of the Arch-Fiend ! No sooner had the reverberation of my blows sunk into silence, than I was answered by a voice from within the tomb! -- by a cry, at first muffled and broken, like the sobbing of a child, and then quickly swelling into one long, loud, and continuous scream, utterly anomalous and inhuman -- a howl -- a wailing shriek, half of horror and half of triumph, such as might have arisen only out of hell, conjointly from the throats of the dammed in their agony and of the demons that exult in the damnation.

Of my own thoughts it is folly to speak. Swooning, I staggered to the opposite wall. For one instant the party upon the stairs remained motionless, through extremity of terror and of awe. In the next, a dozen stout arms were toiling at the wall. It fell bodily. The corpse, already greatly decayed and clotted with gore, stood erect before the eyes of the spectators. Upon its head, with red extended mouth and solitary eye of fire, sat the hideous beast whose craft had seduced me into murder, and whose informing voice had consigned me to the hangman. I had walled the monster up within the tomb!

The Tell Tale Heart

By Edgar Allan Poe

TRUE! -- nervous -- very, very dreadfully nervous I had been and am; but why will you say that I am mad? The disease had sharpened my senses -- not destroyed -- not dulled them. Above all was the sense of hearing acute. I heard all things in the heaven and in the earth. I heard many things in hell. How, then, am I mad? Hearken! and observe how healthily -- how calmly I can tell you the whole story.

It is impossible to say how first the idea entered my brain; but once conceived, it haunted me day and night. Object there was none. Passion there was none. I loved the old man. He had never wronged me. He had never given me insult. For his gold I had no desire. I think it was his eye! yes, it was this! He had the eye of a vulture --a pale blue eye, with a film over it. Whenever it fell upon me, my blood ran cold; and so by degrees -- very gradually --I made up my mind to take the life of the old man, and thus rid myself of the eye forever.

Now this is the point. You fancy me mad. Madmen know nothing. But you should have seen me. You should have seen how wisely I proceeded --with what caution --with what foresight --with what dissimulation I went to work! I was never kinder to the old man than during the whole week before I killed him. And every night, about midnight, I turned the latch of his door and opened it --oh so gently! And then, when I had made an opening sufficient for my head, I put in a dark lantern, all closed, closed, so that no light shone out, and then I thrust in my head. Oh, you would have laughed to see how cunningly I thrust it in! I moved it slowly --very, very slowly, so that I might not disturb the old man's sleep. It took me an hour to place my whole head within the opening so far that I could see him as he lay upon his bed. Ha! --would a madman have been so wise as this? And then, when my head was well in the room, I undid the lantern cautiously --oh, so cautiously --cautiously (for the hinges creaked) --I undid it just so much that a single thin ray fell upon the vulture eye. And this I did for seven long nights -- every night just at midnight --but I found the eye always closed; and so it was impossible to do the work; for it was not the old man who vexed me, but his Evil Eye. And every morning, when the day broke, I went boldly into the chamber, and spoke

The Tell Tale Heart

courageously to him, calling him by name in a hearty tone, and inquiring how he has passed the night. So you see he would have been a very profound old man, indeed, to suspect that every night, just at twelve, I looked in upon him while he slept.

Upon the eighth night I was more than usually cautious in opening the door. A watch's minute hand moves more quickly than did mine. Never before that night had I felt the extent of my own powers --of my sagacity. I could scarcely contain my feelings of triumph. To think that there I was, opening the door, little by little, and he not even to dream of my secret deeds or thoughts. I fairly chuckled at the idea; and perhaps he heard me; for he moved on the bed suddenly, as if startled. Now you may think that I drew back --but no. His room was as black as pitch with the thick darkness, (for the shutters were close fastened, through fear of robbers,) and so I knew that he could not see the opening of the door, and I kept pushing it on steadily, steadily.

I had my head in, and was about to open the lantern, when my thumb slipped upon the tin fastening, and the old man sprang up in bed, crying out --"Who's there?"

I kept quite still and said nothing. For a whole hour I did not move a muscle, and in the meantime I did not hear him lie down. He was still sitting up in the bed listening; --just as I have done, night after night, hearkening to the death watches in the wall.

Presently I heard a slight groan, and I knew it was the groan of mortal terror. It was not a groan of pain or of grief --oh, no! -- it was the low stifled sound that arises from the bottom of the soul when overcharged with awe. I knew the sound well. Many a night, just at midnight, when all the world slept, it has welled up from my own bosom, deepening, with its dreadful echo, the terrors that distracted me. I say I knew it well. I knew what the old man felt, and pitied him, although I chuckled at heart. I knew that he had been lying awake ever since the first slight noise, when he had turned in the bed. His fears had been ever since growing upon him. He had been trying to fancy them causeless, but could not. He had been saying to himself --"It is nothing but the wind in the chimney --it is only a mouse crossing the floor," or "It is merely a cricket which has made a single chirp." Yes, he had been trying to comfort himself with these suppositions: but he had found all in vain. All in vain; because Death, in approaching him had stalked with his black shadow before him, and enveloped the victim. And it was the mournful influence of the unperceived shadow that caused him to feel --although he neither saw nor heard --to feel the presence of my head within the room.

When I had waited a long time, very patiently, without hearing him lie down, I resolved to open a little --a very, very little crevice in the lantern. So I opened it --you cannot imagine how stealthily, stealthily --until, at length a single dim ray, like the thread of the spider, shot from out the crevice and fell full upon the vulture eye.

It was open --wide, wide open --and I grew furious as I gazed upon it. I saw it with perfect distinctness --all a dull blue, with a hideous veil over it that chilled the very marrow in my bones; but I could see nothing else of the old man's face or person: for I had directed the ray as if by instinct, precisely upon the damned spot.

And have I not told you that what you mistake for madness is but over acuteness of the senses? --now, I say, there came to my ears a low, dull, quick sound, such as a watch makes when enveloped in cotton. I knew that sound well, too. It was the beating of the old man's heart. It increased my fury, as the beating of a drum stimulates the soldier into courage.

But even yet I refrained and kept still. I scarcely breathed. I held the lantern motionless. I tried how steadily I could maintain the ray upon the eye. Meantime the hellish tattoo of the heart increased. It grew quicker and quicker, and louder and louder every instant. The old man's terror must have been extreme! It grew louder, I say, louder every moment! --do you mark me well? I have told you that I am nervous: so I am. And now at the dead hour of the night, amid the dreadful silence of that old house, so strange a noise as this excited me to uncontrollable terror. Yet, for some minutes longer I refrained and stood still. But the beating grew louder, louder! I thought the heart must burst. And now a new anxiety seized me --the sound would be heard by a neighbor! The old man's hour had come! With a loud yell, I threw open the lantern and leaped into the room. He shrieked once --once only. In an instant I dragged him to the floor, and pulled the heavy bed over him. I then smiled gaily, to find the deed so far done. But, for many minutes, the heart beat on with a muffled sound. This, however, did not vex me; it would not be heard through the wall. At length it ceased. The old man was dead. I removed the bed and examined the corpse. Yes, he was stone, stone dead. I placed my hand upon the heart and held it there many minutes. There was no pulsation. He was stone dead. His eye would trouble me no more.

The Tell Tale Heart

If still you think me mad, you will think so no longer when I describe the wise precautions I took for the concealment of the body. The night waned, and I worked hastily, but in silence. First of all I dismembered the corpse. I cut off the head and the arms and the legs.

I then took up three planks from the flooring of the chamber, and deposited all between the scantlings. I then replaced the boards so cleverly, so cunningly, that no human eye -- not even his --could have detected any thing wrong. There was nothing to wash out --no stain of any kind --no blood-spot whatever. I had been too wary for that. A tub had caught all --ha! ha!

When I had made an end of these labors, it was four o'clock --still dark as midnight. As the bell sounded the hour, there came a knocking at the street door. I went down to open it with a light heart, --for what had I now to fear? There entered three men, who introduced themselves, with perfect suavity, as officers of the police. A shriek had been heard by a neighbor during the night; suspicion of foul play had been aroused; information had been lodged at the police office, and they (the officers) had been deputed to search the premises.

I smiled, --for what had I to fear? I bade the gentlemen welcome. The shriek, I said, was my own in a dream. The old man, I mentioned, was absent in the country. I took my visitors all over the house. I bade them search --search well. I led them, at length, to his chamber. I showed them his treasures, secure, undisturbed. In the enthusiasm of my confidence, I brought chairs into the room, and desired them here to rest from their fatigues, while I myself, in the wild audacity of my perfect triumph, placed my own seat upon the very spot beneath which reposed the corpse of the victim.

The officers were satisfied. My manner had convinced them. I was singularly at ease. They sat, and while I answered cheerily, they chatted of familiar things. But, ere long, I felt myself getting pale and wished them gone. My head ached, and I fancied a ringing in my ears: but still they sat and still chatted. The ringing became more distinct: --it continued and became more distinct: I talked more freely to get rid of the feeling: but it continued and gained definiteness --until, at length, I found that the noise was not within my ears.

No doubt I now grew very pale; --but I talked more fluently, and with a heightened voice. Yet the sound increased --and what could I do? It was a low, dull, quick sound --much such a sound as a watch makes when enveloped in cotton. I gasped for breath -- and yet the officers heard it not. I talked more quickly --more vehemently; but the noise steadily increased. I arose and argued about trifles, in a high key and with violent gesticulations; but the noise steadily increased. Why would they not be gone? I paced the floor to and fro with heavy strides, as if excited to fury by the observations of the men -- but the noise steadily increased. Oh God! what could I do? I foamed --I raved --I swore! I swung the chair upon which I had been sitting, and grated it upon the boards, but the noise arose over all and continually increased. It grew louder --louder --louder! And still the men chatted pleasantly, and smiled. Was it possible they heard not? Almighty God! --no, no! They heard! --they suspected! --they knew! --they were making a mockery of my horror! --this I thought, and this I think. But anything was better than this agony! Anything was more tolerable than this derision! I could bear those hypocritical smiles no longer! I felt that I must scream or die! --and now --again! --hark! louder! louder! louder! louder! --

"Villains!" I shrieked, "dissemble no more! I admit the deed! --tear up the planks! --here, here! --it is the beating of his hideous heart!"

A Christmas Carol

By Charles Dickens

PREFACE

I HAVE endeavoured in this Ghostly little book, to raise the Ghost of an Idea, which shall not put my readers out of humour with themselves, with each other, with the season, or with me. May it haunt their houses pleasantly, and no one wish to lay it.

Their faithful Friend and Servant,

C. D.

STAVE ONE.
MARLEY'S GHOST.

Marley was dead: to begin with. There is no doubt whatever about that. The register of his burial was signed by the clergyman, the clerk, the undertaker, and the chief mourner. Scrooge signed it: and Scrooge's name was good upon 'Change, for anything he chose to put his hand to. Old Marley was as dead as a door-nail.

Mind! I don't mean to say that I know, of my own knowledge, what there is particularly dead about a door-nail. I might have been inclined, myself, to regard a coffin-nail as the deadest piece of ironmongery in the trade. But the wisdom of our ancestors is in the simile; and my unhallowed hands shall not disturb it, or the Country's done for. You will therefore permit me to repeat, emphatically, that Marley was as dead as a door-nail.

Scrooge knew he was dead? Of course he did. How could it be otherwise? Scrooge and he were partners for I don't know how many years. Scrooge was his sole executor, his sole administrator, his sole assign, his sole residuary legatee, his sole friend, and sole mourner. And even Scrooge was not so dreadfully cut up by the sad event, but that he was an excellent man of business on the very day of the funeral, and solemnised it with an undoubted bargain.

The mention of Marley's funeral brings me back to the point I started from. There is no doubt that Marley was dead. This must be distinctly understood, or nothing wonderful can come of the story I am going to relate. If we were not perfectly convinced that Hamlet's Father died before the play began, there would be nothing more remarkable in his taking a stroll at night, in an easterly wind, upon his own ramparts, than there would be in any other middle-aged gentleman rashly turning out after dark in a breezy spot — say Saint Paul's Churchyard for instance — literally to astonish his son's weak mind.

Scrooge never painted out Old Marley's name. There it stood, years afterwards, above the warehouse door: Scrooge and Marley. The firm was known as Scrooge and Marley. Sometimes people new to the business called Scrooge Scrooge, and sometimes Marley, but he answered to both names. It was all the same to him.

Oh! But he was a tight-fisted hand at the grindstone, Scrooge! a squeezing, wrenching, grasping, scraping, clutching, covetous, old sinner! Hard and sharp as flint, from which no steel had ever struck out generous fire; secret, and self-contained, and solitary as an oyster. The cold within him froze his old features, nipped his pointed nose, shrivelled his cheek, stiffened his gait; made his eyes red, his thin lips blue; and spoke out shrewdly in his grating voice. A frosty rime was on his head, and on his eyebrows, and his wiry chin. He carried his own low temperature always about with him; he iced his office in the dog-days; and didn't thaw it one degree at Christmas.

External heat and cold had little influence on Scrooge. No warmth could warm, no wintry weather chill him. No wind that blew was bitterer than he, no falling snow was more intent upon its purpose, no pelting rain less open to entreaty. Foul weather didn't know where to have him. The heaviest rain, and snow, and hail, and sleet, could boast of the advantage over him in only one respect. They often "came down" handsomely, and Scrooge never did.

Nobody ever stopped him in the street to say, with gladsome looks, "My dear Scrooge, how are you? When will you come to see me?" No beggars implored him to bestow a trifle, no children asked him what it was o'clock, no man or woman ever once in all his life inquired the way to such and

A Christmas Carol

such a place, of Scrooge. Even the blind men's dogs appeared to know him; and when they saw him coming on, would tug their owners into doorways and up courts; and then would wag their tails as though they said, "No eye at all is better than an evil eye, dark master!"

But what did Scrooge care! It was the very thing he liked. To edge his way along the crowded paths of life, warning all human sympathy to keep its distance, was what the knowing ones call "nuts" to Scrooge.

Once upon a time—of all the good days in the year, on Christmas Eve—old Scrooge sat busy in his counting-house. It was cold, bleak, biting weather: foggy withal: and he could hear the people in the court outside, go wheezing up and down, beating their hands upon their breasts, and stamping their feet upon the pavement stones to warm them. The city clocks had only just gone three, but it was quite dark already—it had not been light all day—and candles were flaring in the windows of the neighbouring offices, like ruddy smears upon the palpable brown air. The fog came pouring in at every chink and keyhole, and was so dense without, that although the court was of the narrowest, the houses opposite were mere phantoms. To see the dingy cloud come drooping down, obscuring everything, one might have thought that Nature lived hard by, and was brewing on a large scale.

The door of Scrooge's counting-house was open that he might keep his eye upon his clerk, who in a dismal little cell beyond, a sort of tank, was copying letters. Scrooge had a very small fire, but the clerk's fire was so very much smaller that it looked like one coal. But he couldn't replenish it, for Scrooge kept the coal-box in his own room; and so surely as the clerk came in with the shovel, the master predicted that it would be necessary for them to part. Wherefore the clerk put on his white comforter, and tried to warm himself at the candle; in which effort, not being a man of a strong imagination, he failed.

"A merry Christmas, uncle! God save you!" cried a cheerful voice. It was the voice of Scrooge's nephew, who came upon him so quickly that this was the first intimation he had of his approach.

"Bah!" said Scrooge, "Humbug!"

He had so heated himself with rapid walking in the fog and frost, this nephew of Scrooge's, that he was all in a glow; his face was ruddy and handsome; his eyes sparkled, and his breath smoked again.

"Christmas a humbug, uncle!" said Scrooge's nephew. "You don't men that, I am sure?"

"I do," said Scrooge. "Merry Christmas! What right have you to be merry? What reason have you to be merry? You're poor enough."

"Come, then," returned the nephew gaily. "What right have you to be dismal? What reason have you to be morose? You're rich enough."

Scrooge having no better answer ready on the spur of the moment, said, "Bah!" again; and followed it up with "Humbug."

"Don't be cross, uncle!" said the nephew.

"What else can I be," returned the uncle, "when I live in such a world of fools as this? Merry Christmas! Out upon merry Christmas! What's Christmas time to you but a time for paying bills without money; a time for finding yourself a year older, but not an hour richer; a time for balancing your books and having every item in 'em through a round dozen of months presented dead against you? If I could work my will," said Scrooge indignantly, "every idiot who goes about with 'Merry Christmas' on his lips, should be boiled with his own pudding, and buried with a stake of holly through his heart. He should!"

"Uncle!" pleaded the nephew.

"Nephew!" returned the uncle sternly, "keep Christmas in your own way, and let me keep it in mine."

"Keep it!" repeated Scrooge's nephew. "But you don't keep it."

"Let me leave it alone, then," said Scrooge. "Much good may it do you! Much good it has ever done you!"

"There are many things from which I might have derived good, by which I have not profited, I dare say," returned the nephew. "Christmas among the rest. But I am sure I have always thought of Christmas time, when it has come round—apart from the veneration due to its sacred name and origin, if anything belonging to it can be apart from that—as a good time; a kind, forgiving, charitable, pleasant time; the only time I know

A Christmas Carol

of, in the long calendar of the year, when men and women seem by one consent to open their shut-up hearts freely, and to think of people below them as if they really were fellow-passengers to the grave, and not another race of creatures bound on other journeys. And therefore, uncle, though it has never put a scrap of gold or silver in my pocket, I believe that it has done me good, and will do me good; and I say, God bless it!"

The clerk in the Tank involuntarily applauded. Becoming immediately sensible of the impropriety, he poked the fire, and extinguished the last frail spark for ever.

"Let me hear another sound from you," said Scrooge, "and you'll keep your Christmas by losing your situation! You're quite a powerful speaker, sir," he added, turning to his nephew. "I wonder you don't go into Parliament."

"Don't be angry, uncle. Come! Dine with us to-morrow."

Scrooge said that he would see him—yes, indeed he did. He went the whole length of the expression, and said that he would see him in that extremity first.

"But why?" cried Scrooge's nephew. "Why?"

"Why did you get married?" said Scrooge.

"Because I fell in love."

"Because you fell in love!" growled Scrooge, as if that were the only one thing in the world more ridiculous than a merry Christmas. "Good afternoon!"

"Nay, uncle, but you never came to see me before that happened. Why give it as a reason for not coming now?"

"Good afternoon," said Scrooge.

"I want nothing from you; I ask nothing of you; why cannot we be friends?"

"Good afternoon," said Scrooge.

"I am sorry, with all my heart, to find you so resolute. We have never had any quarrel, to which I have been a party. But I have made the trial in homage to Christmas, and I'll keep my Christmas humour to the last. So A Merry Christmas, uncle!"

"Good afternoon!" said Scrooge.

"And A Happy New Year!"

"Good afternoon!" said Scrooge.

His nephew left the room without an angry word, notwithstanding. He stopped at the outer door to bestow the greetings of the season on the clerk, who, cold as he was, was warmer than Scrooge; for he returned them cordially.

"There's another fellow," muttered Scrooge; who overheard him: "my clerk, with fifteen shillings a week, and a wife and family, talking about a merry Christmas. I'll retire to Bedlam."

This lunatic, in letting Scrooge's nephew out, had let two other people in. They were portly gentlemen, pleasant to behold, and now stood, with their hats off, in Scrooge's office. They had books and papers in their hands, and bowed to him.

"Scrooge and Marley's, I believe," said one of the gentlemen, referring to his list. "Have I the pleasure of addressing Mr. Scrooge, or Mr. Marley?"

"Mr. Marley has been dead these seven years," Scrooge replied. "He died seven years ago, this very night."

"We have no doubt his liberality is well represented by his surviving partner," said the gentleman, presenting his credentials.

It certainly was; for they had been two kindred spirits. At the ominous word "liberality," Scrooge frowned, and shook his head, and handed the credentials back.

"At this festive season of the year, Mr. Scrooge," said the gentleman, taking up a pen, "it is more than usually desirable that we should make some slight provision for the Poor and destitute, who suffer greatly at the present time. Many thousands are in want of common necessaries; hundreds of thousands are in want of common comforts, sir."

"Are there no prisons?" asked Scrooge.

"Plenty of prisons," said the gentleman, laying down the pen again.

A Christmas Carol

"And the Union workhouses?" demanded Scrooge. "Are they still in operation?"

"They are. Still," returned the gentleman, "I wish I could say they were not."

"The Treadmill and the Poor Law are in full vigour, then?" said Scrooge.

"Both very busy, sir."

"Oh! I was afraid, from what you said at first, that something had occurred to stop them in their useful course," said Scrooge. "I'm very glad to hear it."

"Under the impression that they scarcely furnish Christian cheer of mind or body to the multitude," returned the gentleman, "a few of us are endeavouring to raise a fund to buy the Poor some meat and drink, and means of warmth. We choose this time, because it is a time, of all others, when Want is keenly felt, and Abundance rejoices. What shall I put you down for?"

"Nothing!" Scrooge replied.

"You wish to be anonymous?"

"I wish to be left alone," said Scrooge. "Since you ask me what I wish, gentlemen, that is my answer. I don't make merry myself at Christmas and I can't afford to make idle people merry. I help to support the establishments I have mentioned — they cost enough; and those who are badly off must go there."

"Many can't go there; and many would rather die."

"If they would rather die," said Scrooge, "they had better do it, and decrease the surplus population. Besides — excuse me — I don't know that."

"But you might know it," observed the gentleman.

"It's not my business," Scrooge returned. "It's enough for a man to understand his own business, and not to interfere with other people's. Mine occupies me constantly. Good afternoon, gentlemen!"

Seeing clearly that it would be useless to pursue their point, the gentlemen withdrew. Scrooge resumed his labours with an improved opinion of himself, and in a more facetious temper than was usual with him.

Meanwhile the fog and darkness thickened so, that people ran about with flaring links, proffering their services to go before horses in carriages, and conduct them on their way. The ancient tower of a church, whose gruff old bell was always peeping slily down at Scrooge out of a Gothic window in the wall, became invisible, and struck the hours and quarters in the clouds, with tremulous vibrations afterwards as if its teeth were chattering in its frozen head up there. The cold became intense. In the main street, at the corner of the court, some labourers were repairing the gas-pipes, and had lighted a great fire in a brazier, round which a party of ragged men and boys were gathered: warming their hands and winking their eyes before the blaze in rapture. The water-plug being left in solitude, its overflowings sullenly congealed, and turned to misanthropic ice. The brightness of the shops where holly sprigs and berries crackled in the lamp heat of the windows, made pale faces ruddy as they passed. Poulterers' and grocers' trades became a splendid joke: a glorious pageant, with which it was next to impossible to believe that such dull principles as bargain and sale had anything to do. The Lord Mayor, in the stronghold of the mighty Mansion House, gave orders to his fifty cooks and butlers to keep Christmas as a Lord Mayor's household should; and even the little tailor, whom he had fined five shillings on the previous Monday for being drunk and bloodthirsty in the streets, stirred up to-morrow's pudding in his garret, while his lean wife and the baby sallied out to buy the beef.

Foggier yet, and colder. Piercing, searching, biting cold. If the good Saint Dunstan had but nipped the Evil Spirit's nose with a touch of such weather as that, instead of using his familiar weapons, then indeed he would have roared to lusty purpose. The owner of one scant young nose, gnawed and mumbled by the hungry cold as bones are gnawed by dogs, stooped down at Scrooge's keyhole to regale him with a Christmas carol: but at the first sound of

"God bless you, merry gentleman!

May nothing you dismay!"

Scrooge seized the ruler with such energy of action, that the singer fled in terror, leaving the keyhole to the fog and even more congenial frost.

A Christmas Carol

At length the hour of shutting up the counting-house arrived. With an ill-will Scrooge dismounted from his stool, and tacitly admitted the fact to the expectant clerk in the Tank, who instantly snuffed his candle out, and put on his hat.

"You'll want all day to-morrow, I suppose?" said Scrooge.

"If quite convenient, sir."

"It's not convenient," said Scrooge, "and it's not fair. If I was to stop half-a-crown for it, you'd think yourself ill-used, I'll be bound?"

The clerk smiled faintly.

"And yet," said Scrooge, "you don't think me ill-used, when I pay a day's wages for no work."

The clerk observed that it was only once a year.

"A poor excuse for picking a man's pocket every twenty-fifth of December!" said Scrooge, buttoning his great-coat to the chin. "But I suppose you must have the whole day. Be here all the earlier next morning."

The clerk promised that he would; and Scrooge walked out with a growl. The office was closed in a twinkling, and the clerk, with the long ends of his white comforter dangling below his waist (for he boasted no great-coat), went down a slide on Cornhill, at the end of a lane of boys, twenty times, in honour of its being Christmas Eve, and then ran home to Camden Town as hard as he could pelt, to play at blindman's-buff.

Scrooge took his melancholy dinner in his usual melancholy tavern; and having read all the newspapers, and beguiled the rest of the evening with his banker's-book, went home to bed. He lived in chambers which had once belonged to his deceased partner. They were a gloomy suite of rooms, in a lowering pile of building up a yard, where it had so little business to be, that one could scarcely help fancying it must have run there when it was a young house, playing at hide-and-seek with other houses, and forgotten the way out again. It was old enough now, and dreary enough, for nobody lived in it but Scrooge, the other rooms being all let out as offices. The yard was so dark that even Scrooge, who knew its every stone, was fain to grope with his hands. The fog and frost so hung about the black old gateway of the house, that it seemed as if the Genius of the Weather sat in mournful meditation on the threshold.

Now, it is a fact, that there was nothing at all particular about the knocker on the door, except that it was very large. It is also a fact, that Scrooge had seen it, night and morning, during his whole residence in that place; also that Scrooge had as little of what is called fancy about him as any man in the city of London, even including — which is a bold word — the corporation, aldermen, and livery. Let it also be borne in mind that Scrooge had not bestowed one thought on Marley, since his last mention of his seven years' dead partner that afternoon. And then let any man explain to me, if he can, how it happened that Scrooge, having his key in the lock of the door, saw in the knocker, without its undergoing any intermediate process of change — not a knocker, but Marley's face.

Marley's face. It was not in impenetrable shadow as the other objects in the yard were, but had a dismal light about it, like a bad lobster in a dark cellar. It was not angry or ferocious, but looked at Scrooge as Marley used to look: with ghostly spectacles turned up on its ghostly forehead. The hair was curiously stirred, as if by breath or hot air; and, though the eyes were wide open, they were perfectly motionless. That, and its livid colour, made it horrible; but its horror seemed to be in spite of the face and beyond its control, rather than a part of its own expression.

As Scrooge looked fixedly at this phenomenon, it was a knocker again.

To say that he was not startled, or that his blood was not conscious of a terrible sensation to which it had been a stranger from infancy, would be untrue. But he put his hand upon the key he had relinquished, turned it sturdily, walked in, and lighted his candle.

He did pause, with a moment's irresolution, before he shut the door; and he did look cautiously behind it first, as if he half expected to be terrified with the sight of Marley's pigtail sticking out into the hall. But there was nothing on the back of the door, except the screws and nuts that held the knocker on, so he said "Pooh, pooh!" and closed it with a bang.

The sound resounded through the house like thunder. Every room above, and every cask in the wine-merchant's cellars below, appeared to have a separate peal of echoes of its own. Scrooge was not a man to be frightened by echoes. He fastened the door, and walked across the hall, and up the stairs; slowly too: trimming his candle as he went.

A Christmas Carol

You may talk vaguely about driving a coach-and-six up a good old flight of stairs, or through a bad young Act of Parliament; but I mean to say you might have got a hearse up that staircase, and taken it broadwise, with the splinter-bar towards the wall and the door towards the balustrades: and done it easy. There was plenty of width for that, and room to spare; which is perhaps the reason why Scrooge thought he saw a locomotive hearse going on before him in the gloom. Half-a-dozen gas-lamps out of the street wouldn't have lighted the entry too well, so you may suppose that it was pretty dark with Scrooge's dip.

Up Scrooge went, not caring a button for that. Darkness is cheap, and Scrooge liked it. But before he shut his heavy door, he walked through his rooms to see that all was right. He had just enough recollection of the face to desire to do that.

Sitting-room, bedroom, lumber-room. All as they should be. Nobody under the table, nobody under the sofa; a small fire in the grate; spoon and basin ready; and the little saucepan of gruel (Scrooge had a cold in his head) upon the hob. Nobody under the bed; nobody in the closet; nobody in his dressing-gown, which was hanging up in a suspicious attitude against the wall. Lumber-room as usual. Old fire-guard, old shoes, two fish-baskets, washing-stand on three legs, and a poker.

Quite satisfied, he closed his door, and locked himself in; double-locked himself in, which was not his custom. Thus secured against surprise, he took off his cravat; put on his dressing-gown and slippers, and his nightcap; and sat down before the fire to take his gruel.

It was a very low fire indeed; nothing on such a bitter night. He was obliged to sit close to it, and brood over it, before he could extract the least sensation of warmth from such a handful of fuel. The fireplace was an old one, built by some Dutch merchant long ago, and paved all round with quaint Dutch tiles, designed to illustrate the Scriptures. There were Cains and Abels, Pharaoh's daughters; Queens of Sheba, Angelic messengers descending through the air on clouds like feather-beds, Abrahams, Belshazzars, Apostles putting off to sea in butter-boats, hundreds of figures to attract his thoughts; and yet that face of Marley, seven years dead, came like the ancient Prophet's rod, and swallowed up the whole. If each smooth tile had been a blank at first, with power to shape some picture on its surface from the disjointed fragments of his thoughts, there would have been a copy of old Marley's head on every one.

A Christmas Carol

"Humbug!" said Scrooge; and walked across the room.

After several turns, he sat down again. As he threw his head back in the chair, his glance happened to rest upon a bell, a disused bell, that hung in the room, and communicated for some purpose now forgotten with a chamber in the highest story of the building. It was with great astonishment, and with a strange, inexplicable dread, that as he looked, he saw this bell begin to swing. It swung so softly in the outset that it scarcely made a sound; but soon it rang out loudly, and so did every bell in the house.

This might have lasted half a minute, or a minute, but it seemed an hour. The bells ceased as they had begun, together. They were succeeded by a clanking noise, deep down below; as if some person were dragging a heavy chain over the casks in the wine-merchant's cellar. Scrooge then remembered to have heard that ghosts in haunted houses were described as dragging chains.

The cellar-door flew open with a booming sound, and then he heard the noise much louder, on the floors below; then coming up the stairs; then coming straight towards his door.

"It's humbug still!" said Scrooge. "I won't believe it."

His colour changed though, when, without a pause, it came on through the heavy door, and passed into the room before his eyes. Upon its coming in, the dying flame leaped up, as though it cried, "I know him; Marley's Ghost!" and fell again.

The same face: the very same. Marley in his pigtail, usual waistcoat, tights and boots; the tassels on the latter bristling, like his pigtail, and his coat-skirts, and the hair upon his head. The chain he drew was clasped about his middle. It was long, and wound about him like a tail; and it was made (for Scrooge observed it closely) of cash-boxes, keys, padlocks, ledgers, deeds, and heavy purses wrought in steel. His body was transparent; so that Scrooge, observing him, and looking through his waistcoat, could see the two buttons on his coat behind.

Scrooge had often heard it said that Marley had no bowels, but he had never believed it until now.

No, nor did he believe it even now. Though he looked the phantom through and through, and saw it standing before him; though he felt the chilling influence of its death-cold eyes; and

526

marked the very texture of the folded kerchief bound about its head and chin, which wrapper he had not observed before; he was still incredulous, and fought against his senses.

"How now!" said Scrooge, caustic and cold as ever. "What do you want with me?"

"Much!" — Marley's voice, no doubt about it.

"Who are you?"

"Ask me who I was."

"Who were you then?" said Scrooge, raising his voice. "You're particular, for a shade." He was going to say "to a shade," but substituted this, as more appropriate.

"In life I was your partner, Jacob Marley."

"Can you — can you sit down?" asked Scrooge, looking doubtfully at him.

"I can."

"Do it, then."

Scrooge asked the question, because he didn't know whether a ghost so transparent might find himself in a condition to take a chair; and felt that in the event of its being impossible, it might involve the necessity of an embarrassing explanation. But the ghost sat down on the opposite side of the fireplace, as if he were quite used to it.

"You don't believe in me," observed the Ghost.

"I don't," said Scrooge.

"What evidence would you have of my reality beyond that of your senses?"

"I don't know," said Scrooge.

"Why do you doubt your senses?"

"Because," said Scrooge, "a little thing affects them. A slight disorder of the stomach makes them cheats. You may be an undigested bit of beef, a blot of mustard, a crumb of cheese, a fragment of an underdone potato. There's more of gravy than of grave about you, whatever you are!"

Scrooge was not much in the habit of cracking jokes, nor did he feel, in his heart, by any means waggish then. The truth is, that he tried to be smart, as a means of distracting his own attention, and keeping down his terror; for the spectre's voice disturbed the very marrow in his bones.

To sit, staring at those fixed glazed eyes, in silence for a moment, would play, Scrooge felt, the very deuce with him. There was something very awful, too, in the spectre's being provided with an infernal atmosphere of its own. Scrooge could not feel it himself, but this was clearly the case; for though the Ghost sat perfectly motionless, its hair, and skirts, and tassels, were still agitated as by the hot vapour from an oven.

"You see this toothpick?" said Scrooge, returning quickly to the charge, for the reason just assigned; and wishing, though it were only for a second, to divert the vision's stony gaze from himself.

"I do," replied the Ghost.

"You are not looking at it," said Scrooge.

"But I see it," said the Ghost, "notwithstanding."

"Well!" returned Scrooge, "I have but to swallow this, and be for the rest of my days persecuted by a legion of goblins, all of my own creation. Humbug, I tell you! humbug!"

At this the spirit raised a frightful cry, and shook its chain with such a dismal and appalling noise, that Scrooge held on tight to his chair, to save himself from falling in a swoon. But how much greater was his horror, when the phantom taking off the bandage round its head, as if it were too warm to wear indoors, its lower jaw dropped down upon its breast!

Scrooge fell upon his knees, and clasped his hands before his face.

"Mercy!" he said. "Dreadful apparition, why do you trouble me?"

"Man of the worldly mind!" replied the Ghost, "do you believe in me or not?"

A Christmas Carol

"I do," said Scrooge. "I must. But why do spirits walk the earth, and why do they come to me?"

"It is required of every man," the Ghost returned, "that the spirit within him should walk abroad among his fellowmen, and travel far and wide; and if that spirit goes not forth in life, it is condemned to do so after death. It is doomed to wander through the world — oh, woe is me! — and witness what it cannot share, but might have shared on earth, and turned to happiness!"

Again the spectre raised a cry, and shook its chain and wrung its shadowy hands.

"You are fettered," said Scrooge, trembling. "Tell me why?"

"I wear the chain I forged in life," replied the Ghost. "I made it link by link, and yard by yard; I girded it on of my own free will, and of my own free will I wore it. Is its pattern strange to you?"

Scrooge trembled more and more.

"Or would you know," pursued the Ghost, "the weight and length of the strong coil you bear yourself? It was full as heavy and as long as this, seven Christmas Eves ago. You have laboured on it, since. It is a ponderous chain!"

Scrooge glanced about him on the floor, in the expectation of finding himself surrounded by some fifty or sixty fathoms of iron cable: but he could see nothing.

"Jacob," he said, imploringly. "Old Jacob Marley, tell me more. Speak comfort to me, Jacob!"

"I have none to give," the Ghost replied. "It comes from other regions, Ebenezer Scrooge, and is conveyed by other ministers, to other kinds of men. Nor can I tell you what I would. A very little more is all permitted to me. I cannot rest, I cannot stay, I cannot linger anywhere. My spirit never walked beyond our counting-house — mark me! — in life my spirit never roved beyond the narrow limits of our money-changing hole; and weary journeys lie before me!"

It was a habit with Scrooge, whenever he became thoughtful, to put his hands in his breeches pockets. Pondering on what the Ghost had said, he did so now, but without lifting up his eyes, or getting off his knees.

"You must have been very slow about it, Jacob," Scrooge observed, in a business-like manner, though with humility and deference.

"Slow!" the Ghost repeated.

"Seven years dead," mused Scrooge. "And travelling all the time!"

"The whole time," said the Ghost. "No rest, no peace. Incessant torture of remorse."

"You travel fast?" said Scrooge.

"On the wings of the wind," replied the Ghost.

"You might have got over a great quantity of ground in seven years," said Scrooge.

The Ghost, on hearing this, set up another cry, and clanked its chain so hideously in the dead silence of the night, that the Ward would have been justified in indicting it for a nuisance.

"Oh! captive, bound, and double-ironed," cried the phantom, "not to know, that ages of incessant labour by immortal creatures, for this earth must pass into eternity before the good of which it is susceptible is all developed. Not to know that any Christian spirit working kindly in its little sphere, whatever it may be, will find its mortal life too short for its vast means of usefulness. Not to know that no space of regret can make amends for one life's opportunity misused! Yet such was I! Oh! such was I!"

"But you were always a good man of business, Jacob," faltered Scrooge, who now began to apply this to himself.

"Business!" cried the Ghost, wringing its hands again. "Mankind was my business. The common welfare was my business; charity, mercy, forbearance, and benevolence, were, all, my business. The dealings of my trade were but a drop of water in the comprehensive ocean of my business!"

It held up its chain at arm's length, as if that were the cause of all its unavailing grief, and flung it heavily upon the ground again.

"At this time of the rolling year," the spectre said, "I suffer most. Why did I walk through crowds of fellow-beings with my

A Christmas Carol

eyes turned down, and never raise them to that blessed Star which led the Wise Men to a poor abode! Were there no poor homes to which its light would have conducted me!"

Scrooge was very much dismayed to hear the spectre going on at this rate, and began to quake exceedingly.

"Hear me!" cried the Ghost. "My time is nearly gone."

"I will," said Scrooge. "But don't be hard upon me! Don't be flowery, Jacob! Pray!"

"How it is that I appear before you in a shape that you can see, I may not tell. I have sat invisible beside you many and many a day."

It was not an agreeable idea. Scrooge shivered, and wiped the perspiration from his brow.

"That is no light part of my penance," pursued the Ghost. "I am here to-night to warn you, that you have yet a chance and hope of escaping my fate. A chance and hope of my procuring, Ebenezer."

"You were always a good friend to me," said Scrooge. "Thank'ee!"

"You will be haunted," resumed the Ghost, "by Three Spirits."

Scrooge's countenance fell almost as low as the Ghost's had done.

"Is that the chance and hope you mentioned, Jacob?" he demanded, in a faltering voice.

"It is."

"I—I think I'd rather not," said Scrooge.

"Without their visits," said the Ghost, "you cannot hope to shun the path I tread. Expect the first to-morrow, when the bell tolls One."

"Couldn't I take 'em all at once, and have it over, Jacob?" hinted Scrooge.

"Expect the second on the next night at the same hour. The third upon the next night when the last stroke of Twelve has ceased to vibrate. Look to see me no more; and look that, for your own sake, you remember what has passed between us!"

When it had said these words, the spectre took its wrapper from the table, and bound it round its head, as before. Scrooge knew this, by the smart sound its teeth made, when the jaws were brought together by the bandage. He ventured to raise his eyes again, and found his supernatural visitor confronting him in an erect attitude, with its chain wound over and about its arm.

The apparition walked backward from him; and at every step it took, the window raised itself a little, so that when the spectre reached it, it was wide open.

It beckoned Scrooge to approach, which he did. When they were within two paces of each other, Marley's Ghost held up its hand, warning him to come no nearer. Scrooge stopped.

Not so much in obedience, as in surprise and fear: for on the raising of the hand, he became sensible of confused noises in the air; incoherent sounds of lamentation and regret; wailings inexpressibly sorrowful and self-accusatory. The spectre, after listening for a moment, joined in the mournful dirge; and floated out upon the bleak, dark night.

Scrooge followed to the window: desperate in his curiosity. He looked out.

The air was filled with phantoms, wandering hither and thither in restless haste, and moaning as they went. Every one of them wore chains like Marley's Ghost; some few (they might be guilty governments) were linked together; none were free. Many had been personally known to Scrooge in their lives. He had been quite familiar with one old ghost, in a white waistcoat, with a monstrous iron safe attached to its ankle, who cried piteously at being unable to assist a wretched woman with an infant, whom it saw below, upon a door-step. The misery with them all was, clearly, that they sought to interfere, for good, in human matters, and had lost the power for ever.

Whether these creatures faded into mist, or mist enshrouded them, he could not tell. But they and their spirit voices faded together; and the night became as it had been when he walked home.

A Christmas Carol

Scrooge closed the window, and examined the door by which the Ghost had entered. It was double-locked, as he had locked it with his own hands, and the bolts were undisturbed. He tried to say "Humbug!" but stopped at the first syllable. And being, from the emotion he had undergone, or the fatigues of the day, or his glimpse of the Invisible World, or the dull conversation of the Ghost, or the lateness of the hour, much in need of repose; went straight to bed, without undressing, and fell asleep upon the instant.

STAVE TWO.
THE FIRST OF THE THREE SPIRITS.

When Scrooge awoke, it was so dark, that looking out of bed, he could scarcely distinguish the transparent window from the opaque walls of his chamber. He was endeavouring to pierce the darkness with his ferret eyes, when the chimes of a neighbouring church struck the four quarters. So he listened for the hour.

To his great astonishment the heavy bell went on from six to seven, and from seven to eight, and regularly up to twelve; then stopped. Twelve! It was past two when he went to bed. The clock was wrong. An icicle must have got into the works. Twelve!

He touched the spring of his repeater, to correct this most preposterous clock. Its rapid little pulse beat twelve: and stopped.

"Why, it isn't possible," said Scrooge, "that I can have slept through a whole day and far into another night. It isn't possible that anything has happened to the sun, and this is twelve at noon!"

The idea being an alarming one, he scrambled out of bed, and groped his way to the window. He was obliged to rub the frost off with the sleeve of his dressing-gown before he could see anything; and could see very little then. All he could make out was, that it was still very foggy and extremely cold, and that there was no noise of people running to and fro, and making a great stir, as there unquestionably would have been if night had beaten off bright day, and taken possession of the world. This was a great relief, because "three days after sight of this First of Exchange pay to Mr. Ebenezer Scrooge or his order," and so forth, would have become a mere United States' security if there were no days to count by.

Scrooge went to bed again, and thought, and thought, and thought it over and over and over, and could make nothing of it. The more he thought, the more perplexed he was; and the more he endeavoured not to think, the more he thought.

Marley's Ghost bothered him exceedingly. Every time he resolved within himself, after mature inquiry, that it was all a dream, his mind flew back again, like a strong spring released, to its first position, and presented the same problem to be

A Christmas Carol

worked all through, "Was it a dream or not?"

Scrooge lay in this state until the chime had gone three quarters more, when he remembered, on a sudden, that the Ghost had warned him of a visitation when the bell tolled one. He resolved to lie awake until the hour was passed; and, considering that he could no more go to sleep than go to Heaven, this was perhaps the wisest resolution in his power.

The quarter was so long, that he was more than once convinced he must have sunk into a doze unconsciously, and missed the clock. At length it broke upon his listening ear.

"Ding, dong!"

"A quarter past," said Scrooge, counting.

"Ding, dong!"

"Half-past!" said Scrooge.

"Ding, dong!"

"A quarter to it," said Scrooge.

"Ding, dong!"

"The hour itself," said Scrooge, triumphantly, "and nothing else!"

He spoke before the hour bell sounded, which it now did with a deep, dull, hollow, melancholy One. Light flashed up in the room upon the instant, and the curtains of his bed were drawn.

The curtains of his bed were drawn aside, I tell you, by a hand. Not the curtains at his feet, nor the curtains at his back, but those to which his face was addressed. The curtains of his bed were drawn aside; and Scrooge, starting up into a half-recumbent attitude, found himself face to face with the unearthly visitor who drew them: as close to it as I am now to you, and I am standing in the spirit at your elbow.

It was a strange figure—like a child: yet not so like a child as like an old man, viewed through some supernatural medium, which gave him the appearance of having receded from the view, and being diminished to a child's proportions. Its hair, which hung about its neck and down its back, was white as if with age; and yet the face had not a wrinkle in it, and the tenderest bloom was on the skin. The arms were very long and muscular; the hands the same, as if its hold were of uncommon strength. Its legs and feet, most delicately formed, were, like those upper members, bare. It wore a tunic of the purest white; and round its waist was bound a lustrous belt, the sheen of which was beautiful. It held a branch of fresh green holly in its hand; and, in singular contradiction of that wintry emblem, had its dress trimmed with summer flowers. But the strangest thing about it was, that from the crown of its head there sprung a bright clear jet of light, by which all this was visible; and which was doubtless the occasion of its using, in its duller moments, a great extinguisher for a cap, which it now held under its arm.

Even this, though, when Scrooge looked at it with increasing steadiness, was not its strangest quality. For as its belt sparkled and glittered now in one part and now in another, and what was light one instant, at another time was dark, so the figure itself fluctuated in its distinctness: being now a thing with one arm, now with one leg, now with twenty legs, now a pair of legs without a head, now a head without a body: of which dissolving parts, no outline would be visible in the dense gloom wherein they melted away. And in the very wonder of this, it would be itself again; distinct and clear as ever.

"Are you the Spirit, sir, whose coming was foretold to me?" asked Scrooge.

"I am!"

The voice was soft and gentle. Singularly low, as if instead of being so close beside him, it were at a distance.

"Who, and what are you?" Scrooge demanded.

"I am the Ghost of Christmas Past."

"Long Past?" inquired Scrooge: observant of its dwarfish stature.

"No. Your past."

Perhaps, Scrooge could not have told anybody why, if anybody could have asked him; but he had a special desire to see the Spirit in his cap; and begged him to be covered.

"What!" exclaimed the Ghost, "would you so soon put out, with worldly hands, the light I give? Is it not enough that you are one of those whose passions made this cap, and force me through whole trains of years to wear it low upon my brow!"

Scrooge reverently disclaimed all intention to offend or any knowledge of having wilfully "bonneted" the Spirit at any period of his life. He then made bold to inquire what business brought him there.

"Your welfare!" said the Ghost.

Scrooge expressed himself much obliged, but could not help thinking that a night of unbroken rest would have been more conducive to that end. The Spirit must have heard him thinking, for it said immediately:

"Your reclamation, then. Take heed!"

It put out its strong hand as it spoke, and clasped him gently by the arm.

"Rise! and walk with me!"

It would have been in vain for Scrooge to plead that the weather and the hour were not adapted to pedestrian purposes; that bed was warm, and the thermometer a long way below freezing; that he was clad but lightly in his slippers, dressing-gown, and nightcap; and that he had a cold upon him at that time. The grasp, though gentle as a woman's hand, was not to be resisted. He rose: but finding that the Spirit made towards the window, clasped his robe in supplication.

"I am a mortal," Scrooge remonstrated, "and liable to fall."

"Bear but a touch of my hand there," said the Spirit, laying it upon his heart, "and you shall be upheld in more than this!"

As the words were spoken, they passed through the wall, and stood upon an open country road, with fields on either hand. The city had entirely vanished. Not a vestige of it was to be seen. The darkness and the mist had vanished with it, for it was a clear, cold, winter day, with snow upon the ground.

"Good Heaven!" said Scrooge, clasping his hands together, as he looked about him. "I was bred in this place. I was a boy here!"

The Spirit gazed upon him mildly. Its gentle touch, though it had been light and instantaneous, appeared still present to the old man's sense of feeling. He was conscious of a thousand odours floating in the air, each one connected with a thousand thoughts, and hopes, and joys, and cares long, long, forgotten!

"Your lip is trembling," said the Ghost. "And what is that upon your cheek?"

Scrooge muttered, with an unusual catching in his voice, that it was a pimple; and begged the Ghost to lead him where he would.

"You recollect the way?" inquired the Spirit.

"Remember it!" cried Scrooge with fervour; "I could walk it blindfold."

"Strange to have forgotten it for so many years!" observed the Ghost. "Let us go on."

They walked along the road, Scrooge recognising every gate, and post, and tree; until a little market-town appeared in the distance, with its bridge, its church, and winding river. Some shaggy ponies now were seen trotting towards them with boys upon their backs, who called to other boys in country gigs and carts, driven by farmers. All these boys were in great spirits, and shouted to each other, until the broad fields were so full of merry music, that the crisp air laughed to hear it!

"These are but shadows of the things that have been," said the Ghost. "They have no consciousness of us."

The jocund travellers came on; and as they came, Scrooge knew and named them every one. Why was he rejoiced beyond all bounds to see them! Why did his cold eye glisten, and his heart leap up as they went past! Why was he filled with gladness when he heard them give each other Merry Christmas, as they parted at cross-roads and bye-ways, for their several homes! What was merry Christmas to Scrooge? Out upon merry Christmas! What good had it ever done to him?

"The school is not quite deserted," said the Ghost. "A solitary child, neglected by his friends, is left there still."

Scrooge said he knew it. And he sobbed.

They left the high-road, by a well-remembered lane, and soon approached a mansion of dull red brick, with a little weathercock-surmounted cupola, on the roof, and a bell hanging in it. It was a large house, but one of broken fortunes; for the spacious offices were little used, their walls were damp and mossy, their windows broken, and their gates decayed. Fowls clucked and strutted in the stables; and the coach-houses and sheds were over-run with grass. Nor was it more retentive of its ancient state, within; for entering the dreary hall, and glancing through the open doors of many rooms, they found them poorly furnished, cold, and vast. There was an earthy savour in the air, a chilly bareness in the place, which associated itself somehow with too much getting up by candle-light, and not too much to eat.

They went, the Ghost and Scrooge, across the hall, to a door at the back of the house. It opened before them, and disclosed a long, bare, melancholy room, made barer still by lines of plain deal forms and desks. At one of these a lonely boy was reading near a feeble fire; and Scrooge sat down upon a form, and wept to see his poor forgotten self as he used to be.

Not a latent echo in the house, not a squeak and scuffle from the mice behind the panelling, not a drip from the half-thawed water-spout in the dull yard behind, not a sigh among the leafless boughs of one despondent poplar, not the idle swinging of an empty store-house door, no, not a clicking in the fire, but fell upon the heart of Scrooge with a softening influence, and gave a freer passage to his tears.

The Spirit touched him on the arm, and pointed to his younger self, intent upon his reading. Suddenly a man, in foreign garments: wonderfully real and distinct to look at: stood outside the window, with an axe stuck in his belt, and leading by the bridle an ass laden with wood.

"Why, it's Ali Baba!" Scrooge exclaimed in ecstasy. "It's dear old honest Ali Baba! Yes, yes, I know! One Christmas time, when yonder solitary child was left here all alone, he did come, for the first time, just like that. Poor boy! And Valentine," said Scrooge, "and his wild brother, Orson; there they go! And what's his name, who was put down in his drawers, asleep, at the Gate of Damascus; don't you see him! And the Sultan's Groom turned upside down by the Genii; there he is upon his head! Serve him right. I'm glad of it. What business had he to be married to the Princess!"

To hear Scrooge expending all the earnestness of his nature on such subjects, in a most extraordinary voice between laughing and crying; and to see his heightened and excited face; would have been a surprise to his business friends in the city, indeed.

"There's the Parrot!" cried Scrooge. "Green body and yellow tail, with a thing like a lettuce growing out of the top of his head; there he is! Poor Robin Crusoe, he called him, when he came home again after sailing round the island. 'Poor Robin Crusoe, where have you been, Robin Crusoe?' The man thought he was dreaming, but he wasn't. It was the Parrot, you know. There goes Friday, running for his life to the little creek! Halloa! Hoop! Halloo!"

Then, with a rapidity of transition very foreign to his usual character, he said, in pity for his former self, "Poor boy!" and cried again.

"I wish," Scrooge muttered, putting his hand in his pocket, and looking about him, after drying his eyes with his cuff: "but it's too late now."

"What is the matter?" asked the Spirit.

"Nothing," said Scrooge. "Nothing. There was a boy singing a Christmas Carol at my door last night. I should like to have given him something: that's all."

The Ghost smiled thoughtfully, and waved its hand: saying as it did so, "Let us see another Christmas!"

Scrooge's former self grew larger at the words, and the room became a little darker and more dirty. The panels shrunk, the windows cracked; fragments of plaster fell out of the ceiling, and the naked laths were shown instead; but how all this was brought about, Scrooge knew no more than you do. He only knew that it was quite correct; that everything had happened so; that there he was, alone again, when all the other boys had gone home for the jolly holidays.

He was not reading now, but walking up and down despairingly. Scrooge looked at the Ghost, and with a mournful shaking of his head, glanced anxiously towards the door.

It opened; and a little girl, much younger than the boy, came darting in, and putting her arms about his neck, and often kissing him, addressed him as her "Dear, dear brother."

"I have come to bring you home, dear brother!" said the child, clapping her tiny hands, and bending down to laugh. "To bring you home, home, home!"

A Christmas Carol

"Home, little Fan?" returned the boy.

"Yes!" said the child, brimful of glee. "Home, for good and all. Home, for ever and ever. Father is so much kinder than he used to be, that home's like Heaven! He spoke so gently to me one dear night when I was going to bed, that I was not afraid to ask him once more if you might come home; and he said Yes, you should; and sent me in a coach to bring you. And you're to be a man!" said the child, opening her eyes, "and are never to come back here; but first, we're to be together all the Christmas long, and have the merriest time in all the world."

"You are quite a woman, little Fan!" exclaimed the boy.

She clapped her hands and laughed, and tried to touch his head; but being too little, laughed again, and stood on tiptoe to embrace him. Then she began to drag him, in her childish eagerness, towards the door; and he, nothing loth to go, accompanied her.

A terrible voice in the hall cried, "Bring down Master Scrooge's box, there!" and in the hall appeared the schoolmaster himself, who glared on Master Scrooge with a ferocious condescension, and threw him into a dreadful state of mind by shaking hands with him. He then conveyed him and his sister into the veriest old well of a shivering best-parlour that ever was seen, where the maps upon the wall, and the celestial and terrestrial globes in the windows, were waxy with cold. Here he produced a decanter of curiously light wine, and a block of curiously heavy cake, and administered instalments of those dainties to the young people: at the same time, sending out a meagre servant to offer a glass of "something" to the postboy, who answered that he thanked the gentleman, but if it was the same tap as he had tasted before, he had rather not. Master Scrooge's trunk being by this time tied on to the top of the chaise, the children bade the schoolmaster good-bye right willingly; and getting into it, drove gaily down the garden-sweep: the quick wheels dashing the hoar-frost and snow from off the dark leaves of the evergreens like spray.

"Always a delicate creature, whom a breath might have withered," said the Ghost. "But she had a large heart!"

"So she had," cried Scrooge. "You're right. I will not gainsay it, Spirit. God forbid!"

"She died a woman," said the Ghost, "and had, as I think, children."

"One child," Scrooge returned.

"True," said the Ghost. "Your nephew!"

Scrooge seemed uneasy in his mind; and answered briefly, "Yes."

Although they had but that moment left the school behind them, they were now in the busy thoroughfares of a city, where shadowy passengers passed and repassed; where shadowy carts and coaches battled for the way, and all the strife and tumult of a real city were. It was made plain enough, by the dressing of the shops, that here too it was Christmas time again; but it was evening, and the streets were lighted up.

The Ghost stopped at a certain warehouse door, and asked Scrooge if he knew it.

"Know it!" said Scrooge. "Was I apprenticed here!"

They went in. At sight of an old gentleman in a Welsh wig, sitting behind such a high desk, that if he had been two inches taller he must have knocked his head against the ceiling, Scrooge cried in great excitement:

"Why, it's old Fezziwig! Bless his heart; it's Fezziwig alive again!"

Old Fezziwig laid down his pen, and looked up at the clock, which pointed to the hour of seven. He rubbed his hands; adjusted his capacious waistcoat; laughed all over himself, from his shoes to his organ of benevolence; and called out in a comfortable, oily, rich, fat, jovial voice:

"Yo ho, there! Ebenezer! Dick!"

Scrooge's former self, now grown a young man, came briskly in, accompanied by his fellow-'prentice.

"Dick Wilkins, to be sure!" said Scrooge to the Ghost. "Bless me, yes. There he is. He was very much attached to me, was Dick. Poor Dick! Dear, dear!"

"Yo ho, my boys!" said Fezziwig. "No more work to-night. Christmas Eve, Dick. Christmas, Ebenezer! Let's have the shutters up," cried old Fezziwig, with a sharp clap of his hands, "before a man can say Jack Robinson!"

A Christmas Carol

You wouldn't believe how those two fellows went at it! They charged into the street with the shutters—one, two, three—had 'em up in their places—four, five, six—barred 'em and pinned 'em—seven, eight, nine—and came back before you could have got to twelve, panting like race-horses.

"Hilli-ho!" cried old Fezziwig, skipping down from the high desk, with wonderful agility. "Clear away, my lads, and let's have lots of room here! Hilli-ho, Dick! Chirrup, Ebenezer!"

Clear away! There was nothing they wouldn't have cleared away, or couldn't have cleared away, with old Fezziwig looking on. It was done in a minute. Every movable was packed off, as if it were dismissed from public life for evermore; the floor was swept and watered, the lamps were trimmed, fuel was heaped upon the fire; and the warehouse was as snug, and warm, and dry, and bright a ball-room, as you would desire to see upon a winter's night.

In came a fiddler with a music-book, and went up to the lofty desk, and made an orchestra of it, and tuned like fifty stomach-aches. In came Mrs. Fezziwig, one vast substantial smile. In came the three Miss Fezziwigs, beaming and lovable. In came the six young followers whose hearts they broke. In came all the young men and women employed in the business. In came the housemaid, with her cousin, the baker. In came the cook, with her brother's particular friend, the milkman. In came the boy from over the way, who was suspected of not having board enough from his master; trying to hide himself behind the girl from next door but one, who was proved to have had her ears pulled by her mistress. In they all came, one after another; some shyly, some boldly, some gracefully, some awkwardly, some pushing, some pulling; in they all came, anyhow and everyhow. Away they all went, twenty couple at once; hands half round and back again the other way; down the middle and up again; round and round in various stages of affectionate grouping; old top couple always turning up in the wrong place; new top couple starting off again, as soon as they got there; all top couples at last, and not a bottom one to help them! When this result was brought about, old Fezziwig, clapping his hands to stop the dance, cried out, "Well done!" and the fiddler plunged his hot face into a pot of porter, especially provided for that purpose. But scorning rest, upon his reappearance, he instantly began again, though there were no dancers yet, as if the other fiddler had been carried home, exhausted, on a shutter, and he were a bran-new man resolved to beat him out of sight, or perish.

A Christmas Carol

There were more dances, and there were forfeits, and more dances, and there was cake, and there was negus, and there was a great piece of Cold Roast, and there was a great piece of Cold Boiled, and there were mince-pies, and plenty of beer. But the great effect of the evening came after the Roast and Boiled, when the fiddler (an artful dog, mind! The sort of man who knew his business better than you or I could have told it him!) struck up "Sir Roger de Coverley." Then old Fezziwig stood out to dance with Mrs. Fezziwig. Top couple, too; with a good stiff piece of work cut out for them; three or four and twenty pair of partners; people who were not to be trifled with; people who would dance, and had no notion of walking.

But if they had been twice as many — ah, four times — old Fezziwig would have been a match for them, and so would Mrs. Fezziwig. As to her, she was worthy to be his partner in every sense of the term. If that's not high praise, tell me higher, and I'll use it. A positive light appeared to issue from Fezziwig's calves. They shone in every part of the dance like moons. You couldn't have predicted, at any given time, what would have become of them next. And when old Fezziwig and Mrs. Fezziwig had gone all through the dance; advance and retire, both hands to your partner, bow and curtsey, corkscrew, thread-the-needle, and back again to your place; Fezziwig "cut" — cut so deftly, that he appeared to wink with his legs, and came upon his feet again without a stagger.

When the clock struck eleven, this domestic ball broke up. Mr. and Mrs. Fezziwig took their stations, one on either side of the door, and shaking hands with every person individually as he or she went out, wished him or her a Merry Christmas. When everybody had retired but the two 'prentices, they did the same to them; and thus the cheerful voices died away, and the lads were left to their beds; which were under a counter in the back-shop.

During the whole of this time, Scrooge had acted like a man out of his wits. His heart and soul were in the scene, and with his former self. He corroborated everything, remembered everything, enjoyed everything, and underwent the strangest agitation. It was not until now, when the bright faces of his former self and Dick were turned from them, that he remembered the Ghost, and became conscious that it was looking full upon him, while the light upon its head burnt very clear.

"A small matter," said the Ghost, "to make these silly folks so full of gratitude."

"Small!" echoed Scrooge.

The Spirit signed to him to listen to the two apprentices, who were pouring out their hearts in praise of Fezziwig: and when he had done so, said,

"Why! Is it not? He has spent but a few pounds of your mortal money: three or four perhaps. Is that so much that he deserves this praise?"

"It isn't that," said Scrooge, heated by the remark, and speaking unconsciously like his former, not his latter, self. "It isn't that, Spirit. He has the power to render us happy or unhappy; to make our service light or burdensome; a pleasure or a toil. Say that his power lies in words and looks; in things so slight and insignificant that it is impossible to add and count 'em up: what then? The happiness he gives, is quite as great as if it cost a fortune."

He felt the Spirit's glance, and stopped.

"What is the matter?" asked the Ghost.

"Nothing particular," said Scrooge.

"Something, I think?" the Ghost insisted.

"No," said Scrooge, "No. I should like to be able to say a word or two to my clerk just now. That's all."

His former self turned down the lamps as he gave utterance to the wish; and Scrooge and the Ghost again stood side by side in the open air.

"My time grows short," observed the Spirit. "Quick!"

This was not addressed to Scrooge, or to any one whom he could see, but it produced an immediate effect. For again Scrooge saw himself. He was older now; a man in the prime of life. His face had not the harsh and rigid lines of later years; but it had begun to wear the signs of care and avarice. There was an eager, greedy, restless motion in the eye, which showed the passion that had taken root, and where the shadow of the growing tree would fall.

He was not alone, but sat by the side of a fair young girl in a mourning-dress: in whose eyes there were tears, which sparkled in the light that shone out of the Ghost of Christmas Past.

A Christmas Carol

"It matters little," she said, softly. "To you, very little. Another idol has displaced me; and if it can cheer and comfort you in time to come, as I would have tried to do, I have no just cause to grieve."

"What Idol has displaced you?" he rejoined.

"A golden one."

"This is the even-handed dealing of the world!" he said. "There is nothing on which it is so hard as poverty; and there is nothing it professes to condemn with such severity as the pursuit of wealth!"

"You fear the world too much," she answered, gently. "All your other hopes have merged into the hope of being beyond the chance of its sordid reproach. I have seen your nobler aspirations fall off one by one, until the master-passion, Gain, engrosses you. Have I not?"

"What then?" he retorted. "Even if I have grown so much wiser, what then? I am not changed towards you."

She shook her head.

"Am I?"

"Our contract is an old one. It was made when we were both poor and content to be so, until, in good season, we could improve our worldly fortune by our patient industry. You are changed. When it was made, you were another man."

"I was a boy," he said impatiently.

"Your own feeling tells you that you were not what you are," she returned. "I am. That which promised happiness when we were one in heart, is fraught with misery now that we are two. How often and how keenly I have thought of this, I will not say. It is enough that I have thought of it, and can release you."

"Have I ever sought release?"

"In words. No. Never."

"In what, then?"

546

A Christmas Carol

"In a changed nature; in an altered spirit; in another atmosphere of life; another Hope as its great end. In everything that made my love of any worth or value in your sight. If this had never been between us," said the girl, looking mildly, but with steadiness, upon him; "tell me, would you seek me out and try to win me now? Ah, no!"

He seemed to yield to the justice of this supposition, in spite of himself. But he said with a struggle, "You think not."

"I would gladly think otherwise if I could," she answered, "Heaven knows! When I have learned a Truth like this, I know how strong and irresistible it must be. But if you were free to-day, to-morrow, yesterday, can even I believe that you would choose a dowerless girl—you who, in your very confidence with her, weigh everything by Gain: or, choosing her, if for a moment you were false enough to your one guiding principle to do so, do I not know that your repentance and regret would surely follow? I do; and I release you. With a full heart, for the love of him you once were."

He was about to speak; but with her head turned from him, she resumed.

"You may—the memory of what is past half makes me hope you will—have pain in this. A very, very brief time, and you will dismiss the recollection of it, gladly, as an unprofitable dream, from which it happened well that you awoke. May you be happy in the life you have chosen!"

She left him, and they parted.

"Spirit!" said Scrooge, "show me no more! Conduct me home. Why do you delight to torture me?"

"One shadow more!" exclaimed the Ghost.

"No more!" cried Scrooge. "No more. I don't wish to see it. Show me no more!"

But the relentless Ghost pinioned him in both his arms, and forced him to observe what happened next.

They were in another scene and place; a room, not very large or handsome, but full of comfort. Near to the winter fire sat a beautiful young girl, so like that last that Scrooge believed it was the same, until he saw her, now a comely matron, sitting opposite her daughter. The noise in this room was perfectly tumultuous, for there were more children there, than Scrooge in his agitated state of mind could count; and, unlike the celebrated herd in the poem, they were not forty children conducting themselves like one, but every child was conducting itself like forty. The consequences were uproarious beyond belief; but no one seemed to care; on the contrary, the mother and daughter laughed heartily, and enjoyed it very much; and the latter, soon beginning to mingle in the sports, got pillaged by the young brigands most ruthlessly. What would I not have given to be one of them! Though I never could have been so rude, no, no! I wouldn't for the wealth of all the world have crushed that braided hair, and torn it down; and for the precious little shoe, I wouldn't have plucked it off, God bless my soul! to save my life. As to measuring her waist in sport, as they did, bold young brood, I couldn't have done it; I should have expected my arm to have grown round it for a punishment, and never come straight again. And yet I should have dearly liked, I own, to have touched her lips; to have questioned her, that she might have opened them; to have looked upon the lashes of her downcast eyes, and never raised a blush; to have let loose waves of hair, an inch of which would be a keepsake beyond price: in short, I should have liked, I do confess, to have had the lightest licence of a child, and yet to have been man enough to know its value.

But now a knocking at the door was heard, and such a rush immediately ensued that she with laughing face and plundered dress was borne towards it the centre of a flushed and boisterous group, just in time to greet the father, who came home attended by a man laden with Christmas toys and presents. Then the shouting and the struggling, and the onslaught that was made on the defenceless porter! The scaling him with chairs for ladders to dive into his pockets, despoil him of brown-paper parcels, hold on tight by his cravat, hug him round his neck, pommel his back, and kick his legs in irrepressible affection! The shouts of wonder and delight with which the development of every package was received! The terrible announcement that the baby had been taken in the act of putting a doll's frying-pan into his mouth, and was more than suspected of having swallowed a fictitious turkey, glued on a wooden platter! The immense relief of finding this a false alarm! The joy, and gratitude, and ecstasy! They are all indescribable alike. It is enough that by degrees the children and their emotions got out of the parlour, and by one stair at a time, up to the top of the house; where they went to bed, and so subsided.

And now Scrooge looked on more attentively than ever, when the master of the house, having his daughter leaning fondly on him, sat down with her and her mother at his own fireside; and when he thought that such another creature, quite as graceful and as full of promise, might have called him father, and been a spring-time in the haggard winter of his life, his sight grew very dim indeed.

"Belle," said the husband, turning to his wife with a smile, "I saw an old friend of yours this afternoon."

"Who was it?"

"Guess!"

"How can I? Tut, don't I know?" she added in the same breath, laughing as he laughed. "Mr. Scrooge."

"Mr. Scrooge it was. I passed his office window; and as it was not shut up, and he had a candle inside, I could scarcely help seeing him. His partner lies upon the point of death, I hear; and there he sat alone. Quite alone in the world, I do believe."

"Spirit!" said Scrooge in a broken voice, "remove me from this place."

"I told you these were shadows of the things that have been," said the Ghost. "That they are what they are, do not blame me!"

"Remove me!" Scrooge exclaimed, "I cannot bear it!"

He turned upon the Ghost, and seeing that it looked upon him with a face, in which in some strange way there were fragments of all the faces it had shown him, wrestled with it.

"Leave me! Take me back. Haunt me no longer!"

In the struggle, if that can be called a struggle in which the Ghost with no visible resistance on its own part was undisturbed by any effort of its adversary, Scrooge observed that its light was burning high and bright; and dimly connecting that with its influence over him, he seized the extinguisher-cap, and by a sudden action pressed it down upon its head.

The Spirit dropped beneath it, so that the extinguisher covered its whole form; but though Scrooge pressed it down with all his force, he could not hide the light: which streamed from under it, in an unbroken flood upon the ground.

He was conscious of being exhausted, and overcome by an irresistible drowsiness; and, further, of being in his own bedroom. He gave the cap a parting squeeze, in which his hand relaxed; and had barely time to reel to bed, before he sank into a heavy sleep.

STAVE THREE.
THE SECOND OF THE THREE SPIRITS.

Awaking in the middle of a prodigiously tough snore, and sitting up in bed to get his thoughts together, Scrooge had no occasion to be told that the bell was again upon the stroke of One. He felt that he was restored to consciousness in the right nick of time, for the especial purpose of holding a conference with the second messenger despatched to him through Jacob Marley's intervention. But finding that he turned uncomfortably cold when he began to wonder which of his curtains this new spectre would draw back, he put them every one aside with his own hands; and lying down again, established a sharp look-out all round the bed. For he wished to challenge the Spirit on the moment of its appearance, and did not wish to be taken by surprise, and made nervous.

Gentlemen of the free-and-easy sort, who plume themselves on being acquainted with a move or two, and being usually equal to the time-of-day, express the wide range of their capacity for adventure by observing that they are good for anything from pitch-and-toss to manslaughter; between which opposite extremes, no doubt, there lies a tolerably wide and comprehensive range of subjects. Without venturing for Scrooge quite as hardily as this, I don't mind calling on you to believe that he was ready for a good broad field of strange appearances, and that nothing between a baby and rhinoceros would have astonished him very much.

Now, being prepared for almost anything, he was not by any means prepared for nothing; and, consequently, when the Bell struck One, and no shape appeared, he was taken with a violent fit of trembling. Five minutes, ten minutes, a quarter of an hour went by, yet nothing came. All this time, he lay upon his bed, the very core and centre of a blaze of ruddy light, which streamed upon it when the clock proclaimed the hour; and which, being only light, was more alarming than a dozen ghosts, as he was powerless to make out what it meant, or would be at; and was sometimes apprehensive that he might be at that very moment an interesting case of spontaneous combustion, without having the consolation of knowing it. At last, however, he began to think—as you or I would have thought at first; for it is always the person not in the predicament who knows what ought to have been done in it, and would unquestionably have done it too—at last, I say, he began to think that the source and secret of this ghostly light might be in the adjoining room, from whence, on further tracing it, it seemed to shine. This idea taking full possession of his mind, he got up softly and shuffled in his slippers to the door.

The moment Scrooge's hand was on the lock, a strange voice called him by his name, and bade him enter. He obeyed.

It was his own room. There was no doubt about that. But it had undergone a surprising transformation. The walls and ceiling were so hung with living green, that it looked a perfect grove; from every part of which, bright gleaming berries glistened. The crisp leaves of holly, mistletoe, and ivy reflected back the light, as if so many little mirrors had been scattered there; and such a mighty blaze went roaring up the chimney, as that dull petrification of a hearth had never known in Scrooge's time, or Marley's, or for many and many a winter season gone. Heaped up on the floor, to form a kind of throne, were turkeys, geese, game, poultry, brawn, great joints of meat, sucking-pigs, long wreaths of sausages, mince-pies, plum-puddings, barrels of oysters, red-hot chestnuts, cherry-cheeked apples, juicy oranges, luscious pears, immense twelfth-cakes, and seething bowls of punch, that made the chamber dim with their delicious steam. In easy state upon this couch, there sat a jolly Giant, glorious to see; who bore a glowing torch, in shape not unlike Plenty's horn, and held it up, high up, to shed its light on Scrooge, as he came peeping round the door.

"Come in!" exclaimed the Ghost. "Come in! and know me better, man!"

Scrooge entered timidly, and hung his head before this Spirit. He was not the dogged Scrooge he had been; and though the Spirit's eyes were clear and kind, he did not like to meet them.

"I am the Ghost of Christmas Present," said the Spirit. "Look upon me!"

Scrooge reverently did so. It was clothed in one simple green robe, or mantle, bordered with white fur. This garment hung so loosely on the figure, that its capacious breast was bare, as if disdaining to be warded or concealed by any artifice. Its feet, observable beneath the ample folds of the garment, were also bare; and on its head it wore no other covering than a holly wreath, set here and there with shining icicles. Its dark brown curls were long and free; free as its genial face, its sparkling eye, its open hand, its cheery voice, its unconstrained demeanour, and its joyful air. Girded round its middle was an antique scabbard; but no sword was in it, and the ancient sheath was

A Christmas Carol

eaten up with rust.

"You have never seen the like of me before!" exclaimed the Spirit.

"Never," Scrooge made answer to it.

"Have never walked forth with the younger members of my family; meaning (for I am very young) my elder brothers born in these later years?" pursued the Phantom.

"I don't think I have," said Scrooge. "I am afraid I have not. Have you had many brothers, Spirit?"

"More than eighteen hundred," said the Ghost.

"A tremendous family to provide for!" muttered Scrooge.

The Ghost of Christmas Present rose.

"Spirit," said Scrooge submissively, "conduct me where you will. I went forth last night on compulsion, and I learnt a lesson which is working now. To-night, if you have aught to teach me, let me profit by it."

"Touch my robe!"

Scrooge did as he was told, and held it fast.

Holly, mistletoe, red berries, ivy, turkeys, geese, game, poultry, brawn, meat, pigs, sausages, oysters, pies, puddings, fruit, and punch, all vanished instantly. So did the room, the fire, the ruddy glow, the hour of night, and they stood in the city streets on Christmas morning, where (for the weather was severe) the people made a rough, but brisk and not unpleasant kind of music, in scraping the snow from the pavement in front of their dwellings, and from the tops of their houses, whence it was mad delight to the boys to see it come plumping down into the road below, and splitting into artificial little snow-storms.

The house fronts looked black enough, and the windows blacker, contrasting with the smooth white sheet of snow upon the roofs, and with the dirtier snow upon the ground; which last deposit had been ploughed up in deep furrows by the heavy wheels of carts and waggons; furrows that crossed and re-crossed each other hundreds of times where the great streets branched off; and made intricate channels, hard to trace in the thick yellow mud and icy water. The sky was gloomy, and the shortest streets were choked up with a dingy mist, half thawed, half frozen, whose heavier particles descended in a shower of sooty atoms, as if all the chimneys in Great Britain had, by one consent, caught fire, and were blazing away to their dear hearts' content. There was nothing very cheerful in the climate or the town, and yet was there an air of cheerfulness abroad that the clearest summer air and brightest summer sun might have endeavoured to diffuse in vain.

For, the people who were shovelling away on the housetops were jovial and full of glee; calling out to one another from the parapets, and now and then exchanging a facetious snowball — better-natured missile far than many a wordy jest — laughing heartily if it went right and not less heartily if it went wrong. The poulterers' shops were still half open, and the fruiterers' were radiant in their glory. There were great, round, pot-bellied baskets of chestnuts, shaped like the waistcoats of jolly old gentlemen, lolling at the doors, and tumbling out into the street in their apoplectic opulence. There were ruddy, brown-faced, broad-girthed Spanish Onions, shining in the fatness of their growth like Spanish Friars, and winking from their shelves in wanton slyness at the girls as they went by, and glanced demurely at the hung-up mistletoe. There were pears and apples, clustered high in blooming pyramids; there were bunches of grapes, made, in the shopkeepers' benevolence to dangle from conspicuous hooks, that people's mouths might water gratis as they passed; there were piles of filberts, mossy and brown, recalling, in their fragrance, ancient walks among the woods, and pleasant shufflings ankle deep through withered leaves; there were Norfolk Biffins, squat and swarthy, setting off the yellow of the oranges and lemons, and, in the great compactness of their juicy persons, urgently entreating and beseeching to be carried home in paper bags and eaten after dinner. The very gold and silver fish, set forth among these choice fruits in a bowl, though members of a dull and stagnant-blooded race, appeared to know that there was something going on; and, to a fish, went gasping round and round their little world in slow and passionless excitement.

The Grocers'! oh, the Grocers'! nearly closed, with perhaps two shutters down, or one; but through those gaps such glimpses! It was not alone that the scales descending on the counter made a merry sound, or that the twine and roller parted company so briskly, or that the canisters were rattled up and down like juggling tricks, or even that the blended scents of tea and coffee were so grateful to the nose, or even that the raisins were so plentiful and rare, the almonds so extremely white, the sticks of cinnamon so long and straight, the other spices so delicious, the candied fruits so caked and spotted with molten sugar as to make the coldest lookers-on feel faint and subsequently bilious. Nor was it that the figs were moist and pulpy, or that the French plums blushed in modest tartness from their highly-decorated boxes, or that everything was good to eat and in its Christmas dress; but the customers were all so hurried and so eager in the hopeful promise of the day, that they tumbled up against each other at the door, crashing their wicker baskets wildly, and left their purchases upon the counter, and came running back to fetch them, and committed hundreds of the like mistakes, in the best humour possible; while the Grocer and his people were so frank and fresh that the polished hearts with which they fastened their aprons behind might have been their own, worn outside for general inspection, and for Christmas daws to peck at if they chose.

But soon the steeples called good people all, to church and chapel, and away they came, flocking through the streets in their best clothes, and with their gayest faces. And at the same time there emerged from scores of bye-streets, lanes, and nameless turnings, innumerable people, carrying their dinners to the bakers' shops. The sight of these poor revellers appeared to interest the Spirit very much, for he stood with Scrooge beside him in a baker's doorway, and taking off the covers as their bearers passed, sprinkled incense on their dinners from his torch. And it was a very uncommon kind of torch, for once or twice when there were angry words between some dinner-carriers who had jostled each other, he shed a few drops of water on them from it, and their good humour was restored directly. For they said, it was a shame to quarrel upon Christmas Day. And so it was! God love it, so it was!

In time the bells ceased, and the bakers were shut up; and yet there was a genial shadowing forth of all these dinners and the progress of their cooking, in the thawed blotch of wet above each baker's oven; where the pavement smoked as if its stones were cooking too.

"Is there a peculiar flavour in what you sprinkle from your torch?" asked Scrooge.

"There is. My own."

"Would it apply to any kind of dinner on this day?" asked Scrooge.

"To any kindly given. To a poor one most."

"Why to a poor one most?" asked Scrooge.

"Because it needs it most."

"Spirit," said Scrooge, after a moment's thought, "I wonder you, of all the beings in the many worlds about us, should desire to cramp these people's opportunities of innocent enjoyment."

"I!" cried the Spirit.

"You would deprive them of their means of dining every seventh day, often the only day on which they can be said to dine at all," said Scrooge. "Wouldn't you?"

"I!" cried the Spirit.

"You seek to close these places on the Seventh Day?" said Scrooge. "And it comes to the same thing."

"I seek!" exclaimed the Spirit.

"Forgive me if I am wrong. It has been done in your name, or at least in that of your family," said Scrooge.

"There are some upon this earth of yours," returned the Spirit, "who lay claim to know us, and who do their deeds of passion, pride, ill-will, hatred, envy, bigotry, and selfishness in our name, who are as strange to us and all our kith and kin, as if they had never lived. Remember that, and charge their doings on themselves, not us."

Scrooge promised that he would; and they went on, invisible, as they had been before, into the suburbs of the town. It was a remarkable quality of the Ghost (which Scrooge had observed at the baker's), that notwithstanding his gigantic size, he could accommodate himself to any place with ease; and that he stood beneath a low roof quite as gracefully and like a supernatural creature, as it was possible he could have done in any lofty hall.

And perhaps it was the pleasure the good Spirit had in showing off this power of his, or else it was his own kind, generous, hearty nature, and his sympathy with all poor men, that led him straight to Scrooge's clerk's; for there he went, and took Scrooge with him, holding to his robe; and on the threshold of the door the Spirit smiled, and stopped to bless Bob Cratchit's dwelling with the sprinkling of his torch. Think of

A Christmas Carol

that! Bob had but fifteen "Bob" a-week himself; he pocketed on Saturdays but fifteen copies of his Christian name; and yet the Ghost of Christmas Present blessed his four-roomed house!

Then up rose Mrs. Cratchit, Cratchit's wife, dressed out but poorly in a twice-turned gown, but brave in ribbons, which are cheap and make a goodly show for sixpence; and she laid the cloth, assisted by Belinda Cratchit, second of her daughters, also brave in ribbons; while Master Peter Cratchit plunged a fork into the saucepan of potatoes, and getting the corners of his monstrous shirt collar (Bob's private property, conferred upon his son and heir in honour of the day) into his mouth, rejoiced to find himself so gallantly attired, and yearned to show his linen in the fashionable Parks. And now two smaller Cratchits, boy and girl, came tearing in, screaming that outside the baker's they had smelt the goose, and known it for their own; and basking in luxurious thoughts of sage and onion, these young Cratchits danced about the table, and exalted Master Peter Cratchit to the skies, while he (not proud, although his collars nearly choked him) blew the fire, until the slow potatoes bubbling up, knocked loudly at the saucepan-lid to be let out and peeled.

"What has ever got your precious father then?" said Mrs. Cratchit. "And your brother, Tiny Tim! And Martha warn't as late last Christmas Day by half-an-hour?"

"Here's Martha, mother!" said a girl, appearing as she spoke.

"Here's Martha, mother!" cried the two young Cratchits. "Hurrah! There's such a goose, Martha!"

"Why, bless your heart alive, my dear, how late you are!" said Mrs. Cratchit, kissing her a dozen times, and taking off her shawl and bonnet for her with officious zeal.

"We'd a deal of work to finish up last night," replied the girl, "and had to clear away this morning, mother!"

"Well! Never mind so long as you are come," said Mrs. Cratchit. "Sit ye down before the fire, my dear, and have a warm, Lord bless ye!"

"No, no! There's father coming," cried the two young Cratchits, who were everywhere at once. "Hide, Martha, hide!"

So Martha hid herself, and in came little Bob, the father, with at least three feet of comforter exclusive of the fringe, hanging down before him; and his threadbare clothes darned up and brushed, to look seasonable; and Tiny Tim upon his shoulder. Alas for Tiny Tim, he bore a little crutch, and had his limbs supported by an iron frame!

"Why, where's our Martha?" cried Bob Cratchit, looking round.

"Not coming," said Mrs. Cratchit.

"Not coming!" said Bob, with a sudden declension in his high spirits; for he had been Tim's blood horse all the way from church, and had come home rampant. "Not coming upon Christmas Day!"

Martha didn't like to see him disappointed, if it were only in joke; so she came out prematurely from behind the closet door, and ran into his arms, while the two young Cratchits hustled Tiny Tim, and bore him off into the wash-house, that he might hear the pudding singing in the copper.

"And how did little Tim behave?" asked Mrs. Cratchit, when she had rallied Bob on his credulity, and Bob had hugged his daughter to his heart's content.

"As good as gold," said Bob, "and better. Somehow he gets thoughtful, sitting by himself so much, and thinks the strangest things you ever heard. He told me, coming home, that he hoped the people saw him in the church, because he was a cripple, and it might be pleasant to them to remember upon Christmas Day, who made lame beggars walk, and blind men see."

Bob's voice was tremulous when he told them this, and trembled more when he said that Tiny Tim was growing strong and hearty.

His active little crutch was heard upon the floor, and back came Tiny Tim before another word was spoken, escorted by his brother and sister to his stool before the fire; and while Bob, turning up his cuffs — as if, poor fellow, they were capable of being made more shabby — compounded some hot mixture in a jug with gin and lemons, and stirred it round and round and put it on the hob to simmer; Master Peter, and the two ubiquitous young Cratchits went to fetch the goose, with which they soon returned in high procession.

A Christmas Carol

Such a bustle ensued that you might have thought a goose the rarest of all birds; a feathered phenomenon, to which a black swan was a matter of course—and in truth it was something very like it in that house. Mrs. Cratchit made the gravy (ready beforehand in a little saucepan) hissing hot; Master Peter mashed the potatoes with incredible vigour; Miss Belinda sweetened up the apple-sauce; Martha dusted the hot plates; Bob took Tiny Tim beside him in a tiny corner at the table; the two young Cratchits set chairs for everybody, not forgetting themselves, and mounting guard upon their posts, crammed spoons into their mouths, lest they should shriek for goose before their turn came to be helped. At last the dishes were set on, and grace was said. It was succeeded by a breathless pause, as Mrs. Cratchit, looking slowly all along the carving-knife, prepared to plunge it in the breast; but when she did, and when the long expected gush of stuffing issued forth, one murmur of delight arose all round the board, and even Tiny Tim, excited by the two young Cratchits, beat on the table with the handle of his knife, and feebly cried Hurrah!

There never was such a goose. Bob said he didn't believe there ever was such a goose cooked. Its tenderness and flavour, size and cheapness, were the themes of universal admiration. Eked out by apple-sauce and mashed potatoes, it was a sufficient dinner for the whole family; indeed, as Mrs. Cratchit said with great delight (surveying one small atom of a bone upon the dish), they hadn't ate it all at last! Yet every one had had enough, and the youngest Cratchits in particular, were steeped in sage and onion to the eyebrows! But now, the plates being changed by Miss Belinda, Mrs. Cratchit left the room alone—too nervous to bear witnesses—to take the pudding up and bring it in.

Suppose it should not be done enough! Suppose it should break in turning out! Suppose somebody should have got over the wall of the back-yard, and stolen it, while they were merry with the goose—a supposition at which the two young Cratchits became livid! All sorts of horrors were supposed.

Hallo! A great deal of steam! The pudding was out of the copper. A smell like a washing-day! That was the cloth. A smell like an eating-house and a pastrycook's next door to each other, with a laundress's next door to that! That was the pudding! In half a minute Mrs. Cratchit entered—flushed, but smiling proudly—with the pudding, like a speckled cannon-ball, so hard and firm, blazing in half of half-a-quartern of ignited brandy, and bedight with Christmas holly stuck into the top.

Oh, a wonderful pudding! Bob Cratchit said, and calmly too, that he regarded it as the greatest success achieved by Mrs. Cratchit since their marriage. Mrs. Cratchit said that now the weight was off her mind, she would confess she had had her doubts about the quantity of flour. Everybody had something to say about it, but nobody said or thought it was at all a small pudding for a large family. It would have been flat heresy to do so. Any Cratchit would have blushed to hint at such a thing.

At last the dinner was all done, the cloth was cleared, the hearth swept, and the fire made up. The compound in the jug being tasted, and considered perfect, apples and oranges were put upon the table, and a shovel-full of chestnuts on the fire. Then all the Cratchit family drew round the hearth, in what Bob Cratchit called a circle, meaning half a one; and at Bob Cratchit's elbow stood the family display of glass. Two tumblers, and a custard-cup without a handle.

These held the hot stuff from the jug, however, as well as golden goblets would have done; and Bob served it out with beaming looks, while the chestnuts on the fire sputtered and cracked noisily. Then Bob proposed:

"A Merry Christmas to us all, my dears. God bless us!"

Which all the family re-echoed.

"God bless us every one!" said Tiny Tim, the last of all.

He sat very close to his father's side upon his little stool. Bob held his withered little hand in his, as if he loved the child, and wished to keep him by his side, and dreaded that he might be taken from him.

"Spirit," said Scrooge, with an interest he had never felt before, "tell me if Tiny Tim will live."

"I see a vacant seat," replied the Ghost, "in the poor chimney-corner, and a crutch without an owner, carefully preserved. If these shadows remain unaltered by the Future, the child will die."

"No, no," said Scrooge. "Oh, no, kind Spirit! say he will be spared."

"If these shadows remain unaltered by the Future, none other of my race," returned the Ghost, "will find him here. What then? If he be like to die, he had better do it, and decrease the surplus population."

Scrooge hung his head to hear his own words quoted by the Spirit, and was overcome with penitence and grief.

"Man," said the Ghost, "if man you be in heart, not adamant, forbear that wicked cant until you have discovered What the surplus is, and Where it is. Will you decide what men shall live, what men shall die? It may be, that in the sight of Heaven, you are more worthless and less fit to live than millions like this poor man's child. Oh God! to hear the Insect on the leaf pronouncing on the too much life among his hungry brothers in the dust!"

Scrooge bent before the Ghost's rebuke, and trembling cast his eyes upon the ground. But he raised them speedily, on hearing his own name.

"Mr. Scrooge!" said Bob; "I'll give you Mr. Scrooge, the Founder of the Feast!"

"The Founder of the Feast indeed!" cried Mrs. Cratchit, reddening. "I wish I had him here. I'd give him a piece of my mind to feast upon, and I hope he'd have a good appetite for it."

"My dear," said Bob, "the children! Christmas Day."

"It should be Christmas Day, I am sure," said she, "on which one drinks the health of such an odious, stingy, hard, unfeeling man as Mr. Scrooge. You know he is, Robert! Nobody knows it better than you do, poor fellow!"

"My dear," was Bob's mild answer, "Christmas Day."

"I'll drink his health for your sake and the Day's," said Mrs. Cratchit, "not for his. Long life to him! A merry Christmas and a happy new year! He'll be very merry and very happy, I have no doubt!"

The children drank the toast after her. It was the first of their proceedings which had no heartiness. Tiny Tim drank it last of all, but he didn't care twopence for it. Scrooge was the Ogre of the family. The mention of his name cast a dark shadow on the party, which was not dispelled for full five minutes.

After it had passed away, they were ten times merrier than before, from the mere relief of Scrooge the Baleful being done with. Bob Cratchit told them how he had a situation in his eye for Master Peter, which would bring in, if obtained, full five-and-sixpence weekly. The two young Cratchits laughed tremendously at the idea of Peter's being a man of business; and Peter himself looked thoughtfully at the fire from between his collars, as if he were deliberating what particular investments he should favour when he came into the receipt of that bewildering income. Martha, who was a poor apprentice at a milliner's, then told them what kind of work she had to do, and how many hours she worked at a stretch, and how she meant to lie abed to-morrow morning for a good long rest; to-morrow being a holiday she passed at home. Also how she had seen a countess and a lord some days before, and how the lord "was much about as tall as Peter;" at which Peter pulled up his collars so high that you couldn't have seen his head if you had been there. All this time the chestnuts and the jug went round and round; and by-and-bye they had a song, about a lost child travelling in the snow, from Tiny Tim, who had a plaintive little voice, and sang it very well indeed.

There was nothing of high mark in this. They were not a handsome family; they were not well dressed; their shoes were far from being water-proof; their clothes were scanty; and Peter might have known, and very likely did, the inside of a pawnbroker's. But, they were happy, grateful, pleased with one another, and contented with the time; and when they faded, and looked happier yet in the bright sprinklings of the Spirit's torch at parting, Scrooge had his eye upon them, and especially on Tiny Tim, until the last.

By this time it was getting dark, and snowing pretty heavily; and as Scrooge and the Spirit went along the streets, the brightness of the roaring fires in kitchens, parlours, and all sorts of rooms, was wonderful. Here, the flickering of the blaze showed preparations for a cosy dinner, with hot plates baking through and through before the fire, and deep red curtains, ready to be drawn to shut out cold and darkness. There all the children of the house were running out into the snow to meet their married sisters, brothers, cousins, uncles, aunts, and be the first to greet them. Here, again, were shadows on the window-blind of guests assembling; and there a group of handsome girls, all hooded and fur-booted, and all chattering at once, tripped lightly off to some near neighbour's house; where, woe upon the single man who saw them enter—artful witches, well they knew it—in a glow!

But, if you had judged from the numbers of people on their way to friendly gatherings, you might have thought that no one was at home to give them welcome when they got there, instead

A Christmas Carol

of every house expecting company, and piling up its fires half-chimney high. Blessings on it, how the Ghost exulted! How it bared its breadth of breast, and opened its capacious palm, and floated on, outpouring, with a generous hand, its bright and harmless mirth on everything within its reach! The very lamplighter, who ran on before, dotting the dusky street with specks of light, and who was dressed to spend the evening somewhere, laughed out loudly as the Spirit passed, though little kenned the lamplighter that he had any company but Christmas!

And now, without a word of warning from the Ghost, they stood upon a bleak and desert moor, where monstrous masses of rude stone were cast about, as though it were the burial-place of giants; and water spread itself wheresoever it listed, or would have done so, but for the frost that held it prisoner; and nothing grew but moss and furze, and coarse rank grass. Down in the west the setting sun had left a streak of fiery red, which glared upon the desolation for an instant, like a sullen eye, and frowning lower, lower, lower yet, was lost in the thick gloom of darkest night.

"What place is this?" asked Scrooge.

"A place where Miners live, who labour in the bowels of the earth," returned the Spirit. "But they know me. See!"

A light shone from the window of a hut, and swiftly they advanced towards it. Passing through the wall of mud and stone, they found a cheerful company assembled round a glowing fire. An old, old man and woman, with their children and their children's children, and another generation beyond that, all decked out gaily in their holiday attire. The old man, in a voice that seldom rose above the howling of the wind upon the barren waste, was singing them a Christmas song—it had been a very old song when he was a boy—and from time to time they all joined in the chorus. So surely as they raised their voices, the old man got quite blithe and loud; and so surely as they stopped, his vigour sank again.

The Spirit did not tarry here, but bade Scrooge hold his robe, and passing on above the moor, sped—whither? Not to sea? To sea. To Scrooge's horror, looking back, he saw the last of the land, a frightful range of rocks, behind them; and his ears were deafened by the thundering of water, as it rolled and roared, and raged among the dreadful caverns it had worn, and fiercely tried to undermine the earth.

A Christmas Carol

Built upon a dismal reef of sunken rocks, some league or so from shore, on which the waters chafed and dashed, the wild year through, there stood a solitary lighthouse. Great heaps of sea-weed clung to its base, and storm-birds—born of the wind one might suppose, as sea-weed of the water—rose and fell about it, like the waves they skimmed.

But even here, two men who watched the light had made a fire, that through the loophole in the thick stone wall shed out a ray of brightness on the awful sea. Joining their horny hands over the rough table at which they sat, they wished each other Merry Christmas in their can of grog; and one of them: the elder, too, with his face all damaged and scarred with hard weather, as the figure-head of an old ship might be: struck up a sturdy song that was like a Gale in itself.

Again the Ghost sped on, above the black and heaving sea—on, on—until, being far away, as he told Scrooge, from any shore, they lighted on a ship. They stood beside the helmsman at the wheel, the look-out in the bow, the officers who had the watch; dark, ghostly figures in their several stations; but every man among them hummed a Christmas tune, or had a Christmas thought, or spoke below his breath to his companion of some bygone Christmas Day, with homeward hopes belonging to it. And every man on board, waking or sleeping, good or bad, had had a kinder word for another on that day than on any day in the year; and had shared to some extent in its festivities; and had remembered those he cared for at a distance, and had known that they delighted to remember him.

It was a great surprise to Scrooge, while listening to the moaning of the wind, and thinking what a solemn thing it was to move on through the lonely darkness over an unknown abyss, whose depths were secrets as profound as Death: it was a great surprise to Scrooge, while thus engaged, to hear a hearty laugh. It was a much greater surprise to Scrooge to recognise it as his own nephew's and to find himself in a bright, dry, gleaming room, with the Spirit standing smiling by his side, and looking at that same nephew with approving affability!

"Ha, ha!" laughed Scrooge's nephew. "Ha, ha, ha!"

If you should happen, by any unlikely chance, to know a man more blest in a laugh than Scrooge's nephew, all I can say is, I should like to know him too. Introduce him to me, and I'll cultivate his acquaintance.

A Christmas Carol

It is a fair, even-handed, noble adjustment of things, that while there is infection in disease and sorrow, there is nothing in the world so irresistibly contagious as laughter and good-humour. When Scrooge's nephew laughed in this way: holding his sides, rolling his head, and twisting his face into the most extravagant contortions: Scrooge's niece, by marriage, laughed as heartily as he. And their assembled friends being not a bit behindhand, roared out lustily.

"Ha, ha! Ha, ha, ha, ha!"

"He said that Christmas was a humbug, as I live!" cried Scrooge's nephew. "He believed it too!"

"More shame for him, Fred!" said Scrooge's niece, indignantly. Bless those women; they never do anything by halves. They are always in earnest.

She was very pretty: exceedingly pretty. With a dimpled, surprised-looking, capital face; a ripe little mouth, that seemed made to be kissed—as no doubt it was; all kinds of good little dots about her chin, that melted into one another when she laughed; and the sunniest pair of eyes you ever saw in any little creature's head. Altogether she was what you would have called provoking, you know; but satisfactory, too. Oh, perfectly satisfactory.

"He's a comical old fellow," said Scrooge's nephew, "that's the truth: and not so pleasant as he might be. However, his offences carry their own punishment, and I have nothing to say against him."

"I'm sure he is very rich, Fred," hinted Scrooge's niece. "At least you always tell me so."

"What of that, my dear!" said Scrooge's nephew. "His wealth is of no use to him. He don't do any good with it. He don't make himself comfortable with it. He hasn't the satisfaction of thinking—ha, ha, ha!—that he is ever going to benefit US with it."

"I have no patience with him," observed Scrooge's niece. Scrooge's niece's sisters, and all the other ladies, expressed the same opinion.

"Oh, I have!" said Scrooge's nephew. "I am sorry for him; I couldn't be angry with him if I tried. Who suffers by his ill whims! Himself, always. Here, he takes it into his head to dislike us, and he won't come and dine with us. What's the consequence? He don't lose much of a dinner."

"Indeed, I think he loses a very good dinner," interrupted Scrooge's niece. Everybody else said the same, and they must be allowed to have been competent judges, because they had just had dinner; and, with the dessert upon the table, were clustered round the fire, by lamplight.

"Well! I'm very glad to hear it," said Scrooge's nephew, "because I haven't great faith in these young housekeepers. What do you say, Topper?"

Topper had clearly got his eye upon one of Scrooge's niece's sisters, for he answered that a bachelor was a wretched outcast, who had no right to express an opinion on the subject. Whereat Scrooge's niece's sister—the plump one with the lace tucker: not the one with the roses—blushed.

"Do go on, Fred," said Scrooge's niece, clapping her hands. "He never finishes what he begins to say! He is such a ridiculous fellow!"

Scrooge's nephew revelled in another laugh, and as it was impossible to keep the infection off; though the plump sister tried hard to do it with aromatic vinegar; his example was unanimously followed.

"I was only going to say," said Scrooge's nephew, "that the consequence of his taking a dislike to us, and not making merry with us, is, as I think, that he loses some pleasant moments, which could do him no harm. I am sure he loses pleasanter companions than he can find in his own thoughts, either in his mouldy old office, or his dusty chambers. I mean to give him the same chance every year, whether he likes it or not, for I pity him. He may rail at Christmas till he dies, but he can't help thinking better of it—I defy him—if he finds me going there, in good temper, year after year, and saying Uncle Scrooge, how are you? If it only puts him in the vein to leave his poor clerk fifty pounds, that's something; and I think I shook him yesterday."

It was their turn to laugh now at the notion of his shaking Scrooge. But being thoroughly good-natured, and not much caring what they laughed at, so that they laughed at any rate, he encouraged them in their merriment, and passed the bottle joyously.

A Christmas Carol

After tea, they had some music. For they were a musical family, and knew what they were about, when they sung a Glee or Catch, I can assure you: especially Topper, who could growl away in the bass like a good one, and never swell the large veins in his forehead, or get red in the face over it. Scrooge's niece played well upon the harp; and played among other tunes a simple little air (a mere nothing: you might learn to whistle it in two minutes), which had been familiar to the child who fetched Scrooge from the boarding-school, as he had been reminded by the Ghost of Christmas Past. When this strain of music sounded, all the things that Ghost had shown him, came upon his mind; he softened more and more; and thought that if he could have listened to it often, years ago, he might have cultivated the kindnesses of life for his own happiness with his own hands, without resorting to the sexton's spade that buried Jacob Marley.

But they didn't devote the whole evening to music. After a while they played at forfeits; for it is good to be children sometimes, and never better than at Christmas, when its mighty Founder was a child himself. Stop! There was first a game at blind-man's buff. Of course there was. And I no more believe Topper was really blind than I believe he had eyes in his boots. My opinion is, that it was a done thing between him and Scrooge's nephew; and that the Ghost of Christmas Present knew it. The way he went after that plump sister in the lace tucker, was an outrage on the credulity of human nature. Knocking down the fire-irons, tumbling over the chairs, bumping against the piano, smothering himself among the curtains, wherever she went, there went he! He always knew where the plump sister was. He wouldn't catch anybody else. If you had fallen up against him (as some of them did), on purpose, he would have made a feint of endeavouring to seize you, which would have been an affront to your understanding, and would instantly have sidled off in the direction of the plump sister. She often cried out that it wasn't fair; and it really was not. But when at last, he caught her; when, in spite of all her silken rustlings, and her rapid flutterings past him, he got her into a corner whence there was no escape; then his conduct was the most execrable. For his pretending not to know her; his pretending that it was necessary to touch her head-dress, and further to assure himself of her identity by pressing a certain ring upon her finger, and a certain chain about her neck; was vile, monstrous! No doubt she told him her opinion of it, when, another blind-man being in office, they were so very confidential together, behind the curtains.

Scrooge's niece was not one of the blind-man's buff party, but was made comfortable with a large chair and a footstool, in a snug corner, where the Ghost and Scrooge were close behind her. But she joined in the forfeits, and loved her love to admiration with all the letters of the alphabet. Likewise at the game of How, When, and Where, she was very great, and to the secret joy of Scrooge's nephew, beat her sisters hollow: though they were sharp girls too, as Topper could have told you. There might have been twenty people there, young and old, but they all played, and so did Scrooge; for wholly forgetting in the interest he had in what was going on, that his voice made no sound in their ears, he sometimes came out with his guess quite loud, and very often guessed quite right, too; for the sharpest needle, best Whitechapel, warranted not to cut in the eye, was not sharper than Scrooge; blunt as he took it in his head to be.

The Ghost was greatly pleased to find him in this mood, and looked upon him with such favour, that he begged like a boy to be allowed to stay until the guests departed. But this the Spirit said could not be done.

"Here is a new game," said Scrooge. "One half hour, Spirit, only one!"

It was a Game called Yes and No, where Scrooge's nephew had to think of something, and the rest must find out what; he only answering to their questions yes or no, as the case was. The brisk fire of questioning to which he was exposed, elicited from him that he was thinking of an animal, a live animal, rather a disagreeable animal, a savage animal, an animal that growled and grunted sometimes, and talked sometimes, and lived in London, and walked about the streets, and wasn't made a show of, and wasn't led by anybody, and didn't live in a menagerie, and was never killed in a market, and was not a horse, or an ass, or a cow, or a bull, or a tiger, or a dog, or a pig, or a cat, or a bear. At every fresh question that was put to him, this nephew burst into a fresh roar of laughter; and was so inexpressibly tickled, that he was obliged to get up off the sofa and stamp. At last the plump sister, falling into a similar state, cried out:

"I have found it out! I know what it is, Fred! I know what it is!"

"What is it?" cried Fred.

"It's your Uncle Scro-o-o-o-oge!"

A Christmas Carol

Which it certainly was. Admiration was the universal sentiment, though some objected that the reply to "Is it a bear?" ought to have been "Yes;" inasmuch as an answer in the negative was sufficient to have diverted their thoughts from Mr. Scrooge, supposing they had ever had any tendency that way.

"He has given us plenty of merriment, I am sure," said Fred, "and it would be ungrateful not to drink his health. Here is a glass of mulled wine ready to our hand at the moment; and I say, 'Uncle Scrooge!'"

"Well! Uncle Scrooge!" they cried.

"A Merry Christmas and a Happy New Year to the old man, whatever he is!" said Scrooge's nephew. "He wouldn't take it from me, but may he have it, nevertheless. Uncle Scrooge!"

Uncle Scrooge had imperceptibly become so gay and light of heart, that he would have pledged the unconscious company in return, and thanked them in an inaudible speech, if the Ghost had given him time. But the whole scene passed off in the breath of the last word spoken by his nephew; and he and the Spirit were again upon their travels.

Much they saw, and far they went, and many homes they visited, but always with a happy end. The Spirit stood beside sick beds, and they were cheerful; on foreign lands, and they were close at home; by struggling men, and they were patient in their greater hope; by poverty, and it was rich. In almshouse, hospital, and jail, in misery's every refuge, where vain man in his little brief authority had not made fast the door, and barred the Spirit out, he left his blessing, and taught Scrooge his precepts.

It was a long night, if it were only a night; but Scrooge had his doubts of this, because the Christmas Holidays appeared to be condensed into the space of time they passed together. It was strange, too, that while Scrooge remained unaltered in his outward form, the Ghost grew older, clearly older. Scrooge had observed this change, but never spoke of it, until they left a children's Twelfth Night party, when, looking at the Spirit as they stood together in an open place, he noticed that its hair was grey.

"Are spirits' lives so short?" asked Scrooge.

"My life upon this globe, is very brief," replied the Ghost. "It ends to-night."

"To-night!" cried Scrooge.

"To-night at midnight. Hark! The time is drawing near."

The chimes were ringing the three quarters past eleven at that moment.

"Forgive me if I am not justified in what I ask," said Scrooge, looking intently at the Spirit's robe, "but I see something strange, and not belonging to yourself, protruding from your skirts. Is it a foot or a claw?"

"It might be a claw, for the flesh there is upon it," was the Spirit's sorrowful reply. "Look here."

From the foldings of its robe, it brought two children; wretched, abject, frightful, hideous, miserable. They knelt down at its feet, and clung upon the outside of its garment.

"Oh, Man! look here. Look, look, down here!" exclaimed the Ghost.

They were a boy and girl. Yellow, meagre, ragged, scowling, wolfish; but prostrate, too, in their humility. Where graceful youth should have filled their features out, and touched them with its freshest tints, a stale and shrivelled hand, like that of age, had pinched, and twisted them, and pulled them into shreds. Where angels might have sat enthroned, devils lurked, and glared out menacing. No change, no degradation, no perversion of humanity, in any grade, through all the mysteries of wonderful creation, has monsters half so horrible and dread.

Scrooge started back, appalled. Having them shown to him in this way, he tried to say they were fine children, but the words choked themselves, rather than be parties to a lie of such enormous magnitude.

"Spirit! are they yours?" Scrooge could say no more.

"They are Man's," said the Spirit, looking down upon them. "And they cling to me, appealing from their fathers. This boy is Ignorance. This girl is Want. Beware them both, and all of their degree, but most of all beware this boy, for on his brow I see that written which is Doom, unless the writing be erased. Deny it!" cried the Spirit, stretching out its hand towards the city. "Slander those who tell it ye! Admit it for your factious purposes, and make it worse. And bide the end!"

A Christmas Carol

"Have they no refuge or resource?" cried Scrooge.

"Are there no prisons?" said the Spirit, turning on him for the last time with his own words. "Are there no workhouses?"

The bell struck twelve.

Scrooge looked about him for the Ghost, and saw it not. As the last stroke ceased to vibrate, he remembered the prediction of old Jacob Marley, and lifting up his eyes, beheld a solemn Phantom, draped and hooded, coming, like a mist along the ground, towards him.

STAVE FOUR.
THE LAST OF THE SPIRITS.

The Phantom slowly, gravely, silently, approached. When it came near him, Scrooge bent down upon his knee; for in the very air through which this Spirit moved it seemed to scatter gloom and mystery.

It was shrouded in a deep black garment, which concealed its head, its face, its form, and left nothing of it visible save one outstretched hand. But for this it would have been difficult to detach its figure from the night, and separate it from the darkness by which it was surrounded.

He felt that it was tall and stately when it came beside him, and that its mysterious presence filled him with a solemn dread. He knew no more, for the Spirit neither spoke nor moved.

"I am in the presence of the Ghost of Christmas Yet To Come?" said Scrooge.

The Spirit answered not, but pointed onward with its hand.

"You are about to show me shadows of the things that have not happened, but will happen in the time before us," Scrooge pursued. "Is that so, Spirit?"

The upper portion of the garment was contracted for an instant in its folds, as if the Spirit had inclined its head. That was the only answer he received.

Although well used to ghostly company by this time, Scrooge feared the silent shape so much that his legs trembled beneath him, and he found that he could hardly stand when he prepared to follow it. The Spirit paused a moment, as observing his condition, and giving him time to recover.

But Scrooge was all the worse for this. It thrilled him with a vague uncertain horror, to know that behind the dusky shroud, there were ghostly eyes intently fixed upon him, while he, though he stretched his own to the utmost, could see nothing but a spectral hand and one great heap of black.

"Ghost of the Future!" he exclaimed, "I fear you more than any spectre I have seen. But as I know your purpose is to do me good, and as I hope to live to be another man from what I was, I am prepared to bear you company, and do it with a thankful

A Christmas Carol

heart. Will you not speak to me?"

It gave him no reply. The hand was pointed straight before them.

"Lead on!" said Scrooge. "Lead on! The night is waning fast, and it is precious time to me, I know. Lead on, Spirit!"

The Phantom moved away as it had come towards him. Scrooge followed in the shadow of its dress, which bore him up, he thought, and carried him along.

They scarcely seemed to enter the city; for the city rather seemed to spring up about them, and encompass them of its own act. But there they were, in the heart of it; on 'Change, amongst the merchants; who hurried up and down, and chinked the money in their pockets, and conversed in groups, and looked at their watches, and trifled thoughtfully with their great gold seals; and so forth, as Scrooge had seen them often.

The Spirit stopped beside one little knot of business men. Observing that the hand was pointed to them, Scrooge advanced to listen to their talk.

"No," said a great fat man with a monstrous chin, "I don't know much about it, either way. I only know he's dead."

"When did he die?" inquired another.

"Last night, I believe."

"Why, what was the matter with him?" asked a third, taking a vast quantity of snuff out of a very large snuff-box. "I thought he'd never die."

"God knows," said the first, with a yawn.

"What has he done with his money?" asked a red-faced gentleman with a pendulous excrescence on the end of his nose, that shook like the gills of a turkey-cock.

"I haven't heard," said the man with the large chin, yawning again. "Left it to his company, perhaps. He hasn't left it to me. That's all I know."

This pleasantry was received with a general laugh.

"It's likely to be a very cheap funeral," said the same speaker; "for upon my life I don't know of anybody to go to it. Suppose we make up a party and volunteer?"

"I don't mind going if a lunch is provided," observed the gentleman with the excrescence on his nose. "But I must be fed, if I make one."

Another laugh.

"Well, I am the most disinterested among you, after all," said the first speaker, "for I never wear black gloves, and I never eat lunch. But I'll offer to go, if anybody else will. When I come to think of it, I'm not at all sure that I wasn't his most particular friend; for we used to stop and speak whenever we met. Bye, bye!"

Speakers and listeners strolled away, and mixed with other groups. Scrooge knew the men, and looked towards the Spirit for an explanation.

The Phantom glided on into a street. Its finger pointed to two persons meeting. Scrooge listened again, thinking that the explanation might lie here.

He knew these men, also, perfectly. They were men of business: very wealthy, and of great importance. He had made a point always of standing well in their esteem: in a business point of view, that is; strictly in a business point of view.

"How are you?" said one.

"How are you?" returned the other.

"Well!" said the first. "Old Scratch has got his own at last, hey?"

"So I am told," returned the second. "Cold, isn't it?"

"Seasonable for Christmas time. You're not a skater, I suppose?"

"No. No. Something else to think of. Good morning!"

Not another word. That was their meeting, their conversation, and their parting.

A Christmas Carol

Scrooge was at first inclined to be surprised that the Spirit should attach importance to conversations apparently so trivial; but feeling assured that they must have some hidden purpose, he set himself to consider what it was likely to be. They could scarcely be supposed to have any bearing on the death of Jacob, his old partner, for that was Past, and this Ghost's province was the Future. Nor could he think of any one immediately connected with himself, to whom he could apply them. But nothing doubting that to whomsoever they applied they had some latent moral for his own improvement, he resolved to treasure up every word he heard, and everything he saw; and especially to observe the shadow of himself when it appeared. For he had an expectation that the conduct of his future self would give him the clue he missed, and would render the solution of these riddles easy.

He looked about in that very place for his own image; but another man stood in his accustomed corner, and though the clock pointed to his usual time of day for being there, he saw no likeness of himself among the multitudes that poured in through the Porch. It gave him little surprise, however; for he had been revolving in his mind a change of life, and thought and hoped he saw his new-born resolutions carried out in this.

Quiet and dark, beside him stood the Phantom, with its outstretched hand. When he roused himself from his thoughtful quest, he fancied from the turn of the hand, and its situation in reference to himself, that the Unseen Eyes were looking at him keenly. It made him shudder, and feel very cold.

They left the busy scene, and went into an obscure part of the town, where Scrooge had never penetrated before, although he recognised its situation, and its bad repute. The ways were foul and narrow; the shops and houses wretched; the people half-naked, drunken, slipshod, ugly. Alleys and archways, like so many cesspools, disgorged their offences of smell, and dirt, and life, upon the straggling streets; and the whole quarter reeked with crime, with filth, and misery.

Far in this den of infamous resort, there was a low-browed, beetling shop, below a pent-house roof, where iron, old rags, bottles, bones, and greasy offal, were bought. Upon the floor within, were piled up heaps of rusty keys, nails, chains, hinges, files, scales, weights, and refuse iron of all kinds. Secrets that few would like to scrutinise were bred and hidden in mountains of unseemly rags, masses of corrupted fat, and sepulchres of bones. Sitting in among the wares he dealt in, by a charcoal stove, made of old bricks, was a grey-haired rascal, nearly seventy years of age; who had screened himself from the cold air without, by a frousy curtaining of miscellaneous tatters, hung upon a line; and smoked his pipe in all the luxury of calm retirement.

Scrooge and the Phantom came into the presence of this man, just as a woman with a heavy bundle slunk into the shop. But she had scarcely entered, when another woman, similarly laden, came in too; and she was closely followed by a man in faded black, who was no less startled by the sight of them, than they had been upon the recognition of each other. After a short period of blank astonishment, in which the old man with the pipe had joined them, they all three burst into a laugh.

"Let the charwoman alone to be the first!" cried she who had entered first. "Let the laundress alone to be the second; and let the undertaker's man alone to be the third. Look here, old Joe, here's a chance! If we haven't all three met here without meaning it!"

"You couldn't have met in a better place," said old Joe, removing his pipe from his mouth. "Come into the parlour. You were made free of it long ago, you know; and the other two an't strangers. Stop till I shut the door of the shop. Ah! How it skreeks! There an't such a rusty bit of metal in the place as its own hinges, I believe; and I'm sure there's no such old bones here, as mine. Ha, ha! We're all suitable to our calling, we're well matched. Come into the parlour. Come into the parlour."

The parlour was the space behind the screen of rags. The old man raked the fire together with an old stair-rod, and having trimmed his smoky lamp (for it was night), with the stem of his pipe, put it in his mouth again.

While he did this, the woman who had already spoken threw her bundle on the floor, and sat down in a flaunting manner on a stool; crossing her elbows on her knees, and looking with a bold defiance at the other two.

"What odds then! What odds, Mrs. Dilber?" said the woman. "Every person has a right to take care of themselves. He always did."

"That's true, indeed!" said the laundress. "No man more so."

"Why then, don't stand staring as if you was afraid, woman; who's the wiser? We're not going to pick holes in each other's coats, I suppose?"

A Christmas Carol

"No, indeed!" said Mrs. Dilber and the man together. "We should hope not."

"Very well, then!" cried the woman. "That's enough. Who's the worse for the loss of a few things like these? Not a dead man, I suppose."

"No, indeed," said Mrs. Dilber, laughing.

"If he wanted to keep 'em after he was dead, a wicked old screw," pursued the woman, "why wasn't he natural in his lifetime? If he had been, he'd have had somebody to look after him when he was struck with Death, instead of lying gasping out his last there, alone by himself."

"It's the truest word that ever was spoke," said Mrs. Dilber. "It's a judgment on him."

"I wish it was a little heavier judgment," replied the woman; "and it should have been, you may depend upon it, if I could have laid my hands on anything else. Open that bundle, old Joe, and let me know the value of it. Speak out plain. I'm not afraid to be the first, nor afraid for them to see it. We know pretty well that we were helping ourselves, before we met here, I believe. It's no sin. Open the bundle, Joe."

But the gallantry of her friends would not allow of this; and the man in faded black, mounting the breach first, produced his plunder. It was not extensive. A seal or two, a pencil-case, a pair of sleeve-buttons, and a brooch of no great value, were all. They were severally examined and appraised by old Joe, who chalked the sums he was disposed to give for each, upon the wall, and added them up into a total when he found there was nothing more to come.

"That's your account," said Joe, "and I wouldn't give another sixpence, if I was to be boiled for not doing it. Who's next?"

Mrs. Dilber was next. Sheets and towels, a little wearing apparel, two old-fashioned silver teaspoons, a pair of sugar-tongs, and a few boots. Her account was stated on the wall in the same manner.

"I always give too much to ladies. It's a weakness of mine, and that's the way I ruin myself," said old Joe. "That's your account. If you asked me for another penny, and made it an open question, I'd repent of being so liberal and knock off half-a-crown."

"And now undo my bundle, Joe," said the first woman.

Joe went down on his knees for the greater convenience of opening it, and having unfastened a great many knots, dragged out a large and heavy roll of some dark stuff.

"What do you call this?" said Joe. "Bed-curtains!"

"Ah!" returned the woman, laughing and leaning forward on her crossed arms. "Bed-curtains!"

"You don't mean to say you took 'em down, rings and all, with him lying there?" said Joe.

"Yes I do," replied the woman. "Why not?"

"You were born to make your fortune," said Joe, "and you'll certainly do it."

"I certainly shan't hold my hand, when I can get anything in it by reaching it out, for the sake of such a man as He was, I promise you, Joe," returned the woman coolly. "Don't drop that oil upon the blankets, now."

"His blankets?" asked Joe.

"Whose else's do you think?" replied the woman. "He isn't likely to take cold without 'em, I dare say."

"I hope he didn't die of anything catching? Eh?" said old Joe, stopping in his work, and looking up.

"Don't you be afraid of that," returned the woman. "I an't so fond of his company that I'd loiter about him for such things, if he did. Ah! you may look through that shirt till your eyes ache; but you won't find a hole in it, nor a threadbare place. It's the best he had, and a fine one too. They'd have wasted it, if it hadn't been for me."

"What do you call wasting of it?" asked old Joe.

"Putting it on him to be buried in, to be sure," replied the woman with a laugh. "Somebody was fool enough to do it, but I took it off again. If calico an't good enough for such a purpose, it isn't good enough for anything. It's quite as becoming to the body. He can't look uglier than he did in that one."

A Christmas Carol

Scrooge listened to this dialogue in horror. As they sat grouped about their spoil, in the scanty light afforded by the old man's lamp, he viewed them with a detestation and disgust, which could hardly have been greater, though they had been obscene demons, marketing the corpse itself.

"Ha, ha!" laughed the same woman, when old Joe, producing a flannel bag with money in it, told out their several gains upon the ground. "This is the end of it, you see! He frightened every one away from him when he was alive, to profit us when he was dead! Ha, ha, ha!"

"Spirit!" said Scrooge, shuddering from head to foot. "I see, I see. The case of this unhappy man might be my own. My life tends that way, now. Merciful Heaven, what is this!"

He recoiled in terror, for the scene had changed, and now he almost touched a bed: a bare, uncurtained bed: on which, beneath a ragged sheet, there lay a something covered up, which, though it was dumb, announced itself in awful language.

The room was very dark, too dark to be observed with any accuracy, though Scrooge glanced round it in obedience to a secret impulse, anxious to know what kind of room it was. A pale light, rising in the outer air, fell straight upon the bed; and on it, plundered and bereft, unwatched, unwept, uncared for, was the body of this man.

Scrooge glanced towards the Phantom. Its steady hand was pointed to the head. The cover was so carelessly adjusted that the slightest raising of it, the motion of a finger upon Scrooge's part, would have disclosed the face. He thought of it, felt how easy it would be to do, and longed to do it; but had no more power to withdraw the veil than to dismiss the spectre at his side.

Oh cold, cold, rigid, dreadful Death, set up thine altar here, and dress it with such terrors as thou hast at thy command: for this is thy dominion! But of the loved, revered, and honoured head, thou canst not turn one hair to thy dread purposes, or make one feature odious. It is not that the hand is heavy and will fall down when released; it is not that the heart and pulse are still; but that the hand was open, generous, and true; the heart brave, warm, and tender; and the pulse a man's. Strike, Shadow, strike! And see his good deeds springing from the wound, to sow the world with life immortal!

No voice pronounced these words in Scrooge's ears, and yet he heard them when he looked upon the bed. He thought, if this man could be raised up now, what would be his foremost thoughts? Avarice, hard-dealing, griping cares? They have brought him to a rich end, truly!

He lay, in the dark empty house, with not a man, a woman, or a child, to say that he was kind to me in this or that, and for the memory of one kind word I will be kind to him. A cat was tearing at the door, and there was a sound of gnawing rats beneath the hearth-stone. What they wanted in the room of death, and why they were so restless and disturbed, Scrooge did not dare to think.

"Spirit!" he said, "this is a fearful place. In leaving it, I shall not leave its lesson, trust me. Let us go!"

Still the Ghost pointed with an unmoved finger to the head.

"I understand you," Scrooge returned, "and I would do it, if I could. But I have not the power, Spirit. I have not the power."

Again it seemed to look upon him.

"If there is any person in the town, who feels emotion caused by this man's death," said Scrooge quite agonised, "show that person to me, Spirit, I beseech you!"

The Phantom spread its dark robe before him for a moment, like a wing; and withdrawing it, revealed a room by daylight, where a mother and her children were.

She was expecting some one, and with anxious eagerness; for she walked up and down the room; started at every sound; looked out from the window; glanced at the clock; tried, but in vain, to work with her needle; and could hardly bear the voices of the children in their play.

At length the long-expected knock was heard. She hurried to the door, and met her husband; a man whose face was careworn and depressed, though he was young. There was a remarkable expression in it now; a kind of serious delight of which he felt ashamed, and which he struggled to repress.

He sat down to the dinner that had been hoarding for him by the fire; and when she asked him faintly what news (which was not until after a long silence), he appeared embarrassed how to answer.

A Christmas Carol

"Is it good?" she said, "or bad?"—to help him.

"Bad," he answered.

"We are quite ruined?"

"No. There is hope yet, Caroline."

"If he relents," she said, amazed, "there is! Nothing is past hope, if such a miracle has happened."

"He is past relenting," said her husband. "He is dead."

She was a mild and patient creature if her face spoke truth; but she was thankful in her soul to hear it, and she said so, with clasped hands. She prayed forgiveness the next moment, and was sorry; but the first was the emotion of her heart.

"What the half-drunken woman whom I told you of last night, said to me, when I tried to see him and obtain a week's delay; and what I thought was a mere excuse to avoid me; turns out to have been quite true. He was not only very ill, but dying, then."

"To whom will our debt be transferred?"

"I don't know. But before that time we shall be ready with the money; and even though we were not, it would be a bad fortune indeed to find so merciless a creditor in his successor. We may sleep to-night with light hearts, Caroline!"

Yes. Soften it as they would, their hearts were lighter. The children's faces, hushed and clustered round to hear what they so little understood, were brighter; and it was a happier house for this man's death! The only emotion that the Ghost could show him, caused by the event, was one of pleasure.

"Let me see some tenderness connected with a death," said Scrooge; "or that dark chamber, Spirit, which we left just now, will be for ever present to me."

The Ghost conducted him through several streets familiar to his feet; and as they went along, Scrooge looked here and there to find himself, but nowhere was he to be seen. They entered poor Bob Cratchit's house; the dwelling he had visited before; and found the mother and the children seated round the fire.

Quiet. Very quiet. The noisy little Cratchits were as still as statues in one corner, and sat looking up at Peter, who had a book before him. The mother and her daughters were engaged in sewing. But surely they were very quiet!

" 'And He took a child, and set him in the midst of them.' "

Where had Scrooge heard those words? He had not dreamed them. The boy must have read them out, as he and the Spirit crossed the threshold. Why did he not go on?

The mother laid her work upon the table, and put her hand up to her face.

"The colour hurts my eyes," she said.

The colour? Ah, poor Tiny Tim!

"They're better now again," said Cratchit's wife. "It makes them weak by candle-light; and I wouldn't show weak eyes to your father when he comes home, for the world. It must be near his time."

"Past it rather," Peter answered, shutting up his book. "But I think he has walked a little slower than he used, these few last evenings, mother."

They were very quiet again. At last she said, and in a steady, cheerful voice, that only faltered once:

"I have known him walk with—I have known him walk with Tiny Tim upon his shoulder, very fast indeed."

"And so have I," cried Peter. "Often."

"And so have I," exclaimed another. So had all.

"But he was very light to carry," she resumed, intent upon her work, "and his father loved him so, that it was no trouble: no trouble. And there is your father at the door!"

She hurried out to meet him; and little Bob in his comforter—he had need of it, poor fellow—came in. His tea was ready for him on the hob, and they all tried who should help him to it most. Then the two young Cratchits got upon his knees and laid, each child a little cheek, against his face, as if they said, "Don't mind it, father. Don't be grieved!"

A Christmas Carol

Bob was very cheerful with them, and spoke pleasantly to all the family. He looked at the work upon the table, and praised the industry and speed of Mrs. Cratchit and the girls. They would be done long before Sunday, he said.

"Sunday! You went to-day, then, Robert?" said his wife.

"Yes, my dear," returned Bob. "I wish you could have gone. It would have done you good to see how green a place it is. But you'll see it often. I promised him that I would walk there on a Sunday. My little, little child!" cried Bob. "My little child!"

He broke down all at once. He couldn't help it. If he could have helped it, he and his child would have been farther apart perhaps than they were.

He left the room, and went up-stairs into the room above, which was lighted cheerfully, and hung with Christmas. There was a chair set close beside the child, and there were signs of some one having been there, lately. Poor Bob sat down in it, and when he had thought a little and composed himself, he kissed the little face. He was reconciled to what had happened, and went down again quite happy.

They drew about the fire, and talked; the girls and mother working still. Bob told them of the extraordinary kindness of Mr. Scrooge's nephew, whom he had scarcely seen but once, and who, meeting him in the street that day, and seeing that he looked a little—"just a little down you know," said Bob, inquired what had happened to distress him. "On which," said Bob, "for he is the pleasantest-spoken gentleman you ever heard, I told him. 'I am heartily sorry for it, Mr. Cratchit,' he said, 'and heartily sorry for your good wife.' By the bye, how he ever knew that, I don't know."

"Knew what, my dear?"

"Why, that you were a good wife," replied Bob.

"Everybody knows that!" said Peter.

"Very well observed, my boy!" cried Bob. "I hope they do. 'Heartily sorry,' he said, 'for your good wife. If I can be of service to you in any way,' he said, giving me his card, 'that's where I live. Pray come to me.' Now, it wasn't," cried Bob, "for the sake of anything he might be able to do for us, so much as for his kind way, that this was quite delightful. It really seemed as if he had known our Tiny Tim, and felt with us."

"I'm sure he's a good soul!" said Mrs. Cratchit.

"You would be surer of it, my dear," returned Bob, "if you saw and spoke to him. I shouldn't be at all surprised—mark what I say!—if he got Peter a better situation."

"Only hear that, Peter," said Mrs. Cratchit.

"And then," cried one of the girls, "Peter will be keeping company with some one, and setting up for himself."

"Get along with you!" retorted Peter, grinning.

"It's just as likely as not," said Bob, "one of these days; though there's plenty of time for that, my dear. But however and whenever we part from one another, I am sure we shall none of us forget poor Tiny Tim—shall we—or this first parting that there was among us?"

"Never, father!" cried they all.

"And I know," said Bob, "I know, my dears, that when we recollect how patient and how mild he was; although he was a little, little child; we shall not quarrel easily among ourselves, and forget poor Tiny Tim in doing it."

"No, never, father!" they all cried again.

"I am very happy," said little Bob, "I am very happy!"

Mrs. Cratchit kissed him, his daughters kissed him, the two young Cratchits kissed him, and Peter and himself shook hands. Spirit of Tiny Tim, thy childish essence was from God!

"Spectre," said Scrooge, "something informs me that our parting moment is at hand. I know it, but I know not how. Tell me what man that was whom we saw lying dead?"

The Ghost of Christmas Yet To Come conveyed him, as before—though at a different time, he thought: indeed, there seemed no order in these latter visions, save that they were in the Future—into the resorts of business men, but showed him not himself. Indeed, the Spirit did not stay for anything, but went straight on, as to the end just now desired, until besought by Scrooge to tarry for a moment.

"This court," said Scrooge, "through which we hurry now, is where my place of occupation is, and has been for a length of

A Christmas Carol

time. I see the house. Let me behold what I shall be, in days to come!"

The Spirit stopped; the hand was pointed elsewhere.

"The house is yonder," Scrooge exclaimed. "Why do you point away?"

The inexorable finger underwent no change.

Scrooge hastened to the window of his office, and looked in. It was an office still, but not his. The furniture was not the same, and the figure in the chair was not himself. The Phantom pointed as before.

He joined it once again, and wondering why and whither he had gone, accompanied it until they reached an iron gate. He paused to look round before entering.

A churchyard. Here, then; the wretched man whose name he had now to learn, lay underneath the ground. It was a worthy place. Walled in by houses; overrun by grass and weeds, the growth of vegetation's death, not life; choked up with too much burying; fat with repleted appetite. A worthy place!

The Spirit stood among the graves, and pointed down to One. He advanced towards it trembling. The Phantom was exactly as it had been, but he dreaded that he saw new meaning in its solemn shape.

"Before I draw nearer to that stone to which you point," said Scrooge, "answer me one question. Are these the shadows of the things that Will be, or are they shadows of things that May be, only?"

Still the Ghost pointed downward to the grave by which it stood.

"Men's courses will foreshadow certain ends, to which, if persevered in, they must lead," said Scrooge. "But if the courses be departed from, the ends will change. Say it is thus with what you show me!"

The Spirit was immovable as ever.

Scrooge crept towards it, trembling as he went; and following the finger, read upon the stone of the neglected grave his own name, Ebenezer Scrooge.

"Am I that man who lay upon the bed?" he cried, upon his knees.

The finger pointed from the grave to him, and back again.

"No, Spirit! Oh no, no!"

The finger still was there.

"Spirit!" he cried, tight clutching at its robe, "hear me! I am not the man I was. I will not be the man I must have been but for this intercourse. Why show me this, if I am past all hope!"

For the first time the hand appeared to shake.

"Good Spirit," he pursued, as down upon the ground he fell before it: "Your nature intercedes for me, and pities me. Assure me that I yet may change these shadows you have shown me, by an altered life!"

The kind hand trembled.

"I will honour Christmas in my heart, and try to keep it all the year. I will live in the Past, the Present, and the Future. The Spirits of all Three shall strive within me. I will not shut out the lessons that they teach. Oh, tell me I may sponge away the writing on this stone!"

In his agony, he caught the spectral hand. It sought to free itself, but he was strong in his entreaty, and detained it. The Spirit, stronger yet, repulsed him.

Holding up his hands in a last prayer to have his fate reversed, he saw an alteration in the Phantom's hood and dress. It shrunk, collapsed, and dwindled down into a bedpost.

STAVE FIVE.
THE END OF IT.

Yes! and the bedpost was his own. The bed was his own, the room was his own. Best and happiest of all, the Time before him was his own, to make amends in!

"I will live in the Past, the Present, and the Future!" Scrooge repeated, as he scrambled out of bed. "The Spirits of all Three shall strive within me. Oh Jacob Marley! Heaven, and the Christmas Time be praised for this! I say it on my knees, old Jacob; on my knees!"

He was so fluttered and so glowing with his good intentions, that his broken voice would scarcely answer to his call. He had been sobbing violently in his conflict with the Spirit, and his face was wet with tears.

"They are not torn down," cried Scrooge, folding one of his bed-curtains in his arms, "they are not torn down, rings and all. They are here—I am here—the shadows of the things that would have been, may be dispelled. They will be. I know they will!"

His hands were busy with his garments all this time; turning them inside out, putting them on upside down, tearing them, mislaying them, making them parties to every kind of extravagance.

"I don't know what to do!" cried Scrooge, laughing and crying in the same breath; and making a perfect Laocoön of himself with his stockings. "I am as light as a feather, I am as happy as an angel, I am as merry as a schoolboy. I am as giddy as a drunken man. A merry Christmas to everybody! A happy New Year to all the world. Hallo here! Whoop! Hallo!"

He had frisked into the sitting-room, and was now standing there: perfectly winded.

"There's the saucepan that the gruel was in!" cried Scrooge, starting off again, and going round the fireplace. "There's the door, by which the Ghost of Jacob Marley entered! There's the corner where the Ghost of Christmas Present, sat! There's the window where I saw the wandering Spirits! It's all right, it's all true, it all happened. Ha ha ha!"

Really, for a man who had been out of practice for so many

years, it was a splendid laugh, a most illustrious laugh. The father of a long, long line of brilliant laughs!

"I don't know what day of the month it is!" said Scrooge. "I don't know how long I've been among the Spirits. I don't know anything. I'm quite a baby. Never mind. I don't care. I'd rather be a baby. Hallo! Whoop! Hallo here!"

He was checked in his transports by the churches ringing out the lustiest peals he had ever heard. Clash, clang, hammer; ding, dong, bell. Bell, dong, ding; hammer, clang, clash! Oh, glorious, glorious!

Running to the window, he opened it, and put out his head. No fog, no mist; clear, bright, jovial, stirring, cold; cold, piping for the blood to dance to; Golden sunlight; Heavenly sky; sweet fresh air; merry bells. Oh, glorious! Glorious!

"What's to-day!" cried Scrooge, calling downward to a boy in Sunday clothes, who perhaps had loitered in to look about him.

"Eh?" returned the boy, with all his might of wonder.

"What's to-day, my fine fellow?" said Scrooge.

"To-day!" replied the boy. "Why, Christmas Day."

"It's Christmas Day!" said Scrooge to himself. "I haven't missed it. The Spirits have done it all in one night. They can do anything they like. Of course they can. Of course they can. Hallo, my fine fellow!"

"Hallo!" returned the boy.

"Do you know the Poulterer's, in the next street but one, at the corner?" Scrooge inquired.

"I should hope I did," replied the lad.

"An intelligent boy!" said Scrooge. "A remarkable boy! Do you know whether they've sold the prize Turkey that was hanging up there?—Not the little prize Turkey: the big one?"

"What, the one as big as me?" returned the boy.

"What a delightful boy!" said Scrooge. "It's a pleasure to talk to him. Yes, my buck!"

A Christmas Carol

"It's hanging there now," replied the boy.

"Is it?" said Scrooge. "Go and buy it."

"Walk-er!" exclaimed the boy.

"No, no," said Scrooge, "I am in earnest. Go and buy it, and tell 'em to bring it here, that I may give them the direction where to take it. Come back with the man, and I'll give you a shilling. Come back with him in less than five minutes and I'll give you half-a-crown!"

The boy was off like a shot. He must have had a steady hand at a trigger who could have got a shot off half so fast.

"I'll send it to Bob Cratchit's!" whispered Scrooge, rubbing his hands, and splitting with a laugh. "He sha'n't know who sends it. It's twice the size of Tiny Tim. Joe Miller never made such a joke as sending it to Bob's will be!"

The hand in which he wrote the address was not a steady one, but write it he did, somehow, and went down-stairs to open the street door, ready for the coming of the poulterer's man. As he stood there, waiting his arrival, the knocker caught his eye.

"I shall love it, as long as I live!" cried Scrooge, patting it with his hand. "I scarcely ever looked at it before. What an honest expression it has in its face! It's a wonderful knocker! — Here's the Turkey! Hallo! Whoop! How are you! Merry Christmas!"

It was a Turkey! He never could have stood upon his legs, that bird. He would have snapped 'em short off in a minute, like sticks of sealing-wax.

"Why, it's impossible to carry that to Camden Town," said Scrooge. "You must have a cab."

The chuckle with which he said this, and the chuckle with which he paid for the Turkey, and the chuckle with which he paid for the cab, and the chuckle with which he recompensed the boy, were only to be exceeded by the chuckle with which he sat down breathless in his chair again, and chuckled till he cried.

Shaving was not an easy task, for his hand continued to shake very much; and shaving requires attention, even when you don't dance while you are at it. But if he had cut the end of his nose off, he would have put a piece of sticking-plaister over it, and been quite satisfied.

He dressed himself "all in his best," and at last got out into the streets. The people were by this time pouring forth, as he had seen them with the Ghost of Christmas Present; and walking with his hands behind him, Scrooge regarded every one with a delighted smile. He looked so irresistibly pleasant, in a word, that three or four good-humoured fellows said, "Good morning, sir! A merry Christmas to you!" And Scrooge said often afterwards, that of all the blithe sounds he had ever heard, those were the blithest in his ears.

He had not gone far, when coming on towards him he beheld the portly gentleman, who had walked into his counting-house the day before, and said, "Scrooge and Marley's, I believe?" It sent a pang across his heart to think how this old gentleman would look upon him when they met; but he knew what path lay straight before him, and he took it.

"My dear sir," said Scrooge, quickening his pace, and taking the old gentleman by both his hands. "How do you do? I hope you succeeded yesterday. It was very kind of you. A merry Christmas to you, sir!"

"Mr. Scrooge?"

"Yes," said Scrooge. "That is my name, and I fear it may not be pleasant to you. Allow me to ask your pardon. And will you have the goodness" — here Scrooge whispered in his ear.

"Lord bless me!" cried the gentleman, as if his breath were taken away. "My dear Mr. Scrooge, are you serious?"

"If you please," said Scrooge. "Not a farthing less. A great many back-payments are included in it, I assure you. Will you do me that favour?"

"My dear sir," said the other, shaking hands with him. "I don't know what to say to such munifi —"

"Don't say anything, please," retorted Scrooge. "Come and see me. Will you come and see me?"

"I will!" cried the old gentleman. And it was clear he meant to do it.

590

A Christmas Carol

"Thank'ee," said Scrooge. "I am much obliged to you. I thank you fifty times. Bless you!"

He went to church, and walked about the streets, and watched the people hurrying to and fro, and patted children on the head, and questioned beggars, and looked down into the kitchens of houses, and up to the windows, and found that everything could yield him pleasure. He had never dreamed that any walk—that anything—could give him so much happiness. In the afternoon he turned his steps towards his nephew's house.

He passed the door a dozen times, before he had the courage to go up and knock. But he made a dash, and did it:

"Is your master at home, my dear?" said Scrooge to the girl. Nice girl! Very.

"Yes, sir."

"Where is he, my love?" said Scrooge.

"He's in the dining-room, sir, along with mistress. I'll show you up-stairs, if you please."

"Thank'ee. He knows me," said Scrooge, with his hand already on the dining-room lock. "I'll go in here, my dear."

He turned it gently, and sidled his face in, round the door. They were looking at the table (which was spread out in great array); for these young housekeepers are always nervous on such points, and like to see that everything is right.

"Fred!" said Scrooge.

Dear heart alive, how his niece by marriage started! Scrooge had forgotten, for the moment, about her sitting in the corner with the footstool, or he wouldn't have done it, on any account.

"Why bless my soul!" cried Fred, "who's that?"

"It's I. Your uncle Scrooge. I have come to dinner. Will you let me in, Fred?"

Let him in! It is a mercy he didn't shake his arm off. He was at home in five minutes. Nothing could be heartier. His niece looked just the same. So did Topper when he came. So did the plump sister when she came. So did every one when they came.

Wonderful party, wonderful games, wonderful unanimity, won-der-ful happiness!

But he was early at the office next morning. Oh, he was early there. If he could only be there first, and catch Bob Cratchit coming late! That was the thing he had set his heart upon.

And he did it; yes, he did! The clock struck nine. No Bob. A quarter past. No Bob. He was full eighteen minutes and a half behind his time. Scrooge sat with his door wide open, that he might see him come into the Tank.

His hat was off, before he opened the door; his comforter too. He was on his stool in a jiffy; driving away with his pen, as if he were trying to overtake nine o'clock.

"Hallo!" growled Scrooge, in his accustomed voice, as near as he could feign it. "What do you mean by coming here at this time of day?"

"I am very sorry, sir," said Bob. "I am behind my time."

"You are?" repeated Scrooge. "Yes. I think you are. Step this way, sir, if you please."

"It's only once a year, sir," pleaded Bob, appearing from the Tank. "It shall not be repeated. I was making rather merry yesterday, sir."

"Now, I'll tell you what, my friend," said Scrooge, "I am not going to stand this sort of thing any longer. And therefore," he continued, leaping from his stool, and giving Bob such a dig in the waistcoat that he staggered back into the Tank again; "and therefore I am about to raise your salary!"

Bob trembled, and got a little nearer to the ruler. He had a momentary idea of knocking Scrooge down with it, holding him, and calling to the people in the court for help and a strait-waistcoat.

"A merry Christmas, Bob!" said Scrooge, with an earnestness that could not be mistaken, as he clapped him on the back. "A merrier Christmas, Bob, my good fellow, than I have given you, for many a year! I'll raise your salary, and endeavour to assist your struggling family, and we will discuss your affairs this very afternoon, over a Christmas bowl of smoking bishop, Bob! Make up the fires, and buy another coal-scuttle before you dot another i, Bob Cratchit!"

Scrooge was better than his word. He did it all, and infinitely more; and to Tiny Tim, who did not die, he was a second father. He became as good a friend, as good a master, and as good a man, as the good old city knew, or any other good old city, town, or borough, in the good old world. Some people laughed to see the alteration in him, but he let them laugh, and little heeded them; for he was wise enough to know that nothing ever happened on this globe, for good, at which some people did not have their fill of laughter in the outset; and knowing that such as these would be blind anyway, he thought it quite as well that they should wrinkle up their eyes in grins, as have the malady in less attractive forms. His own heart laughed: and that was quite enough for him.

He had no further intercourse with Spirits, but lived upon the Total Abstinence Principle, ever afterwards; and it was always said of him, that he knew how to keep Christmas well, if any man alive possessed the knowledge. May that be truly said of us, and all of us! And so, as Tiny Tim observed, God bless Us, Every One!